The Autobiography of Fidel Castro

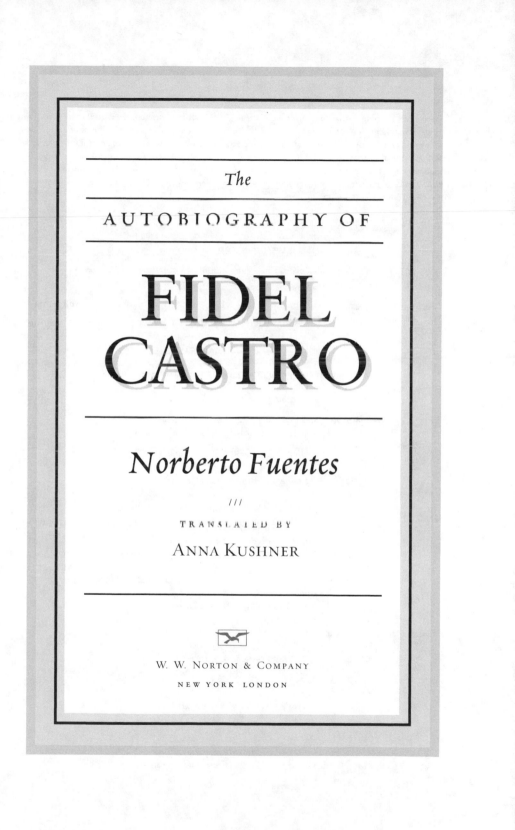

The

AUTOBIOGRAPHY OF

FIDEL
CASTRO

Norberto Fuentes

///

TRANSLATED BY

ANNA KUSHNER

W. W. NORTON & COMPANY

NEW YORK LONDON

Copyright © 20010, 2007, 2004 by Norberto Fuentes
Translation copyright © 2010 by Anna Kushner

This is an abridged version of a two-volume edition originally published in Spanish
as *La Autobiografía de Fidel Castro*

Rights granted by arrangement with Silvia Bastos, S.L. Agencia literaria, in conjunction with Anne Edelstein Literary Agency LLC

All rights reserved
Printed in the United States of America

For information about permission to reproduce selections from this book,
write to Permissions, W. W. Norton & Company, Inc.,
500 Fifth Avenue, New York, NY 10110

For information about special discounts for bulk purchases, please contact
W. W. Norton Special Sales at specialsales@wwnorton.com or 800-233-4830

Manufacturing by RRD Harrisonburg
Book design by Barbara Bachman
Production manager: Julia Druskin

Library of Congress Cataloging-in-Publication Data

Fuentes, Norberto.
[Autobiografía de Fidel Castro. English]
The autobiography of Fidel Castro / Norberto Fuentes ; translated by Anna Kushner.
p. cm.
"This is an abridged version of a two-volume edition originally published in Spanish as
La autobiografía de Fidel Castro"—T.p. verso.
Includes bibliographical references.
ISBN 978-0-393-06899-3 (hardcover)
1. Castro, Fidel, 1926– 2. Cuba—History—20th century. 3. Heads of state—Cuba—Biography. I. Title.
F1788.22.C3F8413 2009
972.9106'4092—dc22
[B]

2009031601

W. W. Norton & Company, Inc.
500 Fifth Avenue, New York, N.Y. 10110
www.wwnorton.com

W. W. Norton & Company Ltd.
Castle House, 75/76 Wells Street, London W1T 3QT

1 2 3 4 5 6 7 8 9 0

What his imagination is to the poet, facts are to the historian. His exercise of judgment comes in their selection, his art in their arrangement.

—BARBARA TUCHMAN,
The Guns of August

MY NAME IS YOUR BLOOD.

CONTENTS

/ / /

BOOK ONE: THE PARADISE OF OTHERS

PART ONE: THE ADVENTURE OF BEING ME

PART TWO: THE PAST OF A MAN WITHOUT A PAST

PART THREE: AS INTIMATE AS CHRIST

BOOK TWO: ABSOLUTE AND
INSUFFICIENT POWER

PART FOUR: A MAN ALONE CAN DO IT ALL

PART FIVE: POWER IS TO BE USED

PART SIX: LIKE THE GUIDE OF THE HORDE

PART SEVEN: WHEN THIS WAR IS OVER

The author has avoided mention of any event of which confirmation,

besides his own testimony, is inaccessible.

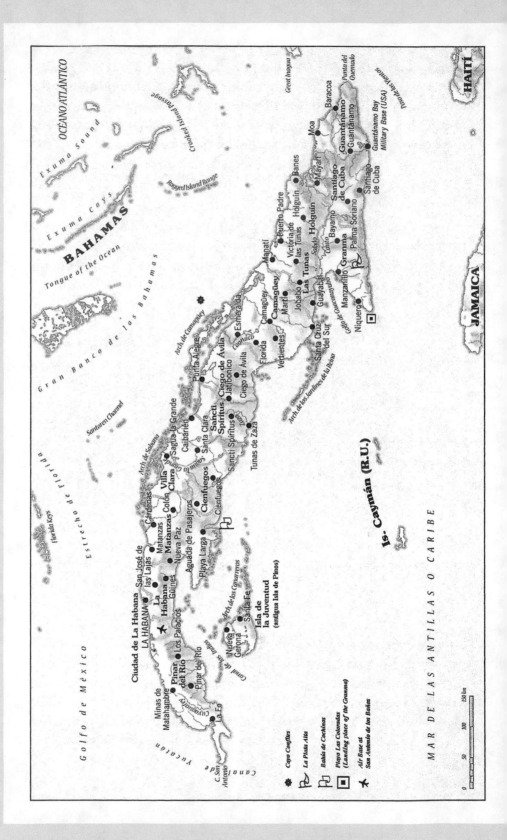

NOTE ON THE CURRENT EDITION

THE ORIGINAL PLAN—OF WAITING UNTIL I WAS ABOUT TO TAKE MY last breath, or was at least close—before allowing the publication of this memoir proved to be a baseless pretension. Two volumes of the first version of this work were published a few years ago already. Editors' requirements and my own impatience to compete on totally new terrain—the literary marketplace—won out. The 869,000 words invested in those two volumes, which comprised more than 2,500 pages, still astound me when I contemplate them, in their solid book form, on the table. Just recently, I said that I had expended tons of paper and tons of breath—the symbolic expression is fitting—on statements, speeches, reports, meetings, interviews and any other verbal form, if such exists.* Well then, a genuine example of that statement can be found precisely in those two volumes. Their weight doesn't quite come to a ton, but in sum they reach about seven net pounds (three for the first volume, four for the second). Nonetheless, that which makes an author proud shouldn't blind him to the chief requirements of his impulse. He wrote for someone. And in my case, logically, the reader in mind is none other than the revolutionary combatant. That's who would be well served by my life experience and whatever other knowledge can be gleaned from my remembrances. As such, the previous edition of *The Autobiography*, whose covers (both) measured 9¼ inches high and 6 inches wide, and the variations of their respective spines (1¾ inches for the first one, 2¾ for the second), make them unfit for battle. Revolutionary works can't be merely objects of display on a high shelf, or designed to be read on a lectern. Understandably, the ideal would be a book that is easy to get rid of in case of a police raid and that fits easily in the pocket of one's field uniform or doesn't

---

* See the newspaper *Granma*, February 29, 2008.

weigh much at the bottom of your backpack. Now I see that my memoirs were excessive for the Revolution's daily duties. And that's without taking into account everything I didn't write!

Since it's a given that revolutions require light communication vehicles, I've prepared the current edition of my book. Its reduced thickness makes it possible to print a pocket-sized edition, which makes for easy transport, without hindrance, and it even fits in a day pack along with smokes, munitions and dry rations.

However, nothing has been lost. All references and largely "historic" materials, which accounted for many of the first version's pages, will be maintained in their natural place: libraries. Specialists and interested parties can consult them there.

I was a healthy man when I finished those books. I hadn't resigned any of my duties and retirement was, if not impossible, then a very remote idea. The energy with which I wrote is clear. Writing back then was quite a challenge. Any word of mine could have jeopardized the country's stability. The same cannot be said about the words of a man who may be isolated in a hospital room somewhere, writhing in agony. Fidel Castro is Fidel Castro's latest prisoner. I am not fooling myself. I know the signs well enough to recognize them. And I know exactly where I am. I am at death's door. But the task has been to preserve my book. And that's all that matters.

Now I realize the date on the calendar of my wristwatch—the date I will have to mark at the bottom of my note—and it's really striking. Should I be surprised? Alarmed? I, who know the arbitrary powers of coincidence? In Rome, 2,052 years ago on a day like today, they killed Caesar. The Ides of March of the year 44 BCE. Poor Roman senator without his proper complement of bodyguards. He offered himself up.

FIDEL CASTRO RUZ
MARCH 15, 2008
4:17 P.M.

. . .

PROLOGUE

I DISMANTLE THEREFORE I WRITE

A MEMOIR? AT THIS POINT?

I've learned something while writing this book. No one owns the past, at least not until it is written. I've learned something else: the Revolution is always creating the past. One more thing: until a certain point in its history, the Revolution won't be able to withstand scrutiny. That point may be when all of its protagonists have died. Meanwhile, the history of the Revolution, and of its men, is in the hands of its enemies—the ones who escape—and any bits of information they were able to obtain.

Random House, Simon & Schuster, Giangiacomo Feltrinelli and nearly all of the world's publishing houses have stubbornly pursued me for years. All this time, I've been courting their offers equally, leading them on. To a certain degree I have resisted the idea because of the inevitable political cost it would carry. If I've decided to do it now it's out of pure boredom. For lack of something new to do. Have you heard of the solitude of power? That doesn't exist. There has never been anyone who keeps more company than I do. Power has provided me with an excess of *compañeros*. Wherever I go, it is usually like moving with a pack. From my impressive height of six feet two inches, I look around as I make my way toward the door of some building—the only time I view anything outside of a car—and what I always see are the concentric circles of those accompanying me and it's like finding yourself at the head of a traveling circus with everyone clearing the way for you as you walk. But it is boring. The boredom is killing me. So writing turns into an unexpected adventure. My fifth discovery. Writing. Literature, they say, is the offspring of bitterness, when it's not the product of defeat. We wouldn't have many of the seminal works of universal literature without bitterness or defeat, or even—what ignominy!—those pages born of the sad tears shed before the powerful so they would employ you again—as is the case with Machiavelli, who has hounded us for five centuries. There's always some kind of ostracism or blacklisting at play. But not with me. I write from a position of absolute power. Out of total fulfillment.

I set out to complete this project now *on my terms*. Let me explain myself. There is no perfect autobiography in existence, since no author has ever put the finishing touches on a work of this magnitude at the exact moment of his death. There is seminal importance about that last breath, when you see that light at the end of the tunnel and try to sit up, and you realize at that exact moment that everything is over. The project consists of seeing these pages published while I am in full enjoyment of my power. The usual method will be employed. I will call upon the world's major editors through the secret channels of my most trustworthy friends and intelligence officials—who only respond to my commands—and say, Here is the material. But I want to go about this in a very specific manner. Let me explain myself. I have to take my cue from the times. So that this doesn't come across as an act of cowardice—the exact opposite of what I am after—or that I am hiding behind the certainty of my death prior to publication. Don't take this the wrong way, but I want to enjoy it. With a close friend, I have arranged for the book to be published a few weeks or a prudent amount of time prior to saying goodbye to this world (in other words, when I calculate that I've got about a week left of life, or at least of lucidity) so that I can find out how it is received. Many times I have said that the only valid judgment over me will be made in a thousand years. Whatever the verdict, the present book should exercise a decisive influence over this, my final judgment.

A Note about the Methodology

It's no secret. The reader knows that I have access to the most extensive collection of documents and papers to write this memoir. This very documentation has been the backbone of my state. It has been useful in ruling and making decisions about some of my affairs on a global level, since the basis of my relations has consisted not only of being well informed but also of having an up-to-date inventory of the favors received and owed. But I am not out to blackmail anyone like that prevaricating financier Robert Vesco—who served a long sentence in our prison system. He tried to publish two books in sequence, one with profiles of his old colleagues and clients, introduced with fictitious names but peppered with revealing details, and the second filled with real names and the most shameless information about the ones who didn't shell out in response to the first book. No, it's not blackmail, it's simply a matter of my wanting to take the first swing. The pile of existing information that will survive and that, I imagine, will come out one day—as with the Czechs or the Germans when the headquarters of their respective intelligence services were attacked or when the Central Committee's files were opened—doesn't alarm me, nor do I pay much attention. While I live, I cannot be blackmailed. And, later, where I'm going to be, I won't care. But I am acting to honor an agreement with my heirs, their protectors and, above all, with Dalia, my companion. Regarding my sources, I've decided to make only careful and measured use of the extensive documentation collected by the Ministry of the Interior and some departments of the Party's Central Committee. In this self-imposed labor of writing, I am trying to go to the root of my own actions—the most well known of them—in the most honest way possible, and since I am in the ranks of memoir writers I don't want to take advantage of documentation which may better serve the Revolution's historians. And since they're going to talk about me anyway—an imagined me that will fill the space of that already intangible me—and they're going to knock me around as they see fit, why should I complicate things for myself by throwing rocks at the sun? So, because of that, and because I want to compete on a level playing field, as if I were in a fishing tournament or on a basketball court, I am resigned to employing the simple method of relying on my memory, the real one, and at a time when, I confess, it isn't as sharp as it used to be. I think this better prepares me for the battle, because, no offense intended, it makes me perfectly human.

November 24, 1958. This provocative billboard is located at the intersection of Thirty-sixth Street and Forty-second Avenue, Northwest Miami, next to the international airport. It's Monday and at the moment of this photo, Fidel Castro is closing in on the main towns in the eastern part of this nearby island, the same one in the ad. In thirty-eight days, he will win the war. The inviting roulette table and rumba dancer are oblivious to the future.

BOOK ONE

The
PARADISE
OF
OTHERS

Fidel in Birán, 1929. Three years old.

PART ONE

The ADVENTURE OF BEING ME

///

IDEAS MUST BE LIVED.

—ANDRÉ MALRAUX

CHAPTER I

The Hurricanes of August

/ / /

A FRIEND GIVES ME THREE BOOKS AS EXAMPLES — *The Autobiography of Alice B. Toklas* by Gertrude Stein, *Memoirs of Hadrian* by Marguerite Yourcenar and the autobiography of Benvenuto Cellini—that all turn out to be literary interpretations, artificial solutions to three types of memoirs, the first two because they take on reality and the last because they say that Cellini made everything up, or a good part of everything. In my case, as you know, I don't need to make up much to attract readers. In addition to having seen myself through the lenses of those authors who have researched my life and published the corresponding treatises—there are hundreds of biographies about me—this volume may provide the experience of seeing myself through my own lens. Me as an object of my own inspection. And I have good material. Not that it always casts the best light on my person and conduct, I must admit. In addition, I have to say something that I've already said in my speeches. I hold myself in very high esteem, as happens with many men unless they suffer from some sort of psychological illness. But I haven't censored myself when it comes to extracting details from the events I've lived that may seem laughable or even reproachable. In reality, I've learned while writing this that those negative details help to establish a subtle range of nuances that not only assure the reader of the credibility of the events but also make the protagonist more likable. Can I give you an example? There's none other than the day I awoke, indignant and angry, after dreaming that I had smoked an excellent Cohiba. And that I had enjoyed it! This happened two or three years after I had kicked

*Line car owned by Don Ángel Castro, used for travel to
the region's mills and the city of Santiago.*

the habit and let it be known to every journalist who passed through Havana. I don't think anyone would have engaged in such critical and harsh introspection about his own behavior as I did that morning of deafening recrimination that led me, for starters, to double the taxes on the public's use of cigarettes and cigars. To keep them from smoking, that was the goal. But what bothered me the most was the fact that I had enjoyed it so thoroughly that I even woke feeling the satisfaction of a professional smoker who just inhaled an entire specimen of this miracle of Cuban industry. They called Zelman, my doctor, and Pepin Naranjo, my secretary and neighbor in the security compound, and it wasn't until the arrival of Captain Núñez Jiménez, a guayabera-wearing sort of scientist with a Rolex on his wrist who has been with me through all of my mad adventures since the beginning of the Revolution, that I managed to calm down. "Ñaco," I said to him, "do you understand what it means that I enjoyed that smoke?"

The original version of *The Autobiography*—consisting of two books, with thirteen chapters per book—was produced occasionally on computers or laptops, but mostly by the traditional use of an old fountain pen gliding over the splendid surface of the presidential notepaper reserved exclusively for my use. I've learned to make excellent use of my time aboard the old and noble Ilyushin Il-62 of my global political wanderings and how to make its retractable food trays infinitely more useful while scribbling out these lines—even learning to take advantage of the inspirational sound of the four formidable turbofan Soloviev D-30KU engines with their ceaseless metallic crunching—and while I take off from Havana at my advanced and respectable age toward any one of the places where I was acclaimed and received as a hero, in Africa or Asia or Latin America, and where the old and living protoplasmic hero that is me is received as a curiosity by young presidents and dignitaries who, on occasion, have the kindness of heart to take me by the arm to help me down the steps, and take me to that part of the runway where the marching band, troops in formation, ambassadors, flags and flowers are waiting. But I take one last look into the inside of my plane and contemplate the tray where I've abandoned my laptop or the stack of papers that Chomi, the diligent secretary, takes care to close up and put safely into his briefcase. Then it's three or four days of official functions, a few witty comments for the ears of journalists, the grasping for and instantaneous invention of a few words of respect and admiration for my hosts and their country, and the whole time I am desperate to find myself again in front of my work in progress, the only thing I should be doing, well dressed and even wearing a scarf, conscious of a cup of tea steaming nearby to accompany me and to take in sips, knowing that I can order more whenever I want, while I go on. Writing.

That is how these pages are not just what other authors have called—in the terrain of literature—a sentimental journey, but have also come into being in unison with the physical sentimental journey of my own existence in this universe, and most of the time it carries the echoes of four Soviet Soloviev engines and the sound of the pilots' professional, neutral voices from the cabin when they radio the control tower and give the location of the CU-T1208, Cubana with a VIP on board—and I lift my gaze from the laptop's screen and direct, as a reflex, my controlling eyes toward the interior of the cockpit. There are only shadows there ahead of me and the occasional flicker of the phosphorescent clocks on the control panel. *Cubana Airlines CU-T1208. Cubana CU-T1208. With a VIP on board. VIP on board. I repeat.* All of my colleagues sleep at twelve kilometers above the Indian Ocean. I write.

The first book spans from August 13, 1926, until January 1, 1959. The second one, from January 1, 1959, until August 13, 2001. The first one, from my birth on Manacas Farm, in Birán, until the flight of the dictator Fulgencio Batista. The second recounts the destruction of the Republic's state apparatus and the precarious installation of revolutionary power and later the height of the Revolution. The author, upon beginning this work, had the secret purpose of using this structure to highlight his fixation with the number thirteen and its multiples. A sort of numerological destiny—which the author has pointed out in various interviews with important foreign journalists—that was able to become a tour de force thanks to the narrative weight of the work resting entirely on the second part. In the present edition, this structure has been not so much abolished as modified to make for lighter reading, but we've still managed to make seven major subdivisions so that we can count on a number related to the cause, seven, the prodigious number seven, which I also identify with and which, at one time, served to tacitly identify the revolutionary movement. The 26th of July Revolutionary Movement. It was on the guerrillas' armbands. It was painted in graffiti. It was whispered and murmured among the clandestine groups. The M-26-7.

In this interpretation of the reasons leading me to write my memoirs and especially to use *The Autobiography of Benvenuto Cellini* as a guide and object of inspiration, I make an observation. Cellini describes or rescues a world where modern communications were nonexistent, everything was still a mystery. There are too many photos and videos in our times. From the moment photography came on the scene, the entire art world moved backward, it had to give up part of the territory. I'm referring to the art of the narrative. As soon as man was able to capture light and stamp it on a piece of paper and reproduce the image, realistic literature and painting had to go in search of other paths. What could I tell you that doesn't already lie in a secret police drawer somewhere or in the pages of any newspaper?

But knowing that there are many biographies about me has liberated me from a long period of indecisiveness. With this book, I am not trying to reject anything or defend myself, but to leave behind an interpretation from my own hands, or rather, from my own mouth, of the events in which I am the protagonist. I repeat, it's not a defense, but rather a way of making it impossible for others to rewrite or to reinterpret. At the very least, they would have to take the events highlighted here as a starting point and acknowledge my commentary and motivations. The truth is that I am not lacking in victories and triumphs and medals and mass acclaim, I may even be the most acclaimed man in the history of the world, the most received by presidents and dignitaries and even the most courageous.

I, *I alone*, have invaded more countries than Alexander the Great, and in even more distant lands; I have defied two empires a thousand times as powerful as Rome, Egypt and all the empires of antiquity and the modern era put together and I've been featured in the global news more times than any other head of state for almost half a century. The flame of my name waves on a flag I signed in the Antarctic (to the extent that a flame could wave on a flag that is frozen), and I was invoked in the conflicts in the Golan Heights, the Western Sahara and in Venezuela's Sierra de Falcón. A Vietnamese battalion used my name as a war cry against the *yanquis* and I proudly carry the marshal's sword of the Soviet Union. But, anyway.

But anyway.

I digress; this text is not an exercise in vanity but rather an intellectual endeavor.

Really, if the end is writing, even if I weren't the captain of this ship,

I wouldn't approve of our old saying that everything ends badly. Because that hasn't been the case.

To write. This was my goal on many occasions. I even wanted to retire to devote myself to this profession. Many learned and important figures have felt obliged to write my life, from Tad Szulc, Herbert Matthews and Anne Geyer to Robert E. Quirk and that Englishman Hugh Thomas, who was knighted by Queen Elizabeth for his book about my Revolution. Che Guevara died thinking of me, and General Arnaldo Ochoa promised to do so when we executed him: to think of me. But when I hand over these pages, I think it is my duty to dedicate them to a soldier of the Cuban Revolution, that young artilleryman Eduardo García Delgado, who wrote my name—Fidel—in blood by dipping his finger in his own open wounds caused by the mercenary bombing of our capital on Saturday, April 15, 1961, in the prelude to the landing at the Bay of Pigs. This isn't about writing out a detailed account of events which are already recorded in not just hundreds, but thousands, of books, not just about me, but about the Cuban Revolution, which are one and the same thing. Rather, I would like to focus and reflect on those moments that I believe are worthy because of their obscurity, to explain them and demonstrate why I've often come across as arrogant and mocking. I've shaped those I've loved. And anyone else, well, yes, I've looked down on them. If any reader in the future—out of the reach of my supposed or probable manipulations or in a far-off latitude or whom I will never meet, which is all the same thing—finds here any explanation useful for his own affairs or adventures or that will help him plan or take action, whatever the case may be, well then, I will include this person in the circle of those who are worthy of my respect.

If I've moved in a world of cowards and weaklings, how can I let myself be influenced by those whom I've betrayed? I need to write for superior beings.

Now let me tell you about what happened after that stormy night in August 1926 when I was born at two in the morning in the house on stilts at Manacas Farm and about the memory I have of my father. My father in the shade of the tamarind tree.

BENEATH THE SHADE OF A TAMARIND TREE IN BLOOM

He was smoking under the tamarind tree while the women skinned the animals and peeled the cassava. Poor thing. I see him getting a breath of fresh air under the tree, a tree overshadowing the whole yard with its twenty-five-foot-thick trunk and the small tamarinds flowering on its branches, its fronds cooling and shading the property, its dense, brilliant green foliage marking its territory from eighty feet high, the extent of its shadow, and its leaves always green even in the dry season and the abundant grace of its five-petaled flowers in orange and yellow bunches with red garlands and purple buds.

I learned about the communion that can exist between a man and his surroundings. I think my first awareness of something tangible was of my father with that veteran tamarind tree, estimated to be over one hundred years old. These were the unmistakable signs of summer. The sugar harvest is over and the field hands' lodgings disappear from the region and out go the chimneys of the nearby sugar mill, Marcané. Then the tamarind tree starts to bloom and my father comes out from his winter refuge up in the attic of the house and begins his long musings, tobacco in hand and stocky legs spread apart under the tree. You can tell by the blooming of the tamarind tree that summer is right around the corner. *La calor*, the intense heat, as the peasants call this season. My father's other ritual begins later, at the beginning of July. At least, that's how I remember it. He voices his admiration for the tree's productivity and incessantly points out the sheer volume of fruit he has picked from it.

The wooden benches, where my father used to sit in those years, surround the thick trunk, like the four cardinal points. And close by, behind him and to the left, is the elevated water tank on its four cement legs, and beyond that, the blackened sticks of *caiguarán* wood holding up the house. As I was saying, I see him. I see him with a Cazador de Pita cigar and the solid diamond adorning his right hand, the one holding the Cazador, not letting it go out and not removing the label until the embers threaten to reach it, close to his lips. Cazador de Pita was his favorite brand of cigars and the *carreros* brought cartloads of them to the front gate of the farm. *Carreros* was what we called traveling salesmen. Later, when my father opened his little store on the other side of the road and across from the house, they would leave the tobacco and the rest of the merchandise there.

And my father has tall rubber boots on and his guayabera shirt is lightly, but visibly, stained with coffee.

Now do you see him? Good, well, this is the bucolic and archetypal Cuban landscape that I myself will destroy thirty years hence. It seems incredible to me. Everywhere I find this scene throughout the country, everywhere, I will destroy it. But not because I hate it, or because it is a premeditated act, or because I think it deserves it, but rather because—this is what I will end up believing—it is the result of an inevitable process. It's something that I myself will raze and that will, little by little, leave me with little power except to adhere to the brute force which I have created and let loose. Because, in all truth, I can't say that things were so bad for me there, in that setting. All my biographers fail on this point. They want to uncover the motives for the Cuban Revolution in my childhood in Manacas, Birán, as if they were watching the behavior of Pavlov's dog. They never want to grant that the Revolution was an intellectual process. First, of balance. Second, of function. Third, of control. They also don't notice that the apparatus I put into motion, or at least stirred, has nothing to do with a happy childhood.

To witness this scene through my eyes—the eyes of a five-year-old—and see my father stand like a chieftain under the tamarind tree and hold out his large hand with the sparkling diamond on it, calling me "son" or "plebeian," is to contemplate the landscape, the world. It's what I'm seeing. The whole world. And, without being able to explain it exactly, I take it as immutable. That is the only landscape that existed. And, I must admit, it was enough for me. A medieval landscape that was to remain unaltered from the time that my father, to establish his sugar colony, tore through mountains and destroyed forests of *ácana*, *majagua*, mahogany and *caíguarán* trees. I feel like I am revolving around my own axis, but in slow motion. The icebox is leaning against the outside of the shack where we keep the pots and the grains and where there is a large table that the older women (my mother, my older sister Angelita and some maid) use to skin the pig, and where they will later put the corn mill, and on that table there is a gutter to carry the animal's blood down the middle toward a bucket on the floor underneath. And since no one knows what's in the icebox, we can still say it's like a medieval landscape.

The house overlooks the road. The road goes to Cueto, half an hour by horse, ten minutes by truck. The windows face the northeast, the direction of the trade winds, if the builder knows what he is doing. My father is smoking his cigar and he has called me over and is saying that since I am turning five, he's going to give me one peso. He adds:

"This year the son of a bitch has given me three hundred and fifty pounds."

Three hundred and fifty pounds of tamarinds.

He uses his cigar to point up at the treetop in which all flowers and fruits have faded until the next spring.

I ask, But Father, why don't you give me five? Five pesos. One for every year. And my father says, *cabrón*, one peso is made up of five pesetas. How can you ask for five pesos? You're too young for that kind of flattery.

The younger women—my sister Juana and maybe Emma or some other seasonal girl, a daughter of the Haitian day laborers who stay around the area after the sugarcane harvest—are peeling cassava in front of my father, and up there, in the house's kitchen, I'm not sure who is making the white rice steeped in black beans. Which aunt, which grandmother, which maid. Little Raúl isn't on the scene yet. Either he's in his crib or he hasn't been born yet. I'll do the math later.

I say that the kitchen was up there because it was built on wooden pillars up to seven feet high. The post office, visible from the farm's front gate, and the little school were also on pillars. Years later I learned why so many houses and public buildings in the Cuban countryside were built on wooden pillars or on cement posts. It was to save on the considerable cost of laying down a foundation and spending a fortune on cement. But it wasn't a cheap Spaniard's invention, as they would have you believe to belittle my father. It was a reasonable habit with its own sound logic that was applied to a lot of buildings in the countryside. As a matter of fact, all of the houses belonging to the United Fruit tycoons in Banes, a nearby town, in the area called "the Americans' neighborhood," were raised up on cement posts. But nobody called those *yanquis* cheap bastards. The truth is that there were all kinds of animals which my father insisted on calling "domestic" animals. This classification included cows, chickens, turkeys, sheep and ducks. But not pigs. Pigs went in the pigpen. Not only had he saved himself the foundation, but simply by using pillars that were a bit longer than were commonly used, he also saved himself the barn.

On with my tour. The kitchen window, facing the opposite direction of the wind to carry away the smells and vapors, is propped open so that the scraps can be thrown out, falling more than nine meters before landing in the bucket waiting below to collect this potluck stew we then feed to the pigs. And the tamarind tree makes the whole yard lovely. And it smells like pure, simple air with a steady wind, and if this keeps up, you'll never notice the smell of sacrificial blood, and the flowers create what my mother calls ambience, and this is something that stays with you. The mud bricks surrounding the thick tamarind tree trunk like a flower bed are also there, brought from the little factory at Cueto that resembles the one in every town in Cuba, with the same oven, the same pile of bricks, the same black men soaked in sweat, shovels in hand, the beads of water on their naked torsos glimmering like after a rainfall.

"Five pesos, my ass!" my father says.

Then he looks me straight in the eye and I notice a rapid flash of mischief in his eyes. I know it's mischief because his face softens and he lowers his voice to make sure that the girls peeling the cassava just twenty meters away from us don't hear what he is about to say, and what he says is something I am not ready for yet, not even to understand it, but as a result I realize suddenly there is a door that can be opened and beyond its threshold, I will encounter a possibility of such magnitude that I feel disturbed for the first time in my life and I forget all about the loss of the four pesos at the mere suggestion of this sinister game.

"You wouldn't want this money for the girls, would you? Hmmm? Are you already feeling the itch? Well, you let me know, because I'll find you a piece of tail for that job and it won't cost me more than four pesetas."

At the edge of the yard is the shack where my father has his RCA Victor and where he takes a nap sometimes and where my brother Ramón, the oldest of the boys, goes to hear Mexican music even though my father only wants to hear the radio serials, when they come in.

Beyond the pigpen are the tractors, Ferguson and Caterpillar.

According to the stories to be fabricated in about sixty years to make me seem like the product of a family of bandits, the United Fruit people, led by their manager Mr. Hodgkins, storm in to where these tractors are parked and chip away at the paint until the original paint underneath reveals the true owner. It is none other than the very same Mr. Hodgkins with his righteous and redeeming switchblade in his pocket, which he brandishes before my father. The stealing of Manacas Farm, which my father cleared with his own hands and in which he only permitted himself three luxuries his entire life—the house wired for electricity, the inexhaustible supply of tobacco (his Cazador de Pita cigars) and the diamond ring on his right hand—is the great lie of my biographers who, having no other way to blemish the story of a boy in the course of his childhood, take it out on a hardworking man born for nothing else. Poor man. If we remember Mr. Hodgkins at all in our family—on the rare occasions on which we gather to evoke the past—it is as a drunk who gave Birán's supply of cognac a good run and who always ended up in some tangled discussion with my father over the sinking of the U.S.S. *Maine*. My father, who first arrived in Cuba as a Spanish soldier, felt it was his duty to blame the Americans for the sinking of their own ship as a pretext to declare war on Spain. Mr. Hodgkins, of course, defended the opposite view. Those cognac-fueled sessions about the *Maine* were just like the two countries declaring war on each other all over again. My father used to wave a daguerreotype—or was it a postcard?—of the remains of the *Maine* in the bay of Havana that he kept on hand in the dining room for these occasions, and gave free range to the mocking tone I never heard at any other time when he said, "You can't possibly deny, my dear *Meester Joquins*, that whoever placed the dynamite there, your guys or ours, was perfectly aware of what this would lead to. Listen here, this is what I call sinking a ship with prescience. Just look at this, my God. What a way to be sunk." Even so, later—and this much I recall—while Mr. Hodgkins stumbled toward his car, my father would say to my brother Ramón, "He still doesn't take me seriously." In my father's mind, the war was still being fought, and it was so easy for him to liberate occupied territory from these Americans, just by repositioning the fences. But no one can prove this little story. To increase his eight hundred hectares at the expense of the United Fruit Company, shifting the fence posts, and doing it at night, is more than my imagination is ready to accept. Although in the end, in my opinion, there is some honor in the legend that a foot soldier of the Spanish army won the war after the war. Pork for you, my father yells to the women, to all the ones surrounding us, in the kitchen, the ones toiling over the cassava, the ones quartering the animal. But for me, bean and sausage stew.

"Did you hear me, women? Dammit. Pork for you. Bean and sausage stew for me."

Up above, in the house, is the vast wooden and leather furniture, big and solid pieces, and with the outhouse being at the edge of the yard there are washbasins under the beds so we can empty our bladders at night and then throw the contents out the window, and here comes the ice cart, Don Hildemaro's cart, pulled by a mule, and there's always an abandoned wagon wheel and always some guy or other who starts calling out to the oxen when he's drunk.

Sunday, August 16, 1931. We're celebrating my birthday three days late so that it's not a workday. *La verbena*, my father calls this, placing a heavy hand on my head. I accept it as a tender caress. That same hand on my head on a stormy night is the first memory I have of real contact with the outside world. I can't say—because I don't know—when I was able to speak for the first time or when I first engaged in what the women in the house called cute little antics, but I remember that hurricane just south of Birán when I was two years old and I associate it with the weight of that powerful Spanish soldier's hand. There was no hurricane over Birán the day I was born, as some writers say. That little gringa Georgie Anne Geyer, despite the disparaging tone and racism of her treatise, can't help but attribute to me some sort of supernatural power capable of unleashing a devastating hurricane over the area in her description of my arrival in this world. There were two very bad hurricanes relatively close by, so they say, and the reddened sky was full of rain and occasional squalls, but that was normal in August. In Cuba, it has never snowed. Only very rarely does a light layer cover the vegetation on the highest peaks of the Sierra Maestra. The temperature is high, but not excessive, and there aren't many completely sunny days and the trade winds always lighten the air. But there are hurricanes. When these let loose, winds can reach up to three hundred kilometers an hour, with torrential downpours and tidal waves. These monsters show up with their hot nucleus (the eye of the hurricane) measuring twenty to fifty kilometers in diameter in the middle of which the temperature can surpass that of the surrounding winds by about ten degrees Celsius. These whirlwinds can get to be five to eight kilometers high and three hundred kilometers across and last an average of eight days. But I couldn't have known I was being pushed into this world on that night of August 13, 1926, around two in the morning, nor that there was a hurricane at a reasonable distance from Birán. But during the hurricane of '28—two years later—I did smell the danger and I could smell the rain and I still hear the rattling of the windows and I still feel the tender heat of the protective hand that was my father's, that strong, tough Spaniard, as he patted my head. My mother has me on her lap and for the first time I am conscious of the tempest and what it's like to be trapped in it and to weather the storm even when you are inside a house, and you hear the winds and the floods and you learn how wonderful it is to be sitting there with a roof over your head while this is happening and you learn this through touch, through your father's hand resting on your head while your mother protects you in her arms. The next day is when you experience the devastation—although now I don't know if I saw it with my own eyes or if I was told about it: the whole settlement in ruins, the sugarcane flattened by the wind, and the cows, the animals— and even people—all drowned.

ONCE, I MENTIONED my mother's fervent religiosity to a little Brazilian priest, Fray Betto, who was taping a long interview with me. He was a revolutionary priest of that jittery and very susceptible Latin American left and with whom I personally sympathized. So I gave him some tidbits to feed his illusions. But I didn't tell him the whole truth. Not even a smidgen of it. Certainly, when I described my mother as a deeply religious woman, I didn't specify which religion she gave herself over to body and soul. She was a *santera*, a follower of Santería. And, in addition, she thought I was destined for greatness. She thought this while I was still a fetus. I was in her womb when it was revealed to her that her unborn child had a very important mission. That my fate was ordained by the gods. She was so convinced that they initiated me into the religion from the womb. She told me this herself, just a few days before the triumph of the Revolution, on December 24, 1958, when I made a quick trip from the Sierra Maestra to see her. Our control over the territory was such that I was able to travel safely within a pretty wide area—through back roads and sugarcane paths, of course—in a well-accompanied four-vehicle convoy. The landscape had changed dramatically in the four years since my last visit and both my father and the big house were gone. But we'll get to that later. Night was falling over Birán and she was waiting for me at the top of the steps, which I ascended while my men, in a state of indecision, milled around at the bottom of the steps. Before Lina Ruz González stood a warrior, his FAL rifle hanging over his shoulder, a beard from two years' growth in the mountains, a slightly worn olive-green uniform with pockets full of cigars and papers, and who took her in his arms and nearly lifted her off the ground when he heard her say, "Aggayú." And almost immediately, as befitting the situation, she began her long list of reproaches. But for once, they were tender reproaches. That I didn't have anyone to iron my uniform. That I had dirt underneath my fingernails. That my men should come out of the orange grove. That my men were eating all the oranges. And the biggest reason I've been waiting for you,

Fidel. How dare you have the audacity to order the burning of my sugarcane fields? At least your father, may he rest in peace, wasn't alive to see it. Fidel. Fidel. Oh, my child. That night, as a side note, I learned the story. I learned that I was a son of the god Aggayú and about the whole process of initiating me into Santería from the womb. She knew I had an important destiny, she told me, and she sent for a Santería priest, and it was he who specified my father was the god Aggayú. "I can tell by your left hand—he told her—because this is blood of your blood and through it I can see your son through you." Being a son of Aggayú complicated everything greatly because Aggayú, who is a top-tier warrior, hadn't had anyone who knew how to perform the saint-making ceremony for him in many years. The old Santería priests were the only ones who knew the ceremony, but all of them had died by the 1920s, taking their ceremonial secrets to the grave. So the saint wasn't one that could be made by its own initiates. In other words, and I am now taking the liberty of using an example from modern medicine, you find the closest saint, which in this case was Changó, whose own Santería father is Aggayú, and you chant the ritual songs to Changó, like a kind of bypass. Do you understand? You initiate him with Changó and you prepare the initiate's head to be dedicated to Aggayú and you ask that Changó transmit this situation to Aggayú. There are saints that go from being *orishas*, gods, to being *ochas*, messengers, and these are very strong, and with the passing of the years their initiation secrets are lost. I understand that even the ceremonies to invoke Aggayú stopped happening years ago; the last ones are rumored to have taken place in Pinar del Río around 1959. Of course, my friend the Brazilian friar will learn the full story if he happens to read these pages. But I remember once, at the beginning of the Revolution, I told one of my classmates at the University of Havana, a black man with intellectual airs named Walterio, whom I later appointed ambassador to Morocco and whose inaugural act there was to take the Cuban Embassy's Mercedes, while drunk, through a busy market and run over the king's tailor, who, by the way, was Her Highness's lover. Walterio Carbonell. *El negro* Walterio.

So that was how my mother had her ceremony, I mean, I made the saint through my mother, who showed up at the ceremony, and they shaved her head and carried out the rest of the ceremonial acts, which are secret. They even brought a Santería priest from Havana, someone very famous. I can't say whether it was Miguelito Febles, who was also a *babalawo* (a priest of the Yoruba religion), or Taita Gaitán, both of them well renowned, or maybe it was Antonio Peñalver, although Peñalver was too young around that time; these are the three names (just names, because they are all dead) that the State Security Forces were able to track down at my request through Bureau Number 3, the one covering culture, religion and sports. Of course, they were also able to uncover the secrets of that famous initiation, but I am keeping that to myself out of the deepest respect. I asked my mother if my father knew. "He paid for everything," she told me

An Aggayú ceremony cost three hundred pesos in those years. That was a fortune at the time. But there were other saints that could be invoked for less. Animals were cheap and abundant in the country-side. Sheep, hens, cocks, doves, chickens, guinea pigs and tortoises. All were sacrificed. I think that sheep were a basic requirement for Aggayú Two cocks are offered. One tortoise, for Changó, who eats tortoise. The animal is sacrificed, and then comes the secret ceremony that can't be revealed. But the animal is killed right there and its blood is given to the saint, and I can't disclose what they do with the animal either, but it follows a different path later.

Almost no biography or story about any historical figure starts with the birth of the protagonist, but focuses instead on the high point of that person's life to lure the reader in before taking a few steps back. Since that whole part about birth and childhood is more or less the same for everyone and the following years spanning youth and careers are the fodder for psychiatrists and studies in personality development, let's get down to those obscure corners in the history of an individual—in this case the individual is me—where we can find the most important unpublished material, since everything else abounds in one way or another in newspapers and libraries and even in film and video stores lately. Take note of the unusual point of departure: my mother's womb. Now let's go into the other area off-limits to all of my biographers until now: my memory. My prodigious memory. If I wanted to precisely describe the place in it where I stockpile the information, I'd have to say that it is on the other side from where the news is produced. There's nothing to read into. Just facts. In any event, with the revelation about Aggayú, my private pantheon of deities or the gods of my fate increased that night, just forty-eight hours before my victory. Saint Fidel of Sigmaringa. He was the first. I remember that when I was a kid my parents told me that April

24 was my patron saint's day, and there was Saint Fidel of Sigmaringa on the almanac.

"There's no such thing as fate. There are decisions," I told my mother that night, around ten, a little bit before leaving to see Ramón Font, the manager of the América Mill, at whose house we had put the commanders in preparation for the siege of Santiago. It was at least two hours' journey. With all the lights out, those back-country roads were very dangerous. "There's no such thing as fate, Mother. There are decisions."

Then I smiled. I had to add something. To make her happy:

"And witchcraft and the University of Havana."

CHAPTER 2

BOUDOIR IN THE GRASS

/ / /

LET'S BE FRANK. I AM ABSOLUTELY CERTAIN THAT THE CUBAN
Revolution would not have existed without me. As a matter of fact,
I've gone to great lengths to ensure that my personal history is also the
modern history of my country. Or, shall we say, the new history of the
new country. Therein lies the reason for the monuments that span our
national territory. They are almost always in places that I attacked in
some commando operation or places in which I was imprisoned. Our
problem was that the last important monuments of our nation, at least
from a historic viewpoint, dated to the time of the war of independence
against Spain, which ended in 1898 upon the intervention of the Americans. José Martí was the great hero of the day. However, half a century
later, when the Cuban Revolution triumphed in 1959, Martí had only
four monuments in the entire country, and these were very modest: one
was just sixty square meters large in a quarry where, when he was practically still a boy, he served a forced-labor sentence as a rock cutter—
the so-called San Lázaro quarry—another was the house where he was
born in one of Havana's side streets (Martí, as you can confirm, was an
habanero, a native son of Havana) and the other two included a moldy
stone tribute erected where he was felled by the Spaniards' bullets in
Dos Ríos, and his grave at the Santa Ifigenia Cemetery in Santiago.
This last one was the most pretentious of all, designed and sculpted, as
a matter of fact, by a sculptor named Mario Santí, whom we harassed
relentlessly at the beginning of the Revolution until we succeeded in
forcing him into exile because of his well-known ties to the Batista

Teenage hunter in the pine woods of Mayarí, near his father's estate in Birán. Winter break, 1943. The pointer appears to be genuine. But no one remembers his name, even Fidel with his famous memory. Nonetheless, he has never forgotten the name of the little horse his father gave him in his adolescence: Careto.

government.* All this marble and a ton of manuscripts, as varied as they were thick, made up for the deficiencies in José Martí's appearance, as he was a short, large-headed man with terrible halitosis due to his miserable dentition in real life. Nevertheless, he fit quite nicely within the parameters of what some described as a saint. Despite his poor physique and stature—he would have come up to my stomach and I would have had to get on all fours to kiss him or to decorate him with our medals—I did not scorn the possibilities (and the inexplicable way Cubans had decided he was a figure to worship) of including him in my entire political program. But I went well beyond his loyal followers in the Republic regarding the monuments. It was out of necessity. We had to create a new historic mythology in a country that had, for the last fifty years, held cigarette, detergent or beer spokesmen as paradigmatic figures or imported them from American baseball clubs or Spanish flamenco bars. Yogi Berra or the Chavales of Spain fell in this group. So I went about the task of creating my own monumentality, ever conscious that it had to be endowed with a sense of pain and sacrifice, allowing every bit of blood I sacrificed to shine brightly. Wherever I had participated in a battle or wherever I had been locked up, I turned these places into ascetic plaster-walled reserves and symbols of my presence in the political sphere of this country. The Moncada Barracks, which once housed a whole regiment, is now a monument to me, because I attacked it. The little ranch in Siboney, an area in the outskirts of Santiago, from whence I departed for the Moncada attack, is another monument; and that whole narrow road between Siboney and Moncada is duly lined with one stone marker after another. The site of my political imprisonment on the Isle of Pines is itself a monument because I spent about three years there of the sentence that was finally commuted for the attack, and which provides me with a forty-thousand-square-meter altar, including its four circular galleries of six levels apiece with a capacity for six thousand prisoners plus the central and administrative buildings, and the stables. The Sierra Maestra, Playa Girón, certain streets and places in Havana—such as the intersection of Twelfth and Twenty-third Streets, where I declared the socialist nature of the Revolution or the apartment that was Abel Santamaría's, one of my *compañeros* in the Moncada attack—are duly converted into monuments. One finds such

* A monument dedicated to José Martí was being erected in an area under construction in Havana—known as the Plaza Cívica, later turned into the Plaza de la Revolución—around 1958.

history no matter where he turns in the country. History, imposing and inaccessible, as history should be, to put it simply, for unhappy mortals, which is a history rivaling that of caesars and emperors. So, whenever an African president or one of the idiotic North American senators comes to visit and I take him on a tour of the Moncada Barracks, I am moved before the very images of myself that line the walls like a revelation, like a being that is, in reality, cast in bronze, but that speaks to you with all familiarity, employing the familiar *tú* and throwing his arm around you, and you suddenly realize that you are anointed by glory, by the weight of his arm resting, fraternally, around your shoulders. In a way, for just an instant, I have allowed you to enter the exclusive domain of the gods. I deliver the coup de grâce at the end of the tour, of course, when I demand the opening of the urn that houses the Remington .30-06 hunting rifle with a scope that I carried with me in the Sierra and which is displayed there in the Moncada Barracks, a little anachronistically since it belongs to another battle. The urn is opened. And I take the Remington off of its pedestal. I cradle it as if it were a babe in arms. I almost rock it. My eyes tear and all of my gestures are evocative. And then—with great care, but without having warned you—I hand it over to you. I place it in your hands. Excalibur. You have the modern equivalent of Excalibur in your hands. Then I know you are mine forever, when I see you babble some phrase of gratitude for that honor which you yourself are calling great and unexpected.

Of course, my birthplace presented a problem. While it's adequate and necessary for every founding father to have a birthplace, in that context Birán is somewhat inconvenient. First of all, there's a certain lack of aesthetics in that house so pragmatically balanced up high so animals could be kept in the space below. Second, it was the strict house of a strict man, where we ate standing up and where I still recall my mother shooing the hens from the armchairs so that the few guests we ever received could sit, and, as a result, the care one had to take to avoid the usual deposits of bird shit. Although, in fact, there is a billboard on the access road— less than a hundred kilometers from Banes—announcing the place of my birth (with the military rank of commander in chief of the Revolution and a phrase that reads, "Historic Site of Birán"), this isn't actually open to the public. All I have there at the moment is a chain that keeps visitors from passing and a patrol of Ministry of the Interior guards. That's how access to that place is being controlled, for now. One aspect that worried me was the cockfighting ring where my brother Raúlito spent half of his youth. He was a die-hard cockfighter. I did away with it, along with all the other cockfighting rings in the country. But he'll also get his monument, a second-rate one, which is, truth be told, what he deserves, and it's the tomb waiting for him on the "Frank País" Second Eastern Front, in the guerrilla zone in the battle against Batista and that he himself gave the orders to prepare. But we've managed to preserve the small school in Birán, where I initially went to school. Inside the school, the desks, the chalkboard and the world map are all the same ones I knew in my childhood

It turns out that a small rural school makes a suitable place to memorialize eminent persons. Although in reality school was the place from which I escaped for my adventures and soon enough—perhaps a little too soon for everyone involved—to go with whores. Note that my first relations with a woman were not paid, nor were they in some rural brothel. But I find it unnecessary to mark the place where I lost my virginity with a commemorative plaque that says, roughly, Historic Site, Where the Commander in Chief Stuck His Cock Between Two Butt Cheeks for the First Time. It was in the copse of a sugarcane reed bed on my father's property, on the grass, with a woman who was a maid in my house and who was, of course, older. I couldn't have been older than seven.

ÁNGEL CASTRO BEGAN his private saga on a desolate crossroads of dry red earth, almost metallic, with crystallized bits of iron. He was already a well-respected landholder when I was born. For as long as I can remember, I heard him talk about his eight hundred hectares and the ten thousand he was renting from some Cuban generals who had fought in the war against Spain. It's difficult, if not impossible, to determine now where these freedom fighters got ten thousand hectares of land to rent to him. As soon as I was a little more aware, I would say to him, Father, you own a country's worth of land. Since he died in 1956, when I was still taking up arms in the Sierra, maybe I saved him some heartache. That of being awakened one morning in his airy room by the sweetish smell of burnt sugarcane when I sent a small group of guerrillas to set fire to the plantation—to lead by example, to show that this was all-out war. In any event, dust returned to dust. I can't assure you that my father would have understood me. Two years later, in the same vein, I carried out the

First Agrarian Reform Law—to do away with *latifundios*, large estates. On my father's estate in Birán, we did exactly what we did in the rest of the country. That was when I learned the full extent of his properties: 777 hectares and another 9,712 hectares that he had permanently rented in neighboring plantations—supposedly those belonging to the generals of the Liberating Army. As far as my mother, Lina Ruz, goes, the Revolutionary Government respected the borders of the family home until she died in 1963. The place now belongs to the State Council—the highest executive government organ—of which I am the president.* The Birán homestead and the house on Manacas Farm will soon be a tourist destination where visitors will pay the entry fee in dollars. However, I have proposed that the entrance for primary and secondary school students be free.

Just recently, as a matter of fact, I decided to make a brief excursion to Birán, but a private one, far from curious eyes. Previously I had gone there with the Colombian writer Gabriel García Márquez.† My goal was to show him that Birán, as concerns its solitude, nature and people, could compete with his native Aracataca. I recall Gabriel's face full of curiosity and even longing while I showed him the inside of the house, as if I were really giving him access to the best-kept secrets of my childhood. It was the day I turned seventy, in 1996. But my aim of comparing Birán to Aracataca was at odds with the Colombian's obstinacy. He was determined to discover the vestiges of my origins, while I was determined to one-up the latent marvels of his little town.

"Gabriel," I said, "no one could imagine you without that place . . . What is it called? Aracataca. Without Aracataca."

"Un-huh," he responded.

"Without those dusty paths that you narrate," I said. "Old, magical recollections of Aracataca."

"Yes," he said.

On top of the table are two photos, in black and white, duly framed. One of them is of my father atop a white horse, with gaiters and a hat. He is serious. The look on his face is that of a man who gives orders. There's a certain arrogance in the photo.

---

* The reader should take January 8, 2003, as the reference point for the book, since that is the date on which the final draft was finished. However, other notes or commentaries may have been added later in the editorial process. [*Author's Note.*]

† A journey between Birán and the provincial capital, Holguín, that lasted from August 13 to 15, 1996.

"They're like revelations of the most obscure regions of your consciousness," I continued in an inspired tone.

"Fidel," he said, his face radiating happiness and a hint of compassion. "Who is this man, Fidel? Is it your father, Fidel?"

"My father," I responded, barely paying attention.

I had to traverse the pungent silence of the large pine-wood house slowly and solemnly, stop at the window to search for the shadow of the high mainstay of my first school amid the intermittent sounds of the telegraph office, and lift my gaze above the cedars until it stopped on the rolling landscape of the Pinares de Mayarí to exhale a tremendous sigh and proclaim, "Birán was my Aracataca."

"Un-huh," Gabriel repeated.

I was going to discourse on the bird rains, the infinite tempests, the mean-spirited or angelical beings, the pathetic stores, the unbearable midday heat devoid of people and the credible levitations of his literature, when he stopped for a second time.

In the other photo, my mother smiles, dressed in white, young, beautiful.

"Your beloved mother, Fidel? Is this her?"

"So this is where I lived, Gabriel," I said. "Surrounded by sugar mill workers and by the brisk dawns, the mudslides and the summer gales. Do you understand, Gabriel? Do you understand me?"

On this last trip, by myself, I wanted to recover awareness of some things, on my own. The most surprising of all the experiences to which I alone have access might just be this, to move through a sort of principality that is a museum dedicated to me. The experience of being able to retrace almost all the steps of your existence, the feeling of almost every object you've ever touched, the trajectory of almost every path you've traveled. This is true of Birán. If I want to sit in the mahogany chair in the living room of my house with the same raggedy ball with which I amused myself, bouncing it against the ceiling seventy years ago, I can do so at my leisure, as many times as I like. The only thing missing would be my mother's voice forcing me to abandon the game lest I break any of her knickknacks, paper flowers, Chinese vases, things that have also lasted seventy years, perhaps lying in wait for the commander in chief to be a boy again and destroy them with a simple ill-aimed *boing* of his ball, as well as the familiar smell of the syrupy plantains, permanent and beloved in my memory, set to fry in a sea of pork fat along with small pieces of bacon. You may think this is a lie. But in the midst of the October Missile Crisis in 1962, my mother sent me a message to remember that she was at home, and that I should endeavor that my "new little war"—these were her words—not affect her property nor her "porcelains," as had happened during the Sierra campaign, when we burned some of—her? our?—sugarcane fields. Following that message, I was plagued by the recurring thought that a half-ton, medium-range *yanqui* nuclear warhead missile would finally shatter the large black Chinese vase with its furious papier-mâché dragon and gold trim over the pantry.

And so I came to Birán and, after opening the windows and waiting for the house to air out, I left my bodyguard outside and went to meet my own ghosts. I don't recall another occasion in my life when I was completely alone in that place. I search. I inspect. I decide.

My father's room. The iron crib where we all spent our first months before being moved out of when it was deemed that we were big enough and had to leave room for the new one on the way, my father's nine children, two from his first marriage, María Luisa's children, and seven from the second, my mother's children, was at the foot of the marital bed, as was de rigueur. It's the crib he had made for just a few pesos at a blacksmith's in Cueto. He placed it at the foot of the same immutable bed where he conceived us all with two different women. It was like a crude fertility symbol, protected with a layer of antioxidant paint, but designed with precision: the crib at the foot of the marital bed. The crib remained there even after my mother had given birth to Agustinita, the last of us. Of course, the day I visited, the bed was empty as well and the presence of those once full of weight and heat and spirit were nothing more than a distant memory and took up no space on the yellowed sheets that had last been changed about thirty years before by a Ministry of the Interior official from some nearby unit to whom the task had been entrusted.

Now I should explain something to you. The truth is that this whole world I moved through in the preceding paragraphs doesn't correspond to any tangible reality, none of those pieces of furniture received anyone's weight, nor were those clothes worn or hung from anyone's shoulders, nor did that food fill anyone's belly. The house is a prop, like a cinematographic set—in which everything is identical but false—reconstructed after the triumph of the Revolution and from which I have always maintained a prudent distance as a gesture that should be interpreted as unequivocal modesty. I understand that the Party's *compañeros* in the region, from the

Armed Forces and the National Cultural Council, in collaboration with my brother Ramón and other available sisters and old house servants, volunteered their memories and some photographs. Because the entire Birán house disappeared in less than an hour on the night of September 3, 1954. Raúl and I were imprisoned on the Isle of Pines and we found out a few days later. The fire supposedly started in the loft. My father forgot to put out one of his cigars on the nightstand, next to the lamp. The cloth under the glass bell was the first thing to go up in flames. The fire immediately spread to the wooden floors and to the house's pine walls. Very few pieces of furniture could be saved. The fire splintered and pulverized all the mirrors and anything made of glass and consumed letters and family photographs and my father's collection of cedar tobacco cases and my mother's holy cards and the planks on the steps leading up to the porch and the *caiguarán* wood beams until these were nothing more than dust. Only the iron crib which saw all of our births maintained its structure, although no one could touch its hot rails for a week.

There were no victims, nor did my father abandon his smoking habit. But that morning—I heard the story later from my mother—he looked at the smoking ruins of his house and the charred *caiguarán* sticks, at least their bark, which were still reaching up toward the sky, and muttered, "It's the beginning of the end." They moved to a two-story house that bordered the backyard of the vanished house and called it *La Paloma*, The Dove, because this was the name of the bar that occupied the first floor, which my father also owned. A neighbor, Cándido Martínez, who was a cabinetmaker, took just three days to make the new divisions in the house above the bar. Later he made huge armoires and dressers, wide mahogany beds and nightstands. Another neighbor, Juan Socarrás, painted everything blue. They transferred the things that had been miraculously saved from the fire while the flames peeled the wall coverings and the floor supports and while the thick railroad spikes that were used as nails became red hot and fell like bullets from the wood where they had been deeply embedded for half a century and everything collapsed. The iron crib, some raggedy balls and a jar full of my mother's souvenirs.

Now that I think about it, I believe that my visit in 1996 only increased the false authenticity of the place, since upon recalling details that everyone else had forgotten—this always happens to me—upon seeking a perfection that exists only in my memory and is subject to the capricious play of shadows and lights, and upon thereby forcing entire brigades of my subordinates to make tangible those pulls of memory that occurred to me as I passed by a window lintel or the projection of a beam of light on the pine floorboards, I was only forcing the reproduction of something that may never have existed in reality and that a man who was already seventy years old believed to recall with exactness. On the other hand, we're talking about very complex tasks. Where was State Security going to find a replica of a toy fire truck from the Edinburgh fireman's brigade, made in 1932 by the Lledo Company, so they could place it under the foot of an armchair in the living room where I remember having always seen it?

The placement of the crib—in the replica of the place where it finds itself today—was guided by a basic principle established by my father. He said that every child of his who was raised in his room, inhaling the same air as he, would be healthy and smart. The crib received the full benefit of those blessed trade winds.

The windows. These demonstrated the wisdom with which my father built his house and designed its interior, especially his bedroom. There he placed one window directly across from another—to create a fluid current of air without any curves or obstacles. One faced the front to the northeast, the reigning direction of the wind, and the other faced the lands to the southwest, providing full and vigorous ventilation. How those uncontrollable winds supplied our intelligence was something difficult for me to accept for many years. I later pondered the effects of the mineral particles and the spirit of wisdom emanating from the pines that the winds we inhaled picked up in the mountain range close to the Pinares de Mayarí before rushing toward our ranch, there where we assimilated them into our bloodstream, and all just a short distance away from where a group of Valeriano Weyler's Spanish conscripts took on the Cubans.

Poor man. Circumstances prevented him from dying in that bed. It would have been better, more comfortable, right there, although those winds were useless and beyond his control that morning of October 21, 1956, on which he would have barely retained a meager mouthful of them in his spoiled lungs, reddened and bloody from the continuous consumption—even on days on which he had a cough or cold—of 90,500 Cazador de Pitas smoked throughout his life before he sank his hard head into the blue-striped pillow and let out a whistle, as if he were deflating. I couldn't be there. I was getting ready in Mexico to disembark with my guerrillas to the Sierra Maestra when I received my mother's telegram.

BIRÁN WAS A COLONY. That was how they called the estates devoted to cultivating sugarcane. Colonies. Birán neighbored the United Fruit colonies, on one side, and those of Fidel Pino Santos, a powerful *criollo*, on the other. Don Fidel Pino Santos, who later became a well-known representative of the Auténtico Party, is the person who really helped my father rise in the world. He lent him money. He advised him. But his loans came with interest that was none too generous—up to 6 percent. Besides (it has to be said), when my father began to have relations with my mother, who had been placed as a servant in the house, Don Fidel was having relations with a pharmacist from Santiago, and both of them took the opportunity to go out partying in Santiago together. My father was married to a woman named María Luisa Argota, with whom he had two children: Lidia Castro Argota, who was known as "Chiquitica," and Pedro Emilio Castro Argota. Yes, my mom was the little maid. I believe—as usually happens in these cases—that it was María Luisa herself who employed her. My mother had come from Pinar del Río, a very poor peasant, practically illiterate, in search of opportunities in the western region of Cuba where there was a sort of gold-rush-like fever with the sugar industry. The house where my mother would work was the fief of Doña María Luisa and my mother would be that girl whom Ángel at last would not be able to just screw right there. Years later, when I had my own fling with another little maid, I would understand the difficulties encountered by an illegitimate couple under a roof partially owned by another. Of course, the house's biggest problem was the sound of footsteps resonating on the wood. The whole house was made of pinewood, except for the furniture, minus our crib, which was made of mahogany, and since the house wasn't cemented down and rested instead on those large posts, there was no natural barrier to absorb sound. Steps resonated in every direction and you could make out when they belonged to one of the maids—of whom one or two were employed every so often to earn their twelve or fifteen pesos per month plus room and board—because they walked barefoot and because their steps were almost always accompanied by the music of their own voices singing Mexican *rancheras*.

In addition, the whole layout of the rooms was basic to the extreme and didn't provide any safe hiding places. On the first floor, in the front room, was where medicines were kept and thus was called the medicine room; then came the bathroom; beyond that, a small pantry followed by a hallway that led to the dining room and the kitchen; and between the dining room and the kitchen were the stairs that led down to the ground. A type of office was added to the first floor. On the second level or mezzanine, on the left side, was the room belonging to my father's four daughters with my mother (Angelita, Juanita, Emma and Agustina); to the right, in another room, was a bed for the eldest, Ramón, and another that I shared with Raúl. At the back, presiding over the whole estate, was the master bedroom. And finally, above a slightly sloped roof, the attic.

As I was saying about Don Fidel Pino Santos. He had a lot of farms in the eastern region of Cuba. And he was one of the people who lent out the most money in mortgages, something he did with extraordinary luck since he tended to mortgage delinquent debtors and thus ended up with many of the properties that he had mortgaged. I loved to see him and my father interact, especially how they exhibited the diamonds on their right hands throughout the course of a dialogue, as if ignoring the flashing jewels. Both of them with their diamonds. Don Fidel and Don Ángel. People in the country wore diamonds in case something bad should happen to them, *wearable insurance*. Don Fidel wore two, *two diamonds*, one on his finger and the other in his tie. The use of these diamonds had its own logic and proved that the speaker was a farsighted man. If by a stroke of bad luck you ran out of cash or everything you carried with you, you had the diamond as a way to make quick money. It was also useful to get through hard times. In that sense, with his two diamonds, Don Fidel could be classified as doubly farsighted. He was my first designated godfather. In Cuba, this was a very important figure within the family structure and reflected a very practical concept. Its origins, of course, lay in friendship. You named a friend the godfather—nearly always naming the child after him—to speak for your child. Well beyond representing him at the time of the baptism, the support he provided throughout the child's life had to prove worthy of the trust placed in him. And, above all, he had to be available to deal with any of the godchild's economic difficulties. So whom to designate as your child's godfather? Who better than your best friend? As a matter of fact, the godfather was invested with the powers of a proxy father. But my father faced other problems regarding my baptism, since he hadn't yet succeeded in divorcing María Luisa, his previous wife, and so Don Fidel's godfathership was slowly forgotten. When the baptismal ceremony was finally able to take place, and the priests had agreed to attend it, Don Fidel Pino Santos was designated Raúl's godfather. I don't know how my father managed to convince him that his godson was now Raúl, that little shit, but that's how it went. In short, I don't think Don Fidel was too worried about which damned godson Don Ángel saddled him with. Luis Hibbert. That's the name of the person who became my godfather in the end. He was the Haitian consul in Santiago and ran a business with my father importing cheap labor from Haiti to work the three or four months of the sugar harvest. Since I was about seven years old by the time of my baptism and had already been officially inscribed in Birán as Fidel Alejandro, my father didn't have much leeway to change my name to Luis Alejandro Castro Ruz. Although I know he considered it. He did ask me one day if it mattered to me to be called Luis. Because, he said, it didn't matter to him. I think what gave him pause was my reply. I asked him how much he was offering to call me Luis.

RECENTLY, I TOLD A PLEASANT Venezuelan journalist who seemed to have bathed in Chanel No. 5 that I lost my virginity at the age of seven with an older woman. I was talking about Nereida. The journalist had tried to surprise me with the most provocative question in her arsenal. "Comandante," she said to me, "are you circumcised?" Of course I am not. But I didn't answer her, at least not right away. I also thought she would probably have to find out for herself, so I signaled the head of my bodyguard—Colonel "Joseíto" Delgado—to prepare the conditions accordingly—in one of my houses in the outskirts of Havana outfitted for such a purpose—in case there was a close encounter with the young lady. Also, at my signal, Joseíto had to set in motion the whole process of deep information-gathering. If she was at a reception with me in the Presidential Palace, she had already successfully passed the first test. She wasn't an assassin hired by the CIA. But now it was a matter of sleeping with her. That had more serious implications. From dispatching a search team (the Secret Search Brigade) to snoop through her hotel room (something that had already happened as a matter of course at least twice, upon her arrival in the country and again when she was invited to the reception) to even calling the Venezuelan ambassador or any of our contacts in that embassy. We try to find out, in a couple of hours, everything from the chances of recruiting the enemy to the chances of acquiring gonorrhea, syphilis and, above all, AIDS, from the foreign subject, Venezuelan in this case.

I should admit that the question of circumcision caught me by surprise. But in addition, everything that has to do with Jewish paraphernalia tends to irritate me, or at least to put me on high alert, ever since my youth when Raúl and I were sent to study at Catholic schools in Santiago and the other kids—to make fun of us, since we hadn't yet been baptized—called us Jews. And anyway, of all the possibilities, the last thing that Birán would have accepted was to have me go under the knife to cut off a piece of skin. My mother, like the majority of Cuban women, was always most concerned with her male offsprings' reproductive apparatus. Not teething, or the first signs of intelligence, or whether we sliced our heads open or broke an arm falling out of a tree. No. Her concerns centered on the equipment always being clean and dusted with talcum powder, and that such had reached satisfactory proportions by the end of our adolescence. I think Cuban mothers get more excited before the presence of newly sprouting pubic hairs of a son than when they contemplated those of the man with whom they were going to sleep for the first time. When all of this happened, when development was considered to have run its full course and they had realized to their satisfaction that their sons had a cock that was consistent with the approved size, width and irascibility, they turned the page forever. In Cuba, a man has reached full maturity not when he takes a woman for the first time, but when his mother stops examining his *pinga*. It's like passing on the torch. For my mother, the only real worry she had after my failed attack on the Moncada Barracks was that Batista's thugs not castrate me. She asked me straight out during the first visit she was allowed to Boniato Prison, just before my trial, "These sons of bitches didn't cut your balls off, right?" It was a possibility. Many of our *compañeros* in the attack were emasculated, and some of their bodies appeared—in the ditches of out-of-the-way roads—with their testicles in their mouths. Also, ever since I was in the Sierra Maestra, my testicles were one of the main objects of the enemy's negative propaganda. Not my testicles themselves, but their absence. Because this was the rumor that Batista's men propagated. That I was a eunuch taking up arms in the Sierra. Evil. But a eunuch.

SHE WAS THE KIND of girl that Cubans call *indiada* because of the trace of Cuban aboriginal features that some people in our country still have, although very few. The Spanish conquistadores wiped out the Cuban Indians. Before that, the Caribs had decimated them. From these mass killings, only a few adolescents survived, the ones that the Spaniards made their wives, their slaves, their whores. Nereida was clearly a descendant of one of these and her looks—copper-skinned, dark eyes, black, straight hair, excessively thin calves and full breasts—were exactly the opposite of the type of women I would demand after Nereida—white, light eyes, blond and, if possible, curly hair, good calves and breasts like halved grapefruits, who could easily withstand giving birth two or three times. She was the maid whose loose, barefoot steps I could hear on the house's wooden floors. My mother was none too fond of her and must have thought that she was trying to take my father away just as she herself had done from her own position as the little maid of the house, although she was never barefoot, as she noted, taking refuge in this statement as a last bastion. But my statement to the journalist slathered in Chanel No. 5 was a lie. The loss of my virginity was limited by the actual means of my virility, such as could be at the age of seven, and by the clear fact that an as-yet-undeveloped device cannot be useful in any way. In other words, there was no penetration. There was a loss of virginity in the sense that the romantic rubbing and touching started lasting longer and became more conscientious, conducted each time more deliberately toward a climax that—with the passing of the years—I've learned to associate with the word orgasm. Something else was happening. Those games tended to be qualified as dirty and I, by mere intuition, knew that I should protect myself from something that was considered dirty. But it was also the case that the same intuition left me somewhat uneasy concerning the possibilities of such dirty games. All of this remained without a ready solution in the small mental archive that one starts to develop between puberty and adolescence, as he waits for answers—convincing ones. Until one day, probably in passing, one sees his first pair of black nipples at the tip of slippery, depraved breasts. Nereida was the little maid for whom my mother or one of my sisters set up a cot in the kitchen when it was time to go to sleep and who lasted an average of one year in our house and who, without any warning, approached me in the solitude of one midday and asked me if I already had "the milk." At last we had our little love nest in a shady corner of the orange grove, on the grass, beyond a border of mango trees, by the left side of the house, up against the path that led to Cueto. She pretended she was going to take the potluck stew to the pigs and I took the opposite route, by the path, as if I were going to hunt pigeons, and then at a given point we each turned, she to the right and I to the left, until we met at the crossroads—invisible, but exact—of our convergence, where the orange trees provided us with shade and coolness, and hid us. The first woman who stuck her tongue in my mouth and touched me between my legs and groped my testicles and did to me what she called a little bud hand job—or a little hand job of the bud, I don't remember where she placed the diminutive now—and who kissed my parts and licked them and stuck them in her mouth and strove to suck me until finally, after weeks of effort, she extracted the first frightful drops of a liquid somewhere between watery and oily which I immediately wrote off as urine and which she, ecstatic before its appearance, proclaimed "your milk," was Nereida. The first woman whose vulva I took the pulse of and in between whose buttocks I inserted my fingers, thus discovering the copper ring she said was her ass and told me to insert my finger without any shame, and whom I brought close to me and rubbed myself up against while I became covered in another liquid, also somewhere between watery and oily, although in her case much more oily than watery, and that had no need of being written off as urine, was Nereida. The first woman with whom I felt immediate remorse and terror over the actions we took part in on that grass carpet, was Nereida. And the first woman for whom I found the need to immediately return to in order to continue the elaboration of such dirty games, since the periods of self-reproach and fear were quickly forgotten, was Nereida. Surely our forefathers were ungrateful to the first Indian women to drive their cocks crazy. There are no statues erected in their honor. They would have to be mounted figures. The women mounting our forefathers. Or our forefathers mounting them. This is no joke. The closest thing to what I'm proposing would be the old Egyptian cemeteries that show up on the banks of the Nile every so often and on whose tombstones husbands who lost their wives inscribed their laments—Oh, sweet wife of mine, now that you walk in the Valley of Shadows, who will cook hippopotamus meat for me the way you did? This is on the tombstones of one of the world's most ancient cultures. Inscribed on the stone. I can't

do any less at this moment, while I use my laptop to write my contempo-
rary version of the tombs of the lower Nile. Well, here goes: Nereida—
wherever you may be—thanks for your ass. Fidel.

IT WAS ALL SUGARCANE. That's what I discovered when the world
expanded beyond the area beneath the shade of a tamarind tree. Ramón,
my older brother by my mother, used to help my father manage things.
In all truth, both spoiled me and I don't remember either of them ever
pressuring me to do any work on the colony. Ramón's chief preoccupa-
tion as my older brother concerning my education as the middle brother
was that I not pick on Raúl as the younger brother. That's as far as he
got in his weak pedagogical control. His other concern was to make
himself into a sort of efficient crown prince of the fief. As far back as I
can remember, I watched Ramón running after my father. During the
harvest— running more or less from December to April—neither one of
them rested because the mill worked six days a week, twenty-four hours
a day, and almost always on Sunday, and sugarcane had to be brought in
from six in the morning to six in the evening so there would be enough
left on the sugar mill's grounds at night. So, relieved of any administrative duties, for me sugarcane was always pure scenery. Scenery that
seemed infinite and monochromatic. Infinite and monochromatic.
Infinite and monochromatic. My father planted fields of sugarcane of
the Jaronú 55 variety when I was between five and six years old that
when the Revolution triumphed—still produced seventy thousand *arrobas** of sugarcane.

Nothing out of the ordinary occurred in our childhoods. It was all
just mechanics. When we got ready to go study in Santiago, it was something major. Everything else, as I've said, was just mechanics. Tangible,
physical mechanics, with set gears that like all true mechanics responded
to a cycle of movements, of connections, of reception and delivery. It
was, perhaps, an explanation of the universe, and as such, probably our
duty or destiny to accept it. Nothing could move it or break it. We could
call it synchronicity, to use a term perfectly suited to mechanics. Or
we could call it harmony, if we wish to interpret it as art. I understood
it in its absolute magnitude the afternoon that my father took me to

* One arroba = 14 kilograms = approximately 30.8 pounds. [*Translator's note.*]

the Preston *batey*, sugar mill village, and showed me those huge metallic masses that in the factory's inner heat ceaselessly ground the torrent of sugarcane that flowed in from all the surrounding colonies and at one precise moment in the system, at one unequivocal instant of creation, consolidated the vegetal tameness of the sugarcane with the metallic imperatives of the factory. *Ba-boom!* Pulled by pairs or a trio of oxen from the countryside to the factory, and hooked onto the tip-platform, the oxcart unloads its five hundred *arrobas* of sugarcane on the feeder belt. The sugarcane will enter the mills mechanically and will be expressed by groups of fifteen or more rollers at least three meters long and almost a meter wide. At the other end of the factory—which is half a kilometer long—sugar will come out without ever having been touched by human hands. It will also produce syrup. The factories have steam boilers to move the mills' groups of rollers and to evaporate the syrup water. The consumption of steam is equal to 50 or 60 percent (eleven hundred pounds of steam per ton of sugarcane) of the weight of the sugarcane. This consumed energy represents ten kilowatts per hour per ton of processed sugarcane. Water is extracted through the various and consecutive processes of clarification, evaporation, condensation, crystallization and centrifugation. The boilers are used to produce electricity when there's no sugarcane being ground, and are fueled by petroleum and *bagazo* sugarcane pulp, the byproduct of sugarcane waste. At the beginning of the last century, when my father cleared and planted his first sugarcane fields, the sugar mills used wood as fuel. They needed 13.42 hectares of forest per year to produce 345 tons of unrefined sugar. The 13.42 hectares of forest produced 12,000 cubic meters of wood. Entire forests of *ácana*, mahogany, *majagua* and cedar were burned to produce sugar. My farsighted father saved his forests for furniture-making industry. *Ba-boom!* Another oxcart unloaded. A hundred *arrobas* of sugarcane brought from the countryside. It will enter the mills mechanically to be expressed by groups of fifteen or more rollers at least three meters long and almost a meter wide and sugar will come out at the other end of the factory.

Ba-boom!

I NEVER HEARD FROM Nereida again. She disappeared into that cheap labor market that existed at the edge of any city or town or village. The girl came from that market and was probably deflowered by her father or her brother, who miraculously did not impregnate her to produce one of those common monsters of incest that seem to be part of the countryside culture, and she submitted to the pressure of the hardened hands of cane cutters, and God knows how many highwaymen stuck their malodorous cocks in her, until my mother placed her in our house—that was the expression, to place—and my father and Ramón would have given her *linga*—a brutal distortion, if you will, of sanding down, in which a piece of sandpaper is used on a wood object which needs to be made smaller—before she came into my hands at the first awakening of puberty and even of pity because a woman just like her, my mother in this case, accepted her only to turn her into her enemy for a whole season and the object of all hypocritical accusations and the mounting suspicions that her husband was being picked off. That was the expression. To pick off someone's husband. I don't know at what moment my mother believed that the girl was a danger—another expression that was in use, to be a danger—enough to do away with her, and I think that she never learned of my goings-about in the orange grove, which would have provided a secondary motive for Nereida's expulsion. My mother. Doña Lina. She lived under the stigma of her own victory.

Two things were clear for me after the disappearance of that girl, and that's the relationship between sex and illegality, or the way that human culture never reveals itself in such a disconcerted form as when it is before its own flesh, and the second thing is that, on the contrary, despite all the infernos assured you lest you not expurgate yourself of the heresy of entrusting that restless subject between your legs to a young woman, the healthiest thing ever is an early relationship with a woman since that keeps you away from masturbation. Once you've tasted that warm skin and felt her slip her hands through your fly, it's very difficult to exceed this experience with your own resources. One day, when I came home from school, she wasn't there. I stopped seeing her around. And I didn't ask about her either. When I was a little older, particularly after I started to frequent the brothels around the edges of Cueto, I understood where her final destination must have been. The whorehouse. Incidentally, she was a presence during those forays since—at least the first few times—I arrived with my money in hand, a condom and the proud declaration that I already had my "milk." In my opinion, I considered it the pertinent statement made in the right place. I say frequent, but there's no need to exaggerate. It probably happened a few times. And the whole transaction could be had for one peso. I stole the condoms from one of Ramón's drawers, and the money if I found it. At eleven years of age I more or less abandoned my passion for horse racing for that of visiting, when I could, *balluses*—the most common term for brothels.

BIRÁN'S "LITTLE SCHOOL" was not the only one in my life. When I married Dalia Soto del Valle, near the house where we lived, in the outskirts of Havana, on the old Santa Fe Highway—the house certain sons of bitches call "Fidel's bunker" (don't think I'm not aware of this, faggots, and that State Security hasn't given me all of your names)—I had a school made for my children, as we started having them, and I named none other than Dalia as the director and teacher of said school. Unconsciously, I think, I was continuing the fief's projection. Dalia has a degree in chemical engineering, so she's competent for that role. If I avoid stating the exact date of our wedding don't take offense, since I held off on marriage until after the death of Celia Sánchez, the Revolution's greatest heroine and the woman who accompanied me for almost the entire Sierra Maestra campaign. She became, of her own merit, the feminine symbol by my side during the first two decades of the revolutionary process. In reality, this was something I had asked of Dalia: that we not marry while Celia was still alive.

Only the children of the very select went to that school—the children of some revolutionary leaders (like Juan Almeida) and some high-level ministers (like Diocles Torralba) and select Ministry of the Interior officials (like one of the de la Guardia twins). Well, what do you make of that? I just cited three nefarious examples: Almeida the mulatto because he's a fool and the other two because they had raised too much trouble since the 1989 proceedings to clean house. Diocles was sentenced to twenty years in prison for corruption, and one of the twins, Antonio de la Guardia, was executed for narco-trafficking. Certainly my father, like me, saw to it that the state provide for the education of his children. He was only able to achieve this up through the fifth grade, more or less, which was as far as Birán's little public school number 15 went. By contrast, I was able to achieve this all the way up through university. And we—my father and I—did the same regarding the decision of our children's careers. My father told me that I was going to become a lawyer, since I was such a talker and chatterbox and since my patron saint—Saint Fidel of Sigmaringa—had received doctorates in canon law and civil law. I accepted this as a matter of course. When it came to Fidelito (the kid I had with Mirta Díaz-Balart, my first wife), I took it upon myself to provide our homeland with a nuclear-issues genius. It was a secret, slow way to get back at the Americans and to reestablish myself as a nuclear threat, something I've been hell-bent on ever since the October Missile Crisis of 1962. I didn't rest until I saw him in Dubna, the closed Soviet city in the outskirts of Moscow, where the future nuclear luminaries of the socialist camp used to study. We even put together a cohort of genius kids, the ones with the best scholastic achievement and highest IQs in all of Cuba—like Jesús Rodríguez Verde—to accompany him in his studies and to serve as a permanent influence on his ideas and imagination. We secretly chose a team of six kids from the nation's school system based on test results. Of these, I remember that little Einstein Rodríguez Verde as the most outstanding. And I designated a proven killer, José Ignacio Rivero, as his permanent guardian until he committed a crime involving two poor boys in Nicaragua, where he was on a training mission, and had to be replaced by Rolando Castañeda Izquierdo (Roli). That Roli was a thug on another level. While he was noble in a way, I ended up putting him in prison for illegal gains, bribery, extortion, contraband and illegal firearms possession during the aforementioned 1989 proceedings. I recall that Antonio—my second-to-last child with Dalia—was the only one I had some trouble with when it came time to set him on his career path. He wanted to be a soccer player. He wanted to devote himself to sports. But his mother wanted him to be a doctor. I said to him, "Son, I think you should study medicine." He insisted that wasn't his vocation. He wanted to be in the Olympics. "There's no soccer at the Olympics," I observed. "And it's not Cuba's national sport either. Baseball is Cuba's national sport." Then, before he could reply with another protest, I said, "Okay. Let's not waste our time on absurd discussions. You'll be a soccer player. But first I'm going to call on you for compulsory military duty and I'm going to send you to Angola for three years. When you return, you'll devote yourself to soccer. You can be the sports guy you want to be, but only upon returning from good old Africa. From good old, black Africa." That same year, this son of mine, Antonio Castro Soto del Valle, a blessing of a kid, entered the "Victoria de Girón" Medical School with the goal of preparing himself through six years of study for a career as a revolutionary doctor, much to his mother's pride and happiness.

As for our education, in the end my father had to send us to Santiago because the little school in Birán had its limits and our mother was convinced that we should have the best training possible.

And so I spent my early years.

CHAPTER 3

THE SOLID TRANSPARENCY OF WALLS

/ / /

Lara was that squealer from Santiago de Cuba whose son—
after the Revolution—would go visit Raúl at the Ministry of Defense,
in Havana; Raúl would never see him. Very early on we converted the
Ministry of Defense into the Ministry of Armed Revolutionary Forces
(Ministerio de las Fuerzas Armadas Revolucionarias, or MINFAR),
and we placed it in a pretty modern building, in the port area, that was
constructed in the early fifties for the naval chief of staff. I think at that
time the navy had more square footage at its disposal in those offices and
hallways than on the decks of all its boats. Raúl went to hide out at Lara's
house after the Moncada attack. Raúl had taken up a strategic position
on the roof of the Saturnino Lora Hospital, from which he controlled the
main access to the barracks, and he took several guards out of combat,
killing them with short bursts from his BAR .30-06 machine gun. But,
having exhausted his meager ammunition, of which he had made excellent use, a noteworthy performance, he tried to find himself a safe place
in a city he supposed would offer him refuge. This man by the last name
of Lara was the one who housed us during our student days at the Dolores School in Santiago, for a sum of money, of course. It only took a few
minutes for him to notify Batista's police. His son, however, had *that certain something*—as we Cubans say—to alert Raúl about his father's actions
and Raúl was able to narrowly escape.

We never had much luck in Santiago. As kids, while we were staying
at the teacher from Birán's house, the drama that our parents weren't
married yet caught up with us, and that (which prevented our baptisms)

Fidel, the favorite student of the Company of Jesus, owners of the prestigious center of learning the Belén School in Havana, where he quickly distinguishes himself in debate and basketball. The picture was taken in May 1945. The young man still doesn't know it, but for the moment he is being mentored by the same order that prepared Stalin in a remote seminary in Georgia. The black sheep that never returned.

led to our being called Jews. Following that began the torment of a radio serial—*The Castros of Birán*—that our half-brother Pedro Emilio paid for on a local station (CMKC), to our scorn and astonishment and to the approval of a growing audience in Santiago, which is villagelike but arrogant.

I have carried these humiliations with me my entire life. But I've managed to put together some slippery and complex ways of talking around them during interviews. I've made up a whole range of evasive arguments, my favorite one being that I found it so strange that they should brand nonbaptized kids "Jews" since "Jews" were a type of very noisy black bird in Cuba. Another story I resorted to was that I was not baptized because there was no church in Birán and the head priest of the municipality Mayarí, about thirty-six kilometers away, only came to the area once a year to perform baptisms, while my designated god-father—Don Fidel Pino Santos—was a very busy man whose schedule never coincided with the priest from Mayarí's visits to Birán. What a rare Spanish fief, without a church and the glimpse of a bell tower. The real reason, that I was a bastard, was avoided.

A lawyer from Santiago, Dr. Manuel Penabaz, owner of the Penabaz Law Firm, represented María Luisa Argota in the divorce proceedings against my father. His son, Manolito Penabaz, who also became a lawyer and studied more or less alongside me at the university, and who rose up with me in the fight against Batista and whom I named as the first civil judge in the liberated territories of the Sierra Maestra, told me that he took advantage of the litigation to show up at María Luisa's house every afternoon for tea. He helped himself to the sweets served solicitously by María Luisa—naturally behind Dr. Penabaz's back—as if this were an unwritten part of the contract. The fact is that while my future comrade-in-arms stuffed himself with meringues and puddings and shortcakes and jams, my parents had to face the harsh reality of having to share their properties, their inheritance and their farm with this fine lady. Then Don Fidel Pino Santos came to the rescue once again. Don Fidel Pino Santos's wisdom and presence. *And his network of amazing relations.* Don Fidel was very good friends with an attorney who was quite the legal eagle. His name was Arturo Vinent Juliá. Don Fidel put him in touch with my father. Things were gaining momentum. On one of the elder Penabaz's visits to Cueto, a town near Birán, on a matter concerning the divorce, shots were fired through his hotel window. That was the

Wild West. Rather, the New Wild West when the old Wild West had already calmed down. There was no more Wyatt Earp and Doc Holliday when the stern Dr. Penabaz, with his solemn black coat, gold pocket watch, straw hat and a bow tie around his neck, drew his Colt .45 with its standard-issue Rural Police long barrel, the one they called a mortar, and shot back at the hessian on my father's payroll who had just fired at him. The problem was that the respectable Dr. Penabaz had the Cueto court secretary in his pocket but he knew the battle was lost because my father—collaborating with Don Fidel as always—had the judge in his pocket. But Penabaz, relentless, played another card and made it so that the case and the subsequent trial were transferred to the attention of Santiago's judge of the court of first instance. This was when Vinent carried out his master stroke. He stuck twenty thousand pesos in a briefcase, but pesos of the lowest denomination, only one- and five-peso bills, so they would weigh a ton and scatter for six or seven meters around when the clasp was unhooked, and he showed up, hidden under the cover of night, at María Luisa's house to carry out that trick and shower her with money on the condition that she stop the proceedings. All she had to do was sign that little piece of paper—and the attached five copies—that he held out to her. She accepted. The trial was over. And that was the end of Manolito Penabaz's succulent afternoon snacks. And the Castros of Birán kept everything. That's when Pedro Emilio, my half-brother, got the idea to produce the serial *The Castros of Birán*. It was a kind of comedy in which he mocked the part of the family with which he had just cut ties. He wasn't in any of the episodes, since he needed to distance himself for his own political ambitions, which consisted of running for representative under the Auténtico Party, a plan which made him quickly exhaust all of his mother's money and coax more out of my father in return for suspending the run of the aforementioned program. The plot development was very simple: Pedro Emilio sat down in a café by the cathedral and said anything that came to mind about the real Castros of Birán to a diligent scriptwriter who listened to the tales of my father's supposed abuses in his diabolical partnership with my mother to strip Pedro Emilio's long-suffering mother of her money and land. Just a few years later, this scriptwriter became very famous and today is one of the few truly venerated icons in the world's history of commercial radio, Félix B. Caignet, who was made famous (and rich) with two radio serials: *The Right to Be Born* and *Angels of the Street*.

Can I tell you something? That was the reason that my presence at the private Catholic school in Santiago ended in disaster. Beyond disaster, for me it was a tragedy. That damned radio serial by my half-brother Pedro Emilio with Félix B. Caignet's script and the star performance—I won't forget it—of Aníbal de Mar (who played the lead role of my father in a farcical tone, as the typical *gallego* of Cuban jester comedies).* It was broadcast on the local station owned by a José Berenguer (Pepín), on a frequency strong enough for everyone within the mountain-enclosed area of Santiago to listen.

It had been quite a battle to allow me to study in Santiago. I wanted to go to the Dolores School, the best of the best of the region's educational institutions, run by the Jesuits. It was a battle because my father refused to spend his money on school for a kid who was so arrogant and disobedient. He finally realized, of course, what he had to do if he wanted to live peacefully in his own house: get rid of me and send me off to study at that damn religious school. There was no other way. It could even be a good move—as my mother argued—for there to be a lawyer in the family. This time, my father sent me to Lara, who was a business friend of his, and at Lara's house I was received along with my brother Raúlito. He was added to the project at the last minute, the project to save Ángel Castro's children from ignorance.

Mr. Lara and his wife and son. He had a small business importing hardware and I think that sometimes he also exported *aguardiente*. In sum, nothing extraordinary, but it was enough to provide him with a house close to Vista Alegre, Santiago's high-class neighborhood. I understand that my father bought Collins machetes from him by the thousands before each harvest, and other farming tools. On occasion, my father could pay him with the excellent *aguardiente* from the sugar mills or with alcohol that he got very cheaply. But with the Lara family I put up with all kinds of shit. In short, despite the money my father, Don Ángel, was paying him for our board, I was not Lara's son, and neither was Raúlito. It was clear that his son was *junior*, a stupid little thing in that stage of youth when he didn't yet have the slightest idea that he would dedicate a large portion of his adult existence and all of his old age to pursuing us in any corner of the Republic where we could be found

* The three main characters of Cuban jester comedy, a sort of creole picaresque, were the *gallego*, the black man and the mulatta.

so that we would give him access to the sinecure of power, and that such actions would oblige Raúl, for that whole period of time, to send an assistant to serve as a barrier.

"Hey, buddy, tell Raúlito that Lara's son is here."

"You mean *compañero* Raúl," they would correct him.

"Buddy, listen, tell *compañero* Raúl that little Laara is here. It's just to see him for a few minutes. Tell him I've spent two years trying to get in to see him."

"You mean Commander Raúl."

"Dammit, *viejo*, make sure Commander Raúl knows that it's me, Lara's son, little Lara. I've been after him for fourteen years now."

"You are referring to the *compañero* minister of the Armed Revolutionary Forces."

"Dammit, for all that is sacred, listen, please, tell the *compañero* minister of the Armed Revolutionary Forces that Lara's son is here. Come on, do me that favor. Tell him I've been trying to see him for twenty-two years. Twenty-two, it's easy enough to say."

"You mean the *compañero* Second Secretary of the Central Committee of the Cuban Communist Party, member of its Politburo and Secretariat, Vice President of the Council of States and Ministers and Minister of the Armed Revolutionary Forces, Army General Raúl Castro Ruz."

EVERYTHING RAÚL AND I did was tightly controlled, down to the twenty-five cents we each received for the weekend. We spent ten cents on the movies, five for a soda, five for a sandwich and the last five for a book of comic strips—*muñequitos*, as we Cubans call them. My favorite ones were from Argentina. They came in a magazine called *El Gorrión, The Sparrow.* Anyway, if we didn't behave, our allowance was cut by five cents for each infraction. But, since I was an expert at disputes and in creating situations, and since I could also count on the ready support of my new sidekick—my brother Raúlito—I decided to organize a brief rebellion of pencils and broken vases and rebellious speeches. I was pondering the tactical proceedings when Raúlito offered to *junior* an infusion made by a "gentle peasant from Birán," when in reality it was a concoction of bellflower (a very, very powerful hallucinogen that is obtained in Cuba with astounding ease from a wildflower by the same name) and that Raúlito had learned to make it in its most concentrated dosage from

Excerpt from a comic strip published in 1962 by the Cuban magazine Mella. *The attack on the Moncada Barracks is the subject. In this excerpt, we see the capture of a fugitive Fidel Castro and his appearance before the judges. The erstwhile reader of the Argentine* El Gorrión *comic strips finds himself transformed into a communist superhero.*

the men who bred fighting cocks and from delinquents from all over the northern end of the province. Junior drank it. He drank the potion. And he was anointed. And the doors of perception opened for him. The two members of the Lara union ran to the dining room and, seeing the state junior was in, rushed to close all the windows to keep such a spectacle inside the four walls of that blocked compartment. Their offspring laughed wildly as he confessed to the most atrocious sins and showed no signs of tiring from a type of Sioux or Cheyenne dance that he was carrying out atop the dining room table while he smashed plates to pieces. Raúlito, who was probably more frightened than anyone else, tried to gain control by running laps around the table. I remained indifferent as I watched the events unfold. And while Lara opened his arms, as if he expected his son to fall like a ball from the sky, I heard his wife say, "Dear, if this wasn't our son, I would say he is on drugs."

We went straight from there to Dolores as boarding students. It cost my father twenty pesos more per month for each of us. The rate for day students, not boarders, was eight or ten pesos. Don't go thinking that for that time it was very expensive, since at Dolores there were no more than a thousand students and there weren't more than thirty of us boarders. A notable difference from other Catholic schools was the absence of black students. Notable because the majority of Santiago's population was mixed-race. The explanation given by the brothers of the Company of Jesus for the absence of black students at Dolores was as impeccable as it was implacable. They said that since there would be so few blacks at the school, they would stand out and they would feel bad and the brothers didn't want to make them—or see them—suffer. At the Belén School in Havana, the Company of Jesus' admission policy was more flexible, especially after Batista's coup d'état in 1952, which brought a wave of high-level government and army workers who were black. Many blacks made a lot of money quickly and wanted their children to attend the most prestigious educational institution in the country—especially since the white bourgeoisie educated their children there.

But the Santiago bourgeoisie were just one step away from erecting a fence around their privileged neighborhood of Vista Alegre. I have never seen, in all of my experience in Cuba, a bourgeoisie that was more segregationist than Santiago's. I think it's inherent to the complexes and feelings of displacement of a provincial aristocracy. At the Dolores School itself, where only the children of moneyed families studied, the difference established between the well-heeled kids from Vista Alegre and the rest of us was marked. They simply refused to have anything to do with us. I don't need to tell you how they judged a student like me, a child of the rural bourgeoisie whose parents broke their backs from sunup to sundown working the land and didn't have time or energy for a social life. Not to mention the pleasure with which one later stripped them of their cement factories and rum distilleries and railroads and port facilities and factories and warehouses and those mansions and their daughters and their wives, and the exultant commanders and captains just come down from the Sierra, still shaking the dust off their boots and long, dark beards, asking them if they were going to allow their girls to go into exile with their virginity intact, charging at these provincial aristocrats of the creole bourgeoisie.

I had a dustup once with a preppy from Vista Alegre. It wasn't a sure thing because he had the advantage of height and muscle over me. But in those days I was already working on my technique of never fighting to lose. I would reinforce this years later with the Vietnamese instructors of our Armed Revolutionary Forces, who never launched a battle against the Americans in the South unless they were guaranteed complete victory two times over. Not once, but twice. Well, anyway, when I saw that I was losing, I would do a surprise leap and start to hit him very quickly in the head, trying to draw blood. Blows to the head are very scary and wounding and drawing blood with those first blows really throws your adversary off. In addition, these little Cuban preppies were in the habit of removing their watches and shirts before throwing the first punch and that's when I took the advantage and pounced on them like a tiger. Then I would beat them to a pulp. At Dolores there were two rules, sanctioned by the priests themselves, that were inviolable. No one could get into a fight after it had started. In other words, you couldn't tip the scale in favor of either of the opponents. The other rule was that when one of the opponents said that's enough, it was recognized that he'd reached the limits of his strength and possibilities, had lost the fight and that it had been a good, honorable fight. But one could never, under any circumstances, continue the struggle, since there was already a loser and he had admitted his defeat. The day of my brawl with the pretty boy from Vista Alegre, one Johnny Suárez, one of my ineffable acolytes of the time was with me. Papito. The three of us were alone and we chose the grove at the back of the courtyard as our battlefield. We were just getting to the place when I acted as if I were bending over to tie my shoe, so that Johnny would get a few paces ahead, which was exactly what I needed in order to hit him with a resounding right hook behind his right ear and let my fist drag across his scalp, opening a wound that practically left his ear dangling off of his head. Johnny turned toward me, as surprised as he was stunned, perhaps intending to ask me why I had betrayed him, but offering his stomach. I took immediate advantage and with my left fist sank a jab into the middle of his stomach that knocked the wind out of him and made him bend over, while he tried to protect himself with moves that were, given those first two punches, completely out of control and purely defensive, and when I withdrew my fist from his stomach he himself offered me his head when he bent forward, just within reach of my right fist, which I slammed into his mouth. The top of his shirt was already soaked in blood and I stuck him with another jab just under his esophagus and two more right hooks right in the face and, for the first time, I felt the blood of one of my adversaries spraying my face. He slumped over without ever having taken a shot at me and he made a gesture with his left hand that was a clear indication that he had had enough. He fell on one knee, then made an effort to stand up. Then he fell back against the wall but made every effort to stay upright. Then he said that's enough. He said it with the word "enough." Papito said to me, "He already said enough." Then I grabbed Johnny Suárez's head with my left hand while I squeezed his throat with my right, pressing all the weight of my body against his, assuming a position that practically twisted his neck, in such a way that I could keep him absolutely defenseless and under my control, and I started to beat the back of his head against the edge of the wall, to crush it right there, my left hand's grip on his hair driving the movement. He had asked me if I knew what a bidel was—the bullheaded Cuban way of referring to a *bidet*.

"Bidel?"

"Then how do the Castros of Birán wash their asses? With their hands?"

That was the root of the fight, which should have ended upon his renewed calls for a cease-fire and Papito's calls for the same. Every time the base of his skull bounced off the wall, Johnny Suárez said, "Enough," and Papito repeated it to me like an echo. I only gave up when I realized that the mass I held with my left hand was all dead weight and I opened my hand and Johnny Suárez slid down the wall, with his eyes rolling back into his head, and collapsed on the ground.

He had to get stitched behind his ear and on his head. The priests, not in my defense but in that of the school, explained to him that it was his fault because he hadn't surrendered, hadn't asked for the fight to end, hadn't articulated the definitive word enough at any moment, something that spoke very highly of the strength of his character and his unbreakable spirit. Papito's word as the only witness was decisive in proving that my adversary never surrendered.

But that afternoon, when they were taking Johnny Suárez to the infirmary, Papito—in a whisper—asked me why I hadn't stopped fighting.

"Papito," I said to him, "he never said 'enough.' "

Papito agreed.

"Look, Papito," I explained, "if a son of a bitch says 'enough,' it's because he's losing. And if he's losing, you can't hear him."

Papito and I became great friends. His full name was Jorge Serguera Riverí. He also became a lawyer, but in Santiago. He was the son of another sugarcane harvester. Old Serguera. In any event, our paths diverged for a while, since I went to Belén in Havana and he was enrolled at a Baptist school, which, incidentally, was the same school where my parents sent Raúlito. Los Colegios Internacionales del Cristo were situated in a mountainous region three hundred meters above sea level and sixteen kilometers from Santiago.

I think Papito has been devoted to the Cuban Revolution ever since he met me at Dolores. At least, since that time, around 1939 or 1940, when we were in fifth or sixth grade, he has followed me without reservation and that's the way it still is.

As for Raúl, he was a couple of grades behind me. The Dolores School—as is known—was run by the Company of Jesus and all of the teachers were Spanish priests, very strict, and whom one learned to respect right away and wanted to follow. There was one in particular, Father Valentino, who led us as if we were little lambs. His greatest ability consisted in playing ball with us, and instead of batting the ball with the recommended device, which is a bat made of *majagua* wood or any other stick as solid, he batted it with his own wrist or fist. I think that my whole world and all I had yet to live opened up the day I understood—at that school in Santiago—the missionary zeal of the Jesuits. It was like the way a vista opens up when you reach the apex of a mountain. The first thing was the military aspect of it all. But the second thing was the mystery and simultaneous underlying need in the mission's concept. The "God exists, therefore I obey" of Ignatius of Loyola's spiritual banner could have been the definitive slogan of our Revolution without changing a single word, not even God, if we understand God as the sum of all the possibilities and ambitions of the men who want to reach Him, in other words, the Revolution as the last mystic possibility for a human being to reach the absolute.

The following is something that I have kept secret for many years. Many. During this time I have covered all of my statements about the Our Lady of Dolores School with the *non plus ultra* veil of a white lie (here I am, defending the brothers of the Company of Jesus before the world's revolutionaries!), although not a straight, explicit lie, rather the use of a bearable truth to divert attention from a reproachable truth. What I will say is that with those saintly men I learned one of the most important mechanics of revolutionary action of all that were subsequently applied in the political process I've led to this day—starting fifty years ago—and which is called the Cuban Revolution. Those robust Spanish priests with the violence they barely contained beneath their frocks only demanded two things: character and conviction. Their stony faces fixed on their cross of fire taught me. Martyrs are only forged by conviction. They taught me that. The necessity of conviction. But they asked my father to take us out of the school. The bad publicity generated by Pedro Emilio's radio serial and the accusation that we were Jews pursued us. My father, in all truth, was outraged. My mother, awash in tears. Brother Salustiano offered a solution. That we be transferred to the Belén School, in Havana. A little farther and more expensive, perhaps, but it was the most prestigious school in the country and it was also run by the Company. Fidel Alejandro would fit right in there. And the other one too. The little mischievous one. What was his name? Raúlillo. That's it. The problem wasn't the Dolores School or the Company, he explained. The problem was Santiago.

At that time I was about to finish my first year of high school, which they let me see through so that my transfer to Belén would seem like an understandable and wise move to pursue a more academically rigorous course of study and to familiarize myself with the Republic's capital, where I would surely practice law once I'd received my degree. (My career had already been decided, as you already know.)

IT WAS ONE OF the best periods of my life. The five years spanning 1940–1945. I was living in Havana and there was a world war in progress. I followed the advances and withdrawals of the forces in the European theater on the maps I cut out of *Carteles* magazine and pasted on the wall of my dormitory at Belén. Nonetheless, I felt distressed that I was not part of the decisions. The events affected me, but were removed from me. They affected everyone all over the globe, but a dozen men, protected in their bunkers, were the ones organizing, moving, deploying. In Cuba, the scale of participation was infinitesimal. It's worth repeating the joke about how Kaiser Wilhelm had to look on a map to find the location of that country with such a peculiar name—Cuba—which was one of forty-four declaring war against him. Our main casualties were the fifty-six Cuban merchant marines who were killed by the sinking of the modest carriers *Mambí, Manzanillo, Santiago* and *Libertad* that were transporting sugar to Morroco, and our main list of services rendered included renting the U.S. the land for the San Julián and San Antonio Air Bases; that Second Lieutenant, Frigate, Mario Ramírez Delgado sank a Nazi submarine off the Cuban coast; and that Mariano Faget, a police sleuth under ex-dictator Gerardo Machado recycled as a sleuth under Fulgencio Batista, captured Hitler's spy Heinz August Lüning and had him executed. I dreamed of martial adventures and imagined myself as Patton or Rommel or even Zhukov, had things gone his way, but it never even occurred to me to imagine myself as Faget, that dark conspiracy genius wearing national police sergeant stripes. I would have more run-ins with him than I could possibly conceive. Mariano Faget. The Party placed him at my disposal during the process of organizing the Revolutionary Forces—in 1959. He was the last piece of the machinery delivered to me (they wavered over whether to hand him over to me or to the KGB) because he was the most precious jewel of their clandestine organization, a man who was already operating in the United States, at the highest level of the CIA, dealing with Cuban files and programs. He had an impeccable pedigree because he had been, for starters, one of the few men who boarded the plane with Batista on the morning he fled Cuba. I was playing war on the walls of the dormitory of the Cuban bourgeoisie's favorite school when the FBI pinned their hopes of controlling Havana on this experienced, hardened policeman, a man made of carbide—as we Cubans say of a man forged in combat—who in the end had not only been recruited by the communists, but answered to this somewhat restless kid, poisoned by reading *Mein Kampf* and other books preapproved by the priests. But you weren't worth a cent to them if they caught you reading *The Communist Manifesto* or *Das Kapital*. You were a dead man if they caught you messing with that. Guaranteed expulsion. On Wednesday, February 3, 1943, I learned that it was all over because the Red Army had annihilated the last pocket of German resistance in Stalingrad. There were 503,650 Germans dead or captured. Three hundred thousand Soviets dead. The siege of Stalingrad started August 25, 1942. It was the German army's finest moment in that year's offensive, which extended to the Kursk-Kharkov-Taganrog line, crushed Voronezh up the Don River and extended to the south as far as the Volga and the Caucasus tributaries. The trophies of war of one of the greatest battles in history were still being tallied at six-thirty p.m. Moscow time, at the moment when the supreme commander in chief sent his congratulatory message to Marshal Nikolai N. Voronof and to the commander of the frontline troops along the Don, Colonel General Konstantin Rokossovsky. Fifty-five locomotives, 1,125 railroad cars, 750 airplanes, 1,150 tanks, 6,700 cannons, 1,462 mortars, 8,135 machine guns, 90,000 rifles, 61,102 trucks, 7,369 motorcycles, 480 cars, tractors and other transport, 320 radio transmitters and 3 armored trains captured at first count. More than 2,300 officials had been captured by then. Twenty-three generals surrendered in the last three weeks. The field marshal, General Friedrich Paulus, commander of the Sixth German Army, had surrendered the previous Saturday along with fifteen of his generals. That last bulletin announced the surrender of Colonel General Walther Heitz, commander of the Sixth Corps of the German army, and of Lieutenant General Streicher, commander of the Eighth Corps.

Each of the reports had at the bottom the unequivocal signature:

J. Stalin.

The Supreme Commander in Chief.

Just eighteen years later, on the night of April 19, 1961, in the Advanced Command Post of the Armed Revolutionary Forces, on location at the Australia Mill, within the very limits of the theater of operations, as I prepared my report on the lightning-fast victory we'd achieved on the shores of Playa Girón in the Bay of Pigs over the Americans and the Cuban mercenaries, I called—by way of a Soviet magnet phone newly put into service—my main executive official in the region, the *gallego* José Ramón Fernández, who was still at Playa Girón counting the captured prisoners and equipment, to ask him a question—of which he was never able to guess the origins:

"Did they bring locomotives?"

"Locomotives, Fidel?"

"Yes, locomotives. We haven't captured any?"

"No, Fidel, no locomotives. But we did capture some Sherman tanks. Five of them."

Not a single locomotive, those faggots. I had to be happy with the nearly two thousand prisoners and their five Sherman tanks. I wrapped up my report about the battle with a general description of the enemy that surrendered en masse and noted that the count was still ongoing of the substantial munitions and armaments captured from the CIA's task force, including tanks and speedboats and their entire felled air fleet and their sunk logistics boats. And I signed it.

Fidel Castro.

Commander in Chief.

The next day, the twentieth, I arrived on the coast with a T–34 tank and an SAU–100 self-propelled cannon and my bodyguards and handful of crew members and in the misty morning we found one of the boats belonging to the mercenary brigade, the *Houston*, which had run aground to the west of Playa Larga. It was trapped there and a heavy column of black smoke rose up from the hold. It had been under fire since the first day of battle, the seventeenth, which was a Monday, and couldn't escape. It ran aground. You could still make out people moving on the deck. The target remained fixed and we fired at it with our two cannons. Then I remembered the walls I had covered at the Belén School with cutouts from *Carteles* magazine and I understood. The two beauties with which we were bombing the hell out of the *Houston* had already rolled through the maps that made my youthful imagination run wild and awakened a longing for something impossible. At last I was deciding the battle. At last it was for real. Once, while reading science fiction writer Ray Bradbury, I understood his infinite sorrow over never being able to travel to a star. He had been writing stories about interplanetary voyages ever since his youth, but he knew that he would never find himself on a spaceship, nor would he ever be able to caress the multicolored tail of a comet. The metallic and tiresome purring of those two heavy death machines that had moved along their mats from the Urals all the way to Berlin, and the violent starts of each cannon shot carried out under my orders in the Bay of Pigs, confirmed that I found myself in the middle of my own stellar voyage.

Then the Cuban CS-13 cutters commanded by Second Lieutenant, Frigate, Mario Ramírez Delgado sank the predatory U-176 that had attacked the four Cuban freighters. The sonar operator aboard the CS-13, *el negro* Norberto Collado, detected its position at a reasonable depth to fire, at a latitude of twenty-three degrees, twenty-one minutes north, eighty degrees longitude, eighteen minutes west, approximately 7.5 miles to the southwest of the lighthouse at Cádiz Bay—on Cuba's northern coast—where they released three depth charges of five hundred pounds apiece, at one hundred, two hundred and three hundred meters and when they were turning around to finish things off, they heard the fourth explosion. *El negro* Norberto Collado heard the explosions louder than anyone, since in the excitement of the chase he forgot to remove his Motorola sonar headphones and concentrated on his eardrums the devastating effect of the expansive waves, so much so that he was deprived of the use of those organs and remained deaf for the rest of his days. Second Lieutenant, Frigate, Ramirez looked at his watch. Five-nineteen p.m., on May 15, 1943. Sonar operator Collado didn't realize he'd become deaf. He merely thought it was silence. He was deaf. This was the only argument the helmsman of the *Granma* offered in his defense when we eighty-two soldiers committed to freedom in Cuba tried to disembark at a point on the southern coast close to the Sierra Maestra in the early morning hours of December 2, 1956. "I'm deaf," Norberto Collado explained to me as he landed the *Granma* atop the mangrove swamp at Las Coloradas Beach. I had already taken out my nine-millimeter Browning to blow his brains out right then and there, and make him into the first martyr of that phase of the Cuban Revolution, and not a martyr for his convictions, of course, when someone yelled, "Airplane!" And we heard the purring of the navy's Catalina off in the distance. I have never been able to remember exactly who it was that recruited Collado as the helmsman of our expedition. Nor have I been able to understand the relationship between being deaf and visually confusing a channel through which to lead one's vessel serenely and without obstruction with an impassable barrier of sordid mangroves.

FATHER AMADO LLORENTE, as many know, was my teacher at Belén. He was about twenty-four years old, had recently arrived from Spain and still hadn't been ordained as a priest. I was a high school boarding student and was about seventeen years old. Llorente taught literature and debate. In addition, he was in charge of the boarders at Belén. I was a devoted sportsman, who received a special medal for my skills in baseball, basketball and swimming. On weekends, when practically all of the boarding students left school to spend time with their families or simply for a change of scenery, I stayed at school. That's how the legend arose that I stayed behind playing basketball by myself or doing exercises to improve my technique or swimming in the school's indoor pool, when the truth was that I didn't have anyone to go see. Birán was more than a thousand kilometers away. This is also the period of another legend: that one time they bet I wouldn't jump on a bicycle and run it into a wall. And I won the bet! Another one was that I was an inveterate liar and that on numerous occasions Father Llorente reproached me, "Why are you lying to me unnecessarily?" To which I responded, "Don't worry, Father, it's just in my nature."

I can say that I had two real friends at Belén. Father Llorente and a kid from Cienfuegos, Eduardo Curbelo. One is deceased—Eduardo—and I understand that Father Llorente is still alive and that he's in Miami at a place called the John Paul II Center, a sort of nursing home for priests—he must be very old by now—and that sometimes he visits the branch of our school Belén that the Company opened there, although it never had the pomp and prestige it had in Cuba. I've never heard a single word of criticism or censure come from Father Llorente; on the contrary, he usually tells anyone who interviews him about his relationship with me and about that evening in 1943 when we took a trip to see the *mogotes* in Pinar del Río, he and about thirty kids, and upon crossing the swollen Taco Taco River, he was almost drowned and I jumped into the turbulent waters to save him. I almost didn't make it. Both of us almost drowned. With a measure of pride, he also says that when we reached the banks and stepped on blessed land again, both of us breathless and practically speechless, I turned to him and said, "Father, it was a miracle that we were saved, let's pray an Our Father and a Hail Mary to give thanks." So we got down on our knees and prayed both prayers out loud with all of our hearts. Why would I contradict him now?

As for Eduardo, he was never in his right mind. He was a poet. Although I think all he ever wrote was one line. Something about an iridescent, graceful lark. Or something like that. I ran into him at the beginning of the Revolution and I named him the manager of the Blanquita Theater, of which we changed the name to Chaplin, where I made my most important indoor speeches. Because of this, State Security had the theater under tight watch. Then one day, toward the end of 1961, there was a short circuit and the lining of one of the lobby's curtains was singed. It was purely accidental and happened at a time of day in which there was no one in the theater. But the *compañeros* at State Security, jealous perhaps, took all of the theater's administrative personnel for questioning at their bureau on Fifth Avenue and Fourteenth Street. This didn't last longer than twenty-four hours, since I knew Eduardo's precarious mental state and ordered his immediate release. It was too late. They caused a bout of schizophrenia that lasted until his death in 1995. I then decreed that he be retired with the highest salary for a theater manager and that he receive all the medical attention he might need. Somewhere among the documents that make up the Special Reserve of the Office of Historical Affairs, there's a photo saved from Belén's billiards room. We're showing our pearly whites and smiling in perfect camaraderie. It's been a while since I last studied that photo. There's Eduardo, so handsome, to my right, still sturdy with his full head of carefully arranged hair, but the look on his face is already that of the poet who is lost without return.

I thought of Eduardo a lot on the eve of an International Labor Day celebration. The parade was looming. It was May 1, 1991. We were facing a lot of problems in Cuba regarding transportation, lack of equipment and lack of fuel, when the miraculous idea of bicycles came up. We acquired close to a million bicycles from the Chinese People's Republic and we started distributing them at workplaces. In just a few months the working class, especially that in the capital, was riding bicycles to work. So much so that the bicycle turned into a kind of symbol of the Revolution. Such was the situation in the days leading up to the May 1 parade. The country was facing a form of survival that we called "the special period in times of peace" and that had been originally designed to keep the country united in case of a military confrontation with or occupation by the Americans. I specifically remember a recording that State Security brought me of a conversation between two Italian journalists staying at the Habana Libre Hotel. They were convinced that they were about to witness the last May 1 under my leadership. I'm telling you this so that you understand how serious the situation was. Meanwhile, our *compañeros* at one of the Personal Security workshops were making a huge assemblage of bicycles in which one, the largest bicycle, was at the head and connected to four other bicycles by a sort of series of tubes that served to carry and support the balance of the one at the head, the largest one, which was, of course, the one on which I would ride, falsely pedaling; in other words, thus your commander in chief would kick off the parade of Cuba's working class on this important date, smiling and experienced and pushed by four of his fiercest bodyguards, who would pedal furiously from one end of the Plaza de la Revolución to the other. In the end, I withdrew from the project. I made the short walk on foot. And then quickly on to the Mercedes. The problem is that I don't want to have anything to do with bicycles ever since December 7 or 8, 1942—that was the date when I broke my nose in a stupid contest to crash bicycles against the Belén School's wall and had to have my nose bandaged up for a fortnight. Ever since then, I've had that aversion. Every time that I run my hand over my nose with its broken septum, now so emblematic of my visage, I remember. That bicycles are for shit. And treacherous. Especially when riding downhill. And I remember Eduardo Curbelo, because he was the only person who was with me and who ran to get help and who stayed by my side, solicitous and kind, trying to stop the blood that ran thick and hot from between my eyes and down and out through my nasal cavities.

At the Modelo Prison in the Isle of Pines, to the south of Havana. A field trip for the law school students. Fidel rules the scene. Under his left arm is Alfredo Esquivel. To his right, Augusto Alfonso Astudillo. The student with the cigar in his mouth remains unidentified. Within seven years, he will go back to this institution to serve a long sentence for his attack on the Moncada Barracks.

PART TWO

The
PAST OF A MAN
WITHOUT A PAST

///

PERHAPS ONE THOROUGHLY DESPISES

THE MAN ONE KILLS.

BUT LESS THAN THE OTHERS . . .

THAN THE ONES WHO DON'T KILL:

THE WEAKLINGS.

Chen, the terrorist,
in *Man's Fate*
—ANDRÉ MALRAUX

4

No One Dies Before His Number Comes Up

/ / /

I WAS ALONE AND I LEARNED TO SURVIVE BY INSTIGATION. I WAS not resigned to the world around me. I discovered the power of words. Not like writers, but the spoken word.

Well, I've gotten off track.

In the story I've told so far, the predominant landscapes have been those of the countryside and the Company of Jesus' monastic buildings. In neither of these cases was my apprenticeship with the word of much importance, except for in Father Llorente's debate class. Now we're entering a new phase. The University of Havana.

I undertook the re-creation of Birán and the setting of my childhood out of the pure pleasure of evoking it and not for the benefit of those who wish to "study" me by any Pavlovian method, since I am not the product of my traumas. I am my actions. My actions to come rather than those of my past, since history and I are one and the same thing. A history released from all of the burdens of childhood and youth, one that began one night in 1952 when I found myself without a single cent in my pockets, alone and with nowhere to go. We'll get to that. Many years later, nonetheless, I discovered something in my battle against small farmers and later with the "Che Guevara" Brigade, which was a type of combat group made up of almost five hundred bulldozers, all heavy devices and sappers, to which I entrusted the task of destroying tens of thousands of hectares of forests, swamps, cultivated and fallow lands; blocking wells and ponds; knocking down public works and homes (relocating their inhabitants first, of course); and destroying everything and anything

Perhaps this was the moment. The discovery of political spectacle and its bewitching effect on the masses. November 3, 1947. Fidel, an obscure student leader, brings by train to Havana—from far-off Manzanillo—the bell with which the patriot Carlos Manuel de Céspedes rang in the rebellion against Spain. He is wearing his ever-present blue suit. And, presto, he leans over to enter the camera's focal point.

that could get in our way and that could be thrown to the ground and flattened—or pulverized by dynamite if they were rocky—by the crushing treads of a bulldozer, like Marshall Zhukov in the Kursk Offensive but supplied with those French, Richard-brand machines. The goal was sugarcane. To undertake the most extensive planting of sugarcane in our history and thus guarantee the 1970 harvest supply, in which we aimed to produce ten million tons of sugar and maintain that level in future harvests until all the other sugar producers in the world market collapsed. To turn the country into a real universal sugar refinery and to relieve myself of all the small farmers while I did so. So, as I was saying, I learned something from them. That a nation's culture is something like the *being* of each of its children, it starts in the smallholdings. In the small farm. In the small tract of land in the country. Why? Because the peasant is the first defender of the ecosystem. He knows where each rock on his land should go, which way the water flows and the wind blows, the months of the year when he should plant what and when he should harvest it, the fruits and flowers that grow best on his land, when and how to make the land fallow, what to do with the livestock's manure, where to tie up the horses and which hive to open up to obtain sweet honeycomb. So wherever he is on the island, he exhales air that you are going to breathe in and fill your lungs with and nourish your entire system with. That's why you are Cuban. Because a *guajiro*, probably crafty and illiterate and very, very slow, who at this very instant is thinking about sacrificing a three-hundred-pound pig he has in the pigpen and about the other thing that keeps him distracted, because the bastard doesn't have a radio, his wife's succulent pussy, he's always thinking about that, he has spent all morning grinding bunches of soy leaves with newly cleared earth to inject it with nitrogen and remove from it any weariness from a previous sowing. Now it's easy to understand why I prevented their proliferation. They personify freedom. Self-sufficiency. But, above all, they are the primary link in our culture. As such, in opposition was the "Che Guevara" Brigade—because I had to divest the nation of that soul and leave it—leave you, the Cubans—defenseless and open to the whims of my designs. Don't consider this cruel or merciless. These are the requirements of a Revolution in its battle to the death: above all, to not allow itself to fade nor to owe anything to another system. You should understand this. In the end, each being is the result of a system. The day when the Revolution respects something, takes something other than itself into account, hesitates or holds back for any reason whatsoever, and above all the day when it finds it necessary to stop for a single moment to choose between what is fair and what is unfair, it's over.

If I've referred to everything above, it is to show that I, Fidel Castro, am not the product of the dark traumas befalling a runny-nosed, marginalized bastard, but rather of the natural surroundings that forged me and of the power of universal concatenation. Either way, and merely as a precautious metaphor—if the secret profile of my basic chemical composition was found among the lumps of that land washed and nourished by rains, caressed by air and cultivated by the hands of farmworkers— I ordered its destruction under the treads and spades and knives of the most powerful demolition brigade known to history—the "Che Guevara" Brigade—which also had (in my opinion) the virtue of forever changing the ecological composition of the Cuban archipelago. It's a general rule. In some cases, it disappears, evaporates, bewilders; in others, it sticks. We started just after the triumph of the Revolution, when *compañera* Celia Sánchez took on the task of collecting all the documentation I produced in two years of battle in the mountains. My messages to column leaders and my usual chidings, my food vouchers and other rations, my notes for speeches on Rebel Radio, my congratulatory message to *el negro* Coroneaux that accompanied two cigars for his splendid management of a .50-caliber in the Guisa battle, my letter to Commander José Quevedo—of Batista's army—so that he would abandon his arms. By documentation, we meant anything that I had left written on any surface. With these materials and others that showed up along the way or that were taped (interviews with battle veterans and witnesses), Celia filled the vaults of a bank in the Havana neighborhood of El Vedado. She named the only known faggot in the entire Rebel Army—Captain René Pacheco Silva—head of the archive and came up with an impressive name for the whole effort: the State Council Office of Historic Matters. Perhaps due to that habit of Pacheco—a man with a very large ass who tended to obesity—of strolling through those vaults with a parrot hooked onto the index finger of his right hand, his elbow at his waist, swinging the hand with the parrot on it to the rhythm of his own movement—"making the little bird dizzy," as he used to say— and to that other habit of letting out a terrified scream every time he thought he had lost one of my little pieces of paper from the Sierra, to be followed by hyperventilating, palpitations and chills, the institution acquired the malicious nickname of the Office of Hysteric Matters. On the other hand, and regarding a different kind of documentation, lest it fall into enemy hands, State Security proceeded to burn all compromising files when the Reagan administration entered the White House—perhaps the most dangerous eight years experienced by the Cuban Revolution, especially after the Soviets advised us that they were not going to embroil themselves in any war on our account. The files that were compromising to us, of course. Not the ones that were still compromising to the counterrevolutionaries. Those were saved. All of them. Pure and disinfected. Every time you hear some Cuban from Miami (or any other place outside of Cuba's jurisdiction) vociferate against us, know that we have a thick file full of his confessions and all of the substantiated denunciations of his brothers-in-arms in a safe place. No one has been released from our prisons without having left us some incriminating document. The others, those who wouldn't speak or who refused to negotiate, those who didn't understand the Revolution's generosity when it was giving them a second chance, make up a large percentage of the executed. The remaining percentage was made up of those who, despite volumes and volumes of their own confessions, denunciations, statements and obliging responses to interrogators and subsequent pleas, tears and requests for mercy and appeals to their youth or the kindness of their captors, were also executed.

A revolution is built on its past. But that which helps it best maintain its vitality is the past of its enemies.

THE COUNTERREVOLUTIONARY paradigm of my childhood—which I will soon put forward—provides clear answers as to why the son of a landholder would rebel against his own class, starting with the strange thesis that he was fed up with inheriting so much land or—what's worse—that he had no interest in owning it or—oh, God, worse still—that it still didn't seem like enough to him and he wanted to take the whole country's land. The great landholder. The ultimate. The absolute. In this paradigm, the imbalance is internal. A childhood enjoyed amid nature isn't taken into account and is replaced instead by the notion that the Americans could stick the segregationist clubs of Banes and of the Preston and Boston Mills up their asses, since all they were really doing was making their own nooses.

The paradigm as they have devised it:

My hostility toward the United States is deeply rooted in my psyche. One, my father was a soldier under Valeriano Weyler, the Spanish general, and was already deeply resentful about Spain's defeat at the hands of the U.S.; two, I was an illegitimate son, something which gave me a deep inferiority complex and is projected in the collective sphere to the relationship between Cuba and the U.S.; and, three, my mother was the servant in the house where the legitimate wife lived with my two half-siblings on the plantation in Birán, the final determining factor for my class resentment.

If to that we add, first, the culture of Banes, dominated by the United Fruit Company, where Cubans were discriminated against in places such as the American Club and where I was snubbed and humiliated; and second, the culture of the Franco-supporting Jesuits who led me to idealize Primo de Rivera and Francisco Franco, it was inevitable that I would be anti-American. If one analyzes the familial, scholarly, historical and social factors that influenced my upbringing, any other result would have been strange. I am not aware of a single influence that would have led me otherwise.

In this way I deceived the Americans and everyone in the counterrevolution, not deliberately, but because I have such an inferiority complex that in my personal interactions I always aim to leave a good impression, agreeing with my interlocutors and repressing my true thoughts and feelings to avoid being antagonistic. Unconsciously, I am obsessed with being accepted. That's why I am so persuasive. Because of that, you should never believe that I really think what I'm telling you.

But that's a counterrevolutionary analysis, for starters because it puts me on the defensive when I'm really a national symbol and a stalwart. In that sense, the Soviets were very refined when they didn't allow me to undertake a self-criticism in 1972, after all the things I said against them from the Missile Crisis through the end of the sixties. But if you want an explanation of what I was and am and how I was tempered, it would have to be practically metaphysical. If I am one of the few visible, identifiable, distinctive and permanent faces in modern history, it's not because my mother slept with my father without the corresponding marriage certificate, making me a bastard or whatever, or because those dogs at the United Fruit Company wouldn't let me into their club, which, incidentally, I was never interested in joining since I was too busy riding horses with Bilito Castellanos—the son of a local pharmacist—or tumbling around in an orange grove with a nice pair of tits. Although if in reality it had all been like that—the Americans in their fortresses at Banes, Preston, Boston—vengeance would be more than justified. Incidentally, that classist story about the spaces the Americans reserved for themselves in the region of my birth comes from Georgie Anne Geyer and the gossip she gathered from some old American ladies she interviewed for her book *Guerrilla Prince*. After realizing they didn't have much to offer—sixty or seventy years later, with a foot in the grave—and that the only thing worth telling about their lives was a small fragment of someone else's life, they gave free rein to the sick minds of that race who made their livings from the ruins of a banana empire and remained determined to prove their superiority, and then they took it out on me. I spent my childhood just a few kilometers from their private neighborhoods. What do you make of it, Miss Georgie Anne? The bastard was so close to us. Would you like another cookie, Miss Georgie Anne? But I understand them. I am—and again, forgive my self-indulgence—the only point of contact with the infinite in their miserable lives full of that human experience that is colorless, odorless and insipid but aspires to one day reach and be anointed by something called glory. I am their glory. Glory that, as you can imagine, swells like a balloon if they confirm that they slammed their doors on my face. Of course, no one is going to pretend that I accepted such testimonies. If you want an earthly explanation, it is that I am always testing myself, I am always facing challenges. I am what I am because of something connected with the gods, with their nature. And when there are no challenges, I invent them. But here we find ourselves in a rhetoric ritornello, since the first quality we recognize in the gods is their relentless availability for a challenge.

FIRST COLT OF THE SERIES

I was speaking of the word and how I learned to use it, going from person to person—pouring words in their ears. Every time I reflect about the five years spanning 1945–1950, I vacillate over which instrument was most effective for my survival, the Colt .45 or the word. For now, I can assure you that both instruments for human understanding were within my control when I entered the University of Havana in September 1945. My father had given me the gun, obtained for a very good price from some American officials on their way through Preston. I had been wanting a gun for years and my father thought it wasn't a crazy idea for me to have my own if I was going to live beyond the walls—that is, outside the protection of Belén's walls—and in a city that seemed to be under rapid combustion due to the political violence unleashed after Batista's departure from the Presidential Palace and the passing of the presidency to the doctor Ramón Grau San Martín. I got my gun. A legitimate U.S. Army Colt.

I would soon develop a habit. I would show up at the FEU* in the evenings. "Just pop in," as they say. My interest was in Manolo Castro, the FEU's president, and some of his acolytes, such as Eufemio Fernández and Rolando Masferrer. I wanted them to notice me. To take me into account. It was essential. You had to conquer the heavens, achieve some position in the FEU, if your goal was politics in Cuba. Thus my nocturnal visits to the FEU. In addition, I have to confess that Manolo Castro was the man with the most influence on me during my university years. While he was the object of my limitless admiration, I was willing to do anything in order to get an approving look or smile from him. It's not that I was willing to kill for him just as a metaphor, it's what I did. Take the two shots I lodged in the stomach of a kid named Leonel Gómez; I did that to get Manolo Castro's attention. I understand we're dealing with a subservience that could only be explained as feminine. Don't be scared away. Calm down, we're not talking about fags here, and besides, it's a very common relationship among the most macho guys. I've seen it so many times among the fiercest combatants who melt in the presence of a dominant figure. It's a relationship that, without my setting out to create it, I see manifest itself toward me among the toughest guys surrounding me, my generals, my commanders, my assassins and my most audacious and daring combatants. But I realize it's something feminine. They blush and everything when I make any gesture of approval—any of my sparse gestures, a slap on the shoulder, a simple word of praise—over some military exploit. Blushing. Yes. Blushing and even jealousy. I suffered both of those things with that son of a bitch Manolo Castro. After having said what I think no other statesman in the world would have the courage to say, I've earned the right to add something: the real reason for my jealousy was that he occupied a

---

* The office of la Federación de Estudiantes Universitarios, the Federation of University Students.

position that belonged to me, or that I should have had and not he. In other words, I thought he was a usurper.

Nothing. There was never anything for me. Sometimes they didn't even bother to respond to my greeting. Sometimes, nonetheless, their comments made their way to me. My problem, they said, was that I had no revolutionary baggage. That I had no history. With the passing of time, on the rare occasions on which I am given to looking back, I see myself entering that FEU office to the right of the Philosophy and Letters Building and I can just barely make them out through the half-open door, some of them resting their feet on the desk, and I hear the secret language in which they communicate with each other, and I hear their laughs of camaraderie that have nothing to do with me, and I console myself and let any lingering resentment dissipate as I remember that Manolo Castro was killed in a side street in Havana in 1948 and that I myself gave the orders to execute Eufemio Fernández in 1961 and that I ordered Masferrer to be blown up in his light blue 1968 Ford Torino in Miami in 1975.

Medium height, olive-skinned, straight hair combed straight back like Valentino. Manolo Castro wasn't strong either. Although I wouldn't call him weak. But he had a lot to say about peasant matters. He had quite a battle over El Vínculo of Guantánamo that resulted in a lot of publicity for him. El Vínculo was a huge farm that the dictator Machado had taken over. There was wild livestock there and a lot of uncultivated land. Manolo Castro would show up at El Vínculo with the guys from the university, after riding a train one-thousand kilometers to the east, where El Vínculo was located, and take the lands and hand them over to the peasants. This turned him into quite the national hero. Needless to say, the university received that spasmodic agrarian reform sympathetically. As opposed to Manolo, Eufemio Fernández was a very elegant individual, good-looking, with careful gestures, and you could tell he wanted to look like a Chicago gangster with his black shirts and thin white ties, or vice versa. But, years later, according to the report I received, he couldn't keep his composure in front of the firing squad. It's very difficult to maintain an elegant demeanor when the barrels of seven FAL rifles are lifted right before your eyes at close range. He lost control of his sphincter and all his functions before they even said, "Ready," and he shit himself and collapsed right there. Masferrer. Rolando Masferrer. This one never shared a thing with the young revolutionary apprentice. He could never stand me. He got in with Manolo—they were very good friends—as a result of those agrarian disputes. Of all of them, the most intense and truly interesting character is Rolando. Or was. He had been a communist and a veteran of the Spanish Civil War, where—in the battle of Majadahonda—he was wounded in one leg, an extremity that he almost lost, but which had the main effect of leaving him with the nickname El Cojo, or "Limpy."

You Have to Aim First

No one knows his killer. I know them all; I'm intimately familiar with them. That Cuban brand of camaraderie practiced by cigar-wielding thugs, so overwhelmingly affectionate. They hug you, they wrinkle your guayabera, they yell it's been so long but you haven't changed a bit, *compadre* (we were all *compadres* in Cuban political society), or you haven't changed a bit, Doctor (all of us doctors), and the hugger and the huggee arrange it to gesticulate to their heart's content, but within safe range of the other's cigar and its ashes. The hug was important because it allowed you to feel where his pistol was beneath his guayabera or jacket, or if it was a revolver, and what caliber shot your back would receive if you dared turn it. It's essential to discern between a pistol and a revolver, because then you know if there's that margin and the warning click of a pistol when it's cocked and the carriage falls back to the top after placing the first bullet in the chamber, *Shaka-nan!* I've spend more time describing it than it takes to brandish a piece, point and rub someone out in real time. Not with the revolver, with the revolver there is perhaps only a *click!* when the trigger has been cocked and by the time a professional takes it out, fires and you're dead, it's about the same amount of time it took you to read from "Not with the revolver" to "perhaps." Perhaps.

The semantics employed are also worth quickly pondering, although there were linguistic nuances in the sector of armed Cuban men that were hard to understand in other idiomatic areas. First of all, due to the enormous difference in social significance that Cubans establish between the common you, *tú*, and the omnipresent formal you, *usted*. So . . . how did he address me? *Usted* or *tú*? Cubans only address people by *usted* who demand a sort of lexical reverence. Damn, he addressed me by *usted*. It's a sign of unequivocal respect for the dearly departed. How are you going to kill someone that you just addressed by *tú*, with whom you're so familiar? Unacceptable. There are codes for everything. It's worth clarifying that these customs were abandoned by the firing squad, where they were better off finishing quickly, *tú*. Hurry up, *tú*, and stand there and stop fucking around.

The first murder attributed to me. Oscar Fernández Caral. He was the head of a kind of investigations unit of the University Police. This police force was created to guarantee absolute autonomy for the University of Havana, which was like an independent island with its own government—including its own police, as you can see!—in the middle of Havana. I was accused of having extorted Professor Ramón Infiesta to give passing grades to someone—I don't remember whom anymore—who belonged to one of the groups. I was trying to win an election. I needed that passing grade so that that someone would owe me a favor. Professor Infiesta, the son of a bitch, accused us, Aramís Taboada (whom I considered a mentor for a while) and me. That we each held guns to his head, one pointed at each temple. That we forced him to sign. Within a few days, I had that detective on my heels and had it out with him verbally. We mutually threatened each other. Days later, Oscar Fernández Caral was murdered at gunpoint near his house. It was late at night on a desolate street in the neighborhood of El Vedado and nobody saw anything. But the suspicions inevitably fell on me. A distinguished judge, Riera Medina, headed up the proceedings. The family hired a very famous defense attorney, Rosa Guyón, who couldn't get anywhere. The case was stayed pending appeal. There was an insurmountable technicality. The murder weapon never showed up. The Central Criminal Lab declared itself incompetent. The same thing happened to me later when Manolo Castro was finally killed. Twice I was accused of the deed and twice the case was stayed. The papers at the time were full of invectives against me in their coverage of the trial. After the Revolution, in the mid-sixties, a small group of rabble-rousers went snooping around the archives of the National Library. One Luis Alfonso Seisdedos—I have the old reports from State Security around here somewhere—who was known as Dracula the Gimp because of a birth defect that forced him to drag his legs, was the main researcher and the one who seemed to really enjoy going through old newspapers. Of course, taking such valuable materials beyond the institution's walls was not permitted and as a result, all of the library's photocopiers broke. It was a time at which I was still not in a position to maximize the censorship machinery, given my courting of Cuban intellectuals and, more importantly, European intellectuals. So I let them look at newspapers for about a decade (which also gave time for Dracula the Gimp, whom I knew was ill, to finally die), until at last I was able to devise an identification system for accessing the National Library's archives, whose complexity and efficiency I doubt is surpassed by that of the CIA's general headquarters in Langley, Virginia. You have to belong to a state organ, either a Party militant or a member of the Communist Youth, outline the purpose of your research and receive the support of a minister or organ chief of a certain level just to *apply* for a limited-time research permit. Oh, and the use of photocopiers is strictly supervised and has to be paid for in dollars. And if they ever push their luck, I'll burn the whole thing down. As a matter of fact, the library and that department in particular called the Enlarged Little Inferno are at the top of the list of objectives to blow up in the event of an American invasion. It's called the Enlarged Little Inferno because there used to be a mere Little Inferno which housed all of the literature of an essentially pornographic nature recovered from Cuban capitalism.

THERE WAS A radio station that broadcast political information almost constantly whose appealing style garnered high audience ratings—"the on-air newspaper"—and was owned by a character typical of Havana and its political ways, very popular besides: Guido García Inclán. I used to show up at his studio window and wave hello. When the audio operator started to turn the acetate placards during commercials and the "On Air" sign went off, Guido would let us in. "What do the restless kids on the hill have to say?" The hill was the University of Havana, which was, sure enough, at the top of an elevation called the San Lázaro Hill. His compassionate manner was part of his job. "No, Guido, look, there's this problem," and you would explain whatever you had to explain, taking your folded speech out of your pocket—the reason for going to see him—and ask Guido for "a chance." He always ceded air time and even urged us on, saying, "Of course, kid. I'll give you the microphone right now. The authorities need to find out about this." The station went by the call sign COCO, so we all called it La Coco. Like the hard fruit of tropical beaches. Although never as hard as García Inclán's well-known tenacity, with which he seemed destined to survive all of our nation's regime changes, social changes and economic changes. All I need tell you is that he made it under our socialist system and La Coco was one of the few semiprivate companies that survived in that environment. It was an explicit order of mine. Do not seize La Coco or nationalize it. Nonetheless, there remained the problem that, because the practice of commercial publicity in the country was finished and capitalist stations operate because of advertising, during socialism they could very well starve and not find any way to pay salaries or electric bills. But I didn't want to hurt the man's dignity. Guido was chubby, straight-haired, and very pale, with a mustache and long nose à la Clark Gable. I wanted him to remain in a position of dignity into his old age, because this would take place during my Revolution, so I ordered a generous state subsidy to cover all of the station and its employees' costs, but under the cover of advertising for sodas and cigarettes and beer, none of which had any distinguishable brands anymore, as all were produced uniformly and according to the supplies the country received—and that the Americans allowed into our ports. It made no difference to say toothpaste or *Pearl*. They all had the same name, *Pearl*, and the tube was blank. No labels. The same thing with sodas. It made no difference to say soft drink or *Son*. They all had the same name. *Son*. In old bottles of Pepsi or Coca-Cola scrubbed of their original brands. Although there were prosperous times in which—depending on the ingredients we received—people could choose between *Son* cola and orange *Son*. We called them *naranjitas*, little oranges. And there were even the occasional, marvelous periods of pineapple *Son. Piñitas*, little pineapples. The diminutive is almost always used in Cuba as an expression of affection, of tenderness. So then La Coco was bombarded with a series of announcements by phantom factories whose only mission was to work as fierce competitors in Guido's imagination upon receiving the book of nine checks issued by the National Bank of Cuba against the account of the Central Planning Board, all for the same amount of one thousand two hundred and fifteen dollars and fifteen cents, national currency, that were dividends of the ten thousand nine hundred and thirty-six dollars and fifteen cents national currency assigned monthly to our old friend. Pineapple *Son* refreshments. Now, that's a pineapple! *Pearl* toothpaste made by the Consolidated Soap and Perfume Company, "Martyrs of Jatibonico," really brushes them for you. Popular Cigarettes. Those are the ones! Et cetera. It was the case sometimes, nonetheless, that one or the other of the products became scarce and we forgot about Guido, so he kept on advertising a product that could take us years to manufacture again, if we even got to it. Nor did I allow anyone to change his editorials, lectures that he delivered daily at midday. He followed a very simple dialectic script, but with his nasal and dramatic voice he could really come out with something that could be interpreted as the very kernel of a counterrevolutionary statement. This happened because his listeners wrote to him or called to complain of any of the many difficulties facing the average citizen in the construction of socialism: a scarcity of everything, an abundance of nothing. Or, as we used to say, an abundance of scarcity, a scarcity of abundance. For example, Guido would read one of those whiny and bitter letters penned by a La Coco listener—recounting how an old house had collapsed and how the old retirees who lived there had devoted their last years asking for better housing and were now both reported to be in critical condition at a clinic lacking in bandages and antibiotics where the director was said to be out partying with the nurses instead of carrying out his duties—and utter a resounding, "Wait until Fidel finds out!" Truly, his faith was unbreakable. I told the Security *compañeros* to pay attention to that program because we'd be able to detect the incipient signs of counterrevolutionary activity there. While you may not believe it, Guido's letters gave me the idea fifteen or twenty years later to take a map of the country and locate the sectors with evidence of counterrevolutionary activity. We used electoral colleges and voting results. In any sector with more than one percent votes annulled or against the government-proposed candidate, we knew what to expect. Pay attention. Just one percent of insubordinate votes, as we called them, was enough for us. A sufficient amount to notice the place and set into motion secret agents, informants, small provocations (for starters) and compromising materials, the planting of bait, tailing suspects and anything that would benefit us to do our detail on the neighborhood.

THE FIRST TIME YOU KILL is the most difficult. I think I've discussed the matter at some point with Papito Serguera, my old *compañero* from the Dolores School in Santiago and later a commander of the Rebel Army. It's very difficult, but has the virtue of clearing the path for the ones that follow. It forces you to overcome lots of internal resistance and the fear of not being able to handle it. But these internal prevention mechanisms are later replaced by a review of what you did well and what you did poorly and then you succumb to a killer's second vehemence: the quest for perfection, and, as such, the need to do it again. That's how killing ceases to be a moral problem and becomes a practical matter. I remember that in the summer of 1986 I was getting ready to travel to Harare, the capital of Zimbabwe—formerly Southern Rhodesia—where the Eighth Summit of Non-Aligned Countries was taking place. Where I would hand over the organization's mandate to Robert Mugabe, the brilliant black president of Zimbabwe, a journey not lacking in danger, particularly given the proximity to South Africa. We prepared ourselves well. Besides reinforcing our troops in Angola and situating the entire battalion of Special Troops in Harare itself, who would permanently patrol all access to the Harare Sheraton, armed with four mobile surface-to-air missile launchers. I also devoted a few days to warming myself up. To losing a few pounds and, especially, to shooting a lot with the 20-shot Soviet pistol. It was then, at the Banes firing range, to the west of Havana, while practicing shots at moving targets, that I noticed my greatest weakness: that I tend to spend more effort watching the objective fall than I do aiming. In other words, I overlook the obligatory mechanics of first taking aim and then pulling the trigger only when the objective is in the center of the scope. It's like saying everything you're going to see has to be through the center of the scope. Extend your arm toward the target, lower your face to your shoulder and aim. Of course, in the end, sometimes it's hard for me to act like a professional soldier instead of the intellectual that I am, thus the unconscious but dominant tendency to contemplate the behavior of the objective that was just shot.

"Listen, Fidel," Papito said to me, in that way he had of always pronouncing my name so properly and deliberately. "Fidel. The first one was so scary."

"You don't need to tell me." That could have been my response. But in situations like that, I don't speak, I've trained myself to listen and not say a word. Before, I had learned the lesson of bringing a cigar to my mouth. When I stopped smoking, I used a Vicks inhaler as a substitute. The cigar was too emblematic to try to convince people that I carried it unlit and only used it to gain time, besides which its presence revealed a mnemonic technique. Stalin usually had an unlit pipe at hand, with its stem macerated by his bite marks, that he raised to his mouth before saying anything to a subordinate. You always need to have a moment for reflection. Never say the first thing that comes to mind. Especially when it comes to expounding on how to kill.

Papito had just come back from Algeria, where he had served as ambassador and—just what we needed—had gotten himself into some hot water internationally in a way that I can only try to explain now and that, to be honest, had happened mostly under my orders, although he was responsible for anything that went badly or went too far. But he was a fine ambassador in Africa and in many ways we owe to him the invention of our internationalist missions that used regular army units and were out in the open. (An armored column that we sent, at his request, from Cuba to support the Algerians in their war against Morocco in 1963.) In fact, Commander Serguera had all the characteristics and courage of a revolutionary ambassador. Restless, congenial, fun-loving and very learned and imaginative. So learned that he was the only Rebel Army officer with whom I could spend hours talking about Rome and Mommsen's books on the subject—which I had studied with Vasconselos. Batista's preeminence over me at any given moment distanced me from Vasconselo's Roman teachings. But what Batista robbed me of by telepathy, he also gave back to me. Papito showed up in my entourage as a valid interlocutor about caesars and empires battling against tyranny.

I bring up all of this because the afternoon we had that conversation about the first people we killed comes to mind. Better said, his monologue. And I remember it because he was mounting an old Bedouin musket on the wall of his home office. He had brought two of them back from Algeria: one for him and the other for me. I had stopped by his house to hear his tales of the desert and to pick up my musket.

"Listen, Fidel. And afterwards it's all the same if it's two or two hundred."

I had been on the verge of saying, It's all the same, don't you realize it? The first one is the only one that matters.

I smiled, almost imperceptibly. I don't remember how the subject came up. But it's the subject on which all conversations with Papito end. Death. But not death under just any circumstance. Death by firing squad. And not just any men. Batista supporters. Many Batista supporters. The Revolution's main prosecutor wouldn't have had it any other way. I changed the subject. The muskets. Papito gave me the one he considered the most valuable and that, he explained, the Bedouins in North

Africa called "Jezail." The short, curved butt is indicative of its use on horseback or camelback. The deep curve at the end of the butt was used to hang the weapon at your side so that it could be fired with one hand while the other hand remained tight on the animal's reins. The musket is from 1821, or earlier, and has an octagonal barrel decorated with a geometric motif and the butt is inlaid with metal, also geometric. Papito kept an eighteenth-century Albanian model.

You, my unknown reader, who may even be one of my bitter enemies, now have access to the confessions that one of my most loyal and determined *compañeros* once heard. But if I refrain from mentioning his name, it's, as we say in the Armed Forces, on a "need-to-know" basis. You are being treated to the privilege of the confessor. What a strange complicity I've discovered between a memoir writer and his reader: I assume you are of comparable intelligence, are understanding of my actions, sympathetic to me and even complicit to a point that is beyond all moral limits.

The first one. I remember that night on which—around three in the morning—I knocked on the door of a friend whose name I shouldn't mention because he lives abroad and I don't know if he could still be charged with obstruction of justice. Although sixty years later the statute of limitations for obstruction of justice should have run out under any jurisdiction.

I needed to shower, change my shirt, smoke a cigar and, above all, talk. I found some dark stains on my shirt collar. Small bits of cranial bone and gray matter had stuck to the fabric. We spoke in whispers and my friend couldn't keep it together.

"We have to figure out a way to burn that shirt," I told him.

After the shower and the first puffs of a Montecristo, I told him that for the second time in my life I needed to talk about something that had happened to me. The first time was when I had a tryst with a peasant girl in the orange grove behind our house. The second time was that night. But there was a difference in sentiments and sensations.

"That first time I had achieved something that all men had already gone through, I just hadn't caught up to them before, and although I was a boy, I was happy and excited about it."

My friend nodded gravely, as he surely thought it was his duty to agree.

"But today I have done something that almost no man does and could die without doing," I said.

"Today, I've crossed a line."

I was pontificating and using my index finger in an admonishing way to help me emphasize this small speech. My index finger as a pointer.

"And do you know how I feel?"

I made a gesture of intimacy while still maintaining a serious tone.

"I feel free."

Casting a Bad Light on Myself

It's 1946 and a young student in search of support to become the law school president tries to curry favor with Manolo Castro by way of a fight with Leonel Gómez, the student leader of secondary schools and Manolo's opponent. He manages to recruit Manolo's acolytes Fausto Antonetti and el Gallego Ángel Vásquez for the task. He hits Leonel with a shot to the abdomen, but Leonel is miraculously saved. The young student has to get rid of the gun that was a gift from his father and turn to his older brother, Ramón, to send him a new gun as a matter of urgency. Of the same caliber, please: .45. Manolo Castro, far from supporting the young student for his act of solidarity and the courage demonstrated in the encounter, sends him a message. "Tell that guy that I'm not going to support *some piece of shit* for law school president" is the spirit and the letter of the message. Without Manolo Castro's support and less still without that of Rolando Masferrer, the young student is left in a precarious position—left dangling from the brush, as we say. Then the situation takes a complicated, tragic, mournful turn when Emilio Tró—the leader of the Insurrectional Revolutionary Union (Unión Insurreccional Revolucionaria, or UIR), the rival faction to Manolo Castro and Masferrer—deems the attack on Leonel a personal offense and decides to carry out a trial against the idiot who shot at him in absentia. What did they say his name is? Fidel Castro. Yes, that one. That son of a bitch. Alfredo "El Chino" Esquivel is the one who tells the young student. Listen, *guajiro,* tonight you're dead.

A medical student—I forget his name, I have to forget one sometime; it's impossible for one to chronicle his own history perfectly—runs into El Chino at a popular Havana intersection, at San Lázaro and Hospital Streets, about eight blocks from the university steps, and says to him, "Hey, man, what are you doing just standing here, giving yourself up like that? Don't you know they're going to kill all of you? Where's Fidel?"

I was at one of our usual coffee shops at the corner of Twelfth and Twenty-third Streets, in El Vedado, one hundred meters from the main door of the Colón Cemetery with its marble carvings.

It's late afternoon and the sun is setting behind the distant and pure Gulf current that serves as the dividing line between the city and the universe when El Chino and that anonymous—let's not say forgotten, which sounds so disparaging—medical student fill me in on the situation and I hear the echoes of my own death at the hands of a pack of crazed, bloodthirsty revolutionaries when an imperfect solution pops up shyly.

"Fats Echeveite," I said.

Fats Echeveite was one of Emilio Tró's associates.

"Or Arcadio Méndez," I added.

Another one of Tró's associates.

"And why the fuck did I get so involved with that Manolo Castro and with the FEU and with the MSR?"* I asked.

I got Fats Echeveite before he left his house, all cologned up and wearing a clean, pressed guayabera as if he were going to see some girl and not to a trial where I would be sentenced to death in absentia. "Tell me where it's happening, Fats. That's all I want to know. You go your way and I'll go mine." At the house of Estrada, an old revolutionary from the Machado days. I don't remember who opened the door, just that he let me pass with a gesture somewhere between resigned and ironic. They were in the living room, settled in on sofas, armchairs and some straight-backed chairs brought from the dining room. The cups of coffee were steaming on the table where they were working, and they all had their cigars already lit, taken out of a box of H. Upmann No. 4's that remained open next to the enormous silver tray with cups and cloth napkins and always taken in a minimum of two, one to smoke now and one—or more—to place next to the Parker pens in the upper left-hand pocket of the spotless white guayaberas they all were wearing.

There were no less than ten men. What my mind retains of that first scan is Guillermo "Billiken" González, Fats Echeveite, José de Jesús Ginjaume, and Arcadio Méndez.The owner of the house, Estrada, wasn't in the living room and didn't show up all night. Then my scan, starting on the left, as the rapid-eye visual compendiums usually do, ended at a point

* Movimiento Socialista Revolucionario.

on the right where I knew that, enthroned on his velvet chair, distant and serene as a caesar who instead of entertaining his palate with grapes taken delicately from a plate held for him has discovered the intoxicating effect of smoking and the unequivocal air of I-order-and-command that only a Cuban cacique can assume completely, who signals or points at his desires with a sweep of the hand, his hand, holding a cigar between his index and middle fingers, was Emilio Tró.

I sensed that I could be saved when José de Jesús Ginjaume broke the ice with:

"Kid, you've got really big *cojones*. Coming here into the jaws of the wolf."

José de Jesús Ginjaume. World War II paratrooper who had made anticommunism his religion. He was the second in command of the UIR and I think he beat Tró in saying what Tró was thinking and that he did so in a flattering way, that suddenly the sequence of events, and with them my destiny, had changed. Ginjaume had shown his boss that he knew how to read him and set the appropriate and honorable conditions for Tró to easily reconsider an opinion he had already expressed in front of everyone.

"Beyond ballsy," said Emilio Tró.

Everyone murmured their approval even before knowing what he would say next.

"Intelligent."

An increase in the approving murmurs and a greater cloud of smoke expelled from the lungs of that crowd of Cubans.

"That's what this asshole is."

The approving murmurs stopped. The sentence was not conclusive. But I was probably the only person there who had realized the weight of anticipated camaraderie with which he had pronounced the word asshole.

Tró was a gentleman, you could tell just by looking at him; a virtuoso, a veteran combatant of the war against the Nazis, head of the UIR, who didn't enrich himself at the cost of the Exchequer, and whose responsibility for certain bloody acts had to be understood in light of the political circumstances in which they took place.

"And we need guys like this."

Sure enough, I was saved.

Nonetheless, I had to satisfy the curiosity of all present, explaining the details of the incident with Leonel and what spurred me to act in such a reckless manner.

When it was over, Emilio Tró himself offered me a cup of coffee, already fairly cold, and grabbed the three cigars that were left in the box. With his own hands he put two in the upper left corner of my striped jacket (I didn't have a guayabera) and placed the other in my right hand. He also struck the match and held it at the end of my cigar while I inhaled with moderate to medium force and made that supreme product of Cuban industry burn. The ceremony was over. I realized that it was the only type of blood pact on the face of the earth lacking in knives and brothers cutting their fingers or slashing their palms or wrists. It was within a race of irreducible sybarites who drank water in great pitchers of fine crystal full of tinkling chunks of ice and who, every night, rubbed up against the silky smooth asses of their wives—the missus—and who, when it came time to kill, got together first under the cover of smoke.

Emilio Tró blew out the burnt match, let it drop into the ashtray and, with an air of resignation, said:

"Ever since I saw you come in, I realized that you already know something. I don't know how you could have learned it. But you know."

I wasn't sure what it was that I was supposed to know. And I never would have guessed correctly. It's one thing for you to think something and another for someone else to say it to you with the same words.

"That no one dies before his number comes up, kid. No one."

His older brother, Ramón Castro, took this photograph in October 1947. Fidel has sought refuge on his parents' property after the Cayo Confites expedition. The scene of his childhood seems unscathed. Behind him, one can see the water tank's cement columns and the caiguarán beams that hold up the house, leaving enough room below for an animal pen, Galician-style.

5

State and Revolution

/ / /

The Cayo Confites Plot

The Cayo Confites adventure—in the summer of 1947—is the one I found most enthralling of all the military operations and plots I witnessed in the whole period prior to the Revolution, and it is the event from which I learned the most useful lessons. As far as plots go, there was nothing like it until the great conspiracies against the revolutionary process began in the summer of 1959, and the only possible comparison to the logistics—including ships and cargo planes and fighter jets—is the 1961 Bay of Pigs invasion organized by the CIA.

Cayo Confites was like a clinic in military intervention. The 1933 revolution in Cuba did not fulfill the internationalist calling of all revolutions at the time and only truly expressed itself fourteen years later on that islet off Cuba's northern coast, a nine-hour journey from the nearest port, Nuevitas, that faced keys and islands inhabited only by wild horses and turtles and thick clouds of mosquitoes. But it had a clear revolutionary basis. If we stop to consider it, the Mexican Revolution accomplished the least, since, it has been said, it was too occupied with its rural component. The Chinese revolution, Mao's, never went beyond its borders for the same reason, besides which the Chinese were too hungry and their cities, starting with Peking, smelled too much like shit for them to worry about what neighboring countries were doing. Not so with the French Revolution. There was no one who was able to export their revolution like the French did until we came along with ours, given that American internationalism manifested itself more like imperialist expansion. I'm not bringing up empire now to slip in a critique. No, what I'm saying is that the French revolutionaries exported ideas, and while the Americans may have exported ideas as well, they did so as they conceived them in tangible forms: machinery, businesses, capital and not going too far out on a limb to bring their revolution outside their borders. Stick the troops in Texas and to hell with everything else. Our *ideas* are the cavalry and the Gatling guns. Of course, not every country you spread internationalism to is the same, nor do you achieve satisfactory results in all of them. The French revolutionaries that contributed to the American Revolution planted the seeds of imperial expansion. The irrepressible desire—highly justifiable, of course—to make universal the concepts of liberty, equality and fraternity found propitious and applicable conditions among the Americans. But, take note, only among the ones in the North. I don't know about this equation when it comes to the slave owners of the South. I say this because of the Haitian experience. In other words, when those same French revolutionary advisors connected with slaves, or at least not with the American landowners and businessmen from the Midwest, but rather with Haitian slave society, what they created was bloody social chaos of such magnitude that two centuries later, things still haven't normalized. And then the Soviets came with all those fleeting European pocket revolutions prior to World War II and their support of the Chinese. But we arrived with an internationalism that has been the least damaging and the least oppressive because we forged the first internationalism in the history of an underdeveloped country with a small population, no industrial or technological base and a mere culture of folk singers and heavy baroque writers, in other words, internationalism in its purest state, without the slightest possibility of imperial projections. Fine, then. I, the head of the Cuban Revolution, undertook my apprenticeship with some very fucked-up but revolutionary guys, leftists in one way or other, and definitively communists, like that limping Rolando Masferrer, or anticommunists, like Manolo Castro. The amazing thing about all of this is that even as I was learning about internationalism, the Cubans were organizing a military operation of the same scope as the CIA would for the Bay of Pigs.

THE GOAL WAS TO overthrow Rafael Leónidas Trujillo in the Dominican Republic. I would say that there was no better reason to call for a revolution than that mulatto. He had already been in power for seventeen years when we began our preparations to overthrow him. He was still there, fourteen years later, in 1961, when he was assassinated by some military people (his close friends just one day prior). Up until then he had managed the Dominican middle class and bourgeoisie's wealth as he pleased. The main sugar mills, the railroads, the hotels, commercial aviation, cattle farms, ports and airports, weapons and munitions factories and any commercial business which would offer him dividends became his personal property. It goes without saying that he controlled all government institutions, beginning with the presidency and, of course, followed by the army, the police, the air force, and the navy. The cadavers of the opposition and political dissidents left by this brutal and disproportionate endeavor have never been duly quantified. But the neon signs (the advertising agencies were also his property) were also vicariates of a potentially divine message. "Dios y Trujillo," they proclaimed everywhere in bright lights. Many cities, avenues, highways and buildings were named after him or some of his close family members. In 1930, the same year in which he became president, a strong hurricane hit Santo Domingo, the country's capital. After rebuilding it, he baptized it with his name and it became officially known as Ciudad Trujillo. In short, to capture that city infested with statues of that mestizo, trained in 1921 under the American Navy infantry, that was our goal.

A thousand men made up the expedition. The invasion was planned for September 25. There was money. The region's countries had come out of World War II rich. God bless sugar. What a lot of sugar those kids, the GIs, needed to face the Panzertruppen. Our Negroes cutting sugarcane and the mills grinding them and those hardworking white guys over there fighting with their Garand .30-06's and swallowing sugar, sweet, noble sugar to energize the soldiers of freedom and to wake up their minds. It was the easiest thing in the world in 1946–47 to find weapons in the United States with little regulatory control, besides those which the Americans themselves provided to governments in the region during World War II. And the troops? Where do you find troops in Cuba for an adventure like the one in Confites? "Very broadly its 'intellectual' background (as the word is used in the Caribbean), is the fetish of revolution which is frequently manifest in feverish form," was the explanation by the American intelligentsia posted at the embassy in Havana. An interpretation—in my opinion—none too far off the mark, by the way. Although its rhetorical delicacy does not negate its racist undertones. For the bulk of the soldiers, it was the idea of revolution, and as always, among Cubans, the possibility of action, of a real adventure that would remove them from the mediocrity of their daily lives. Those Americans were so lazy. They bombarded you all day with Errol Flynn and Tarzan and John Wayne and then they were scared silly when you picked up your weapons. Wherever you went, in the cartoons, at the movie theater, in pulp fiction, there you had them, riding with their weapons at the ready. But they wanted things to go no further than the page. What they needed to put on the covers of their magazines or at the beginning of their movies, right after the notice that they're not responsible for any resemblance to persons living or dead or real-life occurrences, is that the material that follows is for admiration only, not imitation.

MANOLO CASTRO AUTHORIZED IT. Masferrer didn't want to do it at all. In the end, Manolo's criteria for admitting me to the expedition prevailed. I didn't want to be left out, no way. Besides, the expedition was no secret. It was one of those usual shouted secrets among Cubans. I knew that same environment of public secrecy in the days leading up to the October Missile Crisis of 1962. Everyone was in the know about what was happening and if you weren't, all you had to do was open your window in the early dawn hours to see the giant Soviet Kamaz trucks go by taking R-12 (SS4) and R-14 (SS5) medium-range nuclear missiles with which World War III would be initiated. Do you see? For Cubans, the instruments that would decimate all human presence on this earth and would breed faith in the absolute truth of the Einsteinian adage that it would be the last war among men, were nothing more than the source of neighborhood gossip. There were R-12 (SS4)'s being strolled about the outskirts, you could even put your hand under the heavy canvas cloth and touch them, the way you would affectionately tap an elephant's hind leg in the circus's final parade.

The Cayo Confites plan originated in the San Luis Hotel in Havana, where many Dominicans stayed, including Juan Bosch and General Juancito Rodríguez, with whom I was on the friendliest terms and who gave me a gun. Juancito was distantly related to Trujillo, but he was one of the ones who gave the most money for the invasion. Another one who helped a lot was José Manuel Alemán, the Cuban minister of education. All of this began around 1944.

The man in charge of the operation was Manolo Castro and I didn't want to be left out. I hopped a plane to Holguín, a city in the north of Oriente Province, where I knew that the men—all volunteers—were gathered in a huge polytechnic school next to the lands belonging to the Holguín Regiment, one of the two big military units in that province. The Grau administration's commitment to the operation was obvious, since more than a thousand men and their combat aviation mobilized openly. They let you into the polytechnic school. But once in, they wouldn't let you out. It was a given that showing up at that place and passing through its doors was equivalent to taking some kind of Teutonic or Crusaders oath. The six or seven steps invested in going from the sidewalk to the school's interior, to its gardens and wide esplanade in front of the main building, had their own significance in those days, and it was that you assumed, of your own volition, a certain destiny. Someone asked my name. A little while later, he returned with a message from Rolando that I should get the hell out of there. I told him to say that he hadn't seen me again and that he should make up another name for me. But shortly after, I got a message from Manolo. I didn't have to go anywhere. I could stay.

MANOLO HOLDS OUT HIS HAND

July 26, 1947. At dusk, they loaded us into army trucks and took us to Nipe Bay, on the north coast. From there to the barges, in groups of twenty. Thus, they started dropping us off at Cayo Confites.

I disembarked with the seventh or eighth group. The trip took about nine hours from the coast because Confites is one of the most removed islets, in the north, of the Cuban archipelago. They used navy patrol boats with the ID numbers covered over by broad strokes of paint. The sun was setting when we opened the boat's door and the beach appeared before us. There, standing on the sand in a military uniform lacking any insignia, a Thompson slung over his shoulder with the barrel facing down and his hair blown about by the wind coming off the sea, was my commander, Manolo Castro. You could see other men running around in small groups who were lighting bonfires, something we would soon learn was the most effective method against the mosquitoes. Manolo was the welcoming committee. A one-man committee. He greeted us with a smile or a pat on the shoulder when we walked by him and simultaneously made a gesture as if inviting us into his palace. His palace was a sort of Villista camp, with taciturn, silent men around small bonfires beneath the starry night. There was no singing. A curious thing in such a crowd. But the Cuban soldier doesn't sing.

It was my turn to walk by Manolo Castro. Then he stopped me. He grabbed my right wrist with his left hand and extended his free hand, shaking mine.

"I'm so glad you came," he said to me.

I nodded. The gesture caught me by surprise and I didn't know how to respond. But he was singling me out, since he hadn't shaken anyone else's hand.

He let me pass. He was opening the doors of his palace for me.

The wind hadn't died down yet, so the bonfires were bending leeward, in the reigning direction of the wind, which was from west to east, and the Villista camp of my first night as a soldier kept a stable and serene course in the Gulf's current.

NOW WATCH THIS scene carefully. The bow ramp of the old boat has descended onto the beach like a batrachian, and we start to empty out of it. It's the closest we have ever been to Normandy or Inchon. I mean, regarding the use of an LCI* and of taking possession of a beach. Manolo Castro, with his slightly wrinkled but clean khaki uniform, and with his Thompson over his shoulder, receives us. It is his hour. Nothing was ever better for him before and there's no reason to bet on his future. His hour. It's clear from the light in his eyes and the indifference with which he oversees the combatants' arrival and the charming way he directs a smile of approval at everyone as a group and not to anyone in particular. No exaggerated affection. Nothing that would cause a prince to lose his composure. It is we infantrymen who will probably meet death face-

---

* Landing Craft Infantry.

to-face tomorrow, it is we who have this opportunity to offer our lives thanks to him. Then he stops me. With his left hand, he grabs my right wrist, extends his free hand and shakes mine.

"I'm so glad you came," he says.

I nod. The gesture has caught me by surprise and I don't know how to respond. But he is singling me out, since he hasn't shaken anyone else's hand.

Now let me go back. It's just one moment. Rewind. He stops me. With his left hand, he has grabbed my right wrist, extended his free hand and shaken mine.

He still hasn't told me that he's so glad I came and I'm looking at him while I listen to the men bivouacking around their bonfires dispersed beyond the range of sea grape trees that signal the border between the beach and the interior of the key with its thin vegetation; I can hear the din of their conversations and an unexpected chuckle here or there and I know that they are lying around the bonfires and that they are the ones giving the fire shelter, and although the glow is still tenuous since it has not become completely dark yet, I think I can see the sparks reflected in the eyes of my interlocutor Manolo Castro del Campo. It is then that I understand.

It's that simple.

I understand what my entire existence is going to be about. It's the opposite of the sensation they say the dying have when they see the infamous light at the end of the tunnel. What I experienced in that moment might have been a kind of revelation. What flashed before me was not my past but my future.

I think this is the quintessential defining moment of my entire life. I've never told anyone about it. In all truth, this isn't for you. I am telling myself for the first time. I've spent years going over the intricacies of my own being. Every time I try to get to the bottom of my own silent introspection, despite my own natural resistance, and reach that border where matter ceases to be a root particle of energy to become consciousness, what I see before me is a fourth-year engineering student from the University of Havana saying, "I'm so glad you came."

AT LAST I WAS connecting what I learned under the Church's strictest religious order with a possible destiny. Let me explain. When I disembarked there were two levels of understanding for me to come to terms with—two cogs, or two pieces, or two lines of reasoning, that I had always lacked in order to fulfill my dreams. They revealed themselves then, one after another. The most important thing was for me to become aware of the mission. The missionary sensibility learned from the Jesuits had always led me to a void. I had stayed in contact with the Company. I frequently went to the San Juan de Letrán Church in Havana and met with a priest there whose name I won't reveal at this time. But I can say that on these trips I was accompanied by a guy named Mario Jiménez, whom we used to call "Luna Lunera," who is still alive and can be found in Miami to confirm this. Well, at least I can tell you that he used to stand outside the church, keeping guard, and that every once in a while he would come upon me unannounced in the half-dark interior while I read the New Testament with my priest at the back of the church. I am not willing to break my vow of silence with the Jesuits just now. I can only hint that perhaps one day I'll devote an entire book to the story of my extracurricular relations with the Company of Jesus. But there was an imbalance in their proposal. Something was wrong. And it had to do, of course, with the mission. It was in Cayo Confites that I understood my mission could not be to serve God, that my mission had to be earthly. All of those surrounding me there, without exception, were in search of fortune and power, and while they were no less revolutionaries for it, I had to differentiate myself from them. The first thing was recognizing that all of those men ceased to be revolutionaries the moment they reached their desired position. Due to that lesson, I was obliged to keep watch over the revolutionary process, not because of these poor laborers of history, so easily satisfied with any sinecure as long as it left their bellies full, but rather because of my condition. However, this was a lesson I learned after I came to power and it is tied to a device the Soviets discovered that is not exactly Trotsky's permanent revolution, but rather Stalin's spirit of constant civil war. Revolution is directed inward, and in that sense it ends up becoming a very dangerous device for the revolutionaries themselves; not so with civil war, because however you approach it, in a civil war you assume a defensive position and defense is always directed outward. But I was saying that the lesson of Confites was earthly. I realized that I needed to procure some land for myself. That islet led me to the key conclusion that one needs space, some quantity of square kilometers of earth, somewhere to plant the banners of your mission, which was why the Jesuits had restrained me, reasoning that they wanted to keep me for God.

The second thing was the meeting with Manolo Castro. I realized why I had to fight. And that's leadership. A very specific kind of it. It yielded another kind of power, one that didn't allow for discussions or intellectual outbursts and in which you had a chain of command. The chain of command. Damn. That's everything. Therein lies *the thing*. And that's what I learned and felt while I shook Manolo Castro's hand. He didn't notice. What was happening in that moment didn't even occur to him. He thought he was shaking the hand of a subordinate whom he wanted to single out and that I, the subordinate, was accepting his gesture with due gratitude. When we parted, however, from that handshake, I was Fidel Castro who had in that instant completed his revolutionary education and understood that Manolo Castro was just one more accident in Cuba's history and if he was ever to be remembered, it would be due to his relationship with me. In fact, because he had been my adversary. It was better for him to be an adversary so the remembrance would be more intense. But something happened that always awakens my call to rebellion. I know it wasn't a conscious attitude in him. But what does your conscience matter to a lion when you awaken him? It happened that he wanted to show me that he could single me out, and as a matter of fact, he showed anyone who noticed the scene that he was above me. And that was it. The understanding that Manolo Castro and I were at opposite ends of the chain of command and that our roles would be immediately reversed.

SO, WE SPENT two months there. You got an Argentine Mauser for training. There were no blanks. The whole camp was a war zone. We had to return the rifles before bathing, around four in the afternoon. Our bath was a quick dip in the ocean. You also had to take care of your necessities in the water, always noting the direction of the wind so that the material expelled would not go back to the key. If you were on guard duty, you kept the rifle until the next day. The guards were set up at six or seven points around the key. You weren't supposed to smoke on guard duty, but we all did it to ward off the mosquitoes. We slept on that horseshoe-shaped beach. The open part of the horseshoe faced the north and the sea crashed against it, preventing the sand from settling.

The area had sharp reefs and the fishermen who made it out to sell to us their catch said that in winter the waves crashed loudly over them. A row of olive-green wooden boxes on a promontory of sand, a promontory covered by a layer of sea grape leaves, constituted the main barracks. A fat tobacco-chewing mulatto in an undershirt was in charge of the arsenal. He took down all the deliveries and returns of the Mausers in filthy little notebooks. Manolo Castro frequently left the key. So did Masferrer. They say that Manolo would go to Havana and Miami to purchase planes. They even say he was jailed once in Miami and interrogated by the Americans. I don't know what Masferrer was doing when he was gone. It happened on my days off. When he was back in the key, I wouldn't take my eyes off of him. He did the same with me. He sent me messages. We were in plain sight of each other on an islet that was less than one square kilometer long with very few places to hide, but he used the messenger system. "Tell him that as soon as he turns his back on me, I'll kill him," he said to me in one of his messages. In addition, he stood out. He walked around with a Texas hat and aviator sunglasses and, as opposed to Manolo, a small retinue of guards was always with him. Years later, one of the stories that went around the counterrevolutionaries in Miami was that Masferrer stood up to me in Confites and hit me. It's a story that seems to provide them with enormous satisfaction. Of course, I am not going to answer to such stupidities, but I didn't want to leave the detail out, so that you don't think I'm being elusive and thus lend them any credibility. It's best to remember that they made me a squad lieutenant.

THE MOST PRESSING PROBLEM, the one that was quickly breaking down, was supplies. It was a problem of logistics. They deployed the recruits en masse before having all the resources available. To American intelligence, this signaled imminent disaster, although in my opinion assembling without resources isn't always harmful. My experience is different. If we had sat around waiting for the resources, the Cuban Revolution would still be a pipe dream. Or I'd be one of those old party fogies handing over the banner of communism to some impertinent kid. In the Sierra Maestra, we made a rule that to join us you had to bring your own rifle. You have no idea how many guards were killed in the towns and cities around the Sierra to relieve them of their rifles.

I think that there were as many or more than the amount of men killed in combat. There came a time when a guard couldn't go to whorehouses because as soon as he removed his weapons, some kid would sweep in and kill him to make off with his Garand or Springfield. And off to the mountain range he would go. It was sacred. Now that weapon was his and no one could ask him to switch with anyone else. I remember the day we were joined by someone who would later prove to be one of our most valiant and loyal combatants: Antonio Sánchez, whom we called "Pinares" because he was from Pinar del Río. They brought him before me after he was rejected for showing up in the Sierra unarmed. He was truly offended and doing all he could to reason with that group of rebels in a way that was so absurd yet impassioned that he won their sympathy. He came right up to where I was sitting, by some wooden logs, and said, "You're in charge, right? Fidel Castro. Yeah, you. Just like in *Bohemia* magazine. I just want you to answer one question. So tell me. When have you ever seen someone convene a war without weapons?" I have never forgotten Pinares's use of rhetoric. Convene a war without weapons. I have always asked myself where he came up with that word so rare among Cubans. Convene. In any event, I immediately came up with one of those Solomon-esque solutions so appreciated in the Sierra Maestra campaign, the schematic of which, by virtue of seeming fair, established an expeditious principle of justice and helped spread a positive image of the Revolution in which it was no longer just an idea or a lofty goal, but rather the benefit of a state that ran smoothly and had a growing number of citizens who enjoyed this new jurisprudence. Don't forget this because it will be very important later. The basis of the paternalistic Cuban state lies in this quickly executed justice of the Sierra Maestra, and also in the need that forced us to tailor the application of justice, of laws, of rules to any situation. Note that in almost half a century of the revolutionary process we've been decent enough to never make the fleeting claim that the law is the same for everyone. So, Antonio Sánchez Pinares. About eight years later, Che himself would tell me he would appreciate it if I could let Pinares join his Bolivian outfit. And I call him Antonio Sánchez Pinares because it became the habit to add his nom de guerre as a second last name. "Let's do this," I said to him. "And don't disappoint me. I'm going to stick you with Camilo. This is him. One of our finest commanders. Camilo Cienfuegos. And you're going to go with Camilo. But Camilo is going to have to feed you, right? And you won't be able to pay for that food because you don't have any way to fight. In other words, you're like a cane cutter who shows up at the harvest without a machete. Wait. Wait. Let me finish. So, what are you going to do? Well, you're going to carry the sacks of *malanga* and you're going to carry the boxes of bullets we gave to Camilo. Right? You're going to do all of that. Then, when there's a battle, you're going to see how you dodge enemy fire to go after one of the weapons belonging to a *casquito*. What do you think? Do you like that plan? So there's nothing more to discuss. As for the rest of you, get ready, we're marching on. Marching. And you, Camilo. This guy is yours. Here you have him." *Casquitos*, little helmets, was what we usually called Batista's troops. Our disembarkment from the *Granma* provides another example of how our logistical handicaps led us to success nonetheless. There were eighty-two of us—armed however possible—aboard a boat at half mast. Half mast isn't a nautical term, but a Cuban way of saying mediocre. Not completely fucked up, but not completely reliable either. Just half mast. We also had eighty-something men making up the Special Troops we sent to take over Angola. Cortés had fewer men when he set out to conquer Mexico than Pascualito had for the same task. To take over a country eleven times the size of Cuba. Pascualito is Pascual Martínez Gil, who became one of our bravest combatants. He even became division general. Although eventually I had to throw him in jail, when we disbanded the Ministry of the Interior. I'll explain later. Tomás, another general of ours, was good at taking action without waiting for a full complement of resources or troops. He even named his tactical procedure. He called it *"revolico."* "Lots of *revolico, Comandante.* I never wait for the ideal complement because the ideal complement doesn't exist." Tomás was the Division-General Raúl Menéndez Tomassevich, who became famous and even achieved legendary status as the commander who annhilated the counterrevolutionary bands in Escambray.

THE PROBLEM, THEN, is the territory where you deploy your men; if it's an islet, you're finished. But if it's a country or a mountain range, the preassembly logistics need not worry you in excess. See, I took care of the dietary provisions problem in the Sierra with the cows from the ranches on the plains. I told Camilo Cienfuegos to organize some shooters to open up all the corrals and scare the livestock into the mountains, to *agílar* them in that direction. *Agílar*, I think, is a Cuban peasant corruption of *arrear*, to herd. Although it could also come from *agilizar*, to speed up. The herding of stampedes of thousands of head of livestock running into the Sierra on their own hooves was a tactical maneuver that some called "genius." Thus ended hunger on the mountain. Camilo was happy as a kid on those cowboy outings. That's when he started using a Stetson hat. As far as the weapons go, you know all about that. I don't need to repeat myself. Kill a "little helmet," grab his Garand and come join us. In Angola, with the Angolans or the Portuguese, we had different tactics. Rather, variations on a concept. In reality, what we did there in the end was act as a dissuasive and somewhat counterrevolutionary force. If you really look at it closely, from a macrocosmic point of view, it was a revolutionary act because it made inroads vis-à-vis imperialism in the defense of universal revolution, but if you look at it from an Angolan point of view, by preventing the rise of poor peasants' organizations the act left a troubling margin of doubt. But that country and our fifteen-year presence there are a clear example of the subordination of individual concerns to general concerns and I think we'll worry about the rights and wrongs of that later. There we didn't have any other enemy to oppose us. And Exxon and the diamond companies were thrilled with our presence and the way that Cuban tanks scared off the native guerrillas under the Chinese influence, like the ones led by Jonas Savimbi or Holden Roberto. The problem with the Special Troops guys, at least concerning the mission I gave them, was that they got there and occupied the country. They were armed from head to toe. Everything else they had were the normal provisions one would take on a passenger airplane for a transatlantic flight. We weren't concerned with how that enormous country would take care of the logistics. To begin with, if they were hungry upon arrival, they could take over the airport café in Luanda, still fully stocked by a French supply company. Now that I think about it, when I saw him off at the military section of José Martí International Airport, I don't recall having given Pascualito any money.

So of course the Americans, always concerned with how to feed their soldiers, would produce that kind of analysis of Cayo Confites. Applying the Pentagon's logistic rules to a revolutionary enterprise is a strategic error. But it's their nature, and it happens because they don't understand the nature of barbarians. It's better for us if there aren't enough logistics, since that deficiency makes the booty dearer, more desirable and, above all, the men more ruthless at the attack. And they say I don't appreciate individual initiative. The problem isn't individual initiative, it's property. When property is limited to what you can carry in your pockets and rucksack, I have no problem with it. Beyond that, there are other considerations at play. Of course, there were *compañeros* who stuck their paws in other men's rucksacks to make off with a cigar or a can of sweetened condensed milk. In these situations, Che and even Papito Serguera were quite inflexible. They always maintained that theirs was a balanced formula necessary to keep discipline in which not even the modest belongings in a *compañero*'s rucksack could be taken. I think that's how we ended up with more men killed in the Sierra Maestra over cans of sweetened condensed milk than in battle against Batista's troops. You could say that the cans of condensed milk made up for the death toll caused to soldiers in the brothels.

And that concludes my essay about revolution and logistics.

Let's finish up with Cayo Confites.

GENERAL GENOVEVO PÉREZ DÁMERA, head of the Cuban army, couldn't resist two temptations: Trujillo's money and the pressure exerted by R. Henry Norweb, the American ambassador in Havana. It's kind of me to call them "temptations." Pérez Dámera was in Washington for meetings to discuss the preparations for the invasion of the Dominican Republic from Cayo Confites, and had already received the pertinent instructions from the Americans (in addition to hiding Trujillo's money in a safe place), when he retuned to Havana on September 15. His job was to abort the mission. Intercept it however possible. President Grau had decided to remove himself from the matter and delegate all responsibility to the head of the military. So on September 24, General Pérez Dámera declared—"without a doubt," according to the American ambassador—"There is nothing in Cayo Confites." Nothing at that time was fifteen hundred men surrounded by the army and the navy in Cayo Confites. Nothing. But we were surrounded by battleships. The only option was to surrender and be taken—as prisoners—to terra firma.

When the ships came to get us, on September 27, I waited for my chance. I wanted to board one that didn't belong to the navy. They said that two LCIs were heading for Nipe Bay, where there were army trucks to take us as prisoners. Birán was relatively close to Nipe, so I decided my journey would end there. I gave a different name when I boarded the LCI. Things were rather chaotic and there were few sailors. And no less than three hundred men vomiting at once. I said to myself, Get a raft ready with weapons and grenades. We sailed for nine hours. Someone mentioned revolting and taking the LCI on to Santo Domingo and making me the head of a company. But that didn't work out. We took off from the beach at five in the afternoon and it was the dead of night when we made it into Nipe Bay. The navy speedboat was approaching us to escort us. It's impossible to inflate a raft with your own breath, so I stuck my shoes, the grenades and the guns in an oilcloth bag from the blinker light that I had quickly taken in the middle of the entire ruckus. I didn't think anyone saw me jump into the water. The weight of the five or six guns and the grenades acted as a sinker. I was about to release my cargo out of fear that I'd get dragged to the bottom of the bay when I succeeded in stabilizing my position and started to rise. I followed the closest bubbles, which I myself produced with the utmost sense of economy so that I wouldn't pass out or lose my sense of direction. To my right, diagonally, I could make out lights, as big as platters, that seemed to be floating and getting farther away. I later learned these were reflectors being used to search for me. The most agonizing thing about an unassisted night dive is that you have no way to know or approximate where the surface is. The surface surprises you when you emerge from the water. First comes sound and then, immediately, the splashing. Then I heard the voices and saw the reflectors. But they were moving away and the navy speedboat did what I assumed was a brief search maneuver. But immediately the crew halted that project and dedicated itself instead to the easier task of escorting the prisoners. They were searching for me. Or they searched for me. Even if it was only for a few minutes.

I made my way toward the lights that I thought were about half a kilometer distant.

A while later, I felt the swampy bottom on my knees. I reached the coast after about a twenty-minute swim, hauling that bag along the top of the water to air it out and see if it could float. I stood up when the water reached my waist and kept walking until I was on dry land. I decided to wait until dawn, so I could get my bearings and seek out the sugarcane path from Preston to Birán. And so my clothes could dry. In the distance, I heard the barking of dogs. They all seemed to have detected my presence.

AFTER SPENDING A DAY clearing through brush and reaching the Preston road, I was lucky enough to be picked up by the driver of a Plymouth. The thing I remember most precisely—and even with gratitude—about my arrival home was how my older brother Ramón treated me. And the fact that no one reproached me for anything. It was clear that they were up to speed on my adventure even though I hadn't sent them any news of it. My mother hugged me and caressed my cheeks thinking it was the first time she'd seen me with a beard, a mere hint of one, still an adolescent's, sparse and reddish. "My son has a beard," she said. It was pride in that sign of virility that existed only in her perception. My father merely sighed with resignation, "Ay, Fidelillo, these battles of yours cost me so dearly. They're expensive as all hell." Ramón was the one who took the greatest pleasure in my return. Later I found out why. When someone had mentioned at dinner that they hadn't heard from me in weeks, Ramón didn't stop eating his soup while he said, "There's no phone in Cayo Confites." My father corrected Ramón a few days later: "If he hasn't made contact with us from that *cayo* you mentioned, Ramón, it's not because there's no telephone, Mongo. You still don't know your own brother. He hasn't made contact because he doesn't need any money there."

I was still in my mother's arms and Ramón was waiting his turn when I asked him to pay the driver. "I offered to pay him five more than the going rate."

The man asked three or four pesos for the ride—the run, as we called it. Mongo gave him ten above that.

"Here you go," Mongo said. "Plus ten."

I could hear him clearly although he had practically jumped right into the car.

"Wait. Wait a minute. Let me tell you something. If they come looking for my brother, it's because you're a faggot and you reported him. If that happens, I'll kill you. Did you get a good look at my face? Do you have any doubt that I would kill you? Right. Good day, then."

"My little boy has a beard," my mother was saying.

I spent the next few days wandering the yard in Birán, shirtless, and taking care not to stray too far. I followed my father's advice and didn't shave my beard off right away, so as not to hurt my skin. When I finally had to pick up a razor, just before my imminent return to Havana, I was left with pasty skin underneath that differed from the rest of my face, which had tanned during the weeks of my frustrated expedition on an islet off Cuba's north coast.

AFTER CAYO CONFITES CAME communism. My encounter with its literature.

I was getting away from all that foolishness at the university, and increasingly I understood that the sinecures of power are not power—or even an approximation of it—when Alfredo Guevara showed up, then Leonel Soto shortly after and even *el negro* Walterio Carbonell, university buddies who disclosed to me that they were fanatical bolsheviks. From that trio came the initial suggestion that I stop by the Party bookstore or that I accompany one of them there, to see *what new material had come in*. I still made the rounds, going from the mundane bewilderment of a conversation about Primo de Rivera, and its subjugable arrogance, to the folks at the Argentine Embassy who bombarded me with Peronist literature, thus adding a new ideological layer to the previous layers, and then I would swing by the mansion belonging to the Popular Socialist Party (Partido Socialista Popular, or PSP) –"the headquarters"—on the sumptuous Carlos III Avenue. It took three strides to hop up the eight marble steps—I remember it as if it were today—and on the right-hand side was the glass door and through the door and sign shaped like a half-moon, you could see the books.

State and Revolution. I think about reading that on one of the days I stop by. Chapaev. I think I'll read that on another occasion. Until, at last, I make up my mind and grab the little book from the rack. I look quickly from side to side to make sure no one has caught me doing so. No one. There's a clerk, the same one as always, whom people call Limpy or the Cripple, and a few other regular customers. Somebody told me, I think it was Walterio, that this invalid—I insist on calling him that—was one of the most dangerous guys in the combat structures of the Party and that he owed his condition to tuberculosis. Years later, I learned his name—Lalo Carrasco—and we used it to christen one of our best-supplied bookstores, in the lobby of the former Hilton Hotel. In general terms, it was known that in times of social peace, he ran the bookstore with marked reluctance and spent his time there devouring all of the literature that passed through it. But when there was a demonstration, a clash with the police and firemen, he quickly abandoned the pleasures of reading and was the first to go out marching. Armed with a one-inch-thick rebar—one of these pieces of metal was always lying around the corners of the bookstore—he specialized in breaking the ankles, or collarbone, of the first law enforcement official he tussled with. The slogans his comrades shouted didn't matter as long as he could put his crippled foot well up a policeman's ass. I came to a conclusion. His way of leveling the playing field with the rest of humanity was to try and make most people limp or spit blood. Street fights and proletarian barricades gave him an ideal platform for his objectives.

Vladimir I. Lenin. After reading him for the first time—of the hundreds of times I would go back to him—at whatever time it was that I finished his book, I don't think I realized that I had just read the most important book of my life, but I did possess knowledge of far more important things. The bourgeois state must be razed to its foundation. And it's very easy with a revolution. The Revolution. What a collection of symphonies and resonances and fears and echoes coming from the past came together in one single strike and closed like a fist in that one word. The Revolution. What an increasingly subjugable concept. And that ending, in which he tells you that he has to leave the book unfinished because of the events in Russia. And that he is going to live revolution instead of filling notebooks. Because—I know it by heart, I don't even have to look it up—"It is more pleasant and useful to go through the *experience of revolution* than to write about it." Let me tell you something. I still hadn't graduated from law school when I read that pamphlet, but, while I was only nineteen, I had already killed. And I knew something that all men who have killed know from the moment they've killed for the first time. That I had lost God. You're conscious of the loss the moment you've rubbed out the first one—let's have the balls to call it what it is—more than anything else, you've put an end to any dialogue with God. From then on, you're charting your own way in the universe without any assistance. That's why the subsequent attacks are so easy. But. A revolution? What is a man willing to lose to undertake a revolution?

SO ONE DAY I take the little book that has been calling out to me since the first time I saw it, with the big bald head and that cynical little smile on the cover. It had to have dazzled me, like when you learn—at whatever moment in your childhood—that babies don't come from the stork. The bourgeois state must be razed to its foundation. And the Revolution facilitates this. It makes it really easy. Upon assuming the state's power, the Revolution becomes gibberish because the proletarian dictatorship ceases to be a method of government in transit and becomes a method of government in and of itself, at least that's what we do in communist countries, the man seemed to be saying to me, a much more insensitive and screwed-up dictatorship because it lacks the mechanisms and institutions that tie down the bourgeois state. Oh, what a perfected method of all power. The power whose raison d'être is to nullify all powers. Lenin was the only one who could have achieved it. I devoted a lot of time to studying him. Not reading him, but about him. He had the best combination out there, that of a practical politician and a theoretical one, in other words, an intellectual, and you have all the reason in the world to fear intellectuals, because they sacrifice everything in pursuit of an idea. Following the example of the French Revolution, these ideological battles become very bloody affairs. One need only see the frequent use of that machine— the edge of that forty-kilogram blade promulgated by Dr. Joseph-Ignace Guillotin that executioners and their servants can't even bother to wipe clean of the drops left by the blood spurting out under pressure from the approximately forty thousand jugulars and carotid and subclavian arteries cut during the course of the French Revolution in a procedure that took 2/100 of a second from the release of the splendid blade which fell from a height of 2.3 meters at a velocity of 7 meters per second until, with a force of impact of 400 kilograms per square inch, completely decapitating the victim in a further 1/70 of a second— to know exactly what we're talking about. It's bullshit to claim the method is humane when it could take up to thirty seconds for one to lose all consciousness. Forget about the neck. Measure it on your watch. Thirty seconds. Your head, your whole life, your consciousness, rolling around in a basket amid the prints of the clattering dentition of other heads that have chomped like rats, and breathed in air that would have required the lungs now laid out on a separate plank, and the sudden feeling of the incomprehensible lightness of no longer balancing atop a body when the executioner grabs you out of the basket by your hair to show you off to the rowdy masses and the last thing you see is your decapitated body, chest down, and you suddenly experience an autonomy of sensations and feelings that are still yours but that struggle disconnected in dissimilar regions of existence while you remain attached to the plank where your heart continues pumping blood and the reserves of blood still circulating around your brain lead you to believe you are about to vomit when you finally fade into silence. He was a professed follower of the Jacobins, an heir of theirs, magnifying their terror and proclaiming it to all. Lenin. There are orders written in his own hand, kill them all, he says quite frequently. Execute the czar. Do away with this percentage of the Kulaks. Let the Cheka take care of it.

I will record the place where I first read Lenin. It was a setting most favorable to him. It was a guesthouse, of which there were many around the University of Havana, charging very reasonable rates. They had certain rules, about noise, about the volume of radios and conversations, and above all about immorality, in other words, it was expressly forbidden to have young women in the rooms. Almost all of them provided three meals a day—included in the rent, of course—and if there was an inconvenience common to all of them, it was that they had shared bathrooms. Although everything was always in pleasantly pristine condition. I had to move a lot, sometimes for security reasons and other times because the houses found out who I was and threw me out right away. I read *State and Revolution* in a guesthouse that was on a nice street in El Vedado, Seventeenth Street, practically on the corner of L Street, about seven blocks away from the university steps. That day, they served a delicious meat-and-potato dish with a thick layer of black beans made all the better by a pinch of sugar and an immortal and glorious glass of cold water with ice cubes clinking around inside. After I had my coffee, it was essential to send for a cigar. There was usually a kid in those houses who was the errand boy. You placed your order and gave him a dime or a quarter. It was about eight at night. I lit my big cigar, made a seat out of the pillows against the back of my bed, placed my gun on the nightstand, removed my shoes and settled in to read. Two pillows, one gun, an unmade but clean bed, a pair of shoes on the floor and another pair in the wardrobe, a replacement suit and two shirts in that same wardrobe, a few pairs of socks and underwear in the drawers and a pile of change and bills that must have come to about fourteen pesos and constituted the sum of my capital worth at the moment in which I began to read. "What is now happening . . ." I read. "Happening . . ." I got up to look for an ashtray. "What is now happening to Marx's theory . . ." I got comfortable. Perfect. I licked my fingers. I opened the small volume again. "What is now happening to Marx's theory has, in the course of history, happened repeatedly to the theories of revolutionary thinkers . . ."

In wrapping up, I'll offer a comparison. It has been said many times that Machiavelli's *The Prince* is my bedside book. Wrong. This belief must come from the embarrassment its reading causes in the petit bourgeois who spend time analyzing me. Machiavelli is the furthest they can get in their political daring. But Machiavelli was more of a snob than anything else and *The Prince* becomes a second-rate book next to Lenin's and its phenomenal ending that constituted the very border between literature and the demands of an existence without a moment of rest, and in a way, this book —*The Autobiography*—is now taking the same path in reverse: after having lived the Revolution, I come to write about it in these pages. From *The Prince*, I take everything. All Machiavelli. He's the one who says to me, Listen, all of these moral things are like autumn leaves and you have to kiss little old ladies although you find them repulsive. But the guy you beat up once is your enemy forever. Don't forget it. The prince is a realist. A true politician who has to move past the stereotypes in his head. That's what it's about. On the other hand, there's a subliminal message. It's hard to be honest. To write honestly. When I first read him, I said to myself, Someone is finally saying something to me that I want to hear, that I need to hear: get those stereotypes out of your head. Especially the ones having to do with morality.

But Lenin had something else. It was ecstasy, because he didn't have to imbue his arguments with any moral justification. It was fire. It was illumination. Lenin is pure applied mechanics, pure instrument, pure teaching of how to use resources. My greatest discovery in those readings, and I say it many years after having completed them and looking at them as a whole, was that all revolutions were possible if one knew how to identify the causes that led to them. The revolutions. Cause and effect. In our case, the formula would be cause and use. It was the decisive and most important thing I have ever read because it sustained my spirit through all tempests and gave me the only moral shield for my revolutionary project. One cannot be opposed to revolution. One has to be opposed to the causes that lead to revolutions. The Revolution exists, therefore it is obeyed.

The patriot Céspedes' bell and some impetuous speeches. Behind him, to Fidel's left, is Leonel Soto, one of his contacts with the communists; below him, Alfredo "El Chino" Esquivel; resting his hand on Alfredo's shoulder, Rafael del Pino; behind Rafael, Enrique Benavides. Of this group of devoted friends, only Soto will remain by Fidel's side after the first months of the Revolution.

6

The Basket of My Snakes

/ / /

"The guys from the UIR want to kill Manolo and that blood is going to be on my hands."

I remember saying this to Alfredo "El Chino" Esquivel, my closest *compañero* at the university. The UIR was dwindling and in danger of extinction. But they wouldn't give up their quest to avenge Emilio Tró's death. Emilio had been killed on September 15, 1947, while I was in Cayo Confites with the rest of the expedition. I had that feeling once again of being left out of events. Of not controlling events of any goddamned importance. And of being lost to God's hand, on an islet adrift in the Gulf Stream with only five outdated devices cast away by the Cuban army as my only vehicles of communication. The three RCA Victor radios and two Motorola radios connected to truck batteries that just barely brought us news from stations in Havana and Camagüey and the United States amid an unbearable curtain of static. And nine hours away from the nearest port! Through one of those stations we found out that Mario Salabarría's people had made a surprise attach on Emilio. Emilio was having lunch at the house of Morín Dopico, a police commander, when the shooting started. They fought for three hours, in the middle of a residential neighborhood on the west side of Havana, with a newscaster right on the scene, his description of the shooting as enthusiastic as if he were reporting a baseball game. Aurora Soler, Dopico's wife, and then Emilio Tró, went to the door. Behind them was Lieutenant de la Osa. They walked over to the wall surrounding the garden, where there were some well-tended hedges. The shooting began again and the wife was felled. De la Osa took her by the arms to lift her up, while Tró grabbed her ankles. They had barely reached the sidewalk and it was unclear whether Emilio was trying to stand the woman up or whether he was trying to hide behind her voluptuous figure when they opened fire on him again. Emilio collapsed. He fell at Lieutenant de la Osa's feet. He was already dead when he fell. Manolo Castro's head became the most sought-after trophy. They weren't even deterred by the fact that Manolo, like them, was weakened by the failure of Confites. Although in any event he remained the most important man at the University of Havana. Everyone surrounded him. Everyone was attentive to him. Everyone said, "Manolo said this to me," or "Manolo said that." It was enough to use his first name. Manolo. And everyone knew who you were talking about. At the university, he was at the center of everything.

And, although it's true that I had made those kinds of comments to El Chino, in a way I also understood the need to do away with Manolo Castro. His existence had gotten to be bothersome. An obstacle. I don't deny that, within the general context of the UIR's opposition to Manolo's continuing to live, I might have encouraged them. But it was a drop in the bucket. I don't know if you'll understand me. On the night of February 22, 1949, I was traveling in a car on San Lázaro Street, with the university steps behind me, on my way to central Havana with Billiken, Crazy Manolito, and maybe José de Jesús Ginjaume, when I told them to drop me off. I had an exam coming up, I think, and I had to study. Nobody tried to deter me or took offense, since there was no plan and we weren't on our way to any kind of operation. They continued on their way toward the area around the Parque Central, which was the center of life and society in Havana from the beginning of the century more or less until the fifties, and where, in addition, a hundred meters from the park, along what used to be the country's main commercial street, San Rafael Street, a very narrow street constantly packed with cars and buses—stood a small movie theater devoted to the projection of cartoons and matinee showings of Flash Gordon or Hopalong Cassidy. It was called—and still is—Cinecito, and one of its owners was Manolo Castro. It must have been around nine at night when Billiken saw Manolo in front of his establishment. He was drinking a cup of coffee, standing in front of the store on the theater's first floor. They turned their car around and then parked facing the street, leaving enough space for a quick getaway. Somebody, probably Crazy Manolito, stayed at the wheel with the engine running. They say it was Billiken who shot him. Right in the head. From behind. And that Manolo's brains spilled out like scrambled eggs on the pavement. Later, many versions went around. But in almost all of them, I was named. I had the same experience fifteen years later when President Kennedy was assassinated. That of standing accused of a murder I didn't commit, but that could clearly be tied to me in many ways. Well, if I've already said that I didn't discourage any ill will against Manolo Castro, why should I keep from saying that regarding Kennedy? If I didn't quite instigate the execution, I did have enough discernible information about what was in store. Later, I'll go on at length about this subject.

Incidentally, any communist participation in Manolo Castro's murder was always doubtful. At the university there was an eternal student, Manolo Corrales, from an established, moneyed family, who had been recruited by the Party. Manolo Corrales was studying medicine and was assigned the task of "tending to" Manolo Castro and influencing him. I can't say with any certainty whether Manolo Castro knew of his affiliations and whether he accepted them or not. But the story goes that Manolo was inside the theater when this other Manolo, the communist, made him come out to tell him God knows what story. In other words, in a matter of minutes Manolo Castro's brain, which was now lying in the middle of San Rafael Street, had gone from the peripeties of Donald Duck to the idle conversation of a sly communist until it was placed at a comfortable range for a gangster's shot.

But the most astounding version I know of my hypothetical participation is the one offered on December 20, 1957, to the Batista-leaning press by the young Manuel Marques Sterling y Domínguez, son of one of Batista's ministers, determined as they all were to find reasons to discredit me, and which is kept in our historic archives. Manuel maintained that I had acted as the prompting agent for the killers, dressing up as a lottery ticket vendor and taking a strategic position in front of the theater to positively identify the objective.

Although I've gotten considerably ahead of the story, I've done it to close the Manolo Castro case. And—to truly finish, by way of acknowledgment—I should say that the only friend who took the murder as a personal attack was Rolando Masferrer. He made Manolo Castro's death a personal matter. He assumed it as his own, as we say. For example, Eufemio Fernández, who always introduced himself as Manolo

Castro's closest friend, didn't do anything. He didn't lift a single finger to honor the memory of his friend. The one looking for a direct confrontation was Masferrer. He never took comfort. He spent all his days in search of vengeance.

THE SEVENTH PROVINCE

The communists held the deep-seated belief that only an Orthodox Party guy would make a good communist. They used terms of military discipline and attitude to justify themselves. But nobody came to power with Orthodox politics. It yielded good soldiers, not leaders. Even good conspirators. But they were always lacking in imagination. They forgot how essential it was to imbue their activities with adventure and personal initiative.

The Cuban Revolution is a miracle of the imagination. If I had been led by the outline of Marxist mathematics and had waited for the economic contradictions and that whole rigmarole about the gains proceeding to the insurmountable, definitive and total crisis of capitalism, we probably would have had the opposite in Cuba. Things being what they are, today we would be the United States' puppet country, a solidly capitalist emporium of riches. That's the miracle of the imagination I'm talking about. I transformed the country from being a puppet of the United States into a communist bulwark. At the very beginning of his mandate, after the March 10, 1952, coup d'état, Batista could be accused of two or three crimes, and even this is probably an exaggeration. There was a student, Rubén Batista, whom police killed in a protest march. I don't remember any others. It was us who started to kill. The number of dead we produced is infinitely higher than those under Batista's regime. On the basis of the ten killed under Batista, maybe a dozen, if that, we were able to produce, with that reasoning, the quantity of thousands of dead left lying in the fields during the revolutionary process. That's what requires imagination. Marx provided the incentive, especially in the *Manifesto*, not in *Das Kapital*; and Lenin, the methods. But they leave you on your own. They give you the thesis and the tools, but from there it's all you. And that was where the communist recruiters at the University of Havana got fucked.

I've allowed myself the previous paragraph to provide such a clear explanation even knowing that it could hurt some feelings because at this stage of the game I don't think it will seem pathetic or deceptive. The worst thing I could do would be to try to justify more or less deaths in a nation that, against all predictions, has conquered the heavens.

Anytime I saw any of the communists show up at one of our activities, I would say to El Chino Esquivel:

"Don't let him anywhere near us, it's damaging to us."

But, just as the communists projected themselves in the most Orthodox way possible, the repressive forces of anticommunism seemed to suit them. As a matter of fact, the adversaries acted as if they had a tactical agreement that neither group would move on from the positions they already occupied. To the approval of the Cold War FBI, the officials Mariano Faget and José Castaño, today remembered as "gentlemen" and real architects of "scientific interrogation," and the astute, monastic and indefatigable J. Edgar Hoover, the head of the FBI, had established solid collaborative ties between the services of both countries and between themselves personally. Especially Hoover and Faget. Faget came from the former Office for the Investigation of Enemy Activities, activated in Cuba during the Second World War. Hoover called the capture in Havana of Nazi spy Heinz August Lüning a "magnificent piece of police work" and said that Lüning's subsequent confession to Captain Faget that he was working under contract for Admiral Canaris revealed "the most outstanding case of espionage in the Americas [during the Second World War]."

Following the battle against the Third Reich's spies, Hoover, in a move that was characteristic of the start of the Cold War, used Faget in the battle against Cuban communists. But Faget made a mistake: tailing the creole caciques from the Popular Socialist Party (PSP)—a Cuban version of the traditional Communist Party that had dropped the word "communist" from its name to gain easy access to those sectors of the population that could be scared off by the mere mention or memory of the term "Reds"—and ignoring those rebellious university leaders who were regularly at the front of situations with more serious repercussions than merely pondering the exploitation of man.

Faget and his specialists in domestic communism overlooked the important—rather, the very most important—detail they should have taken into account from the beginning: that Cuba has six geographic provinces but the Party had seven. The Party understood the importance that one institution had had in the life of the Republic since the

1930s. The University of Havana and its scientific, intellectual and professional potential as a fief of prioritized attention for the Party. The Seventh Province.

Look at me. However it happened, by a series of coincidences or according to a plan. The fact remains that it started with my friendship with Alfredo Guevara. Then came the books on credit from the Carlos III Bookstore. Then Flavio Bravo, Leonel Soto, Luis Más Martín, and even Walterio. Then my brother Raúlito was sent to Bucharest. It was a long process in which things ran their course. I don't really think that anyone had decided to turn me into the head of the Cuban Revolution. After a certain point, that was the case. After we came to power in January 1959, the Party and the KGB both made it a priority to recruit me. I don't mean recruit in the pejorative sense, since they were subordinate to me and in that sense they self-recruited. But they needed to confirm the objectives. Do you understand? That's the good thing about communists. You only need to commune ideologically with them. Everything else is secondary with that as a given. I can't even say the same of the Church. But if the Party hadn't deliberately planned to train me as a leader, the cultivating field, the Seventh Province, was something deliberate and organized with that purpose in mind.

IN THOSE DAYS, we wore suits. No shirtsleeves. No guayaberas either. The standard dress for law upperclassmen consisted of two pieces, pants and a jacket, cut from the same cloth, a white collared shirt and a tie. El Chino Esquivel and other fellow students had their suits made at El Sol, a store in the center of Havana where all of Havana's professionals were said to outfit themselves. I have never been as finicky as El Chino. I usually bought my suits ready-made. And at any tailor shop where you could get a good cut of cloth cheaply. I mean, the only three suits I had during my entire time at the university. Two were bought at the beginning of my first year, and the third, a gray one, very nice, I bought in New York when I went there with Mirta on our honeymoon. She picked the color out for me. I also bought myself a leather jacket there just like the one in my pictures from the Bogotazo that I had lost. There's also the fact that I don't like to have my measurements taken. It makes me very uneasy. If anything, I would allow some adjustments here or there that, with his yellow measuring tape around his neck, a tailor could do in a minute pedaling his Singer sewing machine, biting his tongue and always in plain view. The whole matter of having someone take your measurements is pretty serious and it's no small thing that since the early sixties I've had my own tailor—*compañero* Esteban Barcárcel—as part of my Personal Security retinue.

El Sol's reputation was due to a method of measuring that they called "anatomic and photometric suits" in their advertisements, a hook that had brought in even the presidents and dictators of the region. The "photometric" technique consisted of taking pictures of the customer from every angle possible and later measuring one with the classic method of measuring tape and a square and chalk mark-ups. They spared no effort in that place, El Chino would say to me. Batista appeared stately and impeccably dressed in the 1950s ads for this prestigious store. The Honorable President of the Republic sports a piece from his summer collection, dressed here in a light 100 percent cotton drill fabric from our exclusive collection for dignitaries, which you can also enjoy, made to El Sol's anatomic and photometric perfection. El Sol. Manzana de Gómez at Monserrate Strect. Tel. 6-7572.

Trujillo also had his suits and uniforms cut there, his embroidered Generalissimo uniforms, short-tailed tuxedoes with gold trimmed epaulets and worsted yarn. I asked around to see if we could slit his neck at that place. I thought he must have made secret shopping trips to Havana. I knew he was also a regular customer at Cuervo y Sobrino, perhaps our capital's most famous jewelry store. But he sent representatives to Havana or received the sellers in Ciudad Trujillo with their samples or catalogues. In many ways, at the end of the forties and well into the fifties, Havana acted as the supercapital of the region's countries, even extending its influence to cities in the south of the United States such as Miami, Fort Lauderdale, Key West. Cuervo y Sobrino proved to serve Trujillo very efficiently, providing the medals and decorations that earned him the nickname among Cubans of Chapitas, "Bottle Caps." Women constituted another area of Cuban importation. Santiago was closest to him for such activities. He loved importing light-skinned mulattas from Santiago for his parties, getting them to sing and later taking them to bed. Nothing excited the Benefactor and Father of the New Nation Generalissimo Rafael Leonidas Trujillo more than a white-looking mulatta singing to him and removing her bra to reveal a pair of black nipples. I know this from a very reputable source, an old friend from Santiago who had been a Spanish-music singer on a local radio station and who embodied this exact body type that cost the Dominican dictator so dearly and whose racial provenance only became apparent when the removal of her clothes revealed the violence of her black nipples, violent and offensive given the whiteness of her breasts and all the more violent and offensive given the amount of time and indecision that passed before allowing themselves to be handled. Regarding the production of the decorations, the Havana establishment favored by the bloodthirsty Rafael guaranteed the purity of the gold and that they would be made with the most sumptuous of metals and the brightest of precious stones. They say that the Cuervo y Sobrino owners had a secretary, a ghastly man always dressed in a black suit, the classic image of a funeral home owner, who was charged with traveling to Ciudad Trujillo and winning over the dictator with a new decoration. First he had to thank His Excellency, the Generalissimo, for being kind enough to give him an audience. Then he would proceed to a sort of careful ceremony in which a jewelry box, lying in the jewelry store representative's left hand on a handkerchief, was opened with a pleasant click of the clasp and the cellophane paper inside was removed to slowly unveil a gold swastika inlaid with one central ruby in a setting of diamonds. The other thing was making up a battle to name the decoration for and dictating an edict or having the Dominican Congress sanction a law establishing the new order or medal.

As far as Cuervo y Sobrino goes, I should say that the majority of their goldsmiths stayed in Cuba. In all truth, goldsmiths, no matter the latitude, have two of the essential qualities of a revolutionary: humble origins and honor. Besides which the owners themselves, after a brief exile in Italy, found it convenient to consider their options and returned to Havana with certain very interesting business propositions. Around the 1980s, when we decided to gather a few tons of gold still in possession of the bourgeois or their remaining family members in the country, we set up—with their help, the goldsmiths' and the owners'—the *casas de cambio*, exchange houses, which the people called the gold and silver houses, in which jewels were appraised. A price was assigned to them and in return one received a voucher to acquire household appliances from a special store outfitted for that purpose. To build trust in the exchangers, we put ads in the press stating that the assessors were the former jewelers Cuervo y Sobrino. I think it's the only time in the whole history of the Revolution that we've resorted to using the prestige of a bourgeois establishment. What we didn't say was that the former owners, or at least their heirs, were also in on the game.

So anyway, however you look at it, with his eyes dazzled or not by the effects of the photometric method, El Chino was a devotee of that shop. He used to say that he got his suits at El Sol and his ties at El Encanto. El Encanto was another legendary institution of the Cuban bourgeoisie. It was a five-story building in the commercial heart of the country, the intersection of Galiano and San Rafael Streets, which people called "the corner of sin," a denomination that, incidentally, is of questionable etymology. For some, it was because married women used the alibi of going shopping in order to meet their lovers there. For others, it was because there used to be prostitution in the streets around there. Nonetheless, all of that frivolity disappeared a few days before the Playa Girón invasion, on April 13, 1961, when the counterrevolutionary Carlos González Vidal threw live phosphorus into the establishment's air-conditioning system and it burned down to the ground in a matter of hours. Incidentally, González Vidal was captured and confessed and we quickly subjected him to the firing squad.

EL SOL. Cuervo y Sobrino. El Encanto.

The city is there, but I never make up my mind to take a stroll through its streets. Though it might be a street that I own, for lack of a better term, in the lands of my dominion, I abstain from strolling through it, even in the predawn hours. It wouldn't make any sense. It would be far worse than a sentimental journey or trying to bring back a past for which I feel nostalgic. In this sense, I wish to be more dignified than my enemies in Miami. They have the excuse of not being allowed back here, of having no entry to the backdrops of their nostalgia. But—as always— I am one step ahead of them. I don't rely on my excuses, but on my arrogance.

The Cubans who fled the Revolution have developed an entire industry based on nostalgia in Miami. They sell tourist postcards, reproduce telephone books from the 1950s and back issues of *Bohemia* magazine, they manufacture the same brands of sodas and beers and christen their restaurants with the same names these had in Havana. You have no idea how many times *a day* the State Security KT* Department detects calls made from Miami to telephone numbers in Havana that have not been in existence for twenty or thirty years. Five- or six-digit telephone numbers that lead to blind lines. Out of sheer curiosity, I've ordered this to be researched. In the majority of cases, they're old business owners calling their former establishments. It's none too rare that the establishments themselves have also disappeared, because they've fallen to the ground or because we've converted them into housing for people in need or even for military units. We've detected calls made to houses in which all of the residents have passed away. On more than one occasion, I've had to keep some of our *compañeros* from responding to these calls as if it were a telephone number and a place still in use. I don't think anyone has the right to turn somebody else's past into a joke. As if I didn't know what hopes people invest in their past.

IN SEPTEMBER 1947, I became affiliated with the Orthodox Party, the best option the Republic offered if the path wasn't going to be a revolution in the end. This last part is something that I only understand now, of course. Nobody noticed that fact at the time. It wasn't even kept a secret from me that the leader in those circumstances didn't like me: Eduardo Chibás. Nobody noticed that I was there to see how much milk I could get out of the cow. The cow of the Republic and its institutions. Of course, you could claim that no one is psychic; besides, I myself didn't know that that political structure wouldn't fit me, and less still my ambitions. They could be right. But only to a certain point. Because if there's something I've learned from my own experience as a novice in Cuban politics, it's to sense who might fuck me over in the future and therefore, whom I need to fuck over first. I understand that the Orthodox Party wasn't going to bow down at my feet upon seeing me walk through the doors. But they didn't kill me either, which in the end is the only solution for people like me. No. They didn't dig too much. They didn't imagine. They didn't conceive. They just let me live and work in their Republic like anyone else. Poor guys.

* The efficient Cuban counterintelligence telephone surveillance system.

ONE OF THE GREAT pleasures of my enemies is thinking that I stay in power to prevent the Pandora's box of my years in office from being opened before it's time. While I remain here, with Cuba under my control, the box is closed. They spend more time imagining my secrets than worrying about the actual retention of power in my hands. I think they're simply justifying their inability to take me out of the game, and above all they think they can judge me morally with a series of abstractions and probabilities that have never been proven. How many unspeakable crimes—they think—must I be hiding in that box? But such a scant appreciation of my abilities as a conspirator still bothers me. As if I would leave a trace of any crime I could commit. Well before Gorbachev brought up the possibility of exhuming the documentation (and while they were at it, the human remains) of a massacre such as the one in Katyn, Poland, we gave the order to burn all compromising documents. This happened as soon as Reagan came to power and the Soviets told us they weren't going to get burned on our account. On the other hand, there are people out there, especially in Miami, still running from the days or years they spent serving the Revolution. Unhappy souls. History's beggars. I am not afraid of any Pandora's box—and believe me—since, for starters, I've burned all the vestiges of compromising situations and left videos of my enemies' antics. For starters, there isn't a single American diplomat posted to our country who hasn't been photographed or videotaped. This material is perfectly conserved. Their taped asses. This is what our *compañeros* in the KJ Brigade call these materials, due to the high quantity of asses of male *and female* diplomats (oh, what a number of lesbians there are among those young women at the State Department) recorded on tapes we keep in metal containers. Of course, no one refers to the accumulated material this way in my presence. The KJ Brigade is one of our specialized units and is in charge of the so-called visual check, taping and taking photos. Since the appearance of video recording, the KJ's operating costs have been reduced and their equipment has also become a lot simpler. We were able to get rid of our photo development labs, which we passed on to ICAIC,* and this gave us the opportunity

---

* The Cuban Institute of Cinematographic Art and Industry (Instituto Cubano del Arte e Industria Cinematográficos).

to expand our personnel and means of transport. Now those *compañeros* are fighting against the normal degradation of the images on magnetic tapes. Digital technology has come to their aid and they're putting everything on DVD discs. The Americans assigned to Cuba after the Interests Section was opened in 1977 seem to follow the lead of so many American magnates and politicians since the instauration of the Republic in 1902 until the end of Batista's days in 1958—of which the most distinguished figure in that class of progressives is John F. Kennedy—of coming to Cuba to tussle about with Cuban flesh. Mr. Kennedy and that whole Camelot tale. King Arthur would have loved to have one of those whores from Casa de Marina call him *"papito rico"* and put a condom on him. We can say that for ourselves, that we had the most hygienic prostitutes in the world, a paradigm at the time of the battle against gonorrhea and syphilis, just like today we can say that the country is a bastion against AIDS, besides which, of course, we do not officially acknowledge that the proliferation of prostitutes is a chronic ill for us. The most distinguished among America's powerful and political families will suffer a blow of unparalleled earthly proportions when that Pandora's box is opened, because we're not talking about rear ends in a state of purity, in other words, at rest; rather, they are all offered up to the public's disposal in proof of the uses to which they are being put. The bedroom is one of the combat areas that almost all of the Asian socialist countries found to be problematic from the start. They didn't have a problem in principle with using hidden cameras to photograph enemy personnel in the country under diplomatic cover, but they had trouble with the idea of their own women being taken to bed. I understand that the Chinese went so far as to execute some poor, unfortunate women who had relations with foreigners. Execution is, according to the code of honor of our brethren in the People's Republic of China, a shot in the back of the skull, from a shotgun or a revolver, but either way they then bill the family for the bullet. Forget about the Vietnamese and the Koreans. It's not just about Americans. They prohibit relations with any foreigner. Even us, the Cubans, their intimate comrades-in-arms. I understand that the only North Vietnamese woman who had relations with a foreigner in Hanoi, during the war, was a doctor who fell in love with one of our heroes at that time, Captain Douglas Rudd y Molé (I cite his whole name now because he has already passed away), who was also the only white Western pilot who participated in air combat against the American Air Force in Southeast Asia aboard a MiG-21PFV under the Vietnamese flag. He was one of the bravest men I've ever known, despite our later having to put him in jail under a twenty-year sentence (a term he didn't get to fully serve). It's not easy to enter into combat and commit to maintaining absolute radio silence (so that a foreigner wouldn't be detected, besides the fact that he wouldn't have shared any common language with the air controller while under his control in the air traffic zone until reaching three kilometers' altitude and being twenty kilometers from the airport, when the air controller would switch him over to the far radar and tell him to change frequency, almost always to channel eight, to become subordinate to the control station navigator, which is the procedure for entering a flight zone and starting the junction). The return was no problem. Nor the detection among their own planes. All of the Soviet planes communicated among themselves automatically by way of the friend-enemy system, which interrogates one with the mere push of a button. The pilot doesn't need to activate any response command. The plane identifies itself. "Radio silence is very nice," Douglas said to me, upon returning from Vietnam. "You're flying low and your only communication is with the engine you're sitting on top of. A formidable, all-powerful R-11F2-300 with 13,118 pounds of horsepower. The 21 isn't known for its radar or its capture abilities, nor for its goal-acquisition equipment or its reach, but it is invariably known as a plane for pilots. It doesn't have computers or sophisticated navigation equipment. It depends on the pilot and (we hope) his good training and experience. For all those reasons, it's my plane. All of a sudden you start to trust in a machine more than your own mother, more than your comrades, more than the Party." Douglas was a real iconoclast, as the rest of really educated combatants usually were. His statement about the Party was a joke he relied on to detract from the bit of poetry he spun when he declared his affectionate dependence on a Soviet R-11F2-300 engine. But I understood him, more than he could have imagined. He probably wasn't even aware of how lonely he was. That's what he was really talking about with me. About his loneliness. I remember that we had sent him on a super-secret mission to buy Western arms, and in the end he had even been in combat. But he also sweet-talked a poor Vietnamese doctor. Of course, he didn't dare tell me that part, nor would I have let him. I found out from Military Counterintelligence (Contra-Inteligencia Militar, or CIM) reports. Always following around everyone's cocks. In any event, I had to ask if our Vietnamese comrades knew about the Douglas affair. No. Quite the contrary. The comrades were delighted with our hero. They're very sensitive, the Vietnamese. We had to be careful with those signs of liberalism, like Douglas's.

What I've been trying to establish for a while here is that our Chinese, Korean and Vietnamese brothers gave up an enormous potential for counterintelligence activity when they prohibited certain affairs between foreigners and nationals.

Of course, the great problem when it comes to talking about many of my life's political maneuvers is that the motives and methods employed remained hidden and the real facts I used were far removed from what the public saw, so that sometimes the truth that has been covered up for so long ends up seeming implausible and the only acceptable thing to do is stick with the old lie, and that distortion is—I think—what creates that thirst—or that imperious need—of mine for secrets, since things turn out so well for me in the end and I've been surviving one ambush after another and it seems like there's not a bullet with my name on it. Nor are there any mysteries. They've run out. There's nowhere to look for them. The delightful thing about Cellini is that he describes or rescues a world in which there were no actual communications, in which everything was a mystery. That's not the present situation. Which stone, which segment, which bush, which layer of subsoil is not classified and plotted out and evaluated and photographed today? Those damn Americans, no matter where we went, had already photographed all the hidden corners of the archipelago since before the triumph of the Revolution. Those maps drawn to one- to fifty-thousand scale that we later used to get rid of the insurgents were the work of the Americans, who left copies of these in the map rooms of Batista's army. That was when we realized we lived in a land that had in a way been taken out from under our very feet and that there wasn't a well or a rock or a sugarcane reed whose existence and even whose name—be it indigenous or Spanish—we didn't share with one of the Pentagon's cartographers. Well, now that I've gotten that essential introduction made, and abounded on mysteries and secrets and tried to persuade you to forget about that salt of the earth—it's not ours to enjoy anymore—I will narrate, or rather, jump ahead chronologically to briefly describe how I fell in love for the first time.

I was married at twenty-two, out of basic courtesy I'll keep Mirta's age to myself, but she had just barely had her *quinceañera*, or at least that's how I saw her, with her dancer's lightness, a lightness I had only seen in the fleeting movements of a deer in the Mayarí forest, so fleeting and elusive before the hunter who couldn't make out whether they had been completely wiped out or if what was passing in front of him and disappearing into the trees was the ghost of the last graceful creature still naively running through Cuba's forests. She had very round, expressive eyes and was haughty and sharp-witted in that noisy way that only white Cuban women can be, and the intensity of her attractiveness was only increased by her being so defenseless, so desolate, such a frail little autumn leaf: a timid Cuban with a proud visage and a descendant of a family of Batista supporters who was about to enter into marriage with the future leader of a communist revolution. The first half of the century had seen three revolutions of considerable international importance—the Mexican, Soviet and Chinese Revolutions—while I was dancing circles around Mirta and she let herself be circled with the sweet attitude of indifference that she assumed so perfectly. Only one Revolution—the Cuban one—would exist in the world while each of us grew old separately, like two strangers destined to never see one another again. We were defeated by two abstractions. For her, it was skepticism. For me, the inability to persuade her. I, who have been able to convince very tough men to request their own execution on our firing walls, didn't have the reasoning or resources to convince her of my love for her and to follow me wherever I went. My little sylvan deer from the forest. My girl who was like the dew that glitters at dawn and who constitutes my most passionate memory, that of the smell of her skin that dusk in Miami Beach while the sun set over a horizon that was beyond the universe while the salt water, upon absorbing the fine particles of light, sparkled over the shoulders of that spoiled girl, spoiled and mine, and who just two days before I had deflowered on the spotless matrimonial bed of an American hotel. They defeated us. Abstractions and time. But, how do you convince a woman that the kingdom you are offering her is but a nascent revolution and that not only are you not planning it yet but that you are still in the process of learning that it is a possible objective, a Perhaps, a Maybe? My God, how to convince Mirta Díaz-Balart that the revolution was all I had to give her?

At first we lived near a factory that made beer called La Tropical in a neighborhood called La Sierra. We were in an apartment that faced a guava-paste factory. The smell of tons of guavas mashed with sugar and boiled in vats was a permanent one throughout the neighborhood and gave it character. I got Mirta pregnant there with my first son, and the only child I had with her. Later, we moved to a building called Frenmar, on Third Street in El Vedado, a much better neighborhood. And less than a hundred meters from the coast. We faced an army camp, where the Corps of Engineers was later located, the embrasures and garrison walls of which were destroyed in the end to make the Havana Riviera, one of the Mafia's hotels in Cuba. Mirta was a real doll who never complained about anything. And a terrible cook. I'm not criticizing her. This was a running joke between us and I hope it makes her smile if she should ever read these pages. Once, I invited El Chino Esquivel over for lunch. "Come on, Chino," I said to him. "Mirta is making meatballs."

"*Guajiro*," he said to me, "since when does Mirta cook?"

Recently, in my first encounter with El Chino in forty years, the first thing he mentioned to me was those meatballs of Mirta's. He said he didn't know how in the devil to swallow those dark little rocks or if he should try to refuse the meal, but he felt bad for Mirta.

OF ALL THESE PEOPLE of secondary importance in my university years, Fernando Florez Ibarra stands out. Old Fernandinito. He was a determined guy. I have to highlight him because among other things he is one of the few people who, according to his own stories, tried to kill me. As the story was told to me, he fired a couple of shots at me from above because I was entering the cafeteria at the School of Philosophy and Letters, which was on a lower level than the portal to the school, where Mirta studied. After the triumph of the Revolution, I had the sense to call him and tell him to stop spreading that story around. I thought he had it made up. As far as I knew, we had had a fistfight once and, I conceded, neither of us was able to claim victory. It was a good fight, employing nothing more than our fists as weapons and in view of the entire student body right in the middle of Plaza Cadenas, the geographic center of the University of Havana. It was then that I found out. Fernando had the balls to confess to me that what had really happened was once he had seen me at the end of the university stadium, perhaps at too far a distance for a short-range shooter. So he fired a couple of shots at me from behind some trees while, he says, I was running laps around the baseball field and at the instant I crossed beneath an enormous scoreboard, with the previous game's nine innings still posted. The home team had made three runs because on the bottom line of the entries, the last box displayed a solid white three on a black background.

Fernandinito says he took that three as a reference point to blow my brains out. He pointed at the three and lowered the gun just a notch. It was midday and I was jogging, lightly, on my own shadow, concentrated under my feet and moving over the grass at my light pace. The sun was fierce and the field was empty. Some student couples were in the stands, seated, looking at their books or wooing each other. Fernandinito came in through a secondary door and quickly realized that I would be a difficult shot with a Colt .45-caliber, but it would have been unforgivable not to even try. He took it out, looked around and when I got below the three,

he fired a couple of times. He hid behind the trees to his right. This movement, which barely took two seconds, didn't allow him to see my reaction. For a moment, his heart beat quickly while he thought he had managed to kill me, because when he focused at the place again where my run should have stopped,

there was no one below the board.

Fernando says that he then took a look at the stands and noticed kids pointing in all directions or picking up their books and leaving. It was obvious that no one had pinpointed where the shots came from, since they weren't looking at the trees. They weren't looking below the scoreboard either. There was no body. Sometimes that happens under the Cuban sun, which is not only blinding, it's also deafening. I say so from experience: the heat also effects how sound travels.

Of course, it hadn't happened at the School of Philosophy and Letters because I never went to see Mirta there. I already knew then not to mix family and politics. It's a principle of double protection. Not only do you keep your loved ones out of the danger zone, but you also keep the enemy from getting to know your routine. You know how it is. The best habit is no habit.

As the years went by, it's obvious that I forgot about those shots. It happened sometimes. A few isolated shots moving through the air around the university. First you drew your gun, then you looked around, and if it had nothing to do with you, you went on your way. That's what must have happened that day. I can't recall the episode in my memory. Fernandinito's memory doesn't help either. If I was running at that hour, in shorts and a T-shirt, one of my buddies—El Chino, Walterio—had to be around, for support and to hold on to my gun, most likely innocently wrapped up in a towel.

"Well, Fernandinito," I remember saying to him, "I don't think those remarks of yours are good for you or for the Revolution."

This conversation would have taken place a few months after the mercenary invasion of Playa Girón in April 1961, because I can clearly remember that Fernando had already distinguished himself in his role as the prosecutor of the Revolutionary Tribunals (Tribunales Revolucionarios, or TR) and sent people to the firing wall. We called them the *Te Erres*. And that was at the time when we executed the most people. Very few came out of the *Te Erres* alive.

UNDERSTAND THAT I am giving you a lesson, and you should take advantage. It would seem that you can't call a murderer by name, at least not too often. But it's about not wasting too many adjectives on your enemy so that the political effect isn't lost. And what's even more dangerous: diluting all of the crimes in a murky stew that you are trying to denounce. Our famous Apostle of Independence, José Martí, had the maxim, "Say everything about the tyrant, say more." You know who he is, right? The Cuban patriot who turned the last decade of the nineteenth century into an obstinate battle against Spain. Of course, he was referring to Spain the way we today refer to Yankee imperialism. But he was playing a false hand. Martí was too internally tortured a man to successfully employ the subtleties of modern propaganda. I learned how to use political incrimination from the much more direct source of revolutionary acts and not from the complicated apostle of a short-statured man with blistered feet and teeth so corroded that no one remembers him ever smiling. To say it as clearly as possible, I learned from street executions. As you know, one of our sayings was that the only hard person to kill is the first one. It's the same when it comes to lifting an accusatory finger. One is enough. Once you have any more, the victim's face is lost. A whole group takes its place. An amorphous, imprecise group. In the end—it doesn't matter how many people you kill—they can only hang you once.

Martí. Sometimes it's difficult to determine how much he acted out of intellectual need or out of resentment at finding himself—and being unable to escape—trapped in such a scrawny, pathetic body so ill-suited to being displayed, for example, at the university pool. I'm reflecting here. Since, as is known, he has been the idiomatic symbol of the Cuban Revolution. The highest and living symbol is me. Fidel Castro, of course. But the presence of his ghost among us endowed us with a sort of common language concerning everything that could be identified as Cuba. José Martí was the creole Jehovah who named all of our things. But who failed in all of his plans, conspiracies and wars. It's in that regard that the Revolution carried out its most brilliant publicity move. We did not take over José Martí. We avenged him. We were victorious on all the fronts in which he was defeated, including that of life span. I've survived hundreds of plans concocted by the CIA while he let himself be killed so easily just shy of forty years of age while dressed in a little blue war suit and mounted atop an imposing immaculately white creole horse given to rushing toward Spanish Mausers. The avenged dead are like boats that you sail at high sea heaving-to with no crew. Our enemies say that we've claimed Martí just to put him at our service. Well, just by suggesting such a thing, they are doing the same, but in their favor. Previously I said this was a reflection. At least part of one. But I don't want you to misinterpret my words. Martí is firmly rooted in my generation. And he has always been worshipped. That's the word commonly used among Cubans regarding their sentiments about José Martí. It's a feeling that should dominate us. Worship. As if we're obliged to suffer certain spiritual tremors upon mentioning him. And I confess that in a way, I also had my sessions of prostration before Martí. Of course, at this point, I don't think I need to subject my listener to the same story again. The problem was that, in a society whose existence was overwhelmed by devotion to Martí, the only way to get ahead was to be the most devout of them all. Pure pragmatism and pure propaganda. I imagine that it wouldn't even be offensive to him. He knew these revolutionary mechanics perfectly well and never stopped using them himself.

MY DENTITION. As opposed to the Apostle, I only had one dental problem. It had to do with my upper middle right tooth that blackened due to a deadened nerve, a fairly common consequence of canal therapy or endodontia, which by a defect in the removal of the pulp leaves you with remains, and that in reality clouded my upper sagittal line. I was already in the Sierra Maestra and was the head of the Rebel Army, when we made a permanent camp in La Plata Alta. The request to bring me a heavy dentist's chair, on mule back, skirting a thousand army ambushes, was one of the first endeavors of my sedentary guerrilla leadership. The movement's command, on their end, sent me a dentist from Santiago: Dr. Pedro Sánchez. The chair came from Manzanillo—one of the largest towns around the Sierra—thanks to the efforts of—by messenger—Celia and her father, who was one of the most well-known doctors in the city, and who found the thing in a forgotten warehouse from the early days of the Republic, probably abandoned by the sanitary authorities of the American Army. It was obvious that we needed an odontological pedal-operated chair that would function without electricity. We installed it at the back of the little house, hidden under the trees, where I had my bed and the few belongings essential in carrying out my campaign: a table, some books and a transoceanic radio. Dr. Pedrito spent half the campaign pedaling and trying to whiten my tooth. When he explained the procedure to follow for *my tooth*, I was absolutely convinced that this had to be modified. It was relatively easy to persuade him to switch the treatment. First, you need to isolate the area you're working on with cotton, so that it stays saliva-free, as dry as possible. You take a round drill mounted on a low-speed counter-angle and bring it down behind the tooth—on the tongue side—until you reach the pulp chamber, where you place a fine layer of zinc phosphate dental cement. In our improvised dispensary, the speed of the instruments depended on the passion with which one pedaled, a fact which led me to ask Celia to oversee my dentist's diet, making sure, above all, that it was rich in fiber (meat) and contained some good, heavy pumpkin purees, since they say that this is an excellent vegetable to strengthen and tone the legs. The issue of nutrition became quite pressing after the time that Pedrito passed out while he was pedaling and was left hanging off the side of my mouth. Let's get back to the treatment. When the cement has hardened, you add a small piece of cotton, very small, soaked in hydrogen peroxide, and wait five minutes, until you're sure that it is completely dry, and you insert a sodium perborate paste in the cavity, wait another five minutes, then rinse it all well and cover the hole with temporary cement. The treatment, known as *recromía*, requires many sessions and is of questionable success. As you will understand, for me it was completely unacceptable upon merely saying that respected word. *Recromía*, bleaching. So I spent a few afternoons analyzing the strategic variants that could be applied in my case and when I had it all sorted out, I told Pedrito how it was going to be. The doctor, a silently obedient mulatto of average height who had shown up for duty with a cardboard case full of tidy white scrubs that he would don to tend to me as proudly as if he were wearing his Sunday best, nodded, approved, was in agreement, thought it appropriate. First, I explained to him, regarding opening a hole in my tooth, no way in hell. Second, the whole treatment will be external. Third, the need to keep the whole work area dry ceased to exist upon implementing my method. And last, he had to pay attention to the planes. Any counterindications? Any collateral damage? No—the tooth puller responded—we're just going to reduce the amount of sodium perborate so that we don't burn you. I spent as much time as I could sitting in that chair, with Pedrito at the pedal, and me with my mouth open, a bib tied around my neck, a lit cigar in my left hand, my saliva welling up because we didn't have an extractor, Dr. Pedrito saying to me, "Spit, Comandante," when he noticed my saliva dribbling from the corners of my mouth, me letting out a few black globs of saliva on the tilted mud floor that were rapidly absorbed by the earth's gravity and, after the third time I spit, Pedrito giving me a chance to take a puff of my stogie—"Smoke, smoke, Comandante," he would say—until he deemed that I had exhaled all of the smoke in my mouth and returned, drill in hand (on the end of which was fixed the rotating soft-cell brush), to leaning over the tooth bathed in hydrogen peroxide with sodium perborate that the movement's New York chapter got from New York University's Dental School, and that he polished as if he were a goldsmith and that his most precious jewel, and pedaling to activate the drill, and spitting, and smoking. We had it timed. Three strokes to polish, one to smoke. And everything was calm, slow, since the procedure can corrupt. If you don't obtain the desired color quickly, the logical tendency would be to insist on more sessions, thus weakening the tooth further until it breaks after being subject to so much of what is, after all, an attack on the enamel. Since we didn't have a water line, either, the liquid available to rinse my mouth rested in two canteens on a tray. One had water in it, the other cognac. After all that, upon the triumph of the Revolution that tooth was as black as it was when we started the campaign. But there came a time when I got to like lying there, with my good cigars and letting out my gobs of spit, while Dr. Sánchez and his whitening drill purred around me and imbued me with a kind of laxness, a daydreaminess, in which I wandered and salivated aplenty.

7

A Military Organization
with a Good Propaganda Apparatus

/ / /

THE ARGENTINES ARRIVED IN MARCH 1948. THEY TAUGHT US SOME-thing that I would use *institutionally* in the Revolution: influence. We still have an active department that operates in the Foreign Ministry but is really a front for the General Intelligence Directorate (Dirección General de Inteligencia, or DGI), what is usually called a work unit disguised as a chancery. That front is the so-called Plana de Influencia, or PI—the Influence Plan—and it essentially focuses on foreign intellectuals, minority movements and things like that. Everything we got right with writers, artists, American blacks, the most eccentric Latin American characters and the support and solidarity we received from everyone from Harry Belafonte to Rigoberta Menchú is the work of the PI, of its recruiting, its approaches, its talk, its patience, its flirtations, its encouragement and its sharp eye. I don't think we've ever gone wrong with any of the PI's files. And if the people in question have money, all the better. Millionaires are the most loyal. Nothing is more satisfying to a millionaire than knowing that a Cuban intelligence organization has his back. For earthly men, as they all are when you come down to it, serving a communist organization, albeit at a distance, gives them a calmness of spirit that can't even be obtained in a church confessional, and since they also enjoy all the security that comes along with it, without worrying about the eventualities of torture and interrogations, it's an intensely romantic type of activism. Everything is in their favor. Of course, we didn't learn our entire methodology from the Argentines. But the Argentines showed up with something

April 8, 1947. Fidel in Colombia. He has organized a student congress to oppose the Ninth Pan-American Conference, sponsored by the United States. It's his first big anti-American operation. The next day, when the populist leader Jorge Eliécer Gaitán is assassinated, he will also come to know his first urban uprising and the excesses of a population over which all control has been lost. That afternoon, however, he is a bored tourist in the outskirts of Bogotá.

coherent, structured. They had an embassy in Cuba. They sent emissaries. They bombarded you with pamphlets and pictures of Juan Domingo Perón. But in addition, they asked about your family and whether you had any pressing needs that they could palliate ever so modestly. And they would even take a few bills out of their pockets and give them to you, without any to-do, without even looking at the denominations of the bills, like you were really friends. Juan Domingo Perón. All of a sudden Juan Domingo Perón became someone familiar among us.

How far did their influence go? Well, it reached our circles, the little coffee shops, the cement benches of Plaza Cadenas, the university steps. Any place with a little shade and some cool air is propitious to conspiring. If you have a cigar to light up, perfect.

They were very dedicated to their mission. I thought this was only possible among communists. But I learned with the Argentines that you could have a consecrated militancy at your disposal to carry out specific tasks without it being necessarily communist. The idea was what was indispensable. If you have an idea, there's possibility. The problem is finding an attractive idea often enough. That's the question.

One night, there we were seated before our steaming cups of café con leche, the whole group: Carlos Iglesias Mónica (one of the Argentines), El Chino Esquivel, Alfredo Guevara, Rafaelito del Pino and me. I was dunking the end of a loaf of Cuban bread bathed in butter, softening up the dough in the milk's steamy residue as my glasses fogged up and enjoying the way the bread got heavier as it absorbed the milk, when Iglesias Mónica complained about what the Americans were going to do in Colombia. We looked at each other. No one knew what the Americans were going to do in Colombia. The Ninth Pan-American Conference, Iglesias Mónica explained. "But it's really an event against the Third Way and President Perón." Without giving it much thought, I said, "Well, let's have our own congress. Let's take advantage of those crooks' conference and let's fuck it up for them with a Pan-American Students' Congress." Iglesias Mónica approved of the idea right away. I could tell by his barely contained excitement. I knew he was going to run right to the embassy, to sell the idea as his. "I'm going to the embassy." "What's at the embassy?" El Chino asked. "Money," I said to El Chino, already in perfect sync with Iglesias Mónica's train of thought. At least at that moment he had to have noticed that I didn't care for his appropriating my idea.

"He has to start looking for money," I explained to El Chino.

That's how our presence in Santa Fe de Bogotá came about and how Juan Domingo Perón came to accrue his first debt with me. I said that it "came about." I should be more precise since I find myself (approximately) about a quarter of the way through my memoirs and it's not inconsiderable that I take advantage of this opportunity to record such achievements as I have had. So, it did not "come about." *I willed it* to happen. It might have been the first time that the use of a counterblow occurred to me. Since this would be the most frequently used weapon during all of the years of the Revolution—even Jean-Paul Sartre extolled the use of a counterblow—its vintage should be noted, like the finest wines.

A few days later we started meeting at the Hotel Nacional, in a more or less methodic way. The Argentines had a room there. They paid for everything. Different committees were organized to visit the countries in the region that would be invited and would negotiate the presence of the student organizations. Mexico wasn't a problem because one of the main Aztec student leaders, Jorge Menvielle Porte-Petit, was in Havana and was already taking part in the meetings at the Hotel Nacional. Bogotá was the destination. To Bogotá to fuck up that chancellor's conference for the Americans, where George C. Marshall himself, the one who came up with the famous plan for Europe's reconstruction, would be present. Alfredito Guevara, at my invitation, took part as the organizing secretary of the FEU at the last Hotel Nacional meetings (I had to find some very "official" support). Then I entrusted to him the task of informing (and inviting, of course), on the side, the president of the FEU. The FEU's real president. Enrique Ovares. Although I asked Alfredo to take his time and not to rush to get to Bogotá.

El Chino was the one who got the airline tickets at an agency located in the Hotel Plaza lobby, where he had a friend.

My first airplane! There was the probability of adventure, and even the mystery of the unfathomable, in trips back then and in the airplanes of the time, when Cubana had two DC–4s called *The Star of Cuba* or *The Star of the East*, while Pan American dreamed its imperial dream and thought it ruled the world under the wings of its clippers called *Belle of the Skies* or *Guiding Star* or *Golden Gate*, which were equipped with rooms containing all the luxuries of a Manhattan hotel. The planes were still DC-3 and C-46 and they were starting with DC-4, and the planes were named as if they were Columbus's vessels and the engines were piston-based and radar was unknown and there wasn't a single artificial satellite out in the earth's orbit and the only navigation help from the ground came from scattered radio control towers whose personnel were guided by the averages of the turn posts and their ability to read the clouds and above all, by the pilots' visual skills, and that they never made the mistake of bursting a cumulonimbus cloud and, resigned themselves to flying under it or around it—around it if it wasn't a cumulus that was so wide it cast a shadow over the Orinoco and if they had enough fuel for this slow multi-hour detour on the edge of a powerful cumulus—because there was not enough power in the engines to overtake it at twelve or thirteen kilometers height and without a pressurized cabin the only thing separating you from the sky is a thin layer of aluminum.

Rafaelito and I arrived in Bogotá on Sunday, April 4, and stayed at the Claridge. Two days later, Enrique Ovares and Alfredito Guevara landed. They brought Jorge Menvielle Porte-Petit, who came from Havana with them on the plane. Jorge boasted that he was a very close friend of Miguelito Alemán, the Mexican president, and of his son, *the other Miguelito*, reason enough to have him always conveniently on our side.

PRAYER FOR PEACE

I remember that we would leave the hotel and go about two or three blocks, reach the Carrera Séptima and then take a left to go to the office where we were meeting or go to the plaza in front of the building where the Pan-American Conference was being held. But Saturday, when we left, people started to show up, people yelling and running, in what could only be described as a frenzy, in all different directions. People who seemed crazed.

Bogotá. April 9, 1948.

Jorge Eliécer Gaitán. His death sparked the whole thing. The Bogotazo. His murderer was a tramp named José Roa Sierra, who would survive his crime for just a few minutes before being practically dismembered by the masses. Almost instantly the motive for the murder ceased to be personal and turned political. Rear Admiral Roscoe H. Hillenkoetter, then head of the CIA, thought it convenient to say that the murder had been "purely a question of personal retaliation," but leaving it clear that they—in the CIA—had sufficient information that something big was in the works that might derail the Pan-American meeting. I've never been able to see what the Americans stood to gain from the Gaitán case. Rear Admiral Hillenkoetter's quickness to show that he had good intelligence about what was supposedly being planned does nothing but prove that they were, in fact, surprised by the events. The exchange of confidential coded messages between Washington and its embassies in Havana and Bogotá reveals the paucity of information at their disposal and President Ospina Pérez had to send tanks in to save Marshall on that fateful afternoon, an afternoon on which it was worth noting that his wife—the Honorable First Lady—tucked a revolver into her waistband, ready to make them pay dearly for her life.

THE COMMONLY ACCEPTED thesis is that there was no political motive behind Gaitán's murder because there was no organization that claimed responsibility, and if there was no organization, then there was no purpose either. That has also been my basic thesis about the matter all these years, and I've used it convincingly and efficiently. But now I will tell you quite the opposite. Look me straight in the eye. Listen to me. Why demand an "organization" when, in fact, disorganization is required for revolution? If you look at things objectively, Gaitán's murder was a vehicle for subversion that was a hundred times more effective than my feigned Latin American students' congress. How could an event planned to disrupt Marshall's meeting compare to Jorge Eliécer Gaitán's head—full of straight black indigenous man's hair combed meticulously back with Vaseline—broken and his brains emptying like egg from a cracked shell? The liberal students put me in touch with him and took me to visit him on April 7, just a little after noon. To his office, on Carrera Séptima; you went up a set of wooden stairs, your steps echoing the whole way, and you could lean on a worn handrail, and the old planks on the stairs were also worn and warped in the middle. Meeting with Gaitán raised suspicions about me, above all because Gaitán went to the trouble of writing my name down in his datebook. As you can imagine, I was motivated by my own interests in that encounter with Gaitán. The main one was to definitively get out from under the Argentines' tutelage. I was not in Bogotá, Colombia, organizing a congress of my own invention just to turn around and offer it up to Peronism. I had used the Argentines to distance myself from and escape the structures of the Cuban FEU and put together a student congress that would leave the FEU in a position equal to that of other Latin American student associations yet all of them subordinate to me as the organizer of the event. Gaitán, I figured, was the man to go to.

But he also fell in love with my student congress. He walked excitedly from one end of his office to the other, already envisioning the event. There we were, following him with our gazes, the two or three Colombians who had arranged the meeting, Rafael del Pino, and me. But none of my companions noticed what was happening, that the congress was on the verge of changing owners for the third time. "A congress with all the bells and whistles," Gaitán was saying. "With a huge mass rally," he was saying. I don't recall ever having seen someone in my entire life who lived up to Martí's concept of the Indian in a frock coat as when I saw Jorge Eliécer Gaitán hold forth dressed in the black frock coat he wore on the eve of his death. "The concept would be to end the congress with a great event for the masses," he insisted. "And, of course, you can be sure that you can count on me to be the keynote speaker. That's a promise."

Before me, I had the perfect man of the bourgeois opposition. The ideal man of the establishment. Never willing to go beyond limits, to modify structures, to threaten order. I'd have to face a similar phenomenon in Cuba soon after in one Eduardo Chibás and his out-of-control popularity. Gaitán was a hindrance to the Revolution. All these leaders who can rise to power by the ballot box are a great impediment to the proletariat's dictatorship. With their victorious electoral campaigns, they legitimize the existence and generosity of the state. In Chibás, there was one factor that was favorable to our cause: that he allowed himself to be carried away by rage and blew himself apart with a shot to the groin—the virtual and unnamable castration. That didn't appear to be the case with Gaitán.

"Here you go, kid," he said to me. "Something like this can be used for our great event's colophon."

He was holding out a pamphlet to me whose cover read, "Prayer for Peace by Jorge Eliécer Gaitán."

There was something of a traveling salesman in his gestures, offering samples of his marvelous products.

"Prayer for Peace," he said, convinced that he needn't say another word. He even raised his eyebrows as a sign of magnificence. My companions, the little Colombians, nodded in agreement, as if Christ himself were delivering a new Psalm or a new chapter of Genesis. Rafaelito del Pino also approved and smiled, perhaps more enthusiastically than anyone else there.

We made a new date for the ninth.

We agreed to that.

I REMEMBER MYSELF with my black leather jacket, like the Cheka officers or the professional Bolsheviks wore, and how surreal it was for me to be twenty-eight hundred meters above sea level, in the central plateau of the Andes Mountains, trying to figure out how to channel that madness by any means and, while it might seem like a joke now, above all weighing the opportunities that would allow me to become the leader of that Revolution right there. I dedicated all of my efforts from the moment that news of Gaitán's murder spread through the streets of Bogotá until the small hours of the next day to exploiting two possibilities in order of their importance: controlling and then commanding. It was like taming a wild beast and then riding it. Of course, I started small. I said to myself: I have to make all of the pieces fit in this puzzle. Then another. Try it.

Rafaelito was walking ahead, with his worn American Army jacket, his Dick Tracy hat and his khaki pants. He had brought his jacket from Havana, aware of Bogotá's altitude. I had to make do with my leather jacket, which was the warmest piece of clothing that could be bought in Havana, the capital—as you know—of a country in which not one speck of snow has ever fallen. Dick Tracy was (or is) a detective in the funnies, published in Cuba in a newspaper called *El País*. I think that supplement in tabloid form came out on Wednesdays. Dick Tracy had a short-brimmed hat and a two-way radio on his wristwatch. I don't know if they still publish him in the United States, but he disappeared from our newspapers in the mid-sixties. We took over those newspapers, threw their editors out of Cuba and never saw Dick Tracy, Superman, Mandrake the Magician or Tarzan again.

Then I saw this short man kicking a typewriter. The tragic symbolism of the scene became clear to me years later, around January 2001, reading a cable about the advance of Kabila's guerrillas on the capital of Zaire. They'd captured a piano in the attack on a convent, lifted the piano's lid, leaving the strings exposed, and generously defecated on it. I always had my deep suspicions about that black lazybones, but Che Guevara was determined to turn him into the paradigm of a guerrilla fighter and bombard him with Cuban weapons and combatants. They shit on the piano. That's how Kabila's troops ended up thirty-three years after Che's death: shitting on pianos. And that was the symbolism of that man descended of diminutive stock who was kicking a heavy Underwood with a Spanish keyboard up Carrera Séptima, around (if I remember it correctly) Sixth Street. I am sure that neither he nor those savages with Kalashnikovs belonging to Kabila's forces had ever heard Goebbels's famous quote about reaching for his gun whenever he heard the word culture, but they were expressing the same sordid resentment toward its instruments.

While I tried not to lose sight of Rafaelito—like a hunter pilot trusting in the protection of his own kind—I spent the rest of the Bogotazo wandering around Carrera Séptima, at times a witness, at times an agitator, a combatant, a fugitive, and even an impromptu barricade theoretician à la Marx, all in the span of a single afternoon. The Colombian plutocracy later used this adventure to support their claim that I had led the revolution and also fomented it. They never learn. They never understand. The only people who brought about the revolution were the Colombians themselves. For years they have been saying that I led international communism in Bogotá. As if, in just four days, I were capable of unleashing all of the hate and madness that fell upon Santa Fe de Bogotá like the lava from Mount Vesuvius on Pompeii.

My theater of operations, then, was practically reduced to Carrera Séptima and thereabouts. The shop windows seemed to explode as we passed. And following the crash and roar of each shop window, there immediately appeared a crowd dressed in brand-new clothing or wearing the splendorous jewelry that had just been ripped from the mannequins. Then a storm of rocks and later cobblestones began, followed by the destruction of streetcars. I remember asking Rafaelito what the hell the leaders of the Liberal Party, Gaitán's party, were doing if not taking control of the situation. I've done a lot of thinking about that moment. It was about 1:30 or 1:35 p.m., when I started to become swayed by the idea. The truth is that they needed a leader. Me. Anyone. It would have been mutually beneficial. As much for those revolting as for the government. That was the problem with Bogotá, if we look at it from the perspective of finding mediation. If we look at it from the perspective of ruining the event for George C. Marshall, I don't even need to say it: the Bogotazo was a resounding success. But once that initial success was achieved, the situation lost all meaning because it spun out of control.

At some point early on, we decided to go to the hostel where Alfredo and Ovares were staying. In Colombia, they called them *pensiones*. In Cuba we call them guesthouses. They were at the *pensión*. Alfredo brought us warm coffee and we started to confer about the events. It was obvious we should forget about the damned student congress. "It would be best to focus on how we get out of here alive," Ovares said. Rafaelito gave him a disparaging look. Rafaelito wasn't a coward, he really wasn't. And he had good training. The best the Americans could give you in their army. But we had to find some way out and I think we all agreed that we had to get to the Cuban Embassy. We were deciding which route to take when a loud procession of people could be heard outside, making the walls shake. Their shapes were visible through the unfurled curtains hanging over the windows and they were going by swiftly and heavily like a herd of bison. I went outside, as they say, to face the stormy sea; they were all armed with devices made of metal or wood, any instrument that could at the very least crack a skull open, lots of crowbars, lots of clubs, the luckiest ones had rifles. This was the procession that I joined and over which I left Alfredito and Ovares in midsentence, the procession through which I sealed my fate, for the second time in my life, with a revolution that didn't belong to me, and as a foot soldier and, to top it off, on this occasion, unarmed. Ah, my guy Rafaelito kept watch for me, peering down and facing five o'clock.

WE ENDED UP at a police station—the Third Station—where I finally got my weapons. The first one was a shotgun to fire tear gas. But a police officer considered himself lucky when he asked me for it in exchange for a model 24/30 Mauser rifle, of Belgian make—a real jewel of European weaponry from before the Americans took over the Latin American market with their .30-06 semiautomatic Garands, which demonstrated, along with the rest of the American weaponry, their versatility and efficiency in the European and Pacific theaters. As the officer retreated with my tear gas shotgun, it was obvious that he had made a separate peace and that he had considered himself to be in mortal danger while the Mauser still hung from his shoulder. I saw him leave the yard of the police station and head out to the street before he lost himself in the uprising's masses. I still think that was the best exchange I've ever made. The Mauser was also .30-06, with an eighteen-inch barrel and a walnut stock and grip coming from the Fabrique Nationale de Herstal, Belgium, along with fourteen bullets, five in the chamber and nine in the pocket, drastically improved my situation. I was happy. At the highest peak of my happiness. And my friend the Mauser took center stage.

My wanderings as a revolutionary agitator began on Carrera Séptima, wanderings that led me to cooperate (unconsciously) with some fellows from the Presidential Guard bent on breaking up one of the protests, until Rafaelito, who had also procured a rifle and a handful of munitions for himself, and who was much better than I was in matters relating to military identification, asked me in passing why I was pushing people and even hitting them with the butt of my rifle if those soldiers were from the Presidential Guard and real sons of bitches; wanderings (really we should say trajectory, the logical trajectory of a budding revolutionary) that continued with the neutralization of a nest of snipers—some Spanish priests—up in the bell tower of the San Bartolomé School or the Montserrat Chapel (I don't remember which); a trajectory that later had me standing before a wall in front of the Ministry of Defense bailing out on about twelve Colombian students who could only agree to a speech about the precariousness of human dignity in times of social crisis and which was where I lost sight of Rafael del Pino, only later finding out that he had been arrested and released after lying—in a perfect Brooklyn accent—and saying that he belonged to Marshall's personal security; and a trajectory that led me to the university with the goal of recruiting an Andean combat battalion (that was the name I thought up), that left me empty-handed, and still left me with enough time to show up at the Liberal Party's central headquarters in search of any available leader, another effort that left me empty-handed and that concluded, at the day's end, with my following some men whose faces have blurred with time to the mountainside of Montserrat, thirty-six hundred meters high, where I remained until the early hours of the morning and where I took the opportunity to exhaust the six or seven rounds I had left, shooting any which way toward the bottom of the valley where the sparks of a thousand bonfires signaled the houses, establishments or offices of a city that was finally something apart from me but which I riddled with bullets from a distance without ever finding out where my shots went.

It was raining. I remember the rain, fine and cold, that afternoon and night in Bogotá and on the mountainside of Montserrat. Due to the city's altitude and the low clouds covering it, the glow of the fires was trapped in the atmosphere. An immovable ceiling of clouds kept the scene a weak, smoky color of red, as if you were looking through the flame of a candle, and that was the spectrum covering the valley, and, at sunset, Bogotá's last rebels, now sheltered on one side of the Montserrat mountain, looked like beggars from another planet.

I didn't have a single bullet left. Some of my companions, whose number, incidentally, was dwindling in this one-night-long uprising, allowed themselves the same useless exercise between the forests and the night, firing at Bogotá's fires, shots that became increasingly more sporadic as the collective reserve of bullets dwindled. So that my Mauser became a useless instrument emptied of its only meaning. I left it on the mountain, leaning up against a tree without a name, without any marks, without shadows—it was the night I realized that the relaxed shadow of lunar light disappears upon being absorbed by the darkness of the ground. I crossed that city as if in a dream, weightless and intangible, where shadows and fire alike were as dangerous as they were surreal. There were still people who seemed to be dancing ancestral warrior dances around the fires. The fires were trolleys and cars and mountains of garbage turned into fuel for the flames. I got to Alfredito and Ovares's *pensión* around three in the morning. Rafaelito still hadn't shown up. He's at the Claridge, I thought. I urged Alfredito and Ovares to try to reach the Cuban Embassy on their own.

Evidently I had distinguished myself, since by the time I arrived at the Claridge I had half of Colombia's secret police on my back in addition to—as a very alarmed Alfredito told me—President Ospina Pérez himself, who had accused me on the radio of being the instigator of the uprising. He said "the Cuban students." The Cuban students was me.

I was in danger. So I had to flee.

And, sure enough, Rafaelito was at the Claridge.

My biographies are brimming with the famous description of my being a delegate or a skilled agent of a foreign power (in some cases the Argentines', in others, the Soviets') and of the mysterious limousines that picked us up at the Claridge to remove us from harm's way. The Colombian press also uses "these facts" in the annual reports it believes itself to be obliged to publish for each commemoration of the Bogotazo. But let's tell them what happened. What happened was that I made it into the Argentine ambassador's car through the window, with a twisting dive as if I were jumping into a pool and which Rafaelito said made me look like Superman. When the Argentines arrived, I told them that they had to get me out of there, and the Argentines said there was no way in hell they were getting me out. They had gone to the hotel in search of I-don't-know-which embassy employee staying there. You have to get me out of here, I said to them. And they could go to hell themselves.

So I made my way in through the window and, once inside, I kicked the door of the Cadillac, I think it was a Cadillac, and I was already lying across the legs of two Argentines in tails, whom I fell on top of, in the backseat, when, at the end where my feet were, I saw Rafaelito in an overcoat, with his short-brimmed hat, halfway through the act of lighting a cigarette, and behind him, beneath the candlelight of a city in the Andes deprived of all electricity, the arcades of the Claridge. Without even sitting up on the diplomats' legs, I said to Rafaelito, "Climb in, Rafa!"

"*Manus militaris*," said the diplomat on the right, as a sidelong comment to the interlocutor on his left, without daring to touch me or demand that I get off his lap, where I seemed to have made myself comfortable.

"*De facto*," said the one on the left, in a similar vein, taking great care not to disturb me or even look below his abdomen, where my torso and head were and where I appeared to still be scrunched up.

The man sitting in the front, next to the driver, also spoke.

"Segismundo."

"As you wish, Your Excellency," the addressed answered.

"Segismundo, kindly drive to the embassy of the gentlemen's choice," I heard the person who responded to the appellation of Your Excellency say.

THE CUBAN AMBASSADOR was named Guillermo Belt. I will always be grateful for his decision, for his quickness. "I'm sending you to Cuba right now, kids," he said to us. There were no regular flights between Havana and Bogotá. But luck was on our side. One month prior, the Cuban government had allowed some bullfights, prohibited by law, to take place in Havana, as a show that they might succeed in convincing legislators to make a favorable judgment on the bullfights and allow their regular occurrence in Cuba. They declared it the *favorite sport* of the motherland—Spain—and claimed that a high percentage of our population was *of peninsular origin*. Such complicated rhetoric to refer to the spectacle and the Spaniards. Another argument, one made by deeply entrenched fans, was that cockfighting was allowed and accepted as perfectly legal. Cockfighting clubs were authorized to exist one per municipality all across the country in addition to as many cockfighting rings as the cock breeders found necessary, the principal difference between the two being that one was called a club and the other a ring. Anyway, the bullfight, held in a baseball stadium called La Tropical, quickly re-equipped for the event, was a real disaster. Two of the six bulls refused to give a good fight. They were Colombian bulls, slow, docile, and to all of the spectators in Havana they looked more like large cargoes of beef shaped like beasts on four legs. The audience went from booing to mutiny. The police intervention was brutal, according to reports in the press the next day, and also according to El Chino Esquivel, who never missed events like that. The only praised and acceptable action came from the bullfight's organizers. They immediately announced that there would be a new fight, with better bulls, and that the same tickets would be valid for the new event. Well then, that was the reason that on the tarmac of Bogotá's Techo Airport there was a Cuban plane, loaded with two Lidia bulls in the cabin, that we were able to board thanks to Ambassador Belt. Five kids didn't add much to the weight of the bulls, the pilot said. The five of us were Alfredito, Ovares, Rafaelito, that Little Mexican Jorge Menvielle Porte-Petit (who came from I-don't-know-where and whom we advised to keep his mouth shut so as not to betray his accent), and me. Eduardo "Guayo" Hernández, a well-known cameraman, also showed up on the runway. He was sweaty, running, with his Bell & Howell Eyemo in his right hand and the pockets of his impoverished cameraman's jacket about to burst with small gray canisters of thirty-five-millimeter film of the Bogotazo to develop. The C-47 cargo plane took off without any difficulties and with the two black beasts conveniently placed in the middle, across the aircraft's main beam, at the point where the wings cross the fuselage, to maintain the balance of the distribution of the cargo, who didn't demonstrate any annoyance or agitation at the change in plans. Bovine, but with mundane resignation, they accepted that the plane should lift its nose and initiate the ascent. I stood the whole way, grabbing on to one of the old parachute harnesses still hanging from the ceiling. I think I recall Guayo doing the same. The others discovered that if they removed the bolts that held them to the fuselage, the transverse seats could be pushed forward and, in sections, these could accommodate up to five men. "They'll take a shit soon and this is going to be fucking unbearable," Ovares grumbled. "Bulls don't shit in space," said that genius Rafael del Pino, as if the old C-47, one of four purchased as leftovers from the war by Expreso Aéreo Interamericano S. A. and full of patches from the bullet holes that riddled it on Omaha Beach the day of the Normandy landing, were going beyond the terrestrial atmosphere, and exactly one second later one of the bulls let loose the first pressurized stream of shit. Shortly after, Ovares asked if there was no way to roll down a window. That was how, according to Rafaelito's description, thirteen years before launching Sputnik, the first manned spaceship to the cosmos took off from Santa Fe de Bogotá.

Two hours into the flight and somewhat accustomed to the effect of the dunghill, I took the seat next to Alfredo Guevara, who was silent, long-suffering, fragile as usual, with his legs crossed at the knee and a white handkerchief held up over his nose and mouth.

He told me exactly what I needed to hear.

His voice was expressionless and muffled through the handkerchief.

"What did you learn in Bogotá, my dear Fidel?"

There were certainly some key things I learned from the revolt. All would be useful to me, especially as they related to a hypothetical revolution in Cuba, all good lessons that I absorbed from that master class on April 9, 1948, in Bogotá and that I shared with an amazed Alfredo Guevara while the CU-T101 left the continental coast behind and crossed the ocean over Cartagena de Indias, entering the Caribbean in search of Santiago. I spent about three hours talking to Alfredo, until the plane entered a zone of light turbulence and you could see through the windows how the wings flexed above a layer of white clouds. I walked to the front of the cabin. It shouldn't have been a problem, since both pilots were smoking and talking animatedly without even paying attention to the controls. We were an hour and a half away from Cuba and the pilot said we were approaching Dominica and if there were no issues and we got to Cuba before the powerful clouds started to make their rounds and there was still no turbulence, we would try to make it to Havana without a stopover in Santiago or Camagüey; since we were going at a good cruising speed, 205 miles per hour, and were moving smoothly at an altitude of eighteen thousand feet, we didn't need anything more due to the good weather, and the work of the two Pratt & Whitney R-1830 twelve-hundred-horsepower engines was steady and sure.

Bogotá was like shock therapy. Alfredo's question forced me to synthesize aspects of my knowledge and learn about my own thoughts. It was like coming to an agreement with my own experience, a sudden crystallization of truth. Perhaps the most important lesson became evident a few years later when I said that the 26th of July Movement was designed like a military organization with a good propaganda apparatus. That was the final refinement of everything I learned that day—with the added luster of my Marxist readings. Lenin once defined communism as Soviet power plus electrification. Today I would paraphrase it, saying that the origins of the Cuban Revolution are the Bogotazo plus *State and Revolution*.

But that was the final refinement—and I would say the perfect one—of a whole series of initial refinements that existed before and that came about, I think, due to a very particular, very specific warning sign. The sign was revealed to me when I saw the out-of-control mobs. And at the moment I knew that they were a revolution's worst enemy, worse than mercenary armies, than the Cossacks, than the White Guard, than the Menshevik government, than the hundred flowers Mao allowed to bloom only to cut them down later, than a counterrevolutionary insurgency, than the CIA. That was the first thing I listed to Alfredo Guevara. I could imagine that crowd if it was given a goal, if it had a leader—especially if it had a leader. The imperious need for a leader. They were in the streets, they had risen up, and it was like a party. But they weren't there to start a revolution. Nothing gets the poor more excited and awakens their imaginations more vigorously than a celebration they haven't paid for. They had a reason. Gaitán. In the future, we would have to look for a substitute for Gaitán. In other words, there's no revolution without a reason. But at that moment, the lesson was a defeatist one, since there were no immediate positive results. Later you learn from that refinement, and when it turns into learning, the results are reversed and turn positive. Do you copy? If you allow actions without crowd control, you waste all opportunities for a revolution. Life and time have proven me right. Colombia won't know the possibility of a true revolution for a long time because any possibility of an attempt was corrupted in a single afternoon by the Colombian people themselves. If the time ever came, this was something that I would never, under any circumstances, allow the Cuban people to get away with. They were on the verge of getting out of hand during the 1933 revolution, but Batista and his cohort of intellectuals put a quick stop to that. It didn't accomplish much more than a few instances of looting and a handful of lynchings.

I just demonstrated the need for keeping the masses under control and the requirement of finding a reason. That covers the two main parts of the refinement for seizing power: the military apparatus that turns into a governing elite, what is known as "the vanguard" in Marxist language, and a reason-producing apparatus to win the public's approval during the course of the war. But there was also Sparta. And this was the final refinement, from an unexpected harvest. Use the army to control the population, but not as an exogenous repressive force, rather as a Spartan-style citadel in which the barriers between civil life and the barracks are never exactly defined. How to turn Cuba, one of the most open and libertine societies in the world, full of prostitutes, gamblers, freewheelers, into an unconquerable, closed plaza, a kingdom of austerity? Well then, let's thank Bogotá. Because that's where I always say many things had their origins.

I DON'T RECALL having talked about the Bogotazo much until the 1980s, when Gabriel García Márquez and his Colombian journalist friends showed up. Then the Bogotazo became an unavoidable reference. The finest moment of those nostalgic gatherings in Gabriel's house in Cuba—well, the house that I placed at his disposal—was one evening when I told the story of the man going around kicking a typewriter in the middle of the revolt, a story I have since repeated a few times, even in the presence of tape recorders. Gabo was taken with the story, so much so that he made me repeat it in front of some of his guests on another occasion, but that time he said to me, in a confessional-type of tone, "Fidel, I bet you don't know who the man kicking the typewriter was? It was me, Fidel! Me!" Poor Gabo. He's very sick now, fighting cancer. But should he still be alive for the publication of this book, he will finally understand why, from that moment on, every time we saw each other I would look right at his feet. Covered as they usually were in white moccasins with no socks, his small feet were white and virginal as an older Cinderella. I ask myself about the effects of the impact of such tiny, oh-so-delicate feet against the armor of an Underwood No. 5 with front-stroke mechanism manufactured after 1910 and how they could possibly not have broken in the attempt.

I WAS WITH ANOTHER woman before marrying Mirta. She was a little older than me. María Laborde. I had a son with that woman. Jorge Ángel. That affair has never been publicized and María has been very respectful of my needs in that sense. I found out that she was pregnant while I was getting ready for my wedding with Mirta. María asked me to let her keep the kid, and in exchange she promised not to cause any problems for me. She has religiously kept her word. I didn't hesitate to give the kid my last name and to help him and his mother all these years. Jorge Ángel Castro is not only my firstborn, but of all my children he is the sweetest and the one with whom I get along best. He is probably not a Castro where it concerns his ambitions and the anguish that my genetic imprint can unleash. Perhaps he favors his mother's genetic makeup. Jorge Ángel graduated with a degree in chemistry, has worked for years at the Academy of Science, is married (I went to his wedding), has a beautiful family and is not wanting for anything. By anything, I mean within the modest possibilities afforded by the Cuban Revolution, in which VCRs, Soviet Lada cars and the two- and three-bedroom houses in the neighborhoods formerly inhabited by the petit bourgeoisie are all considered luxuries. María occupies an important, but discreet, position within the Revolution.

Now I have kept my word to you, my readers, of not eluding any important personal information, but I invite you to hurry up and turn the page, since this is a part of my life that must exist outside the realm of public scrutiny and which I feel obliged to offer as much protection as possible.

I FELL IN LOVE with Mirta Díaz-Balart. Right away. It was the classic love at first sight. And as usually happens in these cases, it was on both of our parts. I was in my first year of law school and we used to study at my classmate Rafael Díaz-Balart's house—another Rafaelito! That's where I met her. In contrast to my usual social misfortunes, her brother Rafaelito seemed to be very pleased with the news. As you know, we honeymooned in Miami and New York. And my father gave me the ten thousand pesos that appear in all the biographies. The sum was more than enough for me to *settle down* as he had planned, that was the real reason for giving me such a gift: ten thousand pesos was a lot of money back then. With that amount, he was hoping I would leave politics, get my professional life together and set up some little side business until I finished my studies. But the main thing was that I abandon the struggle. Of course, that amount was barely enough for us. It was one of the longest honeymoons in history. It lasted almost three months. And we met up with Rafaelito, in New York. That was where, in addition to the gray-toned suit that Mirta picked out for me and the black leather jacket, I bought a used Lincoln Continental. We took it back to Cuba on a ferry. Upon our arrival in Havana, there was no money to pay the customs fees for that monstrosity. Then, once again, El Chino came to the rescue. He mobilized some of our class-mates, the Granados brothers—one of whom, Raúl, was one of our buddies on our outings to the brothels—whose parents owned a farm, and they sold one or two cows to pay the customs fees.

I ASSOCIATE THE END of my honeymoon with the transition to another phase in my life. Perhaps most men have this feeling upon returning from their wedding trip and realizing they are no longer single. But I also associated it with the geographic movement. As I traveled U.S. 1, which took me from New York to Miami, and which would ultimately lead me back to Cuba, I moved toward another point in time while my used Lincoln Continental rolled over the immaculate American federal highway. I raised a lot of money for my honeymoon with Mirta, in addi-tion to the ten thousand pesos from my father, equal to the same sum in dollars, which was a lot of money back then. Other relatives, friends and political figures showered me with money and gifts. Batista gave me a night lamp. He deemed me worthy. At least at the time. I spend about ten days in Miami. Then I call my brother-in-law Rafaelito Díaz-Balart, who had gotten married to a very pretty girl, Hilda, in March, and who was living in New York. They weren't having a very easy time of it there. Rafaelito first tried to be a Baptist minister in a poor neighborhood in Manhattan, in which, following his sermons, he also had to take care of cleaning up the church. He was offered $150 a week. He ended up in an exports company, both he and Hildita, doing some typing. "Where are you?" he asked. "Miami," I told him. "Miami *bich*." "But where?" "At a hotel." "But, which one?" "The best hotel on the beach. The shah stayed here. I want to go up there." "Where should I make you a reservation?" he asked me. "The Waldorf-Astoria?" "No," I told him. "I want to be near you." Rafaelito was living in what was called a *furnished room*. A small, furnished room. A bed, some nightstands, and the hell with it. That was it. And a small kitchen on top of the toilet. Rafaelito, as he himself confessed, had left Cuba fleeing his commitments to the UIR—do you remember them? Emilio Tró's group. We became members of the UIR for many reasons, among them that it protected us. But what worried Rafaelito the most was that one day they would call you out of the blue to go kill someone *and you had to go*. And, Rafaelito reasoned, it was pretty fucked up to kill someone when you didn't know who they were or why. A lot of times, these were due to *cranques*, malicious rumors designed to turn peoples' opinions, the Cuban lexical conversion from the American *crank*, the handle used to start cars before the invention of ignition system engines. "I want to live with you," I said to him. "Unbelievable," he said. "I have money. We'll eat out. And I'll learn English." The super was German. There was just one free room left. But the German guy didn't want to rent it out because it was right next to his own room and the bathroom was wedged between the two. "If they're like you . . ." the German guy said. What he meant was that if we were as neat and responsible as Hilda and Rafaelito, then there would be no problem. That was the condition on which we were rented the room. "They're marvelous people," Rafaelito told the German guy, assuring him of our respectable behavior, though all the while he was perfectly aware that this would be the last civil conversation he had with the German. Dirtball arrived. That's how Rafaelito referred to my arrival at the German guy's building in Manhattan. A dirtball was a citizen averse to washing up much. He was dirty. Very dirty. So dirty that he was literally a ball of dirt. At the time, it was a term of affection. I think it's a very Cuban use of a term that could otherwise be very offensive in certain circumstances. There's nothing that warms the heart more than a good friend calling you a son of a bitch when he wants to show you his admiration and respect. This isn't the same as being a son of a bitch to your enemies, something that would be entirely inadmissible if said to your face and would call for blood, blood and bullets. Rafaelito has always had the luxury of calling me Dirtball in his two absolutely contradictory conditions. As my brother through thick and thin and as my irreconcilable enemy. So, Dirtball got to Manhattan and the German spent a couple of hours explaining the locks on the bathroom's two doors, the door to his room and the door to mine. Four locks in all. Open the bathroom and close my door. Take care of your needs. Open my door and close yours. *Underrrstand?* Close the bathroom from the inside. Your needs. Poop. Finish. Open my door from inside the bathroom. Exit. Close your door from outside the bathroom. *Underrrstand? Opeeen. Clooose.* Poop. *Clooose.* Opeeen. My God, I asked myself at this juncture of history and circumstances: Did Lenin go through this much to take a shit in Vienna? You can imagine how all of that worked out. Well, in the two months we spent in Manhattan, the German didn't get to take a single piss in peace. Rafaelito acted as a sort of emissary during an armistice. While his sister, and my dear wife, Mirta, just turned a blind eye, and the truth is that, though at the time she thought my messiness funny, Rafaelito couldn't refrain any longer from asking me not to ruin everything for him in such a methodic and enthusiastic way. "At least please try, Fidel," he would say to me. Besides my dispute against the Fourth Reich, I did actually spend my time studying. I followed the method of memorization I employed at the university. Read one page, memorize it, rip out the page, roll it into a little ball and throw it out. I was learning English. Learning it like a mother tongue. Rafaelito procured an enormous dictionary for me and I resolved to learn two hundred words a day. I remember that I was at *beaverboard*, halfway through page 101, on the left hand column, when the crisis with the Teuton reached its final stage. Just a few days before, I had bought myself the Lincoln Continental, a used model from the previous year with automatic doors, spending all of the money I had left. Of course, Rafaelito was unaware that I was lacking in funds. But he reproached me for the purchase of that battleship. He said the smart thing would have been to buy a Buick or a Dodge, brand-new, and cheaper. It was then that the German said he wouldn't permit one more transgression and that he wasn't going to allow his bladder—*meine Blase!*—to burst on my account. *Meine Blase!* he charged. "Let's pay what we owe and go," Rafaelito said to me, obviously resigned. "Pay *what?*" I said to him. "I'm so broke I can't pay attention, Rafa." Rafael Díaz-Balart went pale. "Look, Rafa, what we have to do is resist. Wait a few days and you'll see the German guy himself kick us out without our having to pay a single cent. Just wait and see." A few days later we were on the road, en route to Miami. The German's state of indignation just barely gave us enough time to pack. As a souvenir, I left him the dictionary with the first fifty-eight pages ripped out, fifty of the dictionary itself and another eight pages of titles and editor's notes. To this day I still don't know the meaning of *beaverboard* because I had gotten that far, but didn't get to read the entry. I've always imagined it's like a beaver hat or a good-natured anteater on a board. The German guy couldn't take a piss and we were leaving via U.S. 1 South. The Lincoln, as you could expect, would break down every time we reached a new town. That trip lasted five days. The coast was to our left. The United States of America, the whole continental expanse of it, to our right. Behind me, smiling and entertained and taking popcorn out of a bottomless container and crunching it between her small, doll-like teeth, the crumbs sprinkled all over her skirt, was my wife, Mirta, with whom I exchanged funny faces and winks and blown kisses through the rearview mirror. Rafaelito, next to me, was somewhat happy and even anxious to return to Cuba after his failure to conquer New York. Once in a while he took the wheel and drove for a stretch. Hilda, distant and silent, was in the back, to the right. And so we continued.

A black Lincoln town car on U.S. 1 South.

Fidel delivers his October 30, 1955, speech in Palm Garden, New York, in which for the first time he proclaims his commitment to land in Cuba before the end of the following year.

PART THREE

As
INTIMATE
AS CHRIST

8

The Power Yet to Be

/ / /

. . . the old blood which he had not been permitted to choose for himself which had been bequeathed him willy nilly and which had run for so long (and who knew where, battening on what of outrage and savagery and lust) before it came to him.

—WILLIAM FAULKNER,
"BARN BURNING"

GAMAL ABDEL NASSER, SWEPT AWAY BY THE INITIAL FERVOR OF THE Cuban Revolution, once told my ambassador in Cairo that there were two mistakes committed by imperialism in the postwar years. Two strategic errors. The first was the creation of the state of Israel. The second, bringing about Fulgencio Batista's coup d'état in Havana, then accepting his rule. Without the first, he explained, he would have been nothing more than an obscure colonel of the Egyptian army, distinguished perhaps in the Gaza zone. Without the second, I would have been nothing more than an obscure representative clamoring for agrarian reform. It was a way, of course, to paint himself into the picture.

When my ambassador told me about it, I couldn't conceive of this man, who dominated the political spectrum of almost the entire Middle East, engaging in this kind of neo-Stalinist meditation. Later, in the seventies, when our alliance with the Soviets became an inherent part of our way of governing and when I myself was in a way leading that same international communist movement, it became more difficult for me to accept the mental workings of men like Nasser and his view of history

*Fidel's mug shot after the attack on the Moncada Barracks
on the 26th of July, 1953.*

as an enigma, or, worse still, as the product of obscure and unreadable conspiracies. Either way, I could understand why he was interested in coming under our umbrella and why we were so highly esteemed by this hard-line Egyptian leader. In the early sixties, with the Cold War in full swing, Cuba was constantly in the news and my presence in the papers eclipsed almost any other world leader. Only Kennedy and Khrushchev, and later Johnson and Brezhnev, could compete, while Nasser appeared only sporadically with his failed wars against Israel. Don't get angry. I'm merely stating a fact. Confined to that forgotten corner of the world, his reasoning was purely Stalinist, or almost purely, and that's what he let on to the Cuban ambassador in broken English. In reports made by our ambassador, Luis García Guitar, the descriptions that reached me from Cairo were vivid and courtesanlike. And Stalinist. García Guitar was one of those strange products of Cuban homegrown communism, beyond tough, brutal if need be, but entirely dedicated to the cause and very intelligent and able. The perfect man to have at Nasser's side. His reports were the ones my staff gave me when anything came up in the region. He was the first who described Nasser to us as a Stalinist, with a certain note of happiness, as if detached from the fact that our ambassador had found a kindred soul. García Guitar had charmed Nasser as soon as he presented his credentials, October 3, 1964,* when he answered a question about revolutionary Cuba's economy by saying that we were engaged in the daily battle of making soap out of sugarcane. "Soap from sugar, Excellency?" the Egyptian president had asked him, and he answered, as seriously as he could, "Yes, Mr. President, soap from sugar," and from that moment the ceremony turned into an uproar in which Nasser gripped our ambassador's right shoulder as he pitched forward in a fit of laughter, calling out to his whole team of ministers and generals and pointing with his free hand at Ambassador García Guitar's round, but solid body and saying, when the laughter allowed him to catch his breath, "*SOAP FROM SUGAR!*" At least García Guitar didn't tell Nasser that the aforementioned soap was one of my experiments at the time, in which I was trying to save Cuba's main export material in a country whose inhabitants, the Cuban people, felt obliged to wash themselves daily. In that case, Gamal Abdel Nasser might have even laughed

---

* See "Nasser reconfirms his strong support for Cuba. He received the new Cuban Ambassador," in *Hoy*, Havana, Sunday, October 4, 1964. [*Author's note.*]

at our attempts in the soap industry, but he had the same common characteristic that identifies and unites Stalinists across all regions and time periods: nostalgia for revolutions. I detected this in García Guitar's reports when Nasser would take him aboard his yacht at sunset to enjoy iced tea, cigars and a talk about world revolution while the presidential boat cruised slowly down the Nile. "Imperialist mistakes are always more valuable than our successes. Sometimes it's just a matter of sitting at the door of your tent and waiting for them to err," said Nasser. He was afflicted by chronic sinusitis and thus surrounded by diligent adolescents who regularly provided him with lightly perfumed handkerchiefs with which to blow his nose.

It was a deterministic view of history. But—worst of all—it permeated all of his combat structures. Since it was a religious view of history, it was in the hands of officers who were as ruthless as they were fanatical. But this was also their weakness. They ended up succumbing to all of that predestination shit. All of them. In the end, history had nothing to do with it.

In any event, the Nasserist meditation sessions on the Nile, transmitted to me via diplomatic courier, made me think of a certain analogy. One can't help commenting on the fact that we celebrate a common origin. On July 26, 1953, I directed the attack on the Moncada Barracks and on July 26, 1956, he nationalized the Suez Canal. This is where I wanted to start off this chapter about my memories of the Moncada attack. Certainly, despite Nasser and his sophisms, I am pressed to say up front that if the origins of the Cuban Revolution had anything to do with the international communist movement, it was absolutely tangential and something that I directed from a distance, lots of distance. Because the origins came only from my gut. You can call them my aberrations if that suits you. Whatever you want to call my purpose. But note this. It was all personal. No Stalinism or imperialist mistakes or any of that Marxist nonsense.

I.

I am the Revolution.

NONE OF THE MATTERS pertaining to my status as a married man was taken care of when the ferry left the dock at Key West and headed for Havana. It was taking me, along with my wife on deck and the Lincoln

Continental in the hold, to the Republic where I had established my household but to which I was returning with my pockets empty. Everything I could say right now about that time is going to sound like mere whining and not like the description of the final training period of a nascent revolutionary leader debating the injustices of capital society with himself. For the time being, this would be my destiny, the dogma by which I would be forced to live in the years following my wedding. It was the country to which my circumstances fated me. And the future I was forced to accept. The first of September 1949, my second son was born, Fidel Castro Díaz-Balart, whom I thought best to remove from the public eye from 1959 until he received his doctorate in physics in the Soviet Union and who would later go by José Raúl Fernández. For the aforementioned reasons, Fidelito is recognized in history as my firstborn, although I had had that other son, Jorge Ángel Castro, out of my relationship with María Laborde. About seven years after Fidelito was born, and also as a result of an extramarital relationship, with Naty Revuelta, on March 19, 1956, my third child was born, a female in this case: Alina Fernández Revuelta. The last name Fernández (and not Castro) can be explained. Orlando Fernández-Ferrer was the prestigious (and moneyed) doctor whom Naty had married. Moneyed and stoic. Like a determined ship's captain, from the bridge he withstood all the gales and storms his adorable Naty thrust upon his bow. Or was she herself the storm? This production of royal offspring as a result of unions not blessed by the church or by any law has its own explanation, perhaps an all too-obvious one: I can't stand condoms.

MEMORY MAY BE one of the body's functions with the greatest tendency to please. You never have more musculature when you need to lift something very heavy, nor does your vision get any sharper when you want to shoot at a target over a thousand yards away. But when you want to remember something, your memory quickly provides you with a series of remembrances that are *generally pleasant*. It's as if, on demand, it offered you only sweets for your choosing, laid out hurriedly on the plaid tablecloth next to glittering honeys and pastries. But it's the fucked-up material, or the insignificant, that refuses to flourish, to be recalled from the archive. In the case of the fucked-up material, it's there as a negative feeling or as a warning sign and the rest, the insignificant, floats like bottles from a shipwreck in a small sea of calm in which there is no ship in sight. All in your brain. All of it stored from the moment you were born, ready for your personality and life adventures to shape it.

AZPIAZU, CASTRO & RESENDE was an idea that came up on the university steps. We were about to graduate and I had to separate myself from El Chino Esquivel, because he, the son of lawyers, had to take over the business run by his old man, who was suffering from cancer. Esquivel the elder didn't have much time left to train his kid. Rafael Resende, who came from a very poor background and was my same age, had the idea of starting a law firm. Jorge Azpiazu was nine years older than me and had voted against me when I ran for FEU president. But he also grew up in poverty and had taken me for a little rich boy. A preppie. Despite being sprung out of the lower class, which would have so pleased Marx, Azpiazu was always an apolitical man whose only goal in life was to have enough food on his table without committing himself to any party or ideology. With that attitude, he accepted the advent of the Revolution and it is my understanding that he spent the rest of his life as a lawyer in one of our collective law firms. He stayed on there just as he would have stayed on in any obscure legal department pertaining to one of the ministries of Grau or even Batista himself. His monthly paycheck was guaranteed, as well as his food by way of his ration card, a system instituted by our Revolution from 1961 on. What more could he aspire to? In other words, why should he pick up the telephone and call the Central Committee under the pretense of communicating with Fidel or leaving the message—in either of these cases—that his old associate Jorge Azpiazu Núñez de Villavicencio was interested—if it was no bother, of course— in a better job? Resende, in contrast, didn't waste the opportunity given him as soon as the Revolution triumphed to switch to the right until he finally emigrated to Miami. The old hunger pains weren't worth a damn in his case.

We came to an agreement just as we were about to graduate, the three of us seated on the university steps. We leased a small office on the second floor of a building at Number 57 Tejadillo Street, that primarily let out to other law offices. (Cubans say lease. They only say rent when they've emigrated. I do not know the etymological path that such words take in the Cuban mind, distinguishing them from one another). The owner's name was José Alvarez and his building was called Rosario and the rent was sixty pesos a month. Alvarez demanded one month in advance and another as deposit, when we only had eight pesos between the three of us. To be frank, I didn't have to flap my lips much to convince Alvarez to accept the eight pesos so we could set up shop. I also persuaded him to lend us some furniture, at minimum a desk and a chair. It was indispensable—I insisted—to our getting started. If he could also find us a sign maker to write our names on the door, I'd really appreciate it. In alphabetical order, of course.

ASPIAZU, CASTRO & RESENDE

—

DOCTORES EN DERECHO CIVIL Y LICENCIADOS EN DERECHO DIPLOMÁTICO Y CONSULAR

Our first client was Madereras Gancedo. You have no idea how much pleasure I took about ten years later—in 1960—in divesting Gancedo, a typical Spanish immigrant, of his business and his cluttered warehouses. He didn't really have the same spirit as my father, another Spaniard, and the only thing that seemed to interest him were the debts of a myriad of poor Havana carpenters. I still remember his address, Number 3 Concha Street, at Luyanó Street, in a neighborhood southwest of the city, next to a train hub, where almost all the wood wholesalers were. And his telephone numbers. Oh, God, I remember both of his telephone numbers. I prompt my memory and it seems like I am rifling through drawers I had forgotten about, full of old postcards, letters, photos, as if dealing with the discovery of someone else's life. How is that possible? 9 1819 and 9 1529. Gancedo no longer exists, nor do his warehouses or telephones, not even those digits on our communications grid, and I am recalling them with useless precision. It's like looking for your childhood home in a neighborhood that has been completely demolished to make way for new construction.

The work was as a collection agency, but I convinced my associates to take it. At the same time, I convinced Gancedo to pay us—at least partially—in advance and in kind: wood and pieces of plywood so we could finish making furniture for our office. Then we got in touch with the poor devils on his list of debtors and asked them for their own lists, our original plan being to get to the root of all these unmet contractual obligations. That was when we realized the dilemma. I mean, when we actually got something out of the debt-owing carpenters or cabinetmakers in the district, never more than twenty or thirty pesos, we then handed over those discolored, handled and worn-out bills to one of the wretched of the earth only to immediately snatch them away and return them to a well-to-do man made fat on Galician stews. That such a thing should continue its violent course was dependent on what you did with the money. You can imagine what happened, right? That *gallego* Gancedo never recovered a single cent. Nor did he recover the load of wood he advanced us for our furniture. Now let's discuss, *entre nous*, let's discuss *it shorthand,* as we Cubans say, and let's look each other in the eye. Face-to-face. Have you ever enjoyed the look of surprise, initially it's surprise, then it's disconcerted gratitude, when you tell a pariah, a mere serf, a slave, a proletarian, Hey, those twenty pesos are all yours, man? There's no way in hell we're paying that tycoon. Down with the tycoons, man. When you have that experience, on the day that this should happen to you, then and only then will you understand how the education of a revolutionary leader is completed. A pathetic law office in old Havana and a traveling, disorganized band of carpenter-cabinetmakers can be the catalysts for the most stunning historical movement in the twentieth century. That's the moral of the story of the irresponsible little lawyer and his cohort of carpenters. Don't forget the gratitude and the way those hands tremble because they are suddenly putting twenty pesos into their pockets that they hadn't accounted for. Don't forget it, and now spit all the insults you want at me and tell me as many times as you want that I'm a son of a bitch.

It's amazing that Azpiazu, Castro & Resende survived until I left to begin my preparations relating to Moncada. We earned a total of forty-eight hundred pesos in our three years of operation—from our graduation in September 1950 until two months prior to July 1953—a very low sum which would have been embarrassing for any of our other classmates with their own practices already, nearly always prosperous ones. Aramís Taboada had his regal and popular office on San Ignacio Street, if I remember correctly at Number 104, relatively close to our Rosario building on Tejadillo Street. And Rafaelito had set himself up in an ostentatious building called La Metropolitana, on Presidente Zayas Street, the main street in front of the Presidential Palace. Of course, the majority of our clientele, the owners of the small municipal market auctions, peasants from the interior of the province of Havana stripped of their land and students beaten by the police in some demonstration, wouldn't have made us much more. Looking back, what amazes me is how Jorge Azpiazu and Rafael Resende held out for so long.

BATISTA'S COUP D'ÉTAT, March 10, 1952, was the most beneficial action I could have been supplied. By breaking down all of the country's institutions, it did nothing but leave the path open for Revolution. In a way—if circumstances had been friendlier—I should thank him. I'm also able to recognize that, concerning its internal conspiracy, they executed their plan perfectly.

All of the officers suspected of resisting the coup were being watched. Groups of soldiers were assigned to arrest them as soon as they got the signal. March 10 was chosen because it was the day after Carnival in Havana, so the conspirators could blend in with the revelers. Sogo, the officer on duty at Camp Columbia,* allowed Batista's twelve-car motorcade to enter without resistance.† The pictures taken that morning in Columbia of Batista in informal dress and surrounded by a fervent crowd of soldiers in steel helmets symbolized, to my eyes, the frailty of a whole nation. When I gazed at them in the papers, they awoke in me a jealousy that was incomprehensible in theory. That mob of sinewy peasants with yellowish skin and names and surnames that could only belong to the men surrounding Batista—the Sogos, the Tandróns, the Tuñóns, the Cañizares, the Margolles (good God, how could someone who didn't support Batista be called Sogo!)—were celebrating something more than a quick and—if you consider its efficiency and that there were only four deaths—even deserved victory.‡ Their uniforms are soaked in sweat due to their excitement and we can even make out the bitter smell of the soldiers as each one struggles to

---

* This was the main headquarters of the Armed Forces, to the west of Havana. [*Author's note.*]

† Television and radio stations and the telephone company were immediately placed under the control of military personnel with rifles. At nine in the morning, Carlos Prío Socarrás and other members of his government sought asylum at the Mexican Embassy. [*Author's note.*]

‡ The deaths were due to an accidental exchange of gunfire at the door of the Presidential Palace. [*Author's note.*]

appear by General Batista's side in the photograph or to show his loyalty to him with one of those appreciative-underling hugs or ready-
to-serve stances. They're celebrating something that seems to be the
norm among Latin American military men: the occupation of their
own country. Nevertheless, what they're celebrating with even greater
enthusiasm is the fact that while the coup took them by surprise, these
mere army recruits would be running things from now on, in charge
of all the money and sleeping with the ladies and the whores. For the
third time in less than a century, the country had to accommodate an
emerging social group that sought to install itself as the new aristocracy. And that was before our own triumphant arrival seven years later
at that same base at Columbia. But I consider those old photos from
March 1952 and I can't help their becoming an altarpiece of concepts,
a transmutation or displacement of images of philosophic abstraction.
Or perhaps, to those who understand these things, the best way I could
apply the theory of relativity outside the realm of physics would be to
apply it in historical terms. But how could I tell those exalted soldiers
at the height of victory that they were all dead men? What would they
have said if you had told them then that some kid who was just a frustrated and violent nobody, consumed with jealousy when he heard the
news on an old Motorola that someone had beaten him to the punch by
seizing power, was going to end up sending the lot of them to the firing squad and, for good measure, stripping them of all the money and
properties they would steal in the meantime?

SO BATISTA AND HIS MEN carried out their coup and came to power
and I was going to quickly end up poor and disoriented on the steps
of the University of Havana, observing my veins, alone with my own
blood. I took my right hand and beat myself methodically with two fingers, like drumsticks, on the inside of my forearm just under my wrist,
the palest part of my skin, protected as it always was from direct sun-
light, with the goal of stimulating my circulation and trying to register
the latitudes, frequencies, echoes of what I imagined being the closest possible physical manifestation of my own existence. I was alone
against a backdrop that no longer belonged to me. Once more, the sun
set over Cuba. There was a small square in front of me that had been
converted into a parking lot, in the middle of which was a pedestal

with a bronze bust of Julio Antonio Mella, with the indelible trail of white paint stuck on his right side, the side that was invisible to me now, since the university steps, where I found myself, were to the other side of him. Beyond the small square turned into a parking lot was the façade of the Andino Hotel, where my brother Raúl usually stayed. To the left, crossing San Lázaro Street, in a turn-of-the-century mansion, was a large sign announcing the presence, right there, of the "America" Gym.

I didn't even have enough money to buy myself a cigar. There's nothing like a good cigar to get your mind going. There was no cigar. No raucous voices of friends. I was alone. Alone with my own blood. And I was hungry.

A few days ago, I had been running for Representative of the Cuban People's (Orthodox) Party, and simultaneously I was inventing something that was empirically called—or some called it—Radical Orthodox Action (Acción Radical Ortodoxa, or ARO) that obtained the support of no one and quickly dissolved amid more important news. It was not a divisive attempt, although some chose to see it that way. It was merely an attempt to activate an idea about fighting, about combat.

The legal opposition prospects, for the time being, were null. Batista's coup was carried out eighty days before elections were supposed to take place. After the coup, fourteen days later, to be exact, on March 24, 1952, I took the first step in the path of my political future with the appeal I presented before Havana's Emergency Court. I did it as an individual, as a lawyer, while still a member of the Orthodox Party. I was still unaware, of course, that the precepts of legal opposition would have to be annulled forever in the country if I wanted my efforts to succeed.

And it was right there—when I had nothing to take home that night to feed my wife and child, or even enough to have a good smoke (I didn't need anything fancy on that occasion, I would have been happy with anything from a Cazador de Pita to a Romeo & Juliet No. 2), and while carrying on with that investigation of my own pulse, grabbing my own wrist as if, through the flow of my own blood, as if it were an underground current, I could detect the sign I was waiting for, which I knew would come from somewhere, and while my gaze went from the América Gym ad to the bust of Mella and returned to the absurdity of that large hand-painted sign that was probably from the early forties—that I decided to destroy the Republic.

Gimnasio América
San Lázaro 1260
Tel: F 81 11

From then on, that was what set me apart from the rest of humanity: when I was at my all-time low I decided to attack a fortress.

Rebelling against a situation that reduced me to mediocrity is neither a crime nor a sin. The problem, of course, resides in the obligatory extending of these *same rights* that my adversaries—those who become so—are supposedly guaranteed when they in turn reject their own mediocrity under my command. But that's their affair to work out. Now, I want you to pay close attention to this moment. The whole rest of my life after making that decision has been spent justifying it. Because that decision, which was entirely personal, made me drag the whole country along with it, and by country I mean its entire population, history and natural habitats. You should pay attention because, upon realizing the pathetic state of my personal affairs at the time and the circumstances obliging me to find a solution, I made it so that one man, just one, *yo mismo,* should become the neurological center of an entire nation. And this leads to the most reasonable of the theoretical appraisals of the Cuban Revolution. I've told you before. Now my revelations acquire more strength: I am the Revolution. My hunger and my frustration and my bitterness and everything you can think of, my tongue, my eyes, my viscera, they are the Revolution.

Then there was a spark of enthusiasm from the dark ashes of my consciousness. Was it the sign? I had thought it was something abstract, something that probably came from the books of my childhood, from the Knights of the Round Table or even beyond, when I tangled with Niccolò Machiavelli and found that as I raced through the passages of *The Prince*, what lay in my subconscious were medieval castles and men on horseback and strongholds heating up oil in catapults in the early morning mist. The fortress. Attack the fortress. This had been a model of abstraction. The fortresses. The most mistaken and absurd of all military concepts in the history of mankind. Concentrating all available forces in one place to wait for the enemy to strike. Fortresses exist solely to be attacked. Oh, hell, what I wouldn't give for a Partagás cigar. Or even for a Cazador de Pita. Dammit, I've got it. Yes, the idea is there. I've got it, dammit. I've got it. How is it possible that I didn't realize this before? Why, this is a country full of fortresses! No. It can't be Columbia. Too vast, too many troops. So which one, dammit? Which one?

"TRY TO SLEEP, ABEL," I told him.

I was sitting on the floor, leaning against the door lintel, when Abel Santamaría came up to me. I remember that I was thinking about the ten men we had as prisoners in one of the interior rooms, the door immobilized from the outside by a Yale lock. The Revolution was just about to start and we already had our first prisoners, and they didn't come from enemy ranks, they were revolutionaries. Don't think it wasn't a difficult metaphor for me to swallow. But it served as a way to test myself. The lesson I was extracting was that once the process is set into motion, it's unthinkable to allow even a minimal show of hesitation among the revolutionaries and even more unthinkable that I should allow it. The ringleader of the prisoners—for now— was Gustavo Arcos Bergnes. We called those men "the reluctant ones" because that had been their sin: demonstrating reluctance to participate in the plot, which we had explained to the members of our group just a short while before. I was thinking about what in the hell I would do with them when we left for combat. Gustavo himself gave me the most honorable (and if not honorable, then at least reasonable, although right now I couldn't tell you which of the two was better for the cause) of solutions. He knocked at the door and said he had rethought things and was ready for battle. Later he said that his change of heart was due to listening to Lester Rodríguez, one of the leaders of our group, and my brother Raúl, softly singing old Cuban songs until they fell asleep. The remaining nine maintained their refusal to participate and in the end I decided to let them go before we left for combat. They didn't understand the message. Gustavo understood perfectly. Participate or die. Years later, of course, upon describing the absolutely voluntary nature of the men who attacked the Moncada, I've always said that I offered the pusillanimous ones the alternative of waiting a prudent amount of time—half an hour or so—after the last of our cars went out before they left La Granjita. It's unnecessary to explain (to not complicate the positive effects of revolutionary propaganda) that not one of those nine survived and that the army captured them all right at La Gran-jita or around there, and anyway there was no escape possible for them, as they were among unknown mountains and without a single cent in their pockets or means of transportation at their disposal. Participate or die.

The narrow road leading from Santiago to Siboney Beach ran about a hundred meters from the door. There was a red mud flagstone path lead-ing up to the entrance of the farm, lined by areca palms. And it had been at least forty minutes since the last car had passed on the road.

The hours before daybreak passed slowly and the temperature was stifling, since the evening had gone by without any rain and all that water in the clouds was trapped in the middle layers of the atmosphere. Sweat was making my shirt stick to my back and in the clear sky of dawn of July 26, 1953, at the distance we were from Santiago, where the reflection of the city lights didn't block the twinkling of the distant stars, the vault of heaven seemed to expand with the fleetingness of plankton. If the sky remained as clear by midmorning, and no cloud got in the way between the sun's rays and Santiago and its outskirts—I figured—we were going to have a scorching hot July 26.

July 26, 1953. One in the morning.

"One in the morning," I said.

"That's what time your watch says?"

"One in the morning."

"Me too," he said. "My watch also says one."

"Rest, Abel, rest," I insisted.

The volunteers had come in different cars from Artemisa, Matanzas and Havana. I had been sheltering them for days in the Granjita's small wooden house with a mosaic floor, near Siboney Beach, fifteen minutes from Santiago. One hundred twenty-four men and two girls.

Now they were sleeping. Or smoking silently. Or waiting.

I had two hidden sentry posts outside.

"Aren't you tired, Fidel?"

RAFAEL MORALES SÁNCHEZ is in the Carnival's parade. There's a float made up by girls representing the navy, the army and the police. Morales Sánchez is the inspector major of the regiment based at the Moncada. He has two nieces in the float. The float is a decorated truck on which the girls model and dance.

Pedro Sarría Tartabull is on Trocha Street. Trocha Street is the main route authorized for all the Carnival's celebrations and dances and parades. Sarría is a public order lieutenant for Squad Eleven of the Rural Police and leads the peacekeeping effort along with the police. He carries out what he calls—in his slang—"my own service," checking in on the patrol cars he has deployed in the streets. And seated sometimes in a very luxurious kiosk called the Prince. Later he goes on to another kiosk, and on and on, observing everything from twelve at night on.

We get ready to leave. We put on army uniforms. To differentiate me, mine is the only one with sergeant major stripes. It's essential that the combatants be able to locate their leader when it comes time to give the command. I explain the attack plan and ask for volunteers to take Post 3. The weapons are laid out on the ground: .22-caliber rifles, .12-caliber shotguns, .38- and .45-caliber pistols, an MI carbine and an old machine gun. My speech is succinct. "*Compañeros,*" I say, "you may be victorious in a few hours, or be defeated, but either way, pay attention, *compañeros,* either way this movement will be triumphant!" We sing the national anthem very softly.

A while later, with all of our *compañeros* loaded into the cars, I tell Raúl and Pepe Suárez to take off the lock and free the prisoners. But none of them can leave the room for half an hour. I'm not worried about their sounding any alarms because there's not a telephone for twenty kilometers around. The milkmen—with their trucks distributing milk—went by a long time ago and the buses don't start running until six a.m. As for the police and the army, they're all out at the Carnival. Then, amid the shadows, I see Gustavo, either because he's still undecided or because he hasn't been assigned to a car, I don't know which. "You're coming with me," I tell him.

José Izquierdo Rodríguez is in the street, maintaining public order until four-thirty a.m. Izquierdo is the chief of police of Santiago, with the rank of captain. He has closed some cases of the kind that happen in all carnivals, people who drink and get rowdy and get into fights.

Morales Sánchez, as the parade is finishing up, is waiting for the girls and takes them to their houses in his car. Then he goes to his own house and goes to bed. Our convoy departs La Granjita for Santiago. First go the cars that are going to take the Civil Hospital, there are three of them. Then come the cars that are going to take the court, two of them. Thirty-five men. And then, with me on board, come the cars that are going to take the barracks. Fourteen cars. I have about ninety men with me. I'm driving and I've seated Gustavo to my right. We go down Avenida Roosevelt, leaving behind the Vista Alegre subdivision, take Garzón, turn down Moncada Street, which empties out on Post 3. The first car gets ahead of us. At this moment, I take off my glasses and put them away in one of my uniform pockets. I immediately notice the fright that this precaution causes in Gustavo. From then on, he is going to blame the attack's failure on this gesture of mine. Because a few seconds later I've run the car over the curb, right in front of the Moncada. This does not happen, as one would assume, because of my myopia, but rather because of a series of little factors that came together in a negative way and made us lose the element of surprise. Gustavo has never understood that I did not remove my glasses out of vanity but because no one in his right mind, especially in the 1950s, was going to show up wearing glasses for a battle with an army of brutal peasants, all of them with twenty-twenty vision, just like sparrow hawks or lynxes when they discover their prey from the sky or from their observation posts in the branches of baobab trees, which would have been like yelling out a thousand yards away that if there was an intellectual author, somebody who thought all of this up, it had to be—of course—the only one wearing glasses. It was like entering the boxing ring with glasses. Abel and I were the only two in the attack who needed glasses. The two of us entered combat without our lenses. He went into Saturnino Lora. I went into Moncada.

So we leave the Vista Alegre subdivision behind us, take Garzón and turn down Moncada Street, which empties out on Post 3.

The first car goes ahead.

Five-fifteen a.m. There are two soldiers and one corporal at Post 3. We park about ten or fifteen meters away. We all get out. There are eight of us. "Make way, here comes the general," yells Renato Guitart, the only one with us who is a resident of Santiago. The soldiers stand to attention. They present arms. Renato and Pepe Suárez pounce on them and take their guns. Corporal Izquierdo realizes what's happening. He goes toward the alarm bell. Pepe Suárez shoots at him. "*Hijo,* what have you done?" the corporal says, surprised. But as he falls, he succeeds in touching the alarm bell, which sounds shrilly through the entire barracks. Forty-five minutes later, Dr. Erik Juan y Pita, army first lieutenant, doctor on duty, Maceo Rural Police Regiment 1, certifies that at six a.m. today, July 26, 1953, he helps Isidro G. Izquierdo y Rodríguez, corporal of the Maceo Regiment 1, who has a bullet wound in the region of his right cervical. Two bullet wounds caused by a small caliber firearm in his epigastric region. Oral hemorrhage. Prognosis: FATAL.

The men who stormed Post 3 have been under surveillance by the exterior patrol guards, armed with submachine guns, ten meters from there. They haven't seen the guard, but from the second car, I have. "Let's get them," I say. The order is misinterpreted by the occupants of the car's backseat, who are following the movements of a sergeant who is getting closer. The guards are frozen still watching what's happening right in front of them at Post 3.

Morales Sánchez is sleeping.

I bring my car up close—the best Pontiac from the agency in Havana where Abelito was a salesman—to the left curb, half open the door and take out my Luger. The soldiers turn quickly toward the car and point at us with their Thompsons. Gustavo Arcos, about to carry out the order he thinks he heard from me, opens the door, braces his left foot on the curb and yells to the sergeant, "Halt!" In a defensive movement before the Thompsons pointed at me, I accelerate the Pontiac toward the guards, but that's when I crash into the curb and the engine dies. Arcos ends up on the floor. The sergeant instinctively reaches for his holster but falls as a shot hits him from the car. The patrol soldiers start running. The alarm bell keeps sounding.

Morales Sánchez's wife shakes him out of his sleep. His wife says that she heard gunshots. Morales Sánchez attributes it to the Chinese, who were always shooting off firecrackers at Carnival. "It's the Chinese," he tells his wife. "Pay attention," she says, "because it sounds like machine gun fire." Morales Sánchez gets up and calls the barracks and someone identifying himself as Lieutenant Pupo answers and tells him, "Look, Commander, there's a real ruckus going on, there's a bunch of shooting going on with the Armed Forces."

Morales Sánchez gets in his jeep. He arrives at Moncada unscathed. He goes in through the back sentry post. Nobody there. He goes up to the office, where he finds Colonel del Río Chaviano, who is lying on the floor, nervous, between the wall and a desk to protect himself, and talking on the telephone asking for reinforcements from Havana. Then he orders Morales Sánchez: "Ta-take over the defense of the barracks." He stutters. He's clinging to the telephone.

Post 3 is being swept by gunfire and is impassable. After reorganizing my men, I travel the street leading to the barracks, dodging gun-fire, of course, and my *compañeros'* shouts of "Get out of the way, get out of the way!" The surprise attack has failed. It has turned into a battle of positions. Our low-caliber munitions strike the walls of the barracks helplessly.

An hour of combat follows and we've practically exhausted all of our reserves. I realize that if we continue fighting, it will only be because of absurd impulses and perhaps even vanity. But I don't deceive myself about the success of the attack. In battle, broken into small partial actions, only the fate of each individual man counts.

I am already convinced that our efforts to take over the fortress are useless. Pedro Miret, Fidel Labrador and another six snipers prepare to cover our retreat. Miret also understands that the attack has failed and his life—he'll tell me this later—seems *completely lacking in meaning*. We retreat in groups of eight and ten men.

THE BOOK OF IMPOSSIBLES

Vanity? Well, we'd lost and we still didn't want to face it. They were the professionals, not us. Some simple, small-town, working-class men, to whom we would never allow any glory, knew exactly what to do with their submachine guns and repelled us. There were two fundamental reasons to keep them from enjoying a victors' glory. For the victor of a good fight. The first was classic: even though they had won the battle, they wouldn't win the war in the end. The second, which was never obvious nor talked about, remote and Sapphic as it was, hidden away in the most obscure regions of a nation's soul, was racism. The racism of a nation built by slave labor but always under the command of Spaniards or their descendants except for on the two occasions on which a mulatto, who, even worse, was also part Cuban Indian from God knows what decimated tribal group, dared to govern us with an iron fist. So we performed a tangential ser-vice for the ever fearful and volatile white creole bourgeoisie: that of kill-ing soldiers. Don't forget that we were still more commonly known as students than revolutionaries, as "the kids from the university." And in Cuba, students were always white. The mechanics of this line of thinking would have to be adjusted in the foreseeable future, since I couldn't carry out a proletarian revolution if I was fighting against an army of mulattos and blacks and poor peasants. Furthermore, the truly bourgeois and imperialist army was brought down by Batista in his March 10, 1952, coup d'état and absolutely destroyed in April 1956, after the Moncada attack, when he wiped out the CIA-supported conspiracy led by Colonel Ramón Barquín. So I had to work out the designs and plots of my propaganda as best I could to turn those "armed institutes"—as they were known—into an imperialist and upper-class instrument of repression instead of the way of life that it was—with clean clothing, fresh linens, three meals a day and a Christmas bonus—for fifty thousand or seventy thousand Cubans who would otherwise be unemployed, fifty thousand or seventy thousand destitute families with barefoot children and stomachs full of worms. It was all very complicated. Very complicated. But it was something to settle later since I needed them right now—both bourgeois and imperialists—and I couldn't make them enemies just yet. The tactical alliance with my future enemies was made, and without my tactical allies ever knowing what they had signed on to. For the time being, I had to make use of a group that is present in every army: its criminals. Not the other group, the mercenaries, who are the majority.

I saw how Cuban army professionals moved, I saw them spread out at Moncada under fire, never ducking or jumping involuntarily, standing up straight and in complete control of their actions, even though, for many of them, this was a baptism by fire, and I saw them capture me, I saw them disarm and arrest my friends, and there was not a single case, listen closely, not a single case of those officers—I'm talking about the ones who assumed positions in the battle—raising their voices or hitting any of our men, they even displayed the integrity to overlook the fact that we had just killed a brother or a good friend in a surprise attack without prior declaration of hostilities.

That was their job, and true to form, it seemed to be in one of the clauses (ascribed in spirit if not in words) of their military contract (*if they attack, counterattack*) and, with us, they were upright, efficient, professional, prepared. While Alberto del Río Chaviano's hounds reveled in their bloodbath, none of the old officers let himself be carried away by his emotions. They disappeared into the same anonymity from which they surged, at the specified time, to fight against us and defeat us. That is the story of Maceo Regiment 1 Inspector Commander Rafael Morales Sánchez; of the Chief of the National Police, Division 1, Santiago, José

Izquierdo Rodríguez; of the Chief Lieutenant of Maceo Regiment 1, Rural Police Squad 11, Pedro Sarría Tartabull.

In the end, in the *vivac** of Santiago—where prisoners were arraigned right after being captured—and surrounded by Izquierdo, Sarría, Morales Sánchez and Colonel Alberto del Río Chaviano himself, along with two or three stenographers, the only thing those men reproached me for was having jumped into such an adventure with such inadequate weapons. What in the end became one of the primary assets of our propaganda—having confronted the army with those low-caliber rifles and hunting shotguns—was in reality the most condemnable part of our enterprise from the military's point of view. That was the only thing they made sure to point out to me. I could take it however I liked every time they said to me, "Are you crazy, kid? How were you going to attack barracks like Moncada with those little rifles?" But it was also like a warning, like saying to me, Listen kid, next time get yourself a better arsenal. Not for del Río Chaviano, of course. For del Río Chaviano, his firepower—compared to ours, of course—was the basis for his arrogance and the carte blanche for his abuses.

We had to find a strategic equivalent to the adversary's logistical supremacy. My experience now is that you can't put a bastion in its place if you don't exceed its firepower and capacity for destruction, and the strategy of supplying yourself with the enemy's weapons works in guerrilla warfare, but not when you're dependent on the powder magazine of the fortress itself that you intend to conquer. It doesn't work because it causes you to fall into your own trap. It means throwing yourself inside the palisade and seeing, in your final hour, how the drawbridges are raised, or having to stay outside without being able to even scratch at the wall.

While there, in that *vivac* in Santiago, and feeling somewhat protected by the presence of Commanders Morales Sánchez and Izquierdo and especially Lieutenant Sarría, with whom I had established a good rapport—in addition to the fact that he had made me complicit in a secret that would allow me to appear calm and controlled before the sinister del Río Chaviano—I resumed the operation. It was August 1, 1953, around eleven in the morning. It hadn't been a full week since Renato Guitart

---

* A Cubanism for "prevention." [*Author's note.*]

yelled, "Make way, here comes the general," and since Corporal Izquierdo made his way to the alarm bell and Pepe Suárez, upon firing at him, carried out the first shot of the Cuban Revolution and hit a live target. Now I had to work on the propaganda, of course. In short, it was the only resource still intact and at my disposal at that moment.

Then it was time to get used to prison. In my case, it was not a state of resignation, rather of reconnoitering the territory and beginning to move around in it. An exquisite opportunity to test one of our revered patriot José Martí's sayings. He said that a just idea at the back of a cave was worth more than an army. For me it was like an admonishing Christ saying that a camel would go through the eye of a needle before a rich man would enter heaven. I must admit, the more impossible the turns of rhetoric, the more drawn I am to its implicit challenge—with all its imaginative pirouettes—because it raises the bar that much higher. Because of that, I tended to see myself taking on the challenge, kicking the camel's ass, squeezing him through the eye of the needle.

Well, it was time to test out the chemical balance. I was already at the back of the cave. And the whole army was surrounding me.

I UNDERSTAND THAT General Francisco "Pancho" Tabernilla, head of the Armed Forces, had the radiogram that announced our capture and biographical details framed. His goal was to make a present of it for Batista to hang in his office. But Batista didn't pay much attention to the gift and slipped it into one of his drawers, although he thanked his old friend with a pat on the back. The bitter truth was that our existence as a trophy of war lasted a very short time in his imagination.

Republic of Cuba
OFFICIAL RADIOGRAM

CONSTITUTIONAL ARMY

Doctor Fidel Castro, aged 26 years, was arrested along with his colleagues José Suárez Blanco, from Artemisa, aged 23 years; Oscar Alcalde Valls, aged 31 years, a resident of El Cotorro; Armando Mestre Martínez, aged 24 years, a resident of the Poey Subdivision; Eduardo Montano Benítez, resident of La Ceiba neighborhood, Marianao; Juan Almeida Pozo,* aged 27 years, of the Poey Subdivision; Francisco González Hernández, aged 22 years, of La Ceiba, Marianao; and Mario Chacón Armas.† aged 26 years, of the same place.

---

* It should say Juan Almeida Bosque.
† Mario Chanes de Armas.

9

HAVANA FOR THE LAST TIME

/ / /

Mᵧ PARENTS WERE ALREADY IN TOUCH WITH (AND SPENDING A pretty penny for) Monsignor Enrique Pérez Serante, the archbishop of Santiago, to come to our rescue. That was when the priest decided to invest his powers "as an ecclesiastic authority" and became interested in the search for us and took action along with some of Santiago's other cit-izens of note, of which he was the most illustrious, to save our lives. He had an audience, of course, with all of the farm owners in the region, and that was how the message got to us to turn ourselves in. *But he wanted us to turn ourselves in to him,* and only him –to Pérez Serante. José Sotelo, one of those farmers who had also helped hide us and given us a little bit of food, transmitted this message to us. At that moment, as you can see, there were three forces in the area competing to get their claws in us: Pérez Serante, so he could line his pockets with the ten thousand pesos my parents offered as well as assume the role of magnanimous peace-maker; the Party's clandestine group through Sarría (of whose secret connection to the communists I was still not aware) and their interest in saving me for any future eventualities given the enormous leadership potential I had demonstrated in the preceding hours (they didn't hide their enthusiasm to recruit me); and the army officers, the ones from del Río Chaviano's band, because the only outstanding part of Batista's order was to have me killed. Pérez Serante's message improved our situation and offered a new perspective.

In the countless retellings of the Moncada attack, I've said that a group of six or seven *compañeros* who were with me, all of them worse off

Fidel Ángel Castro Díaz-Balart kisses his mother,
Mirta Francisca de la Caridad Díaz-Balart y Gutiérrez.

than me physically, handed themselves over to the authorities by way of the archbishop, which contains only a small piece of the whole truth. In reality, I had also decided to turn myself in. But this initial group would go first, as a test. It was like a reconnaissance mission. I would stay behind with a couple of *compañeros*, the strongest and most determined ones, and wait for news of the first surrender. I spoke with José Sotelo to agree to the meeting between that group and the archbishop. Then we left them waiting for sunrise and the archbishop, and we withdrew about two kilometers, on the border of Las Delicias, the neighboring farm owned by Juan Leizán, in a place they call Mampriva.

I hadn't figured out yet that the Military Intelligence Service was intercepting all communications and that they'd heard a telephone conversation between Sotelo and the archbishop and were sending out patrol cars all over the area, near the main road, well before dawn. But the army in turn didn't anticipate making a similar mistake: having Lieutenant Pedro Sarría in command of that patrol in the foothills of the Gran Piedra.

We were a bit tired and had to sleep on the mountainside, without any blankets or anything, and once inside Leizán's property, the Las Delicias farm, we found a small hut, about four meters long and three meters wide, what they call a *vara en tierra*, really a place where they kept the farming tools, and we decided to protect ourselves against the fog, the dampness and the cold, and stay until dawn. And what happened, at dawn and before we could wake up, was that a patrol of soldiers made their way into the hut and woke us up by shoving rifles into our chests.

We had gotten too confident. We had spent a week at that game of cat-and-mouse without the soldiers finding us. They had dragged the area looking for us while we mocked their efforts for almost an entire week, thinking this could go on forever. We underestimated the enemy. We made a mistake and fell right into their hands.

Then a coincidence occurred. Pedro Sarría. A man of great energy, as I've described in some interviews, but not a killer. The soldiers wanted to kill us, they were worked up, waiting for the slightest pretext, and they had their guns loaded with bullets, and they tied us up. At first they asked us to identify ourselves and we gave fake names. But I was still unaware that Sarría had received two sets of instructions, from two different groups, and that he was trying to reconcile them. I could sense the orders that came from his superior officers in the army, but could never imagine the task assigned to him by "the people" specific to me. I was unaware that he had these other instructions and that in reality, he was going to offer me a lesson that I would frequently use later, especially with Che, when he surrendered to the Bolivian army on October 8, 1967. Don't allow yourself to surrender to the enemy and become fodder for their malicious propaganda. In Che's case, he had to be killed so he wouldn't become a public and notorious traitor, and could continue serving the cause, at least as a symbol, raised to the more useful category of martyr. An infallible method for preserving a revolutionary. It's a perfectly justifiable act from an ethical viewpoint: don't let a symbol be snatched away from you to be similarly used as a symbol by the enemy.

Those soldiers, for some reason, wanted to kill us anyway; and if we had properly identified ourselves, the gunshots would have happened simultaneously to our doing so. I then began to argue with them, to put an end to the situation, since I didn't consider our survival even a remote possibility. Since they were calling us killers and saying that we were there to kill soldiers, they who were the successors of the Liberating Army, I told them that they were the successors of the Spanish army, that we were the true successors of the Liberating Army, which made them even more furious.*

We really thought we were as good as dead when Sarría intervened and said, "Don't shoot, don't shoot," and pressured the soldiers, and while saying that repeated in a lower voice, "Don't shoot, ideas can't be killed, ideas can't be killed." The things that came out of that man's mouth. He said, "Ideas can't be killed" about three times. I was starting to like that more than Martí's phrase. It was simpler and more direct.

But the important thing was, at that moment, I realized that a door was opening and that in the immediate battle unexpectedly before me, the battle for survival, I had found an ally in that sweaty lieutenant who had stepped between his colleagues' Springfield rifles and my two *compañeros* and me. While the plan to turn ourselves in to the archbishop failed, the sudden change in situation could end up being much more advantageous. In less than sixty seconds I'd gone from preparing myself for death, furious and indignant, to devising a new plan, as if, lined up

---

* It really pleases me to leave a record of this fact, in any event. That I, Fidel Castro, at about six in the morning of August 1, 1953, at the moment of my life in which I thought myself closest to death, started arguing about those two distant armies of our war of independence. [*Author's note.*]

already at the firing wall, on the brink of being blindfolded, the firing squad were to open up a folding table, unroll some maps on it, give me a pencil and ask, "Now where do we go?"

We came out ahead with Sarría's entry into our sphere. We were no longer surrendering to an obese and spineless provincial archbishop who was just going to place us at the disposal of the Santiago military authorities and who in the coming weeks would appear along with His Excellency the Bishop and the vain colonel photographed in the society pages, with their cheeks full of grease from some banquet at the Rotary Club or with the Bacardis. There was no surrender. There was no handing us over. We were captured when sleep had conquered us. In other words, we could claim that we had been still in the trenches. We could still describe the situation as reversible. The conditions more than allowed us to start seeing ourselves as heroes— nothing less than what, in fact, we were. There's nothing more powerful for generating compassion and the need for solidarity than the vision of a fallen gladiator. And there lies the great significance of Pedro Sarría Tartabull in the origins of the Cuban Revolution. He cleaned up an image. Ours.

And damn, did that *negro* know how to negotiate.

I remember, as if I were looking at myself right now, lying on the cot in my cell, those hours spent reevaluating the battle and how it ended. I was still getting ready for my trial and taking notes for my opening statement. But I had to start separating information from reasoning. Because my reasoning –if I really saw it through to its natural conclusion—had no place whatsoever in the defense. I did all of this work in my head. In the end, the only thing that made it on to the memo pad was information that could be used in the statement.

Sarría's basis for negotiation—which he came up with in the scant forty-minute truck ride over to the *vivac* in Santiago—was that the military men themselves were impressed by our act, you could say that they had even expressed certain respect for what we had done, plus there was the psychological element: they were already suffering pangs of conscience because at the time they had killed seventy to eighty prisoners and everyone around knew it. So, if the invincible army had won the battle against the hapless attackers, and in addition to that had the enemy's leader among their prisoners, safe and sound and ready to confess, what could they possibly gain by sending another dozen corpses to the Santiago morgue?

Excellent negotiation. And an even better lesson. Even in the worst military confrontation and combat, you can negotiate. The only thing you need is something to put on the table. Nothing big, don't go above what's warranted by the situation, and never offer dreams or chimeras. The real asset in negotiating under almost desperate conditions is to throw a card of equal value on the table that can be cashed in immediately. If you don't lose sight of the fact that every negotiation is nothing more than a maneuver of abstractions against an objective situational background, you've already won half the battle. The mere fact that you're negotiating is already a victory. Let me tell you that from all of this stems one of the basic principles of our intelligence and counterintelligence operatives: when you are able to sit down with your worst and most bitter enemy to talk, you have already screwed him. I say *sit*. This is something we've studied and documented through thousands of interrogations. When you call in a suspect to your office or meet him out in the street or make an appointment with him at a secure location, never offer him a seat. Wait until he asks you to sit down. The officer or interrogator can be standing or not, and seats, of course, should be at hand, but you need to wait to hear the magic words, "May I sit down?" or "Why don't we sit down?" to know that he is all yours. Not a single man who has sat down with us in over forty years of Revolution was later able to get away without compromising himself. In any event, we should concede that there's not a single case on record of an unbreakable guy asking us to sit down—never.

DURING MY STAY at the Reclusorio Nacional para Hombres prison in the Isle of Pines,* I undertook intense literary tasks. I can divide the output into three phases. The first phase was reconstructing my self-defense statement, now universally recognized as "History Will Absolve Me"—right? Isn't it universally recognized? I had a stroke of luck in the beginning: that the house belonging to the parents of one of my *compañeros* in the thwarted attack on the Moncada Barracks, Chucho Montané, was in Nueva Gerona, the closest town to the prison, in reality the only real town in existence on that island, I mean, with paved streets and electricity and a couple of hotels. The ferries that traveled

---

* Indiscriminately called "Modelo" or "Reclusorio para Hombres."

to the isle, two old wooden monstrosities that made the eight-hour trip from Batabanó—a similar town on Havana's southern coast—docked just a short distance away from the wooden Montané family home. Through their house, I was able to send, among other things, my coded letters with instructions for the *compañeros* who were available and not in prison, especially Melba Hernández and Haydee Santamaría, who had been sentenced to seven months at the Guanajay Prison for Women, about sixty kilometers west of Havana, and were now free. It was also the house where our families found a sure welcome when they came to see us at the detention center. But, from the beginning, it was the place where I slowly stored the pages of my writing. It's a real problem to write under those circumstances, when you're not able to review the preceding pages. It creates a kind of uneasiness, like finding yourself on the border between a blurry past and a future with its usual unknowns. The writing exists only in your memory until you receive the first printed copy. In any event, that uneasiness was relieved by the certainty that the pages were in a safe place and that they were no longer with me where I could be caught with them on my person.

The second phase was my political correspondence, part of it coded, about what was taking shape as the 26th of July Movement, and the other part, letters of a more public nature and directed almost always to a journalist called Luis Conte Agüero. The majority of that material has been lost. What was saved is now in a book* of my compiled letters published by this character, perhaps the most foolish of all my useful fools, and in truth very useful under those circumstances. He had a radio program that he called *The Top Voice in Oriente* because upon moving his original radio station from Santiago to Havana, he thought it convenient to be backed up by such a grandiloquent slogan. It's obvious that my fiery proclamations and letters from the Isle of Pines improved his ratings. Nonetheless, there was a time when I respected him. I even included him—without his knowledge, of course—in my plans for Moncada. I had anticipated giving a speech on his radio program to the people of Santiago while we occupied the barracks.

It would be very hard for me to read those letters today—that Luisito published, incidentally, without my permission—in the first place because they were sent to him and were loaded with all the praises I felt obliged

---

* Luis Conte Agüero, *Cartas del Presidio. Anticipo de una Biografía de Fidel Castro* (Editorial Lex, La Habana, 1959).

to lavish on him. Pure political duty, as political as it was repulsive. ("Luis . . . you are so intelligent, so brave, so noble . . ."* Or: "Dear brother: Neither bars, nor solitude, nor solitary confinement, nor the rage of tyrants can prevent these lines from reaching you with my warmest support as you harvest the applause and affection that your civic battles have garnered you")† Was I really obliged or *did I merely believe I was obliged* and am in reality reproaching myself now for the amount of useless adulations that I lavished on him? Perhaps I could reread a few lines today in order to show how certain passages contained the same truths I've expressed so much more clearly and concisely in these memoirs. A few gems, by way of example:

> . . . it would be fantastic if on Oriente Radio you could announce daily the amount of time I've been in solitary confinement: so many months, ten days, so many months, eleven days, and on and on. (Remember Cato who always finished his speeches asking for the destruction of Carthage.)‡

Pay attention to the following first line. It's something we've already talked about previously, but I want you to confirm it now as a thought in its rawest but clearest state.

> We can't forget about propaganda for a single minute because it's the heart and soul of our entire battle.§

And, in the same letter, perhaps the most prescient of all and which was overlooked by all of the intelligence services on my ass, since it was Luis Conte Agüero who had the original document in my own handwriting without a copy filed away in his drawer (the two underlines were mine).

> <u>Lots of hand waving and smiling</u>. Follow the same tactics that we followed during the trial: defend our points of view without rais-

---

* Letter to Luis Conte Agüero dated December 12, 1953 (ibid., p. 20).
† Letter to Luis Conte Agüero dated June 12, 1954 (ibid., p. 25).
‡ Letter to Luis Conte Agüero dated June 19, 1954 (ibid., p. 35).
§ Letter to Luis Conte Agüero dated April 17, 1954 (ibid., p. 37).

ing any hackles. <u>There will be time enough later to crush all of</u> <u>those cockroaches together.</u>*

And finally this line, which surprises even me upon reading it now:

The conditions necessary for the creation of a social movement: ideology, discipline and leadership. The three are essential, but leadership is basic.†

The third phase of my output in prison had to do with the circumstances that forced me to break up with Mirta and divorce her. It's all articulated in one of those letters: when what I took to calling "the only private ideal in my life"—and to whom I was moved to serve blindly and without hesitation‡—was snatched away from me. Mirta. Dammit, it still hurts me here, right in the middle of my chest. Do you know what a man's chest is, of a man like me? I still choke up when I remember the evening of Saturday, July 17, 1954, when I heard the CMQ broadcast around eleven at night that "the Ministry of Government has provided for Mirta Díaz-Balart's severance pay." Yes, those Batista-supporting bastards let me have a radio. They were hitting me below the belt. Not only had they defeated me militarily and killed fifty or so of my *compañeros* and sentenced me to fifteen years in prison, they had also announced that my wife was on the payroll of a public office where she had never worked. Perhaps it was best that I was in prison, because if I had been free with the same obligations that had me in prison, that is to say, with the leadership of a revolutionary movement, the pain would have been much greater. Prison mitigated my anguish because it allowed me to use it as a shield against myself, against the truth that I discerned amid all the cumulative layers of my own rhetoric, the truth of taking Mirta in my arms and letting her head fall against my chest, under my chin, and inhaling the smell of her meticulously washed hair with its schoolgirl bangs falling just over her temples and listening to the voice, somewhere between imploring and spoiled, of a girl waiting to be scolded for

---

* Letter to Luis Conte Agüero dated April 17, 1954 (ibid., p. 38).
† Letter to Luis Conte Agüero dated August 14, 1954 (ibid., p. 61).
‡ I hold the 26th of July above my own self and the instant I realize I can no longer be useful to the cause—for which I have suffered so much—I will take my own life without hesitation, more so now that I do not even have any private ideals to serve." (Letter to Luis Conte Agüero dated July 31, 1954 [ibid., p. 52].)

some prank but who knows herself to be safe from any worse fate, safe from a cruel and uncontrollable world under my protection, under my care, under my attentions. I was better off in jail, with its insurmountable walls. Had I been free, had I had Mirta before me, that fragile, frightened creature, and if my unrelenting hands, those of a stubborn and savage *gallego*, could have grabbed on to her, what would I have done that night, my God, what would I have done knowing that I wouldn't kill her and that the only thing I would have desperately desired would have been to give in, to give in to Mirta Díaz-Balart? My spirit died that night. I know that I died that night. And so it happened that between men and Mirta, I chose men, because from that moment on they would know the price of my choice, because they would pay, they would know without any room for pity or truce.

Cuba is one of those rare countries in which revolutionary leaders have accepted the death of a son before lowering their political banners. We know that Carlos Manuel de Céspedes, our first president of the Republic in Arms, from his hideaway in the Sierra Maestra, listened to the shot that cut short the life of his son, whom the Spaniards had offered him in exchange for his surrender. Stalin is another one. From the remote Soviet Union and in another century, but the same behavior nonetheless. You'll recall that when the Nazis offered to exchange a son of his they had captured for a German general who in turn was in Soviet hands, the response Stalin sent was that he wouldn't trade generals for captains. So I am perfectly aware of the significance of that type of loss because I also had to choose, and it's not a feeling that can be described by approximation. If I abide by the language of the classics, and I've never forgotten Engels's aphorism that a man loves more the children of the woman he loves most, it justifies my assertions. Even more so since Mirta wasn't in enemy hands, but within reach of my forgiveness.

That constitutes the third part of my literary output while in prison: my letters once I learned that Mirta and the sinecure arranged by her brother Rafael were public knowledge.* That night and this hurt live on for me, and a few snippets remain ("Don't worry about me; you know that

* A well-cultivated friendship with Batista and his own shrewdness as a politician allowed Rafael to become the leader of the Batista Youth (Juventudes Batistianas) and later to become the parliamentary majority leader of the Republic's Congress. [*Author's note.*]

I have a heart of steel and I'll act with dignity until the end of my days. Nothing is lost!")* that were nothing more than lamentable bravado.

Nothing was lost?

ISLE OF PINES, SATURDAY, JULY 17, 1954

Mirta:

I just heard the announcement on the C.M.Q. 11 o'clock news that "the Ministry of Government has provided for Mirta Díaz-Balart's severance pay . . ." Since I am loath to believe under any circumstances that you were ever an employee of that Ministry, it follows that you should immediately initiate a criminal suit for defamation against that gentleman, represented by Rosa Ravelo or any other lawyer. Perhaps they forged your signature or perhaps someone has been cashing checks in your name, but that can all be easily proven. If this situation is of your brother Rafael's doing, you should demand nothing less than that he publicly elucidate the matter with [the Government Minister Ramón] Hermida even if it costs him his job and even his life. It's your name on the line and you can't allow him to evade responsibility when he knows how serious this is for his only sister, who is an orphan and whose husband is in prison.

It is now more urgent than ever that you show the document to Miguel Quevedo [the editor of Bohemia *magazine]. Act firmly and don't hesitate to confront the situation. Ask Luis Conte [Agüero] for advice; I'm also dropping him a line about this. I imagine that your shame and your sadness is [sic] great but you can count on my unconditional trust and love.†*

Fidel

A highly convenient interpretation: that's what I would call the preceding pages, especially for one caught up in counterrevolutionary lies. Observe my experience as a prisoner so that you understand how much I am moved by the coarseness and suffocation of the great number of years we condemn people to in our own prisons. On the other hand, that

---

* Letter to my sister Lidia dated July 22, 1954 (Agüero, *Cartas*, p. 47).
† Letter to Mirta Díaz-Balart dated July 17, 1954 (ibid., p. 43).

fierce and relentless persecution and the lack of a moment of peace even while in solitary confinement were useful to me six or seven years later when I had to orchestrate my own prison regimen. They allowed me to understand firsthand that prison isn't just a building where you lock up a guy for a certain amount of time to isolate him from society and prevent him, at least during that time, from going back to his old ways. No. Our prisons had to be a system, a web of punishment, that reached out to encompass the prisoner's whole family, and in many ways was morally defeating.

PRISON WAS NECESSARY for my introspection. I've said introspection and not self-analysis. I always rejected the idea of self-analysis because I considered it a dangerous practice in those circumstances. It doesn't make much sense to go over your own shortcomings if in the end you're just facing a wall. So why torment yourself? Even today, with more than seventy years on my back, it is not a luxury that I allow myself. But in any event, if anything was self-flagellating, practically akin to self-analysis, and forced me to lose hours of sleep while thinking about it, it was Mirta and her Ministry of Government sinecure.

Our marriage could have survived without that money. In truth, we didn't have any pressing needs and my father, under pressure from my mother or not, would always end up giving in and sending me whatever money I asked for. There were times, many times, when we asked for two or three thousand pesos, a real fortune back then, and my father sent them. That was more than the annual salary of the vast majority of Cubans. Mirta never made any reference to my obvious knowledge of the whole matter regarding the sinecure and—even more embarrassing for me—she withstood my abjuration with silent integrity, and I know that she did it all for me. That she did it all for—that one little word is so difficult for me, even just to write it—love. The greatest act of cowardice of my whole life—and I honestly don't think a greater one can be attributed to me—and she allowed me to turn it into a virtue in the eyes of the masses. I abjured Mirta so I could meet my destiny absolutely free of any fault. And Mirta remained silent. She had the strength and character and determination to absorb all of the negative reverberations of that episode and leave the glory of blamelessness to me, even as she knew that from that moment on there would exist no hope of a reunion for us or even forgiveness, because it had to be that I, the blameless one, would never again be able to look her in the eye.

A friend, El Chino Esquivel, says that my divorce from Mirta had a decisive influence on me. Same with the damage produced by my break with Rafaelito. The divorce signified—in his exact words—that the "sweetness so necessary in every man's life" was snatched away from me and that this was later reflected in certain coarse and harsh actions I undertook when I came to power. As far as Rafaelito goes, I've always been convinced that he didn't want me to get out of prison.

But I had made a tactical error when I sang the July 26 anthem to Batista. That kept me separated from my *compañeros* almost the whole time I was imprisoned and in a way weakened our possibilities. Since I was alone, I could only count on the incidental visits I was allowed. But had I been with the rest of my *compañeros* in prison, I would have multiplied the opportunities for communication with the outside world. This was why I was so insistent with Conte Agüero that he use the press to get me out of solitary confinement. This also delayed the struggle for an amnesty because I had to invest some time in resolving the matter of my confinement.

Meanwhile, I was trying to rebuild my amorous possibilities with another woman. I began to idealize Naty Revuelta. At the time, I was not aware that one love is not the same as another and that there's a whole chemistry to it—as I have later said, even in press interviews—that there are as many loves as there are chemistries. I began to draft some letters of forced rhetoric addressed to Naty in which I went so far as saying, "Some things are eternal and cannot be erased, such as my memories of you, which I will carry to the grave," or other, somewhat improved variations, "I feel as I did when I read Victor Hugo's *Les Misérables*, I wish this would last forever," whose real value in the end was for the consumption of historians and biographers—that I was a Hugo aficionado. Of course, who the hell else are you going to be an aficionado of when you are locked up and rotting in a jail cell at the mercy of savage and melancholy jailers? There was something that I realized then: why I feel sorry for men from other centuries. Not the ones from very remote centuries, because I'm really out of touch with them. But I would say the ones that come more or less from the end of the eighteenth century and especially from the middle of the nineteenth century, I feel like I know them because they look like older family members who died when

I was a boy. I feel sorry for them because I imagine them living in dark places with dusty clothes and poor hygiene. They live in palaces but are unaware of toothpaste and running water. And I think the blame for that train of thought can be attributed not to Victor Hugo but to my reading Victor Hugo. In other words, if I read his work in its entirety, it was because I was stuck in a cell and had all the time in the world. These huge tomes from the eighteenth and nineteenth centuries were born of a similar situation. They emerged in winter and from boredom. And that is the great legacy of their literature: writing for the prison population of one or two centuries later, and in the best of cases, for political prisoners or prisoners of conscience, and not con men, murderers, rapists, and the whole gamut of marginal proletariat. And always taking into account, with exceptions, that there is no television in those precincts. Wherever electronic devices make their presence known, Victor Hugo is screwed. On the other hand, and now I'm talking about women, jail forces you to operate on the basis of memories. You remember old girlfriends or rely on any other point in your amorous past, maybe replay the last fling you had before you were imprisoned. You interact only with yourself and according to your own ability to extract remembrances from your memory. You can't go out in search of women in the here and now. The real world is on the other side of that moldy, impassable wall. That's when the fervor of hope comes about. And the making of sacred commitments with females canonized by your own necessity of holding on to them while at the very moment of your idealizing them they are actually on all fours on a bed with their asses raised in shameful proximity to the cock belonging to the first son of a bitch who happened to wink at them on the street.

I found out that an amnesty was a possibility when I received three visitors from the government. The tip-off was that they removed me from solitary confinement and took me back to Pavilion One, where twenty-eight of my *compañeros* were.

Nonetheless, two problems came up regarding the use of rhetoric as soon as the government showed its predisposition for negotiation. It was somewhat similar to what I would later encounter in my battle against the Americans and the ongoing subject of the embargo, once in power. In Batista's case, I had to get out of prison. In the Americans' case, it was the opposite; I needed them to keep the embargo against us in place. But, from a propaganda point of view, the challenge was the same: how to publicly declare a resolution that was in fact its very opposite. The July 31, 1954, visit I received in my cell from Senators Gastón Godoy and Marino López-Blanco and in the end the minister of government himself, Ramón Hermida, called on all of my skills when I had to describe it for publication.* If Hermida was holding out his hand cordially to me, I only described his gesture and abstained from describing my own. *My own gesture*: the one in which I responded with corresponding cordiality. That's how I left it in the text, just his gesture, while in the reader's imagination I stood up like a great dignified gentleman. Since we were dealing with my text, with my version, I could arrange the words and even the intentions as I saw fit so that I would never come across as vulgar or even intransigent to the point of refusing to reason with him and so that it would look like they all came to answer to me instead of the harsh reality that they had initiated the dialogue and that the only thing standing in the way of my freedom was me.

I left prison on May 15, 1955, as a result of the amnesty Batista signed on the sixth, following elections that he won with a large enough margin to allow himself the luxury of benevolence. They opened the doors of the prison at noon for us and we gave our first press conference at the Montanés' wooden house. Late that night, we boarded the dilapidated ferry *El Pinero* to make the slow trip across the shallow waters between the Isle of Pines and Cuba. We docked at the Surgidero de Batabanó at dawn.

My sister Lidia let me stay at her house in the neighborhood of El Vedado. She had an apartment that was right on Le Printemps garden, at the intersection of Twenty-third and Eighteenth Streets. It was full of people. El Chino Esquivel, as I expected, came the minute I sent for him. We gave each other a hug and then I took him to one of the rooms and said to him, "Have you seen how many *guajiros* there are out there?" I recall that I used that term, which, as is known, is a Cubanism for a peasant but never quite has a derogatory connotation, and which probably depends on the tone used or on the person qualified as such. "Yes," responded El Chino, who seemed not to have noticed that my visitors were peasants. "Well, they're all mad at me for not leading them to their deaths." They were part of the Moncada troops who were left out, nearly all of the serfs from the outskirts of Havana. "Listen, Chino, did you bring your car? Well, go get your car and honk in a few min-

---

* See my letter to Luis Conte Agüero in ibid., pp. 55–57.

utes. Don't take too long, let me see if I can get these people out of here. Especially Luis Conte Agüero, who's on his way, I don't even want to see him." Just like old times. There went El Chino to go get his car. I went back to the living room and spent a little more time talking with my *guajiros* and, suddenly adopting a conspiratory tone, said that "some people" were coming to get me soon and that I would have to leave. But, when the horn blew as the signal, it was imperative that none of them move for at least ten minutes after my depature. Only then could they start leaving. And only in groups of two.

That morning, when we stepped on firm ground at the Batabanó dock, just freed from the Isle of Pines, I told Ciro Redondo García that if he had time to go to Artemisa, his town, to see his family, that he should go, no problem, but he should make it to my sister Lidia's house later, in the early evening, and he should procure a car and some artillery for himself. And there he was, later that evening, waiting for me on my sister's balcony, like a sentinel in his watch tower.

I signaled him to go downstairs and meet me on the sidewalk and then I scanned the area for a public phone. There was one at the entrance to Le Printemps Garden. I still find the strong scent of those funereal gladiolas under the arch cloying in my memory. I deposited my five-cent coin in the slot and dialed the digits belonging to the device installed by the Cuban Telephone Company at the residence at 910 Eleventh Street, in El Vedado. The second ring at 30 11 91 hadn't yet finished before a voice quavered on the other end. Is it possible that it happened that way, the quavering before the sound? I was also very nervous and had just found Ciro before me, who was already acting like a bodyguard, and who was smiling at me with complicity while he tapped one side of his abdomen twice to show me that he was armed.

Naty had answered the phone and waited all day for that call and I still didn't realize it. I was making my calculations and taking my precautions. Jail doesn't train you to act any other way. Although it's probable that that evening—and only that evening—I could have gone without so much protection and so many subjective signals.

"Oíga," I said. "Listen."

Silence.

The use of the highly respectful *oíga* instead of *oye* was deliberate and, as usually happens so many times in Cuban popular speech, was one of those expressions that should be taken to mean the opposite. In this case, the implicit distance of the expression in its imperative mode meant the exact opposite in intimacy.

"Listen, little girl," I repeated. "Are you the person who wanted Fidel Castro to die of obesity when you sent him so many sweets?"

"Señor," she said at last. "My señor." Then I heard her take a deep breath. And she said, "Ay, Fidel." She was crying inconsolably. And saying, "Fidel, Fidel." She was repeating, "Fidel, Fidel."

Ciro, out of obvious consideration, and in the most discreet way possible, had taken a few steps back and turned his gaze to the cars running up and down Twenty-third Street.

"Well, Naty," I said dryly and with a note of brusqueness, trying to take control of the situation, "don't waste any of your tears while we're apart. I want them all for myself. When do you think we can see each other?"

I knew what her immediate answer would be. I knew she would have her alibi ready to get away from her husband since the minute she learned we had docked at Batanabó.

"In twenty minutes, you know where," she said.

In twenty minutes. In an apartment we had available to us since before Moncada. I won't mention the address here so that no one gets the great idea to make a museum out of it. And also because the people who loaned it to us ended up being fierce enemies of the Revolution and I don't think that they deserve any credit, even as mere innkeepers.

"Do we have a car?" I asked Ciro.

Ciro nodded yes.

Chucho Montané had gotten a car that very afternoon through his friends at General Motors of Cuba. It was a secondhand Pontiac in very good condition.

I remember what I was thinking as I got in the car and Ciro started the engine. I was thinking of Naty's eyes. For the first time, I thought of them as something within reach, of something that would be tangible in just a few minutes. The proximity of their unforgotten brightness served as the vector of all my fears. I was still very young, but I was coming from two years of forced chastity and I couldn't avoid the agony that all ex-prisoners feel on their first day of freedom. I wasn't sure I would be able to respond appropriately before a woman. And while you may not believe this, nothing makes me weaker or more vulnerable than a woman's green or blue eyes, preferably green. And I was telling myself that, to the extent that I could, I should avoid meeting her gaze, wherever she may direct it. And the only way to maintain the necessary animal aggressiveness was, in my case, by avoiding looking directly in her eyes. Later it turned out that I passed that test without incident and what really caught me by surprise upon closing the door behind me and hugging her was the scent of her skin, that fragrance which I hadn't remembered and which I hadn't counted on in any of my plans. And suddenly, the warmth of her tears on the collar of my shirt and her longing breath and her shaking body. And my saying to her, softly tipping her chin up, I want to see the tears in your eyes. Welling up in those eyes.

On the way to Naty's, without taking my eyes off the rearview and side mirrors to keep track of everything happening around us, Ciro told me that we had guaranteed weapons. Two Colt .45-caliber guns and four boxes of twenty-five cartridges. My gun and my two boxes of cartridges were under the seat. Ramiro Valdés had gotten everything through his Artemisa contacts. Ramiro and Ciro had barely gotten to town and were already in business. I confirmed that they were all proud of themselves, and that pleased me. They were enjoying a hero's welcome for the first time ever. And that allowed them to recognize themselves as the real thing. Something had happened that I would soon learn to describe with precise Marxist terminology. A great leap forward had taken place.

May 16, 1955, around seven in the evening. We had just been amnestied and I made my way to the secret den where I was about to sleep with a woman for the first time in one year and ten months when I became fully conscious that we were a handful of men with a right to be arrogant. Ciro, the peasant boy from the outskirts of Artemisa, who had earned a living as a clerk at a small-town dime store paradoxically called the Revolution, was driving a car, happy and even excited after serving a prison sentence to be spending his second night of freedom keeping watch on the street while another man was gallivanting around with a woman whom he couldn't even, due to a problem of basic discipline, look in the eye.

"Do you have a watch?" I asked.

Ciro had just pulled over the Pontiac.

The inside of the car was already in semidarkness, so Ciro raised his left hand from the wheel and turned his wrist so that I could see the cheap contraption he was wearing.

"And you made sure no one was following us?"

"I made sure, Fidel. No one."

"Good. Are you going to wait for me or are you going to leave?"

"I'll stay, Fidel."

"That's better," I said.

Then I tapped my index finger against my watch and calculated out loud:

"It's seven-ten. If I haven't come out by eleven, honk twice. I'm in apartment three-oh-three. It's the window where the light just went on. If there's any danger, honk three times or come and get me right away. Okay?"

"Okay, Fidel. But don't worry."

I stuck my hand under the seat and pulled out the gun. I knew right away, by its weight, that it was loaded. In any event, I slipped the magazine out of the grip and, with my index finger, pushed the first round into the magazine. It wouldn't go down. Perfect. At the same time, by the position of the trigger, resting on the hammer, I could tell it wasn't cocked, but nonetheless, I made sure by pulling the slide to the middle of the chamber and proving that it was empty. I released the slide, which fell against the catch, where it stopped with a click, and I placed the magazine back in the hollow grip. I put the gun at my waist, under my guayabera, just as I was getting out of the Pontiac and standing up on the sidewalk. Then I straightened my guayabera and repeated:

"At eleven, Ciro."

"At eleven, chief," he responded.

IF I MANAGED to avoid the calming effect of her eyes whichever way she looked at me, I said to myself, the first thing to do would be to try to reconstruct all of the pirouettes I had imagined while I was locked up. It would be like following a script that I myself had written and that was necessary to follow line by line, down to the dialogue, until I completed all of the possibilities that had built up in my imagination. Strictly speaking, I had fulfilled the period of chasitity required for my revolutionary priesthood. Yes, it was a limited-time period of chastity, and I could have easily broken it by slipping some money to the guard on duty or to the sentry so that I could help myself to any of the prostitutes abounding in Nueva Gerona's red-light district, but I abstained from asking for it for the same reason I broke up with Mirta: to not give the enemy any fodder. Now I was finding enlightenment amid the breasts and thighs of this woman, because with each wave of my powerful orgasms and each tremble I felt coming from that Cuban woman in my arms, I entered that reality where everything is suddenly clear and in which your own thoughts rise to the surface with all the power of revelations. Only men who have experienced long periods of abstinence—I think that in this sense, the most spiritually united are sailors and ex-prisoners—and who have not given in to the temptations of pederasty, or worse still, the idiocies of masturbation, can know the meaning of the presence of a naked woman and how it can fill your eyes and intoxicate you, and know the challenge of those raised nipples against soft breasts and the half-opened, longing mouth as you approach her on your knees between her legs as they spread open in a movement that you intuitively know coincides with the opening of her labia under the obscenity of her pubic hair, made even more obscene the more innocent her skin and spontaneous her gestures. But she has to be lying on her back, dammit, with her arms extended, inert, at her sides, so that she is completely submissive. Understand that every intention, every moment of suffering, all energy, has been focused on obtaining something that is perhaps too quickly defined as power and that I, on my knees but already leaning forward to bring my lips to her mouth and her tongue as I hang on to that freshly bathed white woman's hips who is slightly raising her pelvis expectantly up to me to be penetrated knowing that I am going to come from below and without need for her to help me place my glans with her hand at the threshold of her vagina where we will simultaneously establish that initial contact of the flesh while I continue to dominate her masterfully, grasping her hips with my steel hands as I am about to hammer a dick into her that cannot possibly expand to make room for one more cubic millimeter of blood under pressure, made red by the torrents of lust pumping through it, not only am I the symbol of myself, of myself possessing others, but right here, I am the leader that jumps out of the trenches first, raising his Mauser Parabellum gun over his head at the yell of attack to lead his troops, I begin the process of my attack on the heavens.

10

THE FORESTS MOVE

/ / /

STALIN: *To bring about a revolution a leading revolutionary minority is required; but the most talented, devoted and energetic minority would be helpless if it did not rely upon the at least passive support of millions.*

H. G. WELLS: *At least passive? Perhaps sub-conscious?*

STALIN: *Partly also the semi-instinctive and semiconscious, but without the support of millions, the best minority is impotent.*

(*Bolshevik,* ISSUE 17, 1934)

WE HAD TO MOVE QUICKLY THAT SUMMER. IT WAS ESSENTIAL, AND very urgent, to effect a change in what we called the political climate because Batista was winning the war of calming down the masses, making businesses prosper and money flow, and the possibility or not of a Revolution depended on his successes in these areas. Besides which, the sugar industry and the whole country were about to achieve one of their best sugar harvests, and tourism was becoming very dangerous for our plans. That's when the American Mob entered the scene. They had made their initial plans with Batista around 1950 in Daytona Beach, north of Miami, where Batista had a house and where he had spent almost his entire voluntary exile after leaving the presidency in 1945. They were known as—by their own designation—"the Gaming Syndicate" and their main spokesperson for Cuban issues was a small man with black plastic-rimmed glasses and a slim-line diamond-beveled

March 10, 1952. Camp Columbia, the country's main military facility, to the west of Havana. Fulgencio Batista has just carried out his coup d'état. The journalist Alberto Salas Amaro, one of his faithful, advises him.

Waltham watch on his left wrist who boasted about having a Cuban grandmother, while the rest of his ancestry was Italian, whose name was Santos Trafficante but who was known as the Don of Tampa. I am relying on the "historical" information file about Santos provided to me by State Security that accompanies the fat operative information file. He's one character that we never took our eyes off of, with good reason. We have since identified his ties to the Kennedy assassination as well as his proven participation in a dozen assassination attempts against my own person. Batista opened the doors to them by signing the so-called Game Law that allowed the establishment of casinos in buildings whose construction could be valued at no less than one million pesos. This measure was supposed to prevent the entry of poor Cubans to gaming halls, since these buildings could only be found in high-class neighborhoods or the most modern areas of the city, and in this way casinos would be reserved for the use of American tourists and wealthy Cubans. The presence of the "Syndicate" was making a favorable impact on the service and construction sectors. A host of neon ads inundated the city, casting a spell on everything under the night and the trade winds, while the flux of prostitutes coming from thousands of peasant families and poor neighborhoods did not have to make their last, obligatory stop in the brothels of the neighborhoods of Colón, La Victoria, Pajarito. Now they had the opportunity to become a rumba dancer or a model in any of the hundreds of little cabarets that proliferated everywhere. Because of all of this, the potential revolutionary situation in Cuba was teetering. The Cuban Revolution was never as weak as when Havana was having a roaring time. I, who enjoyed myself employing terms like objective and subjective conditions, was surprised upon reading in Lenin that one of the most propitious vectors to create objective conditions was a natural disaster. Was that the only possibility left to me? A tidal wave? An earthquake? A hurricane? No. It wasn't anything we could just sit around and wait for. That was akin to waiting for it to snow in the Sahara. Cuba was not on a fault line, except for maybe on the edge of Oriente Province, in front of the Bartle pit. Nor do we have volcanoes. We'd have to wait for hurricane season and for one of those meteors to decide to pass over the island, but for that we'd require a very well structured political apparatus, to raise the whole population up in arms over the rubble of a hurricane before the government got ahead of us with its resources and won more sympathizers with its assistance plans that could then be turned into juicy profits. So the best we could do was be a hurricane ourselves. Incidentally, it was after the Revolution that we discovered the economic value of hurricanes and the enormous amount of international aid that's received in those instances. The poor Soviets, who have never known a hurricane in their expansive territory, had to pay for the devastating effects of those tempests on our Caribbean island. That feast of donations lasted until Hurricane Kate passed through seven of our provinces on November 19–22, 1985, after the end of hurricane season, and Gorbachev himself called me from the Kremlin to say, "*Strasvítye, tavaríshe Fidela.*" He just wanted to know with greater precision how to help us. Concrete numbers. Specific things. Nails. Wood. Wire. How many nails? How much wood? In planks or in trunks? How many kilometers of wire? How thick? So, you know, I didn't like that conversation at all, the first one we had on our direct line, one of only two direct lines from the Kremlin to the American continent. The other one was to the White House, of course. But our line had the advantage of relying on the best voice scrambler then in existence on the planet, which went from the Palace of the Revolution to the base at Lourdes, in the outskirts of Havana—where the voice was received completely deformed and unintelligible—and from there to the military satellites, which in turn transmitted the voice to the Kremlin, where the sounds were put back together. For the transmission from Moscow to Havana the same ingenuity was applied. This always forced you to have a slow conversation (which was very convenient, since it gave you time, or rather it forced you to have time, to think), which was slower because of the time it took the interpreter to prepare his translation.

The donations from Gorbachev were adjusted, precise: 30,000 tons of rice, 20,000 tons of wheat flour, 10,000 sheets of zinc, 5,000 sheets of aluminum, 2 million slates of asbestos cement, and 1,000 tons of long-fibered asbestos. From my friend Brezhnev, we would've gotten a whole squadron of MiGs out of that hurricane.

We hung up our telephones.

Уточните.

I was in the soundproof cabin on the fourth floor of the Central Committee designed—furniture-wise—for our main Russian translator, Jesús Rensolí, who was one of Raúl's men. The facility still exists. It's useless, dark and silent, silent forever now. Without anyone at the Kremlin to pick up on the other end and with Rensolí having escaped to Finland in the early nineties and then to Washington, where he became a big fish at the World Bank. Its design consisted of the softest carpet I've ever walked on in my life, beige-colored, a softness that I imagine to be about six inches deep, into which my boots seemed to sink, plus two red leather armchairs—one for Rensolí himself and the other one for me, the only two people authorized to park our derrieres there—and a small nickel-plated table on which the tape recorder and two telephones rested—one for Rensolí and one for me, the only two people authorized to take them off the hook, and even then only always in unison.

"What the hell was that *utachnitye* that he kept repeating?"

Rensolí seemed to hesitate before answering. Then I realized he was trying to find the nicest way to tell me something that he knew, beforehand, would upset me.

He finally made up his mind.

"Comandante, it's a lapidary expression. It means 'be precise.' Or it could also be translated as 'tell me exactly.'"

IN THE FACE of the argument that the conditions for a revolution weren't there and that we'd have to wait for these to mature, we had to improvise. In short, I was forced to look for the philosopher's stone of the Cuban Revolution. In other words, I had the beginning of the story and the end, but the middle was missing. The filling. We could use shortcuts, certainly. But a shortcut regarding the tactic. Yes, that. Because I had the concept of a shortcut straight. And there's nothing in Marxism to disqualify shortcuts. No one has ever denied the scientific validity that the shortest distance between two points is a straight line, so what if that shortest distance is covered via shortcut and not the highway? Fine, then, the shortcut.

On the other hand, I was starting to realize that I was no longer the man I had been on the university steps that evening when the attack on Moncada became my raison d'être for the months that followed, with the added difference that I now had that failure to my name. Not failure in a negative sense. (Never let yourself get carried away by those echoes of defeat. It's the only way to turn the most hopeless or humiliating of situations into a simple step on a long path.) In reality, that time, while I was preparing the attack, I had devised some strange sophisms about a general strike that would occur along with the Moncada plot, and in some way I had to outline that step, maybe that was where I could find the force I needed. I had to take my Marxist readings more seriously. That heterogeneous mass that I had glimpsed was without a doubt the urban population. The peasants had been nothing more than decoration and dramatic emphasis for my defense statement in "History Will Absolve Me." The possibilities of a general strike among the urban population began to call out to me like twinkling stars in the night sky.

Many years after these ruminations, I uttered one of my favorite sentences—"It never would have occurred to us to initiate a revolutionary struggle in a country without large landholders"—in truth, a sentence that was made up to serve as the theoretical justification for our origins, since when we began the struggle we were barely conscious of how useful the large landholders would end up being for us. We had an excellent backdrop to work against. A backdrop of misfortune and shit and social inequalities that were starting to cast a shadow over the map of the Republic. If ever a writer said that literature was fed by social carrion* I can tell you that the Revolution discovered the equation many years before. At least it was something that Stalin mentioned in the preamble to the October Revolution when he talked about exacerbating contradictions. Later, without a hint of embarrassment, when he found himself in charge of the Soviet Union, he made it an inherent part of his foreign policy. Did you hear me? Exacerbate contradictions. They already exist. But we exacerbate them.

So I began to consider that such conditions had to be created but that we had to do so by fighting. In short, the attack on the Moncada Barracks fit into that logical framework. In other words, in our case, getting hung up on finding a revolutionary theory was like putting the cart before the ox. That's when I arrived at my best theoretical moment, which was, actually, a sort of anti-theory with no preconceived assumptions, and which I would later pair with the music from *The Force of Destiny* and even some mysticism. Acting on the go. Lenin would have gotten a fever just listening to me. *The Force of Destiny*. That was a title I picked up from our novelist Alejo Carpentier. I don't think I've ever heard it. I imagine there should be a recording. The title was enough for me.

I heard Alejo mention it in passing one night—perhaps in 1964. We were at a reception at the Palace of the Revolution and I took him aside

* Our "little friend" Mario Vargas Llosa. [*Author's note.*]

to congratulate him for his book *Explosion in a Cathedral*, which made such an impression on me that I recommended it to Raúl, and Raúl had recommended it to some *compañeros* who for various reasons had ended up imprisoned at La Cabaña—the fortress the Spanish built at the entry to the port. I'm not talking about counterrevolutionaries, rather *compañeros* from our ranks who had to be disciplined. I clearly remember that at least two of them received copies of the book in their cells that were sent by Raúl. One went to Captain Armando Torres and the other to *el negrito* Carlos Jesús Menéndez. Both of them were in a special area of that prison, where we had provided certain comforts, beds and not cots, blankets for the cold, good food and porcelain service, glasses and silverware.

I sympathized with Armando Torres, whom we called "Frenchy." We had him locked up—"kept away," as we more commonly said—because he had gone to Paris and from Paris to Algiers with the goal in mind of fomenting guerrilla insurrection in God knows what African country, all of his own doing. He was one of those sons of the Cuban bourgeoisie who had gone to all the best schools and who, just as he was about to start his career—opening a high-class law office, a private clinic, an architectural firm, an engineering firm—discovers that his true calling is in the Revolution, an adventure promising to give him all the power in the world. Armando had studied philology at the Sorbonne— hence his nickname "Frenchy"—and he returned to Cuba to join one of the rebel columns under my brother Raúl's command, in the area that we called the "Frank País" Second Eastern Front. When the Revolution triumphed, he was one of the first leaders of the units in the War Against the Bandits in the province of Oriente. The first sign that things weren't going well with Armando was when he threw half of his staff out the door of an Mi–4 helicopter in what he called "high-altitude heli-disembarkment practice" with all their equipment except for their parachutes and which left nine cadavers crushed against the hard floor of the Sierra Cristal. We had him under psychiatric treatment in Havana when he escaped and we didn't hear another word from him until the Algerians told us that they had detected a Cuban organizing a group of Bedouins near the Moroccan border and they wanted to know if they should shoot him on the spot or send him to us on the first flight out. "On the first flight," I ordered through Papito Serguera, our ambassador to our sister Algerian Republic. "But in accordance with the established security requirements," I added. The requirements were to have him in a plaster cast from his chin to his ankles.

The other guy, a minor figure—with whom I have never sympathized—was Carlos Jesús Menéndez, a lieutenant, a combat pilot from the first group that was trained in Czechoslovakia to fly MiG-15s. The lieutenant's true claim to fame was being the son of the famous Jesús Menéndez, the sugar union leader murdered on January 22, 1948, by an assassin named Joaquín Casillas Lumpuy. But he became a liability despite being the son of a great martyr. It never even occurred to him to thank us for executing his father's assassin the very day that the Revolution triumphed. Che's people captured the guilty party amid the Plana Mayor of the "Leoncio Vidal" Regiment of Santa Clara and—under my direct orders—not only was he denied the possibility of a trial, but also that of a de rigueur execution, since a horde of rebels placed him bound by his hands and feet on the bed of a truck and halfway to their destination applied the escape rule, right there, "*sancochado*"—as we used to say—riddling his back with San Cristobal carbine submachine gun bullets. Nor did that *negrito* Carlos Jesús Menéndez take into account that he was an official of the Revolutionary Armed Forces and that Raúl had publicly introduced him as one of the pilots who would shoot down half of the *yanqui* aviation if they should dare invade us, a sort of hero in advance. His problem was that he gave shelter to a fugitive from one of our common prisoner rehabilitation farms. So when my brother Raúl told me that the favorite among our sons of communist martyrs was hiding a criminal, I responded (word for word), "Who the hell does he think he is? Break his balls." In all truth, he had fallen in love with the fugitive's sister, and the guy was a common criminal with a long track record and a file half a foot thick, to whom—it seemed—it had been necessary to administer a beating across the buttocks with a bayonet as a means of reeducation and punishment. I will add this supplemental information: It was halfway through 1961 when the orders were given to arm the prison guards with all of the Springfield and "Crack," Krag-Jørgensen, rifle bayonets from the First World War that were piled up in our arsenals of material inherited from the Republic's former army. A guard with that huge bayonet of almost half a meter in length at his waist was a consistent and adequate symbol of discipline, and even more so when the penal population could show the effects of their submission to the rigors of prison on their glutei.

Anyway, this individual was able to escape somehow and he showed up with his still-fresh scars before one of our first combat pilots, who suddenly decided to illegally shelter him. It didn't last very long, of course, because our excellent State Security apparatus immediately detected them and detained them both. The fugitive returned to his prison camp, with an additional sentence of ten years to serve, and Carlos Jesús Menéndez, after a few days of proceedings at the Villa Marista Prosecution Center, was sent to La Cabaña, to that five-star dungeon we set up there for certain *compañeros*. Raúl was the one who insisted we go easy on the aviator, and who sent him a copy of *Explosion in the Cathedral*. I understand Raúl's reasons for sending that book to our dearest prisoners, since it required them to think about the Caribbean at the time of the French Revolution. It was like saying, a true revolutionary is offering other revolutionaries a paper substitute as a simulation of a revolutionary experience, or perhaps, even better, to say to them, your little mess is not my fault, it's just that we're dealing with a common situation sanctified by all modern revolutions. In regards to Lieutenant Carlos Jesús Menéndez, I recall having sent an interrogator to ask him his motives. Menéndez's response proved to be disappointing while also indicative of behavior that could repeat itself among other members of our own ranks. He said that he didn't want to sully himself with blood. That, at least, he found it prudent to gain some distance from the revolutionary process if it started to beat unarmed prisoners with bayonets. "It's nothing," Raúl said, "it's just that these pilots are somewhat reluctant when it comes to blood. Pilots die with their necks clean and surrounded by air-conditioning. That's the difference between killing a man when you destroy his machine from ten thousand feet in the air and the bloody short-range combat of an infantry." I rejected the notion. "Raúl, the case is that he's weak and a son of a bitch. He's a half-ass revolutionary. He's imposing conditions on us. Break his balls."

Fine, then, Alejo told me that he felt overwhelmed by the weight of using two titles coming from musical pieces. He was desperate to use them in his next novel. Both of them. But he wasn't sure which. *The Consecration of Spring* is one, he told me. "*The Force of Destiny* is the other one." I was crazy about this last one. *The Consecration of Spring* didn't do much for me when he mentioned it. In any event, I remained emotionless in the face of his explanation, with my small glass of cognac in my right hand while my left hand was posed in my habitual defensive gesture (when I want to avoid a situation that will expose my ignorance about any matter, I touch the person speaking to me), I acted as if I were fixing the knot of his tie, a knot that was irreproachably knotted. What perturbed me was the excess of abstraction in the first phrase and not knowing how to tell someone who was one of our great cultural icons—the most distinguished of them all, without a doubt, since he knew all about art, music, novels, essays, urbanism, architecture—that *The Consecration of Spring* was a shitty title. That *The Force of Destiny* was the one that was good.

MY SAFETY WAS becoming a problem, and worrisome to my *compañeros*. You can't go around publicly proclaiming an insurrection with impunity. At the beginning of June, Raúl, Antonio "Ñico" López and Chucho Montané moved to Lidia's house with their weapons, while I decided not to ever spend two nights in a row in the same place. It was excellent training for moving through the Sierra later and, even better, for battling with the CIA and the counterrevolution and their more than six hundred attack plans hatched, and many of them carried out, over the course of forty-three years of the Revolution. Then Batista's henchmen beat up an opposition leader named Juan Manuel Márquez and killed ex-Commander of the Navy Jorge Agostini, who had just returned from exile—a settling of old Batista accounts. Then in one single night, seven bombs exploded across Havana. The person accused of having placed one of the bombs, the one at the Payret Theater, was my brother Raúl. Then the attack on the newspaper *La Calle* followed, the paper where my old friend Luis Orlando Rodríguez published my inflammatory articles. Despite all of this, on the night of June 12, we held the most formal meeting possible, given our underground status, constituting the National Board of Directors of the 26th of July Movement, made up of eleven members.* On June 17, I ordered Raúl, who was the object of two search-and-capture orders, to seek asylum at the Mexican Embassy. Raúl traveled to Mexico on June 24. Then I ordered the departure of a handful of other *compañeros*. The invading force began to gather itself outside of Cuba.

---

* Fidel Castro, Pedro Miret, Jesús Montané, Melba Hernández, Haydee Santamaría, José Suárez Blanco, Pedro Celestino Aguilera, Antonio "Ñico" López, Armando Hart, Faustino Pérez and Luis Bonito.

ON JULY 7, 1955, when I left for Mexico, I made a declaration at Havana's Rancho Boyeros Airport—hiding my satisfaction over the realization of my new goals with a sad tone—that I was forced into exile "to prepare an armed uprising against Fulgencio Batista's tyrannical rule. Since all opportunities for civic battle were closed off to the people"—I was the people!—"the only solution left was that of '68 and '95 (the wars for independence unleashed by our liberators, the *mambises*, against Spain)." I left a rosary of convenient phrases perhaps too grandiloquent to later repeat but very effective at the time (it's like trying to dance one of the ballroom dances from Louis XIV's court in a modern discotheque: that's the problem the historian has with his own history if he doesn't have the right sense of humor when it comes to distinguishing "the values" of the past). "Cuban patience has its limits." "One doesn't return from trips like this, and if he does, it's only with tyranny beheaded at my feet."

THE PROPHECY OF THE FORESTS

A large part of the time, I was training the group that would accompany us on what would later be the odyssey. I was trying to get all of the material resources for this, but propaganda continued to be my main concern. I devoted myself to preparing a series of manifestos to the Cuban people. On August 8, I finished the first M-26-7 manifesto. I still didn't aim the cannons at the PPC (the Orthodox Party), but rather, I devoted myself to the exorcism of my own exile and why I had chosen the path of armed resistance. With a run of fifty thousand copies, my first pamphlet should have been in circulation on August 16, 1955, the fifth anniversary of Chibás's death, to be distributed at the cemetery by the thousands. "You'll see how we break the wall of silence and open the path to a new strategy," I wrote on August 3 of that year. The second pamphlet criticized the previous ways of fighting and launched once and for all "the first slogans of *insurrection and general strike*." I considered this last manifesto so vital that I recommended making a hundred thousand copies.

The general strike? Of course this denies by its own weight any talk of a more or less prolonged guerrilla war. The theory of a rapid punch. This was what percolated in my head. In some way I was conscious that it was like repeating Moncada but with some very important variations. For years I have been able to make all those who study me dizzy with the thesis that in Mexico I had already defined the guerrilla struggle as the direct option to follow immediately upon disembarkation, when in reality it was the last option. In short, what it came down to, as I had been thinking since the *vivac* at Santiago, was that I had to find a strategic equivalent to the logistical supremacy of our adversary, and perhaps (it was still a perhaps) that equivalent would be in the use of time (perhaps a policy of prolonged struggle) and in not betting all our capital on a rapid strike like Moncada. What was truly surprising about Hitler's axiom that history is written by the victors is not the brutality of its truth but that they write it as they see fit. That goes for those who write my history. As for me, I learned a long time ago to only share my thoughts with myself. I tend to portray the result of my meditations, no matter the subject, like Macduff's armies in *Macbeth*, disguised as trees—the forests moving as the witches prophesied to Macbeth—as they approached the fortress of Dunsinane. Nobody should know about them until the siege is complete.

So I left for Mexico with a discreet tourist visa, arriving on Mexicana de Aviación flight 566 from Havana to Mérida, Yucatán. I didn't go directly to Mexico City, because I was short on cash, and my sister Lidia had to sell her refrigerator to pay for my ticket. My brother Raúl, Calixto García and a few other *compañeros* were already waiting for me there. From there, I moved on to the port at Veracruz, where I spent the night, and from the port to Mexico City, where I arrived via highway on the eighth, traveling the whole way in my old and worn gray suit and carrying a suitcase full of books, plus my guayabera and I think two or three pairs of socks.

How the Steel Was Tempered

/ / /

Che, for a man whom I had initially rejected and who later gave me more than enough reasons to realize my intuition had been right, I think I made adequate use of him to the benefit of the Revolution. He was a poor devil. But the true biography of that poor devil whom everyone knows as Che and who was named Ernesto Guevara de la Serna is hardly compatible with the character created after the Cuban Revolution. I know that it will be a bitter pill for all of you to swallow, to recognize that you've spent nearly forty years prostrated before a man who only exists as propaganda.

Biographers seem to agree that the origin of his revolutionary convictions date to his travels around the Latin American subcontinent. It is alleged that, while traveling from Argentina to Guatemala, he discovered the misery and exploitation of peoples and the voraciousness of North American imperialism. These were trips, as is known, that took place at different times, starting at the end of his adolescence. Every year he ventured a little farther and was away from home a little longer. With time, these excursions became a type of ideological ministry, an apprenticeship *on the terrain* of the vectors of a revolution. But if there's something I know perfectly well, after countless hours of conversation with Che, it's the casual nature of those trips and that if any literature informed their spirit, it was Emilio Salgari's action-adventure novels and not Marx's pamphlets. And, more than anything else, if he pushed himself to go farther each time and to attempt the most extreme situations, he did it as a challenge to himself, due to the ter-

Fidel gets ready to leave "Miguel Schultz," the prison in Mexico City, after one of his many run-ins with the local police while training his revolutionary expedition to overthrow Batista. He has to leave Ernesto Guevara behind. The Mexicans want to squeeze him a little more. They're not persuaded by this Argentine who is rumored to be a communist who suddenly appears connected to the Cubans.

rible asthma that plagued him since his childhood. Many years later—
and as a direct result of my observations about Che—I understood that
the force of his convictions and his stoicism in the face of danger and his
iron will had nothing to do with authentic convictions, stoicism or will.
It was asthma. And it's an inherent thing with asthmatics. That permanent sense of suffocation and especially the body's constant response
to it, those hits of adrenaline issued in abundance by the autonomic
system, toughen one up daily to withstand any wave of fear so consis-
tently that one could be on a Japanese blockhouse under the artillery
fire of the *yanqui* Seventh Fleet during the War of the Pacific. In other
words, every time that Che demanded our combatants in the Sierra do
the nearly impossible, I was forced to look the other way and pretend I
didn't care. But, in my deepest convictions, I knew what I was looking
at. I was looking at a sick man forcing a group of happy, healthy Cuban
kids to be ruled according to the canons of his illness. In any event, the
whole experience ended up being beneficial, since the *compañeros* were
forced to reach for goals that were ever higher, and that strengthened
them and gave them a sense of pride.

So Che's supposed revolutionary apprenticeship continued, with a
few deviations, in Guatemala. To earn a living, he went around the streets
of Guatemala City selling images of the Christ of Esquipulas, a black
Christ brought by the Spaniards, to whom the Guatemalans attributed
miraculous powers. Then he met Ñico López. I was in prison on the Isle
of Pines and Nico, who had escaped the July 26 actions unharmed, was
kicking around between Mexico and Guatemala, doing what we hoped
was propaganda work and fund-raising, but in reality was just poor Ñico
trying to survive by conning the natives. You can guess the low-class
kind of business Che and Ñico were involved in if one of them was selling little statues to the Indians and the other one was the representative
of a revolutionary movement whose members were all behind bars in
Cuba. Only an enormous leap of imagination would allow one to guess
that in just five years, Che would become one of the most venerated men
in the history of our civilization.

On those Guatemalan wanderings, Ñico told the Argentine with his
Christ of Esquipulas on his shoulders about our attack on Moncada. And
the Argentine responded, with that ironic tone, of permanent incredu-
lity, that characterized him, "Tell me another cowboy tale." He didn't
believe a single word. It ended up being paradoxical, viewed through the

current perspective, that the second most important icon of the Cuban Revolution (the most important, of course, can only be me) should have his first encounter with the process through a story that he considered beneath his intelligence.

But when I heard about Che for the first time, I was very resistant to having him introduced to me. In a way, this established a balance in the origin of our relations, which was a sort of common unconscious rejection. Like two magnetized heads at the top of a metal bar who repel each other when placed face-to-face. He didn't believe in the Moncada story. I didn't want to meet him. My reasoning? Well, this took place at an intuitive level. I explained it to Raúl, because my brother was the first person who mentioned Che to me, the first person to try to sell him to me. We were in Mexico. He said there was an Argentine who was a doctor and he wanted to introduce him to me, which was when I said (and this is what I mean when I talk about intuition), "*Coño*, Raúl, remember that the whole of Latin America is full of Trotskyites. The only party to do away with that was the Cuban one. Why bring Trotskyism into the Cuban Revolution?"

I'll have you know that up until this Guatemala phase, Ñico and Che were men of scant political education. I can guarantee that since I knew them both perfectly well. Perhaps Ñico—a poor devil who, in the course of his whole life, never enjoyed anything more than the most vulgar of all pleasures, that of leaning over a bowl full to the rim with meat stew and eating until he could eat no more—was naturally inclined toward social change, what in Marxist terms is known as class struggle. But Che was still a little preppy looking for an adventure, although by that time he had already gotten his hands on some revolutionary literature, which he used largely for his own personal benefit: by memorizing some key terms and using them later to impress his friends. Then it so happened that the Americans overthrew Jacobo Árbenz. A government elected by the people in elections that were completely democratic was brought down. Arbenz had been president of Guatemala for three years. On June 16, 1954, the bombing of the Presidential Palace began. Che's legend grew in connection to the Guatemalan disaster. Thus, upon waking, the traveling salesman of Christs of Esquipulas turned into the prototypical hero. A counterrevolution appeared right before Che's eyes, and worst of all was that Arbenz hadn't done a thing to arm his own people. Che would repeat this all over and over again, his indignation at the Guatemalan government's incompetence at mobilizing the people.

The thing is that a period of time went by in which Che and Ñico fell completely out of touch with each other, since they had to get out of Guatemala quickly. Perhaps Che fell out of touch because he had taken his interest in revolutionary literature too far and made personal contact with communists *and other revolutionary groups*, according to what he himself would tell me. Because when we met and he told me his tale, what drew my attention was that mention of other revolutionary groups. And that confirmed my intuition about his probable Trotskyite training.

About a year passed and Ñico and Che ran into each other again at a hospital in Mexico.

"What are you doing here?" Ñico asked.

"I'm here as a doctor, *¿y vos?*"

He wasn't conning the Guatemalans anymore. Now he was conning the Mexicans. "I'm here as a doctor," Che said clearly.

Where did he suddenly get, as if by magic, a degree in medicine?

"We're still preparing the Revolution, we're going to return to Cuba. We get together at María Antonia's house. Come see us," Ñico supposedly said to the Argentine. And the Argentine went, and the person he found there was Raúl. Later Raúl mentioned him to me. His main rationale was that we didn't have any doctors for the invasion. The Argentine could be useful to us. Finally, I agreed. I told him to bring him by María Antonia's house one night. It happened in the second week of July 1955. Years later, he would write that that night he discovered we thought just like each other. "Everything that Fidel says is the same as things I've thought," he said. That I think just like he does! But I don't even remember anymore what I could have talked about, seated on the floor of María Antonia's kitchen all night, but Che, sitting there right next to me, heard it all and believed it.

It still exists. An old, narrow kitchen. The *compañeros* who pass through there say that it is kept in very good condition and that the Cuban Embassy takes care of the maintenance.

CHE HAD MARRIED a certain Hilda Gadea on August 18, 1955, and they had a small apartment. One of my fleeting romances of the time period came about in that house. I was already a regular visitor and I met Lucila Velásquez there, a friend of Hilda's, during a goodbye party in my honor, since I was leaving for the United States to raise the funds needed for the movement. Lucila was very attractive and had a penchant for poetry. Can you respect a paragraph in which I write that such and such person *had a penchant for poetry*? Little Lucila and I had many encounters and it would seem that she fell in love. Hilda, now deceased as you should know, told me that the girl once asked her, "Hilda, tell me, what did you do to snag Ernesto?" Che, who was listening to the conversation, responded with his usual irony: "It was like this: they were looking for me in Guatemala to throw me in jail and she was imprisoned for not revealing my whereabouts. I married her as a sign of my appreciation." In addition to irony, there was, of course, an element of invented heroism that made its way into everything he said. He was actually very good at sending subliminal messages. Where did that Argentine get the idea that anyone was looking for him in Guatemala to throw him in jail? You had to understand him. Anyway. For the first time in his life he was involved with an authentic group of revolutionaries, who had attacked military barracks and been commandos and served prison sentences. It's difficult for an Argentine to be around a group of truly valiant men and not have a single scar to show off. For now, he was the only one of us who couldn't make any reference to revolutionary actions. In that sense, Guatemala fit like a glove. Who in the hell could really determine what he had really done or not done there? What always surprised me, nonetheless, was that he never noticed that I let him tell these lies and that he didn't know that everything has its price, even telling that little lie about the Guatemalans who rose up against Arbenz wanting to imprison him. In other words, he really believed he was fooling me. It's a bad thing, a very bad thing, to try to fool me. But it's even worse to convince yourself that you have succeeded in doing so. Because that's the kind of insult I'll never forget.

On October 20, I left for the United States. The *yanquis* didn't give me any trouble about my visa. My first stop was Philadelphia. Then I went to Union City, New Jersey, and Bridgeport, Connecticut, to talk to Cubans and put a big cowboy hat on the table to collect money. I got to New York on October 23. On October 30, 1955, I spoke at Palm Garden, on Fifty-second Street and Eighth Avenue, and uttered my slogan for the first time that we would either be martyrs or be free the following year. Juan Manuel Márquez accompanied me almost everywhere; he was charismatic, fat and a good speaker and had the ability to submit to my leadership without complaint. I had just named him second in command when the guards captured him after our disembarkation from the *Granma* and shot him. The poor guy, he didn't know (and neither did I, for that matter) that he was going to be one of the first martyrs of our cause. But he was a little on the heavy side. He would have been enormously useful to cover my flank from the ambitions of all the second-tier chiefs and leaders who came up through the revolutionary process, especially during the war. Juan Manuel would have worked marvelously in my favor as the second in command. But the only thing he bequeathed me, in addition to a few months of useful service, was the knowledge that an overweight man can really devastate a guerrilla army if you don't get rid of him in time, or if he himself—as was the case with Juan Manuel—gets left behind. The maxim is that the guerrilla movement can only advance at the pace of its slowest member. But these were subsequent considerations. In the course of our U.S. fund-raising trip, he was always the spirited associate and the one with the best capacity for public speaking. In this case, I think his girth contributed positively. I, for one, don't know of any more intoxicating oratory than that of chubby men, perhaps due to the vibration of their flesh when they speak or how convincing a fat-faced man with flushed cheeks is when he makes a call to arms or sacrifice. I represented something else entirely, and in addition wore a field uniform and had a beard and was practicing a vehement oratory of terror, the oratory of every revolution. But in our pilgrimage to North American cities, we wore suits, with double-breasted jackets and ties, to convey a certain elegance. In that sense, Juan Manuel was irreplaceable.

By November 20, I was already in Miami and that evening I spoke at the Flagler Theater. I saw my son Fidelito in that city. My sister Lidia brought him to me—via airplane from Havana—after I asked Mirta. For the first time, I was tempted to keep him. I've experienced pain and I associate it with Friedrich Engels. Although in *The Origin of the Family, Private Property and the State*, his treatise on human relations, in which he establishes guidelines as if he were a Darwin of filial mechanics,* he doesn't describe paternal feelings in the first exchange with his son following a divorce with the attention to detail of my own experience, I still rely on his revealing aphorism that men love more the children of

---

* And which I tend to quote every time I want to come across as an expert on the matter. [*Author's note.*]

the women they love most to propose a correlating theory. That there is no pain like that felt for a son that one believes to be defenseless and in need of care to the degree that one plans and in certain instances even carries out the kidnapping of a child born of the woman a man loves most, not because of the child himself but as an act that reflects the desperate love still existent for his mother. Do you understand? That one doesn't give a damn about his children. That one is still slobbering over the *cabrona* who is sleeping with God knows whom now. Oh, God, that flat abdomen and the crop of pubic hair that I thought would be mine for eternity and those honey-colored thighs that parted to receive only me, smeared now with the semen of any old slob and the drops of sweat glistening like precious gems under the light of an electric bulb. No. Engels didn't discuss this either, nor did any of the other Marxists. As far as I know, the effect—which is permanent, by the way—of the postmarital relations of the woman a man has most loved on the psyche of the founders of the first socialist states has never been studied. It's difficult to discern, for example, the effect that a similar phenomenon would have had on Vladimir Ilyich Ulianov if Krupskaia had been his most beloved. One idea leads to another. I am asking myself at this very moment if ever in his meetings as skilled conspirator in Vienna or Petrograd did comrade Lenin feel Krupskaia sliding her hand under the table in search of his fly.

Well, for the time being, Fidelito's kidnapping was put on hold. I had him with me in Miami for a few days, then I sent him back. I went to Tampa and Key West, the traditional Cuban acts of faith since it's the same pilgrimage José Martí made when he was organizing the battle against Spain at the end of the previous century. In all, I was able to collect an initial sum of $10,000. The trip was also useful for organizing the Patriotic Clubs and the 26th of July Houses. I spent ten days in Key West, resting at a guesthouse. I think that was the last time I enjoyed that light human pleasure called a vacation.

I returned to Mexico City and during Christmas, 1955, at María Antonia's house I allowed myself the pleasure of cooking and I invited some *compañeros* over, including the Argentine, who for the time being was an exotic and somewhat pleasant figure among my future expeditionaries. After dinner was over, following the *turróns* and the coffee, what I missed most was not having a Partagás cigar between my teeth.

In the summer of 1956, I was already divorced from Mirta and was in Mexico preparing the expedition to Cuba with the purpose of over-throwing the dictator Fulgencio Batista, who had been in power since 1952. But Mirta was on the verge of marrying Emilio Núñez Blanco, the son of the then–Cuban ambassador to the United Nations. Upon learning that Mirta was marrying a conservative and that my son, Fidel-ito, would grow up under the influence of my ex-wife's family, I devised a plan—which seemed perfect to me at the time—to prevent my son from staying at his mother's side. I called Mirta on the phone in Miami, where she was with Fidelito, and asked her to allow the kid to spend two weeks with me in Mexico.

Fidelito had to be back in two weeks. I had given Mirta's father my word that I would return the boy with my sister Lidia, who was a good friend of Mirta's. Fidelito arrived in Mexico from Miami on September 17, 1956. I immediately placed him in the care of a married couple: Alfonso "Fofó" Gutiérrez, a Mexican civil engineer, and Orquídea Pino, a Cuban nightclub singer. The boy's name was changed to Juan Ramírez, and he became a Boy Scout. He started a new life at the Gutiérrezes' comfortable villa, which was surrounded by a high wall and had a pool. I visited him there, honking the horn of my car loudly upon arrival.*

FIVE WEEKS AFTER his arrival, Fidelito hadn't been returned and Mirta hadn't received any word of her son—nor of me. Finally, she was able to get in touch with Lidia, in Mexico. Lidia said she was very sorry but I had decided that my son would not grow up in a family of *esbirros*, "thugs," a word that was very commonly used in Cuba and which came into being as a reference to ex-dictator Gerardo Machado's assassins.

---

* On December 8, with the help of the Mexican police and security forces, Mirta recovered Fidelito, who was taken to the Cuban Embassy in Mexico and from there to Cuba. I had disembarked six days prior and the army had dec-imated my troops and was on my trail. There was nothing I could do at the time to keep Fidelito. Before leaving Mexico, I had taken care to put together a document in which I asked the Mexican people and authorities to take care of the upbringing of my son. If the Díaz-Balart family, to this day, labels that fact a kidnapping, I likewise understand that my behavior forty years later will seem paradoxical to the common reader in relation to the very well-known case of the child Elián González, who was kidnapped and taken to Miami on a raft on which all those on board perished except for Elián. Do you remember the case? It was on *Time* magazine's first cover of the new millennium. I contributed in such a decisive way to the boy being returned to his father, who was still in Cuba, and to the Clinton administration ignoring the vehement insistence of Miami's Cuban exile community to keep him on American soil. But there was one difference. The difference that Miami took up the dilemma as a challenge to the Revolution. In both cases, it was a political affair, certainly, but in one of them the Revolution's power was at stake. Miami challenged me to face the moral dilemma that I had once created a similar situation with my own son. But now we were dealing with a battle in defense of the Revolution, and in that theater of operations there was no room for dilemmas or morals: winning was the only objective. [*Author's note.*]

———

IT'S UNNECESSARY to keep going on about these episodes in Mexico and the two following years of battle in the Sierra Maestra, since there is an overwhelming amount of literature about all of these events. And I'm not writing a history of the Cuban Revolution, but my own personal history. The abundance of texts about this period, according to my understanding, is due to the fact that their authors left Cuba very early on and were witnesses or participants in these two or three years. And in reality, they are unaware of the true revolutionary process, the one after 1959, which they were absent from and which is when things really got going. Do you want to know the truth? The only truly important thing to have happened in all these thirty-three years up until the triumph of the Revolution is that I was born. Everything else is the story that the counter-revolutionary *gusanos* never tire of repeating and publishing in their vain editorials in Miami. In any event, I have used the preceding pages to give my version of certain events and how those events fit together to give me a vision of revolutionary mechanics and how to set certain things into motion. But it's high time for me to wrap up these chapters, lest I become yet another chronicler of that epic which my enemies have wanted to claim for themselves.

BETWEEN THE MONTHS of August and October 1956, Frank País had visited Havana five times and held meetings with the movement's leaders in preparation for my landing. During his last visit, having just arrived from Mexico and been named the national chief of Action and Sabotage, Frank specified the missions that Havana would carry out in support of the disembarkation: mainly the sabotage and neutralization of the electrical system and telephone services.

In Mexico, on November 22, I ordered my lieutenants to send the orders to different groups who, spread out across Mexico City, would participate in the departure for Cuba. We would all meet two days later on a dock on the Tuxpan River, a few kilometers from Veracruz.

On November 27, a cable was received in Havana from Mexico directed to a worker at the Royal Palm Hotel, but whose true addressee was Aldo Santamaría Cuadrado, that said, "Set aside hotel room." It was the order of disembarkation support for the M-26-7 in Havana, Matan-zas and Pinar del Río.

On the highway from Mexico City to Tuxpan, we were stopped by a police barrier and I asked them if they wanted the Cuban Revolution to begin in Mexico.

Then we killed one last traitor. And this is not something I've ever told anyone, nor has anyone in the participating group; it is only because of a drunken afternoon that loosened Raúl's tongue in February of 1987 that we have the information. It was on Raúl's little farm—where the Dominican Caamaño Deño had been living—that he told Norberto Fuentes the entire story. We dug a hole in a nearby beach, in Cancún, and we dug the hole before we set sail, and before we set sail we took the traitor there and killed him. This was who was present: Cándido González; *el negro* Héctor Aldama Acosta, one-eyed Agustín Aldama's brother; Gustavo Arcos; and Raúl Castro, who was the one who shot him in the head. That's exactly how he told it to Norberto Fuentes. "I killed him." Name? Well, now I can't specify because there aren't any papers or any other kind of testimony, nor can you expect me to ask *el negro* Aldama at this point if he remembers the names of the sons of bitches we killed in Mexico, and it's even less likely that I can ask Gustavo Arcos, who has now gone over to the side of the most open and confrontational dissidents. But I can be sure enough to provide you with three names, all three proven to be Batista spies: Jesús Bello Melgarejo, Arturo Ávalos Marcos and Cirilo Guerra. I think there was a fourth man executed, but I can't be certain who he was. I say this because it seems like we buried two at the training camp. Then Orlando Piedra, Batista's chief of police who pursued us most viciously in Mexico, stated in Havana that Arturo and Cirilo were buried in the Lions' Desert, in an extension of the Avenida de Insurgentes, Mexico City, and while the case was never investigated, I can't confirm it or deny it because I never participated in burials. I took great care not to be present at that type of task, not because I felt terrified or was reluctant, but sim-ply because I considered it my duty not to sully the name of the high-est leader of the nascent Revolution. It would appear that I did that for myself, but in reality I did it for everyone. Jesús Bello Melgarejo. That's the one whom I think we executed in Tuxpan, before the departure of the *Granma*. Bello Melgarejo was an American citizen and a veteran of the Second World War and no one ever heard from him again. According to a version that differed from ours, they bought him a few beers, then tricked him into driving to a meeting and finally killed him with a shot to the back of the head. To make him disappear, he was thrown down a ravine only accessible to vultures and coyotes. Make-believe. Pure make-believe. He's buried in a little beach to the south of Tuxpan. If you go there now and if fifty years of the sea beating over it hasn't made the inlet disappear, you'll find him.

We began our journey on the Tuxpan River toward the Gulf of Mexico. The leaders of Batista's army, who were aware of the operation, were prepared to meet us in Cuba. In the small hours of November 25, 1956, as my watch struck one-thirty, we left the city of Tuxpan. The yacht was anchored in front of the city, on the opposite bank of the river, at a place known as Santiago de las Peñas. When we embarked, we did so with the lights off; the yacht separated from the breakwater and the prow pointed downriver, in the direction of the coastal port. All of the occupants on board remained silent. It had been raining quite hard since the previous afternoon. The port was closed to all kinds of navigation due to the bad weather. The yacht sailed calmly down the Tuxpan River's estuary for half an hour, the time it took to go from the dock toward the coast. At the entrance to the port, the lighthouse that protected it was the only witness to the craft's battle against the intense wind and undertow.

Eighty-two men aboard. The *Granma*'s prow pointed toward Cuba. Che was at my side. He was silent. I would say resigned. Or like a lapdog. For the first—and I believe only—time in my life, I felt sorry for him. Che had spent two years and three months of his life in Mexico, which he would never see again.

The *Granma*, a craft built for the transport of fifteen people, twenty-five maximum, had eighty-two men, in the middle of a storm—a storm of such forceful winds that it was doubtful not only that we would make it to Cuba, but even the small distance separating us from the Gulf—and departed toward the east, in the direction of some very remote beaches that the maps said was Niquero. Midmorning on the twenty-sixth, while we tried out our weapons shooting at the horizon, an asthma attack invaded the lungs of then–Medical Lieutenant Ernesto Guevara, who wasn't able to pack his medicines in his bags because of the urgency and excitement of our departure. Faustino Pérez gave him an adrenaline injection and the suffocation passed. A large part of the food destined for the trip had also remained behind on land. A few bags with oranges and crackers and some strips of meat hanging in the ship's hold made up the provisions which I myself would ration out strictly during the whole trip.

The Gulf waters started beating strongly against the craft and it seemed to give in. The yacht and its dangerous lurching back and forth under a black sky and wintry drizzle sparked dizziness and extreme nausea in all of us. One of the expeditionaries, Faustino Pérez, asked, "We only have one engine, right?"

Just one engine. But we were consumed by an intense and silent excitement. For one moment I held my breath, since I was afraid that the slightest noise could abort the whole mission. We entered the Gulf of Mexico and I saw the dim lights of Tuxpan recede; we all felt that the silence of our departure was unnecessary and, as if agreed-upon beforehand, the Cuban national anthem rang out, in unison.

The wind was blowing harshly and the waves crashed against the hull violently. Save for two or three sailors and four or five other people, the crew was dizzy. But on the fourth or fifth day the general outlook got a little better.

Overloaded, the *Granma* was sailing at an average speed of six knots, about four less than we had anticipated, and, with the seawater above the craft's flotation level, the pressure caused water to leak into the ship through the head as well as through the cabins.

We lost our way. The currents and bad weather threw the *Granma* off course and took it farther and farther away from Niquero's beaches.

While this appeared to be the beginning of our misfortunes, we didn't know that in Havana there was a student protest on November 27. Jesús Suárez Gayol, one of the movement's national leaders, and Otto Díaz, from the business school, were wounded by bullets in the street riots, and on the other side, fifteen policemen sustained injuries from beatings and contusions, among them two captains. We didn't know it then, but the protest constituted a propitious prologue to the rebellion in Santiago. The news would have been quite encouraging had it reached us.

And on November 30, as we had agreed on with Frank País, the uprising broke out. The large number of M-26-7 members that carried out different actions in Santiago that day to facilitate the disembarkation of the expedition was decisive. The operation began at five forty-five a.m., but the combatants weren't able to stay in the streets past noon, although some snipers harassed the soldiers for a little longer. For the first time, the olive-green uniform and red and black bracelets with white lettering (M-26-7) that would characterize our combatants were used. The operation was carried out three days after receiving our cable with the agreed upon code.

As far as the 26th of July in Havana, Aldo Santamaría would end up in prison and had to eat the piece of paper with the cable received from Mexico so that the thugs wouldn't learn its contents. Before this, he had shared the contents of it with *compañeros* Enrique Hart and Héctor Ravelo, leader of the M-26-7 on Havana Campo. The 26th of July Movement relied on a plan devised by the engineer Federico Bell-Lloch to paralyze the whole country's communications and electrical networks. But this was never carried out and later no one could figure out what in the hell happened to that plan and where the infamous engineer Bell-Lloch ended up. Enrique Hart Dávalos seemed to be the sharpest and most conscientious of the Havana leaders. At the very least he repeated ad infinitum, "We must do as much as we can with whatever we have." Well, it wasn't a lightning paralyzation of all of the country's energy and communications activities, but it was something. One of his commando units, made up of Paco Chavarry, Miguel Fernández Roa and Eduardo Sorribes, had stolen a large quantity of phosphorous from the Belén School and they had a good amount of dynamite, some brought from Matanzas by Jesús Suárez Gayol and other quantities obtained by Roberto Yepe, as well as some handguns and a few grenades made in Regla, with which they wreaked havoc. In Havana, the use of phosphorous bombs in movie theaters, stores and buses was so great that Minister of Government Santiago Rey and the dictator himself referred to these events on three occasions in the month of December, in official statements to the press.

In any event, this activity and the outbreak in Santiago mainly occurred while I and my men were far away from the events. The revolt in Santiago was finally contained by the police and the army, but not before resulting in many dead, injured and detained people. Those men had squandered a popular revolt in support of a disembarkation that still hadn't happened. And we still had to take care of the problem that Batista's security forces had been alerted and were probably waiting for us. I wasn't wrong: someone had ratted us out. Someone who, to this day, forty years later, still hasn't been discovered. My only hope is that it was the squealer that Raúl killed in Tuxpan. It's not easy to spend more than forty years trying to figure out which of your *compañeros* in the shrinking leadership group is the traitor. The proof, the tip of my Ariadne's thread, is the following communiqué from Batista's Chiefs of Staff to all of the sea and air units:

ARRANGE SEARCH FOR A WHITE YACHT, 65 FEET LONG, NAME LESS, MEXICAN FLAG, WITH A CHAIN COVERING THE ENTIRE BOAT, DEPARTED TUXPAN, VERACRUZ, MEXICO, THIS PAST NOVEMBER 25. INFORM THIS CEN OF RESULTS. GENERAL RODRÍGUEZ ÁVILA.

After 172 hours of crossing, we made out Cuba on the horizon and I decided to land on a desolate beach located to the southwest of Niquero, of which I would later learn the name. Las Coloradas.

The *Granma* was full of water and would only be able to stay afloat for a few hours. That's why I gave the order to head for the island at full speed. We would get off wherever the *Granma* decided to rest its prow, I said, and the old craft chose to sink in a swamp called Belic, about two kilometers off the coast of Las Coloradas and a similar distance from Niquero. The closer we were to reaching the dark horizon we had identified as firm ground, the more we realized how wrong our estimate was. We were approaching a swamp that barely allowed us to move forward toward a line of coconut trees where we sensed the ground was solid. It was December 2, 1956 and René Rodríguez was the first one to jump in the water in search of a beach. He couldn't reach the bottom and he yelled out to me, "Shit, I'm drowning!" My response produced an unexpected effect in René. I yelled to him, "Walk, goddammit!" And like a Christ on the water, he began to move forward. That day I understood what it was to command and for the first time since the Bogotazo, I knew what it was to prevail over an out-of-control crowd. Then I jumped.

A Cuban naval torpedo boat that appeared somewhere in the horizon fired several shots on the rear guard that, under Raúl Castro's command, was still aboard the *Granma*. The torpedo boat was backed up by a plane that began to release bombs indiscriminately across the whole swampy region. I don't know how but suddenly we were in the swamp and we split up and started looking for escape routes in small groups. While I tried to go into the scrub or find a pool of water to calm my thirst, in Havana the United Press International announced my death in combat. I still didn't know what was happening. I still believed that the majority of my men were deploying around me, into the thickness of the reed beds. In reality, I had just lost almost my entire expeditionary force, with the exception of sixteen men, who in turn were going to be slaughtered in three skirmishes. Now I went into a reed bed and bullets whistled by me and the sharp edges of Jaronú sugarcane cut my face and in that tiny struggle of mine against adversity what I was thinking of most vehemently was not the triumph of the social Revolution but that I was dying to drink a Coca-Cola.

NOW I RECALL that a few hours before departing, I had been paging through my favorite work by Lenin. At a given moment, in the rush of packing, I had thrown it in the pocket of my field jacket and forgotten about it. I remembered it in the early morning hours of December 2, while I was rifling through my pockets in search of a forgotten cigar. This type of literature was dangerous. We'd had enough trouble already as a result of the copy of *Imperialism: The Highest Stage of Capitalism* that was found in Haydee and Abel's apartment a few days after the Moncada attack. So I decided to get rid of my little book. Before throwing it in the water, I opened it to the last page, knowing what I would find there. Nonetheless, it was like a rush of adrenaline. I have never forgotten that phrase I illuminated on the *Granma*'s bridge with a marine flashlight. *To live the "experience of revolution."* Then, to throw the slim volume like a wedding bouquet, without any of my companions noticing, was like a kind of ritual. It was something intimate. Something exclusive between the gods, the Gulf current and me. The book opened softly like a dove, in the air, and I lost it in the sea's darkness—or couldn't see it any longer through my glasses misty with salt water and the inclement rain.

FINAL NOTE TO THE FIRST EDITION

This pamphlet was written during the months of August and September 1917. I had already outlined plans for the next chapter, VII: "The Experience of the Russian Revolutions of 1905 and 1917." However, besides the title, I was unable to write a single line of this chapter: a political crisis "disturbed" me, the eve of the October Rev-

olution of 1917. One can only welcome such a "disturbance." But the writing of the second part of this pamphlet (devoted to "The Experience of the Russian Revolutions of 1905 and 1917") must be put off for a very long time; it is more pleasant and useful to live the "experience of revolution" than to write about it.

The Author

Petrograd

November 30, 1917

La Plata Alta, where Fidel moved the Rebel Army's General Command in May 1958. Its facilities were constructed in such a way that they would not be detected by the enemy's air reconnaissance. This photo was taken in October or November 1958, just before the guerrillas descended from the mountains for the final offensive against Batista's army. Fidel is seated to the left.

NOMADS AND THE NIGHT

/ / /

My BROTHER RAMÓN TOOK A PICTURE OF ME. IT IS NOW BLURRY and the shades of gray fade into each other. I don't know what things are like now with photos, what kinds of emulsions are being used to achieve such vivid and firm colors. But those images prior to the 1950s seem to grow old along with the people and objects in them. To such a degree that one can always tell when one is looking at a photograph of a dead person. They were dusty and sometimes moth-eaten at the corners and in them, everyone felt obliged to show his most severe face. In effect, they gave one the sensation that they were withered and would release nothing but dust if one were to shake them. Or did mites actually accumulate in the stillness of those gloomy albums? My photo is from October 1947.[*] Ramón said to me, "Stand there, Fidel." *Stand there* meant I should stop what I was doing. "Look over here." I am shirtless, with my arms hanging at my sides, and behind me are the cement columns holding up the water tank at the Birán farm. My shadow points in the direction of the *caiguarán* sticks—the hardened *caiguaránes* that couldn't be pierced by nails of any diameter—that held up my house. The vague shadow on my face is the extent of the beard I could grow in those days. I look at the photo now, with the passing of the years, to recompose the scene for myself as I write this passage.

Applying my hard-won knowledge of medicine, I contemplate a young

---

[*] See page 90.

body that grew so satisfactorily, a sweet, healthy and splendid adolescence. All of my male features are well established, the facial hair, the developed muscles, the well-proportioned distribution of fat and the well-defined pecs. If I have a light beard, it's a matter of family phenotype, of genetic information, but the shadow that covers my face, the one in that photo, is adequate and sufficient for my age. The human experience is so full of oddities. The symbol by which I will stand out historically, my guerrilla beard, has always been a struggle for my body to produce.

So don't believe that it's easy for me to grow a beard. On the whole, I am rather smooth-cheeked, with a sparse beard that grows very slowly but whose presence is noticeable. Nor do I have hair on my chest. And my beard tends to come in before my mustache. And when this does grow, it looks like a Chinaman's mustache, all straight and hanging over the corners of my mouth.

But I was talking about the photo. I had just returned from Cayo Confites, a veteran of the war that never existed, but for the first time, there existed a natural association between my bellic efforts and the growth, although slight, of that beard of mine. The second time was in the Sierra Maestra, ten years after that photo, and from then on I would never shave again. I'm so thin in that photo, and my face is tanned from the sun, from which I had no shelter at Confites and the saltwater spray. It isn't the burnt skin of a peasant, which is earth-colored and sallow, but that of a seaman—in my case, a young man exposed to the elements that beat upon a small ungarrisoned islet facing the Great Bahama Bank, which makes the skin golden or a coppery red.

The important thing—and the reason that this photo is now, among papers and notes, on my desk and the reason that I am employing it as one of my informational documents—is the significance and value of the beard that I will grow in the days following the *Granma* disembarkation; and why I wanted to compare the Confites one, which was timid and shaved, to the Sierra one, which has been everlasting. My beards have appeared rather by the imperatives of the circumstances and not by an express will, and far less in the service of some publicity symbol or the pride of a guerrilla attribute. It goes without saying that I speak from my personal viewpoint. A newly cultivated beard is also indicative of small changes in habits and the acquisition of new gestures, as I would notice soon after Cayo Confites.

THE LAST THING I remembered was Norberto Collado. He was our erratic helmsman who, at the first light of dawn, tried to follow the best route through the labyrinth signaled by buoys, and who twice had to return to his starting point. He was trying to do it a third time when I took my Browning out and pointed it at his left temple. We only had a few liters of gas left. It was already broad daylight. The enemy was scanning the sea and the airspace. The ship was running a great risk of being destroyed just a few kilometers from the shore with everyone on board. I could see the nearby coast getting lower. "Come on, faggot. Head for the coast. Directly. At full force, faggot," I said. The *Granma* stopped sixty meters from the shore. The men and their weapons disembarked. Our advance—for lack of a better term for our sad pirouettes—took place in a practically stagnant pool of water atop shifting mud that threatened to swallow all of the men and their heavy bags while I brandished the 9mm Browning I was going to use to shoot Norberto's brains out at point-blank range. Someone, I think my brother Raúl, yelling, "Airplane," had a much more powerful effect on my psyche than the unrestrainable urge to kill him, a distinct homicidal impulse. I hit the water with the Browning raised high and the telescopic-sight Remington rifle in my other hand. This was, if you will, a rather uncomfortable and quite precariously balanced position. I sank into that muddy bottom up to my collarbone, although the weight of my backpack helped to keep me upright. If we consider the fact that my height at the time was six-foot-two, then there were about five feet of water on the side where I jumped off the boat. I could hear the splashes as the rest of my *compañeros* jumped in the water and I immediately confirmed that there is no greater command for a group of novices in their first real disembarkation maneuver than the notice of an airplane. Then I had this last view of the helmsman, still on the bridge, as pale as if his blood had just drained out of him, although I've never ascertained whether it was because of how close the plane was or because he had just escaped my firing a gun at his brain. Passing by the *Granma*, run aground at the edge of that mangrove swamp with its engine cut off, was like watching the agony of a beached whale up close. Surrounded by the choking agony of eighty-two men and wearing a brand-new pair of combat boots filling with mud and water like sponges with each step, this was, for me, a vision that was as phantasmagoric as it was incomprehensible; the *Granma*, dying. And why in the hell wasn't anyone singing the national anthem now?

At the risk of seeming pretentious and coming across as a cultural snob, I need to say that the whole thing seemed like an image captured by that crazy guy with the pointy mustache who made clocks melt and eyes float. And that's what I thought about, briefly, while I was making my way up one side of the yacht. Because of the surrealness, but especially because of the unexpected behavior of objects and the dose of arbitrary perspective, it resembled one of his paintings.

Incidentally, if there was really a plane that morning, its effects were not made visible on our ship, nor were the shots that a Batista frigate supposedly showered on it, because the fact is that a few days later, the *Granma*, without a single scratch, was towed out by the prow. The *Granma*, full of gas and running on its own engine, was taken to the navy docks in the Havana port, in front of the town of Casablanca, where it stayed afloat, tied to a jetty, until the triumph of the Revolution.

As far as Collado was concerned, I don't know how he managed to jump from the yacht, avoid the checkpoints that guards set up all over the region and get to Havana. Seeing as no one followed him, and police patrol cars passed by him as if he were just one more mulatto in his forties of which there are so many in that city, and he wasn't recognized as a World War II hero (remember how he was the sonar operator of the Cuban CS-13 antisubmarine under the command of Mario Ramírez Delgado?), nor as the helmsman of a revolutionary expedition, and even less so as a future—near future, two years—commander of the revolutionary navy, he became a bricklayer in one of the teams working on the construction of a majestic condominium building in the neighborhood of El Vedado that would become one of Havana's most emblematic structures, the FOCSA building.

ON DECEMBER 5, in Alegría de Pío, in the Ojo del Toro region, we made a considerable number of mistakes. The first two. We left the yacht aground at the same site of our disembarkation, instead of sinking it or leaving it adrift. And my new boots.

That yacht we left stuck in a mangrove swamp, a white ship, of all signs was the clearest one we could leave, for the enemy, of the site of our landing. All they had to do was follow our tracks. And that's what they did. Tracks in a barrier of mangroves and on swampy ground? Of course, if you are coming after us and you arrive in no less than a day at the place, the swamp still hasn't had time to fill in all of our tracks and wipe them away, and leaves the site marked like a dotted line on a map, and I don't even need to tell you about the mangroves, when eighty-two men stumble through them, breaking their roots and crushing the leaves. One thing in our favor was that, until we reached Alegría del Pío, I think we were quite disciplined in not leaving any waste along the way nor lightening our loads and unconsciously giving ourselves away.

Alegría del Pío is about twenty kilometers to the east of Las Colora-das. We arrived there on the third day of a three-day march, two of these by night, which proves how slow we were. The place where we made our bivouac was flat, bordered by sugarcane reed beds to the north and the edge of the mountains to the south, separated by a broad swath of bare earth. The position wasn't high or dominant, leaving us vulnerable to the enemy's sight and eventual fire. The desertion of our guide—Tato Vega, a *guajiro* we found the day before—at daybreak, and the presence of air-planes were insufficient to alert us that the army was getting close.

Regarding our defense, we were supposed to be organized in three groups. Three groups that (we realized immediately) only existed in our minds, in the haze of our exhaustion. The first squad, under Juan Almei-da's command, faced the east. The second one, covered by Raúl's squad, faced the northeast. And the third, which was José René Smith Comas's responsibility, covered the south. I was at the center of the bivouac. I needed to sleep a little, in all truth. A little before four p.m., someone woke me up and gave me a slice of chorizo, a couple of crackers and a sip of condensed milk straight out of the can that was being passed around from one man to another. It was the same ration all the other *compañeros* had received, they told me. I began to think that I should stretch my legs and clear my head and spend a few minutes organizing my ideas about our maneuvers. I was primarily concerned with two things in the days previous: one was getting out of those plains as soon as possible and, even better, much better, if we could do so by finding Celia Sánchez's people and their welcoming committee trucks, as we had agreed to do in Mexico. The other thing was, at least that first afternoon, I wanted my clothes and my holster to dry already so that I could put my Browning away and leave my two hands free for the rifle. Two additional calamities quickly fell upon us as the hours went by: thirst and hunger. In any event, the unfinished gesture of killing Norberto Collado the helmsman and later keeping my Browning unholstered until my clothing felt like cardboard served the purpose of my gun being the only one of those brought from Mexico to survive intact, without degradation, until the end of the war.

At 4:05 p.m. I still hadn't noticed the danger. I had placed the three defense squads too close to the site where we had chosen to camp out, thus reducing the possibilities of an early warning before the enemy's approach. Nor did I notice a first symptom of disciplinary apathy in the trail of pieces of sugarcane the members of our group left on the ground after sucking all the juice out of them while marching the night before, a trail which led directly to us.

The Second Battalion Company of the Constitutional Army's Mountain Artillery Division, under the command of Captain Juan Moreno Bravo and led by that little traitor Tato Vega came within fifty meters of us unnoticed. They moved without an organized scout team, with their detachment actually looking toward the east, while we were to the north of them. Their surprise run-in with us prompted a series of sudden and chaotic shots. While we weren't prepared, both sides were so equally disconcerted that many of us were able to get away and thus save ourselves. Che himself would say (and turned this in a way into one of his personal legends) that he had to choose between leaving behind a backpack full of bullets and one full of medicine. After hesitating for a moment, he grabbed the one that had the munitions. In short, this decision would save his life, since a bullet from a .45-caliber machine gun aimed at his chest would bounce off his backpack and end up flying by the side of his neck.

The result of that meeting was disastrous—for us. Some of us were captured and executed by a superior and better-trained military force that was strategically prepared to take on a Soviet invasion. Che recounts that upon feeling cornered by the governmental forces, one of the guerrillas dared to propose a surrender to his comrades, among which were Ramiro Valdés, Camilo Cienfuegos and the head of the group, Juan Almeida. Almeida's voice rose above the noise of the shrapnel and orders, "No one here surrenders, dammit!" while he emptied the magazine of his machine gun at an invisible enemy in the sugarcane surrounding him.

I ended up in the adjoining sugarcane reed bed. I was alone. Later,

Universo Sánchez and Faustino Pérez joined me. Universo carried his boots around his neck. He had decided to continue barefoot before submitting himself to the torture of breaking in new shoes. Then I learned a couple of the longest-lasting lessons of this kind of war. One is that you should avoid taming a new pair of boots in the mountains during the first days of a campaign. Two, no friendship is more lasting than that made in such situations. There are those whom I will value for eternity, like Faustino. I would forgive him all of the times he conspired against me following the triumph of the Revolution. Each time we discovered some CIA or counterrevolution activity, Faustino's name came up. But how could I do anything to one of the two *compañeros* who lived through the agony of that escape in the reed bed with me, the cane swaying meekly around us as bullets flew through the air and from which the charred bodies of three of our *compañeros* would later have to be removed? How do you order the execution of one of the three men who at 4:35 p.m. on that afternoon of December 5, 1956, made up the only existing assets of the Cuban Revolution? Faustino was ahead and Universo was next to me. Now I recall that the sugarcane leaves practically smothered me. They kept falling on me and Universo. who was trying to protect me, rather than move them aside, was throwing them on me. Universo, *cojones*! They killed me! Universo, with his boots around his neck, had shown up about ten minutes after the battle began. Faustino, with his hat pulled down over his ears, his nerdy glasses and his Remington with the telescopic sight, showed up a little later. That's why I'm telling you that at that moment, the Cuban Revolution was Universo, Faustino and me, just the three of us.

The siege was getting narrower. They say that later the guards and the airplanes leveled the little Alegría del Pío mountain. Leveled it with bullets.

According to the stories that reached me later, a peasant by the name of Augusto went to take his beasts, probably a pair of oxen, out of the battle zone. As was their habit, they had let the beasts loose in the cut sugarcane fields to feed. It just so happened that this peasant had let his loose through a little sugarcane field that was near Alegría del Pío. A little removed from Alegría del Pío, but not much. The animals weren't his either, to make the situation even worse, they had been lent to him for plowing, which was when he ran into one of our *compañeros* from the disembarkation. According to my calculations, the one he ran into was Juan

Manuel Márquez, who was with a group, all of them hairy, thin, covered in mud and blood and who proclaimed right away that they were lost. This peasant by the name of Augusto invited them to his house. But others followed and his house filled up. Later Augusto told us that the kids "were gross." Beyond the guards on their heels and the accumulated filth, what broke Augusto's heart was their hunger. He said that he served them honey and lemon drinks since he didn't have anything else and that they could hear the humming of the light reconnaissance aircraft.

This was the last we heard of Juan Manuel being seen alive. It's probable, as well, based on the information gathered, that Ñico López was one of the expedition members wandering with that group. That's also the last available information about him alive.

Tato Vega. A few weeks later, one of the men under the command of Crescencio Pérez, the local peasant leader—our most valuable ally in those days—gave the traitor his just desserts, an execution which took place as the result of an agreement I made with the people of the Sierra Maestra. I didn't really remember his name. But I asked Raúl, who had a list in the notebook he carried. Almost all of them were peasants who had helped us and whom we should compensate in some way upon the triumph of the Revolution. But there was a special list. That of people who never made it to that triumphant day.

MANY YEARS AFTER Alegría del Pío, I would read that I came across very badly in the eyes of my *compañeros* due to the sequence of mistakes and setbacks.* But I don't buy it. That's not how I see things. Let me tell you that there we were creating the groundwork for a long-lasting government. Luck and the positions we later assumed determined the spots we occupied in the revolutionary institution, in its government apparatus—and even in history; depending on the roll of the dice on the green carpet. Ramiro, Guillermo, Universo, Faustino, Ciro, Che, Raúl.

In any event, if this had been true, that my moral position before my comrades was compromised, no one ever told me to my face. But I would have sensed it, nonetheless. For the time being, what counted was that we were able to go deep into the mountains in search of the protecting heights of the Sierra. And that I remained the leader. That meant that

* See Lucas Morán Arce's book *The Cuban Revolution: A Rebel Version*.

in those current circumstances I was the axis around which you should place yourself should you wish to survive. First I was my own leader. Then I was Universo's and my own leader. Then I was also Faustino's leader. Compromised moral position? The virtue of any strategist is not merely acknowledging his mistakes but rather knowing them. In the days to come, when I was able to regroup a handful of these loyal followers, adding up to twenty in total, all I would be able to offer were words of encouragement. I left phrases professing my faith in a victory wherever I went. These could have a praiseworthy permanent effect if the war was won later. There, as we were, three thirsty men with their clothes in tatters, one of them barefoot, famished and pursued, in Purial de Vicana, at the foot of the Sierra Maestra, when I asked a peasant about the name of a mountain we could see off in the distance, haughty and blue, with clouds resting upon its summit, and he told me it was called "Caracas Hill," I responded, "If we make it there, we'll win the war." Likewise, when I met up with Raúl and asked him how many men he escaped the army's siege with, and if he had been able to save any of his weapons, and he told me there were five of them and all five with their weapons, I said: "Now we really will win the war."

These phrases, and the backdrop of defeat and death against which I pronounced them, are true miracles of rhetoric, inconceivable oxymorons of men at the limits of their physical resistance, whose actions until then had not resulted in a single enemy casualty, not even one wounded, and to whom the only thing remaining was the reasonable and understandable act of surrendering unconditionally.

THE MAGNETIC EAST OF THE REVOLUTION

I won't specify where we slept, but I remember that the next morning we went looking for water. Universo went down. He brought three canteens. But we heard noises. "Let's get going," I said. After that I spent a lot of time obsessing about water. We had to walk on foot for about twelve whole nights, walking only by night, breaking through the scrub with our chests because we didn't have machetes and making sure we left no trail. I don't recall having drunk water that entire time.

Without food, in unknown territory, discouraged by the sequence of events and uncertain of the fate of my *compañeros*, with whom we had lost all contact, I went in search of the mountain range to the east. In turn, each one of the three surviving parties would travel these same mountains and reed beds all the way from the *Granma* disembarkation point for sixteen agonizing days.

The only thing that kept me going was the vision, off in the distance, of what at times looked like a mountain range but later faded into the horizon or was mistaken for a line of clouds. I was convinced that if I could make it to the mountain range, I would be saved.

I still wasn't aware of what was before me: that this was the stage of my final battle, that this was where the Revolution would come into being. These comparisons may be daring, but Lenin and the Bolsheviks had the same need to go east. And analogies are too compelling to bypass. One of the most important turning points in the history of communism was the 1921 Baku Congress of the Peoples of the East. Facing the reality that the long-awaited German revolution wasn't going to happen, the Bolsheviks decided to turn their backs on the west—no favorable situation could arise there—and take care of themselves while they directed their gazes eastward. They turned toward themselves so decisively that they proclaimed a new doctrine, that of socialism in one country. And they turned eastward as Baku changed the emphasis from a world system of proletarian revolutions in industrialized countries to an anti-imperialist struggle by colonized or semi-colonized countries. The same poverty and shit I would find throughout the Sierra Maestra, ignored by the industrialized and modern west of my country, would be the equivalent of the fuel that the Soviets found in their eastward search. From the moment I disembarked at Las Coloradas until the attack on the El Uvero garrison more than six months later, I wouldn't do anything but direct myself eastward in a permanent and sustained way, to the Sierra.

ON DECEMBER 17, we arrived at the Cinco Palmas Farm, in Purial de Vicana. Cinco Palmas, about thirty-five miles to the northeast of Alegría del Pio, was the farm belonging to Ramón Pérez, who was known as "Mongo." From the summit I took over with Faustino and Universo, I took only two security measures: I kept the house under watch through the scope of my rifle until I was sure, after several hours, that there was no army presence, and later, sending Universo, barefoot and everything, to tell the owner of the house to prepare food for a troop of twenty men, and that he would be generously compensated. That's when I saw Universo return with that peasant. I stood up, with my rifle at the ready, and told him, "My name is Alejandro." The man's face lit up and he smiled like a saint, throwing his arms out to me and exclaiming, "Shit, Fidel!"

They were waiting for us by the foothills, he said. For days, he said. They call us "the disembarked," he said. He is Mongo Pérez. Crescencio Pérez's brother, he said. Crescencio was racing around the whole area like a madman, looking for us. Crescencio and Guillermo and Crescencio's two grown sons. Sergio Pérez is the oldest. Ignacio Pérez is the second oldest. We have to let Crescencio know you're here. At his brother Mongo's farm. "Shit, Fidel," he said.

Crescencio Pérez arrived at Purial de Vicana in the early hours of December 19. He and his men have gathered twelve rifles that the *compañeros* had left behind. There are the kids bringing them, he said, He's a patriarch. He had just barely come into the house where I was allowing myself the luxury of a freshly brewed cup of coffee, when everyone present stood up and you could hear his labored breathing as he cut straight to the chase and asked, "Which of the men here is Fidel Castro?" All eyes fell on me at once, giving Crescencio the information he requested. I left my coffee on the table and walked toward that man—now I'm the one holding my arms out with my most resolved expression of approval. We hugged. The old man also looked at me with approval. His eyes became small—they went "Chinese," as we say, smiling. I even allowed myself to make a joke. "*Usted*, Don Crescencio, don't take offense at the smell. I haven't had a change of clothes in sixteen days." Then I looked all around, as if checking whether I could divulge the following confession. "Or a bath, either." Laughs all around under that guano-leaf roof. Crescencio's laugh was the heartiest one. I'd hit exactly the right note. A bearded, dirty man who due to the circumstances hasn't been able to bathe in the last two weeks and who was still able to joke about his deplorable state of hygiene was not some preppy boy from the big city. He was someone with whom you can find common ground.

CHE ONCE SAID that we had all felt the limitless affection of the local peasants; they had tended to us and led us through a large clandestine mountain range, from the places where they rescued us to the meeting point at Crescencio Pérez's brother's house.

On December 23, a jeep arrived with two couples sent by the head of the Manzanillo Movement to find out if I was alive. One of the girls was the daughter of Mongo Pérez. Mongo himself had sent to Manzanillo the message that I was alive. Eugenia Verdecia, the other woman, brought three hundred submachine gun bullets and nine sticks of dynamite hidden in her skirt. Right away I decided that Faustino should clean himself up a little and take advantage of getting a ride back. Off to Havana with Faustino. I wanted him to find me an American journalist. I wanted publicity. He left in the jeep dressed like a dirty *guajiro* and had dinner with Celia Sánchez that very night in Manzanillo. Cream of asparagus soup. He would always remember that first dish. The next day he traveled to Santiago and had a meeting with Frank País, Vilma Espín, María Antonia Figueroa, Armando Hart and Haydee Santamaría. The following morning, he was on the daily Cubana flight en route to Havana.

IT WAS CHRISTMAS EVE. December 24, 1956. A Sunday. We would roast a yearling on the barbecue, and feast on the semi-raw meat all night. I was sitting on a stool in Mongo Pérez's yard, contemplating my arsenal. It contained Johnson rifles, a Thompson, a Mexican Mendoza model, numerous Remington .22 shotguns and some telescopic-sight Remingtons. All of the recovered equipment was given back to the combatants. We now had twenty rifles and seventeen insurgents. Crescencio let me know that there were thirty young guys from the Sierra who insisted on joining the guerrilla movement. I offered to talk to them. I called on my trade as a lawyer. The speech was about the end of the Revolution, the sacrifices of armed struggle, the need to redeem the peasantry from poverty and give them their own land. When I was done, I picked fifteen of them to fill out the ranks as assistants to the combatants and I asked the rest to wait until we had enough weapons.

I had forgotten the island's shades of yellow and the ever-present smell of salt water that mixes with the humidity at dawn and the smell of firewood and how it crackles when flames break some knot of the timber's stored memory and the trembling light of the oil lamps and the bonfires when night falls. I would then admit the first two peasants into our troops. Guillermo García and Manuel Fajardo. It's a common point of our historiography that Guillermo García was the first peasant to join the Rebel Army. This was entirely true, but only by a fraction of a second. We had already had a few warm and plentiful meals and I was going over my plans to carry on toward Caracas Hill and the group was in the yard outside of Mongo's hut and new cigars showed up and a cloud of smoke enveloped us all when I said to the peasant Guillermo García, a man of advanced years already, "Guillermo, take this rifle. If you don't know how to use it, we'll show you right away." Then I did the same with Manuel Fajardo. Now we were nineteen men and twenty guns. We didn't give gun number twenty to anyone, it was a Mendoza. Symbolically, it was assigned to old Crescencio Pérez, whom we had decided would remain in the foothills of the Sierra Maestra serving us as a sort of liaison and keeping an eye out for any of our group who could still be coming behind us. The Mendoza was passed around by all of us until we left on the twenty-fifth. But Crescencio left with our small group of men, just another soldier, and went into the mountains. Of course, he took his Mendoza with him. He broke it in on January 17, 1957, when he fought for the first time in La Plata, and used it again on the twenty-first in Arroyos del Infierno. Crescencio jumped in anytime we needed anything. Later, he formally joined our little troop, and soon we even assigned him a geographic area to cover. In those days, in which the number making up our forces fluctuated between eighteen and twenty men, and in an effort to lift everyone's spirits, I christened the recently reunited troops with the pompous title of Reunified Revolutionary Army. There's a detail I don't see mentioned very often. No one remembers.

ON JANUARY 15, 1957, we were close to our objective. I watched the movement of the enemy troops. At nightfall on the sixteenth, we crossed the La Plata River with precise information about the positions of the defense and the number of forces that the military garrison had at its disposal. A chance encounter with a collaborator from Batista's army allowed me to obtain more information about the troops' positions and the names of some of the peasants collaborating with the Rural Police. Chicho Osorio worked as the foreman on one of the most extensive private properties in the area. When we met him, I introduced myself as a "Commander González" of Batista's army. The man was so soused with alcohol that he was incapable of identifying me and didn't even notice that I immediately recognized the Mexican boots belonging to one of our *compañeros* that disappeared after the disembarkation. In my role as a Rural Police official, I began to interrogate him. The informant was oblivious, and I convinced him to take us to the very doors of the La Plata military detachment. The second shot fired by the rebels in the attack on the barracks was aimed at Chicho Osorio's head, and he died instantly, bouncing against the rocks in the river. I fired at the sentry and blew his brains out, an incident Che later mentioned in his books. We had so few weapons that there weren't enough for everyone, and some Brazilian-made grenades didn't explode when Che threw them. The attack group warned the soldiers to surrender, but they responded with a spray of bullets. I gave the order to attack and burn down all of the houses protecting any enemy soldiers. The first to try it was Camilo Cienfuegos, who was stopped halfway there by enemy fire. Universo Sánchez did manage to ignite one of the houses. A group of sailors resisted Almeida's charge. It didn't take long for us to hear them surrender. We won. We had just won the battle. We captured shotguns, a machine gun, supplies and ammunition. Batista's army had suffered two casualties and five wounded. Zero injuries among the rebels. Che offered his medical services to the enemy soldiers wounded in battle, and then we left in the direction of the Sierra Maestra, in search of the protection of its thick mountains. I already knew that, sooner or later, the leaders of Batista's army would order a large-scale pursuit and I prepared my defense. I decided to meet my persecutors in an ambush at Arroyo del Infierno. They rushed in for the kill on January 26. I shot down the first soldier belonging to the vanguard of the regular troops who approached the rebel ambush. Che shot down his first adversary, killing him with a bullet to the chest. The rest of our persecutors opened fire on the trees and bushes. We won the second battle. We just won it.

FOR THE MEETING with the American, I moved toward Epifanio Díaz's farm. We started our march on February 12, 1957, from up high on the Sierra. The interview was with *The New York Times* correspondent Herbert Matthews and it would be important propaganda for us. When asked how many men the Revolution had in its ranks, I introduced him to my veterans, calling them my "staff." What I didn't say was that in addition to belonging to my staff, they were also the whole of my troops, engineer corps, cooking staff, latrine diggers, officials, subofficals, communications staff, military police, major sergeants and soldiers. What I hid was that that reduced group of men was all I had in order to stand up to a professional army with more than five thousand troops. The publication of the interview I gave to *The New York Times* provoked an immediate reaction from the government authorities. They labeled the report imaginary, and at first they even insisted that I was dead. Days later, the American media published photos of Matthews and me posing together.

In the end, what remains in my memory is a moment of enjoyment. I had been recognized. That's why I say that there are occasions you can enjoy after the fact. I didn't really know who Herbert Matthews was. I only saw an older gentleman, of the kind Cubans would call *un americano viejo*, an old American. He wore a Lenin-style hat. The only thing missing was a little puffball on top to make it a golfer's hat. Matthews's behavior was affable and proper. At first sight, I knew I was dealing with someone who sympathized with our cause. Later I found out that he was a veteran of the Spanish Civil War and that before returning to his country he had paid a courtesy visit to Ernest Hemingway at the house the novelist kept in one of the hills outside Havana. Of course, I didn't know this part then.

The old man had barely said goodbye at Epifanio's farm when Faustino told me that Matthews had been an enthusiastic supporter of the Spanish Republicans. He's mine, I thought.

Experience placed me on a level I hadn't anticipated: that of literary character, and even that of a living literary character, if you understand what I mean. I had read *For Whom the Bell Tolls* and its pages had made me ponder the attraction of war. Being stuck in a cave with your comrades while they roll a cigarette or prepare some concoction can be an experience you never move past. The guerrilla army. That's the human grouping that has no before or after. No one ever gets himself ready to be a guerrilla. And if he survives, no one can overcome the memory or the longing for its intensity. I glimpsed the guerrilla life through Hemingway. It was like anticipated nostalgia. Or perhaps I saw myself in those scenes. I was the character in a novel he never got to write who in real life was reading the novel Hemingway did write. Look at the picture. Matthews and I were smoking some cigars just rolled by one of Epifanio's sons under that guano shed facing the road. Independent of the fact that we were sharing a session of revolutionary propaganda—for him, perhaps unconsciously so; for me, purposely so—a legend is born. Matthews took detailed notes of every little thing that ran through my head. I was in complete control of the role demanded of me, including only saying what Matthews wanted to hear. That we were practically a functioning army and that the enemy officers didn't have anywhere to hide from us. God may have the Apocalypse. But we were much quicker and the instrument of our divinity was a .30-06 Remington.

In the long run, we were using a method with Matthews that we would later repeat to exhaustion. There were never more than twelve patrol cars available to State Security in Havana. This was an urban center of two million inhabitants and we kept order by the constant circulation of that ridiculously low quantity of cream-colored vehicles. Their tireless rounds fed the illusion that there were thousands of them, with their State Security emblems in white ovals on the front doors. First we had the 1958 Ford Fairlanes taken from the Batista police forces. After almost fifteen years of service, we replaced them with a dozen Alfa Romeos, but these weren't up to the same abuse and we switched them for Soviet Ladas six or seven years later. The same Special Troops, that legendary group of commandos from the General Leadership of Special Troops, with which we supposedly would stop the waves of *yanqui* Marines, at their moment of greatest splendor, barely had six Soviet jeeps, six trucks of the same provenance, two Ural motorcycles with sidecars and a Zodiac blimp. The blimp had been captured from the Americans themselves and was designated for the most refined special infiltration missions on the coasts of neighboring countries. They kept it, breaded in talcum powder, in an air-conditioned warehouse so it wouldn't rot. The talcum powder, Micocilen brand, was made by a Cuban pharmaceutical company for athlete's foot and was the only kind available in the whole country. Regarding the rolling stock, three of the jeeps had B-10 anti-attack missile launchers on them; the other three were armed with 14.5-caliber antiaircraft machine guns; two of the trucks had K-30 double antiaircraft cannons, known by their technical nomenclature as ZU-23 R antiaircraft guns, and the other four trucks were for transporting the company of troops. Ever since my interview with Matthews, for me the value of military resources, in bodies as well as weapons, lies not in their actual power but in their powers of deterrence. Universo Sánchez or Luis Crespo or Camilo crossing in front of the shack where I had my interview with Matthews once and again after exchanging the occa-

sional tip of their hats or modeling their weapons on their shoulders produced the same effect in me as elephants did for Hannibal.

Matthews and Hemingway gossiped at Finca Vigía, the house in
the hills to the southwest of Havana. And both of them mentioned me,
according to reports. And both of them were content reliving memories and conjuring the miseries of a guerrilla partisan without any true
resemblance to the formidable and veteran mountain forces that Matthews thought he had just met. Happy as a result of meeting with me. It
was me. And it was Spain all over again.

So you saw him?
And what is he like?
And is he handsome?
You saw him, right?
You saw him.
The Cuban chap.
Oh, God.
Good.
You saw him, right?
Good.

WHILE HAVANA CONTINUED to deny the existence of the guerrillas, I
participated in a second interview with North American journalists in
the Sierra Maestra. This time, it was with Robert Taber. The diligent
Celia Sánchez, of whom I've already said enough, was the emissary who
accompanied them.

With Bob Taber, we filmed ourselves raising our guns after having
sung the national anthem. I remember having Raúl and Universo Sánchez at my sides. We had just sung the national anthem at the top of the
Pico Turquino, Cuba's highest mountain, and the happiness we felt was
obvious, it was a bit childish to start singing the anthem but it was probably because of that that we look so happy. Behind us is a bust of José
Martí on a rock pedestal raised four years prior by a group of aficiona-
dos of patriotic literature and of the Cuban independence movement
who crowned the peak after an arduous journey and the help of brawny
peasants who carried that heavy bronze bust. They didn't use any mules
so that no beast would leave behind footprints. The effort's main protagonist was Dr. Manuel Sánchez Silveira, the father of the young girl

who would later welcome my Mexican expedition and go on to become my assistant for the rest of the Sierra Maestra campaign. Between the expedition to raise this bust and the arrival of the guerrillas, there is no record of any additional ceremonial acts at that sacred peak.

This same skinny girl was the one with whom I would become intimate. Celia, an apostle; Christ, what were His intimate encounters like? Didn't Mary Magdalene ever take a turn with his joystick?

I told Celia it would behoove us for her to stay and appear in Taber's film in representation of the Cuban woman. A woman with a rifle on her shoulder, marching through the Sierra, was unpublished in the world. Besides, I told her, I need an assistant. You understand, *hmmm?*

You'll always be with me, I told her later. And don't you worry about a thing.

I called Fajardo, Guillermo and Ciro. I told them in front of her:

You'll be responsible for taking care of her and making sure she has everything she needs. Any questions?

THE ARMIES OF THE NIGHT

On May 18, 1957, the weapons and bullets we were expecting from Frank País, and that I was thinking of using in the attack on the El Uvero Barracks, arrived. They came from Santiago in oil drums and that very night, the men assigned to that risky mission—in reality, a labor of infiltration and clandestinity—Gilberto Cardero, Enrique López, Lalo Pupo and his son Héctor Pupo, took them up to the mountains. I picked two or three men from each squadron, eighteen in all, and sent them to receive the weapons, wipe the oil off of them and take them up. Sergio and Ignacio Pérez, Crescencio's sons, were among the chosen.

On May 27, 1957 we began our nocturnal march toward El Uvero. This small Batista military detachment was in a plain leading to the sea on a beach covered with boulders. There were women and children in a sawmill close to the place and this worried me greatly. No civilians should be wounded.

It was still nighttime when I ordered the groups to take their positions on the morning of May 28, strategically placed atop a hill from which we controlled all the surrounding territory.

I told Celia to stay by my side.

"Do you have your MI?"

She nodded nervously.

The M1 had come in Frank's shipment.

"Stay by my side," I told her. "And always shoot from the ground, just like I taught you. Don't stand up for anything. Only when I tell you to. You hear me?"

Che was wearing a machine gun with which he would cover Camilo Cienfuegos's advance on one of the flanks. Raúl was to be in the center of the attack commanding the squad with the most combatants.

Five in the morning. The first rays of light appeared and illuminated the coast. Some of the barracks' zinc planks reflected the sun's rays. From my position, I started firing on the roof, and the sleeping sentries of the El Uvero detachment went from being asleep to being sprayed with machine gun fire. I saw a man look out one of the windows, surprised, and I made him the object of my second shot and knew immediately that I had killed him. I later found out that he was the telegrapher. Eighty men participated in the attack. The guards responded. Che received reinforcements; Manuel Acuña and Mario Leal joined his flank. Celia Sánchez shot her M1 from her position until she emptied all the magazines. She was shooting too quickly.

Che threw himself at the barracks without calculating the risks. From his position, Almeida saw Che run toward the fortress firing his weapon, followed by the four combatants who made up his group. Leal, who was advancing behind Che, took a bullet in the head. Che placed a piece of paper over the wound in an effort to stop the flow of blood. The advance stopped because the plains offered no further defense beyond some sparse shrubs between the attacking forces and the fort's defenses. The situation was becoming unsustainable and I became impatient. I had to decide the exact moment in which our forces would reach their limit and should thus withdraw. I was once again reaching the limits of my reserves. In other words, the limits of my strategy. Various members of the rebel column were felled by the enemy fire that kept them at a distance. To the left, I saw that a sector of the enemy defense was going silent. I heard the unmistakable shots of a Garand about fifty yards in front of the guards. From my position, I was able to make out the familiar figure of Guillermo García, Guillermo working with his Garand. I ordered Almeida to advance on the enemy position with his squadron and take it, no matter the cost. The group went out and was welcomed by a barrage of shots that brought down five of its members, including

Almeida himself, who received a shot to the chest that was miraculously diverted to his shoulder when it ricocheted off a spoon and pierced a can of condensed milk. Upon seeing that Almeida was down, Che stood up and walked toward the enemy positions while firing; Joel Iglesias and Acuña followed him, falling wounded by enemy fire shortly thereafter. Che's decision made Raúl and his center squad join the attack and they quickly made it to the first defenses of the barracks. Guillermo García and Almeida's actions decided the fate of the battle. García's aim brought down various men on the enemy side, thus debilitating their forces, and Almeida opened a direct path to the doors of the barracks. The calls of surrender started to break out one after another. The fort was taken with a total of fourteen dead Batista soldiers and nineteen wounded, tended to by Che, since the regular army doctor, out of fear, had forgotten everything having to do with medicine and could only think about his personal safety. I ordered the release of all the prisoners, sixteen in total.

Nearly three hours of battle left a total of fourteen casualties among the rebels, all entrusted to Che's care. Meanwhile, I tried to climb up to the Sierra, convinced that this attack on the Uvero Barracks would have repercussions. We traveled in a Diamond T truck stationed nearby, used for hauling wood from the Babún. Che began to transport the wounded. Low-level flights indicated that the army was conducting a large-scale search of the area. Che understood that he needed to find a safe place to hide the wounded until they'd recovered enough to walk. He found this at the house of Guile Pardo, who gave them all shelter in his hut. Not only did Che hide with his men at that house, he also took advantage of that time to piece together a network of collaborators. David, a foreman at one of the estates in the area, started out by providing the group with food, and with time became a liaison to Santiago. The lack of medications gave Che a powerful asthma attack. He went from being the doctor to being one more sick person in need of his *compañeros'* care.

SERGIO PÉREZ ZAMORA, Crescencio Pérez's oldest son, became the owner of one of the Springfield rifles taken in the battle at La Plata. Above all, I did it for Crescencio's sake, so he would feel valued. But what every rebel in the Sierra dreamed of owning was a Garand. They called it el Garantizado, Guaranteed, or el Garañon, the Stud. And apparently Sergio wasn't completely satisfied with his Springfield. Sure, it was uncomfortable to be messing around with the bolt action in the middle of combat, but that didn't make it any less fearsome in the hands of a guerrilla willing to wreak real havoc on the enemy ranks. Its effective range was more than that of a normal man's vision and it could be fired at a troop of infantry from very far away. They would have to sweep the area with grenades or with planes to try to find the sniper who was just a single man fighting with maximum returns against an entire force. Go and try to explain that, if you can, to a man of Crescencio Pérez's ilk whose newest fixation in addition to owning his country was being the owner of a Garand. He wouldn't listen to reason. Such that when the party sent to pick up Frank's weaponry for the attack on the Uvero Barracks returned to their rendezvous point, I couldn't help but notice that Sergio had gotten rid of his Springfield and taken possession of one of the new Garands from the shipment. Some dark intuition told me to turn a blind eye on the matter. While it was wholly unacceptable that he should be allowed to distribute the Revolution's resources to his liking, I had the strange feeling that I should leave things be. At the end of the day, disciplinary infractions only take place when you actually notice them.

I admit that he had fought very well in El Uvero with Camilo's squad and that afterward he was an able driver of the Diamond T lumber truck. But he and I had already had our first run-in that morning. Two run-ins. One was because of the greed, anxiety and even violence with which he leapt on what he considered to be the war booty. This included relieving wounded soldiers, or even the ones who were merely surrendering, of whatever object he fancied, be it a cheap watch or a box of cigarettes. "Listen, Sergio," I told him, "the war booty is the military equipment that's on the floor and not the prisoners' personal effects." I looked for Camilo in the confusion that followed the end of the battle and said to him, "Set things straight here, Camilo. They're your men, aren't they? Do me a favor."

The second run-in was over the fact that Celia, who was at my side, told him to bring one of the lumber trucks that was in the sugar mill town—there were three total—and load it with all the arms taken from the enemy. The equipment belonged to the company under the direction of the Babunes, the owners of almost everything in the Sierra. Sergio and Ignacio, both of them, had been truck drivers before taking up arms, expert mountain drivers, by their account. Sergio brought the truck up to the barracks and they started to pick up the weapons and put them in the back, on the bed. Once this was wrapped up, I told Sergio to wait. He gave me lip. He couldn't keep his mouth shut. He told me it wouldn't be long before the enemy's planes showed up and did I mean for them to wipe us all out right there. I cut him off midsentence and turned to Celia, who was in charge of checking on the wounded. Then I ordered the *compañeros* aboard. I helped Celia up to the cabin and I put her in the middle, between Sergio and the place to the right that I immediately occupied. "Let's roll, Sergio," I said. Some of our *compañeros* were hanging on to the mud flaps—and whatever else they could find—and we took off to return to the mountains.

Gilberto Cardero was driving the second truck, with the corpses of our people and a squadron of combatants. Ignacio was driving the third truck, which followed us in the afternoon, and in it went our wounded, cared for by Che, and Raúl Castro's squad.

DAYS LATER, WHEN the trucks had been abandoned and we were on a break, practically all of us sitting on the floor, leaning back on our packs, we were getting ready to start the march toward the western section of the Pico Turquino when Sergio, who was standing, asked about the route we'd be following. In theory this question didn't seem appropriate. Nobody asked the course. Later I found out that the matter had to do with nothing less than a woman. He kept one around Sevilla or El Lomón and was hoping our guerrillas would pass through the outskirts. In any event, I responded with a fair amount of acrimony.

"Since when does anyone here, in this army, ask where we're going?"

Sergio, for his part, didn't like my response at all.

I think the only person who understood what could have happened next was my brother Raúl. Because, without even standing up, he undid the shoulder straps of his backpack and stayed alert.

I didn't realize that I would be further humiliating Sergio with my next order.

"You stop asking where we're going and grab that sack."

I had seen that jute sack by his feet. The contents could have been grenades or canned food. I was ordering him to throw it over his shoulder because we were about to start our march.

He was speechless. Stunned. All the guerrillas were silent.

"The sack," I said, while I looked right into his eyes, which were sparkling with a dazzling intensity in the night's shadows.

It was just this sort of impertinence that pushed Sergio Pérez Zamora over the edge, causing him to draw the Garand and point it at my thorax, ready to fire at me from less than thirteen feet away. His finger was already pulling the trigger when Raúl jumped up from where he was and, with his arms wide open, like a cross, stepped between the gun and me, where I was still sitting on the grass. Raúl cried out, alarmed, "What are you going to do, Sergio? You're going to kill the Cuban Revolution!" He waited. Sergio hesitated. It was all very slow and difficult for him to digest. But he hesitated.

He lowered the barrel at no one's request. Raúl still had his arms spread out like a cross. The other *compañeros* breathed again and entered the scene. The sound of words of reconciliation, pats on the back, friendships being proffered and the typical Cuban expressions apt for these circumstances could be heard. *Coño, caballeros,* how could this happen? *Coño, caballeros,* we're all brothers here. *Coño, caballeros,* we're all here for the same thing. *Coño, caballeros.*

Raúl had lowered his arms, but he remained in front of me, like a live shield. Ciro, with his usual solicitousness and without showing off in any way, approached the damned jute sack and started to throw it over his shoulder when Sergio stopped him with animated gestures and said to him, "It was me who was told to carry it." Sergio shouldered the Garand and with his free hand took the sack and placed it over his other shoulder. He turned in the least forced way he could until he had his back to me.

Crescencio and his other kid, Ignacio, had stayed out of the argument, observing discreetly. I got up slowly. The guide designated to take us to the west of the Pico Turquino—because he said he knew the way—was Manuel Fajardo. I said, "Let's move it, *compañeros,* the night is long."

I suggested we convert this area around the Turquino into our principal refuge and hiding place, at least for a time.

Raúl arranged to have a tête-à-tête with me the next day while we were tying up the hammocks in the little forest of mastic trees where we had chosen to camp and told me we had to kill Sergio that night.

I forced a smile, in case anyone was watching us, and said, "Now it's you who wants to kill the Revolution?"

He would have to be crazy to lay a single finger on that man. Everyone in the Sierra Maestra would be on us. If we killed him, the army could calmly retreat to their barracks. Crescencio and his band would take it upon themselves to get rid of us. Raúl understood right away. I admit that, of all our *compañeros*, Raúl was one of those who most quickly embraced what was practical and didn't waste his time on cerebral nonsense. At the end of the day, when you act in the name of justice or an ideology or to satisfy a vengeance, you're merely massaging words. But that playing with abstractions can cost you dearly.

It's true that a guerrilla can never allow himself the luxury of leaving a traitor behind. But Sergio was in a different category because he didn't stay behind. He moved with us. And besides, he had the balls to turn his back on me and continue on with us the whole time as if nothing had happened. In other words, in many ways he trusted us and believed everything was behind us. In any event, it helped me conceive of a maneuver that, until the present day, is of utmost utility to the Cuban Revolution. I call it the system of captive alliances. What I mean is, while Sergio was with us, he was under control. But the situation would become much more favorable when we abandoned our nomadic ways and became sedentary, because we would immediately establish a zone of responsibility for Crescencio and we would tell him that that was his area of combat. Of course, Cresencio's sons would follow their executive officers. And in that case there is no need to oblige someone to march alongside you or to kill him. In that case you absorb him into the territory under your command. He's your ally, but captive. You should know that type of alliance is easier to manipulate and infinitely more trustworthy than voluntary or good-faith alliances.

I don't want to leave a single detail out. Before leaving El Uvero, I told all three drivers that, when we reached a point at which the trucks couldn't continue, either because of the road's rough condition or because we were out of gas, they should make the trucks disappear, either burning them or pushing them off a cliff. Not a single one of the three of them followed my orders. I found out about this years later. The three arranged to hide them under the foliage or leave them in the care of some relative at the edge of a farm and went back to recover them as soon as the Revolution triumphed. I came to learn of this matter on Thursday, May 28, 1987, when I saw the report in the evening *Juventud Rebelde* newspaper about the thirtieth anniversary of the attack on the Uvero Barracks and the first thing they showed was Sergio Pérez Zamora pleased as punch with himself in his olive-green uniform, sitting atop the immutable Diamond T, saying it was the very one that took Celia and me up to the Sierra that morning.

IT WAS THE HISTORY of human uprisings. The classic circumstances in which needs and demands lose their shape in the pursuit of following a leader. I saw myself crossing the paths of the Sierra like a Christ, or like one of the conquistadores, like Attila or Alexander the Great, and there was a beam of light that I thought I was receiving from on high. But even so, as all of those men grew to trust me and found a need to protect me and be protected by me, I was realizing that I needed to gain some distance, some privacy, which meant, for the sake of unity, I had to be both distant and withdrawn. How would this contribute to unity? Because I could not be accessible to everyone and all ideas. In other words, I couldn't belong to anyone. I had to stay at a distance from which I could decide which way the scales tipped or where things should go. In some way, symbolically, I had to find a certain royal physical height. I realized that when Sergio Pérez grabbed his Garand and was on the verge of killing me. On account of being with them, I had allowed myself to take part in one of their vulgar conversations and I almost compromised the Cuban Revolution's entire process by subjecting it to the finger of a mule like Sergio Pérez. I said to myself, Oh, I need to be with them, but apart from them. As a result, that was what the camp at La Plata Alta, or the command, turned into symbolically. A sort of sanctuary up there, inaccessible, where I lived.

The past is never finished. Even a moment as fleeting as when Sergio pointed the barrel of a Garand at me is one for which I control the details, the significance. It was the moment at which history could have not existed. Sergio Pérez Zamora, Crescencio's son, still had that solid hand of his wrapped around the gun and I thought I was as good as dead when the whole movement was paralyzed by Raúl imploring with his arms wide open not to kill me and calling on the goodwill of my potential assassin. I don't believe I recall another moment at which I truly thought my life would be over.

IN MY CAMP at La Plata Alta, we achieved a certain standard of living before the summer offensive. Remote, inaccessible. In rapid succession, I acquired (a) a wood-burning stove; (b) a battery of pots and pans; (c) a long-haired cook known as Miguelito; (d) a small diesel generator; (e) a kerosene refrigerator and (f) the first ration of steak and eggs in eighteen months. Throughout the entire campaign I had slept under the open sky like everyone else, with the only difference being a mosquito net over my hammock. But in La Plata Alta, the windows had wooden blinds and a woman slept at my side. Celia Sánchez. She was older than me, and, in a way, wiser than I was, wise about mundane things, social graces, you understand. I am not aware of the reason, but the interest of all the women I've been with in teaching me to use silverware and to bathe daily is manifest. Perhaps it was because they preferred to draw out of me all of the sexual fantasies spurred by the good savage and try to avoid my projection as an intellectual. Celia was quiet and fanatical. In addition, Celia had that air of a manly or, quite frankly, lesbian woman, but the impression was immediately erased by her sweetness, and I let her be, and she was obliging. She was also on the ugly side. All of which I realized were characteristics of latent homosexuality, something which, of course, would consume me for a large portion of the months I spent in the Sierra Maestra and which didn't allow me to fully enjoy our resounding victories after the summer offensive. Don't think that it was easy for me to assimilate this information. I was finally able to obtain some sexology manuals in Havana—readings I undertook after the triumph of the Revolution, of course—and those studies exonerated me of all blame for Celia's proclivities. There was no indication of homosexuality in the fact that I had a good time with a woman of Celia's characteristics in those Sierra nights, even less so if she was the solution for a matter as sorrowful as the absence of someone for sexual release, besides which, these knowledgeable manuals say that as a last resort, homosexuality is found in insects and lesser animals. So there was no reason to worry. If a cockroach allows itself to take it up the ass, why should I be ashamed of my Celia in the Sierra? The reason I didn't ask for those manuals in the Sierra Maestra is that none of the *compañeros* from the urban resistance or from the chapters in exile would have understood the nature of my request. Can you imagine the scandal it would have caused? Fidel asking for a book about faggots from the Sierra. On the other hand, there was also Celia's sensitivity to consider. I didn't want to hurt her, nor would it have been very gallant of me. So if I never showed her off as my partner during the course of the campaign it was in the interest of service and because of the utmost condition of austerity and abstinence I demanded from my troops. Celia believed in our pact of extramarital silence, or at least that's what she made me think. The important thing, for me, was to keep her far from the very pernicious idea that I was using her, and in truth, that's what it was about. That instead of giving free rein to my sexual impulses with a *mariconcito*, I did so with a woman who, by all accounts, wanted to be more of a man than I was, but who, in the end, at night, in the privacy we shared at La Plata Alta, submitted to me. Any woman understands that you, at her side, may commit a crime, that you may turn your back on the law, and morals, and even God, but she will never accept your rejecting her because of her looks. She wouldn't understand it, nor would she forgive it. Ever. One more reflection to finish up on this subject. Once again in my life, and especially in matters relating to or associated with my participation in the revolutionary battle, the obvious and the apparent had to be kept secret from the public eye and resolved through complicated uses of rhetoric, of real conceptual twists and even the conversion of the most banal things into a matter of the greatest tactical-strategic reserve.

"*Fidel Castro guerrillero,*" *by artist Eladio Rivadulla, was the first poster alluding to the Cuban Revolution. On the morning of January 1, 1959, Rivadulla—who had focused on posters for Italian movies being shown in Cuba until then—of his own initiative made and printed this colorful poster of the revolutionary leader who had just triumphed that very morning and who had already begun his march to Havana.*

The Republic and Its Capital Are My Boots

///

Prince of the Ambushes

Allow me to tell you what I have learned in this area of human activity. One writes on reflection but acts on impulse. Good or bad, moral or immoral, just or unjust, that which is relayed here is a fragment of life and what happened. One isn't always a son of meditation, but rather of decisions and intuitions that surge like part of your intelligence, from the intelligence behind your decisions, the intelligence that is not only the product of a certain order of a more or less well-organized encephalic mass, but is also the daughter of information and, above all, unconscious information.

I'll give you an example about intuition and its reflection on the autonomic system.

One time, one of many, my mouth became dry during the guerrilla war in the Sierra Maestra, toward the end of 1958. It was in the battle at Guisa, a small town in the foothills of the Sierra. There I was surprised at the behavior of my own nervous system, since I wasn't feeling any fear but my mouth was dry as a stone. I had just prepared an ambush with my squad of Marianas, the girls to whom we had given the best weapons and spent months training. I placed them near a pass that the enemy reinforcements had to go by and I went on to check other positions when all of my internal alarms went off. That day I learned what intuition was. It is the sign of the subconscious sending information. It is a group of synapses that seem to be at rest. Then that group awakens. And it doesn't fail. At least that afternoon, as the first guards barely appeared, right down the road, and you could hear the engines of their tanks and reinforcement trucks, the Marianas, all of them, scattered, and I can say that the most heroic ones were the two or three that didn't abandon their weapons. Wasted weaponry has never hurt me as much as those M2 carbines and San Cristobals. Seventeen of the finest weapons in our arsenal abandoned. I haven't forgotten the quantity. Three M2 carbines, five MIs and nine San Cristobals. In addition, they handed over that entire flank to the enemy. They each played a part in the life I am narrating now when they were never anything more than a mere part of our propaganda project, a cheap part at that, who then turned into historic fact. There is no depth nor width of thinking in many of the monuments of the past. The Marianas. Never confound hope with necessity. Learn from this. And the excitement that surrounded that first unit of Cuban female combatants. Cowardly bitches.

I remember that, years later, at the beginning of July 1979, I believe, I ordered all of the commanders we had on the ground in Nicaragua to be brought to Cuba. We were on the verge of taking out dictator Anastasio Somoza and I had meticulously directed the offensive from Havana. Our purpose was to finalize the details of the final offensive when I lectured them at length about the use of ambushes and their benefits. Then—without mentioning the Marianas, of course, to not tarnish the image of one of our propaganda icons—I told them that the main enemy of the guerrilla movement is confounding hope with necessity.

IT IS INDISPENSABLE that we go back to an explanation of something, shall we say, of a strategic nature. Months before going down to Guisa, and as a consequence of the summer offensive in which Batista's men closed in on us almost to the point of surrounding us—in La Plata Alta, around July 20—along a front of less than two kilometers, I had made the decision to order my men to dissolve the columns in fear that Batista's men would capture or destroy the only part of the Revolution we could save at that moment: the Revolution itself, as a symbol, and on a much more vulgar but entirely practical level, all of the money we had amassed, coming from voluntary contribution and certain taxes on the war zone. I learned then that the Revolution is a bastion, although abstract, and in any event it should make itself inaccessible. Because of this—no matter how much we expanded territorially—I decided to keep gaining distance from the rest of the troops by instituting a kind of floating Chiefs of Staff. Broadly speaking, this was the method that, years later, after the triumph of the Revolution, would be established in Cuba as our defense policy,* which simply consists of the permanent and calculated dispersion of all of our military resources and the autonomy of all of the territorial commands, with the combat order given beforehand. You don't even need to pick up a phone to ask if you should open fire on the invader.† This will surely explain to you why I had up to four hundred men around me in the Sierra Maestra at my finest hour, but whom I quickly dispatched to carry out missions on increasingly remote fronts. Raúl to the "Frank País" Second Eastern Front. Almeida to Santiago. Camilo to the plains of Oriente first and later to Pinar del Río. Che to the Escambray Mountains, in Las Villas—the center of the island. Huber Matos to the area surrounding Santiago—in what we would designate as the Third Front. Likewise that's how another one of our innovative military doctrines came about: the deployment of fronts on far-off borders. Something we accomplished, first with the guerrillas in Latin America and then with the use of regular forces in Africa and Angola, when we deployed our first combat line fifteen thousand kilometers from Cuba's coasts. All of my old *compañeros* will recall my unwillingness to accept new recruits in the guerrilla army almost from the very beginning of the struggle. At the time I uttered certain expressions that I should not repeat today, given my investiture as the head of state. There are so many of us, goddammit, that based on how much we shit, the guards will have no problem finding us: I said that. A recurring expression of the time. And I really was unwilling to accept new recruits. On the other hand, there was the matter of a shortage of weapons, and so I gave the order that no one should be admitted who didn't bring his own gun.

Speaking of unarmed volunteers. I remember that once, before the offensive, a peasant came from Pinar del Río, on the westernmost side of the island, who said his name was Antonio Sánchez, quickly nicknamed Pinares because of his province of origin and who, brought directly by

---

* The military doctrine now known as the War of All the People (*Guerra de Todo el Pueblo*).
† This last one came from the Six-Day War in 1967 when the Israelis intercepted Egyptian communications and achieved a real military victory. It was experience enough for us: if you see a guy on the beach in camouflage with foreign weapons, kill him. This is the most famous and consistent of our military concepts—never accept the order to surrender—and is known among our men as the commander in chief's Order Number One.

Che, upon coming face-to-face with me and my rejecting him because he showed up in the Sierra without a weapon, said with the utmost indignation I've ever witnessed in my life, "When have you ever seen someone convene a war without weapons?" *Convene.* He used that verb. Do you remember this story? I told you in a previous chapter. Pinares had made his way to the Sierra by himself, and traveling by the cheapest public buses all the way to a small town in the foothills. He approached the guerrillas with a picture of me raised in his hand from Bob Taber's report that had appeared the previous year in the magazine *Bohemia.* The order to not accept recruits if they didn't bring their own weapons had yielded us good dividends with the kids from the surrounding towns who ambushed guards in the brothels, killing them by throwing stones or with machetes or simply stealing their Springfields or San Cristobals at the foot of the bed. But the man from Pinar del Río brought only my picture, and a considerable hunger. The fact is that Che ran into him and decided to bring him before me. That was when the man stuck his hand in his pocket to take out the wrinkled picture printed on rotogravure, compared the image in the picture to the original (in other words, me) and exclaimed, "He looks exactly like him, man." I decided to light a cigar (or relight the one I had been chewing on), sit down on a tree stump at the edge of the path and steel myself to hear what could be coming. "What should we do with the *pibe*, the kid, Fidel?" "What do you mean, what should we do, *Argentino*?" "Yeah, look, Fidel, it's just that the *pibe* has some rationale." Oh, that famous *pibe.* And with rationale. "And what could that rationale be?" "Tell him, *pibe.* Tell him your rationale." Then he came out with the war *convened* without weapons. That only I would think of convening a war without weapons!* I later delivered my sermon with Solomon-esque touches about having to get hold of a weapon in battle, and just in case, I didn't assign him to Che, but to Camilo. I've never liked to put men together who sympathize with each other so readily.

ON DECEMBER 1, in the Sierra Escambray, the mountainous range that covers almost the entire southern region of the province, Che and Rolando Cubelas—the leader of the March 13 Revolutionary Directorate—signed

* Antonio "Pinares" Sánchez was one of the internationalist combatants felled in 1967 along with Che Guevara in his Bolivian guerrilla war. Although at the time he was using the pseudonym "Marcos."

a document they called the Pedreros Pact, which was, in short, the arrangement that served as preparation for the final offensive in Las Villas. On the other side, in Dos Arroyos, Che had a meeting with Alfredo Peña, from the Second National Front of Escambray. They neither reached nor signed an agreement, although there was a tacit acceptance of collaboration. This Second Front was a detachment of the Revolutionary Directorate's guerrilla army and quickly became the most nonconformist guerrilla group under our leadership and of the most obvious right-wing affiliation.

If there was any good to all of this it was that, under Che's leadership, the first of December, at the start of the rebel offensive in Las Villas, with the base of departure in the mountains next to Sancti Spíritus and with the Revolutionary Directorate and the Second National Front of Escambray subordinate to that of the 26th of July, by degree or by force I remained protected, there in my Sierra Maestra peaks, while the bait was cast in Las Villas to lure any remaining troops from Batista's army. While I was kept safe in my sanctuary, I also threw into the battle the best of our revolutionary troops, who until then had been against me and challenged my leadership—the Directorate and the Second Front—ideal cannon fodder. I recognize that they had shown wisdom, those bastards, upon rising up in Escambray and not trying to carve out a place for themselves in the Sierra Maestra, where they would have had to assimilate to our guerrillas, although not as an allied force with their own identity, but as rank-and-file soldiers (and perhaps one or the other of them as officers, but few and far between); or we would have gone to look for them in their hiding places and executed them like bandits, which ended up being the fate of the independent little guerrilla armies that tried to enter the Sierra Maestra. It's so easy to discover the crimes a group of rebels commits in their quest to survive, to begin with because they have to eat. At the first hen they take from a yard or the few sweet potatoes that they extract from the larder, they're already committing the crime of theft. Later they fill their bellies and a bottle of rum comes out of God knows where and next thing you know they're ripping apart the ass of the little peasant girl who is the oldest daughter of the owner of the place. And that's rape. In other times, it was part of the simple matrimonial rites of the Cuban peasantry. You ripped apart her ass and you took the girl a little further along to where you set up your own hut and burned down some forest and started your planting. But under the revolutionary battle conditions and due to the need to establish our prerogatives as the dominant group in the area and to discourage the appearance of any of those free-agent guerrillas, we started to execute these men. The peasant girls themselves were discovering the attraction of the spectacle for the first time. There was no real rape committed with any one of them, since none of them were forced to spread their legs or buttocks or whatever muscles or extremities could be parted open. But when they saw themselves before a squad in troop formation and even at times before American journalists—although in some cases it was necessary to explain what a journalist was and what a foreigner was—it was inevitable that they would take a stand against the fleetingness of those pairings and suddenly play the role of victim. The other thing we did was tie the violators to a *guásima* tree and riddle them with bullets. "*Mamita*, you won't be getting any more cock!" These were the only words of defiance I heard in the middle of one of these executions in the mountains. They were uttered by a kid named El Maestro, who cast his eyes on the young girl who had just abandoned him to his fate after she testified to rape.

As I was saying about Che. Che's tactic—following my exact instructions, as you'll understand—was to block the highways between the main towns. He started with the highway from Sancti Spíritus to Trinidad, which Batista had just constructed, followed by the Central Highway at the point where the bridge ran over the Tuinicú River.

Later they rendered the bridges over the central railroad lines useless. Thus interrupting the "life and war" supplies from Havana to the province of Oriente, which then you could only reach by air and sea.

The rebels first attacked and took over the least fortified points and then gradually moved toward the most fortified ones. The attacks on the barracks started at night, after setting up ambushes against possible reinforcement troops on all the access routes.

Of powerful influence. Las Villas. Although I've never thought it convenient to say so in such an unequivocal way, the war was decided there, in that territory that demarcates the middle of Cuba. Located more than three hundred kilometers to the east of Havana, which is the political and administrative center of the country and where Batista made decisions and tried to conduct the war to his benefit, and about five hundred kilometers to the west of the Sierra Maestra and its neighboring territories, where I had been able to establish the foundations of a well-organized guerrilla movement and where this war's main theater of operations was located, the city of Santa Clara—which is the capital of the province of Las Villas—turned into the focal point where the fate of the Republic was decided.

FINE, THEN, WHEN we came down for the final offensive in Oriente with the idea in mind to start at Guisa, I—due to everything explained above—didn't have more than twenty men with me, the ones that were in La Plata Alta, and with the ones I was able to gather from Vegas de Jibacoa we came to forty. There were no weapons. But that was a minor problem and that's how I explained it to my silent followers. "The enemy has the weapons."

The truth was that we were extracting weapons here and there from the mangled remains of trucks that had hit a land mine or been ambushed, scraping the charred skin of the cadavers off of the wood of the rifles, until December 7, the date on which a plane from Caracas landed at our clandestine strip in Cienaguilla and dropped off a dazzling shipment of fresh weapons. This signified not just guaranteed access to a batch of brand new Garands, but the immediate increase of the, shall we say, hygienic aspect of our troops. The problem was that some *compañeros* were not very meticulous when it came to removing the flesh encrusted on their San Cristobals and these pieces started to rot in the gaps of the wood and to smell badly. Even at a distance, sometimes you could detect those of our troops who were armed with the remains of an ambush and it was as if the ghosts of all of those poor devils we killed for their weapons were still tied to their minuscule lumps of cartilage or nerves.

That whole scenario made such an impression on me that even today I feel a certain reluctance to approach one of the San Cristobals we have exhibited in the so-called Museums of Combat Glory that make the rounds in our military units as souvenirs of the Rebel Army's battles.

The bitter reality, given that our weapons provisions depended on enemy depots, is that the San Cristobals were an outstanding part of our meager arsenal. That carbine was the emblematic rifle of the Rebel Army. Although to the present day there exists no exhaustive study about the captured weaponry and consequently our use of such, I can assure you without any fear of being mistaken that the San Cristobal was necessarily the weapon of choice of the guerrillas, just as it was necessarily the weapon of Batista's troops: in other words, out of necessity in both cases. At the last minute—and while waiting for the first shipment of almost twenty thousand FAL rifles from Belgium in the face of the *yanquis'* weapons embargo—Batista had acquired about five thousand of these double-trigger Dominican carbines, which, incidentally, were not dependable in the least; "very zealous," that was how we referred to these weapons that would go off at the slightest thing and had metal parts that were only good for a very short while in combat; in reality, you understood that it was a weapon that was really made for the needs of repression—shooting against street rioters or executing opponents—but not for withstanding the rigors of combat, and even less so, prolonged combat. It was decidedly not an FAL or an AK-47. The FAL had its own defects, you know. It got stuck with just a bit of the salty air of our coasts, or perhaps it was the fine sand. But, damn, that Kalashnikov, when the barrel is red hot, you can stick it in a bucket of water and it whistles on contact, and you take it out and it keeps on shooting as if nothing had happened, as if firing thirteen or fourteen magazines of thirty bullets each without pause were nothing. You won't believe me, but in Angola our most seasoned combatants had a bucket of water at their feet when they were entrenched, to cool off their Kalashnikovs from time to time. Not because it was required or because this was in any maintenance manual, but because of the service calling that every true soldier owes his weapon.

A curious thing comes to mind now. It seems strange—or perhaps it was a consequence of excessive confidence in governing a peaceful Republic amid friendly nations—that no Cuban government prior to the Revolution—not even Batista's—made infantry weapons. This was not the case, as can be proven, with Generalissimo Rafael Leónidas Trujillo on our neighboring island. Trujillo faced—although much earlier—the same difficulties Batista did to obtain weapons and munitions, which was why he considered the idea of producing them himself. We did the same later because we didn't consider sufficient what we were receiving from the socialist camp. And so we began our own production of Kalashnikov carbines, under Soviet license, in the Mambí factory in the province of Camagüey. It was a real gem. We called it the Black AK, due to the severe dark tones of its woodwork, which was molded from mahogony trees from the Sierra. The last mahogony trees of our forests were carefully reserved to carve the autochthonous pieces of our—for the time being—irregular daily production of carbines; let me explain, irregular regarding their quantity, sometimes a hundred, sometimes a dozen.

IN DECEMBER, YOU COULD only travel the Central Highway by convoy in the three easternmost provinces of the island. The train didn't go all the way to Santiago anymore. The La Cubana bus line had suspended its service with a total loss of twenty-five buses valued at twenty thousand pesos each.

I imposed revolutionary taxes on the large business owners of the three easternmost provinces (fifteen cents per bag of sugar). The 26th of July Movement delegates, mainly Pastorita Núñez and Alberto Fernández, collected those duties, which amounted to more than $3 million. The large sugar, cattle and agricultural landowners were forced to make an agreement with me and pay to continue running their businesses. Since only thirty-six were North American–owned sugar mills responsible for 37 percent of the country's production, the rest of the mills being primarily in Cuban hands, the probable drama was limited to our backyard. The landowners, sugar colonists and cattle farmers brought Che about $700,000 in Las Villas, in the form of voluntary taxes in advance, through Rebel Captain Antonio Núñez Jiménez, after the president of the association made a pact with me in Guisa.

Three-quarters of the country's sugar production and half of the livestock were located in the territories in the east and in Las Villas, under our control. The cutting off of the national highway and railway lines in the central region of Las Villas cut the island in two, breaking up the regime's physical base. Havana's factories resented the loss of their markets in the three easternmost provinces. In an article by Andrew St. George about one of the ranches in the Sierra at the end of the campaign, he estimated that after December 15, each day represented a 2 percent loss on the total return on the sugar harvest.

Very early on, the large Cuban and North American business owners in Cuba were pressing the American government to force a political solution "without Batista or Castro." In the end, the powerful sugar interests lobbied in Washington for an unofficial liaison with me through a trustworthy emissary capable of negotiating a truce that would guarantee the protection of the sugar harvest that was due to begin on January

15. The sugar magnates were begging me on their knees to let them carry out their penultimate sugar harvest as landowners, given that the one in 1961 would take place with all of the mills and surrounding territories under my control.

ON BEHALF OF HIS government, Ambassador Earl T. Smith asked Batista to give up power and leave the country, but without proposing any formula to fill the vacuum of power that would create. It was a case of raw political intervention, one that would become catastrophic due to the manner in which it was carried out. All foreign mediation or intervention can be positive or negative, can be helpful or damaging. American political action in this case was, quite frankly, imprudent, as it precipitated the fall of a regime without stimulating the formation of a transitional government with middle-class representatives able to sway public opinion enough and raise the morale of the Armed Forces.

The subsecretary of state for Latin American Affairs, Mr. Roy Rubutton, declared at the time in Washington that there was no evidence of organized communism within the Castro movement, nor that I was under any communist influence. Mr. Rubutton's declarations represented the best assurance for those who were active in the revolutionary ranks and the guerrilla fighting against Batista's regime.

On the other hand, Ambassador Smith seemed convinced that the revolutionary groups under my command were infiltrated by communists. At least, that was his reasoning. But he was powerless to do anything to make this truth or reasoning—which could and should be different matters—duly recognized. Smith would have tried to achieve, the suspension of the arms embargo if the army had made a show of strength by winning some decisive battles; but his hopes proved vain because after the June offensive it wasn't even possible for any of the operation units to win a simple skirmish.

Nonetheless, the government's last efforts were taking place. Batista still thought—and continued to think until that fateful and frustrating December 17 on which Ambassador Smith dashed his hopes—that he could avoid a disaster if despite everything the weapons he ordered from Europe arrived in time and events allowed him to reorganize the Armed Forces.

At the end of it all, Batista held on to the belief that the electoral efforts carried out by his regime would yield the satisfactory results he longed for, especially regarding the Americans, but no one believed him. The events did not favor the coming to office and retention of power by "the candidate-elect" (in other words, Batista's handpicked successor) Dr. Andrés Rivero Agüero, which made it doubtful that the American government would recognize him.

By the information Ambassador Smith had picked up "from military and revolutionary sources," according to his interpretation, the army wouldn't last until the president-elect was to be inaugurated and the deterioration of authority was "considerable."

At the end of the meeting with Ambassador Smith, the night of December 17, Batista held an emergency meeting of his Joint Chiefs of Staff to inform them that the government of the United States was withdrawing its support of the regime and would not recognize the presidential candidate-elect, who was to be inaugurated on February 24, 1959. Batista emphasized how critical the situation was and asked the high military leaders to help him find a national solution that would allow him to leave the country, in keeping with Mr. Smith's recommendations.

He demanded absolute secrecy so that the news wouldn't spread beyond the political officers, adducing that it could precipitate a collapse of the Armed Forces.

USING THE HELICOPTER that General Francisco Tabernilla had sent from Havana (a Bell 47G-2 piloted by Lieutenant Orlando Izquierdo), on the morning of December 28, General Eulogio Cantillo—head of the forces in the province—moved from the Moncada Barracks in Santiago to the demolished Oriente Sugar Mill in San Luis, where my command post was. At eight in the morning we shook hands. We carried out an exhaustive analysis of the national situation, the course of the Revolution and the state of the Armed Forces at that moment. We agreed to a joint movement that would be carried out starting at three in the afternoon on December 31, starting with the revolt of the Moncada and Matanzas troops, at the same time that the rebel groups made their entry into the city of Santiago. Soldiers, rebels and the general public would fraternize while a national proclamation would announce a revolutionary coup d'état and invite the remaining military garrisons in the country to second the movement. If the regime offered resistance, the tanks based at the Moncada Barracks would head a joint advance on the Republic's capital, trying to cover nine hundred kilometers (Santiago to Havana) in thirty-six hours.

The ones who agreed to go along with me were José Rego Rubido (second chief of Oriente); Naval Commodore M. Camero, head of the Southern Naval District; Brigadier Carlos Cantillo González (General Eulogio A. Cantillo's half-brother), head of the province of Matanzas, and Colonel Arcadio Casillas, head of operations in the region of Guantánamo. At the end of the meeting, Cantillo returned to Santiago, where he relayed the agreement and dictated instructions to Colonel Rubido:

"I'll be here [for the agreed-upon date of December 31], but if for any reason I have to stay in Havana, you'll be in charge of carrying out these instructions. You and Commodore Carrera will go ahead to receive Fidel Castro in the outskirts of the city."

THAT NIGHT OF FREEDOM

On the afternoon of the twenty-eighth, Raúl showed up with Vilma Espín at Huber Matos's camp, in some abandoned school buildings. Raúl, following my instructions, told Huber that I had a conversation with Cantillo and that I'd sent him to say that there was an important role for Huber to play. Huber went to see me at the América Sugar Mill, where I'd moved my command post, and told me that there was euphoria in the air and that they were already savoring victory. I said, Look, Huber, forget about all the plans of attacking Santiago and all of that. That's all null and void. We've reached an agreement with Cantillo. Which is as follows. On January first at three in the afternoon in the Moncada Barracks, there will be a joint rebellion with the Rebel Army and the Constitutional Army and there we will say that the battle is over, that the forces have come together and that the Revolution has triumphed, and that a period of pacification is beginning, and on and on. But you're the man who will represent me there with Cantillo. For obvious reasons, I can't go. Furthermore, you're going to go with three hundred very well chosen men from your troops, they should be well dressed, you're the one who is going to be there and I am going to be somewhere else with a good number of troops. In case I have to come to your rescue.

"That, Huber," I told him, "is to see if we can march into Santiago without any problems and see if, by extension, we succeed in getting the capital to submit to us. But don't worry if anything gets fucked up. If things turn out badly or don't go according to plan, the country we belong to is, in any event, the sliver of land where we've planted our boots. Now get your men together. Explain the delicate nature of your mission and ask them to make themselves presentable."

ON THE NIGHT OF the thirty-first, I was at the house of Ramón Font, the manager of the América Sugar Mill, when I heard gunshots. A captain had had a few drinks and fired his .30-caliber BAR up in the air to celebrate the new year. He had carried out his little celebration about two blocks from where I was. The town was full of rebels wandering about in search of women or a bottle of rum or something to keep them warm while they slept. I went to look for the captain and told the kids who were my bodyguards, I think Aníbal and Nengue, "Tie him up and take off his shirt because we're going to execute him in the morning. I'm going to execute him myself." I went back to Ramón Font's house, where they were making me a pot full of arroz con pollo.

SO LIEUTENANT PEDRO BOCANEGRA, one of the president's bodyguards, received the order from Batista, a gesture of approval, to close the airplane door, and Air Force Colonel Antonio Soto Rodríguez, seated before the C-46's controls, was told the destination airport: "Jacksonville," Batista said. They lifted off from Camp Columbia, which as of tomorrow would be called Liberty City, and a while later the air traffic controllers in Miami would deny them entry to American territory. Then they would turn off toward Ciudad Trujillo. "Ciudad Trujillo," Batista said. He had wanted to go to Jacksonville because it was the usual port of entry when he headed for his house in Daytona.

Now the C-46 flew along the southern coast, at dawn, and required two hours of flying in cruise control before the Sierra Maestra spread out before its belly just as the first rays of that winter sun hit its silver fuselage and emitted a flash visible from the ground.

I heard, up high, the unmistakable sound of an airplane engine. Up high. The sun continued to rise, slowly, over the island.

I was going to execute the drunk captain at daybreak. I couldn't miss with that shot. While they had him tied up there, to the tree.

I was trying to imagine how things would be the next day when Santiago surrendered and if Hubert was capable of assuring my place. But I don't think I had gotten very far in my speculations. I've always thought that I would have gone crazy had I been able to glimpse what the future had in store for me, a future that would begin in three hours. As I made my way to a potful of arroz con pollo at the América Mill village in those early morning hours, how could I have possibly imagined my armored regiments advancing across the African high plateau or using the best airplanes of the Soviet fleet to travel around the world or being received by hundreds of foreign dignitaries or taking foreign visitors around our combat forces' drill fields or seeing my picture in posters covering the walls of all the towns and cities and that there would be a state at my feet and that I would dispose of a Praetorian Guard and that there would even be a new type of culture radiating out with me as the axis and that sports would even be invented and we would be able to inject Hellenic athletic excellence into the game played by kids on neighborhood streets, which is baseball.

The sound of the airplane alarmed me. It echoed in the Sierra. I realized it wasn't a warplane and that the sound didn't resemble Batista's light B-26 bombers. It was very high. It wasn't a combat plane, but Cubana Airlines planes didn't fly at that hour, either. There was something that eluded my system of connections and reflection, and while I approached Ramón Font's house, with Celia and my bodyguards in tow, I said to myself:

"How strange, that plane."

The MacArthur Causeway in Miami, January 18, 1959. Fidel Castro entered Havana ten days before. Bill Webster, the billboard czar, wants to show his admiration for the Cubans and pays all costs for the ad out of his own pocket. The reaction of the main newspaper, The Miami Herald, *is as unexpected as it is hurtful: "WELCOME TO CUBA . . . AND TO THE CASINOS." The paper has decided to wage war.*

BOOK TWO

ABSOLUTE

and

INSUFFICIENT POWER

Fidel launches his second war in the mountains. One of the first incidents is the pursuit of ringleader Manuel Beatón. In the Sierra Maestra, winter of 1959, Commander Aldo Sanamaría, head of the Minas de Frío school of recruits, receives instructions from El Comandante to deploy his men.

PART FOUR

A
MAN ALONE
CAN DO IT ALL

///

UNDERSTANDING THE REVOLUTION
IS MORE DIFFICULT THAN
DYING FOR THE REVOLUTION.

—From a speech delivered by Fidel Castro
in Santiago during the public commemoration
of the ninth anniversary of the attack
on the Moncada Barracks, July 1962

My State, the Revolution

///

I MUST CONFESS THAT IT WAS IMPOSSIBLE TO RESIST THE TEMP-
tation of visiting my mother. I decided to go on December 24, 1958.
Raúl had been there—Birán, our parents' farm, where we had grown
up—the day before. So that we were not together, for security reasons,
he left. As far as I could remember, it was the first time that—as a protective measure—we were deliberately not in the same place. From then
on, we adopted that tactic of never being together anywhere we could be
easily located by the enemy.

I hadn't seen her in years. I knew that Raúl had her under his protection in some way, as well as our lands, since the area under his command—called the Second Front "Frank País"—ran beyond the limits of
Banés.

A bit of background. The heart of the guerrilla army—the emblematic "José Martí" Column One, subordinate to me personally—broke
up in March 1958 under Commander Raúl Castro's leadership to permanently operate to the north of the eastern region's valley between the
mountains. From this group sprang the organization called the Second
Front "Frank País," which took its name from the second leader of the
26th of July Movement who was shot down by Batista's police the previous July 30th in an alley in Santiago, the Callejón del Muro. The use
of Frank's name was meant to attract the greatest number possible of
restless (and often detestable) young inhabitants of Santiago to the Second Front and get them far away from my domain, in addition to rendering unsustainable the theory that I was the one who had reported to

The first column of the Rebel Army enters Havana on January 8, 1959. The history of the Americas, including the United States, was changed at this exact moment.

the authorities Frank's presence in the back alley where he was killed. A stratagem that was as innocent as it was effective.

We traveled to Birán in four or five jeeps, full of rebels. We left from La Rinconada. Crespo, El Guajiro, who was driving one of the jeeps, didn't notice, due to the high grass, a small bridge and went tumbling down into a canal. In the end, I don't know how they managed to get there, but I remember them with their Willys sputtering smoke from under the hood, as if it were braying, and despite this, the imperturbable happiness with which they arrived at Birán.

Following my mother's hug and her damning complaint about two of my bodyguards who—in her own words—were "sacking" her orange grove, I found out about the men that Ramón killed. Ramón Castro Ruz. The bastard had racked up quite a death toll.

Mongo, my brother. By the look of things, he'd gone too far with some tenant farmers, the poor wretches, with whom he'd had some problems regarding the lease of the land, or some payments that were behind, or some woman or some cockfighting debt, who the hell really knows. Ramón had quite the cockfighting habit. Both of my brothers did, to be fair. But Ramón was the one who got Raúlito addicted.

The fact is that a little while after basking in my mother's indulgences and all of her Christmas sweets, I learned that a committee of peasants had shown up at the house to speak with me. Word of my arrival had gotten out and they came in search of justice. My mother had already warned me that Ramón was in Holguín, doing some business. But even if he had been there, I would not have subjected the current head of my family to one of those instantaneous guerrilla trials which, as everyone knows, invariably consisted of applying the death penalty to anyone accused of prescribed crimes, "prescribed crimes" referring to any behavior leading to the moral or material weakening of the guerrilla columns or that could result in bad propaganda for our cause. It was not the right time to execute Ramón because it would have created the worst possible image for the Revolution just as it was about to triumph. Nobody would have noticed my equanimity in carrying out justice even against that savage brute, my brother. No, what they would have noticed would have been that I was even willing to kill my own brother.

Of course, this was not what I said to the peasants in my speech. First I invited them to a meeting at the little school. There were about a hundred peasants. An easy audience to sway, as the rural Cubans tended to be, especially back then when the majority of them were illiterate. I could hypnotize them easily enough by taking their side and uttering a few curse words—nothing makes you closer to an audience of the poor than the use of bad words or expressions in poor taste. But in addition, I also had going for me that I was the son of the area's landholder and that I was educated, a lawyer, and soon they would discover that this Being on High was receiving them, listening to them, nodding in understanding before their complaints and not becoming visibly angry even when he was told of *his own brother's* excesses. I took advantage of the moment and became, to them, then and forever larger than Christ. Because not only had I listened to them, I was also speaking to them. I appealed to the simple logic of blood to silence them. What should I do in such a situation, defend a brother of mine at all costs or turn my back on him? Who among them hadn't had to hide or protect a brother who was unruly or a drunk or even a fugitive? The rest of my rhetoric rested on the base of that shared blame and, of course, in principle it was about no crime occurring with impunity, even if committed by the brother of the most exalted of the revolutionary leaders. I immediately made the obligatory references to the repressive forces of tyranny, the beatings, the abuses, the hunger, the parasites in the stomachs of their children, who had never worn shoes or felt soap run across their skin. It was indispensable to touch on all these themes to remind them of the injustice and hunger that they lived with daily, to make them forget any previous wrongs and to focus on what was really wrong. The problem was not that impulsive brother of mine Ramón, although the case may be that a few days before he had slit a farmworker's throat. The problem was capitalism. The full force of my speech was aimed at that objective. That we do away with the root of the problem. Do you all understand? First we need to win this war. Then will come the next agrarian reform and we will hand over the land to you freely. The land. The possession of the land. Although none of this means that we will evade a thorough investigation of the formal complaints against my brother, and if what the *compañeros*—at this point in the speech, they were already our *compañeros*—say should be true, then Ramón will be duly punished. In any event, the problem now is the war. Finishing it. But finishing it victoriously.

Do the *compañeros* agree with me?

ONCE THE MEETING with the peasants was over, the trial against my brother was delayed until after the triumph of the Revolution, and I returned home. My mother agreed to have two or three of the guerrilla army's main commanders to dinner, but she asked them to wash their hands first. I don't remember how many of my sisters were present, but I do remember their coming and going and that two or three little peasant girls were helping them with the pots of rice and the huge steaming pots of black beans and the overflowing trays of succulent pork. The peasant girls had wide skirts on and differed from my sisters because, without a trace of embarrassment, they wandered barefoot across the house's wooden floors. The rest of my group was tended to in the yard under the frond of the old tamarind tree. There they placed the heavy mahogany tables assembled with the leftover lumber from my father's first sugarcane railroad and spread the tablecloths and my comrades were dutifully attended by a team of young peasant girls and someone said it was like some kind of *verbena*, a festival. My mother was seated next to me at the new table in the dining room, and we could hear the party below between my guards and the peasant girls. She barely took a bite and didn't let go of my hand, atop of the table, although she was directing all of the servants with the imperious silence of her gaze.

We returned at midnight.

Celia didn't go on that trip. I thought it wise not to show up at my mother's house with a woman.

She was waiting for me with part of my unit under a bridge close to Palma Soriano. She was bivouacking in the shadows. I could hear her gaiters, her camping things, her whispered conversations. Knowing that we were on the Central Highway—although it was closed to traffic— and that my men were moving without taking any precautions and as if in a slow-motion dance—made me realize, for the first time, with all its intensity, that we were on the verge of winning the war.

I found her immediately by the nervous light of her cigarette. She was serious and restless. She was sad. "Celia," I said to her. "I brought you a little container with food." I knew what she was going to say to me. That she wasn't hungry although she might have a bite later.

"I'm not hungry, Fidel," she said to me. "But I might have a bite later."

And not to worry.

"Don't worry, Fidel."

"It's not that I worry. It's that you should eat something."

Later, later.

"Later, Fidel. Later."

Then I saw the porters. They were two young guys, rather hunch-backed, Indians, as we Cubans say, probably of Yucatán descent or maybe even of Cuban aboriginals. Despite exaggerated scoliosis, they were carrying two enormous backpacks which contained all of the Cuban Revolution's money and papers at the time. They were the only ones who knew where I was going. Celia would whisper it in one of their ears. They marched about three hours' distance from us. Although sometimes, if I traveled in the Land Rover, it could take them up to a day and a half to catch up to us. I greeted them, asked if they'd had dinner yet and gave them some cigars. It was how I was able to avoid Celia and her silent reproaches.

The night was humid and there wasn't a soul on the highway. I told Celia we were leaving. We had to start getting close to the ruins of old central Oriente, near San Luis, the town to the west of Palma Soriano, where I had an appointment to spend the next two days with General Cantillo, the main head of Batista's forces in the theater of operations.

"Let's get going, *caballeros*," I said. "I don't want to still be at this camp at dawn."

COLONEL RAMÓN M. BARQUÍN had an elitist vision of the conspiracies against Batista in which the common people had no role. Barquín, himself a conspirator, and as is known safely hidden away behind bars in Isle of Pines since 1956, received word of Castroist movements without being able to do a thing. As the leader of the so-called Conspiracy of the Pure which Batista's high-ranking officers to this day claim as the CIA's first attempt to overthrow Batista, Barquín watched all his own political possibilities disintegrate from behind bars. The truth is that the CIA did everything possible to use him before handing over the whole country to me. Almost all of their possible coup plots involved a plan to free Barquín and place him at the head of a military junta. Thus, it is surprising, and puzzling, that at the end of the war, Batista's last order should reveal his desire to withhold all possibilities of power from the Americans, the country's bourgeoisie and—of course—his disowned officers: before fleeing the country in the early hours of January 1, 1959, right from the airplane's steps he ordered Cantillo not to release Barquín under any circumstances and bring him to Havana.

The plan was to snatch power out of Batista's hands and put Barquín at the head of a government junta. The junta would be joined by General Eulogio Cantillo, head of Oriente's Armed Forces. The junta would operate provisionally and "only to guarantee the country's stability and public order" during the period of time between the fall of Batista's regime and the formation of a Civil Government of National Unity, which would include well-known politicians of the era *"and would include Fidel Castro"*—according to the original documents that have survived to this day—and other *representatives* of the opposition that clashed with Batista. How generous! Or should I say what an undeserved honor? They *included* me! On the other hand, Colonel Rosell, head of the Engineer Corps, was being controlled remotely—and this under the CIA's express orders—to meet with an Ismael Suárez de la Paz—or "Commander Echemendía," of the 26th of July Movement in Havana. The instructions came from Jack Anderson himself, who was the CIA's man in Havana, so obeying him was the same as obeying the leadership in Langley directly. The CIA's purpose was to try to create some kind of link, even just as a start, between the army and the clandestine structures of the 26th of July Movement in Havana. If they succeeded, they held that this would give them a privileged position of monitoring and godfathering any type of conspiracy that could result from those contacts. Upon choosing the insipid Ismael Suárez de la Paz, or "Commander Echemendía," they were revealing—without realizing it, of course—the paltry degree to which they'd penetrated our movement. I remember that I was in the Sierra when the information reached me that the Americans had made contact with the 26th of July leaders in Havana and that Commander Echemendía was meeting with them. They were asking how to proceed. I sent a response that they should listen to what the Americans had to say. I also remember that at that moment, with the little slip of paper still in my hands, seated on that bench of palm strips that I had at the entrance to the La Plata Alta camp, I turned to Celia and asked her, "And who in the hell is this Commander Echemendía, *chica?*"

So they were on a mission to establish contacts so that the rescue of Barquín from prison on the Isle of Pines would be successful. Of course,

I was removed from all of this. I was coming down from the Sierra for my last offensive while those bastards conspired not only behind Batista's back, but also behind my own.

AN AUDIENCE, OF AN urgent nature, was granted by Batista to Lieutenant Colonel José Martínez Suárez, who wished to speak to el Señor Presidente "about an important matter." Batista agreed to meet with him at eight o'clock at night. Martínez Suárez informed him that General Eulogio Cantillo had left for Oriente that day under orders from General Tabernilla—the head of the Joint Chiefs of Staff. Since Cantillo was in the habit of seeing the president before returning to his post whenever he came to Havana to deal with the Chiefs of Staff, Batista told Colonel Martínez Suárez that he found it strange that Cantillo should leave before speaking with him.

"He couldn't do it, Señor Presidente. He received the orders to go to Oriente as quickly as possible and take a helicopter from Santiago to the place where he had a meeting with Fidel Castro."

"If what you're telling me is true, I will remove the army's leaders this very night," Batista supposedly responded.

"I am sure that General Cantillo left for Oriente and that he is going to carry out those orders. You know that in all of the posts, from Las Villas to Oriente, the units that have not been taken or surrendered are damaged or incommunicado. I beg you, Señor Presidente, not to mention my name because it could cost me my life; but I spoke with General Cantillo before he left for Santiago. I believe, Señor Presidente, that it's a little late to order the head of the army, Colonel Rego Rubido, and the chief of the naval district, Commodore Carnero, to negotiate a truce with Fidel Castro."

When that meeting was over, Batista immediately called the head of the army's staff, General Pedro Rodríguez Ávila, in order to find out whether General Cantillo had actually left for Oriente. He confirmed it, saying that the head of the Joint Chiefs of Staff gave the orders, stipulating, in addition, that the head of the air force, Brigadier General Carlos Tabernilla, should provide the plane and helicopter he needed.

Then Batista called a meeting and asked General Tabernilla, in front of the other chiefs, who had offered to negotiate and facilitate a truce. Tabernilla answered that he was not aware of these negotiations and, upon telling the president that he had no knowledge of the orders given to General Cantillo regarding his plans to confer with the lead rebel in Oriente, coughing nervously, trying to offer up his vague explanations, he said that General Cantillo had communicated his intention of speaking with a priest who had contact with Fidel Castro and for that reason he wanted to go to Santiago; but that he hadn't authorized any meeting. Then Batista gave direct orders to the head of the Chiefs of Staff, General Pedro Rodríguez Ávila, to immediately send a coded radiogram ordering General Cantillo to call off any meeting he had arranged, directly or indirectly, with rebel leaders and that he had orders to appear before the Chiefs of Staff as soon as he was settled. General Eulogio Cantillo didn't answer the dispatch, nor did he return the following day. Batista ordered Rodríguez Ávila to investigate and keep tabs on Cantillo's return. But when he didn't receive a response to the radiogram, Rodríguez Ávila decided to send a messenger by plane and designated Colonel Martínez Suárez.

The next day, the plane was broken, there was a delay in fixing it and at last they took off. Around ten, when Martínez Suárez arrived in Santiago, Cantillo had already gone to the Sierra Maestra and in the afternoon when Cantillo arrived via helicopter, with Izquierdo, the best helicopter pilot they had and whom the head of the air force, "Winsy," ordered, "Prepare the helicopter, make sure it doesn't cause any problems"—Martínez Suárez said that Cantillo told him, in English, "*It's too late, Martínez,*" it's too late, like a girl getting up from the bed where she lost her virginity, with the same sweet mischief and perhaps embarrassment: too late, Martínez.

And Martínez Suárez returned to Havana telling the story that according to Cantillo he never received the telegram from the Chiefs of Staff to call off the meeting with Fidel Castro, that he had never received it, despite Cantillo having left an assistant on call in case a counter-order should arrive and that the counter-order never came.

THE ATTACK ON SANTIAGO, planned for December 30 or 31 at the latest, had been postponed due to solemn promises from General Cantillo, agreed to in the meeting with him on December 28, which took place in the center of Oriente Province, in Palma Soriano. We spoke for four hours. A Catholic priest and several officers witnessed the dialogue, in which an agreement was reached to carry out the revolutionary military movement, all synchronized. It was the most mixed group I had at hand and whose only purpose was propaganda. To that end, the presence of Raúl Chibás was especially helpful at the negotiating table with Cantillo. Raúl, the brother of the deceased Orthodox leader Eduardo Chibás, had already grown a rather bushy beard and I had made him a commander overnight, and I think we got the priest Francisco Guzmán out of one of the surrounding churches. Of course, the finishing touch was to show off the two commanders, José Quevedo and Francisco Sierra—both limpid and enthusiastic—who had come over to our side, the two of them with weapons at their waists, U.S. Army regulation Colt .45s with plenty of ammo—Quevedo with a new pack of Raleigh tobacco for his pipe—and both of them with the stars of their commander rank at the points of the collars of their army jackets. What better proof of his promising future could Cantillo ask for?

There was coffee, as well as cigars and the exchanging of pleasantries. But I overlooked all of Cantillo's references to the army's support and "representativeness," and above all I didn't act impressed by any of his name-dropping. I wanted to make him see that we should cut right to the chase and once and for all get rid of that whole lot of commitments that would only work against his freedom of choice. Something happened with him, in that meeting, something that I've seen shine through with monotonous frequency in my interlocutors. I was hit by a blinding understanding of the phenomenon a few days after that meeting with Cantillo while I was advancing toward Havana with my triumphant caravan. And the worst of it is that very few people realized what was happening, that as my Sherman tank hit those streets, I was truly bringing freedom, not just the freedom with which I live and that I value, but that which I give my followers the opportunity to enjoy. The group. Such is the simple mathematics of my statement. Power is the group. But people tie themselves to things that prevent them from being free. The concept of honor, moral concepts, ethical concepts, economic or political concepts, all kinds of concepts. All of this is bullshit. The problem is what you need. And it's not even, as the French philosopher Louis Althusser said, in a phrase—that I have underlined—in his mammoth volume about freedom, that freedom is the comprehension of need. Is that so? And did he write that before or after strangling his wife? Well, I offered people the absolute comprehension of their needs and *power too*. In other words, you're never freer than when you have power. As a minister in my cabinet, it would have taken a lot for Althusser to spend even two days in jail. During these discussions Cantillo tried, without any luck, to get me to agree to a cease-fire. But to tell you the truth, the only time he hesitated was over the matter of putting Batista in a safe place. I realized something. Cantillo was unaware of two essential things. The first, that I couldn't give a shit about Batista himself. But second, the truly noteworthy thing, was that I needed to capture him alive for reasons of public spectacle.*

In Havana—on the twenty-eighth at nightfall, according to my information—the head of the Chiefs of Staff informed Batista that Cantillo would leave Santiago. Batista sent an assistant to Cantillo at the airport, with the instructions to accompany him to Batista's own house, at the Kuquine farm, without contacting any other headquarters.

Batista received General Cantillo in the library behind closed doors. Upon asking why he had left for Oriente without going to see him first, Cantillo answered that when he informed the head of the Joint Chiefs of Staff of the problems regarding his post, General Tabernilla insisted that he make contact with Fidel Castro. He remembered at the time that a priest, Father Guzmán, had sent him a message saying he could serve as an intermediary to speak with the rebel leader. And that General Tabernilla ordered him to leave immediately to make contact with said priest and try to meet with Fidel Castro personally to "find out what he wanted."

I recognized that Cantillo was on the razor's edge. When he arrived at Kuquine and met with Batista (and came under his command, I would say), Cantillo wanted to tell him about the meeting with me and Batista rejected the notion. "No, don't tell me anything," he said to him, adding, "*It's too late.*" This time, he was the one who said it, and gave the following order. "*Usted,* don't report to General Tabernilla, *usted,* go home." But before dismissing him, he revealed his plan to Cantillo to flee Cuba on January 6 and then ordered him to go to Oriente the next day and call off any agreement with me.

---

* And then there was money. Between $300 million and $900 million were deposited abroad and we were going to force him to return it in exchange for vague promises not to execute him. The opposition to submitting him to the rigors of revolutionary justice lasted for years—in fact, for the rest of his life. A meticulous operative from the General Direction of Special Operations (DGOE) to kidnap the ex-dictator in Palma de Mallorca was called off the very same morning of August 6, 1971, on which international cables informed us that he had died as the consequence of a heart attack. [*Author's note.*]

The reader will have guessed that this information about Batista's inner circle came into my hands after the triumph of the Revolution. I've also benefited from some material that was meticulously compiled in recent years. Through this material, I've learned that before the general got into his car, a blue Buick, Batista took Cantillo by the arm and asked him—or perhaps it was just a thought that escaped from between his lips involuntarily:

"The strange thing is," he said, "if Fidel Castro practically has the war won since the summer offensive, why would he have any interest in negotiating?"

Let's go back to where we began. Batista didn't understand. If I'd won the war, why would I be open to dialogue, even encouraging it? Perhaps, he estimated, these last two years of battle had also been hard on me. Was I exhausted? Were there problems among my ranks? Mistake. A grave mistake. The guerrilla army is the most flexible military formation on earth. But, in any event—and this was what Batista never got—I was opening the lines of communication with the army. *Not with him.*

Why couldn't Batista, that great negotiator, find a middle ground with me, another great negotiator? It's disappointing that Batista wouldn't realize it. The point is that he was a loser and that he would have only been in the way of my achieving power. He had to be brushed off, like a stupid insect.

"I have no answer, Presidente," Cantillo supposedly said. "None."

A little after Cantillo returned from his meeting with Batista in Kuquine, Tabernilla showed up at Cantillo's house in the confines of Camp Columbia, and old Pancho said to him, "But, Canti, what happened with Fidel . . . ?" And he said, "I'm sorry, General, but I'm under orders from the president not to report to you."

I WAS IN LA PLATA ALTA one afternoon and they notified me that José Pardo Llada had arrived with another gentleman. I remember that it was my brilliant new secretary who told me: Antonio Llibre. That there he was, on the rustic benches at the camp's entrance, José Pardo Llada and a lawyer from Holguín, Manuel Penabaz. Pardo brought me a bottle of cognac. I don't know how he managed to transport it all the way to La Plata Alta without breaking it. Manolito Penabaz, whom I knew perfectly well, brought me other presents: Hershey's chocolate bars and books, if I remember correctly, four books: one by Josip Broz Tito about guerrilla warfare, Máximo Gómez's campaign diary and two little volumes by Mao Tse Tung: *On the Correct Handling of Contradictions Among the People* and *On Guerrilla Warfare*. Then Manolito removed a green box with gold trim from a rather coarse-looking bag that contained the first Rolex diving watch I would have in my life and, from the bottom of the bag, a Minox camera. Then he gave me a copy of *Selecciones**—the last item to come out of that magical bag—and opened the cover to reveal a Rolex ad on the first page with an admiral honorably seated on a battleship above a caption saying, "Men who control the fate of the world wear Rolex." With that literature, he was trying to make me appreciate the jewel that had just been given to me in all its intensity.

Days later, Pardo Llada and I were seated at the wooden doorjamb of the house occupied by La Plata Alta's little hospital and talking about Mao. The aroma of coffee reached us from inside the house. Celia was in the kitchen, watching the liquid as it bubbled. I was twirling an excellent Montecristo No. 4 unlit in my fingers. I was savoring the anticipation of lighting it after drinking my coffee.

For me it was clear that Mao, as much as the Americans did, worked out his thesis within the confines of his experience. But this was particularly disastrous for the Americans because they made their inferences after we devoted ourselves to subverting Latin America during the sixties. They were really scared. They truly believed that we were trying to take power in that whole group of countries. They concentrated their vast resources and all of their efforts on the creation of specialized forces to combat counterinsurgents and in filling the continent's police commissaries with their intelligence advisors and interrogation specialists (in other words, brutal torturers, with their briefcases full of the latest electronic devices to shock your balls, empty your eyes out or burn your tongue to a crisp). They never realized that this was no more than the Cuban Revolution's low-cost defensive maneuver. At that time, we set up our guerrilla army to extend the borders of our country beyond the island. We forced the Pentagon and the CIA to defeat a hypothetical continental revolution and to turn their backs on us, where nothing hypothetical was going on, since we were conducting a real revolution. While some of our Latin American brothers in solidarity fell in com-

* The Spanish version of *Reader's Digest*.

bat against gringo-trained rangers, we, in Havana, became the conspirational center of world revolution. I don't know if they ever realized it. But they were so absorbed by the idea that low-intensity warfare wasn't enough to seize power that—I imagine—they must have felt somewhat peaceful.

"You know what?" I recall having said that afternoon from the little hospital's doorjamb at La Plata Alta.

Pardo and Manolito remained silent.

"When the Revolution triumphs, we're going to need an army of 300,000 men. We need to be ready to spend no less than twenty years in power."

Pardo paled at the news. In that instant, it became clear to me that he would never be my ally and that the distance he would travel with me on this path would be very short. Upon seeing the blood suddenly drain from his face, I understood the underlying reason for that phenomenon known as the solitude of power. It lies in no one being willing to risk blindly following unrestrained imagination.

Pardo stammered, "What about the Americans, Fidel?"

The worst enemy of all possibilities is fear.

"The Americans are shit-eaters, Pardo," I told him. "And they're not going to lift a finger against us. They'll be paralyzed. Look at what Raúl has done to them in the Second Front. He kidnapped fifty of their marines and they haven't done a thing. Not only that, Raúl has demanded fifty new Garand rifles from them to initiate any kind of negotiations and they gave them to him. These were flown directly from the Guantánamo Naval Base to the Second Front's landing strip.

Look, there's a fact that had never come to light before.

Well, so then I find out that, behind my back, Pardo says to Penabaz, "Listen, man, Bolas has gone crazy." Bolas was the old nickname I picked up at the University of Havana. Well, in reality, it was only half, since the full nickname, as I said before, was Bola de Churre, "Dirtball," due to the rumor that I was no friend of personal hygiene. I would never forgive Pardo for that. I would never forget. There was something Pardo didn't know: that the only thing you can't allow yourself to do is suddenly pale as a reaction to one of my statements because I know that that signals the inevitable birth of an enemy. From then on, and until we got rid of him after the Revolution, Pardo never uttered a single word of which I was not duly informed. Not a single one escaped my knowledge. Not even in the tangled mountains or in the cities or in Moscow, Peking or New York (where, among many other places, I had sent him as a traveling ambassador) or in airplanes or bathrooms. Not a single one.

IT WAS AT ABOUT six in the morning. I was walking on the streets of the América Sugar Mill's complex—a mill is the sugar factory as well as the complex, the housing—accompanied by Celia Sánchez and some of the kids who were bodyguards and I was thinking about the captain of our troops whom I had left tied up and shirtless so I could execute him myself when the sun came up and as I approached the wooden house on stilts that belonged to the mill's manager, Mr. Ramón Font, I was reflecting for no one but myself on the fact that I couldn't miss with that shot. I couldn't miss, I was thinking, due to the number of people who would be gathered there to see the execution. The captain had fired in the air for New Year's because—they told me— he'd had too much to drink.

It was important for me to impose strict discipline on my forces now that the fall of Batista's dictatorship was clear. I couldn't allow this group of sallow-skinned peasants on the verge of freedom the luxury of celebration. Until that moment, one of my greatest achievements had been to shape that army up high in the mountains with men who differed from bandits and highway robbers only in that I kept them in line through the use of firing squads. Their cohesion as a revolutionary guerrilla army lay in making them aware that they couldn't just do as they pleased. On one end were the rifles of Batista's men and on the other end were mine.

I am pressed to declare, nonetheless, that the peasants were usually peaceful people of limited ambition. Despite lacking almost all of the conveniences of modern life that came about with the Industrial Revolution in the dawn of another century, in Cuba they had the bare necessities of survival, in other words, some chickens, a pig eating scraps in his pen and some rice seeds and beans planted, and as such they didn't agonize over the future. In reality, they didn't have any reason to torment themselves with a fixation on the future if when they looked at things they weren't even aware that yesterday they had a past. But the attachment to their surroundings turned them into one of the perfect cogs in the Cuban rural economy. Because the surroundings gave them their habitat and their habitat gave them material peace and material peace gave them that eternally serene temperament. Nothing had happened before and nothing would happen after. This was how it was until one fine day they joined one of our guerrilla units. The mere possession of a rifle was transformative.

The kid was still tied to one of the trees in the sugar mill complex's little park. He was going to be executed at the appointed hour, but when I looked for him through the sight of my FAL I couldn't see clearly because I had removed my glasses and it didn't seem appropriate to take them back out of my pocket because there were already a lot of people gathered behind me. I definitely didn't want to miss, with all of them following the movement of my rifle while I pointed it at the poor devil's head, and I was waiting for the signal from Celia or any of my officers to get me out of this jam—it didn't come—when I said that they should leave him tied up there. Of course, this was going to be the first time I used my FAL, which Rear Admiral Wolfgang Larrázabal* had sent as a gift from Venezuela with a generous provision of ammunition, and I didn't know that at that distance, which was very short, the rifle's firing power would have surely decapitated him and his body would have lost all control of its functions, thus turning a public act of justice into a very unpleasant public spectacle. I have found that a man knocked down by the shots of a firing squad can bleed to death on the ground and even go into convulsions after receiving as many as three or four coups de grâce without causing an unfavorable reaction in the public there assembled. But should his brains or guts spill out because the shot has opened his flesh, it's enough for the crowd to start vomiting and making other expressions of disgust. I say it was the first time using my gun *against a live target* because in the previous days, having been at the General Command Center at La Rinconada, before moving to the América Sugar Mill, I devoted various hours to familiarizing myself with the rifle and to shooting it at the army's light aircrafts.

The sun was coming up on that Cuban winter morning and I was making my way to my arroz con pollo. It had gotten cold overnight and I ordered that a shirt be put on the captain who was awaiting his execution. Something was wrong. I had a feeling that something was going on and I feared the worst. The truth is that one is never more alone than

---

* Larrázabal was the revolutionary movement leader who came to power after the fall of dictator Marcos Pérez Jiménez.

before the waves of your own unconscious information. The religion of atheists is superstition. Or at least that's the closest they get to metaphysics. But I believe that, in turn, superstition is a generalized form of intuition. The thing is that I was receiving a very strong, yet still undeciphered, vibe of premonition while taking long strides across the exterior hall of our resting place and taking deep drags of my cigar and softly muttering my thoughts out loud.

"Fidel."

For a moment, I didn't even recognize Celia's voice.

"Why are you out here?"

She took me by the arm, a gesture that was more fraternal than feminine.

"Don't keep walking around at this hour, Fidel. Look at how damp your shirt is. The night watchman."

When I heard the plane, in an instinctive gesture, I made a visor out of my hand, facing the east to protect myself from the sun's rays, almost horizontal at this hour, looking upward. I immediately identified the plane not as a bomber, but a transport or cargo plane. But why was it flying so high? The nearest airport in the area was in Santiago and at that distance it should already have the landing gear out and be almost touching the tops of these mountains.

"How strange, that plane," I told myself.

CRAZY HORSE WITH NO NAME, RED DAWN

Manolito Penabaz arrived at Los Negros on horseback. A horse he took at Guisa. It belonged to a little bourgeois woman named Evorita Arca and had won prizes. Manolito seized it at the Arca-Villa Évora farm. So from there he went on horseback to Los Negros, on a dark golden horse, very elegant, a mix with Arabian horses, with tremendous spirit. It wasn't easy to ride him. He took a very uncomfortable English saddle. Los Negros. He had the mission of collecting taxes from the Arabs and there, in the company of René Pacheco Silva and Remigio Samé, things turned into an investigation of what ended up being called The Mexican's excesses. The trio of investigators included Pacheco and Samé. They had gone to collect taxes and now they wanted to execute a son of a bitch they called The Mexican. He had declared himself the boss of the area and was stealing money, until Sorí Marín ordered his arrest a year prior. These three horsemen passed judgment on him and Mano-lito designated Pacheco as the defense counsel, while Pacheco was dying of laughter. The Mexican denied it all and since everyone in the place was deathly afraid of him, nobody testified against him. The Mexican was exonerated.

That night, Manolito himself told me, he slept next to Pacheco, at the home of a Moor named Alejandro Zaitún, who had a coffee warehouse. When he woke up, the radio announced the news that Batista had left. He didn't need the horse. Pacheco had a jeep. He gave the horse away to a totally idiotic kid, who went nuts when Manolito handed over the reins. The roads were really bad. It was already dawn when he got rid of the horse and people were up in Los Negros. "Let's go to the América Mill," Manolito said. Everyone went out on the street to celebrate in Los Negros. They arrived at the América Mill. Pacheco left Manolito there, in front of the manager's house, where I was, and Pacheco said, "I'm leaving before this *loco* names me president of the Republic." There was no excitement or anything in the sleepy streets of the América Mill's *batey*. Everything was normal. Pardo was calm. Seated on the terrace, rock-ing in his chair, perhaps waiting to be called in and have some arroz con pollo. Nobody realized that we had won. "Listen, Pardo, the radio is say-ing that Batista left," Manolito said. They came into the dining room where I was sitting before my arroz con pollo. They hadn't finished tell-ing me that Batista had left Cuba before I was standing and slapping the table and yelling, "That son of a bitch has launched a coup d'état against me!" My first reaction was incendiary, literally. "Call the cap-tains in Santiago," I yelled. "Call them! And get all of the trucks with gas in them and take all of the gas out of the garages. We're going to set Santiago on fire. Fifty-five-gallon tanks." Set Santiago on fire. Arroz con pollo. Betrayal. In some of my biographies (the detail appears in many of them), I've read that once, when I was a child, I asked my father for some money, probably a couple of cents, and before his refusal to part with these little coins, I tried to cause a fire in the house at Birán, set fire to it, reduce it to ashes. If I remember correctly, they even mention some charred wood, some damage that I was able to unleash before they found me with a torch in hand. In the end, the house was burned down years later in the blink of an eye because of a lit cigar that the old man had for-gotten in the loft. I'm amused that my biographers should be unaware of what I wanted to do to Santiago the day of the triumph of the Revolution because it would have allowed them to explain my pyromaniacal tendencies when I don't get what I want, whether it be some coins from my father or the surrender of the Republic.

PERHAPS BURNING DOWN the country's second-largest city was dramatic to an extreme and I accept that I had images of a crazed Nero and the Chicago fire of October 8, 1871, going through my head. Let's be serious now: it's not that I give free rein to my imagination, to my temper tantrums; but it so happens that sometimes people don't realize that I'm just like everyone else, except that I can do whatever I please and am able to do it all. Who's going to hold me back? The same thing happened with that kid, that captain of ours, whom I was going to execute. Looking at it very closely now: how was I going to kill a brave guy in front of an entire town, regardless of how fascinated the people would be by the spectacle? That head—which was where I was going to shoot him— exploding like a pumpkin under the fire of my FAL, who would erase that from the history of the Cuban Revolution? In any event it was about doing something noteworthy because I really didn't know what was happening in the capital.

The Cuban Revolution has never been more vulnerable than at that moment, when it was victorious. The hours that passed between my hearing Batista's plane and my being able to sit down in the capital and control the Directorate and dissolve the army, when all ends were still loose, those were the most fucked-up hours.

In the end, we were never going to be more like each other, at least at that stage: Fulgencio Batista and me. The general spoiling his army, I flattering it with promises of sinecures even when I arrived at Columbia, the country's main military facility, to the west of Havana, and joked with the soldiers in my speech when I told them we aspired to a disciplined army—the racket with which they had welcomed me didn't allow me to speak—and they, amused and hopeful, cheered for me; they didn't stop cheering for me. But I had to calm them down, bring down all of their defenses and any reason for suspicion with my fraternal rhetoric. They were still armed, still organized in companies and battalions. Let me tell you: from the darkest days of the Sierra Maestra, I had needed that army to guarantee Havana. On March 13, 1957, when the Directorate attacked the Presidential Palace, I realized that I was still nine hundred kilometers from power. By way of our brand-spanking-new battery-operated Zenith radio—which Celia had sent—I found out that a commando unit had tried to assassinate Batista and failed. For me, that was the news that most alarmed me during the entire campaign. It caused me to understand as never before how far I really was from the centers of power and that any reckless person could ruin the whole setup I had worked so hard to achieve and could even allow himself the luxury of killing Batista, taking power and calling elections whenever the hell he felt like it, while I rotted up there in the Sierra without anyone giving me a second thought. They say that two or three officers of the palace guard stood with their backs to the door of the presidential office and didn't allow any of the attackers to come close. No one has ever valued the service those men did to the Revolution. At that moment, in a paradox of our history, they were impeding the triumph of what was going to immediately become a counterrevolution had the attackers achieved their objectives. They accused me of being a putschist day in and day out and here they go pulling a putsch that made all of my previous actions pale in comparison. And they almost succeeded, dammit.

And I understood in that one moment that I was going to lose the war due to how far away I was—my distance was formidable only as a defense strategy—and then I started to plot my ties with the army. The concept of the maneuver was as follows: use the enemy troops themselves to represent our presence in Havana's government buildings, given the impossibility of filling them with my guerrillas due to the distance between us. It was a possibility, but only if I could open channels of communication and, at the opportune moment, throw sparks of hope their way. In short, it was a matter of circumstances. To add the army at some point didn't mean anything but defeating it but under a different name than defeat: assimilation.

Because I was still in the midst of these negotiations, December 31 caught me by surprise.

That was when I conceived of making Santiago the capital, because it was about the Revolution having its identity wherever I was and not where the ministry buildings were, and there was the danger that a coup d'etat would be forged in Havana and that the Directorate, already aiming to take over the palace, would sabotage my taking of power. The problem wasn't the symbol of a palace, the problem was me. That's why I named Santiago the capital and started to move slowly toward Havana, until I reached Columbia. It wasn't about reducing the city to ashes any-more, quite the contrary. Santiago, provisional capital on January first; in short, what I had finally done was run toward Havana, but left my capital in the rear guard. You are familiar with the images from January 8, 1959. On the few occasions in which I deal with cash or finger a one-peso bill, I contemplate the scene. I am on a war tank being acclaimed by the cit-izens while I advance amid the city's skyscrapers. It's all idyllic. It can't be anything but idyllic, since this sketch of our entrance to Havana was drawn up in Prague, at the beginning of 1961, when we commissioned the Czechs to make our new Cuban paper money. I won't hide my anx-iety from you, atop my tank, surrounded by my officers and by Batista's leaders. My last memory of Havana was El Chino Esquivel the afternoon before my trip to Mexico to prepare the *Granma* expedition. I recall that the horizon appeared suddenly on the descent to a town called San Fran-cisco de Paula, about fifteen kilometers to the southwest of the city, by the Central Highway. I saw it as if for the first time this January after-noon and didn't recognize it. And I said, "*Cojones.* What a country I've conquered. And all of this is mine?" I was going to immediately inundate it with my filthy bearded men. Many things came together. It's not for my health that I'm opposed to all kinds of clandestinity in Havana, and even in Santiago we had to start cleaning house among my followers. We had to break the will of each city so that the guerrilla force could main-tain its supremacy. Once this objective was achieved, we had to attack the army, which was still intact. It ended up being an indispensable act for the existence of the Revolution. Because of that we started the close-range executions. But first I gave the order to kick out the three North American military missions. I knew the moral effect this would have on the high military leaders and even on the national bourgeois class. For the first time since the instauration of the Republic of Cuba, the mili-tary caste was going to have to manage on its own.

The festivities dubbed the "Freedom Carnival." The triumph of the Revolution occurred the previous fortnight. Commander Camilo Cienfuegos, head of the Rebel Army, participated in the revelry.

15

THE REPUBLIC FROM THE GALLOWS

/ / /

The classes which must abandon the stage of history,
are the last to believe that their game is ended.

—JOSEPH STALIN
TO H. G. WELLS,
July 23, 1934*

I HAD A GENERAL NOTION OF MY OBJECTIVES IN MIND WHEN HAVANA appeared over the horizon just as my convoy started to descend on the Central Highway about fifteen kilometers to the east. The unexpectedness of the skyscrapers made the view dazzling. It was clear that we needed revenge to maintain our honor—or what we started to call *los pueblos dignos*, "the honorable peoples"—and that revenge required the prior existence of an affront. Ergo, if objective and palpable affronts did not exist, we would have had to make them up. You should know that the first order of the day when the Revolution triumphed was the desperate search for an enemy to fill the vacancy left by Batista, and if we could get one with whom we shared a long history, all the better. We were already realizing that we were running out of henchmen who worked for Batista to execute, and that in the end, mass executions provide negative press.

And you can't be changing enemies every day. The most convenient enemy is a strategic one. That famous note of mine to Celia in which I

---

* Joseph Stalin and H. G. Wells, *Marxism vs. Liberalism* (New York: New Century, September 1937; reprinted October 1950).

swore to start a war against the Americans after we got rid of Batista was prescient. But it would be foolish to claim that we were already creating the conditions at that moment to have a more substantial enemy than Batista. Foolish and a useless exercise in cynicism. But a poor peasant's home reduced to ashes by American rockets is just the type of data worth storing for the future.* Lenin said that a revolution is worth what you know how to defend. We expanded on the concept: a revolution, at least one like the Cuban one, is worth knowing how to create enemies to justify your defense.

I already said that we were never more vulnerable than right after we won. In that sense I mean there were factions against our being in power before we had consolidated it. But after power was consolidated, we recognized that we were vulnerable because we didn't have an enemy. Disbanding the army and the parallel guerrilla groups and immediately destroying the country's economic plutocracy was nothing more than the conscious application of Leninist methods. But my enemy, that creature to justify all of my offensives, where was that bloodthirsty, cruel and ruthless entity? And that is no longer Leninism, patient reader. That is already—and forgive me the indulgence and what could appear as excessive vanity—pure Fidelismo.

THE FIRST TIME THAT I was sure we had won, that victory was unquestionably mine, was when I noticed how carefully Celia was styling her hair. It took me a while to understand what was going through her mind. We had left the América Mill, heading toward Palma Soriano, where I was expected to address the nation over the radio, and the *compañeros* at Radio Rebelde, with Carlos Franqui at the head of the operation, already had the equipment ready. Another common tale of our historiography is that the primeval group of the guerrilla was composed of twelve men. In reality, this was something made up by Carlos Franqui, the journalist who published our clandestine newspaper—*Revolución*—in Havana and who was very agile with publicity. When he arrived in the Sierra, he was charged with taking Radio Rebelde on the air. The idea of The Twelve, to put us on a par with the apostles, occurred to him after the triumph of the Revolution. At first, only a jeep followed us, with Pacheco at the wheel

---

* See page 550.

and Pardo Llada and Penabaz inside. The same personnel who always went in my Land Rover. Celia in the front seat, between the driver and me, and the four bodyguards in the back, with the top down. But vehicles started joining us all along the way, from all the farms, from all the roads that emptied out onto the narrow highway that went from América to Palma Soriano. They joined us in tractors, in sugarcane trucks, in rental cars. Then I noticed Celia and her badly disguised worry. In addition, I noticed that she had adjusted a handkerchief on her head, knotting it at the nape of her neck. Before, I had seen her with a beret. Then with her hair loose, falling to her shoulders. Now she was adjusting the rearview mirror and looking into it. I thought for a moment that she was taking some security precaution and that she wanted to make sure everything was in order behind us. But instead she took out a small tube of lipstick and started to apply it to her lips, taking great care that the inevitable bumps on the road not make her smear it. This woman, I said to myself. This poor woman. In the years to come and until the day of her death, more than two decades later, Celia Sánchez Manduley would be the most powerful woman in Cuba. Probably in all the Americas. And perhaps even in the world. She would be the great mediator in the course of our revolutionary process and the person to whom revolutionaries and citizens and even bourgeois people fallen from power would come by the thousands in search of jobs, houses, cars, justice, the commuting of death penalties or lessening of prison sentences, medicine, money, works of art, exit permits, scholarships, hospital admittances and any other thing for which someone would think her intervention necessary. She would be an institution. But she knew that, with the triumph of the Revolution, I was going to leave her. That the triumph of my political ideals was the loss of her romantic ones. The institution would be no more than a fragile little lady from the obscure semirural bourgeoisie who was desperate to be a woman lying at my side, pitifully obedient and demure. In addition, I had made an unforgivable mistake. The problem is that I have always thought that my balls are of an exaggerated size. I've discussed the matter with some of my doctors and specialists and they've told me that my observation lacks all scientific validity. I deduced, nonetheless, that it was a real burden to me when my sack got too full of semen. It's not the same to walk around light in the balls when you're going up and down mountains as it is when you're weighed down. That's why the presence of this *compañera* in the Sierra was so beneficial to me: not only as an executive assistant, I mean, also to keep me unburdened. Of course, I never told her that my permanent sexual willingness in the mountains was a function of what I deemed to be a requirement of my capacity of movement. A woman will forgive you for treating her like a prostitute—Celia was no exception to this rule—but not for asking her to suck your dick because your balls hurt. They're whores, not medication. Then it just so happens that we go down to the plains and sure enough there's a change in altitude and the weight of my testicles no longer demands my attention and as a result I begin to space out my furtive nocturnal encounters with Celia and to require her applied favors to a lesser degree.

My quick response to the sadness Celia wanted to stamp on that morning created a much more regrettable situation.

She had already put the lipstick away in her pocket, over her left breast, when I patted her thigh and uttered what we Cubans call a *bravuconada*.

"*Coño de su madre.*"

"What's wrong, Fidel?"

I wasn't looking at anyone in particular. I wasn't looking at her. I was looking at the road in front of us and the people hurrying to the curb to see us pass and greet us with a wave of their hands.

"What do you think could be wrong?"

This was supposed to be the triumph of the Cuban Revolution. I said, And what do we have? We have the Directorate, the communists from the PSP and Gutiérrez Menoyo's forces, those sons of bitches from the National Second Front of Escambray, all lined up to challenge my coming to power and Batista is landing in Santo Domingo and Cantillo is planning a coup d'état in Columbia. Is this victory, Celia? Tell me the truth. Is this victory or is this a piece of shit?

PALMA SORIANO. Its entire population had come out onto the streets and everywhere you looked there seemed to be armed civilians—with two-toned 26th of July bracelets as their only valid identification. I would have to get used to moving though large crowds in the coming years. I still couldn't imagine that it would be more than forty years. I don't think anyone has ever heard his own name called out so many times as he passes as I've heard mine since January 1, 1959. As I advanced in my Land Rover I saw the first revolutionary fashions come out. The girls had arranged it to dress themselves with red blouses and full black skirts, the two colors of the movement's aforementioned bracelets. The men, eventually abandoning the use of razors, wanted to suddenly appear dirty and austere and each one of them was willing to join a firing squad, perhaps the last opportunity to kill in this war. A country that until that moment had demanded its citizens shave and in which tubes of under-arm deodorant were one of the products in highest demand from the two large soap factories—Crusellas and Sabatés—became accepting of half-shaven men, and even the body odor associated with wandering through the mountains ended up taking on a certain elegance in society. I would say that that air of the wild life is part and parcel of a victorious guerrilla revolution. And wherever I went, the people chanted my name. Fidel. Fidel. Fidel. I'm telling you that even Christ didn't enjoy such exalta-tion. And when I say this, I'm relying on scientific studies that I've done. If Palma Soriano had 25,421 inhabitants— according to the 1953 cen-sus (the last one carried out in Cuba before the Revolution)—and we add another 5,000 for the day of our triumph, thus bringing us to about 30,000 people in Palma on that date, and compare it to a maximum of 25,000 inhabitants in Jerusalem on the day of Christ's crucifixion, and if we add the detail that not everyone in Jerusalem or in those popula-tions of Judea went out onto the dusty streets to greet the Lord when He arrived there, but that without a doubt the entire population of Palma Soriano spilled out onto the streets to cheer me on, you will easily con-clude that I always, from the very first day of the Revolution, had more spectators than the Son of God. My facts, I repeat, have a scientific basis. The initial estimates—of 55,000 to 95,000 inhabitants in Jerusalem—were severely reduced to half or a quarter upon concluding that the water supply to that city from all of the possible sources would have only been enough for a maximum of 70,000 consumers, assuming that five gallons per day were available per person. Palma Soriano, in turn, was a prosper-ous municipality—prosperity stimulated by the presence of three sugar mills, América, Miranda and Palma—located on the wide part of the depression that extends from the high valley of the Cauto River to the Cuenca of Guantánamo and the mountains of the Sierra Maestra—on the south—and where there were never any water shortages.

Once the equipment for Radio Rebelde was ready—in the studios of a modest local station—and all the stations in the country had promised to tune us in, I was ready to deliver the first of my "official" communi-qués, as a statesman in the strict meaning of the word, still scratching at the doors of power, but a statesman nonetheless. The atmosphere in the place—I have no other way to describe it—was electrifying and all eyes were on me.

I was trying to get settled when someone told me that General Eulogio Cantillo was trying to get in touch with me. They showed me a telephone or a microphone or some headphones. I know it was some kind of phonic device.

"I'm not crazy," I said.

I made eye contact with the man whom I had designated as president in my speeches on Radio Rebelde, Magistrate Manuel Urrutia, and saw more commanders than I knew the Rebel Army had. They told me again that Cantillo was calling me from Havana. I knew I was not crazy. I remember thinking that: I am not crazy. But I didn't remember that I had also said it. As I reviewed the notes now that Celia took that morning, I discover a comment. "I am not crazy," I said. "Don't you realize that only crazy people speak with things that don't exist? And since Cantillo is the head of the army's Chiefs of Staff, a thing which does not exist, I am not going to speak with him, because I am not crazy. All power is for the Revolution."

That ending was perfect. All power is for the Revolution.

I HAD COMMANDER Huber Matos in Alto del Villalón. I assigned him the attack on Santiago. Colonel Rego Rubido and Commander Bonifacio Haza showed up before him a little before noon. They raised the two largest white parliament flags in the world. They had a Protestant minister with them, Pastor González. Bonifacio Haza, who had been put under Huber's orders a few weeks before, would later be executed under Raúl's orders. He would be the last one in the line mowed down by machine gun fire at the edge of a mass grave bulldozed the night of January 12 at the foot of San Juan Hill. Rego Rubido and Haza showed up at Alto de Villalón to see what they should do, given Batista's flight. Huber said, Well, the battle may be over but if there's no agreement, I attack. The only possible agreement was for Batista's supporters to surrender. Unconditionally. Fidel wants to set Santiago on fire, he said. Today. Rego seemed to shrink in his seat and just then Raúl arrived and joined the talk and finally Rego said that he couldn't assume responsibility for the rest of the officers and Raúl said, Then let's go to Santiago and speak with them there. They went to Moncada in different jeeps and once there invited the officers and told them to go speak with me. Before they left for Moncada, I had told Huber by a hand-crank phone that I found on the way out of Palma—still intact and functioning like a live relic on the demolished and singed wall of the small barracks of the Highway Surveillance Service, which we had attacked on Monday—to take his officers and place them on the road from Cancy to Santiago, and I told him to tell his officers to place all of their columns along the road and to gather as many cars or trucks as they could seize. It was only later that I realized: they were going into the jaws of the wolf. It was incredible, I thought, but my primary skill as a combatant had been the ability to avoid death, to elude it, to fight it at a distance. Yet Raúl and Huber, whom I sent as an advance party to Santiago, were willing to assume this dance of evasion that would ordinarily belong to me. In other words, sacrifice What has always surprised me is how readily those who surround me accept me as a chosen being and the quickness with which they are willing to sacrifice themselves.

There were about four hundred cars, jeeps and pickup trucks and no less than three thousand rebel soldiers occupying the strip of highway that went from Santiago to El Escandel. Rego and his officers saw that one-kilometer mass of troops while they went toward the place where I was waiting. They moved in two buses and our guys, at nightfall, seemed like ten thousand men. What could they have felt—in the chiaroscuro of that winter nightfall in the outskirts of Santiago—that the Romans wouldn't have also known as they were besieged by barbarians? "Fidel has good plans for you," Raúl, who was on one of the buses was telling them. "The Revolution has triumphed," he was saying, "but you are also triumphant."

I spoke to them from atop a table in the school at El Escandel. I said, "There won't be any more Praetorian Guards, just one army." Even the thugs that we later executed were there—and me up on a table. And from there to Santiago. We were hungry and I told Celia to go find us food. When we were entering Santiago, I told Huber, Don't leave my side.

That night we were in Santiago and, from the balcony of City Hall, I said, "We have arrived at last!" Thirty minutes later, I proclaimed Urrutia president and that city as the provisional capital of the island. Urrutia was sworn in before the crowds. I left then and there. I said, "I'm leaving for Havana right now. By highway." Huber is still at my side. He hadn't gone anywhere. "Of your guys," I told Huber, "I'm taking Duque with his troops, one hundred and some-odd men. You have to occupy the city, all the high points." In the morning, he went back to Moncada. To take care of the plaza, as the head of the district.

I asked about Rego Rubido. The colonel showed up with his high school teacher glasses, good-natured and docile, but without the slightest awareness that his promised ascent to the leadership of the Armed Forces would be over as soon as we reached Havana. I'd instructed Rego to quickly organize a motorized column made up of an infantry battalion, a campaign artillery battery and tanks. The Freedom Caravan. Toward Havana. I was accompanied by a total of one thousand insurgents and two thousand soldiers from the army. "Come with me, Rego," I said to him, with the warmest, most unpretentious tone and even with a touch of abandonment. A slow, calculated journey made not as much for the purpose of being seen atop my tank, as to go winning over pockets of resistance, lots of negotiating, lots of speaking, although the hardest nuts to crack would be the city of Cienfuegos, which had been taken by the Second Front of Escambray folks, and all of the positions in Havana on which outskirts the Revolutionary Directorate had already deployed and claimed as theirs. Well, I was taking the army with me, and Rego Rubido, who still didn't know he was my hostage.

Raúl, in the company of Vilma Espín, came to say goodbye. I was below the arcade of the Moncada Barracks, the same one that I had tried to force my way into by gunshot with my commandos six years prior, and Rego's column and my rebels had already formed a column with the vehicles and I was coming from City Hall. I tried to ignore the memory of my own hesitant steps the morning of the attack, and I headed toward the tank that would supposedly lead the march. Out of the corner of my eye, I saw that Raúl was saying something to Vilma, clearly that she let him have a tête-à-tête alone with me, because he moved away from her to cover the ten or twelve steps separating us and Vilma didn't move. I waved at Vilma and smiled with a gesture of complicity, as if to tell her that I approved of her relationship with my brother. She looked young and sweet with her olive-green uniform and her heavy gun at her waist and a white gladiola hooked flirtatiously on the side of her thick black hair. I was informed very early on about the relationship consummated by the two of them in Mayarí, where Raúl spent his time receiving, on the one hand, all of the combatants who were *burning up* from Santiago's underground, and, on the other hand, the majority of the communists that the Party sent us ever since it approved its support of an armed struggle. I accepted half a dozen, but Raúl took the rest of them. Regarding the *quemados* from Santiago, the "burnt" combatants, Vilma was very useful to Raúl. *Quemado*, "burnt," was what we called the *compañeros* who stood out in the city by placing bombs or executing policemen, and for whatever reason their names became known by the police and they started to close in on them. Vilma exercised great influence over them, since she came from one of the oldest families of the Santiago aristocracy and because her father had been the manager of the largest factory in the area—the Bacardi liquor factory—in the forties. I don't know what relationship of dutiful respect the *compañeros* in Santiago established with this family of provincial patricians. A few days after this goodbye—I still hadn't made it to Havana—they married in a civil ceremony.

Raúl had his long mane pulled back with a brooch Vilma had lent him and it fell from behind his black beret. It fell all the way to his first spinal vertebra. The violence of this stark female attribute in his military package was, for me, a revelation of what I call the equivocal personality of my brother. Before Vilma, who was also sent by the Santiago Movement as a *quemada*, the news reached me that Raúl had selected a group of young boys to be his bodyguards in the Second Eastern Front. They stood out for being mulattos who were over six feet tall, some with green eyes, all of them criminals. The best of their race. In this sense, Vilma's ascent in the Second Front and especially her obvious coupling with Raúl was excellent news. But then the triumph came and those commanders coming from the Santiago Movement began to stand out in the Revolutionary Tribunals, issuing death sentences prodigiously. And I would see them in the newspaper photos and in the trials that were transmitted live on television and what caught my eye were their manes and how they wore them loose and how ruthless they were and that many of them—as opposed to my brother—if they weren't smooth-faced, managed to shave meticulously but never touched their manes. Being white and from good families, their straight pageboys shone next to the nappy buns of the large mulattos who constituted the majority of my troops in the Sierra Maestra, another, coarser race of killers.

I put my arm around him, to further close off the Faraday cage effect of our street conference.

I lowered my voice to make certain clarifications. Indispensable clarifications.

"You're staying here with Haza, right?"

Raúl nodded.

"Well, don't lose track of any of these officers. You need to stay alert. And start purging them."

"Haza is a dead man, Fidel. He's getting the ax tonight."

"*Coño*, Raúl. Don't be hasty."

"We've got to execute him, Fidel. He's a son of a bitch. It pisses off the movement's people to see him walk around the city so haughtily with his Twenty-sixth of July bracelet."

"Okay. Execute him, but only once I've gotten a bit ahead with the convoy. When I get to, maybe, Camagüey. Do you understand me? We have to dissolve the army, Raúl. I'll take care of Rego and the garrisons that have yet to surrender. Your mission now is to hit those structures."

"And the squealers, too," he was pressed to tell me, as if he needed something in his favor. The execution of squealers also seemed to be his cards in this game.

"Do whatever you want with the squealers, Raúl. But please listen to me regarding Haza. Wait until I am far away."

"Haza is a son of a bitch," he said.

I nodded and in a smooth transition, with my arm still around my brother's shoulder, I walked over to Rego Rubido, pressing Raúl under my arm. Walk, kid.

IN ITS FINEST HOUR the Cuban army was made up of seventy thousand men. I looked at this force from atop an old wooden platform at the Columbia complex. Camilo had ordered an inspection of the platform to make sure the posts would hold the weight of my committee and the public pushing against us. That stage didn't come crashing down because Camilo took the precaution of surrounding it with the brawniest combatants in his column. They stood with their backs pressed up against the structure, wielding the butts of their Thompson rifles blindly against the senseless crowd. The Thompsons were more compact and therefore more maneuverable for keeping that human ocean in check. For me, one of the great mysteries of my arrival in Havana is that there weren't any accidents. First, from the turret of my Sherman tank, I saw how a kind of trench opened up amid the people pouring out onto the streets applauding me and how the people moved around the exterior sides of that hunk of iron whose driver was under orders not to stop. I didn't want to look behind me, convinced as I was that if I were to turn around, I would look over the hatch and see the flattened bodies of some of those idiots, I mean, those poor devils. Another miracle was that the driver was able to drive through those streets without any reference points and without even going up on the curb at all, surrounded by that compact crowd that barely got out of the way, and that he did so at the level on which the driver of a Sherman is located, his visibility always below the average height of a man despite the tank being a rather high structure and not one of those splendid Soviet machines we operated later, from the T-52 series, and the ones that came after, that seem to march as if they were flat against the ground, which made me say they were crouching. He was one of Batista's men and I didn't get a chance to congratulate him when we arrived in front of Columbia. I feel quite sorry as I write this because it is only now that I ponder his skills as a driver. I could have offered him some position. Even left him in the new Armed Forces. We had left the city of Matanzas —a gem on the north coast, full of slow canals and an abundance of bridges and colonial mansions, one hundred kilometers to the east of Havana—before noon. The crucial moment for me, speaking personally, and which I have always kept to myself, of my approach to Havana and my entrance into it, took place in a small town called El Cotorro. I accept that a town with such a name is an unfortunate location for a moment worthy perhaps of a caesar. But I don't think that I could convey with words the emotion I felt, so I'll just record it. So, it was when I discovered that the whole clan of my sisters was blocking the road out of El Cotorro and holding a small boy over their heads who was hastily dressed in an olive-green uniform—to confirm that that small child was smiling at me and holding his arms out to me from a distance of perhaps three hundred meters separating us—I chose to put on my glasses, the first time in the whole journey that I allowed myself that luxury. "My, how the kid has grown!" I said above the metallic din of the engine to Rego Rubido, who was at my right, stoically suffering the brunt of a nine-hundred-kilometer journey by Sherman tank on rough roads from Santiago to Havana. "Huber, it's Fidelito!" I said to Huber, who was directly behind me, leaning one hand against the hatch to keep his balance, since the tank's exterior chassis was overflowing with people who had jumped on. "Fidelito!" I repeated, pointing ahead. Then I patted the shoulder of one of my bodyguards, Aníbal, who was seated at my left with his right arm leaning on the cannon, and I said, "Look at how much that kid has grown in two years!" Nobody answered me verbally. They just nodded. How my son came into my arms, up there to where I was presiding from the tank's turret, is something I'm not sure of now. I only remember that it seemed—and still seems—that I made contact with his tender bones. That was what I felt of his body upon hugging him. Each and every one of his bones. Have you heard enough? Don't think that I am going to prolong this sentimental little soap opera. I'll only add, for the record, that my first talk with Fidelito is never going to be worthy of a place in the frescoes. "Did you miss me?" was the only thing, I must confess, that I thought to ask him. And he, of course, at age nine, didn't improve the dialectic level. "Didn't you bring me anything? I want a machine gun." Mirta was in Cuba that day—I found out later. They had Fidelito in Miami until the fifth, but she sent for him so that I could see him upon entering Havana. "What did you say you want?" I asked him. "A machine gun," he said, as he greedily eyed all of the weapons my *compañeros* had raised in the air. I pressed him against my chest again. The scent of his skin. That's the other thing I remember in addition to the contact with his bones. I'll clarify now, to organize this reading properly, that a few kilometers ahead I made them stop the convoy so I could hand the kid over to Celia, who was traveling in one of the jeeps behind me, so she could take care of him for what remained of our journey and find a way to get him back to his relatives later. Champ, I'll come get you later. And we'll spend a lot of time together. I promise. Oh, yeah, and the machine gun.

The convoy's journey and entrance to Havana is one of the obligatory icons of modern history and is an episode that has always belonged to the world of visual images. I cannot compete against it with written words now, although there would be, modesty aside, sufficient material for a great epic poem—or at least that is what many visiting writers have made me believe. The first one was Pablo Neruda, incidentally. But much later, he sent us the bill. That *Song of Protest*, or whatever it's called, cost us about ten thousand dollars. But I have learned, from hanging around so much with other artists and poets, and especially cameramen, that when historical events first occur before the lens of a camera operated by someone of average skill, there's not much space left for the amenities of artistic leisure. Existing documentary film and television kinescope footage of that march, as well as thousands of thirty-five-millimeter negatives, of which we were only able to recover about forty percent, since the rest is in the archives of American publications—at the time Havana was flooded with *yanqui* photojournalists—is our unacknowledged equivalent to the poetry of Homer. It wasn't all that bad anyway, the image of our marching into Havana. What happened was that I—still—was a little old-fashioned. But that very night my speech from Columbia was transmitted via television all over the country. And the next night I appeared on another program. One called *Meet the Press* that had a solid reputation as a political interest program and which was a faithful copy of an American program by the same name. And I was even excited by that word. Appear. Appearance. We would soon leave behind the era of radio transmissions as the end-all, be-all of Cuban politics and perhaps even finish off the leading articles in the Friday edition of *Bohemia* magazine. On the other hand, while moving toward Columbia, I had seen my picture on some posters people were holding up as I passed and I had also seen them hung out on balconies and up on walls. It was the first time in my life that I saw myself reproduced on posters. What I mean to say is that the use of these images grabbed my attention in such a way that I would use them however I could as my main propaganda tool.* I had just discovered something. I was the first guerrilla in a field uniform with a beard to introduce myself, live, before any country's television cameras. For that matter, I was the only guerrilla in a field uniform and with a beard in existence in the world. In and of itself, that Rebel Army look and its imprint were completely unknown in history, a real mix of feudal bearded guys with FAL shotguns or ultramodern telescopic-sight Remington hunting carbines and huge cigars between their teeth and the straps of their machine guns slung across their chests and reminiscent of Robin Hood or Emiliano Zapata. It was, in the end, the triumph of subversion. I'll tell you something else: the Cuban counterrevolution's only constant is the mimetic projection of that afternoon. Just take a look at their speeches, documents and propaganda. Their goal is a counterrevolutionary restoration taking place on a single day and the only mode in which they contemplate the disappearance of our regime is as a "collapse." Not a single possibility for negotiation or reform. They

---

* Made by the artist Eladio Rivadulla, who also paid for the printing.

only see themselves knocking me out of my place on that tank and raising my rifle themselves. In truth it's an image that is as attractive as it is unique. That's why, at the beginning of 1961, when we sent the first bills we issued to Czechloslovakia for printing, I told Che, then president of the National Bank, "*Oye, argentino*, on the most widely circulated bills, the one-peso bills, put the drawing of our entrance with the rebels in Havana."

Getting back to Columbia. I watched the crowd of military men who were unsure about the chain of command and the thousands of civilians from nearby neighborhoods flooding the camp and the unmanned barracks to take anything at all—steel helmets, gaiters, white ceremonial gloves, canteens, even cot mattresses. The soldiers wore an expression of pitiful hope and I tried to joke with them and convince them that in our estimation they were still military men in service. It was also an unprecedented use of language with great tactical flexibility because it didn't respond to any of the needs of the past. Those officers and soldiers, nonetheless, couldn't understand that they were discharged and that many of them were even as good as executed. It took a lot to get them to let me begin. Nor had there been anything else to listen to since my entrance into Havana, besides the noisy crowd like a rough sea whose waves never recede and remain on the shore. Finally there was some calm in the audience, although just barely contained. Now imagine the next four hours. I was going on with my spiel about the difficult years ahead of us. I was just getting warmed up and Camilo's officers, two meters below us, were attacking anyone who approached the platform with the butts of their rifles, when, with a surprise flap of their wings and the glow of their flight below the spotlights, doves released by someone in the audience landed—two of them—on my shoulders. Since then I have maintained that the doves were in search of the highest point in the place, which was me—with my six-foot-two stature. Some joker, nonetheless, one with very poor taste, said that the doves were attracted by the strange odor that emanated from me. I controlled any abrupt motions to not scare them away and drive the photographers to ecstasy over the scene and also because I knew the spell they would cast on the audience. They spent half of my speech sitting on my shoulders and I had to withstand their shitting on my epaulets. I don't know if doves piss, but if they piss, then they also pissed on me. I remember that Hugh Thomas, in his fat book about us (rather, *against* us), said that it was an omen of peace, in other words, according to his point of view and in keeping with what would happen later, a mistaken omen. Of course, Thomas ignored the fact that one of the most deeply rooted Cuban superstitions defines the dove as the tangible emissary of misfortune, even death, although I imagine that he consulted with some *babalawo** while carrying out his historical research in Cuba. Even so, I sensed that it was a very good sign. My religious knowledge at the time was scant, but I did know some rudimentary things, especially those learned from my mother, so that in their approaching flight toward my shoulders I did a quick visual check of their feet, which were already facing my epaulets to complete their landing maneuver, and I had time to confirm that they weren't carrier pigeons because they didn't have bands, without a doubt the best of signs, since in the Santería religion you can never work with an animal that has been tied in any way, no rope, no band, to impede its freedom. Later, in the course of the Revolution, as some of my *compañeros* know, I've developed a close relationship with the Yorubas and have even participated in their ceremonies. These doves on January 8 decisively opened the doors to many of their secrets for me, since the dove is the little animal offered in never-revealed quantities to Olofi, the earthly representative of Oloddumare, the supreme god of the Yorubas, in the impenetrable initiation rites of a *babalawo*.

Commander Camilo Cienfuegos was to my left on the stage, scrawny, flat-bellied, his emblematic Stetson cowboy hat and washed and decently pressed olive-green uniform. "Am I doing okay, Camilo?" I asked him surprisingly, with the required tone of camaraderie in the middle of my speech about the dangers that the future held. Camilo nodded, without any affectation, just two short movements of his head but in a gesture that was accentuated by the horizontal tilt of the wide brim of his hat. It was the moment in which the first truly significant event of everything that would be the Cuban Revolution happened. In that exchange with Camilo, the revolutionary process staged its first open rebellion: the rebellion of language. Interrupting a speech of such obliged solemnity by telling an army still armed before you that you've defeated them and interrupting yourself to make an aside to one of your guerrilla *compañeros*, like two kids sharing a snack, meant that for the first time in Cuba's five-

---

* Or *babalao*, a priest of the Yoruba religion.

century-long civilized existence, the language of power was being implemented. Tomorrow, the firing squad.

I SPENT THE FIRST night in Havana at the Hotel Monserrate. It was really a facility halfway between a student guesthouse and a cheap motel. On the first floor there was a good diner, with a counter where they sold Cuban coffee, cigars and lottery tickets, another counter which was the reception proper of the hotel and a third counter where interprovincial train and bus tickets were sold. Some of the bus companies used the Monserrate as a stop. There was even a massive bell on the wall to announce the departure of the Matanzas line. Two rows of solid mahogany chairs were at the disposal of the guests as well as the passengers waiting to board the next bus. Many times, as you will have guessed, I escaped on one of those buses, with the police on my tail, out to the provinces. You can imagine why I wanted to spend my first night as the victorious head of a Revolution in one of the Monserrate's cheap rooms. We arrived alone, a little after midnight, Celia, Captain Pupo, Leoncito the driver and me. Celia told me she had left Fidelito with one of my sisters (she wasn't sure which one at the time) well before entering Columbia and had slipped two hundred pesos into my sister's pocket for anything she might need. That first night, the rest of the bodyguards were practically kidnapped by the people. The people wanted to have us. I don't know how else to explain it. To have us. To appropriate us. Probably—this is my guess—more than half of my kids lost their virginity that night. The street in front of the Monserrate was deserted and I remember that I signed the guest book. The guest book never showed up again despite the time Celia spent trying to track it down with the idea in mind of exhibiting it in one of our museums. The next day, Celia called Camilo on the telephone to tell him where we were and to have him send some cars and men with rifles. Camilo was at Columbia and had dispatched patrol cars around all of Havana to find me. At noon I was able to regather part of my group of bodyguards. In the afternoon, I decided to move to the Havana Hilton, which had just opened a few weeks prior. We took up the entire twenty-third floor. Since the walls were sliding and interchangeable—we discovered this later—we came up with an ingenious defense plan consisting of changing the location of my room daily. There was no control. The rest of the floors were also occupied. Then, after we'd been there about a month, the owners wanted to charge us thousands and thousands of pesos and I asked the hotel chain to intervene. But we had to start thinking about moving on already. Celia was the one exerting the most pressure. The idea of moving turned into an obsession of hers. Of course, a twenty-five-story building, with almost five hundred rooms and all of that infrastructure at my disposal, including telephone operators, waitresses, maids and office workers, in addition to all the other women milling around the hotel to meet me, led to a situation that became harder and harder for her to control. Then the guards moved to the San Luis Hotel, on a second-class commercial avenue called Belascoaín. Celia was friends with the owner of the San Luis and he offered to charge us a modest amount for the lodging of about forty of my men—the guards were constantly increasing their staff. I spent a few more days at the Hilton until I traveled to Venezuela—from January 23 to 27.

Around that time my brother Raúl, whom we had already sent for, picked three rebel officers in his trust, Orlando Pupo, Pedro García and Valle Lazo, to purge the guard (there were a lot of reports of debauchery, drunkenness and shooting, to tell you the truth) and ordered them to prepare a garrison in Cojímar, the little fishing village to the east of Havana that everyone knows because of the book *The Old Man and the Sea*. At the entrance to this village there was a hill, from which you could see the mouth of the Cojímar River, which the fishermen had turned into an enclosed bay, and to the left there was a complete view of the town, and on top of the hill was a house. The house was taken over and immediately outfitted with new furniture and air-conditioning units and on the barren piece of land in front of it a foundation was poured and then the garrison's barracks hut was built and at the access road to the facility two cement posts were placed along with a horizontal chain to prevent the entry of unauthorized vehicles—an entry that was cleared in a very simple way, with the mere lifting of the hooked end of the chain that was attached to a ring fitted into one of the posts and letting the chain fall to the ground, over which the vehicles' tires would cross, leaving the road free.

Raúl was an organizer par excellence, and the effects of his heavy hand were immediately felt, not only in the improvements in my bodyguards but also because in just a few weeks I started to realize that we were building a new army. You started to detect a bearing, the shined shoes, the beards that, while not shaven, were at least groomed, the ranks of the officers placed with a certain meticulousness on the points of their collars or on their epaulets, and fewer and fewer men with rifles in the streets. Raúl was the one who surprised me one day with the proud declaration that he slept with his wife in Batista's bed, his reasoning being that you've got to seize everything from your enemy, even his bed. Well, I've always believed that he is a man of a medieval nature. He is in transit between barbarism and Renaissance culture. Perhaps that is the root of his ruthless nature, but, in turn, it also explains his need to give an honorable and wordy explanation for his darkest actions.

CELIA SPENT A WHILE removing the contents of the four large campaign pockets of my uniform—two front ones over the army jacket's breast and one on each side of my pants—the night of our arrival at the capital, while we were getting settled, for better or for worse, at the Hotel Monserrate. She removed crumbling cigars, lighters, two pairs of glasses and all kinds of papers. I precisely remember the cardboard back of a pack of Competidora Gaditana cigarettes on which someone had written for me the six or seven names of guards he was going to execute and that there were a couple of names crossed out because he decided to switch them out for two other ones. It was clear that the fellow was more concerned with the number of people he would dispose of than his reason for applying the sanction in the first place.

I estimate that in those first days we executed no less than five hundred of Batista's officers and soldiers. The consensus was that the most famous one was Colonel Cornelio Rojas, a heavyset man who gave a master class on oratory. Cornelio was one of the heads of the Batista regiment in Santa Clara and known for his cruelty. At least he walked determinedly to the firing wall, with his short-brimmed hat and his shirt hanging out of his pants. Placed in front of the barrels of different-caliber rifles of various provenances—I think an American MI carbine, a Dominican San Cristobal carbine, an American Springfield and Garand and an Italian Beretta submachine gun—he raised his right arm in a stately courtlike gesture and told his executors in a booming voice without a single note of agony or fear that they already had their revolution and that it was their duty to protect it, a very convincing and flowing speech that was interrupted by the storm of bullets that split his head open and emptied it of its contents, leaving a trail of encephalic mass and bones on the wall. They brought me a film they took of it about ten days later. Although it was silent, one could hear his voice in the spirit of his gestures, and in any event his speech was reported by the journalists present and became known all over the country. *You've got your revolution already, kids. You should protect it.* And the whole country learned of his aplomb in the face of death. I, at least, have never forgotten the determined way he lifted his right arm to accentuate his pronouncements, and how the nobility of his conduct was adulterated by the involuntary gesture of his hands, which flapped like a chicken's wings when he received the impact. His brain was already a bloody stain etched on the pores of the wall when his body suddenly lost gravity and crumpled to the right but with his little hands at the level of his chest like when Chaplin undertakes the dance of the potatoes in *The Gold Rush*. The first instance of deliberate censorship under my government may have been due to the filming of Colonel Rojas's execution. From then on, I prohibited the presence of photographers at any execution. I mean, photographers who were not under our control. Shortly after, we had to extend that type of censorship to include the personnel we were putting on trial. We had tried Jesús Sosa Blanco, another colonel under Batista, with Papito Serguera—my old *compañero* from my grade school days in Santiago—acting as the indefatigable revolutionary prosecutor, the living image of a Jacobin in the shade of our palm trees, and the decision was, of course, to execute Sosa, even though public opinion seemed to lean dangerously in favor of this Batista man. According to the study we carried out later, the soldier presented an impeccable show of courage and absolute serenity in the court of his death, and this had ended up being very bad propaganda for us. All he did was show the handcuffs we kept on his wrists and make them visible for the television cameras, smile indifferently and say, "I'm in the Roman circus," making reference to the crowd that filled the sports complex, where he was on trial, and who insulted him and asked for his execution. Finally we also had to prohibit there being any photographic evidence of the prisoners in the funeral chapel—in other words, after the trial and before the execution—because a photographer had snuck into one of the passageways of La Cabaña prison and had taken an excellent snapshot of Jesús Sosa himself extending his arms from between the medieval bars of his cell, in a useless attempt to caress his youngest daughter, who was allowed one last visit in her mother's arms.

The photo showed up on the front page of an evening newspaper called *Prensa Líbre* and caused a kind of national consternation. I used the situation, of course, so the public would fully understand how far we were about to come in the revolutionary process and I gave the relevant orders to Che, who was put in charge of La Cabaña, so that that very night, or the next morning—I don't quite remember—Sosa would be executed. Then I used a television appearance around that time to express my own consternation over the way that the media took advantage of the understandable pain of a man who was about to be executed when he saw his small child for the last time.

Let me tell you that our determination to sink our claws into Batista was paralleled by that of other *compañeros* to execute well-known thugs who had fled the country—especially to Miami. There were two colonels—Esteban Ventura Novo and Orlando Piedra Negueruela—who caught our eye. I don't know the number of times that their victims—independently—and even highly specialized sections of our intelligence services came to tell me that they had located Ventura or Piedra and had a chance to take them out. I always rejected such plans because we seemed to have little to gain from them. Nobody in the world knew these minor thugs, no matter how much they had tortured our *compañeros* or how much they had emasculated them or scratched their eyes out with a pair of scissors. The Revolution wouldn't receive any good propaganda from gunning them down at their favorite café; on the contrary, we would have raised the red flag for the American police to start keeping tabs on our clandestine structures in Miami. I always said, Focus on Batista. If I wanted to kidnap Batista, it was to make a bigger ruckus than the Israelis did with Eichmann. I explained it over and over to the people at the Ministry of the Interior. Who the hell was Esteban Ventura Nova to public international opinion? This showed me—and I write it now so my experience can serve some nascent leader—how far I had come in my learning and how much I had matured in the last few years, since my impulses and all of the human pain I could be informed of were subordinate to the praxis of propaganda and its usefulness. There was a woman in particular, named Verena del Pino Moré, from the clandestine ranks of the 26th of July Movement in Havana, who had fallen into Colonel Piedra's claws and he had raped her on some kind of gymnastics vaulting horse that seemed to have been installed by the police chief for activities of that nature in his torture chamber. Verena never overcame the traumatic episode and spent her days knocking at the doors of all of our espionage offices waving her ripped underwear with the yellowed bloodstains as irrefutable proof of her need for revenge.

There were other cases, although of a different nature. One afternoon —this was still in the early days of the Revolution—Raúl was going very slowly with one of his motorcades through the streets bordering the University of Havana when the side mirror of his Buick showed him a girl sitting on a cement block, crying inconsolably with her head in her hands. I won't name her for her own protection, but she was someone we knew. She was crying because she had lost her job and also because she feared for her life. To summarize, she confessed to Raúl that she had become the lover of the terrible Ventura to save the life of a brother whom the thug had picked up for some clandestine activities. Now everyone was alive and well. Her brother was one of the new captains in the Revolutionary National Police. Ventura, in Miami, was setting up a security company with armored trucks for the transportation of money and guards armed with sawed-off shotguns. Meanwhile, she had been disowned by her brother, ignored by Ventura, accused of being a whore and a supporter of Batista and kicked out of her job at our Treasury Department. It goes without saying that Raúl, in a quixotic gesture (which I gladly approved immediately, as soon as I got the news), took care of her, got her her job back or got her a new one in the army (I'm being vague to prevent her being identified) and gave her a phone number she could call should anything else befall her. "Raúl," I said when I ran into him, "the only thing we have to be careful of is Verena finding out."

Raúl. My brother Raúl. I don't think he'll execute anyone else in the time he has left on this earth. I mean him administering the coup de grâce himself. He's too old for that type of thing now. So I don't think I'll have another opportunity to talk to him about the matter or even reproach him for it. He led the guerrilla territories under his command with such a firm hand. I don't think anyone has executed as many people in Cuba as he did. And after the triumph of the Revolution, in January 1959, as the head of the former province of Oriente, he sent Batista-supporting journalists to their deaths in a field on the outskirts of the city. A very quick, irregular, uneven thing. A bulldozer arrived, opened up a ditch, then a truck arrived with some poor devils piled up in the back and some others on a public bus, seventy in all, who were piled out, shouting, with Raúl himself giving the order to open fire and taking out his own gun and starting to shoot at close range, so that his ten or twelve *compañeros* reacted with a certain delay and each one fired when he was ready and with the weapon available to him, a Thompson machine gun here, a revolver there, then kicking the ones whose extremities remained outside the pit, so they would fall in completely and so that when the bulldozer returned to cover and rake the ground, it wouldn't cut the bodies into pieces and leave some outside the ditch. The newspaper Raúl had pulled his victims from supported Masferrer more than Batista. Rolando Masferrer's guys. Rolando had that characteristic. It didn't matter what task he was deployed to, no matter if it was as senator of the Republic or as the head of a paramilitary force, the Tigers of Masferrer—who gave us a few bloody noses while fighting in the Sierra—he also ran a newspaper out of his camp. He wanted to kill me. He kept up the struggle. He organized the Tigers, with about three thousand men, and deployed them in the Sierra Maestra with the sole objective of hunting me. When it came to me, Rolando didn't forget a thing from our days at the university.

16

Rumor of a Besieged Plaza

///

EL AIRE LIBRE HAD BEEN OUR FAVORITE MEETING SPOT EVER since our days at the university. If we overlook the fact that it was half a block away from the Colón Cemetery, the main facility of that kind in Cuba, and the negative vibes that those places tend to have, the little café provided the appeal of being located in a strategic part of the city because the intersection was a public transportation hub, with routes coming from the four cardinal points, and because the first bundles of Havana's evening-edition newspapers were dispatched to the vendors set up there. Around three in the afternoon you could probably already get a paper, its ink fresh and its commanding red headlines announcing news that at times had just happened an hour before and of which you were often the protagonist, so you could sit down with your friends and spread that sheet open before your eyes—an *Avance*, a *Prensa Libre*, an *El País*, this last one undaunted in the solidity of its black typeface, never having the luxury of a headline in red—and you could read something in which you were mentioned or that you yourself had written while cups full of café con leche, with spoons tinkling against their edges after you'd sunk sugar into the milky brew, not only steamed but called out to you from the middle of a marble table. That was the sign of our generation and of the three or four generations of politicians and Cuban dilettantes that came before us in the Republic: the generous and excessively sweet cup of café con leche. Our plans were not the products of wine or beer, or in the tradition of Bohemian Europe of open-air cafés. We never knew the link between alcohol and dilettantism, only that of

San Julián Air Base, western Cuba, August 22, 1960, during a parade of the first military detachments. From the left: Captain Pablo Ribalta, Fidel, Che and Commander Dermidio Escalona. Escalona is the head of the provincial regiment and Che was just named military political head of the region. Ribalta would later be named Ambassador to Tanzania. But for now his assignment was to not lose sight of the Argentine.

infusions poured over pasteurized, homogenized milk and the addition of no less than three spoonfuls of refined sugar. Besides, El Aire Libre was covered—a necessary protection against the alternating inclemencies of sun and rain—at first by green awnings, then aluminum siding, and if the Revolution hadn't triumphed in January 1959, the owners were planning to install a Westinghouse air-conditioning system. You'd have to wonder if the name of the café would have survived the installation of those devices because, I think, the concept of *aire libre*, "open air," would be lost as soon as those huge vertical consoles started up. Another unforgettable part of our gatherings was the pervasive scent of flowers. All of the gardens—as the flower shop and floral arrangement businesses were known—were concentrated in that area, alternating with tombstone workshops. The employees at the gardens, to preserve the plants' vivacity, would serve them water methodically in their metallic display containers or flower beds, and protected them in the shade or under cover from the sun's inclemency. But, I estimate, the regular misting of water on the flowers was responsible for scattering their natural fragrance and spreading it around the surrounding neighborhood, while keeping the pavements slick and covered with the occasional puddle, as if a hard rain had just fallen.

Of course, greater forces caused later generations to be unaware of the mundane life that took place at El Aire Libre, our much-loved little café. To begin with, we found ourselves experiencing the need, toward the end of 1961, to ration coffee and milk, and reductions in the distribution of these products are still in place today. *Caballeros*, it's hard to believe, but it's been more than forty years of coffee with rationed milk. And, of course, public transportation was also significantly reduced and the evening newspapers were reduced to just one for a few years until finally we had to do away with that one too, the only one that was left in circulation. Problems with paper supply, you understand? Nonetheless, the glorious fact remains that that intersection of Twelfth and Twenty-third Streets was the place where, on April 16, 1961, with my entire staff on the bed of a truck set up as a platform, facing fifty thousand members of the militia making up the funeral procession for those felled the previous morning by the surprise air raid on three of our aviation bases as a prelude to the invasion of the Bay of Pigs, I declared the socialist nature of the Cuban Revolution. There's a frieze there, on the corner facing El Aire Libre, now renamed La Pelota, commemorating the event.

THIS IS THE STORY El Chino Esquivel told me, a few days before my departure for Mexico, the last time I saw him until after the triumph of the Revolution. We were at El Aire Libre, in front of our usual cups of café con leche. This was what happened in Havana while I, more than a thousand kilometers away, tried to reach the mountains close to the little Siboney ranch. I'd managed to escape the shooting in front of the walls of the Moncada Barracks and now I was headed for the mountains. If I made it to the dense forest of the mountain range, then I could decide whether to use the mountains as a refuge or an escape route. But for the time being I was in need of some shade, a jar of cold water and, if possible, a cigar. Those would be the most valued means momentarily to calm me down and allow me to think.

Such were my main existential goals around eight in the morning on Sunday, July 26, 1953—shade, water and tobacco—when Aramís Taboada, our old *compañero* from law school, called El Chino and told him that something very serious was going on in Santiago. Since it was a Sunday, El Chino thought it was too early for such a phone call. But, he told me, he felt an inexplicable fright when he heard Aramís' voice. *Something very serious is going on in Santiago.*

Aramís didn't have a car, but El Chino had a secondhand Ford that he always described as "*un forcito ahí*," but in which he had already installed one of the first air-conditioning units that came to the country. El Chino went to pick up Aramís, they greeted each other somberly, as if they alone were responsible for anything that could take place on the island, and since they weren't really certain where to go that morning on the deserted streets of Havana, they decided to go to the offices of the *Pueblo* newspaper, where another mutual friend, Luis Ortega, was the owner and director. There they met up with Fernández Macho, the former councilman of Havana and mayor of the city by statutory substitution in President Grau's time, and a lawyer, Raúl Sorí Marín, a classmate of all of ours and the brother of Humberto Sorí Marín, who was also a lawyer and a classmate and who years later I would receive as a guest in the Sierra Maestra and who, as a lot of people know, I put to work drafting the First Agrarian Reform Law and who, after the triumph of the Revolution, was caught having strange dealings with the CIA and of whom I ordered the execution along with the news of the disembarkation of the mercenary brigade at Playa Girón on April 17, 1961. So then, Luis Ortega was standing behind his desk and talking on the phone with his correspondent in Santiago. He was transmitting to those present the details of a battle that, in actuality, was already over. Luis Ortega was saying that it was a squabble between the soldiers themselves when he was interrupted by El Chino, who said, to everyone's surprise including his own, something that he had just sensed and that he blurted out without being able to control himself: "That's not the army, gentlemen. That's Fidel Castro."

"It's not?"

"It's not them."

Ortega's right hand, poised to accompany some speech, froze, and Ortega looked at El Chino, intrigued.

"It's not the army at all, gentlemen," El Chino insisted.

"El Señor Fidel Castro," he repeated.

El Chino didn't think he could delay going to my house. Aramís decided to accompany him.

I lived in the apartment in the neighborhood of Almendares, behind the guava paste factory—Dulces Villaclara—and close to La Tropical, a very well-known beer and malt manufacturer. But the dominant smell was not that of brewer's yeast but of guava, and wherever you went in that area you could feel the heavy viscosity of that product which, in the usual advertising euphemism, they called "fine creams of guava, orange, mango and fruit *turróns*," but which represented for all the residents around a heavy and solidly cloying atmosphere in which oxygen seemed to barely seep in. There were no police when El Chino arrived with Aramís. Mirta was dragging Fidelito by the arm. Mirta's expression and the careful slowness with which she opened the door, and the relief she felt upon identifying her visitors, confirmed all of El Chino's suspicions. "I have never seen so much terror in one expression," El Chino told me. "Never."

El Chino avoided all of the evasive devices of rhetoric that could be used in a conversation of this type. He was direct.

"Mirta, *this* is Fidel."

"Yes," Mirta said. Or rather, nodded in agreement.

El Chino turned to Aramís.

"Didn't I tell you that this was Fidel's doing?"

Satisfied with his wise declaration, he turned his gaze back on Mirta.

"Well, Mirta, what did he tell you?"

"He came by a few days ago and picked up two pairs of underwear and told me he was going to Pinar del Río."

Pinar del Río is in the diametric opposite direction to Santiago. Complete opposite.

"Chino," Mirta told him, "I don't have any food and I owe rent on the house."

El Chino gave her all the loose change he had on him.

El Chino was telling me this story and I was thinking about how right I was in leaving for Moncada and not worrying about anything I was leaving behind; a simple blink of the eyes, a simple moment of hesitation, and the Cuban Revolution would have never existed. Here you have the naked truth about the origins of a movement of historic dimensions: that I picked up a couple pairs of briefs at my house and told my wife I was going in the complete opposite direction of where I was really headed. To renounce and distance yourself from the most basic earthly details and their probable, small rewards. I don't know any other vocation that ignores more human possibilities than that of revolutionary leadership. Perhaps at the beginning there is some hope that at a given stage in the process there will be a rest, like the landing in a flight of stairs, and you reestablish your position as a mere mortal. Well, that never happens, let me tell you. There are no landings on the stairs. In any event, the attack on Moncada taught me to leave domestic logistics in the hands of others. You concentrate on the battle, it's up to God to provide soup to the hungry mouths back at home.

"What about *el retiro*, Mirta? Do you have the *retiro* papers?"

At this point, Mirta was on the verge of losing control and she started to sob from deep within her chest and her eyes were blinded by a veil of tears. She had understood the situation El Chino was warning her about without any room for misinterpretation. The *retiro* became, upon the death of its bearer, the spouse's pension.

Prevented from using her voice by the intensity of the emotions overtaking her, Mirta could only nod and, in an absentminded gesture, cover her upper lip with the lower one.

El Chino decided to carry out his mission to gather contributions by knocking on all the doors he could. He was in the middle of this when two cars blocked his way that afternoon. Rafaelito Díaz-Balart and his bodyguard. "I've been looking for you all day," he said to him. Rafaelito had a plan. "An idea," as he described it to El Chino. The idea was to get a group of four or five young guys together. People who were more or less known in politics, to go to the nunciature and request an urgent meeting with Arteaga, the only existing cardinal in Cuba at the time, so that he would intercede with Batista and not have me killed. Meanwhile, Rafaelito said, he would go "talk to the chief"—Batista.

So El Chino convened the group proposed by Rafaelito and took them to the nunciature, a carefully maintained colonial-era building located in the city's historic district. Seminarian Raúl del Valle saw them first and asked them to sit in the hall and wait. The seminarian left them, closing the door behind him. Silence. Ten or twelve minutes passed. Steps outside the door. The seminarian returned and asked his distinguished visitors to please follow him. They took a set of wooden stairs up to the second floor. There was a door at the end of a hallway. The cardinal received them on an inner terrace. He was seated on a wooden armchair and didn't stand to greet them. He was a thin man with severe scoliosis that kept him facing down at the floor, and the play of light shining through the areca palm leaves behind the back of his chair made him appear ghostly. A scar from a hastily stitched wound crossed his face from the edge of his red beret to just between his brows. Each man went to him, knelt before him and kissed his cardinal's ring. Arteaga extended his hand coldly to facilitate the transaction. Arteaga displayed the last vestige of the wardrobe before the reform initiated by Paul VI between 1963 and 1978 which would do away with the privilege of the train and abolish the use of the hat, in addition to the sublime weave of the undergarments and the silk beret, except for the trapezoid-shaped headdress that the popes imposed on their eminencies to symbolize the rank of cardinal, which would remain the only souvenir of the golden age of ecclesiastic fashion. And such was the adornment that Cardinal Manuel Arteaga Betancourt, with a slow, bored gesture, adjusted over himself, perhaps to fix its position on his bony head. Then he placed his tired hands on the folds of his cassock, where a cheap cardboard fan rested. The delegates quickly launched into their explanation and the cardinal didn't show any sign of wanting to come out of his torpor until, with all of his dialectic skill, Aramís mentioned the fact that I was the son of one of the wealthiest families in the north of Oriente. Upon realizing the immediate success of his stratagem— a flash of light in His Eminence's eyes—Aramís began to describe my father's sugarcane estate as if it were the Spanish Empire in the century following the discovery of America, on which the sun never set. "The kid is a little crazy, Your Eminence," Aramís said, "but he comes from a good family." "Youthful recklessness, my child. Youthful recklessness," the revitalized cardinal remarked. Then he immediately suggested he call the first lady himself, Martha Fernández Miranda de Batista; the solemn and vain Colonel Alberto del Río Chaviano, commander of the Moncada Regiment; and His Eminence and his very dear friend, Bishop of Santiago, Monsignor Pérez Serante. At least the call to Pérez Serante was made in front of them. The young seminarian who obviously acted as his assistant placed the white telephone on a little table to Arteaga's left. The device was connected by a long cable, also white, to some socket out of view in the adjoining room. "Please connect me with His Eminence the Bishop of Santiago." As could be assumed, His Eminence the Bishop of Santiago was up to speed on what had happened, and not only that, but, with the help of the Almighty, had already taken the first steps in an effort to restore peace and concord among the Cuban people. At least the Cubans in his region. The cardinal instructed the bishop to do everything in his power to preserve the life of Dr. Fidel Castro, the well-loved son of the illustrious Castro Ruz family of Birán. An impetuous lad, for lack of a better term, but a fervent Catholic educated under the wings of the wisdom and guidance of the brothers of the Company of Jesus—all information, as you can assume, that had just been supplied by the group before him. Then, waving his fan in an effort to provide his tired head with a bit of fresh air, the cardinal told them that his secretary, the young seminarian, would be in touch with them by telephone regarding the next steps to take. He kept his promise with startling efficiency. That afternoon they were informed to appear at Camp Columbia the next day, where they would be taken by military plane to be present at what would supposedly be my capture, and an immediate negotiation to prevent my being lynched. As you can assume, that was as far as his negotiations went. Because the next day, upon arriving at Columbia, they were met by a lieutenant assigned to inform them that the trip had been called off and—he added—the truth was that the troops in Santiago were threatening to revolt if anyone dared capture me alive.

It's strange that no one has ever relayed this story about the cardinal's intercession. The publication of some of these details would have been difficult to manage from a publicity standpoint, unless I had been willing to offend the sensibilities of many of my followers or at least held back from attacking Rolando Amador, Rafaelito and the cardinal. These three all ended up going over to the side of the counterrevolution almost at the beginning of the process, and since then, thanks to the files compiled on them, I would not even hesitate before the dilemma of whether to forgive them for old times' sake or break their balls like anyone else. I'm not talking about El Chino, because he was never a counterrevolutionary activist. Nor will I dwell on Rolando Amador, because he was a small-time enemy to me. Cardinal Arteaga, however, was one of the early standard-bearers of the Cuban bourgeoisie in their fight against the Revolution, and he himself offered to distribute the first of the Church's pastoral letters against me and to organize a National Catholic Congress in November 1959 that in reality was a well-planned attempt at urban rebellion and a warning to us. Although its message could appear very confusing to those who hadn't been warned, I took all due precautions. Thousands of Catholics turned out—from the provinces to Havana— staying at the houses of thousands of other parishioners, all under the control of the prelates and the neighborhood churches that abounded at the time. They also made excellent use of the schools and charitable institutions they owned or managed for logistical support. The plan they developed included taking La Virgen de la Caridad del Cobre* across the island. To achieve this, they undertook a relay marathon, leaving the Sanctuary of el Cobre, in Oriente Province, and, advancing before the float with the image of the Virgin, members of Catholic Youth, and believers in general, they passed a torch that supposedly identified their counterrevolutionary yearnings. In sum, it was about placing the Virgen de la Caridad in competition against me. At least, the journey from the outskirts of Santiago—where the Sanctuary of el Cobre is located—to Havana was the same as my Freedom Caravan of eleven months before. At sunset on November 28, the marathon ended on the esplanade called the Civic Plaza (rechristened a few months later as the Plaza of the Revolution), where they managed to bring together five hundred thousand parishioners for a mass before this venerated image. At the appearance of the plaster statue, carried on the shoulders of a squadron of visionaries, applause resounded loudly all through the plaza.

---

* Our Lady of Charity, the patron saint of Cuba. [*Translator's note.*]

This was the moment in which my *compañeros* began to show their nervousness. We were at the Armed Revolutionary Forces Ministry, which had already been set up perfectly in the former naval chief of staff building, and we watched the ceremony on a couple of televisions we had there. Raúl wanted to plow tanks over them. His opinion was seconded by a dozen commanders who were gathered there. I had to ask them to calm down and reflect. In the first place, what tanks were we talking about? We had to extend the lives of the fifteen old pieces of junk that we had at Camp Managua, to the southwest of Havana. And how did they wish to carry out this massacre? In front of television cameras and in plain sight of the whole world? They didn't understand. That's the kind of battle one is never allowed to accept. They're the battles that are avoided because you win them after the fact, when the conditions and the terrain are favorable to you. And that happens when you later grab them, one by one, all alone in their homes. The closing ceremony was planned for the following day, with a procession down a centrally located avenue and ending at the baseball stadium, before some forty thousand members of the organization Acción Católica (I myself have no idea how many members of that organization we executed in later years). Up until that moment, they hadn't had the courtesy to invite me to any of their events. But I beat them to the avenue and made my way smoothly through the crowd and got in front of the procession. I had taken out all of my scapularies, chains and religious medals that I wore around my neck in the Sierra Maestra to receive American photographers and I put them on again for the occasion. But they were lucky. Another way to say it: their luck lay in the coldness of my calculations. There wasn't a single priest killed in Cuba then, nor has there ever been as a result of revolutionary violence throughout our entire process. I even took that possibility of martyrdom away from them. "I don't want any of these faggots killed," I made it very clear to the officers in charge of operatives or street demonstrations against the churches. "You can kill an altar boy. But this has to happen outside the church. Preferably on his way home and in a distant neighborhood."

I'll tell you something. There is no work requiring greater precision and the exercise of painstaking control than that of dealing with street demonstrations. If just one detail were to escape us, like, for example, that a civilian be carrying an unnoticed firearm and that he take it out and use it in a moment of confrontation, or that the crowds manage to break the doors, or the gates, or the windows, and enter buildings to siege them, we would be on our way to a civil war. Almost all civil wars begin as a demonstration that goes out of control. In this case our tactics were consistent. (1) Stay ahead of the game by organizing our own demonstrations; in other words, carry out in practice the theory that was institutionalized through the revolutionary process, which is winning the streets, or, if you will, controlling the streets. Don't ever forget this when the time comes to study the Revolution, because it has been the basic concept of our uninterrupted path of victories: *winning the streets*. (2) The only people authorized to carry firearms—*and only small ones*—were those belonging to police or security forces, and the use was only and strictly allowed in extreme cases and to fire into the air. This team of personnel was responsible for establishing the topographical limits of the demonstration and enforcing their investiture as agents of order. In regard to the demonstrators, they're only there to yell, until the blood vessels in their necks burst if they wish, and to act angry with their left fists raised up over their heads. The range of violence, of course, is carefully controlled by our own agitation personnel and through the tactical distribution of propaganda through the crowd. The corporal punishment exerted on our adversary—and only against carefully defined and situated objectives—couldn't exceed a few kicks. Never shoot. And never—please, never!—carry rifles, or at least don't let them be seen outside of patrol cars. They're not necessary, and besides give the undesirable impression of a state of siege. (3) Prevent the enemy or adversary from gathering in groups of more than two or three individuals and from setting up his own demonstration unit. Those embryos had to be destroyed before they were even set up and that's a procedure we called group-breaking. They're easily identified because it always happens on the outsides of our mass of demonstrators and because through unconscious nonverbal language they're communicating their growing suicidal impulse, typical of the petit bourgeois' eagerness to play the leading role. So a few days after this fervor and possible increase in clerical hope, in one of my television appearances I brought up the subject in order to snuff it out. I remember that I whispered something in very poor taste to Raúl before sitting down in front of the cameras. I'm going to repeat it here because it's a strictly historical detail. And while I don't think even Raúl would remember it now, in which case history could well do without the phrase, I don't want to leave any loose ends, not even floating in the nebulousness of a recollection that is more than fifty years old. I reiterate my apologies for the vulgarity. But I said to Raúl, "I'm going to make Cardinal Arteaga shit through his mouth." I knew that he had colon cancer and that he'd had a colostomy. My statement that night that we had in our possession hundreds of bank checks in the sum of thousands of dollars made out in the name of Cardinal Arteaga in the bloodthirsty dictator Fulgencio Batista's own handwriting and that photographs of such would be published the next day in the newspaper *Revolución* caused a succession of intestinal obstructions and a deterioration in the prelate's general health. Whether he literally found himself obliged to take care of his necessities through his throat or not remained in the strength of his pyloric sphincter. Damn. This paragraph is such an unpleasant tirade. But that's how things were. And it couldn't have been any other way with the consequences of his use of his rectal tube, his macerated rectal tube.

I doubt that foreign readers or Cubans born after the Revolution are aware of one of the greatest scandals of Cuban high society in the 1950s— an episode apropos of this behavior. Héctor Duarte, a gunman who used to supplement his earnings as the favorite of the cardinal's sexual fancies, did not receive the fee he thought he had earned on one occasion and, without even giving the cardinal time to yell, he removed the cardinal ring from His Eminency's finger and using it as a sharp instrument of perforation or perhaps as a five-inch dagger, ripped open Arteaga's skin with a wound that went from the edge of where his beret normally sat to just between his brows, causing the Cardinal to fall to the floor unconscious and covered in blood, while Héctor put the ring in his pocket and went to the closest pawnshop. They didn't give him much, according to my information, about forty pesos. These dark details about Arteaga's personal life could appear excessive, reasonably so to some readers. But in my opinion they're indispensable to understanding the dubious morals of characters like this, the high cost it had in national public opinion, and its subsequent responsibility for weakening the Cuban Church. Before turning the page, let me tell you about this old man's last dirty trick. It was April 17, 1961, when Arteaga entered the grounds of the Argentine Embassy in Havana and requested diplomatic protection out of fear of being arrested and executed. It was already public knowledge that that morning an enemy group had disembarked in the Bay of Pigs, and what haunted the Cuban clergyman was a mix of bloody episodes that amplified themselves, such as the Spanish Civil War and the number of priests, always increasing, *shot down from the belfries* by my own hand during the Bogotazo in Colombia. Cardinal Arteaga's polished black Cadillac rolling through the gravel path up to the door of the mansion occupied by the Argentine chancery and the doors opening to reveal a squadron of diplomats and servants, and surely Monsignor Raúl del Valle, falling all over themselves to extract the exhausted Cardinal Arteaga with the least damage possible, this is surely the end of Catholicism in Cuba.

The seminarian. As far as my information goes, he was ordained as a priest at some point and in the late fifties he had already been recompensed with the title of monsignor, although he stayed on as Cardinal Arteaga's secretary more or less until the latter's death at a Havana hospital in 1963. Then he left Cuba and ended up in New York. And there he became Cardinal O'Connor's secretary. A true promotion in his functions as an ecclesiastic aide-de-camp, rising to the shadow of the head of New York's archdiocese. But, sometime in the late eighties, the priest got cancer, although I'm not sure what kind. The fact is that Cardinal John O'Connor was a very good friend of ours and used to fly to Havana from New York in his Learjet, almost always with some message from the pope or other Vatican official and always accompanied by the priest who was now a monsignor. O'Connor was, for example, the person who pushed Mother Teresa of Calcutta's visit on me; in other words, he practically forced me to receive her in Havana, although he was also skillful enough to tell me that I would have her in my pocket if I let her set up half a dozen of her hospices in Cuba. Those Catholic institutions, staffed with nuns, are something that have always benefited us, not only because it's excellent propaganda to demonstrate our tolerance in religious matters, but also because those little nuns solved some social problems with a portion of our elderly, beside the fact that the Church itself takes care of supplies. I also do my part, of course. I remember that in the early sixties, when the first batch of twenty-five Soviet Volga cars arrived, which Aníbal Escalante and other communists distributed between the Central Committee and the *Noticias de Hoy* newspaper, which was reporting to them as their official organ, I set aside some of those cars and sent them free of cost to the little nuns at the hospices. I did the same with some television sets that came to our port and some refrigerators and blenders. So Madame Teresa of Calcutta was going to be well received and we would immediately accept all of the hospices she wished to set up and supply and the number of nuns she thought convenient to bring to staff these facilities. One thing in our favor: in Cuba, there's no leprosy or tuberculosis, so her nuns would have a less stressful job. Regarding that poor devil the monsignor, hopelessly sentenced to death, he understood that the situation entitled him to one last wish, so he spoke to Cardinal O'Connor and asked O'Connor to come up with an excuse to send him to Havana, for any reason. His last wish was to wander the streets of his childhood neighborhood. All it took was one telephone conference between O'Connor and me for his Learjet to receive the authorization to land in Havana.

That O'Connor was a very funny guy. I remember that they patched his call through to me on one of those devices connected to the battery of telephones behind the back of my reclining chair. "The cardinal," he said to me, referring to himself in the third person, "has the weekend free and is pondering the convenience of hopping on down to Cuba." He just wanted to know if His Excellency, the Cuban President, was in disposition to receive him. We would follow our usual program. Go to Cayo Piedra and devote a few afternoons to drinking wine from my finest reserve, taste cheeses, and he would smoke a dozen Cohiba Lanceros. And while he submitted to gourmet pleasures, he would force me, hilariously, to repeat once and again all of the bad things I had done to the Catholic Church in Cuba. Then, the Cuban cigars crammed into his Learjet—around which no New York customs agent ever dared sniff—we would say goodbye. My convoy of armored Mercedes would cross the tarmac up to the stairs of his plane and there I would receive, with an unpretentious smile, his blessing. "Goodbye, dear friend," I would say to him. "Goodbye, my beloved son," he would reply.

I DON'T WANT TO come across as cynical, and especially not when it comes to retelling my life and all of its accompanying commotion, but the speed with which I am forced to explain some things might lead you to that conclusion. When you begin by telling the ending, it's like only showing that which lies on the surface of liquid poured into a container and you don't express everything that was inside, the material at the heart of it, and if you don't explain that your actions arose from your needs, then you can make a very bad impression. Let's just assume that I say I killed General Arnaldo Ochoa or sent Che to his death and withhold my reasons from the reader. I would come across very badly if I didn't first explain the reasons that led me to act, and if the evidence didn't convince the reader and get him to take my side and say, Damn, he left him no other option, I myself would have volunteered for the coup de grâce. But in reality, at times the writing of this chapter about the first months of the Revolution has been almost as hard for me as controlling the development of events as they were happening in real life. After Bay of Pigs, it doesn't happen that way, because from then on my power is absolutely consolidated and let's say that beginning with that battle my existence has been a series of more or less happy anecdotes with the scales tipped in my favor. Oh, the reasoning. You don't know the miracles I've worked with my very efficient use of reasoning in combination with my powers of discourse. The struggle in the Sierra was my best lab, in that sense. And my best example is that of a kid they called Menguado Echavarría and who—in the periphery of the territories already under our control— went around with a small guerrilla team of three or four acolytes, attacking isolated farms and engaging in a sufficient quantity of affairs with the peasant girls to qualify before them and especially their fathers as a confirmed rapist. There were other guerrillas who went around as "free agents"—as we said—and they were starting to damage our reputation and affect our finances by acting out of control and pocketing their earnings. I sent Camilo to arrest them for me. He brought about fifty of them from three bands that were running around scattered in the plains: to our knowledge, the band led by Chino—Chino being the nickname used in Cuba for anyone with almond-shaped eyes—a certain Merengue's band, and that belonging to Echavarría. The trial, which had to be one of the quickest in the campaign, took an unexpected turn. The idea was to execute the leaders and incorporate the rest into our columns. But the attitude of this Echavarría complicated things. He became really contrarian. Before the trial he acted aggressive, intolerant and despotic. That's my most elegant translation of the five or six ways he told us to go to hell. I immediately gave orders to prevent his escape, in other words, to have him tied up. We had another problem with Echavarría: that two of his brothers were captains of our columns and that his parents had given us shelter and food in our most difficult days. To forgive him or make him the recipient of a more benign sentence was entirely impossible if we needed to make an example of him and, given the circumstances, executing the other two leaders was necessary. This was the first challenge: how to make sure that young man was taken to his death while I remained as innocent as a lamb in the eyes of his parents and two valiant brothers. The other challenge was caused by his own attitude of disrespect. Then I decided to reason. This was the main thread of my dialectic development: "You know that your whole family is in the Revolution. That you yourself got to be a lieutenant because of your acts of valor and because of your sacrifices. Your brothers are heroes and your parents are proud of their participation. I would like you, and no one but you, as a revolutionary, as an active revolutionary militant, to be the one to say whether I should execute you or not." We had to rob him of the feeling of being wronged—of seeing his old *compañeros* lift the barrels of their carbines to kill him—and replace it with that of a patriot rendering a service that is highly valued. Even so, don't think it was easy for me. Those who were with me during that process know that I spent more than a day—I would guess twenty-five hours, approximately—in trying to convince him that what was going to happen to him was fair. First I ordered the removal of Chino's and Merengue's dead bodies. I took him below a *guásima* tree and told them to untie him and leave us alone. I had already managed to get him to stop looking at me suspiciously and mistrustfully, which I had achieved by sending for cigarettes for him—I remember that he told me he smoked Trinidad & Hermanos—and a plate of vegetables with a little bit of meat. Echavarría reached the conclusion that he should be executed upon finishing the fourth pack of those harsh cigarettes, in other words, sixty-four cigarettes from one day to the next, since there were sixteen cigarettes in each pack. But I realized that he had made a pact with me when the heavy streams of sweat began to dissipate and the smell of his skin became tolerable. I talked nonstop during those twenty-five hours and my reasoning centered on the single notion that even if he were executed he would still be a revolutionary and that there was something differentiating him from the other two we had executed (Chino and Merengue): that he was one of ours. The notion of death in and of itself, of its own terror, was absolutely secondary in our shared conversation. Or what I thought was a conversation, since such a thing doesn't exist if only one person is speaking. But the situation couldn't have been any more propitious to obtaining the necessary results: the *jefe máximo* of the Revolution seated on the ground at your side beneath a *guásima* tree devotes more than a day to explaining his detailed reasoning in regards to a decision concerning you and makes you feel how intensely he needs your cooperation. In reality what was being asked of him was a slight change in the order of things at an execution: instead of being in the firing squad, he would be in front of it. His breath had noticeably stabilized when he stood up slowly, wiped off the seat of his pants and said to me, "Do me one last favor, send for them to get me a few more cigarettes and to give me a few sheets of paper and a pencil. I'd like to write to my folks." It was the first time that a man sentenced to death in the Sierra asked to write his farewell. I couldn't help but show my admiration. It must have been because we were executing the first peasant who wasn't illiterate. A small detail. I remember that, upon his rising, his stiff blue pants, of the type used in Cuba to work in the fields, remained above his ankles, perhaps due to the effect of having been seated for so long, and since the fabric was so impregnated with sweat and earth and the dampness of nights in the Sierra after weeks of not being washed, it meant he had to shake his legs vigorously for the cuffs to fall back to their usual position above the tongue of his very cheap boots. The detail I want to share with you is that I felt inexplicably unsettled upon realizing that Echavarría didn't have any socks on. That there was no layer of protection between his feet and the coarse interior of his shoe. And the inexplicability of the effect of this detail is that no one in the Sierra wore socks around then and probably weren't even aware of their existence, so I've always asked myself why I felt such anguish when I saw his thin, earth-covered ankles. I'll finish up on this note. Echavarría wrote extensive letters to his parents and brothers, forgave his judges and executioners in them, and considered their actions just. I told Camilo to execute him himself. It was, perhaps, a spurious consideration, but a consideration all the same. Because in some strange way we thought that if it was Camilo who killed him, something of Camilo's smile and sweet presence would have a soothing effect on the execution. Then a number of *compañeros* approached me with Echavarría's letters in their hands. I didn't want to read them until after he had been executed. Camilo, given his sensitive nature, cried like a boy during the two or three minutes it took to execute him.

MY SECOND NIGHT in the capital, I got away from the hotel and took a motorcade of two or three Cadillacs—I was still using Batista's and would continue to do so for a few more weeks—to go do some reconnaissance. What I saw in the city that night spurred me to draw up immediate plans. I had a very clear idea of what I had to do. First I must destroy the plutocracy, because the only formula for absolute government in this country is for everyone to be equal. I had conceived of their annhilation when I was still in the Sierra Maestra. Of course, I would not destroy them with tanks because that would surely be unnecessary, in addition to creating very bad propaganda. The other thing was to place under siege this dazzling and freewheeling city that I was rediscovering and that had been filling me with negative premonitions since receiving me as a hero just a few hours ago. This city, I reasoned, was the only one that could rise up against me. And right away, I was telling Camilo to place the units he captured at the service of this mission, but to remove them from Columbia and deploy them to, for example, Managua—a town about fifteen minutes away, where the army's barracks were for the time being next to the Cadets' School—and to only admit men from Oriente for training. Then I realized that Camilo wasn't really the man for the job, because, among other things, he was also from Havana.* From the start we called it Operation Budapest, with our objectives clearly determined. Resentment hit me head-on the previous afternoon when our convoy arrived at the city's main intersection. It was the new main intersection because the city center appeared to have moved from the neocolonial center of streets with Castillian names like Galiano, Neptuno or San Rafael to that area of new skyscrapers and television towers known as La Rampa. My arrival at that new neurological center of the country's capital would later receive the benefit of the modern equivalent of Greek friezes: its reproduction on the bills in current circulation. There I am, on what is supposed to be my Sherman tank, with my arm raised and surrounded by my rebel *compañeros*, receiving the acclaim of an entire people as I arrive at the intersection of L and Twenty-third Streets. What that scene drawn by Czech National Bank artists, to whom we entrusted the issuing of our

---

* Besides, Camilo was already proving to be quite problematic. The dance put on by his friend, a guy by the name of El Coyote, or Humbertico Núñez, plus a heterogeneous crowd of distinguished potheads from the Havana neighborhood of Lawton, only seemed to hint at stormy times with our Gentleman of the Vanguard—such was the princelike name our guerrilla had bestowed upon him. Gentleman of the Vanguard. A beauty of a name. Battle-hardened. On the other hand, an old man with glasses, Captain Lázaro Soltura, his assistant from the Sierra, whom I personally asked to help me guide Camilo down the right path, given his youth and the inevitable temptations of being young and powerful, decided it was better to corrupt himself with Camilo—if it came to that—than to collaborate on my regenerative effort. "We have a better time with Camilo than with Fidel," was the expression that reached my ears through Captain Soltura while he pontificated on a binge of whores and rebels. [*Author's note.*]

new paper money, does not register is, from the top of my tank and basking in the nation's attention, I was a man with deep suspicions.

AND WE WENT TO WORK. On January 9, in the morning, once the headache of moving from the Hotel Monserrate to the Havana Hilton was done, I started a series of meetings of a secret nature. I already had some ideas about how to run my government. I knew, especially since mid-1958, when I first planned my conspiratorial flirtations with the leadership of Batista's army, that you shouldn't leave the enemy completely bereft of a leader. I sent for some kids who had stood out in the underground battle but who had common origins. I wanted them to be petit bourgeois, with some disciplinary issues and who had no knowledge of ideology. With Celia's help, I picked five or six of them and we set the meetings, but at different times so that they wouldn't see each other. In any event, there was such a ruckus of people going to and fro in the hallway leading to my suite at the Hilton that it was like trying to point someone out in Times Square, so I shouldn't have been too concerned about their recognizing each other later. And nobody noticed their neighbor in a crowd. All eyes were on me. The task, I told each kid as Celia locked him in the room—prepared for the effect with the suite's interchangeable panels and manned on the other side by a rebel armed with a bipod BAR and two strips of bullets crossed over his chest to prevent the entrance of any unauthorized personnel—and which I entered through a side door—also interchangeable—the task, as I was saying, was to return to their provinces or neighborhoods of origin and start to carry out small sabotage jobs. *Small to begin with.* I remember one of their names: Luis Felipe Bernaza, who later achieved a certain level of fame as filmmaker. Their jaws dropped when I proposed the mission. I had to explain to them what was going to happen in Cuba in the coming months, which was the development of virulent conspiracies to overthrow the Revolution. Although none of them realized at the time that they were receiving a lesson in historical materialism, especially the chapters describing the confrontation of classes, and that the situation which I was starting to describe to them first as an unending struggle against Batista's supporters, squealers and other collaborators with the old regime—to which we would add large landholders two or three months later and then expand to include tycoons a few months after

that, until in the end it was this big bag where we would put the imperialists and all of their henchmen—was the counterrevolution. The goal
was for them to start to make a name for themselves with these activities
so that they would attract a following. The goal was that when the counterrevolution awoke and was willing to fight, we would have their leaders ready for them. The objective was to stay ahead of the game. There
was a very big war coming—I explained—and when this should happen, they were not going to surprise us because we'd already be waiting
for them, and with the ability to provide their leaders. We were going
to direct the counterrevolution. I must confess that it was a stratagem
with a twofold purpose. The reality of kids like Luis Felipe Bernaza
was that, because of their class conditions, they were authentic counterrevolutionaries, and that's why I asked Celia to help me pick them
out according to the names that some of the resistance leaders gave me.
I knew the characteristics I was looking for, as I said above: undisci-
plined (in other words, inherently irreverent), lacking in ideology (in
other words, not predisposed to being morally broken) and petit bourgeois (in other words, not necessarily tied to an economic group and
with a relationship to the bourgeois that had more to do with envy than
attraction). They ended up being the best. I understand the key to their
success was that they made a game of what they would have actually
done if I hadn't recruited them beforehand. But, in addition, the risk
they ran was minimal. They were on the side of power and at the same
time they enjoyed the last sinecures of the Cuban bourgeois. In that
sense, I also got ahead of them. With an enormous amount of time on
my side, I snatched them away from the adversary's forces. But in addition we were dealing with very dangerous men, of proven courage and
with a considerable death toll produced in each of their places of origin,
and it wasn't at all advisable to leave them at the disposal of the counterrevolution. They each had the prospectus of a young killer who had
populated the ranks of the underground battle. All of them had killed.
From a very young age.

In *compañero* Bernaza's case, after conversing with me, he headed
toward Santiago's Instituto—the high school where he was studying—
and set some trash cans on fire and tarred and feathered a janitor. A good
start. So much so that, two years later, by the disembarkation at Playa
Girón, he was the head of the schools sector of the counterrevolutionary
organizations operating clandestinely in Santiago.

THE SITUATION REGARDING armored matériel was disappointing. Using one of my favorite of Stalin's axioms as an instrument for reflection —that strategy is reserve—I was realizing that we wouldn't get very far with the tanks we inherited from Batista. Although there certainly were enough of them to control a situation—*for the time being.* The choice of the horse-raising center in Managua, at the foot of the mountains to the southwest of the capital, was a good one. In the first place because it was twenty minutes from access to the city, on the west end. One of those tanks, by its treads, needed just one hour to make it to the city center and start shooting down anything it was ordered to shoot. Over the course of the following years, we took various measures to speed up the journey to the city. The main one was the design and construction of the so-called First Ring bypass of Havana, an eight-lane highway that allowed us to send the tank regiments from the western theater of operations—destined to defend the city of Havana—by any of its approaches, except for, of course, from the ocean, and to make the permanent location of these forces more efficient by making a first-class highway pass right by their main doors. Also—and this information is little known—a considerable portion of the First Ring was designed to be used as a combat aviation runway and included the construction of subterranean shelters in the farms lining the highway for the eventual preservation of our MiGs. It's incredible, but all of this dissipated, as I tend to tell my *compañeros*, like a midsummer night's dream. That was the apex of our military deployment, when we were one of the few countries in the world who spoke of geopolitics in our own terms and with over five hundred tanks deployed in the southern cone of Africa to guarantee these pretensions of ours, even forcing Ronald Reagan to describe us as a little mouse with imperialist airs. What a son of a bitch. I remember that I would stand at the end of one of those stretches of highway closed off to traffic and in five minutes it was turned into a combat aviation runway and the MiG-21bis would start to come out from beneath the surrounding hills and take off into the air one after another with the familiar hum of a take-off and I, at the height of my power, always a real joker, would turn toward the Soviet staff officers who were with me and say to them, "We don't want you to come tell us later that we're a Soviet aircraft carrier anchored off American shores." After the disappearance of the USSR, understandably, we'd return to the policy of the obsolete tanks. I would say that with a medium T-55 or T-62 tank, we could control the streets of Havana. Geopolitics has been dramatically simplified. The second basic principle of using the tanks—and you'll see it written here for the first time—is that if a mass deployment is what's needed to conquer a territory, an armored company dispersed in the city is enough to smash any urban uprising.

The fifteen A34 Comets arrived in Cuba before our triumph, along with fifteen Sea Fury combat planes. Although, as is known, none of this equipment ended up being operable for Batista's final battles, we were the beneficiaries; at least it allowed us to have an initial supply of new non-American matériel and whet our appetite for European matériel. Even better, it showed us that the American market was expendable and that we had nothing to fear from its embargos. That's something we owe Batista and his negotiators and this is the first time that I allow myself to accept this publicly. The Belgian FAL rifles were also on their way. They bought a first lot of twenty thousand and we bought another twenty thousand. But, at the end of 1959, when Foreign Minister Raúl Roa landed in London as my special envoy, Prime Minister Harold Macmillan received him with a diatribe that England emphatically condemned the death penalty, a none-too-subliminal reference to our massive executions of Batista supporters. I had hoped to exchange the lot of Sea Furys for reaction engine planes, but then he started harping on this. Roa, in any event, was delighted. "What?" he exclaimed. "You've finally decided to oppose the executioner's ax? I must inform Havana immediately. Because you've really made heads roll around *here*!" Macmillan didn't offer any condolences for the Sea Fury planes and the Comet tanks sold to Batista. As long as the armaments were to wipe out revolutionaries! Nor would any tears be shed two years later when those same machines, recycled for my benefit, were used—at least the Furys—to crush the Bay of Pigs invasion. But Batista's soldiers and confidants fell like flies before the armaments of North American and Dominican provenance. We blew Cornelio Rojas's brains out and smeared them across a Santa Clara wall as a result of the combined firing power of magnificent American MI carbines handed over to Cuba by virtue of the Mutual Economic Aid Pact and some Dominican San Cristobal carbines and no one complained to the providers, nor did the executioners doing the executing complain to the previous executioners. That's the problem with countries like us that don't produce weapons, we're later subject to the provider's capricious critiques. And British engineers—imperturbable with their plaid scarves around their necks and pipes in their mouths—kept arriving each morning to assemble tanks without taking into account that right under their noses those tanks had been deposed from the battlefields of one army and that another army had taken possession of the same.

May 15, 1960. Fidel and Che participate in a Hemingway Fishing Tournament, off the coast of Havana. Fidel fishes for marlin while Che participates as a reader of Stendhal. Later, he moves on to Konstantin Simonov.

17

THE SACRED BRETHREN

///

It was, if you will, the outline of a theory about man and his powers; restored by means of a counterblow; no one had devised it, but it already contained the root of radicalism, since it should facilitate the Cubans' way of thinking about their condition and changing it.

—JEAN-PAUL SARTRE:
"IDEOLOGY AND
REVOLUTION"

I EXPERIENCED A SERIOUS SETBACK REGARDING POPULAR SENTI-
ment in the early weeks of the Revolution. In one of my televised appearances, a journalist asked me if I considered it appropriate for a black
man to *piropear*, "make flirtatious comments," to a white woman. The
question was so absurd and so inherently racist that I nearly jumped
on the idiot's jugular. But I must confess that it caught me by surprise,
and this resulted in an absurd and poorly thought-out response on my
part. I said it was as reprehensible as a white man to *piropear* with a black
woman and that the best thing, in short, would be if nobody engaged
in any *piropos* with anyone. Allow me to explain to my foreign readers
who may not be familiar with the custom of flirting as a particularly
Cuban art with deep roots and, in the end, as a demonstration of wit
and popular imagination as well as an indisputable celebration of feminine beauty. A man was expected to say *something* to beautiful girls when
they passed in front of him, and it was even more expected from a group

of men. Although there was no shortage of crude comments and certain uncalled-for expressions, the best competed for their poetic qualities. You had to smother a girl with attention as she passed. It was even known that women dressed up and put on their finest in order to be the objects of a good *piropo,* an innocent and imaginative game played by an entire population, if you will. And it so happened that I went and made that stupid comment on television. I think the only time in my entire political career that I have gone back on something I've said was regarding *piropos.* But I was just short of provoking a national uprising. I called Commander Efigenio Amejeiras, who had just been named chief of the National Revolutionary Police, and gave him exact instructions. "*Coño*, Efigenio, I beg you, please, don't arrest anyone for making a *piropo.*" Efigenio's response was symptomatic of how the country felt. "Listen, Fidel, is it true that you're going to forbid *piropos?* Fidel. Fidel. Have you gone crazy, Fidel?" I recalled how many police and uniformed men called out *piropos* at women on Cuba's streets, and I ran to a television station to emphatically declare that it had all been a misunderstanding. Apropos of the subject, I will say that I've never been the best at coming up with *piropos.*

I do recall that years later—around 1965, according to my memory—my convoy of Oldsmobiles was going slowly up a coastal road, in an area the people of Havana call La Rampa, when I saw a white Cuban woman with a solid pair of calves, soft round buttocks under her red cotton dress, a waist so small you could put your hands around it and your fingers would meet, loose black hair and who was clearly enjoying her own majestic gait and the way she was ruthlessly punishing humanity by radiating her beauty. Stupefied, I turned my head, my mouth hanging open, and lost all control, spitting out, "Son of a bitch!" You could have heard me in any corner of the city and anyone who had seen her would have agreed with me. Of course, she saw me in the middle of all the traffic due to the unmistakable presence of my three wine-colored Oldsmobiles and responded with a wide, healthy and pleasant smile. She even gestured to me, waving her finger as if to say, Yours, Fidel. Yours.

Later, in a series of setbacks and poorly considered administrative decisions, the minister of government, my old friend Luis Orlando Rodríguez, whom I named to the position, said he was going to eliminate gaming in Cuba. He was referring to gaming in the casinos still under North American management. I was keeping the casinos open as part of my stratagem of feigned indecisions and flirtations with the *yan-quis*, when this crazy bastard Luis Orlando decided the time had come to stop the spinning of the roulette tables and the rolling of the red die down the green blackjack cloths all across the country. It was still true that those casinos were supposedly operated by people reputed to be Mafiosos and that the main heads of the organization had been picked up under my orders at their luxurious apartments in El Vedado to be sent to Tiscornia, an establishment used since the beginning of the Republic for people who were waiting to be deported. It was in a corner of Havana's port and its most illustrious guest was Santos Trafficante, known as the Don of Tampa, and the highest representative in Havana of the so-called Syndicate. Having him in Tiscornia was another part of my stratagem with the *yanquis*. The FBI was dying to get their hands on Santos and had publicly proclaimed their interest in our handing him over to them. I had responded—using our dialectic logic of revolution-ary give-and-take for the first time—that on our end there was no prob-lem if on their end they would hand over the thugs they had given refuge to when Batista fled the country. It was the first time not only that the Cuban people understood that the Americans didn't intimidate us, but that the Americans heard someone speaking to them in the same tone they were in the habit of using. If they didn't fully understand the sig-nificance of our reaction, it's because of my tacit belief that they didn't know how to deal with equals. And that was the worst thing that could happen to them. Because it prevented them from knowing the enemy. So, while they tried to decipher my reaction, I made Santos the most eminent citizen of Tiscornia. Perhaps he never would have believed it, but we also had him there as a security precaution. I would get news that there were FBI agents poking around the city and any of them could have attempted a kidnapping, no difficult feat to carry out in Havana back then. But if they wanted that big fish, they would have to negotiate with me. I also did it to distance him from Frank Fiorini (or Sturgis, as he was also called), the ineffable chief of the military police of the Rebel Air Force and, according to one of my jokes at the time, who didn't know exactly which *yanqui* service to serve—the CIA, the FBI, the army's G-2, the navy's S-2. I had rolled my eyes when I heard that Fiorini had been appointed as the head of the nonexistent military police corps, but I told Camilo to call him and offer to name him auditor of the Mafia casi-nos. It put him in proximity to the person he was truly afraid of: Santos Trafficante. Santos and his Italian-American entourage had moved their Chiefs of Staff from the Sans Souci cabaret, which had originally been a rural club, to the Comodoro Hotel, on the west side. Sans Souci had been furiously looted at the announcement of the triumph of the Revolution. It is my understanding that no other Mafia facility weathered a greater insult on January 1, 1959. Less than three years later, we used the buildings to set up a repair shop for 12.5-caliber four-barrel Czech antiaircraft machine guns. Anyway, the first week of June 1959, the news was published that the *compañero* minister of government, Commander Luis Orlando Rodríguez, had announced that he would be expelling Santos Trafficante from the country in a few hours. And that's the last we heard of Luis Orlando as the minister of government. On June 10, I named José "Pepín" Naranjo to the office. The guidelines I gave him regarding Santos were that he should allow him to find a solution with his lawyers to leave whenever he wanted and to wherever he wanted, but on two conditions: that he not allow my name to be publicly linked to any of his affairs and that he never accept any money to carry out official negotiations.

Another piece of disquieting news regarding Santos was that Rolando Cubelas, the commander of the Directorate, was going to see him at Tiscornia. I called Pepín to cut off those contacts as a matter of urgency. Rolando's visits to Santos stopped. The last thing I needed was an alliance between the Directorate and the Mafia. The CIA had already worked with the Mafia to try to infiltrate Frank Fiorini into the Sierra Maestra.* Although I imagine that all Rolando was looking for was to see how he could get in on some of Santos's properties so that he could manage them. That Fiorini was a disaster, incidentally. A fool. I have never mocked someone and the *bosses* who controlled him at a distance as much as the renowned Frank Fiorini (or Frank Sturgis and all the other names he used.) In any event, before Santos left Cuba I sent him the message that next time he should get himself a brighter emissary.

Frank Fiorini nearly jumped out of his skin when I sent for him to come to the command post at La Plata Alta, uncorked a bottle of rum in his honor, filled a coffee cup with the liquor and told him:

"Shit, Frank, I've been watching you and I've realized that you're

---

* He took a shipment of weapons via airplane—with the Cuban pilot Pedro Luis Díaz Lanz—to the Sierra Maestra and stayed in rebel territory for weeks.

a man with experience. The kind of man you only see in intelligence services."

The cup was about to go flying out of his hand like a Ping-Pong ball.

He tried to babble an explanation. I cut him off with a wave of my hand. Then I served myself a finger of rum, in another cup. Frank's shirt was immediately soaked in sweat. He looked like he had just been through a storm. Or worse, that he had taken a shower with all of his clothes on. I overlooked those nervous emanations. It was obvious that he thought he was facing a death sentence. At least, every time I have seen a man sweat that way, it has been on his way to the firing squad. Because of that, I hastened to convey an idea that would calm him down.

"I'm not saying it in a bad way, Frank. I'm saying it because you are exactly the kind of man I needed here, in the Sierra."

"So you say," he whimpered.

"Let me explain, Frank. Let me explain. A little more?"

I showed him the bottle of rum. Frank nodded. Yes, a little more.

"Look at what's going on, Frank. What's going on is that I am convinced that the guerrilla army has been infiltrated by communists. Those bastards must be lying low somewhere. So I was watching you, ever since you arrived with Pedro Luis, wandering around here, around the command post, and I said to myself, Shit, this American is what I needed; he's the man who is going to help me. What I need, Frank, is for you to determine whether it's true that there are communists here or not. I'm going to give you the rank of captain, you know. Captain of the Rebel Army. And I'm going to give you a pass, or safe conduct, so that you can inspect all of the columns for me. You're free to move as you wish. But I want results, Frank. I want communists exposed. Do you understand? That's what I want. Do you agree with me? Are you going to help me?"

The bottle of Bacardi was in my hands again. I raised it high.

"One for the road, Frank?"

ONE KGB REVOLUTION

My alliance with the communists—or what some have lately been calling the "Secret Pact at Cojímar," as if they had made a big discovery—is essential to my rapprochement with the USSR and to my receiving weapons and gas, for starters. It is entirely understandable that some of my enemies would wish to read into these sessions in Cojímar a complicit relationship. Remember that there are two parallel governments, Urrutia's and the Cojímar one. Urrutia's—the one in the Presidential Palace, with its Council of Ministers and all of the usual government paraphernalia—is for the peace of mind of the bourgeoisie and the Americans; the Cojímar one, given its secret intentions, was of an eminently conspiratory nature that could not exhibit its power lest it lose its effectiveness, and it was to keep the communists and other revolutionaries in the spirit of conspiring with me anonymously to consolidate the revolution.

I warn you that there was nothing humiliating in the way we treated the communists. Quite the contrary. Almost any kind of settlement would have been a relief to them. The reality is that we found ourselves with a Party that Batista had practically done away with. Their other sources of income had been closed off to them, especially in the unions—all of these were moved under the control of Batista-supporting representatives—and the newspaper *Hoy* was definitively shut down. In this way, it was the Revolution that came to the rescue and gave them the printing press from *Alerta*, the Batista newspaper, for the printing of *Hoy*, and opened a few secret accounts so they could pay their debts; because on top of this series of misfortunes, the early months of our process meant a financial crisis for them. Another form of assistance were the Party's debts, which we began to absorb into the Armed and Security Forces. I have a very clear memory of a scene which I saw repeat itself at Raúl's house that whole year of 1959. Raúl and fifty of those old communists-turned-G-2-officers sitting around the dining room table which had once been Batista's. On the table there was a pile of bills of almost every denomination that the government ministers had brought just a few hours earlier. Raúl had called them on the telephone and told them to bring him all of the leftover money after settling their payroll. The handout followed the basic principle of distributing the money not only on the basis of what was available but on individual needs. And never going over two hundred pesos per head. Don't go thinking there was enough to pay more than that. And if anything was left over, it was kept for the following month. At a level higher than the recruitment of those personnel—as is already known, more or less—I had placed Aníbal Escalante and Osvaldo Sánchez under my protection while Raúl covered Flavio Bravo and Joaquín Ordoqui. Raúl was even bold enough to name them captains of the Rebel Army and elevate them in the rudiments of what would soon be the all-powerful General Chiefs of Staff.

You had to know how to coordinate things very well with new allies. Keeping them subordinate but at the same time giving them an air of leading role. Understand. Communism is what allowed me to insert the country into world history. Better put: it's what allowed me to insert Cuba in the ever-critical struggle of the Cold War. If we had not inserted ourselves in the context of the most encompassing and expensive confrontation in the history of humanity, we wouldn't have been anything more than a memory—if even a memory—of a quick slap by the Americans. Upon placing ourselves under the Soviet Union's wing and making a proclamation of faith in Marxism-Leninism, we substantially altered the value of our presence.

This achievement was barely noticeable at the beginning.

The still rusty cars owned by the communists started to make the rounds of Cojímar. Osvaldo Sánchez and Aníbal Escalante were a permanent presence. Osvaldo was a veteran of the KGB activities who met with me numerous times in the Sierra. Aníbal was the Party's hard-liner. I was living in Cojímar because I liked the view and I could shoot with my FAL from the doorway. I was going to live there until I returned from New York, on a trip I was planning, although it would continue to be a meeting point with the Party's people. Celia was finishing putting together an apartment for me to accommodate *all of my needs* in a neighborhood in Havana—El Vedado. The famous bunker on Eleventh Street. What she really wanted was to create a comfortable surrounding where, she guessed, I would feel at home and not need to go anywhere else to satisfy my whims. In short, a trap where she thought I would meekly fall.

A SUBJECT THAT I haven't seen explored at length or even mentioned in all of those books that I call "the literature of debacle" published in the West and in Russia itself on the occasion of the opening of the KGB's archives and the Soviet party's most sensitive files, is that of intelligence-sharing. At least in Vasili Mitrokhin's book, you're not going to find anything substantial in reference to Cuba and its maneuvers in this field.* The absence of this information can be explained. First of all, despite everything, we knew to keep the most sensitive operative games to ourselves. Despite Mitrokhin's belief and that of other high-ranking KGB officers that the Cuban service—the General Intelligence Directorate (Dirección General de Inteligencia, or DGI)—passed all of the most sensitive information on to them, the reality was that we were very conservative and never opened anyone's files. There was good cooperative work done, to be sure, and excellent institutional relations. Once, I recall, as a result of Kennedy's assassination, there was an indiscreet question on their part about our operatives who had infiltrated the CIA or the Cuban counterrevolutionaries involved in the so-called Dallas *magnicidio*, the murder of the president. Our response was that we would also be very interested in knowing who they had infiltrated at Langley and especially that we were desperate to have information about the years that Lee Harvey Oswald spent in the USSR. Game over. I don't think there was ever another incident worth mentioning. On the contrary. They—I mean the KGB—even had a tracking station in Cuba for their exclusive use. I'm not talking about the ultrafamous "Lourdes" signals intelligence facility to the southwest of Havana, which was a part of the SALT agreement, and operated by the Soviet Ministry of Defense. The station I am referring to, operated by the KGB in association with our services, was called the Organization and Automated Systems Department (Departamento de Organización y Sistemas Automatizados, or DOSA) and had its own bunker, an enormous subterranean building half a kilometer from the road that leads to Havana's international airport.

On the other hand, we were the ones who supplied the Soviets with the most sensitive technical-scientific information produced by the Americans. We kept them informed of any invention, modification or application coming out of scientific labs and institutions—secret ones in many instances—in the United States. You may not believe me, but that information came to us in huge cardboard boxes, of the size of a normal seaman's trunk, and sometimes even in wooden crates. We took a cursory look and pulled out any little thing that could be of interest to us, especially in the fields of medicine or biotechnology and of the

* Christopher Andrew and Vasili Mitrokhin, *The Sword and the Shield: The Mitrokhin Archive and the Secret History of the KGB*, Basic Books, New York, 1999.

fight against cancer. But everything that was of military interest, especially concerning nuclear matters, was put on a plane to Moscow. On
more than one occasion, we even chose to send Minister of the Interior
José Abrantes with the shipment, especially when we thought that the
intelligence material we were sending was of such strategic importance
or sensitivity that it required an escort from our Ministry of the Interior. The truth is that we didn't have any trained staff, nor staff in the
required quantity, to process all that information. If there's a Cold War
secret left unrevealed and of considerable importance, it's what I just
placed before your eyes as a reader. Of course the most basic of principles of loyalty prevent me from revealing the names of the very selfless
compañeros of both sexes who provided this precious information, above
all because they still work for us. I still have in my memory the image of
Raúl's office in the Party's Central Committee blocked by those boxes
when they had been collecting for a few weeks. The habit was to deposit
them there until we sent them off. Likewise, I imagine that if there's
something they miss in many academic facilities in modern Russia, it's
the wooden crates from Havana. And to think that Ethel and Julius
Rosenberg were burnt to a crisp for the trifle they passed on to Moscow. I say trifle in comparison to what we had been sending them since
the end of the sixties. Given the sum total of highly classified scientific information from the United States that we put in the hands of
the Soviet Union, we wouldn't pay for our faults even if the Americans were to burn the entire population of Cuba to a crisp three times.
We would have melted all the electric chairs in their inventory from so
much use. But the most curious thing about all of it is that the agents
themselves emphatically refused to work for the Soviets or to hand over
the same intelligence. You can even be sure that only now, in reading
these pages, will they find out the final result of their efforts and the
risks they took.

There are cases significantly absent in the bibliography of the dissolution of the USSR that have to do with one of our most sensitive units,
the Plan de Influencia (Influence Plan, or PI).* For example, not a single
word about the blank check the Soviets gave us so that the PI would take
care of Philip Agee, the CIA deserter whom we've had living in Cuba

---

* Remember? The Plan de Influencia was the intelligence department dedicated to North American minorities,
journalists, writers and artists. [*Author's note.*]

since the mid-eighties. A blank check and authorization to put whatever sum we chose.

Don't think that I'm criticizing Moscow. It doesn't even matter that the USSR has disappeared or that Vladimir Putin thinks he can toy with capitalism with impunity. What I did viscerally hate was having to depend—at the beginning of the Revolution—on Blas Roca, one of the leading communists at the time, and that whole group to vouch for me with the Soviets. That's what I'll never forgive. It was unacceptable that Blas had to vouch for Fidel Castro with Moscow. In the long run, that favor of Blas resulted in a life sentence for himself. And it so happens that by 1962, I was rubbing elbows directly with the Soviets, and due to this rubbing of elbows, I even had atomic missiles and then it was time to dissipate the PSP (Partido Socialista Popular), dissipate that force, before it was conscious of its power or importance. But I am getting ahead of events. It tends to happen to me. Whenever I get angry, I get ahead of myself.

Since we are still in the scene of the secret meetings of Cojímar, one afternoon I said to them—I think to Blas and Aníbal—that we should invite the *compañeros* from the Directorate to make them think that they were part of the real revolutionary direction and thus start recruiting them. Of course, I warned, it wouldn't be all of them. But there were some I found appropriate to invite. It seemed essential to me to incorporate them, I said. In any event they were going to find out and they were going to feel excluded, passed over, and it would be an unnecessary source of problems. In the end, I always aimed to keep the Directorate under my protection. It was a more cohesive force than the remnants of the 26th of July Movement and the PSP was never going to be mine. In other words, I was perfectly aware that I didn't have any political group at my disposal that would answer to me like the Party answered to Blas or the Directorate to Rolando. The 26th of July being what it was, an abstraction, every time I referred to the union of the three main organizations that had fought against Batista, in reality I was mentioning two organizations and me personally. So I always ended up flirting with the Directorate and even felt a certain compassion for them, because they were like the Cinderella of the process. Now, don't think we were going to hurry up and send invitations out to all of the people in the Directorate. What I wanted, simply, was to start getting Aníbal and Blas worried. After turning off the light and sticking the wolf in the room with them,

I told them, "There's no need to hurry, not at all. We should think about this and soon we'll have a very good idea of whom we'll invite. I've only brought it up to you as a concern."

On the other hand, I also knew that taking two or three commanders from the Directorate to Cojímar was like inviting the American ambassador himself. Maybe I could get a couple of them to compromise themselves. They had to be the most ambitious ones, not the most trustworthy ones. Because ambitious people leave aside their ideological convictions more easily if power is in the balance. Trustworthy people don't, because as a general rule they're idealistic. Faure Chomón, the Directorate's *jefe máximo*, was ambitious. We had to consider him as a probable candidate for the Cojímar meetings. Rolando Cubelas, in contrast, was trustworthy. I couldn't even consider inviting him as a joke to a meeting that would appear to be under the communists' control.

Then, one afternoon, in Cojímar, during a break, I saw Aníbal Escalante through the blinds with Celia, visibly trying too hard to be friendly with her.

They were outside, on the porch. Aníbal was in front of her trying to, I imagine, piece together some anecdote, because he burst out laughing at some point. Celia's reception of whatever story he told was cold. She barely cracked a smile. It's no less an embarrassing situation for Aníbal, since Celia's smile, or anything she could say to him—on the few occasions on which she removed the ever-present American cigarette from her lips—was merely a requisite gesture of politeness. And she was letting the seasoned communist leader know this.

I realized that Celia was enjoying her own impudence. Knowing she was safe under my protection and the awesome power I delegated to her, she gave free rein to her contempt for the country's communist leadership, an attitude which, I must confess to you, always seemed irrational and disproportionate to me.

Celia and her family were rare birds in the Manzanillo area because of their unadulterated anticommunism. It wasn't easy to find that type of people in an area habitually controlled by communists, although you could find them in other parts of the country and it was practically the norm in the western part. Although their anticommunism was a bit facile and lacking in serious reasoning, it was well suited to the cultural needs of the last crop of the Cuban petit and middling bourgeoisie, especially the new generation of professionals, for whom communism—

especially homegrown communism—was a step backward when what they really wanted was to get ahead. Communists meant blacks, strikes, tobacco-pickers, poor neighborhoods, the port unions, and the memory of the Party's alliance with that mulatto Batista.* In an axiomatic way, in the minds of thousands of Cuban professionals in the mid-fifties, being a communist or a Batista supporter was the same thing, quite a convincing view to accept and an even easier one to sustain. No recently graduated young Cuban professional turning on the air-conditioning in his office and lighting his Parliament or Marlboro or Salem cigarette would find attractive the image of a black Cuban seasonal farmworker, sweaty and toothless, whom the Communist Party claimed to redeem. Such an abstract effort exceeds the parameters of all demands.

I smiled to myself while I observed Aníbal Escalante through the blinds trying to get any kind of friendly gesture out of Celia.

Son of a bitch, I thought. So you're trying to wear down her defenses.

I had made a promise to Celia. I made it many times in the Sierra. I had told her that when all of that was over, she and I could lead a normal life. I am repeating it verbatim. *When all of this is over, you and I can lead a normal life.* Did I say anywhere in there that we would get married? Would you come away from that thinking I had asked her to marry me? Well, I don't know where she got such an idea. So she began to pressure me about it. The solution to my problem—or at least a long-term distraction—came to me when I witnessed that scene between Aníbal and her on the porch in Cojímar.

I had to remark on the scene that very night.

I got to the Eleventh Street bunker. I took off my gun. I asked Celia about Gumersinda, whether Gumersinda hadn't left yet. Gumersinda was the cook. No, Gumersinda hadn't left yet. Why? Listen, Celia, I'm dying to have some *frituritas de bacalao.* Do you think it's too late for her to make them for me? I casually grabbed one of the newspapers from the neatly arranged pile on my desk and the file with the summary of the international cables and, without taking my eyes off of these papers, I said to her, "You wanna know something, Celia? You know what? These communists seem to be taking off. They're feeling very powerful. Wouldn't you know that today they told me that if I'm ever to get married, whenever that might be, that I can't marry you. They say you come

---

* During the Second World War. What they called "a strategic alliance." [*Author's note.*]

from one of the most anticommunist families in the whole area of Manzanillo. What do you make of that? Listen, Celia, these sons of bitches are really getting full of themselves.

I was flipping through my newspaper.

"Who told you that?"

"Who else, Celia?" I said, shrugging my shoulders and continuing with my supposed reading.

"Aníbal," I say. "Aníbal told me so."

ON APRIL 15, 1959, at the invitation of the Press Club, I arrived in the United States. Jules Dubois, the Latin America correspondent for the *Chicago Tribune*, who had interviewed us during our days in the Sierra, handled all the invitations and bent over backward to show us off as his prize before all of the American tycoons. We let him lead us around like little lambs and introduce us to the moguls of the American press. You could look at it as the same game we played with other Americans, but in Jules Dubois' case, our role was more passive. The game was convenient for us, for the time being, in that it didn't reveal any of our economic or social demands to people in the United States. On this trip, I repeated over and over again on television that I was not a communist. On the nineteenth, I met with Nixon in the Capitol building. Nixon would describe me as "incredibly naive" regarding communism. Naive is the exact word used in his report. On the other hand, the date will serve to remind me that symbols work, they come true. Two years later, exactly two years, on April 19, 1961, we carried out a devastating defeat of the *yanquis* on the sands of Playa Girón, the embarrassing failure of a plan to destroy us through military action that Nixon himself began to plot when that three-and-a-half-hour conversation of ours at the Capitol ended.

I made just one demand: that my secretary, Captain Chicho, accompany me. That was the name I came up with for Luis Más Martín, one of the communists from the university group. He turned out to be my best choice, given his status as an old communist in that team of pretty petit-bourgeois that accompanied me on my first trip to the U.S. as the leader of Free Cuba. He was the only communist I had there and only coincidentally part of the delegation, I believe as one of the legal advisors who was included in case we needed to sign any treaties; another act of concealment, since in reality he was at the head of one of the Revolutionary Armed Forces units overseeing the execution of Batista's men.

At the meeting, which took place in the vice president's office in the Capitol building, besides Richard Nixon, Luis Más and me, there were two members of Nixon's staff present. They and Luis Más remained in an antechamber until the end of the conversation, in which they were allowed to participate for a few minutes. From the beginning, I agreed to speak in English and rejected the use of any interpreter. I am convinced that the entire conversation was taped by a hidden microphone. But it must have been solely for Nixon's use and he must have kept the recording later. That allowed him to frame things as he saw fit in the report he wrote of the conversation. Whatever was done with the recording, one thing is certain, we couldn't care less if it has been kept in some official American government file.

Rough draft of summary of conversation between the Vice President and Fidel Castro:

When Castro arrived for the conference he seemed somewhat nervous and tense. He apparently felt that he had not done as well on "Meet the Press" as he had hoped. He was particularly concerned about whether he might have irritated Senator Smathers for the comments he made with regard to him. I reassured him at the beginning of the conversation that "Meet the Press" was one of the most difficult programs a public official could go on and that he had done extremely well -- particularly having in mind the fact that he had the courage to go on in English rather than to speak through a translator.

The subjects we discussed were no different from those on which he had made public statements on several other occasions. A brief summary, however, might be of interest, particularly in view of the comments I made with regard to the positions he took.

The war hadn't even begun yet and I already knew that I'd won. They're lost, I told myself. They don't know me. They can't estimate me. They don't know what I want or what I am going to do. From now on, it will always be this way. And in this moment, I understand that I have the advantage and that in their superficiality, as well as their way of underestimating me, lies—and will lie—my victory.

I understood, despite everything, the impression that the Americans had of me, a young Mr. Nobody, dressed with my guerrilla fatigues, in a world in which revolution always meant breaking with the status quo in Latin America, in other words with the Americans themselves, and whose most recent memory of revolution was Arbenz's in Guatemala, and all of this together was quite an obstacle. For many years it has been said that I felt offended because I wasn't received by anyone of consequence. I imagine they're referring to the fact that President Dwight D. Eisenhower wouldn't see me and that he felt obliged to make up I don't know what strange excuse about a previous commitment—that was, in addition, unavoidable—to a golf tournament. I didn't see things that way. It was a public relations trip due to that whole matter of executions and if it failed in any way, the failure was mutual, both sides failed, since not seeing anyone important meant that Nixon wasn't important, and that I was being told that the furthest I could go was that Mr. Nobody. He immediately started in on that harangue about having elections every four years. At this point, as in the rest of the conversation, I believe that I was extremely clear. *There would not be any elections for a long time.* I said it quite frankly. The most basic of my reasons—that in the past, elections in Cuba had only produced bad government—seemed to make a lasting impression on him because he highlighted my words, "*the people did not want elections because the elections in the past have produced bad government.*"

I tried to explain that I wasn't interested in sugar and that they would not be able to use our main industry to blackmail us. Because my goals were otherwise, not the economy, not sugar—an industry I planned to quickly eliminate to gain distance from the Americans and integration with Latin America. Cuba would be destined for great things: not for planting and harvesting sugarcane. Was it clear to him that I wasn't interested in sugar, that we would later make it lose value? From the start, I saw the reason for America's blackmailing of the Cuban economy: the sugar industry. When Senator Smathers later declared the policy of lowering the sugar quota, he proved us right in not focusing too much on that product.

Nonetheless, to make a revolution, you don't need to know anything about economics, just about guiding or controlling the masses. The Revolution suppressed elections as the sine qua non of its own existence. I didn't say this to Nixon, but for me, once more, Lenin's aphorism about a revolution being worth what it knows how to defend was clear. Convening elections in the middle of a Revolution is akin to surrendering.

I repeated that there would be no elections in Cuba. Regarding his oh-so-illuminating lesson about democracy, freedom of the press and trials that should not end in the summary execution of Batista's thugs, I withstood it all without batting an eyelash, the same smile frozen on my face, for the entire length of his diatribe. Then he launched into a seemingly endless stream of rhetoric in which he tried, according to his own words, to pressure me with the fact that even if you believe in majority-rule governments, there are majorities that can be tyrannical and that there are certain individual rights that a majority should not be given the power to destroy. I will never forget that portion of his gibberish. Years later, with the fall of the Soviet Union, I mimicked Nixon's speech behind closed doors at one of the Party's congresses by saying that we should prepare ourselves to govern as a minority. In the vice-president's Capitol building office, I learned that opportune words are more powerful than all the laws in the world. Allow me to be more specific. It's not that I learned all that gibberish about majorities and minorities from Nixon. What I learned was something else: that events are what prevail in politics. I knew that the terrain dictates the battle. Applied to politics, I would say that opportunity dictates policy.

I will add that—for me—the finest moment of the meeting took place just as we were wrapping up our exhausting two-hour-and-thirty-two-minute exchange. After authorizing our assistants to come partake in the meeting, he, Nixon, hoping to catch me with my guard down, suddenly expressed his concern over the unprecedented amount of communists in key positions in the Rebel Army and gave me several stapled sheets containing an endless list of the Party's *compañeros* lending their services to the incipient Armed Forces. I was giving it the once-over when I saw that on the third or fourth line of the third page or so, under the letter M, was none other than Luis Más Martín's name. "Hey, Chicho, take a look at this," I said, surprised. "Luis Más is a communist." "Let me see," Luis Más Martín said with great interest. "Look," I said, pointing out the name:

Más, Luis. Rank: Captain

"*Coño*, Fidel," he said. "Luis Más is a communist." "What a son of a bitch," I said. "Chicho, did you know he was a communist?" "No, Fidel, no. This is news to me."

But I decided to cut that exchange with Luis Más Martín off imme-diately because I noticed that Nixon was bristling. He may not have understood a single word of Spanish, but he could sense that we were mocking him. I saw his muscles tense up under his well-known five o'clock shadow. In any event, it's obvious that he was aware of the scope of our mockery, since not a single word about the incident made it into his report to President Eisenhower. In other words, he felt sufficiently humiliated that he preferred to turn a blind eye to the matter and not mention it at all to his superior. Also, much later, I found out that one of the two members of Nixon's staff was later apprised of the true iden-tity of my assistant by some member of our delegation—I never knew which one. It appears that they explained the extent of our mockery to Nixon, that the hypothetical Captain Chicho was none other than the list's Captain Luis Más. *The fucking Cubans.*

STRANGERS IN THE NIGHT

Neither side has thought it advisable to refer to a meeting that I had on April 21—two days after the one with Nixon. I am referring to an offi-cial encounter, but of a strictly classified nature. It was at our embassy, in the wee hours of the night. Gerry Droller was the Agency's main expert on communism in Latin America—a man in his fifties, weighing about 185 pounds, of medium build, who smoked a pipe, wore glasses, spoke in a calm manner and paid the utmost attention to everything I said, but without ever making me feel like I was being scrutinized. During the course of our conversation—lasting *three hours*—he displayed an impec-cable knowledge of modern history. I could detect the slightest hint of a foreign accent when he spoke. It wasn't the usual rhythm of con-versation I had been listening to throughout my travels in the United States. ("*¿Cómo está, señor?*" he said to me, in Spanish, upon shaking my hand.) The reports I've received after the fact confirm that my meet-ing with Droller was the height of my popularity with the CIA. Later I realized that my ambassador Ernesto Dihigo and one of the members of my delegation, the minister of revenues (or of finances, as the rest of the world says), Rufo López Fresquet, were aware of the CIA's request for an appointment, or at least sensed that it was coming. I could tell by their excitement and by the expectations they voiced about the matter in the hours leading up to the emissary's arrival. Right then and there I understood for whom the sons of bitches were working. It was one of the characteristics of almost the whole of my Council of Ministers and of my diplomatic corps at the beginning of the Revolution. They served as the Americans' antennas. And that was the best-case scenario, assuming they hadn't already been recruited. But it ended up being a highly convenient sign for me, not only because they identified themselves as agents, but also because they would tell me about the enemy's projected course of action. That's how I learned, for example, that they were desperate for me to request economic aid from the *yanquis*—all kinds of loans, investments, capital. Besides which, their presence around me acted as a Praetorian Guard arranged by the counterrevolution. I liked to imagine them as being like the pioneers in the Old West who would circle the wagons to repel the furious attack of the mounted Cheyennes. They had to go wherever I went and because of that, their hopes were pinned on the shy advice they let fall on my ears. But the fact that I remained discreetly silent about the anxiously awaited economic aid request placed them in a situation that can only be described as that of helplessness, and the atmosphere of uncertainty increased by the day in Washington's circles of power. My minister of revenues watched the hours go by without my making any mention of the matter. Until, at a given moment, he somehow found a way to convince another member of my delegation, the president of the National Bank of Cuba, Felipe Pazos, to bring up the subject with me. "*Coño*, Fidel," Pazos said to me, and he spared no vulgar words in expressing his idea, "hurry up and ask the Americans for something, they're dying to give it to you up the ass." I took my time, and surely paused to take a few puffs of my cigar before responding. "No," I said to him, in a way that was as calm as it was reflective, and without it being necessary to offer a reason. "No. Let's wait, Felipito. This isn't the trip for it. Next time." *Next time!* You can imagine that I had already given determined and precise thought to this strategy. Allowing North American aid—in any form, be it loans, donations or investments—would have only served to empower those characters among my first Council of Ministers, who would turn into the direct managers of the money, in addition to the American businessmen and the Cuban bourgeoisie, who would be the natural beneficiaries of these revenues. Nothing could be more counterproductive to my strategy of doing away with the country's plutocratic groups than allowing an influx of hundreds of millions of dollars. Money to fill my enemies' pockets? Next time, Felipito. Next time.

The CIA's car arrived—with official U.S. GOVERNMENT plates—at the wrought-iron gates of the Cuban Embassy, which were open. There was a cement path running next to the old three-story house and the car stopped in front of the porch. They escorted a man to the private elevator that led right to the ambassador's office door. The carpets were green and I still remember them today as dusty, a cloud of dust mites rising up in the wake of our diplomats' steps. I received him with the door to the office half open, in my usual field uniform, with a book in hand. I had my finger on one of the last pages of this small volume, as if I were completely immersed in it. It was *The Bridges at Toko-Rí*, in English, which I had taken down from the ambassador's shelf and which I had seen in the movie theater, but at the moment I don't remember the author.* He came over to me and extended his hand when he was just a few short steps away from me and said, not without a certain seriousness, "¿Cómo está, señor?" My response consisted of a warm, "Finally! Someone who understands me!" This was delivered with infectious happiness, me looking him right in the eye, but taking great care not to express hardness and much less suspicion, keeping all of my gestures under strict control. He had to think I was receiving him as I would any comrade. But I was forced to suppress my disgust upon making contact with his right hand, a small, fat and I would say flabby hand that left a trail of sweat on my skin. I had ordered Ambassador Dihigo's office be vacated and that I should have an acceptable supply of alcohol and cigars on hand. There were two wide leather armchairs in front of the walnut desk and I took care to mark the page I had supposedly stopped reading by dog-earing the upper right corner. The fact that I was not occupying the extremely expensive, heavy reclining chair behind the desk—belonging to our Washington representative—was a gesture of deliberate courtesy to my guest. It was also symbolic. It showed my caller that I didn't place anything before our exchange and that I was not a man given to the protocol or the stiff customs of the diplomatic world. I made a quick estimate of his background based on his apparent age. Fiftyish, right? World War II Veteran, I told myself. On the other hand, there was something unmistakable in his accent, something that would lead me—like a DNA test—to determine his national origin. That hooked nose, I

* James A. Michener, *The Bridges at Toko-Ri*. Before coming out in book form, the novel appeared as a serial in *Life* magazine in its July 6, 1953, edition.

noticed. That nose and the Coke-bottle lenses of his glasses. That's it, I told myself. Just a few seconds later, the definitive detail confirming his provenance came in the sharpness of his look, typical of myopics. The son of a bitch was Jewish, I told myself. With the speed of an interrogator, I made a tally of all the elements to determine with relative certainty whom I was up against. Let's see, I told myself. If he was in the war and he's a Jew born outside the United States and if the CIA trusts him enough to let him detect any moving communist between the Pentagon and the Rio Grande, he is one of the Jews recruited by William Joseph Donovan on the German border. In Switzerland, surely. And, of course, the accent is German. Or some related language. A fugitive from Nazi Germany. Oh, God, what I have in front of me is a veteran of Donovan's group from the Office of Strategic Services. They can't fuck with me. This is one of the CIA's founders. *Hueso*, I said. This guy is *hueso*. The expression is probably a Cuban-style contraction of a hard bone to gnaw, our equivalent of a hard nut to crack, which is not used in its entirety among us due to how strange the word gnaw probably is to the majority of my compatriots. A certain affection was established between us ever since I revealed my relief at finally having someone to understand me. I proceeded to expand upon this notion. It's so easy with a war veteran. "Military man?" I asked him. The satisfaction my question brought him was accompanied by a gesture of false modesty and a phrase that went something like, "More or less, Comandante Castro. More or less." This is typical of someone who spent a war operating as a vile rat for any of the special services. They really appreciate your comparing them to a line officer. "More or less what you would consider a military man, certainly. At least, since my youth, all I've done is take orders." The response continued in perfect Spanish, although with the same remote accent of an uncomfortable rigidness that was more pronounced here and there. I asked him to sit down, pointing to the armchair. I tried to maintain an attitude in line with his calmness and repeated to myself that I shouldn't raise my voice or interrupt him under any circumstance. Above all, upon taking my own seat, I told myself that it would be inappropriate to follow the Cuban custom—of which I am such a fan—of moving my testicles with an ostentatious motion over my pants as I sat down. A gesture of unmistakable camaraderie followed. Something you could even take as a show of tenderness. From the top of the desk, within my reach without having to get up, to my right, I took the open box of H. Uppman No. 4s and placed them in front of Droller, right at eye level, and said to him jokingly, "Let's give some use to this war booty." Then I noticed the pipe. Droller also seemed surprised at that moment by his own accessory and by the fact that, with the opened cedar lid of a box of H. Uppman No. 4s in front of him, his pipe was a nuisance, so he immediately sought out an ashtray, conveniently located on a small table to his right, and with two or three skillful taps emptied the bowl of his pipe and left it leaning there with its stem tipped toward the bottom of the ashtray. Emptying it, in any event, had been unnecessary, since the pipe wasn't lit. He probably carried it in his hand—I guessed—as a remedy for anxiety, or out of pure habit. I encouraged him to take more than one of the cigars. I explained that they were the ambassador's special reserve. The thrill of theft. I myself took five or six of those exalted products of the homeland, leaving one out and putting the rest in my jacket pocket. Shyly, but completely committed to me in carrying out the crime, he took four cigars. He kept one in hand and the other three went right into the pocket of his checked jacket with its leather elbow patches. "In a little while, we'll grab some more," I said to him, with a wink and my best possible attempt at a mischievous smile. We laughed in unison again. I hit his shoulder a couple of times with a kind of slow-motion jab. We tried to contain our laughter, so we wouldn't be heard outside. Our cheeks hurt from the pressure of laughing so much. He was looking at me. He was happy. The rabbi was radiant. We lit our cigars and fell under the smoke's spell and were ready to chat and, after getting off to a start like that and establishing that we were in the trenches together, to get down to discussing where our interests met. All of them. There wasn't going to be a single thing left that we wouldn't agree on, to be sure. I had no problem, of course, in feeding him the story that he—it was obvious—had set forth to get from me. In that sense, it was a very easy conversation for me to lead. Because I knew exactly what he was looking for, exactly what he wanted to hear. Ever since they asked for a meeting with me, I was able to pinpoint their objectives. Anticommunism and open field for investments. And don't forget about the suspicions raised about Che and my brother Raúl. First I was on guard, as a logical defensive reaction. But I acceded to the request. Nixon had not been satisfied with me, not satisfied in the least, and was reacting very negatively. Not so much because of the way I explained my revolutionary projects, but because of the contempt with which I treated him. Both of us—and you have no idea how much it bothers me to confess this—turned a political matter into something personal. But Richard Nixon also really came down on me! And that was what set the CIA in motion. They had to find an immediate reason, but in keeping with their interests at the moment, to balance against Nixon's visceral reaction. Probably I had barely taken my leave and walked through the door of his office in the Capitol building when he picked up his secure line and asked to be connected to Allen Dulles immediately to demand my head on a platter. That's how, just a few hours after my meeting with Nixon, and many years before the famous report of my visit was declassified, I knew what kind of impression I had made. And now I had to help the CIA construct a more positive image of me. I had to throw them a bone so they could save face. Fine, then, there, right in front of my face, I had the staff member who was going to return to Allen Dulles's office with a report that would serve to refute the one that Nixon had already prepared and on which the entire structure of North American policy toward Cuba would definitively rest for the next half a century. Gerry Droller, the man who, in just a few short months, would appear before the eyes of the world as one of my staunchest enemies, who would show up in Miami as the famous Frank Bender, or "Mr. B.," the CIA's operational leader during the preparations for the Bay of Pigs invasion. The one in charge of everything. The one responsible for every piece. All you have to do is type the name of Gerry Droller or Frank Bender into your computer to get an overwhelming amount of Web sites citing him, describing him, featuring him, and almost none of them in a positive light. Jewish. Of Austrian background. Born in Germany around 1905. Worked closely with the Office for Strategic Services and with the French Maquis. I was very confident and quick in my commitments. I decided that for him, rooting out all of the communists that had infiltrated the Rebel Army would be imperative and that I would have to get rid of Che too, however I could. I rehearsed a kind of apology for having admitted him into my Revolutionary Forces. "We couldn't find another doctor willing to go with us." I talked about enacting laws favoring private businesses immediately and ended with a veiled attack (we were talking about my brother!) against Raúl, an "extremely reckless" young man. I even floated the idea of a commission that would make sure the communists were duly reprimanded. "You can really help us clean up the Cuban political landscape," I said with absolute conviction. "Who has more experience than you when it comes to that?" Whatever the opinion of analysts and historians may be about the strategic value of his mission, one thing is sure, and that's that he walked away from those three hours with me saying that the revolution *was theirs*. I understand that in retrospect, it was one of the CIA's great inside jokes. All the same, he told our minister of finance, and later a well-known counterrevolutionary, Rufo López Fresquet, who was waiting for him at the embassy's door, "Not only is Castro not a communist, he's a staunch anticommunist crusader." It was a serious mistake to think that I had left the man convinced by the strength of my reasoning and by my loquaciousness. I was dealing with a professional. He limited himself to fulfilling the needs of his office. What did they need? A report? That was favorable to Castro? When did they need it? He had alerted me when our conversation had barely begun. Since my youth, all I've done is taken orders. That's it. A simple task.

As a result of what I would call my "commitments to Nixon" (I called them that upon my return to Cuba, although they were really a result of my April 23 conversation with Frank Bender, not Nixon), I removed all of the communists from the Rebel Army . . . to relocate them (and this didn't have anything to do with my "commitments to Nixon") in the nascent revolutionary G2, which was quickly placed under partial control of the veterans of the former Communist Party, the Aníbal Escalantes, the Osvaldo Sánchezes and the Isidoro Malmiercas.* And Sánchez and Malmierca, at least, were positively identified as KGB. But Aníbal Escalante was the one at the head of things, at least nominally so, for the time being.

THE MATTER OF Urrutia was easier to implement. All I had to do was show up in the wee hours one morning at *Revolución* and write up a headline in typeface that would take up the entire front page, which, the guys at the newspaper's workshop explained to me, was called *"tipos de palo."* Since the letters didn't already exist in the size I requested, they had to make them out of wood. In the July 17, 1959, edition, with all the vio-

---

* The G2 would become—halfway through 1961—the Department of State Security. Although out of habit it was still called the G2.

lence of the best and heaviest red ink that could be procured from the warehouses, my *tipos de palo* shouted out:

FIDEL RESIGNS

And on TV that night, I delivered a speech denouncing it. A made-up resignation of my own—from the position of prime minister—to forcibly effect the real resignation of the citizen president. And just what in the hell was I resigning from? Well, the post that I had held since February 16. During that month and a half after the rebel troops arrived in Havana, I had tried to keep myself under the government's protection so I could enjoy complete freedom of movement and not appear responsible for any official activity that would tie my name to matters that could cost me or force me to employ any of my conspiratorial moves. But I was already starting to run the risk that executive power would be completely out of my hands. Up until that moment, the palace had allowed me to pay my dues to the politicians who had joined me in one way or another during the course of the revolutionary war and with whom I had contracted unavoidable obligations. Their parade through the halls of power in that brief time period helped me show people the ineptitude of those men in commanding a revolution. And finally, for the first time, I was testing the validity of Lenin's thesis that the best way to destroy a political line is to give it power. And so I told that fine gentleman José Miró Cardona that he could cease his duties as prime minister in the Revolutionary Government and asked how he felt about going to the embassy in Madrid. This was how, after having ordered fresh coffee to be brewed and biting at a cigar to rip the tip off and allow the smoke to flow freely, unhindered, I assumed the premiership. I still can't imagine how that man faced up, first, to those politicians of ours who shit themselves in fear in front of the Americans, when I snatched the premiership away from him like candy out of a kid's lunch box and he had to deliver the bad news himself to the embassy; and then, in Francoist Spain, when Generalissimo Francisco Franco received him in person, to conspire against the Americans! "Tell Comandante Castro on my behalf," Franco explained, as if imparting advice, "that you always say yes to the Americans and later you do whatever the fuck you want." Franco, of course, was looking at things from the old school point of view. He didn't understand, for the time being, that my policy was based on confronting the Americans and not on avoiding them. As far as Miró was concerned, the poor guy, the end of his political career in alliance with the *yanquis* ended in a rather symbolic way. Of course, I guessed that he wouldn't take long to abandon our diplomatic quarters in Madrid and end up in American territory. It was a deliberate way of making asylum easier for him. I've always subscribed to the idea of keeping my surroundings free as possible of enemies, and never keeping those characters who appeal to a public of such narrow interests. And however you look at it, to the Americans he seemed like the right guy to lead the civil government they were preparing in conjunction with the military invasion plans that led to the Playa Girón disaster, well known by all, in which our forces captured almost two thousand members of the expedition after they'd been left to their fate by the North American authorities who had promised them all kinds of naval and air support, and among those captured was Miró Cardona's son. If I had kept old Miró in jail for a couple of hours or executed him, today he would be more famous than Our Lady of Fátima. The very same innocuous old man turned international deity thanks to a repressive measure of mine. Do you understand the moral of the story?

My reasons to get rid of Manuel Urrutia were legitimate, nonetheless. Urrutia turned out to be an impediment to the revolutionary process. He was too straitlaced, too clean, too decent. So we had to deal with him. He was rather lucky in any case: he became the first president on the continent whose mandate was abruptly cut short without shedding a single drop of blood. For just one naive moment, Dr. Urrutia believed it was possible not only for him to govern, but for him to do so in a Republic whose highest aspiration was progress and stability. And nothing was more reactionary, at given stages of the process, than those aspirations. Besides, there's the inexorable axiom that all participation in a process such as ours is that of the man who is assigned tasks, one at a time. Your duty is to carry out the assigned task. The Revolution's duty is not to assign you more than one at a time.

The only task that Urrutia was able to carry out to a tee was that of resigning that very night, urgently signing a little piece of paper with the Presidential Palace stamp that had been placed on the table in his office while I was going off on him on every TV channel in the country. I have reports that it took a while for him to blame me for his misfortune. During my televised condemnation of him, he kept saying that I was acting under pressure of other forces and at first he identified Raúl as the main instigator. It wasn't until past midnight that he started to hit himself on the head and scream, "I've been so stupid!" And after beating himself up for a good long while, he tuned his thoughts to another frequency. This flagellation session took place in front of Esperanza Llaguno Aguirre de Urrutia, his wife, who, incidentally, didn't do anything to stop him or even to calm him down.

By that time, Urrutia had another worry. It was whether he would get out alive, whether I hadn't stirred up a million people in Havana to attack the palace. But all precautions were made, as you can imagine, and Commander Efigenio Amejeiras had cordoned off the palace's exterior perimeter with Revolutionary National Police companies armed with FAL rifles. They had the dual purpose of not letting anyone reckless get too close as well as not letting the president and his entourage out until I gave the order. That order came late the next day, to leave them rotting inside that building where, in addition, there wasn't a single phone left with an outside line. So there would be no doubts that they shouldn't return. I think it was Commander Amejeiras himself who showed up at the palace, reviewed the board from the Services office on the ground floor of the palace where all of the keys to the cars in the presidential fleet were hanging, picked a Cadillac and took the Urrutia family away.

(Later Efigenio would tell me that the pathetic part took place when he showed up at Services to pick a key and saw an old mulatto dressed in an olive-green uniform with enormous dark plastic glasses and enormous captain bars on his collar. A quick check alerted Efigenio that he was wearing a Colt .45 at his waist, on the right side. At first the man gave Efigenio the impression of being a wax figure. He seemed to have an inexplicably satisfied permanent smile that could have been taken for mockery or stupidity. And—what was disconcerting to my chief of police—this inscrutable figure, who didn't seem to mind being treating like one more item in a warehouse, seemed immune to the dramatic intensity of the events developing around him. Until Efigenio understood who he was. "Captain," he said to him. The man instinctively moved his head toward the sound of the voice. "Yes?" he said. "How are you, Captain?" Efigenio said. "It's Commander Amejeiras speaking. Do you remember me?" "At your service, Commander. At your service," responded the man, who had already turned his head again toward the spot where he must have calculated the approximate center of the axis running between the eyes down to the chin over the straight body was. "Everything's in order, Captain. Everything's in order," Efigenio said. "Just a regular check." "I'm here, at your service," the man insisted. "Don't bother yourself," Efigenio said, keys to Cadillac 03 already jingling in his hands. "Oh, good," the man said, "very good." "I'm going to take my leave, Captain," Efigenio explained. "Is there anything I can do for you?" "No. I don't need anything," he responded. "I'm very satisfied." "Well, Captain—" Efigenio started to say, with the usual Cuban rhetoric for an informal goodbye (what's not informal in our linguistic precepts?) when the man, with his head still firmly placed over the established axis, asked, "And what did you say your name was?" For one moment, Efigenio thought of giving another name, just as a joke. Surely any name would have done. But he felt sorry for the man, and besides, Efigenio knew he was under a kind of protection of mine, there was no other way to explain a blind man carrying a .45-caliber gun at his waist. Nor was it permissible to disrespect Pedro Sarría Tartabull, public order lieutenant for Squad 11 of the Rural Police, who saved my life after the attack on Moncada and whom I had designated as the permanent assisting captain to the president of the Republic. The presidents could be removed, but Sarría's post was for life. He was already suffering from glaucoma when the Revolution triumphed, but I acted as if I were none the wiser about his ailment and went to his house personally to name him to the post. Batista had kicked him out of the army and didn't even allow him his retirement pension. I ordered that he be paid everything the army could owe him. "Commander Efigenio Amejeiras," Efigenio identified himself again. "Could you do me a favor?" Sarría said, and started to feel around the top of the desk, looking for pen and paper. "Please do me the favor of signing a receipt for the keys you just put in your pocket."

First—at his own request—Urrutia was taken to the house of some of his relatives, where he wanted to "rest" awhile, and they agreed that Efigenio would pick him up the next day to take him to the airport. Efigenio was under very specific orders of mine to address him as Presidente the whole time, even on the steps to the plane, and to swear on his life and everything else not to light up any marijuana on the way.

"And in case you get the urge," I advised him, "smoke it now."

"In the final chaos of water and eternal nights, the only vestige of what was once life will be the cock-roaches." García Márquez's description of the world after the nuclear war meets with Fidel's approval, but falls into oblivion. September 9, 1962. The intermediate range R-12 missiles that he authorized to install in Cuba are moving along a secondary road. Final chaos lies waiting in those trucks.

PART FIVE

POWER IS
TO BE USED

IN EVERY STATE THAT IS WEAK IN THE FACE OF A
WAR OF OBVIOUS ANNIHILATION, BUT WHOSE IN-
CONCLUSIVE HOUR HAS YET TO COME, IT IS THE
DUTY OF SENSIBLE, STEADY AND UNBIASED MEN TO
BE READY FOR THE INEVITABLE BATTLE, TO UNDER-
TAKE IT AT THE MOST FAVORABLE MOMENT AND
TO FORTIFY THE CALCULATIONS OF ITS DEFENSE
POLICY THROUGH STRATEGIC OFFENSE, BUT THEY
ARE SURROUNDED EVERYWHERE BY THE LAZY AND
COWARDLY MULTITUDES OF THOSE WHO WORSHIP
THE GOLDEN CALF, WHO ARE OLD, WHO ARE DEBILI-
TATED BY AGE AND BY LIGHTHEARTED MEN WHO,
ONLY DESIRING TO LIVE AND DIE IN PEACE, DELAY
THE FINAL BATTLE AT WHATEVER COST.

—THEODOR MOMMSEN, *The History of Rome*

Is Defeat Such an Orphan?

///

Raúl was pressuring me to proclaim the revolution's socialist objectives. But there was something he just didn't get. I'll concede that he was concerned about my ideological azimuth as he watched my flirtations with one revolutionary group, then another, then certain groups within the bourgeoisie, then the communists, then the Americans, and a little bit later even with the Soviets. Perhaps many of my readers won't believe me, but you should know that even Raúl didn't have access to my most private thoughts—what now could be considered "conspiracy"—and had even less access, of course, to my tactical plans. Since by this point I've already met almost all of the goals I set out for myself, I'll tell you something else. Not even I knew exactly which ideology I was going to adopt, nor where my tactical plans would take me. Everything—to put it simply—was dependent on the offers I received. Who was making them and whether they assured me power. Holding on to it. Consolidating it. Power would show up along the way and I would have to be able to recognize it. In the meantime, then, I navigated, or I should say I was heaving-to amid, all the political currents of modern history, in search of my haven. My brother, of course, from the start thought that if we raised the red socialist banner over the Revolution, we would experience a complete and total victory that would allow us spiritual rest, but that would also allow him a kind of power over me. Being the orthodox and methodical guy that he was, whether he was espousing the Soviet, Chinese or any other existing socialism in the world at that time, he wanted to bring me into his fold. There was something really fucked

A world-famous philosopher wanders through the Ciénaga de Zapata's works under construction. Jean-Paul Sartre, with aplomb and good humor, removes his jacket and faces the torpor of the embankment lining the swamp. The ambitious project is that of his host, Fidel Castro. To dry out this immense territory—a million acres of miasma, insects and reptiles— and turn it into a sweet plain of fruit trees and cattle pastures.

up that he didn't understand, and it was what would happen in the long run. Like all Latin American communists at that time, Raúl had that tunnel vision in which the international communist movement was rooted in Marx's theories about the Paris Commune. That's also a consequence of the movement's Stalinist methods, which marked it with those religious characteristics so vital to the vision of socialism in one country. Don't ever forget this assertion when you study the first years of the Cuban Revolution. *The construction of socialism in one country.* I won't deny that in its time the concept allowed for, first of all, the existence of the October Revolution. In other words, the Bolsheviks considered the construction of socialism in one country an attainable reality and this allowed them to survive. They already knew then that they couldn't count on anyone and that they'd have to manage on their own. But that was the beast against which we'd have to fight. Besides a few enthusiasts from the early days who didn't yet occupy positions of any importance, it wasn't easy to convince our heavy military/political machinery to move generously and benevolently in our favor. The truth is that our main ally and supplier had been conditioned to exist in a situation of absolute seclusion for almost five decades. The only luxury its strategic thesis of socialism-in-one-country would allow was to include the so-called popular democracies, also known as Eastern European countries, which in reality were managed like other Soviet republics, within its borders. But if the locales were just a little bit removed or didn't owe their independence to Red Army tanks—Yugoslavia, China—look at all the problems they caused. Now imagine if you will this little island in the middle of nowhere, more than ten thousand kilometers away and lacking in the usual natural resources, at least the most basic one, namely oil, wanting to make such a dangerous and costly alliance. In sum, the only thing Stalinism could offer was death, a sure way out of this shit hole called life, since, in the end, comrade, your execution will help us achieve our proletarian paradise, oh, and one last thing, don't forget to shout out, *Viva Stalin*, when they give the signal to fire. Yes. All together. It would be excellent if it were in unison. Will you remember? *Viva la Patria. Viva Stalin.* So you can guess how interested the Kremlin was in the martyrs piling up far from its icy borders. Who in the Kremlin would feel any sorrow over the deaths of any of our *compañeros?* Who among them would be moved? And so, from my point of view, Raúl's plan of turning Cuba into a sort of Ukraine by the beaches of Miami was an innate part—but in the opposite sense—of what I've come to call the second-day effect: the *yanquis* wiping us out, while they—Raúl and his men—achieved martyrdom. "All that education has only prepared you for death," I said to him.

I think that's why he was so crazy about giving the coups de grâce. That's why he killed so much. In the end, it was like taking a shorter path to a place where souls like his were already in limbo and where it wasn't at all inconvenient to receive new recruits. He was very much a Stalinist in that regard. I mean that he had Stalin's same sense of humanism. And he tended to see the act of killing a man as a sort of severed connection, and even when he talked about executions he made a gesture with his hand as if he were turning off a light switch.

I especially remember one of these conversations in my office in the National Institute of Agrarian Reform (Instituto Nacional de Reforma Agraria, or INRA) building. Raúl, looking very young, fresh and light in his gabardine uniform, already wearing short sleeves as was the new custom, his commander star in a silver circle the only mark of his military rank on both epaulets, low-top shoes with the laces tied meticulously, his Browning Hi-Power at his waist in a black leather holster, very seldom wearing a hat or beret, but his thick, straight black hair cut and combed with great care.

"Raúl, you don't want the palace. What you want is a mass grave. That's what's going to happen."

"Fidel, we've got to take a position," he would say to me, his voice taking on a deep, serious tone. "Take a position."

I would listen to him and the first thing I thought was, Shit, this guy is going to get cancer of the vocal cords.

"We don't have to do shit, Raúl."

He still didn't understand.

A strategy would have fixed our course, would have made us collapsible.

"Raúl," I tried to explain to him. "Why do you want direction? You must mean a strategy."

"Of course, Fidel."

"A strategy?"

"Uh-huh."

"That's what you want? A strategy?"

"A strategy."

"But don't you understand that if we map out a strategy and fix our course, we'll immediately fall into an ambush? The only thing the enemy needs to know is where we're going so that they can take their positions and ambush us. Do you understand?"

He went mute. Another battle lost to me.

I changed the subject immediately to an innocuous topic, but chose it with utmost care so it wouldn't seem humiliating. This tactic can be counterproductive in the dialectic of a conversation between conspirators, and especially when it's with someone who considers himself to be in a position of power and importance but who, at the same time, recognizes that he is at a permanent intellectual disadvantage. From that assumption, you, the superior, are never going to be regarded as the boss, but rather as the object of envy and resentment, and you should learn to manage things very tactfully because at any moment the spirit of normal communications implied in a chain of command can break and lead to a relationship of suppressed but very visceral doubts, always building up and always tending toward betrayal. Such that, when it comes to bringing up an innocuous topic, you should do so quickly, as if it were something you're really concerned about, and that shows your interest in even the simplest aspects of your interlocutor's personal life.

"How's Vilma's pregnancy going?" I asked him. "How many months along is she now?"

Right away, of course, you take on a conspiratorial tone again. But this time, it's not to reject his suggestions, but rather to share a task. In Raúl's case, the subject that most intensely focused him was political repression.

"Look, Raúl." I slid my arm over his shoulder and spoke right into his ear, in that kind of Faraday cage that we habitually make of our bodies, without it mattering that we were by ourselves in the office I'd made for myself at INRA and that no one else was authorized to come in.

Upon re-creating this scene, my arm over Raúl's shoulder, whispering another task in his ear, I thought of the number of times that I'd commissioned all kinds of tasks to thousands of *compañeros* with this same gesture. It's practically an automatic impulse: where there's a task and a man to whom to entrust it, the muscles of my right shoulder are already raising my arm and extending it toward his upper torso to establish a communion between us. I think that if I had to choose the expression of my body language with the greatest symbolic meaning in the history of my revolutionary leadership, I would choose this one without hesitation.

Well, rest assured that I have conducted almost all of the Cuban Revolution by placing men under the weight of my right arm, and this has not at all been an uncomfortable position for me due to my six-foot-two stature, when the average height of my compatriots is well below this. In other words, I was basically resting on them while I whispered whatever task it is that I was assigning them.

"Our problem," I told Raúl in that de rigueur confessional tone, "our problem is that we have to maintain control over two fronts: the Revolution and the counterrevolution."

His eyes lit up. He immediately agreed.

"Two fronts," he repeated.

"Do you see?" I said. "Two fronts to control."

"Two. Two," he said.

Now, as I write this, I think that from very early on we learned not to speak very clearly and to keep a hand in everything to keep people guessing; and it has especially been that way in the eyes of the Americans, and later the Soviets, and with Raúl himself and Che and even with my lead bodyguards, to whom I frequently say as they're leaving my house, "Let's go to my office at the Palace of the Revolution," and, halfway there, leaning back in the backseat of my Mercedes limousine, I tap Colonel Mainé's shoulder or that of Colonel Joseíto, depending on who's in the front, and say, "Let's go to Mampostón instead," which is in the absolute opposite direction. I remember that once, around 1966, when I had authorized the relentless persecution of the last bastion of old communists that I was given to calling "the microfraction," I sent one of our *compañeros*—Captain Osmany Cienfuegos—to speak at a function at the Ñico López National School of the Party about the topic "Who said we're socialists?" Raúl acted very offended when he found out about this conference. He thought my actions were sacrilegious, since I had declared the socialist character of the Revolution a few years prior—on the eve of the Bay of Pigs battle. On April 16, 1961, in the memorials in Havana for the victims of the bombings of our airports as a prelude to the military invasion, I declared—at last—the socialist character of the Revolution. I had chosen the right moment, the unequivocal and essential opportunity to do so. With the whole country inflamed by that cowardly aggression and my troops on a war footing—all of my followers at that moment being part of the enormous military structure that had become the Revolution—and before the imminent attack, who was going to oppose me? In the end, our die was cast. To not leave any wiggle room for any of the doubtful, I decreed a maximum state of alert for the whole country.

Five years later, Raúl was complaining to me. I was telling him not to worry, that we also had martyrs from the previous ideological battles. And everyone dies when his time has come for what he believes in.

"Do you see?" I kept saying to him.

HE WAS BULLHEADED. Obstinate. Single-minded. But like all men with these qualities, he barely considered the suitability of a new idea before he allowed himself to be captivated by it and invested all of his stubbornness and determination in that new direction. But you had to be patient and persuasive to make him give up his old ideas. The hard part was making him change. From my point of view, the origins of his ideas were not in any way political and it was essential to find them in the deepest part of his psyche. It was his constant need to amass enemies. He didn't measure his successes by the allies that joined him but by the enemies that confronted him. I think that the only explanation for this can be found in the dominant feminine side of his personality. Raúl is insecure. Raúl hits below the belt. Raúl is shadowy.

In all truth, many years ago I tried to teach him one of the basic principles of strategic conduct. The principle is that you yourself pick your own enemies. It's about establishing a kind of category, a kind of select aristocracy or private club in which only people that you have determined are your fiercest and most irreconcilable adversaries are allowed in. *You yourself pick your own enemies.* Wrap your brain around that and you'll enjoy many years of imperturbable leadership. So . . . what about the rest of them? you may ask. What do we do with the rest of them? Nothing. The rest don't exist. At most, the rest of them are those hysterical little lapdogs that you hear barking—rather yapping—when you go by. If I gave up on educating Raúl on this principle it was because I also realized that it is best to keep the men in your inner circle feeling surrounded by enemies. Nothing makes them weaker or more easily frightened. It's also an excellent way to use them as live shields by diverting your potential attacker's attentions to them. At this stage, I don't think I need to explain that in terms of the process of power in the Cuban Revolution the blood relation between my brother and me carries no importance.

You can be sure that it is the thinnest blood in history. Since this is the case, what matters isn't that Raúl is fully conscious that I wouldn't forgive him the slightest show of disloyalty but that everyone around us knows it.

Upon reflecting over these aforementioned matters, I can't ignore the fact that the Cuban Revolution is more a victory of Raúl's than my own. Its communist nature, I mean. I acknowledge that he was always trying to provide me with a basic working ideology and that at the time it was just emerging to replace all of the nation's previous foundations. In some way—although perhaps unconsciously and by virtue of his obstinate militancy; in other words, he acted more out of provocation than conscience, God only knows what interior demons he was trying to dispel—he was offering me an ideological support system. In short, it ended up being entirely beneficial and was never an impediment to any of the paths that I could have chosen, and its utility and efficacy was equal to that of the army that I was putting together for myself. The thing was knowing how to use his orthodoxy as a launching pad to do whatever I wanted; to say it less harshly: his immaculate orthodoxy allowed for my limitless irreverence.

I CONTINUE WRITING these paragraphs with a heavy heart. I am anxious to get to the parts with high military content, like the Bay of Pigs or the October Missile Crisis. But I shouldn't leave any loose ends. Because it's here, in these events, that the entire Revolution is gathered. There was something deep that I became aware of when I was able to put myself nominally and physically at the head of the government, in other words, when I assumed the office of prime minister. What I learned, for starters, was that there is no other form of government that isn't conservative. The more we dedicated ourselves to perfecting a system of government, the more impediments we ourselves created for the unfolding of the Revolution. We had already met all of the Leninist requirements about the destruction of the bourgeois state. But would any manual tell us what procedure to follow on the second day of the Revolution besides Jacobin- or Bolshevik-style bloodletting? The mere low-grade killing of Batista supporters that we carried out—only a few dozen or so—generated such bad propaganda, what would happen if we had carried out a wholesale execution of the entire opposition? To use the words of Mussolini or

Getúlio Vargas or António de Oliveira Salazar, perhaps we were going through the experience of "Estado Novo," although surely of an intensity and a dimension that none of these predecessors of mine ever knew. Yes, in fact, it was an Estado Novo, but only by virtue of the fact that we had destroyed the old one. Such was the situation. We were forced to start from scratch. We started with a government that functioned exclusively around a Council of Ministers, a body that was primarily comprised of notable revolutionaries—the ministers—and that in turn took on the functions of the Cuban House and Senate. And this political fiction forced us to make some adjustments. The Council of Ministers was given legislative and executive powers six weeks after the triumph of the Revolution. In other words, it was given authority in the absence of a Congress to govern through decree-laws.* On the other hand, there was that masterly invention of the Ministry of Revolutionary Laws, at the head of which was none other than Osvaldo Dorticós, which considerably alleviated the workload created by the absence of both the House and Senate. There was no Congress, but we were trying to reproduce the Republic. You understand me. *Trying to act* like a Republic. A little later, in May, I sign the Agrarian Reform Law, which gave birth to the National Institute of Agrarian Reform—the instantly famous INRA (Instituto Nacional de Reforma Agraria). This was the moment in which I realized that I had the solution at hand. INRA turned into my parallel government. From there—under the innocent excuse that we were busy dealing with the complexities of the agrarian reform—I started to duplicate all of the state's functions. Now I started to govern on two fronts. And, best of all, I'd automatically gained an army of more than a million men who were going to blindly obey me: the peasants, to whom we'd just given the deeds to their land without any further ado. Of course, when I resigned from my post as prime minister to force Urrutia's own resignation, that mass of grateful peasants was the first thing I had in mind. Haven't I told you how I returned to the post? Well, I filled the capital with close to a million peasants, brought from all over the country and given lodging by the people of Havana in their own homes, so that on July 26 they would attend the first commemoration held to celebrate the anniversary of the attack on the Moncada Barracks. At four in the afternoon the

---

* Regarding the decree laws, this was the sweetest-sounding name we found for what in practice were authentic and final ukases. [*Author's note.*]

Plaza Cívica (it was still called that; it would later become the Plaza de la Revolución) was a sea of people and hats woven out of palm leaves, the traditional attire in our fields, with their machetes raised like charging warriors. When I appeared onstage, the peasants suddenly, of their own initiative, greeted me in a most peculiar way: they clanged their machetes in the air, making them sing. It was a very strange, and I would say never-before-heard, sound. And it remained etched in many of our memories for a long time. "I obey the majority will of the people who demand that I return to the post of prime minister," I said, at the end of my speech. Of course it was a sentence said for effect, a theatrical blow. But I had to carry out my return to the post somehow, and that histrionic declaration was almost de rigueur against that background of hissing and menacing steel filling the plaza. I remember those machetes clanging against each other because it was symbolic from any point of view and I know that it made quite an impression on my enemies. Perhaps they like no one else understood that the country was moving out from under the control of all of the institutions used for better or for worse until then. It was the second time in a period of no greater than seven months that I invaded the Republic's capital with an army of unkempt peasants. And that wailing of machetes as night started to fall over Cuba did not bode well for my enemies.

Back then, we occupied the enormous unused building that a mayor in Batista's camp, Justo Luis del Pozo, a greedy and bureacratic old man, had built as his city hall. That's where we put the INRA headquarters. I very quickly had an apartment made up for me next to my office as president of the institution, on the top floor, the eighteenth floor, from which you could see almost the whole city. Celia, as usual, took care of the details and the furnishing. It pleased me to see our captains and lieutenants at the head of the first state farms or one of the Agrarian Development Zones. In fact, that was where I wanted to see them: our uniformed men on the wide paths of our sugarcane fields or our first experimental crops. Or operating a bulldozer. Or putting together an irrigation system. We were achieving the creation of something beyond an image. Something that was a concept in and of itself and that, at the same time, because of its own rudimentary beauty, was its own magnificent propaganda vehicle. It meant that, in the end, belonging either to the Rebel Army or INRA had no importance, since all that mattered was belonging to the Revolution. We in Cuba acknowledged the value of the communist reliance on the man with a task. And one task at a time. Although we learned this last part with the passing of time. The multiplicity of tasks should be the province of only a few chosen ones among the greatest leaders; and, much more conveniently, of my own exclusive province. Two tasks—or more—entrusted to one revolutionary cell signified a multiplication of its authority and, if successful, would give it influence over a greater number of subordinates. On the contrary, the assignment of one sole, indivisible task allowed greater control over the *compañeros'* work as well as an understandable increase in the demands to which they were subject.

This scene of combatants taking part in the Agrarian Reform vaguely reminded me of a phrase I had read in one of Mao's pamphlets—which Raúl would give me every once in a while—and it pleased me to remember it, however far off it may have seemed. The people's army as a quarry of leaders.

The scene, nonetheless, cannot be repeated. All I have left is the possibility of enjoying it while I contemplate my fading memories.

In all that hoopla, everyone seemed to have his own style or to have his own favorite tailor at his disposal. No two uniforms were of the same cut. There weren't two belts of the same weave, nor two holsters or even two pistols—or revolvers—that were similar or even of the same caliber. All of the world's existing weapons were on display on the waists of our combatants. It was also normal, and for some people it was even in good taste, to go about your normal life while brandishing an M1 carbine or a Thompson machine gun. One of the last times that I saw Camilo—the head of our army—I even saw that he was wearing an eye-catching black leather cartridge belt with a Colt .45 pistol hanging from it with a mother-of-pearl grip and, just to the left of his belt buckle, toward the middle of the belt, as part of his guerrilla outfit, in a very novel and highly personalized design, he had a .38-caliber Cobra revolver, also with a mother-of-pearl grip. Well, Camilo had studied graphic arts and knew something about those things, but I couldn't help making a joke at his expense and saying that he reminded me of Bat Masterson, the hero of one of those western shows that Cuban TV had started to broadcast when I was still in the Sierra—and most people don't know that in those early months of the Revolution I arranged for a private projection of all the episodes. In real life, Bat Masterson was one of Wyatt Earp's deputies. But on this half-hour TV show, he was an ex-sheriff who took part in different western adventures. His trademarks were a black walking stick, which actually concealed a saber, and a revolver, which he carried in a peculiar fashion that differed greatly from the rest of the legendary gunmen on the screen—not on the side, but in front, in the manner that Camilo was probably imitating, although Camilo's Cobra was of a lower caliber while the real revolver belonging to the real Bat Masterson, a .45-caliber single-action Colt—and, according to Masterson's written instructions to the manufacturer, with the barrel equal in length to that of the ejector rod and a nickel-plated finish and gutta-percha grips—was heavier and had more presence. One sure thing is that Camilo became legendary, among other things because of that medium-brim Stetson hat, which was the most distinguished headpiece in the whole Rebel Army, and not just because of the way it evoked a Tombstone sheriff. There simply wasn't a hat or cap like it in Cuba. Nor boots, whether they were tall or short. Nothing mattered, nonetheless, as long as the uniform's cloth was olive-green. You could add all of whatever pockets, buttons, zippers, epaulets and pleats you could think of to the basic cloth. So, with an olive-green uniform, a cigar in your mouth and an assigned task, you were invested of all the powers the Revolution gave you. That I—Fidel Castro—gave you.

AS FAR AS THE Agrarian Reform Law was concerned, like all laws, it was something that we distrusted. We felt it was a straitjacket, even though it was our own doing. We began to understand quickly that the survival of a revolution is compatible with its attachment to opportunism. Here's where I would spend hours debating Darwin, because I believe the chief attribute necessary to survival is having the good sense to take advantage of certain opportunities or to determine when you should remain inconspicuous; this speaks to your ability to be adaptable and flexible and not in any way to your strength. You can be as strong as you want, but the chameleon is going to last longer under his rock than the lion, despite its roaring and lean muscles. And that's how we found out that all laws, even revolutionary ones, have their limits. Because of that I added a final paragraph to all of our laws and orders unequivocally revoking all previous laws and orders. In other words, I created the perfect legal limbo by promoting a system whose basic order lay outside regular jurisprudence. Legality that becomes illegal every time it's reviewed. My God, to what degree could we perfect the state of power above the law this way? We never violated laws because, just before they got in the way of our objectives, we repealed them. That's why I wasn't too worried about that First Agrarian Reform Law, as far as its scope was concerned, since I knew that in any event we would pass many more versions of it in the near future and that each one would more aggressively reduce the amount of land allowed as property. For the time being, we left the size of the farms at about thirty *caballerías.** About three years later—the Second Agrarian Reform Law—we established the limit as five. But be advised that in May 1959 we didn't go beyond the agrarian reform imposed by MacArthur— very astutely—in Japan to destroy the feudal relations in that economy. I was following a similar path. My goal was to break all of the possible vectors of the Cuban plutocracy. So I signed that piece of paper in front of the entire Council of Ministers that we had taken kicking and screaming all the way to La Plata Alta.

JUST A SMALL, perturbing note. I arrived at La Plata Alta after having already been informed that Fidelito—my son with Mirta Díaz-Balart— had had a car accident and was in serious condition. One of my guards, an irresponsible twit whom I will refrain from naming right now, let the kid drive one of my cars. To be fair, the little *compañero* from my guard was just a kid himself; he was one of those adolescents who joined the Rebel Army and served as a barefoot messenger or as one of the sappers who blew up the enemy army's convoys. In short, Fidelito's car was going over a hundred kilometers an hour and got tangled up in some trees near my residential compound in Cojímar. Afterward, on top of the agony and uncertainty produced by the fact that my son's end could be near, I had my first encounter with Mirta since our divorce. I had returned to Havana, going as quickly as the pilots of the *Sierra Maestra*, as we had rebaptized the presidential plane, could go. It was about nine at night and I was entering the hospital's parking area when I saw her. Celia was next to me, inside the car, when she noticed the change in my breathing. She still hadn't seen Mirta. I heard Celia say to me, "Fidel, what's wrong?" Then she must have seen Mirta, because I didn't hear her say anything else. Emilio Núñez Blanco had his arm around Mirta very

---

* One *caballería* equals thirty-three acres. [*Translator's note.*]

noticeably and he led her into one of the entrance halls of the facility, where they were setting I don't know how many of Fidelito's fractured bones. Before entering the hallway, he lowered his arm and grabbed her by the waist. He put his hand on Mirta's hip. Emilio was an old colleague of mine from the Orthodox Party. A real bland type. But he had the balls to marry Mirta and take her to Paris on their honeymoon in 1956, while I was in Mexico getting ready for the Revolution. This was the first time I was seeing Mirta since just before the Revolution. Emilio had the balls to stay in Cuba with her for almost five years, ignoring the Revolution's triumphant rise to power, in other words, my rise to power. Now he was strutting around with her in front of me, consoling her, caressing her waist, opening doors for her. I stayed in the parking lot. Of course, there was a moment, one so ephemeral that it left as much of a trace as a small star extinguished forever millions of years ago somewhere in the confines of the universe, when—before entering the hall—her eyes scanned the parking lot and met mine. Not even the news, received shortly thereafter, that Fidelito seemed to be out of danger affected my spirit more deeply than that look. Celia, with her usual discipline—more so than discretion—remained a few steps behind me. She was still silent. Her silence extended to all of my bodyguards. Then I realized how alone I was. And I reacted childishly. I began to beat the hood of my car. I don't remember if it was one of my guards—Aníbal Hidalgo—or the driver—Leoncito—who took my arm very gently and, in a gesture of solidarity, said to me, "Let's go, Comandante." I remember that gesture with extraordinary gratitude, although I can't pinpoint in my hazy memory the person who was kind enough to console me. "Let's go," he said to me. "We'll come back later." I followed him, strangely obedient, while he took me to one of Fulgencio Batista's old Cadillacs.

THE COLLAPSE OF THE legal system. This was another one of our problems, and it took time and energy. The jurisdiction of the Revolutionary Tribunals was created, which fell under the command of the Rebel Army leadership. These were military tribunals and—at a level above our organization—they would become the Court for Crimes Against State Security. I put a lot of emphasis on the Revolutionary Tribunals because I was aware that all of the national agitation engendered by the Revolution should be circumscribed by exact boundaries and that the best way to do so was to make the firing wall the outer limit. There was a Tribunal Revolucionario, or TR, as the Tribunals were known, for each province. I already mentioned before that we started to call them that. *Te Erres.* Even so, if the TRs decisively contributed to controlling the counterrevolutionary element within society, it's also true that the minister of justice and the judicial power lost their edge and importance in fighting common criminality for a long time. It was a front that we gave up—due to the demands of the process itself—and that resulted in a crime rate increase. But the need existed to concentrate our human material resources—especially our most talented—on the battle against imperialism and the counterrevolution. A few years later we created the TR2, for crimes of corruption ("misuse of funds" as we called it). Finally, around 1963, as an expedited way to curb criminality, we extended the use of the death penalty to common criminals. In that sense, we can't deny that we raised their status and made them equal to the bourgeois. You could say that we started to treat them the same way. Well, to be honest, I shouldn't keep beating around the bush. I'm referring to the all-too-obvious situation that the majority of criminals were black. And because we gave them the same sentences as the white counterrevolutionaries, an equilibrium was reached. That was the joke among some of our *compañeros* at the time, that we were giving equal treatment to blacks and whites. Of course, it's easily explainable—all the more in light of Marxist political economy—why the black Cuban population was more disposed to criminality than the white population. It was due to the poverty in which they found themselves and to discrimination and all of that capitalist garbage that we couldn't help but inherit. Let me tell you something curious that came out regarding the firing wall. It so happened that the level of enthusiasm and decisiveness among the members of the firing squad was not the same when it came to asking for volunteers to kill La Cabaña's counterrevolutionaries or at another prison where inmates would be executed. There were more than enough volunteers to execute counterrevolutionaries. But, as far as criminals were concerned, we practically had to force the executioners even after explaining how atrocious the crimes of the accused had been. That was our experience and I've never forgotten the lesson about class solidarity that can be drawn from it. And when I say class, I'm not saying that the majority of cases—and believe me, I say it sorrowfully—came from the ranks of the working class or the peasantry. Rather, the executioners and the convicted alike come from a group that abounds in Cuba: the lumpen. Finally, I'll add that the main thrust of the battle against common criminality during that period was left in the hands of one man: Héctor Aldama Acosta, who participated in the task of executing that guy in Tuxpan, Mexico, just before the *Granma*'s departure. He's a huge, mean black man like all huge, mean black men and with the most authoritative use of his hands that I have ever seen. Authoritative and convincing and in many ways perceptive. We put him at the head of something we called DTI (Department of Technical Investigations, or Departamento Técnico de Investigaciones), a sort of poor man's FBI, and it was really something to see him rest those heavy hands on the shoulders of the poor devils just recently admitted into the facility, a gesture not lacking in affection and intimacy, and to hear the tone of his voice when he told the criminal, practically right in his ear, "Don't talk to the instructors. They're just little white guys who don't know shit about life. They have no street smarts. None at all. And just between us, I want to see what I can do to help you. They're asking for your head on a platter, did you know that? *Coño*, you killed an old lady. And she was unarmed. It's okay, it's okay. That's what I want to talk to you about. Of course. Of course. I'm sure she put up a fight. Of course. What did you say the lady's name was? Pilar? Of course. Of course. So you knew her. That's why she opened the door for you. Of course." In short, all of that is water under the bridge and it's no longer important how Captain Aldama won a criminal's goodwill and how the criminal agreed to everything Aldama said to him, so readily, given Aldama's way with words and the understanding he showed the poor devil, the very same guy whom, perhaps fifteen days on, he would lead to the scene with sandbags and searchlights at the center of which was the famous execution post. Water under the bridge because here I am putting together this part of my memoirs in an effort to explain to the reader the considerable sum of government matters that took up our time. Especially all the personnel I had to deal with to raise the beams of the new Republic.

ON JUNE 9, I DECIDED to get Che out of Cuba. We made up a strange diplomatic mission and searched for new markets. We were not quite sure what kind of merchandise we'd be offering, but the reasoning was as solid as it was daring. Searching out new markets subliminally meant that we wanted to get away from the *yanqui* commercial guardianship.

Although my primary and true purpose, as you'll understand, was to separate the Argentine from Raúl, breaking up that alliance. Also, since they were the two main supporters of the communists, it also weakened our good friends' possibilities. Likewise, it was a way to fulfill one of the agreements I made with Frank Bender—getting Che off my back, at least for a spell, by sending him off on this long tour.

So Che was ready for his first official mission abroad. Under the designation of traveling ambassador, he traveled light. Zero machine guns, revolvers, grenades, ammo. If he needed weapons, he could get them from the Cuban embassies where he would spend the night. But he took cigars. I ordered that a shipment be deposited in the plane's hold—some for his own consumption, some to take as gifts. So he was going to distribute some very expensive boxes of cigars—with the state emblem of the Republic of Cuba stamped on the cedar lids—among princes and leaders of what was yet to be called the Third World, who would accept them with more enthusiasm than I would have anticipated, greedy sybarites that they were. What I had considered a poor man's gift—anyone in Cuba can afford to bring an H. Uppman No. 4 to his lips—turned into a splendid present. We didn't have the same view of our product that people abroad did, nor did we know what it cost in European capitals and much less in the Middle East, or farther still, in Asia or Oceania. Now it's not just Winston Churchill who can appear in his portraits smoking a splendid Monarch cigar rolled especially for him by H. Upmann. Thanks to a kind of international prosetylization led by Che, our first messenger to those parts of the world, Jawaharlal Nehru, Josip Broz Tito and Gamal Abdel Nasser—in addition to a dozen other statesmen—all had cigars on par with the British ex-premier. Their capriciousness followed, I'll have you know. Nasser preferred cigars that were a little smaller and shorter, like a cigarette, while Tito the marshal favored Partagás Lonsdales. Not Nehru, though. Nehru had no preference. As long as his "reserve" didn't run out, he was happy. His "reserve" was a humidor—with the same Cuban shields stamped in gold—in which there were no less than two hundred cigars *permanently* at his disposal. You have no idea what benefits we reaped in the realm of international relations thanks to tobacco. I don't know a single leader in the world who hasn't considered our usual tobacco supply before making a decision regarding Cuba. I mean, in the United Nations or in the Non-Aligned Movement nations. I'm not kidding.

Perhaps you're not aware that John Fitzgerald Kennedy was reluctant to approve attack measures against us—the Bay of Pigs or the embargo of all Cuban products—before his friend Pierre Salinger, whom he had named the White House's press secretary, was able to guarantee a crate of twelve hundred of his favorite kind of cigars: the H. Upmann Petit.* What an idiot. He could have asked me for them. With Bay of Pigs and the whole *yanqui* fleet surrounding the island, you can be sure I would have sent them. Amid the bombardment and my shouting insults at the skies, I still would have taken Celia aside for a moment to say, "Don't forget about Kennedy's cigars." It's a bond. Cigar-smoking is a bond that doesn't fail among the powerful. And, damn. How I long for one of my Lanceros now. Right now, as I write this. Oh, to slowly roll a puff of smoke over my tongue, meditating on it, because meditating on smoke when you're the one in power—preferably ruling with an iron fist—has been the experience of very few men. Of course, I knew how to take due notice of the greediness with which these dignitaries accepted the gift. As soon as Che told me, I took him out of the game and the doling out of tobacco to foreign dignitaries became my sole province. From then on, the supply of cigars became a personal affair of mine directly with each leader. A permanent supply, free of cost to them, of course. Without a doubt, not everyone has the privilege of making the $50, $70 or $100 that these magnificent cigars cost go up in smoke in just one sitting, and also the ability to tell the person across the table from them that it's a gift from Fidel Castro.

There was a problem, however, with Che's final trip. The ration of cigars designated for the group's consumption started to decline. The tour went beyond what was originally planned and Che ordered the confiscation of what ended up being precious cargo. Only he and the oldest person in the delegation, whom I myself had taken care to include in that little group—Dr. Salvador Vilaseca, a university professor in his fifties, an expert in advanced mathematics and a veteran supporter of the Com-

* If this information had been in my possession at the beginning of his mandate, I would have been put at ease. I would have immediately come to this conclusion: he wanted to have such a large stock at hand because he wasn't convinced that the actions they had undertaken would be successful. If he was going to bring our country to its knees and immediately occupy it, all in just a matter of days, a few weeks at most, this occupation would logically include all of our tobacco farms and the factories where our artisans rolled the coveted H. Upmann Petit. So, why worry about having a two-year supply of cigars at hand? Because evidently that was the amount of time he thought the start, development and happy conclusion of his negotiations with me would take. And I'll tell you something: think of all the good cigars we would have smoked during those chats! Not peace pipes, but peace cigars, hmmmm. [*Author's note.*]

munist Party, for whom Che held special deference—were authorized to smoke them. Vilaseca, as I understand it, appreciated the decision. Now that they're both dead, I'll say that I was interested in including Vilaseca in that savage team so he could win Che over and keep an eye on him at close range, both of which expectations were met completely. The reasons I gave Che took the form of a conspiratory order: "Look, Che," I said to him, "take this old guy with you to give your mission an air of respectability. So that it really looks like a business trip." Che accepted in good humor. And I was left feeling satisfied by how one conspiracy covered another.

And everywhere he went, Che descended the airplane steps in his baggy olive-green uniform, never mind that it was American Army Infantry clothing that Batista's army wore until their defeat, his shirt regularly hanging out of his pants, his boots tied only halfway up his calves, sporting a black beret sometimes and not others, his sparse beard with those gaps under his sideburns where his beard refused to grow and his hair meticulously combed at times, and other times flowing freely like Prince Valiant's pageboy. Che came out first, with that moody smile, and behind him his seven or eight companions, who were also bearded and uniformed, although they were more rigorous about wearing their jackets all pressed and proper, tucked into their pants, and finally Professor Vilaseca, with his sober dark suit, white shirt and tie. And so it was, without our having set out to do so, that we inaugurated that shabby diplomacy that has become such a deep part of the history of the Cuban Revolution. I was about to say unpretentious, but no. I was the one who was unpretentious. I was the one who later lent things a touch of unpretentiousness because I did so within the confines of my studied elegance. Che wasn't elegant. He was scruffy because he thought that was the poster child for rebellion to the extreme. I, on the other hand, knew that there was no more effective rebelliousness than that which came from the seat of power. And that power requires given attributes, given manners. But, I must admit, in the end Che's worn and crumpled clothing would give things a fresh air that we hadn't conceived of beforehand. That has been the way with many things within our process. We've been surprised as we go. I think that in our time we've been one of the best-read governing teams, and in the classics at that. Very few of our actions were taken without first consulting Machiavelli, Lenin, Napoleon, Gramsci, Marx. But sometimes the results appear to have been pulled out of a magician's hat. Do you follow? The origins of our actions usually lie in a classic option that we have learned from books. Because it so happens that along the way, we've had the wisdom to act with extreme tactical flexibility. It's not a bad combination, I assure you: the classic starting point and iconoclast development. Try it. And tell me how it goes.

HAVANA, OPEN CITY

The bohemians smiled upon us. Every revolution, no matter how bloody its path may have been at its start—and I'm not saying ours was particularly so, just using other revolutions as a point of reference—has been able to count on the tender warmth and appeal of irresponsibility that surges at tables around which friends and good wine are gathered. A strange thing: we Cubans toasted with café con leche. Our open-air cafés, soon to be covered and invaded by air conditioners and surrounded by glass walls, were our equivalent of the attics where the French or American revolutionaries put together their first cabarets. El Aire Libre. I stopped being able to enjoy those talks at the end of 1959. It had to do with the exile of my friends and some plastic explosives from the CIA. The scene had ceded all of its charm—the chitchat, the glasses of steaming café con leche, the intoxicating cigars—before the lugubrious spectacle of the people's army marching and of my own voice, serious and resounding, with which I called for resistance and with which, in many ways, I protected my compatriots while I spoke from a truck bed parked across the road. You may recall that the café was on one of the four corners, the northeast one, at the crossroads of Havana's most traveled streets—Twelfth Street, running north-south, and Twenty-third Street, running east-west—and, being about a hundred meters away from the main gate to the Colón Cemetery, it was a kind of obligatory witness to the funeral processions that came from all of the city's funeral parlors. The first time that I showed up on that stage, I had before me—amid the crowd—101 coffins. The explosion of the French freighter *La Coubre* deprived our national defense of 44 tons of grenades and 31 tons of munitions for FAL rifles. The devices installed by the CIA at the port, Amberes, were a pressure relief detonator and a delayed-release one, which made part of the 1,492 boxes of grenades and munitions carried by the ship explode. Following that, there was no reason for me to return to that little café to show my devotion. As a matter of fact, I have stopped before its doors very few times. Probably no more than three times in the last forty years. The next time would be for the burial of the artillerymen fallen in the surprise air raid that served as a prelude to the Bay of Pigs invasion, and forty years later for the unveiling of a commemorative marker of those events. Well, in any case, I've managed to do something for El Aire Libre, later rebaptized La Pelota: I've never allowed it to be closed down. I have not allowed that even in our moments of greatest penury. There's no milk? There's no coffee? Well then, serve water. What more could any fellow traveler be grateful for? And why have a socialist revolution if you can't also take care of the noble and eternal travelers? We've spent millions on upkeep of the facilities relating to a history of the revolutionary process and my own life: the prison in Isle of Pines, the Moncada Barracks, the camp at La Plata Alta, the careful reconstruction of the house in Birán and the permanent repopulation of the forests of the Sierra Maestra, always trying to achieve the impossible feat of an anticipated immortality, or perhaps—as Celia must have planned at the time—that I would foresee the places my ghost would one day haunt. Death's a real bitch, *coño*.

On the afternoon of March 5, 1960, my eardrums were still ringing from the freighter's explosion the day before. This was the second explosion, which caught me in front of the Pan American dock, where the freighter was berthed, at the very moment I was getting out of my car as I headed toward the rescue teams with visions of the *Maine* going through my head and in disbelief that something similar to what my father experienced half a century before in the same port could happen in my lifetime. I got up on the improvised stage of the truck bed where I was going to deliver my speech. Shortly after, that famous snapshot of Che was taken. Right away, I realized that my order had been carried out to place two black cylinders containing two FAL antitank grenade launchers on the inside of my armored podium, below the shelf with the microphones. There were about fifty people atop the truck bed and I remember that, a few minutes later, while I was wrapped up in my impassioned speech, I saw that the Argentine was falling all over himself to flatter Jean-Paul Sartre and his wife, Simone de Beauvoir, who were traveling the country as our special guests. Sartre's excitement that afternoon was noticeable—and it had nothing to do with the Argentine. When I raised my arms up over my head, those two black cylinders containing the FAL antitank grenades in my hands, Sartre—as he himself explained to me later, if the translation was right—understood that, being on that stage, to my right, while I raised those cases, hundreds of which had been blown to pieces the previous afternoon, he had attained the ecstasy of the revolutionary experience for a writer. On that improvised little plaza on the bed of a Mack B-61 Hauler, he was suddenly at the same risk of death that we were. In some way, without anyone having planned it, we shared an incomparable fate, that of the first day of war in Cuba and on which I, as is necessary for islands standing up to entire continents, pronounced my Cuban equivalent of Churchill's offer to the people of blood, sweat and tears. For the first time, I delivered the slogan "Patria o muerte," with its ability to exorcise the enemy. I don't know the moment at which Korda panned the stage with his M3 Leica. I just know that after 1967 the legend came into being—unstoppable to the present day—of what a revelation it was for Alberto Korda to discover Che's face through the viewfinder of his Leica. A poorly framed picture in dull shades became one of the iconic images of our time by virtue of the Argentine turning away from Sartre for just one moment, annoyed by the hysterical shrieking of some woman who had lost her husband in that tragedy at the port and was unleashing her intense sorrow at the foot of our stage. That was the moment at which Korda had clicked the shutter of his Leica. That was the moment in which a photo practically made to appear on the society pages was on the verge of turning into the currency of a glorious and eternal process. I say society pages because this was the era in which Carlos Franqui, the director of *Revolución*, was sending me photographers in his employ to capture graphic proof of whom I invited onto my stage. But still it was not a definitive operation. We still had to wait for Giangiacomo Feltrinelli to land in Havana seven years later in search of the right photo of Che for the cover of one of his books. That's when he discovered, amid Korda's archived contact sheets, the Argentine's saddened face. A poet would say that it seems like he is looking off in the distance. The visionary's eyes reach you and pull you to him. The far-off and weightless Che Guevara of that photo was already a dead man. "This one," Feltrinelli said. "This is my photo. Tell me how much it is, Signore Korda." Of course, Feltrinelli couldn't hear the chaotic screams of these fat mulattas from the neighborhoods around the port who just became widows the previous afternoon, their flesh once belonging to stevedores or sailors, all of them women hardened by life, whores, or daughters or granddaughters or great-granddaughters of whores. The only thing Feltrinelli knew was that that photo would make a fortune after he cropped it the right way. Che's image had to be isolated from this big-nosed guy (unidentified) standing between him and what appeared to be areca palm leaves. The silence of his photograph was hermetic, invulnerable. Every photo contains a story as the viewer wants to imagine it, never the true story, never what actually happened. Everything that happened before the instant in which the shutter clicked is the past, but an unfathomable, unknown one of which all knowledge will always be forbidden. I'll tell you something, I was two meters away from the spot on the stage where that photograph was taken and, as always, I was in a state of alert and had kept Che and the two French people under strict watch, not because I was worried about them as it concerned my security, but because of how annoying I found it to see Che so attentive with our guests and trying to sabotage my delegation in a way, constantly commanding Sartre's attention and not leaving him alone for one single second so he could listen to me. And I can assure you that there was no drama. I was the drama. I was in the middle of the stage and not reflected in Che's face. I was demonstrating the two cylinders containing the FAL antitank grenades that that very morning I had ordered be dropped from a helicopter at varying altitudes, seven hundred feet, four hundred feet, three hundred feet, to prove their safety and to firmly establish that we were dealing with sabotage. And shortly after, I would abandon this menacing pose with arms in the air and grenades in hand to take up the analogy with the *Maine* again, when Alberto Korda took his famous shot, one of his three hundred shots of the stage. That's Che: those are the posters based on the casual picture of a guy with a black beret and an American-made McGregor-brand olive-green oilskin jacket, photographed by the Cuban Alberto Korda, master of those pin-ups featuring splendid Cuban women—always lying across that same white plush rug in his studio and always strategically placed to prevent the sight of their nipples—and whose real name was Alberto Gutiérrez but who decided to adopt Korda as a last name because of its familiar resonance with the makers of Kodak film. In the decidedly post-American industrial culture—Kodak, pin-ups and McGregor—communism's most powerful modern icon and the one most reproduced in postcards and textiles, more so than the Mona Lisa or than all of the Catholic Church's saints put together, was created. Che was one lucky bastard to always show a serious face at decisive moments. The same thing would happen to him the morning of October 9, 1967, a few minutes before a Bolivian army sergeant killed him with an American M2 carbine. Félix Rodríguez, the CIA operative of Cuban origins who was interrogating him at the little school in La Higuera—and who tells this story any time he can— asked if the Argentine would be good enough to go outside and allow him to take a photo of them together as a souvenir, which Che agreed to unquestioningly. He got up from the bed where he lay slightly wounded (oh, so slightly, it seems), on the dirt floor of the little school and walked outside. Rodríguez put his thirty-five-millimeter Pentax camera in the hands of Bolivian Major Jaime Niño de Guzmán and briefed him on how it worked. Because he was a helicopter pilot—Rodríguez guessed— Niño de Guzmán had the sufficient ability to handle his very expensive camera. Right away, Rodríguez stood next to Che and said to him, "Look at the birdie," drawing a spontaneous and pleasing smile out of the prisoner. But a cloud suddenly came over Ernesto Guevara's face, at the very moment that the Bolivian official clicked the shutter button to take the last picture of Che Guevara alive.

THE FREIGHTER WAS tied to the so-called jetty at the Pan American dock. It had been called that for thirty years because Pan American's clippers coming out of Key West anchored in this part of the port and let their passengers off on this dock. Their terminal had luxurious art nouveau decorations, as the *compañeros* from Museums and Monuments have explained to me, although without specifying exactly what in the hell this art nouveau they cite so regularly is. Pan American dock. 3:10 p.m. March 4, 1960. The security measures for the shipment of grenades and munitions were extraordinary, they came packed inside a parquet wooden box, inside a zinc box and inside a cardboard case. Each munition was kept separate, in a fixed case. If two workers were going to pick up a box, they did so at waist level, to keep it stable and distribute the weight. The personnel came from the war matériel section of logistical unit G4, which was headquartered in an old military warehouse—from the Spanish—called the San Ambrosio Barracks, near the docks. The person in charge of unloading it was First Lieutenant Eduardo Calvert Horta. It was the same group of personnel that would soon work receiving Soviet troops, including the nuclear arms that sparked the October

1962 Missile Crisis. They unloaded the first freighter, this very same *La Coubre* at the Pan American dock in October 1959. It had Belgian weapons, the FAL rifles. They were missing a few munitions and other military supplies, which would come in the first quarter of the following year. They unloaded the second freighter, with munitions coming from Europe—the *Puntinia*—in December 1959. The personnel was trained. The personnel were in hold number 6 of *La Coubre*. The boxes of munitions had already been unloaded and were on the dock. The boxes with the grenades were in a compartment above the hold. There were thirty tons in the boxes. Twenty of these boxes had already been unstowed and unloaded. 3:09 p.m. They were about to go on to box twenty-one. They were about to go on. 3:10 p.m. The pressure relief detonator between boxes twenty-one and twenty-two was freed. The action took place in hold number six but time stopped in the whole city. The mushroom cloud still hadn't dissipated when my cars screeched to a stop at the entrance to the ill-fated Pan American dock. I'd already gotten out of my car and I started toward the base of the mushroom, walking to the back of the jetty along with hundreds of citizens there to lend their assistance, who began to notice my presence amid the ruins and the cylinders of grenades that hadn't exploded yet and the human remains, bloody masses of decapitated torsos and arms and legs with ligaments and bones hanging off of them, still trembling. 3:22 p.m. There was a hand, on the floor to my left, cut off at the wrist, that was still trying to hang on to the last object it had had contact with, and when I lifted my gaze in front of me, and tried to search between the heavy smoke of lime that was getting hotter by the minute, I saw the ghosts dancing in a forest of fireworks, which was when the mushroom seemed to revive itself and reproduced. 3:23 p.m. The second explosion. The electromagnetic load claimed its space, established its own death row. With thirteen minutes in between explosions, the sequence established by CIA specialists.

The spectacle before my eyes in that old Havana port neighborhood connected all of my emotional receptors. The vision I had, in sequence, of the two mushroom clouds rising up toward the vault of a pristine sky and the people gathering at the death scene, touched a very personal, very intimate chord. I was the one responsible for everything happening around me. I was the one who had pushed circumstances to the limits of the impossible in our country's history. And this afternoon, between 3:10 and 3:23 p.m. local time, I'd taken the Cuban people to the point of no return. A memory came to me then. This isn't a literary device. It really came to me. It surfaced in my mind like those breaking news banners that run at the bottom of the TV news programs. I remembered the words—which I knew so well—of Lieutenant Colonel Paul Tibbets, commander of the *Enola Gay*, after having made a violent 155-degree diving turn to the right, a move which caused him to drop 1,700 feet in altitude, to escape the effects of a uranium bomb that he had just dropped over Hiroshima and which led him to say, "My God, what have we done?" and also to write it in a notebook he had open on his right thigh. *My God! What have we done?* Tibbets was on the verge of a mystical experience, and that's understandable, when a very bright light fills the inside of the plane and a first shock wave reaches them one minute later from nine miles away, and the tailgunner, Bob Caron, sees the shock wave come rushing toward them at 1,100 feet per second, and below, at seven o'clock in the narrow visual field that the cabin of the B-29 Superfortress allows behind them, Lieutenant Colonel Tibbets, his eyes squinting behind protective glasses, confirms for the first time that Hiroshima is no longer visible at the base of the cloud rising as a column that is already 27,000 feet high, propelling radioactive material into the atmosphere, and the mushroom cloud is still visible behind them for 90 minutes, with the plane almost 400 miles away. I would say that, after that spectacle, and knowing themselves to be directly responsible for the deaths of more than 120,000 people, the crew of the *Enola Gay* was closer to God than any man up until that point. But it was a crew of twelve poor Americans. From 8:16 a.m. on August 6, 1945, only God could intercede between them and eternity. But I remembered the phrase as a mechanism of contrary action. I hadn't carried out the sabotage. But I had supplied the circumstances. At last, the enemy had decided to offer me something truly significant. And that was the reason that Lieutenant Colonel Tibbets's phrase, as a negative reflection, came to mind. The words were his, certainly, along with the possibility of a mystical experience. But the violence served as a confirmation of what I had done right strategically. And I understand why I thought of Tibbets as my convoy left the docks, and, in the backseat, I saw Alfredo Gamonal gushing blood and noted, not without some surprise, that there were still people in the streets who were spirited enough to raise their hands and greet me as I passed. The thing is that I was fully aware that *I had done all of this.* Nonetheless, as opposed to the crew of the *Enola Gay*, I didn't feel any kind of sorrow or guilty conscience. In the end, the demands to which I was subjecting the people started from mutual needs. Satisfaction. I felt satisfaction. And once again, don't take me to be heartless or allow yourself to be swayed by the ignorance of counterrevolutionary propaganda. That would be the most indelible sign that you haven't understood a word of what I've written so far. And of my great efforts to be as clear and sincere as possible. It's simply about my being the great architect of destruction. And the great provider of death. We wouldn't have been able to exist any other way. Ruins and blood are our work. Years before, there was an afternoon of despair, hunger and loneliness. I found myself on the steps of the University of Havana and I knew that the only path to appease my desires was a Revolution of the Cuban people. All of the opportunities offered to me until then made me into something second-rate: lawyer, radio journalist, Orthodox Party representative, university gangster, American baseball team pitcher, heartthrob. So my personal salvation project came to fruition on the splendid afternoon of March 4, 1960. But there was a cost to this kind of pact with the devil: the only currency with which I was allowed to pay for my entrance to History was ruins and blood. That explains my vast rewards as we left the scene of that atrocious sabotage. And God knows, I was responsible for all of that.

Building of the General Staff of the Revolutionary Air Force. Cuidad Libertad Base (west of Havana).
Eight a.m. April 15, 1961.

*Daybreak at Bay of Pigs, April 20, 1961. The pose is strangely feminine, per-
haps accentuated by the paunch or by the sagging of the shoulders. But do not
doubt they hide a man in a state of deserved relaxation, absolute relaxation,
and of spiritual indifference. He has just destroyed invading Brigade 2506 and
has delivered to the United States the most humiliating military defeat in its
history. And they say that glory is intangible.*

The Empire in Spring

/ / /

AN INESCAPABLE FIGURE IN THE CUBAN REVOLUTION'S HISTORY, as well as my own, is the CIA, or "La Sia" as the average Cuban calls it. In all honesty, they never had much to teach us. When I named Manuel Piñeiro Losada, Commander Red Beard, to infiltrate the CIA and told him that I hadn't chosen him to develop political strategies but to act like an utter son of a bitch, it was clear what our basic approach would be. A little later on, I established for all of our State Security and Intelligence divisions what they now call their motto: when it comes to your analysis, you can't take sides. We were clear on that point. You don't carry out an analysis to defend your ideas, because then it just turns into a discourse of your ideas. Motto. These kids I have in Intelligence have such a suspicious passion for the English language.

To prove how vulnerable the CIA was, I have thousands of pages of confessions in our State Security Prosecution Center, in Villa Marista, to the southwest of Havana. The trove of visual material—photographs and films—is equally vast, although it was mostly produced in the eighties. (If you don't want to watch hours of footage of tough CIA officials bawling their eyes out and/or down on their knees, their arms extended, begging us not to execute them, don't ever ask us to declassify our files.) In the sixties and seventies, video and digital recording technology wasn't as widely available as it is now, so we don't have very much on record from that time period. That technology started to come into our country in the eighties, brought directly from Japan or through Panama.

A lot of it was sophisticated Sony equipment for which we paid a premium. Sony didn't lower their prices even though we condemned the *yanquis* for Hiroshima and Nagasaki. I was starting to realize that the world was moving in the direction of an *ahistorical* business language. It was the beginning of what would quickly be known as globalization.

So, the CIA's incompetence. It's admirable how they understood us and found us puzzling at the same time. And despite their puzzlement, in other words, the uncertainty that we caused in them, they insisted on coming within close range. Not out of an encyclopedic eagerness but rather as a strategic need.* The number of texts written about Cuba and about me in the United States is already in the thousands. But one thing is certain, this enormous list seems to generally follow the same premise: we're the unsociable men from the woods who have been discovered in the West Indies. Allen Dulles himself, the head of "the Company," our irreducible enemy, our sleepless nemesis until the days (fateful for him, so fateful) of Bay of Pigs—was the first gringo to seem conciliatory and even understanding. On January 10, 1959 (according to my reports), when the Senate Foreign Relations Committee demanded an explanation of what was happening in Cuba—the massacre of Batista's supporters that we were carrying out in the open—he explained:

> *When you have a revolution, you kill your enemies. There were many instances of cruelty and oppression by the Cuban army, and they have the goods on some of those people. Now there probably will be a lot of justice. It will probably go much too far, but they have to go through this.*†

---

* I would say that up to the time of Bay of Pigs, after which we consolidated the process and turned into an affair just below the Floridian peninsula that was in many ways incomprehensible, the literature about Cuba produced in the United States was a kind of pamphlet on the order of C. Wright Mills's *Listen, Yankee*. Only after 1964—and their understanding that they would be dealing with us for a long time—was there a marked interest in looking for explanations. The first presenter was *The Invisible Government*, by David Wise and Thomas B. Ross. Although Wise and Ross concentrated on the CIA's mechanisms, questions started getting asked after the disastrous Cuban operation. This information-gathering purpose became the norm from then on in the administration, the State Department and, it goes without saying, academia, and included right-wing think tanks. For the time being, I took advantage of how well we came off in *The Invisible Government* and ordered its immediate translation and publication in Cuba. It wasn't because they had any particular interest in weighing in on our behalf, since I recognized that the book was the outcome of some internal American intelligence battle and that we were used to prove one side's poor judgment. Or perhaps it was a text that was goaded into being by the Kennedy administration as the culmination of its policy to remove Langley's old leadership, the Dulles brothers and the Bissells in particular. But I could use it as internal propaganda to show off my astuteness in front of my followers in Cuba. This was something the book overflowed with. [*Author's note.*]

† Allen Dulles, director of the CIA, testifying before the Senate Foreign Relations Committee. Quoted in Robert E. Quirk, *Fidel Castro*, W. W. Norton, New York, 1993.

I understand him. I understand him perfectly. It was the best way to get ahead of his detractors. What at first glance appears to justify our behavior, really justifies his own. It was his way of shifting the blame from himself, passing the buck because he had been unable to control us. To his enemies within Eisenhower's government, he could even argue that his moderately tolerant conduct provided a way to get close to us, in addition to demonstrating that he had our Revolutionary Government infiltrated down to the last clerk. At least this was what we could decipher upon our initial analysis of his statements. Nonetheless, very few were able to see the truth: that the ghost of institutional cooperation between us hung over us unseen but in front of us all.

Note that Dulles only represented one tactic. He was part of the initial group focused on figuring us out. Soon after, a whole team of his brainy specialists began to focus on the same thing. You know what? I haven't mentioned the Great Prophet of the U.S. Embassy—the chargé d'affaires—who had been skillful enough to see what I saw, but from his own point of view. I have his documents around here, that son of a bitch.

In a previous chapter, I said that we were never more vulnerable than when we overthrew Batista. Because victory left us without an enemy to confront and reduced the possibilities of social mobilization practically to nothing. Do you remember this? Well, Daniel M. Braddock *realized this.* He was the American Embassy in Havana's chargé d'affaires who had the foresight to prepare this analysis for his ambassador after my appearance on the TV program *Meet the Press* on February 19, 1959. The underline is mine.

Castro was clearly speaking for his audience, and his statements are extreme. But he was also speaking freely and without restraint, and his remarks reflect his underlying convictions. There can be little doubt that his basic attitude toward the United States is one of distrust and unfriendliness. Also, the downfall of Batista has left him and his movement without a convenient whipping-boy, and consciously or not he tends to fill that void with the United States and certain Latin American governments. At heart he is still, and unfortunately may always be, a revolutionary, with the revolutionary's need for something to attack or at least to oppose.

For the present at any rate he finds the needed symbols in the
United States and in "dictatorial" governments.*

Nonetheless, there was something he couldn't see clearly. My attack
didn't come out of nowhere. It wasn't a matter of my not being aware
that my true enemies would be the *yanquis* in the long run, it was that I
couldn't designate them as such so early on. I had to let them declare it.
They had to make the first move. Allen Dulles was different. He had
proved himself to be quite supportive of us in the Senate and held back
considerably before bringing down a heavy hand. As I understand it, he
took the position at that time that his intuition allowed him: in other
words, he was saying, Okay, kid, we'll stay in touch.

Dulles and his flirtations. I must confess that we encouraged him.
The situation was a relief compared to the harshness in relations that
had begun after my meeting with Nixon, even while we knew that Nixon
had that very afternoon assigned to the CIA the mission of overthrowing
me. It was a dialogue between Dulles's emissaries and mine. Although it
would soon prove to be an unworkable game for the Americans, it turned
out to be very productive for us both while it lasted. It didn't directly
affect them, it didn't affect them at all, because it forced me to limit my
quarrel with the *yanquis* to civil institutions, I mean, the White House
or the Capitol building, not Langley. Although I understand that this
allowed the CIA to present themselves as extremely trustworthy medi-
ators when necessary. On my part, once I had achieved my purpose of
coming to power, all I wanted afterward was that they not interfere in its
consolidation.

Meanwhile, they were stuffed with extremely expensive boxes of
cigars and we in turn were supplied with generous loads of scotch. Of
course, this doesn't mean that they weren't preparing their own conspiracies, and we, ours. But we communicated about the essential things
and established an open line between their distinguished officials in
Havana and Celia on my behalf. Without a doubt, Celia proved most
trustworthy, and a person with the appropriate level of anticommunism
to represent me. Celia set up meetings with them at one of the first safe
houses we set up in Nuevo Vedado, at a rather desolate spot next to the

* See: "Excerpts from the Appearance of Fidel Castro before the press (CMQ Television program) on February 19,
1959," http://lanic.utexas.edu/la/cb/cuba/castro/1959/19590219.1 of the Castro Speech Database.

Colón Cemetery, and showed up in her olive-green field uniform with her black ballet flats, a black ribbon in her hair, her gold-beveled white steel twenty-six-millimeter Lady Datejust Rolex and, tied around her left ankle, a very thin anklet, also gold, which had replaced an ID bracelet with her name and date of birth on one side and the delicate inscription, UN SOLO AMOR on the other, plus a light sprinkling of her favorite perfume—Narcisse Noir, by Caron. These were the coquettish touches that were not just permissible, but seemed called-for. She would leave her gun in the glove compartment of her car and, with the determination of a general, open the door to the house where the gringos had already been served coffee and finger sandwiches. Mr. Roger. Mr. César. They were pleased to be tended to by someone of Celia's importance. And I was at peace. None of my commanders could offer me the certainty that he wouldn't run out of there to go gossip to Raúl or, worse still, that he wouldn't come to an agreement with the *yanquis* and turn into their own emissary. In addition to the fact that I have always guarded my relations with the CIA very jealously. I don't share them with anyone. You can be very sure of the following: a considerable part of power in countries like ours, where instability is a common factor and where you find yourself at the center of international attention —is held in relations with the CIA. Merely being in touch with them provides this.

I'm trying to make a point here. What a revolution needs is dialogue with the CIA. The Revolution doesn't need a State Department. None of those structures is necessary. But at the very least, it should have an army, a ruthless path (the more ruthless, the more attractive it is) and the appeal of secret meetings with its most bitter enemies—the CIA. Look at where the Soviets got with all of their foolishness concerning diplomatic disaffectation.

So they send us their emissaries. Of course, I'd had that meeting with Frank Bender on April 21 in Washington that had spurred later meetings in Havana.

But where did these Havana-based sessions come from? I'm trying to remember. You could say they started with Max Lesnik. Old Polish Max. He was the messenger! From the beginning—I'm talking about the first two weeks of 1959 here—he reminded us of our promises to the CIA. "*Coño*, Fidel. The Americans want to see you." As a function of his position as head of the urban capital (Havana) of the Second National Front of Escambray, he had made some very good contacts with the CIA. He went from one of the movement's clandestine groups to another in Havana—the few left that hadn't yet been raided by the police—and picked up whatever information he could. I have to commend him, however, for his ability to avoid the misfortune that befell Jack Stewart, old Jack Stewart. I don't know whether to deem the fate of "deputy" Stewart, the embassy's assistant attaché who lived at Calle 12, Number 29, Apartment 19-b, telephone 31 1932 (we kept his calling card), as tragic or laughable. On New Year's Eve, Stewart and Max were drinking cheap Old Kentucky bourbon with water and ice on the balcony of Stewart's apartment. Stewart was a level above Max in the CIA's Cuban operation, but he wasn't quite the reclusive and cunning John L. Topping, his chief at the CIA station in Havana. By the next morning, the situation had dramatically changed. Max now had the upper hand. In one way or another, Max was the one who belonged to the forces that were coming to power. Stewart had gone nuts trying to find the Pole. He had orders from Washington to make contact with the rebels. Max did what he could at the time for his friend. He handed over thirty printed safe conducts to put inside the windshields of the cars requiring a *vía libre* through the Second National Front of Escambray.

VIA LIBRE

Segundo Frente Nacional del Escambray

My curiosity is still piqued by the question of where he got those impeccably printed pieces of cardboard. But I marvel all the more at the thought that the CIA station chief was issued a *vía libre* in a city without any kind of government and where all of the state's ministries and administrative offices were empty and crowds were looting casinos and destroying parking meters and attacking police officers who dared still wear their uniforms.

AT THE END OF October 1959, when the CIA's emissaries cut off all contact without warning and didn't set up any new lines of communication, I was getting sufficient firsthand information to confirm that we had lost Allen Dulles. Around that time, Ramiro Valdés received my guidelines to change the way he tailed those two Embassy employees—Roger and César—who had been meeting regularly with Celia. He was advised to switch from checking up on them secretly to doing so "Japanese-style"—as we called demonstrative monitoring. "I want you to make things impossible for them, Ramirito," I said to him. "I want them to feel our boys breathing down their necks twenty-four hours a day." As far as John L. Topping and his new deputy in Havana, Robert D. Wiecha, were concerned, the order for the time being was not to take his eyes off of them, but to loosen the noose. No demonstrative monitoring with them. Just give them a wide berth of movement and take careful note of each one of their steps.

I was obsessed, nonetheless, with one question: why had they cut off contact with me? There had to be someone better, someone they thought they would get more out of. *Coño*, if these people were going to cut me off, it had to be due to something I wasn't getting. Information started to slowly come in a few weeks later. Eisenhower had joined the game, but—according to initial reports—he was pressured by Nixon, who had noticed the CIA's sluggishness with us. It was purely a visceral reaction of Nixon's, since we had yet to issue our most radical revolutionary economic acts, we hadn't nationalized anything and the only thing we had dared to implement was a generous agrarian reform, and there wasn't even a glimpse of Anastas Mikoyan in Cuba; in other words, zero Soviet presence. But Eisenhower called Allen Dulles and scolded him. He said he wanted to see an "extensive" Cuba program. This was going to mean a substantial gain for us in the long run because this was the moment when they committed egregious force. The establishment of a nonspecific combat group for a battle that had yet to be ordered. But the questions kept circling around in my head. What fools. The contact with them held me back. And now they had cut me off. What the hell? It didn't make sense. For the time being, my government was simply feeling its way, a little too unevenly for me at times, and I couldn't be accused of committing myself to any ideological orientation. Enough years have gone by for you to accept that at the time there wasn't a group with any dominant ideology except for my enemies. Of course, I accept that I was a Marxist. And I could have even been called procommunist. But exclusively from the perspective of being a studied application of its mechanisms. No revolutionary who reads Lenin—and especially Stalin—is immune to his teachings about seizing power. That's why these readings are so dangerous and tend toward street riots and violence, and it's thus understandable that their printing and distribution would be repressed. But it doesn't necessarily entail—as Che and especially my brother Raúl would think—the immediate construction of a socialist state in Cuba. In sum, my communist strategy was no more than a dialectic I kept in reserve. History has become warped from having been manipulated so much, and worse still, since we were the victors, there's a tendency for us to be viewed as opportunists.

I WOULD LIKE for you to explain to me how it could affect an American consortium if I planted a eucalyptus tree or tamarind tree (the Forest Repopulation Plan) in a desolate (and rather eroded) savanna in the San Antonio de Río Blanco municipality or if I put a snot-nosed kid, a petty criminal, one of the thousands abandoned to their fate on Cuba's streets, in a reform school, giving him food and clothing in the process. Other acts were low-budget concessions that I passed to contain the masses. How could the American military-industrial complex teeter as a result of our lowering housing costs—on apartments in general—for Cuba's poor and middle classes? Even Ambassador Philip Bonsal encouraged us to nationalize the telephone and electric companies, both *yanqui* properties, because the *yanquis* would take care of the compensation. I could laugh at him and even mentally anticipate the joy of expropriating every last piece of property, down to the nails. But this was never used as political material because it didn't go any further than the confines of my imagination. Likewise, we could have gone a lot more slowly or come to mutually beneficial arrangements. Just like I made concessions to the masses, I was willing to work with the capitalists in the pursuit of balance. None of what we were doing up to that point was that serious. What possible cause for complaint could they raise? We had carefully tiptoed around the areas close to their true interests, and I brought Raúl and Che under control. But it was clear then that there would be no defense planes, that they wouldn't let us buy new infantry weapons and that they had declared a tacit war on us. No one in the world knew it yet. It was even difficult for us to grasp that idea in its full scope. But Cuba was at war with the United States of America!

So why the change in attitude? The information came later. Eisenhower had suffered various cerebral vascular accidents and had had a heart attack. He was partially paralyzed and had ceded almost entire control of all the CIA's clandestine activities against the "Red Terror" to Nixon. I am now reviewing one of the files on enemy information from that time period. According to a note written by Gordon Gray, President Eisenhower's special assistant for National Security matters, when the CIA's director Allen Dulles presented the Agency's proposal to sabotage Cuban sugar mills to the president, the president—who was already more or less Nixon's rag doll by then—said "I am not satisfied with what has been done about Cuba up until now," and asked Dulles to come back "with a more extensive program." Nixon was already focused on the elections and knew that the subject of Cuba would be inevitable. With the passing of time, it was something I considered a basic lesson in our struggle against the *yanquis*: Nixon's Achilles' heel was the CIA's dependence on the shortsightedness of North American democracy. Did you write that down? It's extremely difficult to outline any kind of strategy when you're always thinking about the elections that take place at least every two years. At the beginning, I saw the U.S. as being much more monolithic than it actually is. And the day I discovered that the empire's greatest inefficiency came from its origins in the idea of the republic, I gave up on them.

AT DUSK ON AUGUST 12, 1959, the first DC-3 landed on the village of Trinidad's grassy runway. The primitive airport and the nearby village and surrounding area and the access roads to the Escambray Mountains, all of it, supposedly, was in rebel hands. A priest by the last name of Velasco (he later identified himself), was on board and was Generalissimo Trujillo's emissary. The men who approached the aircraft had the unequivocal air of guerrillas: grim faces, dark uniforms, munitions strapped across their chests. The plane had stopped, but the pilot took the precaution of not cutting the engine. His silhouette was visible within the DC-3's raised nose, his presence, in the left-hand seat, occasionally lit up by the phosphorescent control panel in the cabin's semidarkness. He put the engines on low and didn't move. Caps and berets had been blown off by the effects of the turbulence and some were pressing their hats to their heads with one hand. I could see the priest's black frock flapping in the plane's doorway as he waited for the stairs to be brought over, and he made that feminine gesture of trying to keep a dress from blowing up in the wind. And then, in a miracle of choral virtuosity, that centurion of crazy people started to proclaim, *Viva, Trujillo* and *Down with Fidel*—right to me, goddammit. I can't forget the scene because of the meaning of those booming voices imposed over the rumbling of the DC-3 engines and that pale, scrawny priest struggling to keep his soutane from flying up over his waist and flashing everyone his cream-colored underpants. Their backs were turned to me. I could see how, with the hands not taking care of their hats, they lifted their rifles and offered those war cries I just told you about. I was hiding in a *bohío*, a hut, about two hundred meters away, when I thought I saw the priest give a sudden reaction of pleasure. The priest and the fuselage's left side were in front of me. Then I turned my head to the inside of the hut, where resting on a table was the Viking Valiant radio with which we had been in direct communication with Trujillo for hours and which was one of three Viking Valiant transmitters with a twenty-meter directional antenna that the Dominican intelligence service provided us for the operation. To my right was Commander Camilo Cienfuegos, peaceful and happy, his permanent disposition before battles. He had his cotton olive-green uniform, his unmistakable Stetson hat, his pockets full of tobacco and his FAL on his shoulder. Happy and stable Camilo. A few steps to the left, Commanders Eloy Gutiérrez Menoyo and William Morgan, who served to speak with Santo Domingo and of whose betrayal—of course—Trujillo was still unaware. And farther back, both leaning on stools, Celia and Commander Almeida seemed distant and lacking in emotion. I would say bored. I would say that *el negrito* Almeida was even nodding off; with his FAL across his lap, of course. I had turned my head seeking the approving gestures of my *compañeros* for that magisterial ambush of mine. Eloy and William had the best smiles. The best in the world. That's what I noticed in their expressions. That we were the best in the world. Here we were, no less than five of my men for each one of the newly arrived party, Thompsons and FALs in hand, according to my men's preferences, with bullets for all of their targets, knowing which head they were assigned to shoot at the slightest false move and displaying those forced smiles of delight.

IT WAS THE FIRST serious counterrevolutionary attempt to which we had to respond. The warning came from a combatant named Yamil Ismael Gendi. He had been contacted by Gutiérrez Menoyo's people to—as Cubans commonly say—"get him excited about something." Yamil was the assistant of Commander Filiberto Olivera, the *disputed* head of the Tactical Forces of the Center (Fuerzas Tácticas del Centro, or FTC). I say disputed because I had Commander Juan Abrantes* placed there. Raúl was an obstacle because he coveted that position for one of his men. As everyone knew, he was never sympathetic to the Revolutionary Directorate's people. So then, Filiberto passed Yamil Ismael Gendi's information on to Ramirito Valdés, the head of the Rebel Army Intelligence Agency (Departamento de Investigaciones del Ejército Rebelde, or DIER). I told Ramirito to tell Filiberto to tell the *compañero* Gendi to keep a close watch on the case and to meticulously report on everything. How much schooling did Gendi have? Was he an assistant? Filiberto's assistant? A typist? Perfect. Tell him to sit down at his typewriter as soon as he knows something new and to write it all down for me. He shouldn't wait until the next day. Got it? Does he smoke? Does the *compañero* smoke? Great, send him these cigars on my behalf. Fresh information. There's no greater privilege. It's one of the norms to establish with the heads of State Security. I used to say it was like a bucket you pulled from the well. If you walk too far with it, you spill half of the water along the way. According to the later statements we compiled, Batista had nothing to do with the conspiracy. The word was that Trujillo was

---

* The older brother of José "Pepe" Abrantes. Juan died in an aviation accident very early on in the process: on September 23, 1959. I brought Pepe Abrantes under my wing shortly after. He quickly became the most solicitous and charismatic assistant of mine. He later became head of State Security and minister of the interior. [*Author's note.*]

still training his troops of almost three thousand mercenaries, a task group he had designated as the Anti-Communist Legion of the Caribbean. The CIA—through its Havana outpost—was leaking some information to us. In addition, we were getting supplementary information through our friends in Ciudad Trujillo and what we could get by following Eloy and William in their constant trips to Miami and their meetings there with Trujillo's son-in-law, that little pretty boy Porfirio Rubirosa. At the time, if my memory serves me right, there were thirty regular daily flights between Miami and Havana, and Cubans weren't required to have a visa to enter the United States if they weren't going to stay for more than twenty-nine days. You only had to show your Cuban passport to the immigration officer. In many respects, we were still moving in that sphere of banana republic intrigues that the *yanquis* allowed in their own backyard. We were still in that stage with cardboard palm trees and white drill suits whose primordial ideology was Ernest Hemingway's *To Have and Have Not*. Yes, sir. I've seen the movie enough times, of which I am more a fan than the novel. Now I'm asking myself what nationality Eloy and William were using to travel. Well, the fact is that their round-trip Havana-Miami trips happened on a regular basis. Eloy and William had been won over by Trujillo's diplomatic missions in both cities with regular payments of $10,000 and promises of high-ranking positions in the new Cuban government. My God, what a state of permanent transgression my country had been fated to. A Dominican satrap who set out to place a *gallego* and a gringo in Cuba's government, to take the country's reins. And then it bothers them when I try to send guerrillas or troops to any corner of the world. Or are you going to deny the fact that for the last five centuries they've wanted to turn us into a freeway for greedy adventurers? And I haven't even gotten to the *yanquis* yet. Eloy and William's contact in Havana was Paul Duane Bethel, a CIA official with a front as a press attaché at the American Embassy, who lived at Calle 11, Number 612, Alturas de Miramar.

Looking at things calmly and with a certain distance, it was a marvelous plot for all those implicated, at least in its initial phase. It seemed as if everyone involved stood to gain something. As I've told you, Frank Bender (or "Gerry Droller" or "Don Francisco" or "Mr. B.") supervised the operation where it began, in situ, in Ciudad Trujillo, and made the recommendation to his superiors at the CIA to let things run their course and see what happened. Nonetheless, I should acknowledge that the Agency's attitude at all times was like that of observers, and in the end they seemed to be briefly inclined toward us. Of course, it wasn't in their interest for Trujillo to win. Nonetheless, the mere fact that they sent their emissary to the Dominican Republic had been perceived by Trujillo as a good sign, and because of this he felt gratified. There was nothing better than having the *yanquis* circling around, even if it was just waiting, in an adventure of that kind. In turn, as far as the CIA was concerned, they were offered the chance to pass some virtually classified information on to us and be thus owed a favor. Eloy and William and the people from the Second National Front of Escambray would get the juicy sinecures that came with being double agents. They acted to Trujillo's benefit and took all the money they could from him while passing along information about his escapades to the Americans. In the end, they were triple agents because they were also in my service. Bethel warned them to report to the authorities the conspiratorial offer Santo Domingo was making them. In other words, that they let me know about the matter. As far as I was concerned, my participation in the conspiracy (which was forced in a way) meant I was up to speed on everything and made it so that, in its way, everything revolved around me.

The first thing to do was reveal that some of my men were involved. I wanted some idiots who could be useful to me—for propaganda (as a way to prevent seditious acts)—making them look like tough enemies, I mean. The landholders who seemed the most affected by the recently enacted Agrarian Reform Law were conspiring with Trujillo and thus had to confront the harshness of the Revolution. I had to use them as a warning to the rest of the landholding bourgeoisie. It was the first time in the history of the continent that I was going to place a dozen healthy, and in all truth innocuous, landowners in prison for up to thirty years. It ended up being extremely simple to get them to carry out their conspiracies under the watchful eyes of butlers and secretaries that we had previously recruited to our cause, and especially their *queridas*, the generic term we used for "kept" women. Batista's soldiers made up another group. Between August 6 and 11, there was a wide-scale arrest of hundreds of ex-soldiers and ex-policemen across the country. Of those personnel, the ones who didn't get a significant prison sentence were scared out of their minds and it was made clear to them that they were being very closely watched.

So I let Trujillo's machinations run until they sent the second plane. That priest Velasco, upon returning to the San Isidro base, to the east of the Dominican capital, captivated Trujillo with his enthusiasm. The second plane, loaded down with a squad of characters and equipment, landed on my birthday, August 13, 1959. Trinidad's grassy runway turned into an international airport. We didn't demand visas either. But I told Camilo, "I think we're going to put an end to this right here." I estimated that the next dispatch would consist of more than one plane and would already have the Anti-Communist Legion of the Caribbean in call to action stations. Likewise, we could predict air strikes by Trujillo's de Havilland Vampire jets. I had ordered the airport be surrounded with .50-caliber machine guns and some 60mm and 81mm mortars, from the weapons founded in Batista's arsenal. I located most of the pieces myself. The direct fire of sixty or seventy .50-caliber machine guns placed in a half moon against an infantry group that disembarked from a supposedly allied airfield was a battle that was already won beforehand. The massacre was guaranteed. But it left an important part of our defense naked: our airspace. Then I had the sense that I was being hasty in responding to the ruse of a little banana republic war and that it was going to get out of hand. Now let me tell you one of my cardinal rules: there comes a time when all conspiracies acquire a sort of critical mass. It's the point just before fission. To say it another way, the point of no return in a conspiracy occurs when it becomes impossible not to draw your guns because you can fool your enemy no longer. Do you understand the context? The critical mass about to fission. A situation on the verge of getting out of control.

William Morgan (under the pseudonym "Henry") kept in radio contact with Trujillo and convinced him that everything was in order. We were supposedly completely demoralized because we hadn't reacted when we saw his plane. That Thursday, my birthday, I gave William the script for his next message. What hung in the balance was the possibility of neutralizing—either via bloodbath or imprisonment—the cream of the crop of the Anti-Communist Legion of the Caribbean. Night was falling when I squeezed William's shoulder—he was seated before the microphone—so that he not drop the communication. And I whispered in his ear so that he practically took on the artful role of simultaneous interpreter to transmit the coda of our message. Attention. Attention. This is Henry. Tell me if you read me. Attention, Pantera. Henry to Pantera. Attention. The troops of the Second Front

advanced on Manicaragua and then descended on Santa Clara. A counterattack by Fidel's forces allowed them to recapture the *batey* at the
Soledad Mill, but Río Hondo, Cumanayagua, El Salto and Caonao are
still under our control. We should take advantage of the enemy's low
morale to disembark our legion and prepare for the final battle. This is
Henry. Tell me if you copy. Trujillo's response was typical of his modus
operandi. The legion would be dispatched when the conditions were
more favorable. In the meantime, he would send another plane with supplies, advisors and a personal emissary. "Son of a bitch," I said, "you're
a son of a bitch." My cigar at my lips—as usual, converted into the focal
point of everyone present—I paced around the table. "You're going to
wait for Santa Clara to fall. You're going to do that to then decide to
send a symbolic force. And in the process, you'll save millions of dollars. Millions in operational costs." It was beyond axiomatic. The Anti-
Communist Legion of the Caribbean wasn't coming. Oh, you little son
of a bitch, I thought. Oh, Rafaelito. So I made the decision to capture
the plane and finish off the operation. Camilo made a disgusted face.
"*Coño*, Fidel, weren't we going to capture Trujillo?" It had been the second time (though not the last) that the idea had occurred to me to
arrest a sitting president (Batista had been the first). The environment
was such that at any moment, Trujillo could touch down in Trinidad to
rouse his troops. "Forget about that, Camilo. It's over. Leave it to the
Americans. Now it's their business. Call Artola."

Commander Lázaro Artola received my order to capture the plane.
The plane landed fifty minutes after the close of communications with
Santo Domingo. With my entourage, I left the hut next to the landing strip and went to the barracks to give Artola's men room for con-
ferring in the hut. I couldn't see from there the site where the DC-3
was parked, but I was able to hear clearly how the vessel taxied with its
engines lowered and, at the end of the trajectory, I was surprised to hear
the engines shut off entirely. I looked at the two Rolexes I had dancing around my left wrist. The fluorescent spheres said the same time:
eight p.m. The plane had eleven men on it. The pilot was Lieutenant
Colonel Antonio Soto Rodríguez, the same one who had taken Batista
and his fleeing delegation to Ciudad Trujillo in the early hours of January 1, 1959. Another two characters on board: Rolando del Pozo Jiménez, the son of Justo Luis del Pozo y del Puerto, the ex-mayor of Havana
under Batista, and Roberto Martín Pérez, the son of Lutgardo Mar-

tín Pérez, the ex-police lieutenant colonel and one of the most well-known Cuban war criminals. Following them: Carlos Vals, the copilot; ex-captain Francisco Betancourt, a fugitive from revolutionary justice; Pedro Rivero Moreno, ex-soldier and also a fugitive; Alfredo Malibrán Moreno, a Spanish mercenary who was a bazooka specialist; and the Cuban mercenaries Raúl Díaz Prieto, Armando Valera Salgado, Raúl Carvajal Hernández and Sigifredo Rodríguez Díaz. Six of them were planning to stay and the others to return. That stupid little son of Havana's ex-mayor would introduce himself as Trujillo's personal envoy. He had barely stepped on firm ground when he noticed the face of his friend Eloy Gutiérrez Menoyo among the welcoming committee. They had been friends when they were younger and—according to my reports—del Pozo had given Eloy the money to open a nightclub around 1955, or at least for the initial payments, about fifteen thousand pesos. Eloy was quick to introduce him to some of the people around him as the fastest and least violent way to release himself from his embrace. Then del Pozo took a map out of his pocket and asked where they wanted Trujillo to send the two bombers he had ready. Shit, what he had in mind was getting some use out of those things. The de Havilland Vampire was kept in reserve. The man refused to retire his two B–17s before allowing himself the luxury of at least approving a long-range bombing mission for himself. "The bombers can come tomorrow, Eloy," Trujillo's emissary said, "when there's a target to hit. Tell me where you want it. Mark it on this map. And sign it."

They told me that later Artola clapped his enormous farmworker's hands twice and yelled, "*¡Arríba!*" to hurry up the unloading, when a little lieutenant of ours named Oscar Reytor, who wasn't part of the initial group chosen by Artola, thought that "*¡Arríba!*" was the signal and placed his hand on his gun to draw it. Silence. "Don't you hear the silence, Camilo?" I was saying this to Camilo. "Silence. They've turned off the engines. He is completely trustworthy, Camilo. Completely." This little lieutenant of ours didn't know the real signal that was agreed upon. *Look at how good these grenades are!* That was the signal. The little lieutenant heard Artola say, "*¡Arríba!*" and thought that was the signal and placed his hand on his gun to draw it. Supposedly, immediately thereafter, a member of the plane's crew fired the first shot, which triggered a shoot-out. Since the exchange happened within the loading cabin and all the participants were reaching for their guns and riddling each other with bullets, in just a few seconds there were four dead and two wounded. That was the immediate output, but the battle lasted about ten minutes. Trujillo's group had two dead: Carlos Valls (who, we later learned, was the first one to try to resist arrest, in other words, the first one who reached for his gun upon seeing Lieutenant Reytor's move) and the Batista ex-captain Francisco Betancourt. On our side, Lieutenant Eliope Paz and the civilian Frank Hidalgo Gato; Lieutenant Oscar Reytor died later as a result of his injuries, his move to draw his gun left unfinished for all of eternity. The wounded one on the other side was Lieutenant Colonel Antonio Soto Rodríguez, the infamous pilot who spirited Batista away. Filiberto Olivera, our other commander deployed on the ground, gun in hand, jumped inside the cabin and detained the rest of the crew, who, as Filiberto explained to me, seemed to be waiting for him with their hands already raised up in the air. So he personally arrested the guys and brought them to me at the barracks and the first thing we saw was Rolando del Pozo Jiménez and Roberto Martín Pérez. Filiberto wanted to take them to the cemetery right away and execute them. There was a time in which we were given to doing that. Executing people on the edges of cemeteries if these had good walls of a certain height. Artola smacked his hands together loudly again. *Arriba*, he said, because later it would be too late. I heard someone ask where the cemetery was around here. "Camilo," I whispered to the head of my army, "stop this drama right now. Stick them in the car and take them to Havana. Tell Filiberto and Artola that they answer to me for the lives of those prisoners. I don't want anyone to die along the way. Do you copy?" "So," he said, "no firing wall?" "No, Camilo." "Uh-huh," Camilo said. "Do you copy?" "Copy, Fidel." "Loud and clear?" "Loud and clear, Fidel." "Pay attention. I want them bathed, shaven and clean for tomorrow. I'm the one who has to appear with them on television."

In fact, my men preserved their necks, although not only in exchange for a television appearance. As I explained to the *compañeros*, it was del Pozo and Martín Pérez's fathers who were being punished, not them. Executing their kids would have caused the ex-mayor and the ex–lieutenant colonel no more than two years of suffering in their Miami refuges. But as long as we kept their sons in Cuba rotting in a colonial-era galley, they would stay connected to the unbearable oppression of that sentence, in addition to becoming the new members of one of the main deterrent forces we could count on against invasions and plots, which we designated as captive allies, who wouldn't be participating in any adventure against us from Miami, lest we decide to blow their sons' brains out in their cells at the sight of the first *yanqui* parachuter landing on our territory.

And that was the end of Trujillo's conspiracy, the most significant attempt to destroy the Cuban Revolution until the battle at Playa Girón and after which—as I've said—the characteristics—or *pattern*, as they say—were established that the CIA would follow as an operative model: internal insurrection and destabilization, mercenary invasions, an Organization of American States (OAS) maneuver with the approval of their regional allies—in other words, at that time, everyone in the region—and legitimization of a U.S. intervention to keep the peace.

Just a few more details and I'll finish up. William was detained on October 17, 1960, for organizing a center for counterrevolutionary bands in Escambray, according to the CIA, and we had to send him to the firing squad. I went to see him at La Cabaña on the afternoon of March 11, 1961, before he was executed. I took my place on an old stone parapet raised above a narrow moat with a grassy bottom, a rectangle surrounded by enormous feudal walls that Spanish military engineers had designed three centuries before to defend the fortress. A chain of heavy links hung from one end to another of the parapet. Access to that site came only through a tunnel that ran through the collection of buildings and which I estimated to be about a hundred meters long. Both ends, of course, were garrisoned by rusty barred doors that squealed painfully when, for my exclusive use, they were opened for the first time in perhaps a century. They required the efforts of my well-built guards and an officer responsible for that part of the prison to permit us a small gap of entry. Héctor. The officer responsible for that special area said his name was Héctor. I remember him. He was a lieutenant. A white man with a thin mustache. He wore his olive-green field uniform, an American gun at his waist and a bunch of keys, each one of which should have been a museum relic, in hand. He was extremely chatty, probably because he was in my presence. He had stood out in La Cabaña from the beginning of the Revolution and was telling me that it was he who carried out Colonel Jesús Sosa Blanco's last wishes. The story was a way of showing me his extreme efficiency as a jailer. He had shown up at the prisoner's cell and informed him that it was his last night and was there anything he could do for him. "*Coño,* *chico. Un* arroz con pollo." As a result, and to carry out the request to the utmost, Héctor went to the cook at the officers' club and asked him to take great pains and not be stingy with the peas or the peppers, much less with the pieces of chicken. Héctor told me that he even got him some napkins and a couple of beers and that when the prisoner had finished, he patted his belly a few times and, visibly gratified, said to him, "You see, *chico*? Now I'm satisfied." Below, diagonally across from me, was the portico that led to the *capilla,* the cell for those awaiting execution and that was kept closed with two enormous, heavy iron planks, its hinges likewise ungreased since time immemorial. I ordered all of the guards and Héctor to leave. They emptied out. I concentrated on my task and on my objectives and it was as if I were alone on the parapet. I lit a cigar with great difficulty. The Lenten winds gathered forcefully within the moat's walls and made me waste several matches. At last I was able to make one stay lit. I had on my olive-green beret, fitted very tightly on my scalp, and I was wearing a field jacket with four front pockets that went down to my mid-thigh. Then the portico opened. I had told them to bring me William through the middle of the moat and to keep him down and about five meters away from me. I signaled the two guards accompanying the prisoner to unlock his handcuffs. William, upon feeling his wrists become free, made a gesture similar to that of boxers when they let their arms fall before a fight. He raised his eyes toward me. The temperature was that of Cuban winter. It didn't make you sweat, but the air could get heavy after night fell. And William was lightly dressed. He was only wearing the short-sleeved khaki shirt in which he would shortly be executed. What I wanted to tell him was that his mother had called from the United States and had asked me to spare his life. "She just called, William. The whole thing wasn't easy for her, since you know that we haven't had relations with the Americans since January second. She spoke with the Swiss business attaché, who is handling all of their affairs now. The Swiss guy got in touch with Dorticós* and Dorticós got in touch with me. The Swiss guy says your mother called from Toledo, Ohio. Her name is Loretta, right? Loretta Morgan? I told Dorticós that I was the one who was going to speak with you because you're the one who is going to make the deci-

---

* Osvaldo Dorticós was appointed president of Cuba by the Council of Ministers—after the resignation of Manuel Urrutia—on July 17, 1959. He served as president from that date until December 2, 1976.

sion. And I want to hear it. And that's what I came here to do. Listen to you." "What decision is that, Fidel?" "Whether I execute you or not, William. You know." "In exchange for something," he said. "Isn't that right, Fidel?" "No, William," I answered. "It's not in exchange for anything. It's just that you are the only one among your conspirators whom I would consider forgiving. If in fact you want me to humor your mother." "I should take that to mean that you're going to execute Jesús anyway." "This very night, William." We were referring to Commander Jesús Carrera, of the Second National Front of Escambray, who had acted as a sort of assistant to William. "In any event," I added, "of the thirteen from your cause who were charged, there were only two death sentences imposed. We were considerate enough to do that." "What about Olga?" He was talking about Olga Rodríguez, his second wife, a Cuban woman, schoolteacher, whom he had been with since his guerrilla days. "She's still in hiding, William. To your satisfaction, we haven't been able to sink our claws into her yet." William nodded, I imagine with justified pride, but in the shadows and the distance between us, I couldn't see his facial movements very clearly. I made use of the gesture to bring the cigar to my mouth and look at my watches. It was a sign of impatience that William was sharp enough to notice. "There's no deal, Fidel." "I know," I answered. "I know there's no deal. I already know." "You understand me, right?" I nodded affirmatively. "I knew beforehand that that would be your response. But I had an obligation to your mother. And my own interest in coming to see you. Poor thing." William didn't respond. "Well, William," I said, "I think that's all. If you change your mind in the little time you have left, let me know. Although I understand that I'm saying this to you as a courtesy, not because I think you'll regret your decision. And I'm not misleading you. I think it's the best decision for all of us." He remained immovable. "As for everything else," I concluded, "I think it would be a joke in very bad taste to wish you good luck." "Can I ask a favor of you, Fidel?" "What would that be?" I asked, a hint of impatience in my question. "When you capture Olguita, don't sentence her too harshly. And when you let her go, tell her that my last wish was that she go live in Toledo with the kids." "Okay, William. You can count on that." My next gesture was directed at the guards, so they would recuff him and take him to the cell. I didn't wait around to watch the whole process of leading a man sentenced to his death. Upon struggling to light my cigar again,

I realized I hadn't been courteous enough to offer some of my good Lanceros to William. But it would have taken all of the dignity out of our exchange if I had turned around then. So I was left with the regret of not having given him cigars on that needy morning.

THE INFORMATION WE have gathered for years about Bay of Pigs—a considerable sum—confirms that the war began almost as soon as my meeting with Vice President Nixon ended on the afternoon of April 19, 1959, in his Capitol building office. His first plan was some kind of disembarkation that would run parallel to my assassination. The design didn't vary much in the following months. One half or another was increased as they went on, but the strategy always rotated on a two-point axis. Disembarkation and assassination. In all scenarios, and until the final hour, the goal of the disembarkation was to fill the momentary power vacuum that would surge after my death. The proposal reflected a pucrile strategic behavior. While an assassin sent me off to the next world, a commando unit of CIA-trained Cubans—not a great many of them, according to the original concept—would seize the Presidential Palace, secure the perimeter, designate any oaf as the provisional president and the next day they would be—as the well-known American saying goes—*"Open for business!"* Allow me to explain something very important. That these initial concepts were so modest was a result of Nixon's operative limits and the fact that he was forced to maintain a very low profile in these actions. The main reason was that had he gone to Eisenhower or the Pentagon, things could have become more complicated or slipped out of his grasp. An intelligence operation with the CIA could be managed at a reasonable price. It was nothing for the CIA to drop a little money under the heading of intelligence-gathering to actually put together a kind of coup d'état and parallel assassination. On the other hand, they were making the same mistake so often criticized by Carl von Clausewitz: they were preparing for wars that had already been fought. That little war in Guatemala—the one they conducted to take Jacobo Árbenz out of power in 1954—had been too easy, too quick and too cheap for them and it was entirely understandable that they would want to repeat it. Even if they hadn't read Clausewitz, I knew him by heart. Besides, it wasn't complicated at all for me to guess where they were headed, because during those two years—between my meeting with Nixon and the disembarkation at Playa Girón—I never got any information that the Pentagon was plotting anything against us. It was a battle in which almost all of their strategic mistakes were made before they even fired the first shots. Of course, mistakes of a strategic nature always lie in the concept. So if not in the Pentagon, then you had to look for the signs in Langley. On the other hand, it was extremely convenient for us to obtain information at all levels of the North American executive, political, military and intelligence communities because they never imagined that we would have the audacity to infiltrate them—us infiltrating them first—with such a competent mass of agents. I say mass quite consciously. It was a massive invasion of spies, many of whom, incidentally, continue reporting to their center in Havana if they haven't died or retired yet. Perhaps one day I'll have the time to write a book about these long-serving agents. While the Cold War is over and our disputes with the United States appear to have diminished, perhaps forever, along with the possibility of war between our two countries, our old spies are still at it. They remain "planted" there, using stale codes and alerting us about the movement of American forces in the Caribbean that nobody cares about anymore. Sometimes I'm even worried that at this stage in the game they'll do something reckless and be discovered and create a real problem in the United States with no possible solution. If they're in Washington, I do what I can so they can go down to Miami and reacquaint themselves with their equals: the old counterrevolutionaries. It's a sphere of activity that doesn't represent any danger for anyone and at the end of the day, who is going to take either of the two sides seriously anyway? But right now, I don't wish to downplay their surprising and efficient activities—especially from 1960 on—when they were highly productive. In those months they were able to infiltrate themselves in the *yanqui* organizations, since all flanks were wide open and the Americans weren't ready to thwart our intelligence activity, in addition to the fact that they themselves, the *yanquis*, on many occasions—as part of their policy to rob the greatest possible number of professionals from us—took care to pay for their plane tickets and place our men inside the United States. Professionals who, of course, we had recruited beforehand. What did they think? That we would make spies out of black cane cutters? So then, Nixon was still set on keeping his penny-pinching operation under control and I was focused on invading American territory with spies when it still remained to be seen where all of this was going.

AS YOU KNOW, March 17, 1960, is a decisive day. The Cuba project, which had already been developed by the CIA and which was backed up by an initial budget of $4.4 million, began to take flight under President Eisenhower. Eisenhower and the previous war. They were still living in the times of overthrowing Jacobo Árbenz. But upon signing that ill-fated piece of shit, they sentenced themselves to a course. A general preparing himself for the previous war. And from that point on, he made the Cuban counterrevolutionaries his hostages, not his allies.

What had really happened at the end of the day? According to the simplistic theories, the United States' own nature and its history of invading Mexico, Haiti, the Dominican Republic, Cuba, Nicaragua and Panama played a role in making the CIA believe that an armed attack was viable. But I've never entirely bought this. I accept that there's a strategic vision problem and that the United States stands out for its ineptitude as an empire. But let me tell you what happened, according to my analysis. The first thing in our favor was our public image. Let's say that we were the prequel to Star Wars. Although both sides —the CIA and Cuba— were equipped only with materials left over from the Second World War, we Cubans entered the battle with our image splashed across every television set in the world. We were more attractive and original than even Kennedy with his out-for-a-good-time-on-Saturday-night air, perfect teeth and reddish-brown coiffed toupee. From the start, his classic propagandistic claims and the accusations against us were worthless. Who cared if this rosy-cheeked, thin-bearded, Greek-profiled, olive-green-uniformed, calf-length-booted, tall-as-Gulliver son of *gallegos* with a long stride and enormous *cojones* bulging through his pants was a communist? No one cared. All anyone wanted to do was follow me. Who in the hell would think of Lenin's baldness or Marx's strawlike beard when faced with a visage like mine with a pair of lips that Jean-Paul Sartre had described to a Western European audience as being of an unnerving sensuality as they closed like a fist on my cigar? Do you realize it now? Therein lies the root of it all. In their losing their image. And that was the reason why, from the beginning, they found themselves forced to plan a covert operation. Something that would happen in the shadows and by surprise. My beauty conquered them. This wasn't my intention. I think there's enough information out there about my lack of personal hygiene and there are exhaustive chapters in the bibliography referring to the dirt I accumulate under my fingernails and what little importance I attach to cleanliness and smelling nice. But in the end, despite it all, I was handsome, and thus political circumstances turned me into an unrivaled exhibit of masculinity.

Another problem—not to be scorned in the least—was that the CIA, under pressure from the executive, was forced to change the course of its original Cuba strategy of dialogue and control, although this was developed on the down-low. They had been able to evade Nixon's pressures for quite a few months and put off all of his fantasies of strike forces and commando teams, their faces blackened by shoe polish, silently cutting my throat, preferably in my sleep. But when Eisenhower started to pressure the CIA as well, they had to design another kind of program. One that required a lot of imagination and a certain complexity. Overthrowing the world's most popular politician, that was the mission.

MOVING OKINAWA FOR THEM

In January 1961, I got out of a helicopter in Isle of Pines, the enclave to the south of Cuba—and the second largest island in the Cuban archipelago—where I had mobilized a task force of fifty thousand men, when I discovered that the local commander, William Gálvez, an eccentric and willful commander, had closed the island's only red-light district. In my usual lilt, I asked Gálvez (who years later relayed this back to me), if he had thought of the consequences of closing off the only possibility of "sexual release" available to so many mobilized men. I don't recall Gálvez's response or whether he lifted the noble troops' forced period of abstinence or not. But this isn't a report about the inevitable need for prostitutes near the steel battalions of the proletariat, rather about the understanding of a revolutionary leader, about the subject of countries prone to this division and in a way—why not admit it?—about the instinct that this same leader had about this other matter and about how these same countries that are divided or segmented have later been a real headache.

In the fifties, in fact, it appeared to be a Cold War requirement that certain countries have an "other," the same country with a different name, North and South Korea, East and West Germany, North and South Vietnam, continental China and Formosa. And each one, more or less onerously, was a dutiful satellite of the White House or the Kremlin, and in some cases—Korea—even of the People's Palace of Peking. The reason that I filled Isle of Pines with my first heavy battalions of Havana's working militias and scores of newly unpacked four-barrel antiaircraft machine guns and planted mines and explosives ready to blow up the two airports and all of the island's bridges plus the prison with all of its political prisoners inside was to avoid the CIA turning it into the Cuban Formosa or the equivalent of the portion of the Korean peninsula that extends to the south of the so-called demarcation line. So here we were in January 1961 and I deployed a task force of fifty thousand men in battalions to the old enclave of corsairs and pirates. It was all too clear. Faced with a counterrevolutionary emigration to Florida that was growing by the day, we had to make it easy for the enemy's strategists to create only one viable plan and dissolve their hope of creating an alternative Cuba in Isle of Pines. We had to force them to disembark in what we could call solid Cuban ground, in other words, the archipelago's other large island, the Cuba we all know. No letting them occupy Isle of Pines to eventually turn it into an emporium of riches, and less still into an anchored aircraft carrier just ten minutes' flight away from the southern coast of Havana Province and twenty from the suburbs of Havana proper. Of course, in the end, the invasion ended up happening at a remote spot called Bay of Pigs, which we now know as the setting for the most humiliating defeat in American history until Vietnam.

Turning Isle of Pines into an impregnable fortress was the first strategic decision we made in 1961. We didn't have planes or ships in reserve. So we were there beforehand. The second one was Escambray, but I'll talk more about that later. In other words, we were closing off the possible disembarkation scenarios one by one for as long as they gave us time to do so. The reactivation of my old master's degree in preparing and mounting an ambush. First lesson: *you* pick the place.

And it was just a short while before we took the rug out from under them, at the Bay of Pigs.

At the end of March 1961, I set out on a tour of the various Revolutionary Government plans under construction. I went to the Ciénaga de Zapata, where they had built various tourist centers in the area of Playa

Girón, Playa Larga and in the Laguna del Tesoro. Girón and Playa Larga were the places in which we had made the largest investments in the Bay of Pigs enclave.

In Girón, the landing strip was finished, in addition to a highway connecting the beach with the town of Jagüey Grande. There was an unusual clarity in the coastal sky in those predawn hours, and at approximately one-thirty a.m., according to the fluorescent sphere of my diving watch, I stopped near the shore. As I contemplated the horizon, I turned to Celia, who, as always, was walking behind me, and I said to her, "You know what? This is an ideal place for a disembarkation."

I rethought this a little, since I'd done some deep-sea fishing in these waters.

"But maybe that's not such a good idea. You see those dark spots over the water? Don't you see them where the moon is shining? Those are coral reef barriers. You see them? Look over there. About fifty meters from us. Do you see them yet?"

I kept walking over the damp sand. Celia and some guards were following me. I told them to turn off the car lights. I concentrated on the sea's surface.

Then I called over Captain Antero, the head of Jagüey Grande's military post, who joined my convoy when we entered the Ciénaga area. He was the highest military authority in the region and the custom was that they join me on my tours.

"Listen, Antero," I told him, "let's put a fifty-caliber machine gun in the water tower"—it was pretty high up—"and another one in front of the landing strip."

I kept talking.

I talked about placing four-barrel antiaircraft machine guns and an infantry battalion. Likewise, reinforcements also needed to be placed in Playa Larga.

Nonetheless, we wouldn't have time to do this. Events got ahead of us. There was no time to carry out my orders. The weapons and the men weren't placed as I'd asked.

But that's the least of it.

I stopped walking on the sand. An affectionate pat on Captain Antero's shoulder meant he knew he should withdraw. I was left alone with Celia, while I listened to the sound of the sea and the moon traced a diagonal line over the Bay of Pigs. Our only luck at this hour was the land breeze, which stopped the plagues of mosquitoes for a while.

"You know what, Celia?"

"Hmm?" she responded.

"I'm making a serious mistake. I just realized it right now."

"You, a mistake, Fidel?" she said.

She was not being ironic. She was merely allowing me to gear up to my reflection, whatever this might be.

"Don't you realize that I'm under siege and I'm repeating the old strategic mistake, that of hunkering down inside the fortresses? Not that I'm French.* I've turned this damned island into a fortress. And what do I get out of it? Nothing. I get that I've trapped myself in my own siege. No way. We have to make a radical change in our defense policy."

"What are you going to do, Fidel? What are you going to do when the sea is your border?"

"It's simple, Celia. Simple. I'll place the fortresses on the other side of the sea. Don't you realize? Don't you see? We have to take our combat fronts out of the island. That's precisely the trap that the Japanese avoided and that's why they spread out all over the Pacific. I'm going to do the same thing, but without the mistake of Pearl Harbor."

"You're crazy, Fidel," she said, and cracked a loving smile.

"Crazy? Oh, you'll see. Starting now, I won't close off any more possible disembarkation areas for the yanquis. From now on, they're going to have to chase me all over the planet."

Then I bent down and picked a polished beach pebble that looked like a piece of marble and wound up my right arm and threw it across the water's surface as I had learned to do as a child, with a delicate but decided inward movement of the wrist, so that the pebble would slide across the surface and skip over the water until it gradually lost all momentum and sank.

There I was, tossing pebbles at Playa Girón in the predawn hours with Celia Sánchez in the background. The battle was coming.

Can't you hear it rolling?

The peacefulness of a beach. A beach at night.

---

* From the time of Pierre Choderlos de Laclos (one of the most acerbic critics of fortresses) to the Maginot Line, the French army seemed to take great pleasure in ceding offensive capacity to the enemy.

THE BATTLE OF Playa Girón (Bay of Pigs to the gringos) was defined by our predictions. The enemy's own actions gave us the exact information about their purposes and enough time to circumvent them. The signs we were able to pick up from their movements were essential because—remember—we were dealing with a covert operation. The very concept defined its own limits. Aviation, for example. Florida was too close to us, they had to come from Nicaragua, reach Cuba's shores, maneuver, then go back at full speed. That's why Playa Girón's airport was so important for them. It had a fairly solid landing strip that we built the year before for the development of the Ciénaga de Zapata tourism plan. The operational effectiveness of their air support depended on them capturing the runway and using it as a base for the B-26s. Once the beachhead was secured, the Revolutionary Council folks, the group created by the CIA to legitimize the excursion, would also arrive via that landing strip. The parachuters were the first sign. Nobody drops a force of parachuters in broad daylight if there's not a massive disembarkation to follow. So when the air strike took place on the morning of April 15, not only did it announce the imminent invasion and clearly reveal that they wanted to destroy all of the aviation we had on the ground, but it also alerted us that they were limited to a couple of rounds of machine-gunning down their objectives—the three airfields where they knew we kept our combat planes—and then trying to return straightaway to Nicaragua; or, in an emergency, to the CIA's displeasure, ditching the planes damaged by our antiaircraft fire in Florida. You can then imagine what happened in Washington when the U-2s revealed that there were still some T-33s intact on a runway. Well, they said these had to be wiped out. But it was really hard for Kennedy to give the order, because nobody knew where those planes were anymore, since we were constantly moving them and making the pilots sleep in the cabins, or, if they were uncomfortable, on cots under the wings, making them take off at dawn, so that there would be no more surprises, and the U-2s saw them here and there. Remember the axiom: slow to policy, but very quick to war. Me and my own blitzkrieg. And if Kennedy had authorized the second air strike, there would have been a straight-out war between the two countries right there, in which there's no doubt that they would have wiped us out but at such a high political cost that not even the United States would have been able to face it, in addition to the threat (which had considerable influence at the time) of Khrushchev coming to our aid, and from then on Kennedy turned into our unwitting ally and of course wouldn't commit himself to the most decidedly reactionary elements in his intelligence service and the Pentagon. Besides which, the boats had already set sail and the planes were necessary to back up the disembarkation. In sum, the time span for a covert operation had run out and as the fleet got closer to Cuba, the veneer of subterfuge disappeared with the same imperturbable speed as the sail of its old carriers, and in the end, when they anchored in the bay and the cranes on board were used to take out the disembarkation speed-boats, the clandestine operation made its quick transition to an open and tangible war maneuver.

ETERNITY IS NOW

We were like a butterfly circling around a lit candle. For a long time, we kept up our unspoken demand, since up to that point, on the whole of the American continent, it was considered absolutely prohibited to make a declaration of communist faith or be publicly associated with this system. If anything, the only acceptable shape of this type of militancy was as a pariah. Don't even think of going Red, because you are as good as overthrown, and in the best of circumstances, you might still escape with your life, but you'd be sentenced to eternal exile. How odd: neither us nor the CIA publicly revealed our true intentions. They were preparing a military invasion in the airtight shadows of clandestineness. We were advancing toward socialism while we kept up our discourse of putting together a democracy on par with Switzerland. When during the course of my conversation with Nixon I realized that he preferred to ignore my barrage of truth, I decided that the most advisable thing, while I could sustain it, was to remain elusive about our intentions. The invasion became for us the point of no return, but they got there first, since they had the option of an invasion available to them. But I knew how to take advantage of that azimuth. I knew how to take advantage of it before the forces even arrived at the meeting point. I knew that either way, if they were defeated, they would justify this military adventure by investing all of their propaganda in showing my ties to communism. So I had only one option: take the words from the tip of their tongues. So I was one step ahead of them, at four p.m. on Sunday, April 17, 1961, when on my truck bed cum stage—a new memorial service, this time for the fallen in the previous day's bombing of three Cuban bases—I paused to give myself time to listen to one of my guards (I had seen him out of the corner of my eye while he made his way to me on the right through that crowded stage), who, whispering in my ear, said, "Comandante, on the horizon—to both the east and west of Havana and on the coast to the north of Oriente—we can see ships." I had a sea of rifles in front of me, part of Havana's heavy battalions, and I carried on with the speech in which I listed all of the matters about which the *yanquis* didn't seem willing to forgive us, and—when I had finally processed the information that had been whispered in my ear—I took the next eleven seconds to proclaim: *Because the imperialists can't forgive us the fact that we're here, they can't forgive us for being dignified, determined and valiant, they can't forgive us our ideological strength, our spirit of sacrifice, the Cuban people's revolutionary spirit. That's what they can't forgive us, that we're here, right under their nose, and that we've carried out a socialist Revolution right in the face of the United States!* and changed something beyond Cuban, U.S. and American history, and in those sixty-nine words (in Spanish) of enraged oratory, I ratified the continent's future for the coming decades, cutting everyone's speech. I got ahead of myself that time and until I'd crushed the last pocket of resistance of the invading brigade at Playa Girón, at around the same hour, but on Wednesday, the nineteenth, our nation's fate remained in the balance. I took another pause before continuing with the last part of my speech when it became obvious to me that the funeral had turned into a celebration and I heard people chanting their rhythmic anthems while raising their FAL rifles and Czech submachine guns in the air. In any event, the reasons I used were in my favor. Upon proclaiming that the Revolution was socialist, I entered a space where the *yanquis* didn't have any footing. My battle was superior. It was for socialism; for utopia and all of the mysteries of something unknown, intangible, while they were left with nothing more than the vulgar attempt to rescue their paltry businesses, their lands, their stores. People will volunteer to die for ideas, for their flags. But not for someone else's capital. That's the aggregate value of socialism to modern mysticism. Socialism not as an economic theory but as a banner of war.

I was surprised. Can someone be surprised by the sound of his own words?

They had just shown me—where did it come from on this improvised stage?—the plank on which someone had written my name in blood. The truck bed is holding up a sea of people, ministers, commanders, all of them fully armed, surrounding me and singing slogans in unison with the audience at our feet. Eduardo García Delgado. I still don't understand what the person is saying to me who shakes the plank before my eyes. "Eduardo," he says. That the artilleryman's name was Eduardo García Delgado. The 50-caliber missile from one of the B-26 planes attacking the base at Ciudad Libertad cut through him, emptying his guts onto his back, and he used his agony as an ink pad and wrote my name on the panel of a door.

It was like a warning, like a finger pointing at me, an affront. But I realized that I belonged to the dead, that I had to answer to them. When a man sees his name written by someone else's agony, he inexorably turns into something godlike. For the first time, at that moment I became conscious of the fact that I had to protect myself from emotions and the call of blood. The people, in their death and agony, were making me weak. The devoted gesture of that antiaircraft machine gun artilleryman Eduardo García Delgado practically forced me to be generous.*

Two sides of the same coin, I told myself. Two sides of the same coin, but substantially different because one side stands for dead and the other for life.

Then I thought I noticed an idea that had at first been elusive to me. An idea or a premonition?

* Eduardo was the kid to whom I considered dedicating these memoirs, I said it from the first chapter and did so when I wrote on the book's first page, as its heraldry, "My name is your blood." [*Author's note.*]

A day in the life of the Iluyshin Il-28, San Julián base, in the westernmost part of Cuba.
Thursday, October 25, 1962. The medium-range Iluyshin Il-28 bombers, carriers of atomic
bombs and nuclear torpedoes which the American spy agencies have deemed inoperable, are
actually assembled and ready for their test flights and to complete their combat missions right
away: in other words, to deliver nuclear strikes to objectives in the U.S.

THE DAY BEFORE

/ / /

WHEN I SAW THAT THE ENEMY FLEET HAD DISAPPEARED, EITHER sunk or fleeing, with combat just barely begun, and when I saw that in just a fraction of a minute those planes—my planes—had overtaken the whole battlefield, on that damned terrain over which it was so difficult for us to advance, under mortars and machine gun fire and pieces of our *compañeros* flying through the air, brains and bones and lungs— and when they tell me that one of the American ships exploded like an atomic bomb (that was the *Río Escondido*, which was bringing the aviation fuel and onto which Carreras had snuck in a pair of rockets in Santa Barbara) and that there was another one with a column of black smoke billowing from it, mortally wounded, the stern sunk and the prow rising up (that was the *Houston*, which was bringing the American reinforcement battalion and their munitions)—I said to myself, *Cojones,* this is how you should run a war. All of it scrap metal. This was all our planes left behind. I had just found the ideal complement for the phrase I often repeat, that time is what's needed for politics, but speed for the battle. That was the crux of the matter. Speed. At that moment I needed, like never before, to act vigorously and gain in speed, because the invaders were establishing a beachhead. Their first goal was to control the sky. There was no other reason for them to prevent our purchase of planes and later destroy the aviation I had on the ground. I had infantry at my disposal, armored cars and sufficient artillery to overtake them in a ratio of a hundred to one, but their aviation could contain me without much effort.* This restraint would signify the greatest danger to me: a delay. I only had five trailers to move the tanks from Managua over to the theater of operations; they would take a long time to arrive. If the enemy controlled the skies, we wouldn't be able to advance by day. So we were forced to gain speed some other way. That's where the aviation came in, my aviation, and it was the first time in my military career that I deployed it in combat. The first target was the enemy fleet. I was leaving my troops exposed on the ground, but it cut off all of the enemy's reinforcements. They had the enemy there in plain view, a much-needed reserve, stranded on a ship with its prow rising up like a shark's jaw and that column of smoke still rising from it. I kept using our ground forces guerrilla-style, forced to move them only by night, guarding them from the firepower of the B-26s under the safe cover of night just like our forests had sheltered us in the Sierra Maestra, until my planes could give them protection.

THE PERSONNEL FROM the American fleet were limited to a few innocuous reconnaissance flights from the *Essex*, ever more desperate as they received the updates from the Brigade's leadership. The Soviets—and now I am referring to the Kremlin itself—at a distance of 9,758.9 kilometers to the northeast of Havana, had the luxury of getting situated through much more trustworthy information. General Vladimir Semichastny, then head of the KGB, had ordered the main specialist on Cuban matters—Nikolai Leonov—to gather all of the information that came into the KGB and to report on the situation every forty minutes and analyze it. Equipped with two large maps, Leonov set himself up in Semichastny's office. On one of these maps he accumulated the information coming from the American information agencies and on the other, how things were being interpreted by his *compañeros* in

* At the start of battle that April 17, 1961, the USSR, Czechoslovakia and China had already supplied us with 125 tanks (IS-2M and T-34-85), 50 self-propelling SAU-100s, 428 pieces of field artillery (from 76mm to 128mm), 170 57mm antitank cannons, 898 heavy machine guns (82mm and 120mm), 920 antiaircraft pieces (120mm and 12.7mm), 7,250 light machine guns and 167,000 rifles and guns, all with munitions. And we were awaiting the previously planned delivery of 41 fighter aircrafts (MiG-19 and MiG-15), 80 additional tanks, 54 pieces of 57mm antiaircraft artillery and 128 pieces of artillery (including the massive 152mm cannons). As far as our adversary was concerned, according to their own estimates, at the time of their disembarkment at Playa Larga and Playa Girón, they had no less than 25,000 reserve weapons on their ships and the largest combat and transport air fleet in all of the Americas, and the necessary equipment to supply the anticipated uprisings that would take place in the country. It goes without saying that they were well trained, well equipped and well supported. [*Author's note.*]

Cuba, whom he immediately instructed to make contact with "Cuban leadership." That's how Yuri P. Gabrikov showed up at my command post at the Australia Sugar Mill, no less than ten kilometers from the front, at sunset on Monday the seventeenth. He came in a Moskvich 407 car that was part of the surplus batch from the USSR which he had appropriated for his own use. "But Yuri!" I exclaimed, with a smile that went from ear to ear, upon seeing this KGB representative arrive at the stuffy manager's office at Australia. "Aren't you also the cultural attaché?" "That too, Fidel," he said to me. "That too." The walls were covered with the 1:50,000 maps of the Ciénaga de Zapata and a dozen of my officers were buzzing around, focused on their watches and compasses and looking at the maps or going over to the swarm of magneto phones that had just been installed that afternoon. It didn't escape me that Yuri was dressed in a National Revolutionary Militia uniform, brand new. Nonetheless, weirdly, he was unarmed. I guessed that he would bring something of the appropriate caliber for his Moskvich. "Yuri, you're not carrying any weapons!" I exclaimed, once again with surprise. "Haven't they given you anything to defend yourself?" "I have what I need, Fidel." "This is important, Yuri. Very important. You have to go into war armed." I immediately put my arm over his shoulders and established that essential bell effect. It's as if, upon covering the other person, you were creating a unique communication center closed off to the outside world. In this sense, *compañeros* who only come up to my armpits make ideal conspirators for me, as I said before. Yuri allowed himself to be led docilely over to the maps held up by staples and tape against the office's cardboard walls and, whispering in his ear the whole time, I showed him the theater of operations and offered him a detailed description of our advances. A mere thirty hours. That was the most they had left. "Moscow needs firsthand information, *compañero* Fidel," he said. "They gave me that task." "Well, this is the information, Yuri." "I know, *compañero* Fidel. I know what I should report." I asked some cursory questions about whether he was driving back to Havana alone. It was a three-hour drive and he should complete it before nightfall. I insisted on this because I was overcome by the worry that any mishap would delay his sending the report. I told him clearly, "It's extremely important that your message reach Moscow, Yuri. So I'm going to have a patrol car accompany you." I also remember that, before he left—to make the most of his presence in the mounting battle and while we could hear the rumbling of the T-34 tanks that made the road in front of us tremble on their painstaking journey from the outskirts of Havana—I made a request. More modern weapons and in greater quantities. "Now the problem we have is that we're going to beat them, Yuri," I said. "Time is running out for our enemies. I should get ready to come face-to-face with them." Our friend Leonov would tell me much later that it was the dead of night in Moscow when he received Yuri's report and that he ran to share with his leaders the assessment that the Americans were going to lose. "Our specialists report from the site of the operation which, according to the Americans' information, the anti-Castro forces have already occupied." Leonov's words allowed Khrushchev to breathe a sigh of relief and call his secretaries. The lights at the Kremlin's Politburo didn't go off until dawn. They drafted their message to President Kennedy, one which sounded like an ultimatum. The bold move of some who thought they had the game in the bag. At noon on April 18, as McGeorge Bundy, the national security advisor, was about to tell Kennedy that the situation in Cuba wasn't good, Khrushchev's message was coming in to the White House. Nonetheless, I think—and I go on the record here—I think the euphoria of that Moscow morning, while Khrushchev and his advisors put together the message for Kennedy, was the driving factor that led to a series of mistakes over the course of our relationship. Since Leonov passed on the request I made through Yuri for new weapons, and an amused and loquacious Khrushchev accepted that it should be resolved without delay—especially due to the obvious demoralization in the American administration—the idea became credible among the Soviet leadership, mainly with Khrushchev, that the United States—following its defeat at Playa Girón—was in no condition to stop an escalation of Soviet military reinforcements in Cuba. The illusion that we had become an invulnerable fortress on that day of victory led us down the other path to perdition.

I was in the rustic yard of the administrator's bungalow at the Australia Mill's office and I said goodbye to Yuri, who had taken the wheel of his Moskvich 407. He had a 1957 Ford Fairlane patrol car belonging to the Revolutionary National Police on his tail that would accompany him to Havana. It had a crew of three policemen armed with Czech submachine guns and they already had the flashing blue lights going. I leaned over slightly and reached through Yuri's open left-hand window to pat him on the shoulder, my habitual way of saying goodbye, when I saw all of the combat supplies that he had brought with him from Havana. He had it all right there within reach and didn't even have to let go of the wheel to grab any of the articles. There was a cloth handkerchief, neatly extended over the seat and on which you could make out embroidery in worsted yarn, and arranged on this were a thermos, a bottle of vodka (half empty), a glass, an apple, an onion, a piece of black bread and a Makarov gun.

I would say that the sea of sugarcane reed beds that surrounded us throughout that conversation looked like a tailor-made backdrop. They comprised the sugarcane fields —mostly of the POJ 2878 variety—of the Australia Mill, a modest sugar factory silent and waiting about five hundred meters from where we were. So that the reader can get the most complete picture possible of the zone of operations, he should know that the Australia Mill had finished its harvest farmwork, in other words, all manufacturing was complete until the beginning of the following winter, usually until the middle of January. It was now the so-called Tiempo Muerto—a period which was used to make repairs and tighten up all of the machinery at the mill and in which the fields were left to rest so the cane would grow again. That's why the cane cutters were absent from the reed beds around us while we were fighting. Because they had gone off to find other crops to work in the country's other regions. I think this detail is indispensable because all labor that comes to life around a mill in times of harvest—the cane cutters facing a wall of cane and the oxen and the tractors pulling the carts with their loads and everything flowing along the paths and trails and roads toward the mill—was not happening at that moment and so didn't create any additional complications for us. The fields were empty, as were the roads, and the tired old oxen were grazing wherever their owners let them. Very few mills were still processing sugar when the invasion happened. The Australia had already gone into Tiempo Muerto and so we had the surrounding landscape—especially its roads—free of any inopportune civilian laborers. Yuri took his leave and, before I returned to the administrator's bungalow, I took a quick look at the factory's chimney. It had to be the tallest marker for 150 kilometers around. I had been listening to Gamonal bellyache about this for a while. And with reason, because it was a matter of concern to the *compañeros* in my guard. The chimney, without a doubt, was a long-range visibility guide for the aviation. All we needed was for them to find out about my advance command post and they would forget about the rest of their mission and concentrate on razing the Australia complex to the ground. There was a plane, nonetheless, that tried to make its approach on the morning of April 19, one of the two B-26s manned by Americans from the CIA's latest crop, since the reserve of exiled Cuban pilots had run out in Puerto Cabezas, or because we had shot them down or because they refused to fly toward that guaranteed slaughterhouse into which we had converted the Cuban skies. If the Americans had any information about my presence at the *batey*, they obtained it via U-2 reconnaissance flight. The *Essex*'s planes never made it as far as the Australia Mill, nor was there the slightest indication of infiltration or exfiltration of personnel among our ranks. I had thought that they could locate me with the U-2 if my three Oldsmobiles showed up in their images, although it would probably take a day and a half for the U-2 and its crew to return, unload its cameras, develop and print the pictures and then analyze them. I leaned more toward the theory that their objective was to bomb the thirty-four-kilometer road separating the Australia Mill from Playa Larga, by which traveled the uncontrollable flood of our troops and equipment. Another reason it was doubtful that they were hunting me from the skies was that they didn't let on that they knew about the impassable ring of four-barrel antiaircraft batteries protecting our command post. It goes without saying that this B-26 was one of the many planes shot down over land. It came into the antiaircraft locations at such a low altitude and speed that it could do nothing to avoid the explosive tracer fire, which perforated the B-26's fuselage before pilot Thomas Willard Ray—who was identified, of course, after the battle—attempted a crash-landing. It hit a reed bed belly-down. Isn't the symbolism of it falling down on our sweet sugarcane obvious? The plane split in half, not lengthwise, but around the middle. The back half went up in flames. The pilot and his companion—navigator-bombadier Leo Francis Baker—jumped out of the cabin and started running before the engines exploded. They didn't get very far. I had designated Commander Oscar Fernández Mell to pounce on them with a small troop of militia that were at hand. In just a few minutes they tracked them down in a narrow trail winding amid the reed beds that led to the mill. One of the men opened fire with a short-barreled .38-caliber revolver and a burst of fire from a FAL immediately threw him up in the air. The other—Thomas Willard Ray—reached for a grenade and was instantaneously slammed in the chest with another spray of bullets and one lone bullet that hit him in the right eye. The grenade, with the safety pin still in place, slipped from his hand and fell to the ground.

When Commander Oscar Fernández Mell—rumored to be the best-looking doctor who took up arms with us in the Sierra Maestra—showed up at the door of my command post, his horde awaiting my congratulations with those two corpses carried on palm tree leafstalks, I immediately realized that his face was seized with agony and that he didn't see any reason to share in the happiness of the occasion. Oscarito's hands were caked with blood when he held them out to me to hand something over. "I was going through their pockets," he said to me. "Uh-huh," I responded, waiting for what followed. "These two are American, Fidel." "Holy shit, Oscarito. Holy shit!" My initial reaction. Cursing. "Damn, Oscarito!" I went on. "Damn. Holy Shit. Fucking hell. This is fucking incredible." He still had his hands held out to me. "You don't say, Oscar ito, You don't say! Do you know what it would have meant to catch even one of them alive? Can you imagine? Tell me, Oscarito." I made a gesture for Gamonal to pick up the materials. "There are all of their documents, Fidel. There's the report. And shit. And damn. And fucking hell. And this is fucking incredible."

I wasn't surprised so much as angry because up until then the Americans had denied any involvement and suddenly I had irrefutable proof of their involvement right in front of me, yet I couldn't go to the international press with the pilots because they were dead. In short, there was nothing to be done about the situation, nothing at all, so I went over to the militiamen and, with a forced smile on my face, I said to them, "Mission accomplished, *compañeros.* Go report to your units now." The corpses were taken by truck to a cemetery in Jagüey Grande, the nearest town, which we were using as the first place to pile up the enemy's dead. Then I invited Oscarito into the bungalow. "Come in." As he passed by me, I decided to give him a pat on the shoulder and show him my recognition. "Don't worry, old man," I said to him. Gamonal cleared off some space on the table, on which there was a map spread out, moving aside telephones and compasses and pencils, to set our small treasure down and take inventory. "This came from the American who took the worst beating," Oscarito told me. "He had on a gray pair of pants, a white shirt and pair of sneakers. I would say he's about five-foot-five and weighs about a hundred and sixty pounds." "Well, now he weighs more," I said, "with all the lead in him. And since when are you a forensic specialist,

Oscarito? Weren't you a surgeon?" There was an American nickel—I imagine it was some kind of good-luck charm—a pilot license, number 0832321-M in the name of Leo Francis Bell, home address 148 Beacon Street, Boston, and a Social Security card, number 014-07-6921 in the name of Leo Francis Baker. There were no documents on the other corpse and Oscarito described him as wearing the same clothing and body type, although a little taller and more robust. I asked Gamonal to take all of the things away and reached for my fountain pen. Shortly, I would have the Revolutionary Government's Communiqué Number Three ready in which, with the corpses of at least two of their nationals in my possession, the involvement of the Americans was revealed as unquestionable.

WE'VE NEVER HAD the exact numbers. But almost half a million counterrevolutionaries or those suspected of leaning that way ended up in improvised prison facilities. In one morning we beheaded the whole fifth column. We didn't let anything move an inch in our rear guard. Half a million prisoners, even if only for a week, out of a population at the time of barely seven million people, yields a percentage that turns us into—and by net numbers too, don't get smart with me—the perpetrators of one of the biggest raids in the history of the Americas and surely one of the most significant in the world, and God bless our resolve to defend ourselves. The three main centers were established in the Ciudad Deportiva, the sports complex; in Havana's two main baseball stadiums; and in Blanquita, a well-known theater in the high-class neighborhood of Miramar. The latter was chosen because it was an easy place to take the bourgeoisie. They could even be walked there. And later it was where Eduardo Curbelo, my noble classmate from Belén, became the manager until he succumbed to the shadows of schizophrenic psychopathy, and which was later called the Chaplin Theater because someone had told me he was kind of communist, but of which name I also stripped the theater one night, late one night, I remember the pavement was slick with rain and there was no one on the streets and while I was going west, I looked through the Oldsmobile's window and saw the theater's marquee on my right and its high red marble façade and I got pissed off and thought, Who does this guy think he is, he never even appreciated this gesture, and what the fuck, in this country everything should be named for the martyrs of the Revolution and maybe for international heroes of the proletariat and as far as I'm concerned Chaplin can shove his derby hat and walking stick up his ass, what the fuck, I repeated, so the theater ended up being called the Karl Marx Theater. It was more appropriate, really, because it was the place where the Cuban bourgeoisie sang their swan song and where a fraction of them, business leaders and eminent figures of industry and banking, died of heart attacks, hypovolemic shocks, dysentery, nervous attacks— have you ever tried spending a week living like a prisoner in the red-velvet-upholstered orchestra seats of a theater that was inaugurated in 1951 with all the fanfare of *Los Chavales de España*? They stayed in Cuba waiting for those task forces—already disintegrating under fire from the 120-millimeter guns— to take power of the country back on their behalf, and died practically suffocating from the stench of their own feces and of the women's menstrual flows, which must have stopped up the toilets of the theater's luxurious bathrooms and which left them no better than military latrines, the women not knowing where to get cloth to make sanitary napkins since they all began to menstruate at once. This last circumstance led us to use trained dogs to detect menstruating women in the service of the Revolution's repressive needs and at the same time to establish a satisfactory reserve of Íntima brand nationally produced sanitary napkins in our detention centers for our female citizens. We confirmed that phenomenon for the first time in those days spent neutralizing the fifth column. But in the years to come, as illegal departures from the country started to happen, we realized that sanitary napkins were often discarded in remote locations on the coast and aroused our search dogs from a considerable distance. The medical explanation for this is that stress creates an increase in sweating, palpitations, anxiety and depression and stimulates the body's systems, causing a biochemical imbalance that releases feminine hormones, estrogen and progesterone, which results in a period. So, once we were aware of this, we were able to better spend our time and resources on getting a leg up on the illegal departures. Simply put, we placed a patrol with dogs in any coastal area where we suspected people were escaping and when the dogs lifted their snouts and started to whine or act excited or get an erection, then we knew that there were *balseros* with females in the group.

ALL THE DEAD PILOTS

A few days after Playa Girón, I showed up at San Antonio de los Baños and gave every one of my pilots a Soviet Stechkin pistol, perhaps the first dozen of these distributed in the country. I talked about instituting the Revolution's first decorations and told them we would start by decorating them. Then, knowing beforehand that every real pilot is a consummate drunk, I proposed we open a bottle of cognac that I had brought in the trunk of one of my Oldsmobiles along with the pistols. I raised the bottle of *Tres Cepas*, one of the last ones left in Cuba, and said, "Let's get started, I know how much you need your fuel!"

I lifted my small rum glass which was full of golden cognac, the Cuban reserve of that *gallego* Domeq's, to toast glory and death.

"Grandpa," one of the pilots said, I think Rafael del Pino.

It had been Grandpa's first mission with a B-26 and the *Houston's* antiaircraft fire or the tail of one of its missiles ripped off his right wing. Poor old guy. In reality, age wasn't on his side. I was about to say that they shouldn't have let him off the ground when I remembered that I myself had transmitted the initial instructions via telephone that morning and had designated the parameters for his flight. The thought of a quick absolution of all recriminations went through my mind. Well, if in addition to being short on pilots we were going to ground them for being old and because they didn't put their glasses on until they were already in the air, so that no one would report them for having poor vision, we were done.

"Pom Pom Silva."

"Grandpa Pom Pom Silva," another one said.

Our *compañero* had a lot of nicknames.

"And little chicken. Little chicken Ulloa," Carreras added.

"Chicken Ulloa," Douglas Rudd Molé said.

Carlos Ulloa. The Nicaraguan that the revolutionary movement in Managua had sent us and whom the invaders had shot down in their first mission over the Bay of Pigs.

"Yes," I said. "All of the *compañeros*."

We were in one of the bases' run-down hangars that was missing a few sheets of zinc on the roof and where one of the B-26s was being repaired. I had asked Captain Victor Pina—a communist of the Old

Guard, and Raúl's personal deputy in the air force—to gather everyone somewhere on the base because I wanted to meet with them privately. As is customary in these cases, the personnel were summoned, but my impending arrival was not revealed to them. The pilots didn't have much to do after the battles and they weren't training because the station was falling quickly into disrepair. The matériel available to fly was kept for an emergency. While the new MiGs were on their way from Moscow, the base acquired the sleepiness again that it had had when spring began.

In sum, the reason for my deciding to meet with my pilots was that, around 5:50 a.m. on the morning of April 17, about four hours after the disembarkment maneuvers began, the enemy had lost almost all of its operational capacity and you could say that at that hour they had practically no supplies or reinforcements and were thus abandoned to their fate on a strip of coast. They could withstand it, no doubt. They had five tanks on the ground and enough .50-caliber machine guns, mortars and nonrecoil cannons. But I know my enemies and I know that sacrifice is not a character trait of the Cuban bourgeoisie's pretty boys. Our paltry combat aviation, which I had barely—and thanks to Captain Victor Pina's pleas—been able to keep in the air, was able to turn the tide of battle to my benefit in a mere twenty minutes. They gave me the advantage of time.

"Well, kids," I said, "this will probably be a museum piece in just a few days."

I was referring to the B-26 at our backs, in the hangar.

"The MiGs are about to arrive. So I came here to propose something to you. Don't fly in these pieces of scrap metal anymore. I don't want you killing yourselves out there. If it's not urgent, if it's not an emergency, with me myself calling because something has come up, then wait for the MiGs."

My meeting with the pilots ended there.

I hugged them one by one and before each hug I used the pilot's names and then gave him a thunderous clap on the wide open-wing emblem on his chest.

"*Álvarito.*"*

---

* Captain Álvaro Prendes Quintana. Thirty-two years old in 1961. Experienced fighter pilot, two thousand flight hours. Eleven missions carried out in Playa Girón. Three planes shot down, plus one motorboat sunk. He became a colonel. Became a dissident in 1992 and went into exile in Miami in 1994. He died of a heart attack in Miami in 2003.

"*A la orden,* Comandante."

"Del Pino."[*]

"*A la orden,* Comandante."

"Carreras."[†]

"*A la orden,* Comandante."

"Alberto."[‡]

"*A la orden,* Comandante."

"*Bouzá.*"[§]

"*A la orden,* Comandante."

"Lagas."[¶]

"*A la orden,* Comandante."

"Guerrero."[**]

"*A la orden,* Comandante."

"*Duglitas.*"[††]

"*A la orden,* Comandante."

I WITHDREW WITH Pina in my car and left the pilots with their cognac glasses empty and the boxes with the pistols inside leaning on their thighs or stuck under their arms. I saw that they were still looking at their little glasses.

"I think I left them thirsty, Pina," I said while the cars left the runway and made their way out of the base.

"They're very good *compañeros,* Fidel. Don't worry."

"One bottle was too little."

---

[*] Lieutenant Rafael del Pino Díaz. Twenty-two years old in 1961. The highest-ranking pilot (brigadier general) that came out of the Revolution. Ten combat missions. One and a half shot down (a B-26 shared with Douglas Rudd). He became a brigadier general. He defected to the United States in 1987.

[†] Captain Enrique Carreras Rolás. Thirty-eight years old in 1961. Specialist in propeller-reactive, combat, bomber and passenger planes. Seven combat missions. Two shot down plus two ships, the *Río Escondido* and the *Houston.* He became a division general.

[‡] Lieutenant Alberto Fernández. Twenty-four years old in 1961. Inexperienced. Nine missions. One shot down, plus objectives on the ground and ships. He became a captain.

[§] Lieutenant Gustavo Bouzac (pronounced "Bou-ZA"). Twenty-seven years old in 1961. Inexperienced. Eight missions. Objectives on the ground, shared the *Houston.* He died in Havana at an unspecified date, but sometime in the late eighties.

[¶] Captain Jack Lagas. A Chilean hired as an instructor. Age unknown. Eight missions. Objectives on the ground. He returned to Chile and died there in a plane accident.

[**] Lieutenant Ernesto Guerrero. Nicaraguan. Age unknown. Four missions. Objectives on the ground, one Sherman tank. He returned to Nicaragua. At the beginning of 2000, he was living in California.

[††] Lieutenant Douglas Rudd Molé. Twenty-seven years old in 1961. Well trained, a natural pilot. Seven missions. One-half shot down (the B-26 he shared with del Pino), plus a munitions truck, objectives on the ground. He became a captain. Arrested in 1968 for counterrevolutionary activities (never proven). Received asylum in the United States in 1991. He died of a heart attack in Miami in 1992.

Pina smiled, his only response. A discreet one, this one is, I thought. What a bastard.

I decided to go on to dictating orders so that I wouldn't have to deal with the complexity of human relations.

"Listen, Pina, let me tell you something," I said. "I noticed certain tensions among that group."

"Tensions?"

He was going to start to excuse them.

" Yes. Listen to me. When I said decorations, that kid, Douglas, made a disapproving face. I don't know if you noticed. But I think that there, in that group, there are some rumblings."

Victor Pina put in his place. He didn't have any choice but to face my questioning. And, at the time, I was referring to the favorite of his disciples.

He hesitated a little at the beginning. Then he dropped the load. In very few words. But he dropped it.

"Yes, Fidel. The thing is that there's a lot of ill will toward Guerrero and with Lagas. They didn't act too decisively in the battles. There's that complaint."

"Hmmmm," I said.

I took a couple of cigars out of my pocket. Pina turned down the one I offered him with a gesture of gratitude. He didn't smoke.

My suspicions would be confirmed in a week when Lieutenant Douglas Rudd rejected the decoration he had been recommended for. He claimed that he didn't want the same medal that would be put on a couple of *pendejos*. Of course, he achieved two things right away. One, that he could forget about receiving any prizes like that forever. Two, it put him in my crosshairs. No one was going to dictate norms of honor to me in a process such as the Cuban one.

All of my intuitive systems were already on alert by the time we left the main gate of the former Campo Batista base. I turned to Victor Pina, who was now practically sitting at attention in the backseat, and said to him:

"What I want, Pina, is that from this moment on you stop spoiling those vagabonds. Put them to work. But above all, be alert. I'm seeing a lot of headaches on the way. There's going to be a real ruckus here in the near future. Do you understand me?"

Pina answered with the most conventional variation of military acceptance that could have come out of his mouth, although I doubt that he had weighed the eventuality that, in turn, it would also serve so that I would feel insulted.

He said:

"*A la orden,* Comandante."

THE REAL THING

The Soviets imposed the transfer of nuclear missiles on me.* The Soviets were, as we say, "upping the ante." We were going to be—although just for a few days, we would later find out—a nuclear power. More than enough time, nonetheless, to put the world on the verge of a real holocaust. It's odd that we were the ones who had those weapons in our territory for the least amount of time, yet we were the ones who were about to destroy the planet most quickly. We shook Western intelligence services out of their prolonged lethargy. I understand that their analysis relied on one thing only: previous experience. Who would have believed that, on this island full of *barbudos* just come down from the Sierra Maestra with uniforms as mismatched as they were wrinkled, the Soviets were going to be sending and installing nuclear weapons? To get the work started and determine the situation for missiles on the island, a delegation of Soviet officials under the command of Army General I. A. Pliev, who traveled to Cuba under the nom de guerre Pavlov, showed up in Havana. They went on the Tu-114's first flight to Cuba on July 10, 1962, with a layover in Conakry, Guinea. The plane was piloted by A. Vitkovsky and they arrived at "José Martí" (Rancho Boyeros) International Airport in the middle of a strong tropical rainstorm. The rain did not prevent the flight from being received by a party of thousands of Havana's residents. You can imagine the surprise, the stupor, the bewilderment—what other adjectives could describe those faces?—of generals used to hermetically secretive lives and who in addition were showing up incognito at a place where they were planning to deploy munitions and their carriers of world destruction, when the plane's door opened and what they found there, on the runway, was a carnival. How to describe on the pages of world his-

---

* On May 29, 1962, Marshall Sergei Biriuzov, head of the Soviet Strategic Missile Forces, was given the mission of proposing to the Cubans, on behalf of Nikita S. Khrushchev, the installation of forty-two mid-range and intermediate missiles equipped with nuclear warheads on the island, in principle as a deterrent measure in the face of American threats.

tory that man's return to the Stone Age started with a rumba? The mere announcement of the arrival of that monster of a vessel mobilized the entire population to come out and greet it. The people greeted *a plane* and not the people traveling on that plane. I am convinced that never before has a population enjoyed the effects of proletarian internationalism as the Cuban people did. Of course, no one attached any great importance to the handful of evasive characters that deplaned among the other passengers and who, at the bottom of the steps, would be picked up by three black Chevrolet Bel Airs belonging to the General Chiefs of Staff and quickly disappear, exempt from all immigration and customs procedures. They were dressed identically with white cotton shirts and beige, short-brimmed straw hats and had stevedore's wrists on which their square one-ruby Poljot watches looked like they were about to burst. The following day, I got to the airport to examine the Tu-114, pleased that the flights were a reality at last. The nuclear war began with the airplane that the Soviets just retired from service as a long-range missile deployment bomber. Their flights over New York or down the East Coast of the United States weren't undertaken to wipe out those quadrants of American territory, but rather to make their way to Havana. After four flights, Guinea was pressured by the Americans, and the Guineans denied permission to refuel in their airports. The altered routes had layovers in Dakar (Senegal) and Algiers (Algeria), who after various flights were also pressured by their local American Embassies and began to deny the Soviets their refueling stops. Despite the Soviet troops in Cuba reaching a sum of 59,874 men accompanied, as planned, by nuclear missiles and other means, such as the personnel and war matériel that comes out in the crisis, we were exposed the whole time, by force, to the risk of making refueling stops with these high-ranking officials who don't travel in ships. Up until then everything had turned out well, although the *yanquis* fell over themselves at all the layovers to photograph the Soviet personnel that got off to stretch their legs. They were even more worried by those dark and silent characters, older men with washboard abs and hair shorn close to their heads, who remained inside the planes by the pilots' cabin and of whom they obtained vague descriptions from the scarce airport service personnel who managed to go aboard the vessels. We couldn't depend on ships for the exchange of emissaries, especially because we were a strategic ally. Nor could we depend on radio or telephone communications. If there was something both our sides knew anything about, it was that there was only one trustworthy, safe and categorical means of conspiring: whispering into each other's ears. The plane, of course, then became our only possibility, although it became necessary—and this was left unresolved until the following year with the so-called Cuban variant of the plane—to close off the layovers. The need for the direct Tu-114D flights was urgent. They emerged from deep within the Ural Mountains and crossed Europe, then the Atlantic, and landed in Havana without being recognized. You can be sure that never before had I looked God straight in the eye. On that afternoon of July 10, 1962, while Army General I. A. Pliev was taking my hand and shaking it kindly and vigorously and showing me his fine lips for a kiss, I looked God in the eye. I have frequently asked myself since then how it is possible that the CIA's flying identification teams didn't realize who was on those planes, how it's possible that they didn't even sense it. There, in that man's corporeal mass—and I was half a head taller than him—in each of his expressions, in every gesture of his hands, in the sound of each of his words, lay concealed the architecture of the inferno and the disappearance of the human race, of perhaps *the only species* you could count on in the universe's vastness; it was something he could carry out as he threw back a glass of vodka, picked at a piece of black bread and pressed a button. I don't think that Einstein would have been able to firmly withstand, as I did, his embrace. Because he would have understood, in the end, that there was a place where time and space came together, not only in the confines of the galaxies but also on earth; in the powers of this energetic and somewhat operatic little man lay the ability to stop all time and space for us. I must confess that there was something that made me uneasy just as I started getting into the war plans with the Kremlin's emissary, and it was the obvious anomaly that initiating the reign of darkness from Cuba signified. The object until then of the world's contempt, I myself doubted that we were worthy of making the oceans boil until they evaporated and broke the earth's crust. Even the bones of the dead in their tombs were going to crackle like firewood.

It would appear not only surprising, but also even obscene that someone with my irregular political record (as almost all of my biographers have made commonplace), the leader of such a hapless country, would be tempted with the magnitude of power that, at least on paper, I was being shown. So, all of a sudden, I understood the nature of another feeling overcoming me. It was a situation of unanticipated happiness and in which I thought myself separated from my own physical presence, and then I knew that I was in a state of very special grace, that of having the absolute consciousness of having attained immortality. Which in that moment I had just achieved. Whose favor had I curried? It was as if I had been tapped on the shoulder with Excalibur and knew that upon joining I was already knighted. I am trying to convey to you the experience exactly as I lived it, exactly as I understood it. I can try to do so in a lesser frequency, in more common language, and tell you that I have never felt as happy and pleased to be Fidel Castro as I did at the moment, of which neither General Pliev nor any of the members of his delegation was aware. Because it was like a convert's experience. I had achieved the miracle of belonging to history, because all of a sudden we, Cuba, were part of the Soviet Union and its war legacy. First I felt diminished in a way by the battles that were as unreachable as the stars. Then I truly knew the course my life would take. Then I. A. Pliev was hugging me and telling me that comrade Nikita Sergeyevich Khrushchev and the Politburo of the Soviet Union's Communist Party, in consideration of the measure adopted to deploy long-range nuclear carriers off the coast of the Republic of Cuba placed him before me to start the research work and fitting out of the territory. In terms of our equipment, we were suddenly moving from World War II to World War III without any transition. To think that here was where the *Enola Gay* trained. In 1945, Squadron 509 was sent from Cuba to Nebraska and from Nebraska to the Mariana Islands and in August they dropped the two bombs, on Hiroshima and Nagasaki. That passing relationship of Cuba's with history suddenly stopped. It must be our geographic location. Real history was always brushing up against it. It passed by its side, bumped up against it. There was always a history in passing, like something that didn't really belong to us and fanned us as if we were foreigners in our own country. It was history that moved like trade winds over Cuba. Coming and going. Coming and going.

We had been the starting point or the destination. Now we were allowed to be the epicenter.

November 15, 1962. San Antonio de los Baños air base. Fidel wants to shoot down one of the low-flying reconnaissance planes commissioned by Kennedy to confirm the withdrawal of Soviet strategic weapons. Fidel reasons that, following Khrushchev's surrender, the plan is to humiliate him. Destroying an American plane—or planning to—would alleviate his wounded pride. Besides, it would strengthen his position to pressure and negotiate with both Washington and Moscow.

THE VISIBLE PART OF GOD

/ / /

So MUCH ACTIVITY WAS UNUSUAL. THE MIG-21S HAD ARRIVED AND were flying low all over the island, and wherever you went the Soviets were stopping traffic. Their convoys occupied the western highways, as if we were being cut off from the outside world like Berlin in 1945. Here's a small secret of mine. Ever since then, the Russian language is the language of the night for me. It was my advice to Pliev and his Chiefs of Staff. "Move by night." My guerrilla experience was proving to be useful again. A pseudo-specialist—Captain Antonio Núñez Jiménez— mentioned that the U-2 optical system had infrared rays. "Get the fuck out of here with your infrared rays," I told him, "U-2 cameras can't even see through a cloud in broad daylight." Besides taking advantage of the cover of night, the Soviets could rely on the dozens of kilometers of old laurel trees hanging over the Central Highway, allowing them to pass under those vaults of sweet shadow without the possibility of their detection from the air. In any event, we were the ones who had warned the Soviets from the start of the operation—and in response to their insistence that all maneuvers be carried out in secret—to count on U-2 planes and their regular reconnaissance flights over our territory. Raúl told Khrushchev himself in Moscow on July 3, 1962, before taking a look at one of the first drafts of the strategic weapons Cuban deployment pact, and that was the reason he persuaded Khrushchev to modify the sequence in the transfer of weapons. The defensive weapons would travel first, mainly the SA-2 surface-to-air missile components, as well as Luna tactical missiles and FKR cruise missiles. Later the offensive weapons would be transported, the R-12 intermediate-range ballistic missiles in the first stage and the R-14 intermediate-range ballistic missiles in the second stage. No strategic matériel would be moved until adequate antiaircraft and anti-naval defense systems had been deployed. With all of that coming into our country, into the atmosphere, I'll admit to you that I was thinking, This is going to be a bitch. Soviet troops where you least expected them and SA-2 surface-to-air missiles coming out of every corner. At some point someone told me he felt like he was watching a movie, I think it was Pepe Abrantes or one of the kids from Havana in my guard, the only film fans in that bunch of butchers. I refrained from asking what kind of movie because I understood what he meant perfectly. All around us images were being projected of a world we weren't ready for. The missile launchers were still supposed to be a state secret. That's when I put Commander Enrique Oropesa in jail because he found out about the existence of the nuclear locations from a drunk Russian general. The mid-range atomic missiles were already tucked somewhere amid our very sparse mountains and there was a strange atmosphere with machinery and dark canvas-covered trucks traveling up Esperón Hill. And through Limonar, Bejucal and San Antonio. I traveled like a ghost along those same roads, allowing myself the chance to enjoy the moments when we had to stop at a barrier and the reflectors of my Oldsmobile shone on Soviet guards, all dressed indistinctly in civvies or olive-green uniforms which resembled ours in color if not in cut and which served as the attire for the Military District of Turkmenistan, in Central Asia, where the climate was most like Cuba's in the whole of the Soviet Union. And with those unmistakable AKMs across their chests. They would warn us to come to a dead stop with that imperious gesture of their hands, lords of the theater of operations: *Stoy! Stoy!* Until their flashlights fell directly on my face and they saw me sitting next to the driver, a cigar in my mouth and wrapped in the silky weave of my Spanish gabardine army jacket and exclaimed, *Eta vii?* Is it you? Those savage figures would pale as if Stalin himself had just been reborn before them, Stalin in all his marvelous significance as the Man of Steel, and without a moment's pause, as can only take place under the ruthless discipline of the world's best army, they would take a step back, click their heels with a skillful snap, salute me with their arms perfectly synchronized and order their comrades to let us through immediately: *Dabai!*

Dabai! Eta on! Eta on! Eta on means "It's him," but said with eerie religious conviction. These were the first vowels I learned of that language of the night. Stop! Stop! *Stoy! Stoy!* Is it you? *Eta vii?* Let's go! Let's go! *Dabai! Dabai!* It's him! It's him! *Eta on! Eta on!* The troops had only been taught two words in Spanish—stop and go—during their stifling journey across the Atlantic, hidden in the holds of those heavy merchant ships with just a short while to go out under cover in small groups to breathe in some fresh air and smoke a few of those terrible Papirosa cigarettes. Stop and go. I traveled and took mental notes—no writing anything down in my notebook—and worked things out in my head. A squadron of Ilyushin Il-28 bombers made up the rest of the nuclear force. There was no missile base in Oriente Province. But at the Holguín base, they were expecting this unit of up to twelve mid-range nuclear bombers. As opposed to the interception and chase squadrons, the bomber units they explained to me were made up of three squadrons of three planes, which are the so-called Troika formations. And the rest are for training and leadership. The Il-28 (as they were commonly known, a shorthand for Ilyushin) were assembled at the San Julián base, in the island's extreme west, where a naval regiment would likewise have to be deployed (thirty-three reactive and mined torpedo-launcher machines plus three for training). When they had finished putting the first ones together and they had carried out their test flights, there would then be six 407N free-falling atomic bombs (weighing twelve kilotons each) at their disposal, which were stored with the rest of the nuclear warheads in a bunker that had just been built under the hills to the south of Havana. The area, full of streams, palm trees and farmers who primarily grew tobacco in fields that the Spaniards had leveled with their machetes against the *bejucales*, which were particularly overgrown there, three centuries before to make their parcels, and which they named, of course, Bejucal, was one of the first sites the Soviets picked for the dispersal of their materials. It had an adequate network of roads around it, due precisely to the proliferation of small farms, and it was a fast and easy trip to the Mariel port, which was where the bulk of the troops and the logistics were disembarking. In turn, the loads assigned to the naval regiment of Il-28—which were not as far from the takeoff strips as the 407N bombs, since they were stored in San Julián itself—contained 150 RAT-52 reactive rocket-propelled torpedoes, and 150 anti-ship mines.

THE NAMES ON MY LIST—which I still have, in my own handwriting—of Cubans who were familiar with the deployment of nuclear weapons do not exceed nine: President Osvaldo Dorticós, Raúl, Che, Ramirito Valdés, Blas Roca, Gamonal, Flavio Bravo, el Gallego Fernández (José Ramon Fernandez), and Fats Emilio Aragonés, whom we had as an important Party leader at the time—organizing secretary—replacing Aníbal Escalante. And that's how we kept the sacrament, within that sacred brotherhood, at least officially, until Kennedy blew the lid off of that Pandora's box with his October 22 speech.

On his July trip to Moscow, Raúl wasn't able to convince Khrushchev to accept our reasoning that it would be better to make what was being planned public, not even when he mentioned the fact that the *yanquis* were going to discover the installations with their constant U-2 flights over our heads. A second delegation, in August, also failed to move him, even though I sent our resident chatterbox, Che, in the company of Fats Aragonés. I was expecting that Argentine's measured, never impassioned, never grandiloquent voice to work a miracle. And perhaps two foreigners would be able to come to a sensible agreement about Cuba. "No, comrades," Nikita Sergeyevich said obstinately. "You don't understand. The right thing, the proper thing, would be for us to wait until November, when I visit Havana, for us to make a public statement." The balls on that guy! Well, I already understood everything all too well and if things kept going like that, along that path, I was going to end up useless, like a puppet. In that sense, Nikita was putting the Cuban Revolution at risk. Didn't he understand that allowing something that would bring discredit on me was the closest equivalent to doing away with the entire Cuban process? Hence my apocalyptic statements—interpreted, perhaps, as defiance at the time—were nothing more than a defense of the Revolution. Because the situation could not be any more clear: while the operation was kept discreet, I'd be kept out of the game. Compare this with having been a signatory in equal standing of a military pact with the Soviet Union. A cigar would help me resolve this. A cigar and a good walk along Santa María Beach at sunset while the October waves spilled over the jagged border drawn by the sand a meter to the right from where I made my path. The cars had stopped under some casuarina trees and, Uzi in hand, Gamonal was walking a few steps behind me discreetly. I had just finished a round through the outskirts south of Havana and had been surprised by the frequency with which the power line poles were cut on town corners and at sharp bends in the roads and how these had been replaced by other poles in places that were noticeably farther away. "What is this, Alfredo?" I asked the head of my guard. Alfredo Gamonal leaned into my ear, from the backseat, to tell me in his usual whisper, "Soviet rockets, Comandante, are more than twenty-three meters high, and the things can't round the corners with those masses on top." "Aren't these typical Cuban *embreado* poles?" "No, Comandante, they're birches." "Birches." "Birches, Comandante." "And where in the hell did you get so much information, Alfredo? Let's see, how do you know what a birch is?" "I've undertaken a permanent and detailed study of all the areas you have to move through, Comandante. And those are birch posts because I've seen them in movies." I responded, as warranted, with an approving smile and the removal of a cigar from my pocket, which I extended to him ostentatiously. "Here, Rin Tin Tin," I told him, in a joke we could allow ourselves, comparing him to the German shepherd from the American adventure show, "have a bone." Later I told him we were going to a beach, that he should pick one, and on the way I was mulling over his explanation in my head until we got to Santa María and I started my walk and let night fall on us. Back then, Cubans stopped going to the beach in mid-September, with the first storms from the north, and didn't go back until the beginning of the following summer, between June and July. So the beach's desolation was guaranteed no matter which one Gamonal had chosen. *Brooom!* The waves were breaking to my right and the wind blew a fine drizzle of salt water on my field jacket. *Brrooommm!* Then a slapping sound. And then the water dragging chunks of sand. The formidable Partagás I'd kept in reserve in my pocket and that was now hanging between my teeth could barely stay lit, despite my helping revive its combustion with a sustained puffing toward my palate. If I could call upon any wisdom in circumstances like those, like an old sailor who knows it's impossible to light a cigar on the bow of a ship, it was that my smoke would get fucked up the minute my attention strayed and I let the cherry go out. And you know what? All of a sudden I was able to enter into complete harmony with my friend at the Kremlin. We were fighting for the same reasons! Before this moment, I had been incapable of understanding that he was as desperate as I was because the *yanquis* had caught him with his hands in the cookie jar, which was exactly what he wanted. That nightfall I spent before the swelling sea produced the exact result I had gone in search of but with the catch that, *compañeros*, a blindness to the mortal challenges of the revolutionary fighter prevailed in me instead of the lucidity and shrewdness of a world-class politician. *Vavoom!* I hadn't understood it. I hadn't seen it coming. I hadn't weighed the convenience, if only temporary, of its seduction. And I had made an opponent out of a real comrade. That's why he was increasingly willing to give us more rockets and tank brigades and bring the submarine fleets close to American shores. Because he was also dying to let them find out, although, understandably, only when it was advisable, in other words, when those fearful missiles capable of killing entire populations were operational. That's why my fiery public diatribes continued regarding our sudden and invincible military shield. There's a running joke from that time period, that the people used to chant along with me, upon listing the new armaments that were obviously making our arsenals swell and after naming the armored cars and planes and cannons and antiaircraft guns, I would conclude with an enigmatic reference to the et ceteras. "We have tanks," I declared. "And planes. And cannons. And antiaircraft guns. And . . ." This was the moment in which I trailed off, waiting for the audience to respond, with all the gaiety of a party, "And et cetera, et cetera, et cetera!" Like an unwritten script between us, I joined in their fun and repeated along with them, "And et cetera, et cetera, et cetera!" And I rounded it off by laughing heartily and joining my people in the enjoyment of that power so difficult to discern and openly name. My responses to "Alejandro"—Ambassador Alexander Alexeyev—to the Soviet concern caused by these speeches was that I had to prepare the country politically. *Ponimai, ponimai*, I understand, I understand, was his resigned response, both of us aware that I was spurred on by the desire to assume a leading role in the affair. I even told Dorticós that he should tell our diplomatic missions out there in the world that there was a new member in the atomic club. Five, there were now five of us. The Soviet Union, the United States, Great Britain, France and Cuba. American intelligence, however, denied it. (Oh, how that reminds me of my conversation with Nixon! They don't know how to listen, dammit. They just don't know.) A careful reading of my statements would have warned them far enough ahead of time, which in many ways was something I was counting on. My attempt—similar to those of a hostage trying to send clandestine messages to the outside world—obtained very poor results, if any.

OCTOBER 22, 1962. In the Command Post of the General Chiefs of Staff, there was a militia lieutenant acting as operative guard officer by the name of José Millán. The General Chiefs of Staff were in the building built by Batista for the Naval Chiefs of Staff. The lieutenant—I later found out—was this fat guy who was just transferred from the San Antonio base, where he had been working in the Propaganda Section on the recommendation of the ineffable Victor Pina for a job that was rather more administrative within the guard corps. You know the old military axiom, that all of history's great generals owe their victories to two things: their tactical genius and their Chief of Staff. The man adjusted marvelously to expectations. A little after four-thirty p.m., he received via telephone and teletype the first intelligence reports about the sudden suspension of a monstrous naval maneuver that the *yanqui* Navy had been conducting in front of the island of Vieques, in Puerto Rico. Like myself, he was awaiting Kennedy's announced appearance on radio and TV; in addition, he was up to speed on the fact that at ten minutes to four in the afternoon, I ordered a Combat Alert. In other words, he was prepared, tense. So he glanced at the teletype page with the report of the suspension of maneuvers in Vieques and made the very daring decision to decree a Combat Alarm for the entire nation. 5:35 p.m. October 22, 1962. Kennedy's appearance had yet to take place when this fat little sybarite issued an order that only I would have been able to consider and, above all, carry out. I don't think even Raúl would have been that brave. It was the slow dusk of a Monday and I was in my office at the Eleventh Street complex, from where I conducted almost all my official business. I was waiting for Kennedy in front of a shortwave radio, with a supply of cigars and coffee and a couple of translators. The expectation of war took up all of our time, all of our reading of reports, all of our thoughts. I was watching the news (or the absence thereof) that came from the United States on the morning and afternoon of that day. You didn't have to expend too much brainpower to understand that all of that rushing about in Washington had to do with the placement of the Soviet missiles. *They had finally discovered them.* I was growing more and more certain of this. Finally! The information was constantly flowing through the battery of telephones and the three teletype machines in my office. The reinforcement of the American base at Guantánamo and the evacuation of family members and civilians started early in the morning and in plain view of our agents within the base and the Border Battalion sentry guards. The reports from the agents were offered to the State Security apparatus. The information coming from the leadership of the Border Battalion, in turn, was of a strictly military nature, full of the usual details that advanced exploration yields. The base was surrounded by hills, which in and of themselves were excellent positions for observation, and located a relatively short distance from the docks and other vital facilities. In addition, we had established a watchtower system with artillery theodolites that allowed us to sniff out anything happening inside the facility, and what the sentry guards were radioing over their magneto phones to the battalion's leadership was that, sure enough, they were seeing unusual movement among the civilians. Nonetheless, what really stood out was that the Marines had traded their funny white shorts for field uniforms and none of them seemed inclined to remove those heavy helmets from their heads and—even more significant and alarming—the frenetic planting of mines on the entire border contiguous to the twenty-eight-kilometer-long demarcation fence that surrounded the base. Raúl and Ramiro couldn't go five minutes without warning me that their respective ministries had received a new report. I, in turn, had Celia running around, getting me coffee or tracking down Alejandro—the Soviet ambassador—or getting Raúl or Ramiro on the line again. I already knew that it was about the missiles, although I couldn't predict exactly what kind of military action they would undertake and where it would take place. I was certain, however, that an attack was imminent. It was at 3:50 p.m. that I made a decision that was within my prerogatives as commander in chief. Placing the Armed Revolutionary Forces on Combat Alert. They weren't going to surprise us. They'd never been able to. It was the beginning of a war that I had been prepared for since 1959. I've always known how to avoid surprises, preparing myself for them and, above all, making sure the *yanquis* know that I am waiting for them, that is my main defensive maneuver. I think that this is the logical training for one who considers himself a master in the art of ambushes. I simply apply the norms in reverse. I know, like no one else does, how to create a silent zone for the enemy to rush into. In the Sierra, those were the shady and kind paths in which not even a leaf moved, which were arrived at from very far away—how many? three hours' journey?—the barking of dogs indicating there were no peasants living in the surrounding area. Do you want to know something? This has been my decisive military asset in forty-some years of Revolution. Me, reading into the silence. Me, scrutinizing its codes. Because silence also has a past. And there is no better key to finding its revelations than memory. The day before, Sunday, October 21, our diplomatic mission to the United Nations in New York didn't find any articles or reports about Cuba in *The New York Times* or in *The Washington Post*, so from that channel the teletypes in Havana remained silent. Hmmm, I told myself. Just like in the Bay of Pigs. They didn't publish a single word after the sustained racket of months prior. Kennedy himself had called the worthy editors on the eve of the invasion so that "national security interests" would obviate the Cuban matter. Well, you already know that when the Americans go quiet, it activates my internal alarm system. On the other hand, we had a swarm of agents placed around the American bases in Florida and even in Virginia and Puerto Rico. Despite being a bit rudimentary when it came to their code systems (using messages such as "many cows are entering the corral," or "no more passes for the students") and transmitting them via long-distance public telephones (to speak with *some relatives* in Havana), they were able to supply us with a considerable amount of information. Let me tell you, they were efficient. Through a basic system that we had designed, we were able to interface those amateurs' reports with tables describing the enemy's means and from there obtain an excellent intelligence evaluation. The Soviets, both in Moscow and in Cuba, were equally well informed, especially by the military Sputniks. But we had the best information and the definitive sign had just come in that afternoon from Vieques. That thunderous maneuver undertaken in the vicinity of our coastline—and to intimidate us, of course—had stopped without any explanation. *And the ships were going back.* I was processing all this before Kennedy's speech and I understood that he was going to let us have it, when the operative guard officer at the command post got ahead of me. The special connection switchboard, to my left, had turned on with a very peculiar and insistent hum and the line was flashing red. Whoever was on the other end of that line didn't recognize my voice. He said, as commanding as he was sharp, "Inform the commander in chief that the Armed Revolutionary Forces just went to Position One." I sensed that the two translators, on the opposite side of my desk, were startled, even before they knew what was happening. I must have transmitted my own tenseness to them. The communication had ended. The second call, a moment later, was from Raúl, also via the special connection phone. He was at his office in the General Chiefs of Staff building itself when he received the call from the command post and was informed as briefly and succinctly as I was of the event. The only difference was the grammatical person: "I inform the minister of the Revolutionary Armed Forces that we are in Position One." Raúl determined that he should only pronounce my name. "Fidel?" "Raúl," I said to him, without letting him put forth another question. "The decision that was made is right. Wait for me at the agreed upon place." "The Monastery?" "Positive," I said, "and don't call the cars, Raúl. Let's keep the radios silent. Even if they're landing. I am going to see them first because I'll be on the street." Then Gamonal came up the stairs in great strides and with an energetic "Comandante, with your permission," asked to enter. The Combat Alarm signal—he explained to me—had just come in on the radios in his Oldsmobile. It was obvious that news of the mobilization was spreading because Celia was hurriedly walking down the hall that led to her apartment and I saw her head pop up behind Gamonal's shoulder. "Well, *compañeros*," I said to the translators, "your work here will have to be canceled for the time being." I stood up from my seat and Gamonal knew my departure was imminent. As an automatic gesture, he grabbed my beret and the cartridge belt with my pistol and the magazine case I had left on the sofa and held them out to me. I put on my beret. While I was fastening my cartridge belt, my daily light battle equipment, I gave Celia instructions to offer the translators a nice afternoon snack and then take care of their transportation back to their offices, I believe in one of State Security's buildings. Before going down the stairs, and at a prudent distance from the translators, so they wouldn't hear me, I told Celia to immediately track down Flavio Bravo—the veteran communist and head of the General Chief of Staff's EMG's Operations—the Argentine, and Ambassador Alexeyev and to send them to the Monastery, the code name in those days for offices of the General Chiefs of Staff. Then, while I was on a lower step and in some way diagonal to her, I put my hand on her left shoulder, with all ease since I was still taller than her, and I moved my lips toward her ear to entrust one more thing to her, when she confused my intention as that of kissing her goodbye. I continued on to her left ear, ignoring her mistake, and said, "When you speak with Alejandro, use the secure line and tell him that we've moved from Combat Alert to Combat Alarm, that I have the country on a war footing and I need him to use his channels to inform Nikita immediately and General Pliev. And tell Che and Flavio for me that radio silence is mandatory. These *yanqui* sons of bitches can track us down by radio-goniometry and we're not going to give ourselves away." I left the Eleventh Street complex with my convoy of three cars and headed toward the General Chiefs of Staff building. We were going at a steady fifty kilometers per hour on the well-paved avenues. I didn't use air-conditioning in the vehicles, so I was happy with the breeze our speed generated. The lack of air-conditioning also made me accessible to passersby, even if I didn't exchange a single word with them. No one leads in seclusion if he leans his elbow through the open window as he travels, dispersing the ashes of his cigar into the street and going into rhapsody at the sight of his fellow *ciudadanas'* asses. The atmosphere of urgency and contained agitation that had reached me in my office extended all along the way and I could see more and more passersby in their militia uniforms and fewer people dressed as civilians. I asked Gamonal to keep going at fifty kilometers per hour to avoid causing the people any alarm or unnecessary worry and I calmly and gently answered each passerby's greeting with a smile. There was a strange sense of excitement but also contained joy in Havana's people, who hurried home to change their outfits, throw some things into their backpacks, lace up their boots, place their berets on their heads and report to their respective combat units. I noticed that their spirits were buoyed by thoughts of our success at Playa Girón rather than concerned with the imminent prospect of disappearing in a nuclear holocaust. Eighteen months before, they had returned victorious. Things didn't need to be any different now. Raúl and Flavio were waiting for me at the command post. When I entered and made my presence known, someone yelled, "Attention!" quite energetically. I delivered a very solemn but good-natured "*Buenas tardes.*" Here I did wear a serious face the whole time. A little while later, Alexeyev arrived, and then Che. The command post was rather rustic but had an excellent climate provided by a high-power air conditioner, if the personnel gathered there stayed under a dozen. There were some maps placed horizontally on tables, while others covered the walls, and long pointers that looked suspiciously like billiard cues were scattered around the place. A combatant rigidly stood watch by a table with coffee thermoses and mugs on it, taking great care to wash and dry it continuously while keeping the ashtrays free of cigarette butts and cigar stubs, and there was a telephone switchboard and a battery of telephones, some with rotary dials and some without—the switchboard's hot phones—and the new (for us) Soviet military magneto phones, which were activated by cranking a handle on the right side. Although I already knew which of the eight or nine officers now in a semi-paralyzed state around the map table—awaiting my order to be at ease—I wanted to address, I asked for him anyway. The man, who had been standing at attention since my arrival, with his arms rigid at his sides, his fists closed, said, "*A la orden, Comandante en Jefe!*" I immediately recognized the voice from the earlier phone call. I looked at him with the calculated scorn that I reserve for these occasions before asking, "What is your name, Lieutenant?" He identified himself as Militia Lieutenant José Millán. A rare feeling of compassion came over me upon seeing him make an effort to maintain an appropriate martial position despite his obesity. "Make yourself comfortable, Lieutenant," I said. And, with my back practically turned to him, while I considered a quadrant to the east of the capital on the map, I aimed my first question at him. "So tell me, Lieutenant, what's the operative situation?" I wasn't going to immediately congratulate him, however, nor did I feel obliged to go beyond the norms of cordiality. I understood that it was enough to affirm that it had been the right decision. "It was the right decision," I said. Then I extended my hand out to him and shook his. And I allowed myself to add, "Thank you very much, Lieutenant." I continued contemplating the maps for a while, asking my usual string of questions here and there—questions which I directed primarily at myself—about movements and the disposal of troops, the enemy's as well as our own. Then, the most important thing, what all of our analyses of that afternoon must highlight, was that we could have declared war almost an hour and a half before they did. Once I had finished my conversation with the obese operative guard officer, the Soviet ambassador thought he had found his opening. Alexeyev made a gesture that I would characterize as timid. In vaguely diplomatic language, he told me that the decision by Cuba's highest commanders to place the Armed Forces first on a state of alert and then complete combat deployment *was known* in Moscow. The rigid Slavic insistence on using the preterite tense always bewildered me. And the depersonalization was even worse. At the beginning of our relationship, I had thought that it was just the way the TASS cables were written. Later experience proved that it wasn't just their way of expressing themselves in "telegraphic services"—

as they called them—but also in their regular interactions. "So, Alejandro, that means that you informed them as I asked Celia to tell you to do." Alejandro agreed. "Fine, then," I said, and patted the Kremlin emissary's shoulder approvingly, indicating that our dialogue was over. I think it was about a quarter to seven and I asked Raúl if there was a translator in the building. There was. So I told him, Alexeyev, the Argentine and Flavio that we were going to Raúl's office, to listen to what Kennedy was going to say to us. As he moved solemnly but at ease in his white, long-sleeved guayabera, Alejandro did not look like an ambassador of the Union of Soviet Socialist Republics. I convened the General Chiefs of Staff that evening because I was dying for him to tell me everything Moscow was thinking, all the information at his disposal. Gossip, details, yelling over the phone, decrees, jokes, little pieces of paper slipped from palm to palm, conspiracies, in sum, everything he heard. Especially what military decisions were coming from Moscow. But we got to the end of Kennedy's speech and our ambassador *compañero* was as mute as ever with the same serious, and even slightly surprised, expression he had had on his face ever since showing up at the command post. It was obvious he didn't know anything and even that the development of events had taken him by surprise. It didn't take much to understand that. So, when Kennedy had finished his seventeen-minute-long speech—*Our goal is not the victory of might, but the vindication of right—not peace at the expense of freedom, but both peace and freedom, here in this hemisphere, and, we hope, around the world. God willing, that goal will be achieved. Thank you and good night*—and Raúl, all paternal, had ordered the young sergeant translating for us to leave, I approached Alexeyev—who had sprung from his chair—put my hand on his shoulder, looked directly into his eyes and said to him, "Well, Alejandro, we obviously just went to war with the United States. Not just Cuba, but the Soviet Union too. From now on, I beg you to keep in touch with us while conditions allow it. And I am officially asking you to tell General Pliev that we are at his complete disposal to assemble a plan together and to maximize cooperation." This meant—and Alexeyev understood it perfectly—that he needed to obtain the latest information from Moscow for me and use it to let the head of the Soviet troops in Cuba know that he should get in touch with us as soon as possible. This last part, however, was unnecessary, since Pliev's emissaries, two generals, had just shown up in the building. We took them right into Raúl's office. They were wearing short-sleeved white shirts tucked into gray pants that had gone out of fashion thirty years before. These tough men, greasy and robust, paled when they saw themselves surrounded by the entire pantheon of Cuba's revolutionary leadership; although they immediately recovered and regained the necessary aplomb to stand at attention and unequivocally offer me—just me—a salute with their flattened palms at an angle against their bare foreheads, automatically recognizing the person of highest political and military rank in that room. They didn't waste any time. Out of his black leather map wallet, one of the generals gave me a sheet written in code and another in teletype, both of them held together with a copper paper clip in the upper left corner. "*Sovershenno sekretno,*" the general said. "Top secret," Alexeyev hurried to translate for me. "*Osoboi vazhnosti,*" the general added. "Special importance," Alexeyev translated mechanically. The first page had groups of paragraphs that mixed numbers and letters from the Cyrillic alphabet. Above what seemed to be phrases in hieroglyphics, someone had penciled in their meaning in Russian. The second page, apparently, had the typed version, or at least something produced by an electronic communication instrument. I handed the document to Alexeyev. I still remember the silence reigning in that room as Alejandro adjusted his glasses, took a look at that document, cleared his throat and finally read it aloud. Pliev reported that in the Soviet command post in Havana a message had been received thirty minutes before the U.S. president began his speech dated the twenty-second of that month from the minister of defense of the USSR, comrade Marshall Rodion Malinovsky, which stated that the Group of Soviet Forces take immediate measures to elevate the state of combat deployment and be ready along with the Cuban army to rebuff the enemy with all of the might of the Soviet forces, except the STATSENKO and all of the BELOBORODOV. Damn, it was a message that started out in such a combative way, only to quickly reach an end that was not quite ambivalent—nothing combative is ambivalent—but extremely careful, measured, unable to commit to the spirit of battle. Alejandro had the discernment to bluntly explain the meaning of what I had just heard. "STATSENKO means Missile Division and the BELOBORODOV refers to the nuclear cargo." It was one of those moments in my life as a revolutionary leader in which it was vital to not show any emotion, in addition to the fact—I confess—that I was still undecided about whether to follow the sirens' song and turn myself over to the Soviets or to trust my intuition that they had me by the balls. This last feeling, above all, forced me to act with great equanimity. "Correct," I said. There was an emphasis on this single word of mine that Alejandro especially must have interpreted as a tacit acceptance of mine of the course of events and the way that the Soviet part was developing.

ТРОСТНИК — товарищу ПАВЛОВУ

В связи с возможным десантированием на о. Куба американцев, проводящих учение в Карибском море, примите немедленные меры к повышению боевой готовности и к отражению противника совместными силами кубинской армии и всеми силами советских войск, исключая средства СТАЦЕНКО и всех грузов БЕЛОБОРОДОВА.

ДИРЕКТОР
№ 4/389
22 октября 1962 г.
23.30

One of the telephones went off. Raúl lifted the receiver and listened to the message. "The *compañeros* from Military Intelligence," Raúl said, to identify the call's origin. "They report that the evacuation of civilians from Guantánamo was completed at the very moment Kennedy went on air." "Translate this for our *compañeros* the Soviet generals so that they don't worry," I cautioned Alejandro. I was tempted to tell them we weren't being bombed yet, but I had the good sense to keep my mouth shut. "And tell them," I continued, "to transmit my appreciation to *compañero* Pliev for keeping us informed." I reserved the right to call them merely *compañeros* and not let a single "comrade" pass my lips. It was essential to retain that sign of independence as part of my verbal strategy. I shook the hands of both generals and they responded with military salutes as soon as I let go of their hands. For Alejandro, another pat on the shoulder, accompanied by one last smile. Alexeyev and the Soviet generals were dismissed. Five of us remained—including Alfredo Gamonal, who didn't have a voice or vote in that conclave. 7:55 p.m. Havana and Washington were in the same time zone. You could confirm that the president of the United States virtually declared war. At 7:59 p.m. I was still struggling to take in some of the words from his speech and perhaps I was resisting the significance of what I had just heard. Then I tried to meet Che's gaze. Until that moment—par for the course for him—he had remained silent. No, better said, in waiting. I needed to find out what the Argentine thought. Those present knew that this was what I was going to immediately do. I settled into the armchair Alexeyev had emptied with the majesty of a judge receiving a jury's decision and I asked Commander Ernesto Guevara, "Che, what do you think?" He smiled. The son of a bitch smiled before asking, "About the Soviets or the Americans?" What a devious one this Argentine was, always so sharp, damn him. "About the Americans, Che. About the Americans," I said, pronouncing my words with clear annoyance. Che looked at me through the rings of smoke of his cigar. He took two or three puffs with obvious pleasure, and he cracked his emblematic smile without releasing the cigar from his lips before responding. He was sprawled out on a sofa with a green vinyl cover next to Raúl's desk and had the laces of his boots tied only halfway up his calf. "He's scared shitless," he said, in a tone so convincingly disparaging, so Buenos Aires, that his proclamation left little room for appeal. "Kennedy?" I asked, to confirm. "Kennedy," he confirmed. Raúl and Flavio both looked at me then. I took two or three good puffs from my cigar as I reflected, then took it out from between my teeth to use as a pointer while I answered. "I wouldn't put it that way, Che. We could make the very serious mistake of underestimating him. I think, however, that he himself has taken his main weapon against us out of play. A surprise attack." As I said this, I was suddenly taken with an idea that filled me with doubt, with the anomaly of agony. Giving up the surprise factor was not the whole equation and much less the whole answer. It was noticeable—since I'd slipped with a small gesture of annoyance—that my brief period of uncertainty had been transmitted to all those present. The idea came from my subconscious as the automatic consequence of a previous thought. Che understood my mental situation immediately. "Then that means that this is no longer our war." Even more annoyed that I'd been discovered, I looked at the Argentine carefully. In an icy tone, I told him, "Look at that battery of phones. All of them silent. Khrushchev hasn't called."

EIGHT P.M. TIME to mobilize. Raúl's Oldsmobiles and Che's cars would travel behind my convoy, although now I can't remember if the Argentine was in an Oldsmobile or one of the two Chevy Impalas that I had given him the year before. I'd outlined the arrangement already. Raúl and Che would take up the positions assigned since the days of Playa Girón, Raúl in Oriente Province and Che in Pinar del Rio. Same positions, but under different circumstances. Commander Juan Almeida's designated position didn't need to be called since he was already at it. I took my leave of Raúl. With my brother, I allowed myself the pride of a Roman legionnaire's goodbye. The die was cast. We hugged each other and said that: The die is cast.

THE NIGHT OF THE twenty-second and the morning of the twenty-third I was calling people to the Eleventh Street complex and handing out missions.

At midnight on the twenty-second, I received Commander Joel Iglesias, secretary general of the recently created Union of Communist Youth. Joel was a product of the Revolution. Che had taken him in his guerrilla group, first as a pack mule, then, when the kid had managed to take a Garand from one of Batista's sergeants, he accepted him as a combatant. Iglesias ended the war with the rank of commander. With the aftereffects of a gunshot that ripped the muscle mass off of his neck and part of his jaw and atrophied his vocal cords, he spoke with great difficulty and with a metallic harshness. But he managed to hide the hollow under his chin with a full beard. Besides myself, he was the only commander who wasn't obligated to shave under our regulations. I told him his task was to get in touch with Armando Hart, then minister of education, pick the best students, and he, Joel, was to then take them to the caves in the Sierra Maestra. He should also speak with Manuel Luzardo García, the interior commerce minister, regarding supplies. It was a measure designed to preserve the finest specimens of our race. At that time, we only had three nuclear shelters, or places designed to that end, and these were still under construction: the bunkers in the hills of Bejucal, where the Soviets stored their nuclear warheads; in Pliev's command post, near San Pedro; and mine, in a lime quarry near the mouth of the Almendares River.

IT MUST HAVE BEEN about three in the morning and I was about to take a catnap when Alejandro's call came in. "Fidel," he said. From the beginning I allowed Alejandro to call me by the informal *tú*. "Fidel, for your information. An hour before President Kennedy's press conference, the American ambassador in Moscow, Foy Kohler, delivered a personal message from the president of the United States to our dear *compañero* Nikita Sergeyevich Khrushchev at the Kremlin along with the public declaration of the discovery of the missiles and the establishment of a naval blockade to Cuba." Alejandro had managed to adjust to our convention of substituting the classic communist appellative, comrade, with the more natural—and I would even say wild—*compañero*. And what could I say at this time of night to the ambassador of the Union of Soviet Socialist Republics as he confirmed that all of the precautions of the previous months had become a harsh reality? So they'd made a public declaration of the discovery of the missiles. I was on the verge of asking him, So, Alejandro, where the fuck do we hide now? Maybe it was time to counter with accusations and sharp questioning. And the only valid question at the time was whether Kennedy or Khrushchev was more of an amateur at this game. But I didn't ask. I held back. What was done, was done. "*Coño*, Alejandro," I said, "I really appreciate the information. No, don't worry. I was awake. If anything else comes up, call me. Yes. No matter the time. Fine, Alejandro. Fine."

Dawn of October 23, 1962. I pored over the newspapers, which Celia had laid out across the bedspread, under which I had slept for less than two hours. There was also a selection of cables from international agencies. As you could expect, it was a mess. Celia's thin hands would soon be holding a steaming cup of coffee. She would soon be asking me if I was having breakfast.

The telephone. A direct line to the Soviet Embassy. It was Celia who heard it and was able to identify them. "The Russians," she said. "I know their ring." My office, where there was an entire battery of telephones, was a level below us in the apartment building that had been turned into a fortress by Celia. But there were extensions of the main lines in her little office, contiguous to her apartment, and this was just across the hall from mine, on the same level. Alejandro was calling, of course. It was about something important. Our dear *compañero* Nikita Sergeyevich had sent me a letter through the automatic code system and it had already been decoded. If I remember correctly, we decided that if the message was political, there was nothing wrong with having it read to me over the phone. Alejandro agreed. It was a long letter (Khrushchev was a fan of epistolary diplomacy) and it took a long time to get to the heart of the matter. This finally showed up in one of the last paragraphs. Nikita Sergeyevich considered the actions undertaken by the American government to be pirate-like, perfidious and aggressive; and in addition he informed me that he had given instructions to the

Soviet military representatives in Cuba to adopt relevant measures and be completely ready. "Repeat that last part to me, Alejandro. Repeat it to me." "You mean the part about him having given instructions to the Soviet military representatives in Cuba to adopt relevant measures and be completely ready?" "That part. Yes. That one." "Well, Fidel"—he cleared his throat—"instructions have been given to the Soviet military representatives in Cuba to adopt relevant measures and be completely ready."

THE COLLISION POINT

At nightfall, I was with Alejandro at the embassy. He spent a few minutes showing me the antiaircraft bunker he had put together in the yard. It didn't smell yet like piss or like rats, so it must have been finished just a few days before. Not a soul could smoke a cigar in that atmosphere full of fresh whitewash and disinfectant, and I asked if we could go up to his office. I never really cared that Alexeyev didn't smoke. "If the smoke bothers you, Alejandro, open a window." "Not at all, Fidel. Not at all," he hastened to tell me. Out of habit, he offered me his reclining chair behind the desk. He set me up behind his plush green blotter with its embossed leather corners and an enormous Murano crystal ashtray at the bottom of which the shield of the Soviet Union was engraved in gold. I did everything I could to keep the column of ash on the unsmoked part of my Grande de España, this excellent seven-inch-long cigar, such great flavor, provided to me by the personal security *compañeros* from the El Rey del Mundo factory. I noticed that Alexeyev took my old smoker's funny little ways as a consideration of mine not to soil the symbol of his homeland, but my goal was to keep up to an inch of ash hanging from the cigar before shaking it off, so it burned better. So. He explained how concerned they were about the *Alexandrovsky*, since the ship was carrying 24 R-14 missile nuclear warheads and the forty-four nuclear warheads remaining from the FKR cruise missiles. But it arrived at port before the quarantine decreed by Kennedy went into effect (which was planned for ten a.m. on Wednesday the twenty-fourth). The *Alexandrovsky*, destined to dock at the Mariel port, changed its course toward Isabela de Sagua. General Pliev didn't want to run the risk of the five or six hours of coastal navigation, bordering the north of Cuba, that would be required to get to Mariel, and ordered (after a hasty consultation with me) them to make it to the nearest port. The nuclear weapons would remain aboard the *Alexandrovsky* for the time being. Since all of the specialized personnel in Cuba were wrapped up in the frenetic endeavor to put into operational mode the R-12 devices that were already installed on the island, as well as the corresponding firing machinery that was in the Mariel port, it was essential that the *Alexandrovsky's* cargo remain in the hold, awaiting the development of events. I asked him about the R-14 missiles. I knew that the FKRs were deployed and that they were operational. But . . . what about the R-14s? We were supposed to be able to reach anywhere in the contiguous United States with them, except for Oregon and Washington State. They were supposed to be able to completely destroy Houston, Texas, or Washington, DC. "Those missiles, Fidel, are on the high seas." "On the high seas." Alexeyev asked me for a minute with a gesture of his hand and took a piece of paper out of a pocket of his guayabera. He read the names he had written down. "They're on the *Almeteevsk, Nicolaeev, Dubna* and *Divno-gorsk* warships. The four have orders to follow their course toward Cuba. Direct orders from the Kremlin."

KENNEDY HAD LEFT that inexplicable opening that gave both Khrush-chev (as I would learn months later) and me the sense that the last thing Kennedy wanted was a real confrontation. Nonetheless, the whole affair proved to be the most dangerous of all games: the one in which I was participating merely as a spectator. Kennedy was giving Khrushchev more than one day's advantage for everything the Sovi-ets could have at sea to arrive in Cuba. And the only thing navigating out there of real strategic value was the *Alexandrovsky*. And this vessel had already moored next to an ancient and practically extinct sugar cargo terminal, in Isabela de Sagua, which up until then had only been important to Cubans due to its provisions of fresh oysters served by restaurants and street carts in Havana. The rest of the cargo—no less than the R-14 intermediate-range ballistic missiles!—was in the holds of four warships still navigating outside the boundary of the American Navy. The Soviet merchant ships were getting dangerously close to the area the *yanquis* were trying to close off. "If they're escorted," I said, by way of reflection, "that's the collision point." And, with my ring finger, I applied the coup de grâce to the Grande de España that I was holding between my thumb and index finger, in this way shaking off the first inch and a half of ash. "Are they escorted?"

"According to intercepted information, there's a submarine," Alejandro said. A masterly response. A real son of a bitch. He wasn't revealing any of his own information, just what, supposedly, the Americans had discovered. "One of our submarines *shadowing it.*"

"Shadowing it," I repeated. The term was of *yanqui* naval provenance. The four were navigating in sync like a Second World War convoy and the submarine was *their shadow*, submerged just a few feet away, with its periscope raised, leaving a wake of foam on the surface. "Now we need to know how far they are from the quarantine line."

"They're pretty close, Fidel. Let's say about a day's journey away."

"One day?"

"Let's say so."

"So we're one day away from war breaking out."

Alexeyev was quick to understand that I had just turned our conversation into an ultimatum, although a low-grade one. *An ultimatum to the Soviets.* His answer was as impeccable as his tone of voice upon declaring it. "The Soviet leadership is following the Cuban Armed Forces' combat deployment."

Now everything seemed to depend on what would happen when the American fleet came face-to-face right in the Atlantic with the four Soviet warships loaded with nuclear payload. Kennedy had given Khrushchev an opportunity and he had taken advantage of it. Now it was the American president's turn. As for me, all I could do was wait for that pack of ships to detect—first by radar, then by sight from the bridge on the prow—that their path was blocked by an American destroyer.

Incidentally, I was noticing Alexeyev's change in tone and all of its significance. I didn't know what he was up to. The *Indigirka*, which sailed from Baku on September 17, was already unloading in the Mariel port. "Let's keep the initiative going," I recall commenting then. "It's ours. *For now.*"

PLIEV EXTENDED AN invitation to me from his command post. It reached me through all of the existing channels: radio, code, Ambassador Alexeyev, the General Chiefs of Staff liaisons and the officers assigned to my bunker. It wasn't that I couldn't just show up at any of his units whenever

I felt like it, but in the case of the GSVK* supreme commander's territory, it was appropriate to await his invitation. He owed me the courtesy. And I had to be very careful not to come across as someone trying to sniff around where he didn't belong. That detracts from your cachet. It makes you look bad.

The Soviet command post was in the old juvenile delinquent reform school called Torrens, an unworthy place for the USSR's glorious forces' command post, but which seemed to them very well located, above all because of the protection offered by the hills, on one side, and it was the place that they themselves chose and wanted from the beginning. I never liked the building, especially that negative air that seemed to hang over it. It seems to be inevitable in prison settings, no matter how regenerative their grounds: they always end up being homosexual colonies. I am aware of the opinion out there about me, that I am extremely prudish about certain sexual habits. Some starving snot-nosed kids, abandoned by their parents God only knows why in the city's darkest corners—never the children of well-to-do families—rounded up from the streets en masse and thrown into these galleys. I still think that such a place should be razed. Pragmatism and necessity, however, prevented this from happening. The Soviet command post required a building with a couple of stories, not too high—to avoid being detected from the air in reconnaissance flights—surrounded by forests and in the shadow of hills to serve as a natural barrier. This place seemed unbeatable. So, to hell with the fags. Now let's turn our attention back to the Third World War. The next day, my convoy headed for Cacahual and went down the other side of the hills toward Torrens. At the time I was not aware that American intelligence reports already mentioned those parcels of land starting on August 22 and that the massive Soviet deployment had not gone unnoticed. I may not have known it, but it was a given. It's in CIA Director John McCone's "Updated Intelligence Memorandum" about the Soviet military presence in Cuba. A gray-walled ship's galley with water-streaked walls was the place to receive the Soviet generals in charge of the world's destruction. There were maps on the walls and tight red strings held at the ends by tacks leading from the west end of Cuba and radiating out to the northern urban centers of the United

---

* Group Soviet Troops in Cuba, or Группа советских войск на Кубе (ГСВК), also known in Spanish as Agrupación de Tropas Soviéticas. [*Translator's note.*]

States. Although I was not able to read the Cyrillic alphabet, I could clearly tell that the strings ended up in New York, Washington, Detroit. If upon entering the complex I had to stop myself from comparing the place to the gates of hell, this impulse was automatically replaced by the sudden realization that this was going to be a real bitch. All of Pliev's command post generals, dressed in their olive-green uniforms, were at attention below the vaulted ceiling. There were no insignia on their uniforms to reveal that they were generals, but Pliev told me so: "*Eti tovarichie moi generali.*" These comrades are my generals. Pliev was to the right and a translator, also in an olive green uniform, had appeared as if by magic between Pliev and me; and I cannot recall now who among my companions was there with me, whether Flavio was, or Commander René Vallejo, or Gamonal, when a young man came out of the formation— there must have been about twenty men—and walked over to us, practically goose-stepping, in a waste of martial effort that must have taken a whole morning's worth of practice before my arrival. The general was not only young, but radiated a strange friendliness. He completed his five steps just in front of us, clicked his heels together energetically and saluted me. His pride was obvious in his voice and even more significant was the paternal look that all of the Soviets present directed at him as he reported that the three regiments of R-12 missiles, with twenty-four nuclear warheads, had just gone to full combat deployment. In the years to follow, this information that had just been relayed to me at the Soviet command post, in the presence of Pliev and almost all of his generals, was going to be debated, examined and doubted to the point of exhaustion by almost all of the American personnel tied to the crisis. The problem was that the White House was acting with a bewildering ignorance that twenty-four missiles from the Forty-third Division of the Smolensk Guard of the Soviet Union's Strategic Missile Troops, under the command of Major General Igor D. Statsenko were already on launchpads, pointing right at them. All the Soviets had to do was fuel the missiles up and place the nuclear warheads on them. We traveled by convoy to Torrens, in San Cristobal, an almost three-hour journey. General Statsenko was waiting for us, wearing one of our olive-green uniforms for the first time, without a cap and with a slice of guava fruit in his tense right hand. He asked us to follow him down a gravel path overgrown with *mangales*. I went at the head of the group, between him and Pliev. First we heard the slam of the jeep doors as we got out. Now you could hear our steps on the gravel. There were no more than thirty of us, the Soviet officers and my companions. But you could hear voices beyond the shaded mountain. Voices unknown in the Cuban wilderness. And for the first time in my life, I was suffocated by the feeling that at the end of that path, I was going to be executed. Then we stopped in front of a concrete parapet. I thought I saw a tank atop a kind of large platform. I was going to continue on when I realized I was looking at the nuclear transporter. The supposed cylinder atop the supposed platform. I had imagined that some heavy military canvas would be drawn to unveil it or that a camouflage mosquito net would be pulled aside. It was Statsenko's gesture, thunderously clapping down on the missile's surface, to my left, that made me stop short. Statsenko hadn't gotten rid of that piece of guava, but rather had just moved it to his other hand. And he kept rhythmically whipping himself with it. Statsenko put his hand on top of the missile's fuselage, which was painted an opaque green color without any insignias, turned to me, his voice serious and proud, and said: "*Tovarich Glavnokomandushie.*" Comrade Commander in Chief. "*Eta Tanya.*" This is Tanya. Pliev's long face, behind Statsenko's shoulder, had an unmistakably satisfied look. Besides, he joined in stroking the nuclear delivery system's fuselage, and even began shining it with a handkerchief extracted from one of his pockets. Statsenko's voice cracked slightly with emotion upon saying to me, "*Eta Niuyorque.*" This is New York.

NOW I'LL TELL YOU something related to the previous scene that happened many years later at Gabriel García Márquez's house and in the presence of Raúl and Vilma and a Cuban writer—whose name I do not care to remember—and a little blonde, with blue eyes, who used to drive me crazy, the writer's wife. I use the euphemism "at García Márquez's house" when I should really say at the house we assigned to García Márquez. Gabriel was putting together a lecture about nuclear holocaust and I said, if a nuclear war is unleashed, that would mean that man's only chance in the universe would be lost forever. The novelist didn't pay any attention to my words. To this day, I am still convinced that it was a better phrase that any of the ones already in his speech, the best of which, mentioning the famous antinuclear resistance ability of cockroaches, couldn't compete with my sentence. He could have quoted me and placed my words within quotes and assured everyone that it was an unpublished thought that I had placed at his exclusive disposal. Not to mention the fact that I was speaking an absolute truth, since at that time I was one of the three main figures, and the only one still alive, who could have been responsible for such a holocaust. As I listened to the long tirade that Gabriel was going to read at some peace congress—and he was very interested in getting my approval—his voice turned ever more distant and I started swimming in my own thoughts. I started calculating the real effects of what he was trying to describe.[*] How in the hell can you write something pretty about everything going to hell in a hand basket? It's like covering a meringue in shit. Have you ever heard Gabriel read something? His words hiss between his front teeth and he tries to pronounce every last syllable and he's punctilious about the spacing of the words before him, on paper, and his mustache quivers— due, I imagine, to the effect of his upper lip moving up—when he wants to emphasize an idea, to which he adds the additional gesture of bringing together the thumb and index finger of his right hand, as if he were catching a written period between them. *A minute after the last explosion, over half of the world's human beings will have died, the dust and smoke of continents in flames will destroy the sun and absolute shadows will reign over the earth again* . . . I heard these words of Gabriel's in their virginal state, twenty-four years, two months, twelve days and eleven hours after my visit to the strategic placements in San Cristobal. *All Creation will have been destroyed* . . . Or at least I was supposed to have been listening with the attention and pleasure of a proud teacher with his favorite student. *In the final chaos of water and eternal nights, the only vestige of what was once life will be the cockroaches.* The atomic bomb detonated over Hiroshima produced an explosion equivalent to 12,500 tons of TNT. Any of *our* one-megaton nuclear warheads launched over any coordinate of the United States' surface had eighty times the power of destruction of that artifact from 1945. Given the R-12's narrow margin of error—its deviation from the target was never greater than 2,400 meters—it barely mattered where it fell. A kilometer here or there, who cares? When the RD-214 engine filled with the propulsion fuel (a compound of nitric acid and kerosene) made that 41,000-kilogram monster take off, it left you enough time to have a Lancero cigar—although not a whole one—while it climbed to its ceiling of 398,000 meters and reached its maximum

---

[*] Gabriel delivered his speech—entitled "The Damocles Cataclysm"—on August 6, 1986, on the forty-first anniversary of Hiroshima, at the so-called Ixtapa Conference in Mexico. [*Author's note.*]

velocity of 12,700 kilometers per hour and rushed toward an American city. I wouldn't finish the Lancero because the R-12's flight time to cover its 1,500-kilometer trajectory is 11.8 minutes and I have confirmed that the burning time of a Lancero cigar, if you know how to smoke it with spaced-out puffs, can be a little over half an hour. You're in San Cristobal and you light your stogie just as the missile takes off and you're counting the minutes on the fluorescent sphere of your Rolex and every once in a while you puff on the Lancero, taking care to keep the ash and the cherry going, you're still only halfway through it when one of the empire's urban enclaves has been wiped off the map. A crater 60.96 meters deep and 304.80 meters wide is left by the missile's impact and all around its edges is highly contaminated radioactive ground and everywhere you look are just ruins. Nothing is recognizable nor left standing in a 975.36-meter area from the center, except, perhaps, the ruins of the basements and foundations. Only the strongest buildings—those built with reinforced concrete—are still standing but only outside, at a radius of 2.74 kilometers. Ninety-eight percent of the population is dead. "*Eta Niuyorque,*" General Statsenko said. Pliev polished the carrier with his handkerchief. Gabriel went on with his speech in praise of cockroaches.

"Man's only opportunity," I insisted. "The last one for the sentient."

It was a strange situation. The time that has passed since October 1962 forces me to introduce substantial changes to my original estimation. The innocuous imprimatur of a Saturday night gathering of Western petit bourgeois replaced that presence of mine before the nuclear delivery system in San Cristobal. I knew then that the biblical predictions of Armageddon and the final battle between the forces of Good and Evil had been mistaken. The end would have come from a decision made by communist leaders and have occurred in a matter of hours.

But it was convenient, almost obligatory, to avoid mentioning the old episodes before the vehemence of speeches such as Gabriel's. "The only opportunity," Gabriel reiterated, although it was obvious that it was a mere courtesy and that I was making it difficult even for him to stay focused on his careful reading.

Well, let me explain something to you: from a purely ideological point of view, there was undoubtedly a final battle between Good (us) and Evil (them) on the verge of taking place. It had nothing to do with divine will.

So no one noticed my phrase. I was trying to awaken the admiration of that small circle and above all—given my failure in getting Gabriel to quote me in his piece—to manage to elicit some spark of admiration in the blue eyes of that girl with the messy golden hair and irresponsible smile. She pertained to a very specific sort of Cuban woman of medium height, full breasts and a beauty that rivaled the Heliades. A real challenge to the gods, those girls.

I was rocking in a chair in front of the rest of the guests, who were on a sofa and perhaps an additional chair so that everyone fit. There was a low table with a glass top with some drinks on it. A long delicate glass was in front of the girl. A lightly bubbling liquid was inside. *Champán*. That's what I thought. *Champán*, which is the regular and systematic way that we Cubans refer to champagne.

A waiter approached me on the right.

"Will El Comandante have something to drink?"

In a very commanding way, I pointed toward the glass of champagne and said:

"I'll have what she's having."

I WAS DEALING WITH the Soviet generals in my nuclear shelter, on the edge of the Almendares River, and one of them was preparing tea in his samovar when the news came over teletype that a U-2 had been downed, that at 10:17 a battery of Soviet antiaircraft missiles took down a U-2 in the north of Oriente Province and the pilot was dead. After the Bay of Pigs, another American pilot was down on Cuban ground. Instinctively, I looked at the calendar on my watch. October 27. I looked at the hands that indicated the time. 10:31 a.m. That American pilot was alive when one of my Soviet generals was engaging in the rites of infusion in front of his copper-colored samovar. And you know what? Almost at the same time this news broke, a stunned Khrushchev who realized the situation was out of control became legend. The crisis had gone completely out of his hands, just as—the parallel legend—the same thing was happening to Kennedy in the White House. An officer by the last name Antonyetz decided to go beyond all political consideration and gave the order to bring down the *yanqui* espionage plane. As I myself would later say, Antonyetz was going to enter history just at the end of all history. All I knew was that from that moment on I felt completely displaced, since it was the Soviets, and not the Cubans, who were shooting down American planes. I had to join that wave. It didn't please me at all that the Soviets were acting more aggressively than me. It turned me into a puppet. That's why for many years I tried to make hazy the details of bringing down that U-2. The truth is that the incident took me by surprise. For the time being, the first thing that made me realize that the situation had undergone a dramatic change was when the Soviet general quit toiling in front of the samovar, opened a little drawer that came up to his knee and removed a bottle of vodka.

I remember that the wooden parquet doors were closed and we were lounging there, in the laziness of the nuclear shelter, when Commander Pedro Luis arrived with a page of military teletype in his hands and said to me, "Listen, Comandante, they downed a U-2." We received reports constantly and Pedro Luis always told me about the most important ones. "Comandante, they downed a U-2 in Banes. The Banes Antiaircraft Group." "But how could that be?" I asked. Then I called the Soviets, the five generals who were in the shelter with me, but they didn't know how to answer. In reality, the Soviet command had placed them there as liaisons and—now I understand—for nothing more than to keep me under observation. There was a compartmentalization among them, impenetrable. Someone gave the order to the head of the Banes missile group. But it hadn't come out of my bunker. Or else someone had misunderstood things. No way. The sequence of events still wasn't clear. The head of the *boyeboy*, combat group, Captain B. Antonyetz, said that he had received the order to shoot down the plane, an order from a superior. That was the remark. The Soviet generals would say to me, "We're going to make inquiries, we're going to make inquiries." I had believed all that talk of communist solidarity, but the shooting down of this U-2 was the first sign that something was fucked up and was always going to be fucked up with my allies, and just a few hours later, the pact with Kennedy was the last straw. That shooting down of the U-2 was the culmination and the end of the October Missile Crisis. It went beyond—I estimated then—what Kennedy and Khrushchev could each handle. Meanwhile, I, submerged in that foul tunnel, said, "Start calling everyone, because tomorrow we'll have the Americans here already. Call the units. They have to be ready for combat in the morning." I didn't have even the vaguest notion that messages were rapidly flying back and forth between Khrushchev and his new toy: Kennedy. I had already taken it as a given that the next day the war would begin, and I said to Captain

Rafael del Pino, now in my crisis entourage as an aviation advisor, "Call the units and make sure they have all the aviation forces in the air at dawn. Note that it's not Position One. It's aviation in the air and ready for combat." Del Pino started to call all of the units. He told Carlos Lamas, the aviation officer we had as the head of Holguín, that war was one day away. "Tomorrow, Carlito. Tomorrow they'll smoke us."

About five Russian generals heard my chatter that night. And Sergio del Valle, Flavio Bravo and Pedro Luis were nearby. I knew that I was triggering the usual admiration for my endurance. I don't recall anyone asking for permission to go sleep in their bunks. A little while later Del Pino showed up, haggard, and relayed a dream to me. "Listen, Comandante, I fall a little bit asleep and I start to dream that I'm coming out of a tunnel, and I've just lived tomorrow morning's war and there are ashes all around me and I ask, Who won? My house, you know, is right over there, on the other side of the river, and I come out of this hole and see that everything is destroyed, it's all ashes and silence and no one answers to tell me who won. Everything is destroyed. The low river, the stones. There was nothing. A nightmare. I woke up and heard that you were still talking."

I was listening to Del Pino, but over his shoulder I saw that an officer had called Pedro Luis from the teletype corner and that now he was coming closer down the hallway, with another page of teletype in his hands. If there's something I can smell a mile away, it's bad news. I could almost guess what he was going to tell me. The news that the Soviet ships en route to Cuba had stopped their engines in the middle of the Atlantic and we were, to put it bluntly, no longer the world's fifth nuclear power, even with borrowed missiles, and that this was always going to be an insurmountable insult. I was convinced that this was what he was going to communicate to me. Goddammit. The Soviets. The only people I ever came to respect.

I TAKE TEN WHILE I write. Taking ten is the latest way to describe a brief respite in the workday. It's the ten minutes that are comfortably long enough for a cigarette and some chatter and, as a norm and habit, is usually extended to a good half hour. I ask that they take me—in my convoy of Mercedes—on a furtive trip, at sunset, to Santa María del Mar. The beach from which in 1962 I expected to see, on the near horizon, the ships with their cargo, sunk in midwater with their delivery platforms bobbing uselessly amid the waves. My day of glory and death. The one that Khrushchev robbed from me. I know I am going to head west, as I walk, slowly, en route to the sand bank where there was once a forest of casuarina trees. The waves will break to my right and the wind will send a fine drizzle of salt water over my raincoat. Gamonal doesn't exist anymore. The old *compañeros* from the guard, if they're still alive, are ancient pensioners who occasionally receive, as their only sinecure for having served me indefatigably and loyally, a monthly supplementary bag with essential items, given the tight times imposed on us by the disappearance of the Soviet Union: a bottle of cooking oil, a few pounds of rice and five or six bars of soap. Nor do I have my pockets full of the wonderful stogies from my reserves. Perhaps the barely audible but cavernous sound of emphysema (which I can detect clearly) coming from my lungs is a reminder that I was once a thoroughbred smoker. I look behind me and memorize my own footprints. They are light and quickly covered by the breaking waves. The marks left by a man weighing more than 220 pounds and wearing calf-length military boots don't exist at my back anymore, determined as I am today that my Italian boots be kept safe from the effects of the salt water. This thinnish and even frail septuagenarian dragging himself along the beach he had once designated for the total destruction of the world is something so trivial and temporary that, beyond reflection, it only causes me a merciful smile. All weightless. All flowing.

At fifty years' distance and in the comforting dampness of the sand, it's difficult even for me to find any connection to the glories of the past, to recover their place in history.

AND IN THE END the world remains divided between idealists and usurers.

Residence of the Cuban ambassador to the USSR, April 29, 1963, 3:35 a.m. in Havana, 11:35 a.m. in Moscow. Fidel's first trip to the USSR. Leonid Brezhnev is the president of the USSR, but he's not the secretary general of the Party. Nikolai Leonov and Alexander Alexeyev, Fidel's Soviet friends, have told him that; nonetheless, he is the one to be courted in Moscow.

PART SIX

LIKE THE GUIDE
OF THE HORDE

/ / /

THE REVOLUTION
IS A WAR THAT
CHANGES ITS FORM.

—From Fidel Castro's speech
to the directors and officials
of the National Revolutionary
Education Schools, June 1962

A March in the Desert

/ / /

Halfway through 1965, it became clear to me that we had to increase our population. I saw it as a strategic necessity for the Revolution. In the blink of an eye, we had lost more than half a million inhabitants—due to the wave of emigration—and my prognosis for the next twenty years of governance indicated that, from a strictly military point of view, we were going to require Armed Forces that were two and half million men strong. We would be in a position to have enough men, women and kids over the age of fourteen by the late seventies if we increased the population to ten million, preferably twelve million. So I needed to pull twice as many inhabitants out of a hat. No one in Cuba would ever consider sexual abstinence or ponder the virtues of preserving their virginity until marriage. And if they did, I would have quickly pegged them as counterrevolutionaries. To increase the population, the government used the simplest and most expeditious method that has ever been put into practice on the planet. All importation of condoms, contraceptive creams and intrauterine devices (IUDs) came to a halt. And we watched the sales of Vaseline, because those sons of bitches would surely find an alternative that went against nature. I remember that the public health minister—I believe it was *compañero* José Ramón Machado Ventura at the time—made an interesting contribution. "We have to discontinue the distribution of K-4 ointment." "What the hell is that, Machadito?" "Comandante, it's an ointment used to treat hemorrhoids." The Ministry of Public Health's statistics showed that said ointment was very popular among the island's fags, who used it as a

El Comandante Castro and General Pinochet in Santiago, Chile, 1971.

lubricant, in addition to using it as preventive medicine. Facing the possibility that, in our attempt to contain sexual deviance, we would leave many *compañeros* and citizens who suffered from this cruel ailment to their fate, we decided that said ointment would still be provided in our pharmacies, but only under doctor's orders. Another measure favoring an accelerated birth rate was a campaign—in which I involved the Cuban Federation of Women (Federacion de Mujeres Cubanas, or FMC)— promoting the respect for and defense of single mothers, and even presenting them favorably in that organization's posters and placards. Just as at the beginning of the Revolution we had ordered the inclusion of a black man—at least one—in all of our political propaganda images, now we had to include a single mother. We had to turn around the nation's morality, which had condemned these poor women, and create slogans that would praise their condition as mothers above any other consideration. It took about two or three years, just that, of restricting contraceptives, if memory serves me correctly. Over that time, there was no significant increase in the anal lacerations of our *compañeras* nor in the case of vaginal infections caused by bacteria brought from the rectum during the period under consideration, so the Ministry of Public Health determined, according to its statistics, that the practice among our population of the so-called abominable crime was *historically* part of its sexual conduct and not necessarily linked to the temporary requirements of the revolutionary process. This led us to consider allowing the unrestricted sale of K-4 ointment to the general population and the elimination of the Hemorrhoid Patient Card which was required to purchase this product.

Just as when, years later, I decided to undertake the national campaign against smoking in the mid-eighties, the first person to stop smoking was me, the birth of Alex, my first son with Dalia—with whom I was living consensually by then—was seen as a result of my secret campaign of accelerated fertilization. It was late, my usual hour of arriving at the nest, about four in the morning. Dalia was smiling, imperturbable in her mastery of accommodating me. A woman full of pride for her warrior, this Attila who briskly pulled open the flaps of her tent and couldn't help but cast a scrutinizing look over the room, forced by his nature to confirm that everything was in its place, lord of everything under that roof, starting with her, and his breath smelling of tobacco and to whom, in any event, she had to present herself as obliging and grateful and to whom she hurried to announce the sweets in which she had invested her waiting: "I made you some pudding, Fidel. I think you'll like it. I put a lot of cinnamon on top." I had had an apartment outfitted on the most removed street of the residential neighborhood inhabited by the Party's leaders, the Kholy neighborhood, a community from which we had removed all of the bourgeois people and suspicious elements, or people in whom we had no political trust. The building contiguous to ours was a house that we restored to use as the Personal Security Clinic, or "Clinic on 49," as it started to be called because of the street where it was located. The building in which we outfitted Dalia's apartment had three stories, one apartment on each floor, and I picked the middle one. The floors both above and below it were left vacant for protection. There was a garage underneath. That's where the three Oldsmobiles in my convoy spent the night. A military guard unit was there permanently, armed at first with Uzi submachine guns and later with Soviet AKs. Captain Araña. I began by mentioning him. I remember that I had my encyclopedic pocket dictionary in my hand and that I sank into an armchair and said, "Listen to this, *mamita*. Captain Araña. 'They call a person who sees people on board and remains on the pier this, in other words, he who encourages or incites people to do something and then doesn't join them.'" Dalia Soto del Valle's face lit up. I tell you, nothing is more pleasing to a woman than something made up. "What have you got up your sleeve today, Fidel?" she said. "When those little Chinese eyes of yours sparkle and you say something like that, it's something big." I was removing my boots as I continued my lecture. "In the year 1812," I said, although I no longer required the pocket encyclopedic dictionary because I knew it all by heart, "the emancipation movement in South America breaks out in the overseas Spanish colonies under the inspiration of men like Bolivar and San Martín." "Fidel. Fidel." "Wait, *mamita*. Wait. Let me finish," I said, without even making the effort to suppress a smile. "Aren't you going to put on that little Chinese silk robe? The black one? The one with the dragon?" "The little robe," she said. "Well," I said, "I'll continue. The war of liberation forced the Spanish crown to recruit great quantities of men to face that insurrection. That's when a guy shows up, a Captain Arana or Araña, who recruited the most Spaniards but who, when it came time to board, disappeared. The earth swallowed him up." "Fidel," she said, in a tone of obvious reproach but that really meant she was playing along with my game. "What does my Chinese silk robe have to do with Simón

Bolivar?" "It has a lot to do with him," I said to her. "It's all part of universal concatenation. Everything flows in its dialectic movements. Flux and reflux. And it's relevant because you wouldn't allow your husband to be known as the second Captain Araña in history. Right, *mamita?*" So, around 1966, upon verifying from the window of my Oldsmobile with satisfaction that the majority of women on Cuba's streets were pregnant, I gave the order to open up the warehouses where we had stockpiled Chinese condoms and a Czech contraceptive gel—which was later very well known among us—called Anti-Jele and that came beautifully presented, in a green box and included a plastic applicator, a very beautiful applicator. Nonetheless, I still don't know what the condoms were called because the writing was in Chinese characters, but I remember perfectly well that they looked like American matchbooks and that they were decorated with multicolored butterflies. Butterflies that were not very appreciated by our consumers. I told the *compañeros* at the Ministry of Foreign Commerce to talk to the Chinese manufacturers about putting a bear or a tiger on them. "What criminally minded black man," I asked, "could possibly like little butterflies?"

RAMIRO HAD THE FILES of a bunch of the leadership's *compañeros* spread out across the backseat of my Oldsmobile. All of them involved in the roguest sexual activities. All of them going against nature. You have no idea what an impression it causes to see photographs of resolved revolutionary combatants getting nailed by citizens of the same sex, or magnificent and heroic *compañeras* naked in the throes of ecstasy atop other *compañeras.* There was something happening around me for which, simply put, I wasn't ready. Ramiro managed to shock me that afternoon.

"*Coño,* Ramirito," I complained. "I didn't make a Revolution to deal with this kind of shit."

Ramiro nodded. He knew me well enough to know that it would depress me to review those files. I was seated in the car's right front seat with the door open, my back to the wheel and my feet on the running board. I was taking the files from the backseat and flipping through them, pausing at some of the photos taken by the technical department's tiny cameras and tossing the files on the car's floor, on the rubber mat. I spent a while on a file on Melba Hernández, one of the most distinguished women of the Revolution and who was known as the heroine of

Moncada. Ramiro was standing in front of me, in his commander's uniform, with his right arm leaning on the door. My three cars and Ramiro's two were parked in a forest of casuarinas growing at the edge of the beach of Santa María del Mar, east of Havana. The sun was setting and the beach was empty because it was off season. We could hear the waves coming and going and my guards weren't taking too many precautions due to the solitude surrounding us.

"A Revolution of dykes and faggots!" I cried. "My God!"

I am relaying this tale literally, hence my repetition of the most common words used to denote lesbians and effeminate men. Dykes. Faggots.

This was when, partly indignant (due to the information in the files) and relieved (at finding a solution), I let out a click that I made by pressing my tongue against my palate. *Chchtt.*

I was going to take these sons of bitches to a cliff. Straight to a cliff. You can't arrest the entire Central Committee. So off to the cliff. That's where I needed to lead them. Like a herd of mammoths.

I stuck two fingers violently in my pocket in search of a pacifying cigar.

"Where the hell did I leave that cigar?"

In reality, I was giving myself time to decide the next step to take.

I made sure to tell Ramiro to hold back on creating these types of files. It would be imprudent and even dangerous to maintain a State Security brigade devoted to photographing the asses of our prominent *compañeros*. These situations arise when a counterintelligence body suddenly finds itself without any clearly defined tasks. Since by that date the internal counterrevolution had been quelled, State Security was slowly turning toward the revolutionaries. And their next objective could be Ramiro himself, or, worse still, me! The desire to keep tabs on the ups and downs of amorous indiscretions via photography, even if it started with some fags, would in the long run end up focusing on any kind of relationship, even the most orthodox of marriages. And another problem was that it turned the makers of these sexual files into unbearable and absurd moral gatekeepers. The worst of all.

So. Ramirito. The orders were given. The last one was that he take all of the files out of my car and make sure they didn't end up in a third party's hands.

"Take all of this out of my car right now, Ramirito," I said to him.

"Don't burn or destroy them. But put them somewhere safe. And don't forget to open a file on all those café con leche Marxists that I told you about."

Then I picked up Melba's thick file from the floor and said to Ramiro, "I'll keep this one."

And now I open it again, after so many years. More out of curiosity than voyeurism. At first glance, these images are identical to the photographs in the pornographic books rampant in Havana before the Revolution. The same semi-naked mattresses with striped lining and cheap furniture and wrinkled, messy sheets. But only the scenery is the same. Since I first looked at a pornographic image as an adolescent, I'm not excited by State Security's furtive shots of my *compañeras* in battle on the threshold of their old age sucking the clitoris of some young recruit in the National Scholarship System. Young girls. Just young girls, sweet and fresh faced girls for the use and pleasure of our prodigious matrons.

PERHAPS THERE'S SOME interest on the part of certain readers to know about my own amorous episodes, especially between 1960 and 1970, the years of my greatest erotic and sentimental activity. Simple. It was something that I tried to keep as private as possible, to keep it from becoming official state business. The most I would allow myself, when I saw some face in the crowd that caught my eye, was to give Chicho* or José Abrantes (one of whom, as a general rule, was always with me) a meaningful look and they knew they had a mission. It wasn't hard to find the object of my sudden admiration. They always started with the blondes, then by narrowing it down to only the women in the crowd with light-colored eyes. They were mistaken on very few occasions, and if they were, it was win-win because they found me a girl who was even better than the one I had initially noticed. And that was the only luxury I allowed myself as head of state. Sending a little message through my guards. In this kind of missions, Pepe Abrantes was always the best. He knew my tastes very well. He said I liked women from the fifties— "wide skirts and thin legs." One thing, I demanded that my men be careful and formal in their approach. "Good evening, *compañera. Mire,*

* The usual way I referred to Captain Bienvenido Pérez. He shouldn't be confused with Luis Más Martín, who was the recipient of the same nickname before the interview with Nixon on April 19, 1959. [*Author's note.*]

the comandante has taken an interest in you and we would like to know if you would like it if he invited you to go out on a date sometime. I mean, if you are free, if you don't have any other obligations." I don't recall anyone ever turning down the invitation. Anyone ever having any other obligations. Being married. Having children. Only one rejected the suggestion Pepe Abrantes made to her one afternoon in 1961 while I was walking around the narrow colonial streets of Trinidad: Dalia Soto del Valle, the woman to whom I am currently married and with whom I have five children. You can imagine that, with the kind of life I lead as a leader, moving day or night under the strictest secrecy through all corners of the country, first Celia then later Dalia were never able to track down my exact whereabouts. The mission assigned to my messengers concluded with getting a name and phone number. I had strictly forbidden taking the women out of wherever we were in one of our cars. I didn't allow my men to write anything down, either. But Chicho and Abrantes had trained themselves to memorize such precise information. If it happened in Plaza Cadenas—the little plaza in the center of Havana University—where the crowd gathered around my cars and stayed standing, since there were no seats there, there was time for Chicho or Abrantes to start their initial inquiries through one of the Oldsmobiles' Motorolas. "Listen," Pepe would say in a voice that was certainly sweet but that made his subordinates in State Security tremble all across the Republic. "Listen. Listen, take a look and see what we have *out there* about a Vivian. Get her phone number. Track her down." So that when my ceremony was finished and I spread out in the backseat of the car, Abrantes passed Security's initial report on my next romantic adventure to me. We let a few days go by to carry out a deep investigation; that was the norm. After that requirement was met, the operation remained under my control and no one else intervened. I arranged the date. Who's speaking? Vivian? Listen, Vivian, it's Fidel. The options, of course, were limited. A day fishing or a stroll around on the yacht. A private movie screening. Hunting in Mampostón. Or a weekend at the beach. Always dinner to start out. For my mental health and self-esteem, the rest of my conquest had to be carried out without the presence of my collaborators, without any other kind of assistance. (Except for their accompanying me to pick her up, naturally.) Sometimes I allowed myself the luxury of showing up at her house with my convoy, if it was somewhere quiet and remote, although the house was never exempt from a secret check of the area hours before. Secret check means that the Personal Security *compañeros* came in civilian attire and old American cars to scout the location. It goes without saying that in a matter of one hour, after we were alone on the yacht or in some remote country house on, for example, the terraces of the valley of Viñales, we were getting it on and I was hammering my cock into her all the way to the base of my *cojones*. But it was essential to make use of my own Don Juan-esque abilities. And when I fell in love, I even wrote poems. When I referred to being "alone" earlier, it should be understood as being inside the perimeter of a room. Because outside—protected by silence and the shadows of the night—I had men waiting as if for battle, with all access sealed off and machine gun emplacements. And if we were in some peaceful crook of the sea, to the east of Varadero, protected by a natural barrier of islets and low reefs, with at least one foot of water, three or four MPK submarine hunters would take possession of the channels, also in full combat mode. I did all I could to seem attentive and delicate, and one of the greatest pleasures—when it occurred— was hearing the women say they didn't know "it could be like this." It's true that they said it quite frequently and I took it as a compliment for not acting like a cannibal. Another thing that brought me great satisfaction was sensing the pleasure they got each time they saw that it was me they had between their legs and it was my cock hammering into them. Do you want to know the difference between fornicating before coming to power and after? It's that I don't recall ever having made love before the triumph of the Revolution to a woman who kept her eyes open the whole time. Santa María del Mar. That beach on Havana's east side was the most frequented for my trysts and was where we eventually made some residences available for my use, always hidden behind some wall or barrier of casuarinas, but without requiring any great investment because we inherited them from the bourgeois in very good condition and in well-protected, set-apart places. The truth is that, even though they weren't revolutionary leaders harassed by history's largest empire, the Cuban bourgeoisie took great pains to take care of themselves. My other favorite leisure sites were similar residences taken from the bourgeoisie in Varadero and the Isle of Pines. My scattered small paradises. In any part of our national territory I had access to a kind of secret fort to consummate my rapid amorous conquests. And we were dealing with places that only I could use. Some were used just once, but it only took their being designated "Fidel's houses" for the Ministry of the Interior's delegations to assign a permanent guard to them, not in every single case, of course, but in the great majority of them, and their maintenance and cleanliness were meticulous, under the permanent supervision of State Security. In reality, I possessed that whole country—and I'm saying that openly now in all its sexual significance.

I THINK THE TIME has come for a description. The moment in which I tell you in detail what things are like, in flesh and bone, in my nether region, or at least what it's like from my point of view. *My nether region.* My victorious cock. The one that all Cuban women, without exception, find so appealing. Come on, dear ladies of Miami. Don't pretend you don't know what I'm talking about. Don't look disgusted or repulsed. Would you like me to publish a list in *Granma* and run it along with your exultant and flirtatious letters? The most legendary cock—and its accompanying *cojones*—in the entire history of Cuba. Fidel Castro's cock. Oh, the political connotations that the people attach to its maximum leader's virile member and to the representative of the man who symbolizes all of their lives' aspirations: the father's cock, the older brother's cock, the chief's cock. You have no idea what that means. Especially when the person behind the accessory is oneself. A considerable amount of women can be consulted regarding the following information. I won't boast by speaking of quantities, nor is this a projection of excessive vanity: I simply say this so you understand that more than enough witnesses exist regarding the following. In a state of repose, or flaccidity—as doctors like to call it—its length is 3.5 inches (8.89 centimeters) and when fully erect, 6.3 inches (16.00 centimeters). This is, of course, with the foreskin pulled back and without any of the guards making his nearby presence known or else I get distracted. In circumference, it's also a beast, it is between 4.9 and 5 inches (12.4 to 12.70 centimeters); all of which speaks very laudably of my masculine endowments, which, as you can see, is above the average—especially in length—for the white race, which is from 5.5 to 6 inches (13.97 to 15.24 centimeters) and 1.5 inches (3.81 centimeters) in circumference; and, in my case, is not so far from that of our black *compañeros*, whose average is from 6.25 to 8 inches (15.88 to 20.32 centimeters) in length and a circumference of 2 inches (5.08 centimeters). In fact, and against all general belief that it is more difficult

and takes more effort and concentration to lift and make hard a member
the size of mine, due to the amount of blood that must pump through the
system, the facts and accompanying statistics show that while it requires
a more forceful irrigation in our cases, the willies that are under three
inches long when at rest must increase their size by 250 percent if they
want to reach the average dimensions of 5.5 or 6 inches while the bearers
of an instrument larger than three inches long only need an increase of
160 percent to reach the average.

Its coloration—one of the young ladies who has explored this area
of my anatomy told me so—gets darker as your vision focuses on my
crotch, perhaps due to the effect of the play of light on my abundant
pubic hair (which is currently not so abundant), and takes root from a
line that's like a dividing equator of the lower abdomen. In sum, the skin
of my cock is darker relative to the rest of my skin and is already decidedly shady and even somewhat mysterious in covering my heavy, bulging *cojones*. I am, in fact, pink skinned and for many years, even well into
the revolutionary era, I was a redhead, and many of my lovers were surprised upon taking my hands and not finding any of the roughness that
they were obviously expecting. Or which, in many cases, they desired,
since it was really about the hands of the man who shows up in a field
uniform and who, if necessary, can use those musician's hands to kill.
Still today, at my current age, I am seized by a disquieting insecurity, as
if I were still an adolescent and not the head of state of the Republic of
Cuba and the most renowned revolutionary leader in the world, when
that young lady comes to mind and I can still hear her, obscene and
indomitable, the descendant of some light-skinned mulatto and a white
whore, while she straddled me naked, facing me, in the cabin of whatever
bourgeois' nationalized yacht or in one of the houses we took over from
the du Ponts, on Hicacos Peninsula, the two of us alone in the room,
after having some lobsters in chocolate sauce—raised up by their whis-
kers from the same iceboxes placed alongside the boats where the fishermen threw them—and I had just tasted one of my Lanceros and a sip
of cognac, the air-conditioning running steadily and silently, some candles arranged tastefully as the only points of light, while she was removed
from the exquisiteness, caring little for any of it, anything not having to
do with devouring me, and who told me, brushing the edges of my ear
with her sweet lips, about the caresses she had in store for me. And she
ran her tongue—which she called "my little tongue"; in other words, that

the tongue was hers in usufruct and came from her mouth but I was its master—across my abdomen and went down to that dark place so desired by her and suddenly she found my cock-"my little cock" she would say—and she wet it, once and again, with her mouth—her "little mouth"—and she would desist for a moment and I would tell her not to be cruel and to come back. But that happened before or after she would describe in her volunteer-teacher way in the greatest detail possible what she considered the highest of earthly pleasures—whichever caress she made up for me for the occasion. Nevertheless, it did make some impact. I continue tasting the bouquet of my Napoleon reserves, even if I've given up smoking, and the occasions on which I go out fishing are few, but that girl hungry only for me, naked and straddling my legs, I've never forgotten her. It's not that I haven't followed up with her nor that I've allowed her to be lacking in anything all these years, in fact, she has even been given the role of vice minister of one of the foreign technical collaboration organs. It's something else, another feeling. Perhaps some of you will understand me. But, for those who have not tasted this ambrosia of the gods, this whole spell made up of a good meal, a good smoke, a good and regal cognac and the trembling light of candles rescuing the skin of an eighteen-year-old Cuban girl from the shadows, you can't come close or have any ability to understand. Our little party had a brew of my invention as dessert. Call it a special alcoholic concoction or a cocktail *por influencia*. I named it myself. Decapitated Pineapple. Although on other occasions we've called it Crown Rum. I have to be feeling very happy and clearheaded and eager to share my treasures to decide to open the small hotel freezer in the cabin and, amid the blast of cold air, extract the pineapple covered in frost that is hard as a rock, although only on the outside. I'll share the recipe. You cut the crown off the pineapple. You can cut up to an inch and a half off the top. Then you take the body, for lack of a better term for the seven-eighths left of the bottom, and start digging the flesh out with a spoon, so that, at the end of this operation, you've got a vessel. Of course, you need the skill to leave sufficient mass on the shell so that it doesn't lose its pineapple shape and to avoid the leaking of the liquid you are now going to pour into it. To the brim. That liquid is rum. Pure rum. Without anything else. Then you're going to put on the upper part, the one with the *penacho*, the one you took off at the beginning, like a hat. You take your pineapple with its belly overflowing with rum and you put it in the freezer. Don't worry about the drink, because alcohol doesn't freeze.

You're not going to make a Popsicle inside the pineapple. And you forget about it. A month is a good amount of time. Two months, if you're really a sybarite. You invite your lady friend with whom you've just fornicated—if you think she's worthy. Back to bed after pouring two servings of rum on the verge of freezing, but not quite, into clean champagne glasses. Now taste that. Take little sips. Taste that and tell me. Don't hurry. Take little sips.

DIFFICULT WOMEN? NO, there weren't that many of them. Antonieta Lorenzo. I would put her at the top. The most difficult of them all. She came from the children's department of the famous Cuban luxury store El Encanto. A respectable number of the wives of our captains and commanders came from El Encanto. Commander René Vallejo, one of my closest and most loyal men, and my personal doctor since the beginning of the Revolution, fell in love with Antonieta, madly in love with that woman. One day he told me he was going to marry her and I told him there was no fucking way he was going to marry Antonieta and I yelled at him and insulted him and practically called him a faggot and that night he had a stroke and died a week later.

Vallejo was a very upstanding man, truly, with very good manners and a thick white beard, and in his commander's uniform and high boots and his eye-catching Stechkin twenty-shot pistol in a black leather holster, he made quite an impression wherever he went. He met Antonieta because I had made him the messenger of my own flirtations, because I had fallen in love with her first. It was a mistake because previously I had used him as a messenger with Margarita Muñoa, a Uruguayan actress of little fame who was involved with the Montoneros and who was in Cuba as a political refugee, I believe, or training for one of that group's clandestine actions and who ended up, logically, landing in one of our theater companies. I saw her. At a meeting of the Montoneros. And from there I sent Vallejo with my message that I would like to "have a more private moment with her" and the messenger was the one with whom the little lady fell in love. In Antonieta's case, it was René who fell down at her feet. As far as I was concerned, I had already cut off all ties with Antonieta Lorenzo, when René started to court her and ended up, as I've told you, asking my permission to marry her. René was a vehement spiritualist—which is to say that he had been ordained as a Yoruba priest, in other words, a *babalawo*—and, as part of his very personal protocols of faith and celebration of spirituality, he had ordered a room be set up on the top floor of his three-story house with a roof that had a large funnel with the wide end pointing toward infinity, through which he said he received the intergalactic influences quickly and directly. The narrowest part pointed toward the inside of the place and hung from about three meters in height toward a place on the floor where he rested his head on the nights that he contemplated the firmament. Then he had that argument with me and a few hours later had the encephalic vascular accident. Let me tell you that when word got out that Vallejo had had the stroke, all of Cuba's *santeros* undertook a simultaneous *toque de tambores* the likes of which had never been seen on the island and which went on nonstop, beating of sacred dreams for a week, during the course of which he continued hemorrhaging but breathing. I myself gave the brothers the order to stop the *toque de los tambores*. We had to let our brother René rest. Another important reason was that René had assumed my death. He told me so himself. He called it "a situation that had presented itself" while he was looking up at the stars through his cosmic funnel, and one that I interpreted as his dialogue with some spirit. In sum, a procedure that the *santeros* call *robo de cabeza*, robbing the head, which consisted of deceiving death, had to take place. The methodology varies widely and there are many different versions employed to ably complete the job. In any event, it's a diversion maneuver. The most commonly used process in Cuba almost always has the goal of saving some terminally ill person and is achieved by taking a rag doll, who looks as much as possible like the dying person, to holy ground and putting it in an open tomb as an offering to Oyá, the *orisha* (goddess) of the spirits and, as such, ruler of cemeteries. Other *santeros* prefer to carry out the robbing the head with somebody who has some kind of illness or weakness that is not necessarily fatal. This is why so many *santeros* prowl around hospital waiting rooms and is also the basis for the Cuban custom of not leaving sick family members alone at a hospital. René's case was quite different. Neither he nor I had any kind of illness. But he saw my death, and, with his vast spiritual powers and his authority as medic commander of the Rebel Army, he made a pact with the *orishas* so that the robbing the head was paid for by his own sacrifice. So it was necessary to ask Havana's main *babalawos* to stop that eerie and sustained *toque de tambores*, since that was the only way to give meaning to Commander Vallejo's sacrifice. I sent the captains from my guard with the message and the plea that they get in touch with the country's remaining *babalawos*. We had to give our brother René's spirit some peace. They had done what they were supposed to. Now it was my turn to give the order to unplug him. We might be sending the wrong signal upon maintaining his body alive artificially if there was no spirit there any longer. Besides which, the *orishas* could become confused and not realize that they already had a head The *babalawos* understood and quieted their drums. On my end, I was there for the autopsy. To relieve the tension, I decided to tell a story about my friend, which was a way of remembering him. Three pathologists started to open up René's corpse. "Vallejo used to say," I said, "that he operated barefoot because he had made a promise to the saints." I wanted to add that he was experiencing his last visit to what could be considered an operating room and that here he was barefoot, and naked besides. And that this was his personal best. But the noise of the electric saw cutting bone would have forced me to speak too loudly. And I wasn't worthy of competing with a saw. There was just one fucked-up moment during the entire autopsy. Even the pathologists couldn't suppress a gesture of surprise. It was when they finished sawing off the top of his head and Vallejo's brain escaped like the contents of a well and slipped right into the autopsy table drain. His encephalic mass had become completely liquid. That was as much as I could take and, using the authority inherent to my position, I told the pathologists I was getting the hell out of there. While avoiding shaking their hands, I thanked them for their attention and left. On the way to our cars, I told Chicho, "Listen to me, dammit. Take me anywhere in this country without a jar of formaldehyde within a hundred-kilometer radius."

SO, WE'VE ARRIVED at the moment you've been waiting for. Dalia Soto del Valle, whom we tend to call Lala in our family circle, my second wife since the early eighties and with whom I have five children, all of them male. She is a teacher and chemical engineer, the daughter of a pharmacist from Ranchuelo, a town in the center of Las Villas Province that used to have just one manufacturing center—the tobacco factory belonging to that bon vivant Diego Trinidad (or "Dieguito")—where the aforementioned Trinidad and Hermanos blunts were made—and was in a permanent state of euphoria over having taken the rural mar-

ket over from the main tobacco industry: Regalías el Cuño, Seal of Privilege (what names we Cubans waste on our products!)—and a girl whom
I met in the following way: My convoy of three purple Oldsmobiles was
slowing circling around the difficult, narrow streets of Trinidad, a town
that is usually known for its counterrevolutionary activity and which, at
the time, in May or June of 1961, I had flooded with militiamen with
machine guns—mostly Soviet machine guns from the Second World
War called PPSh and the more modern Czech M/52 retractable bayonet rifles—and Literacy Campaign brigades. My guards didn't hide their
weapons either and made a great show of casting intimidating looks at
any suspicious passersby. The Escambray Sierra rose up in its somber
majesty over the immediate horizon of the town. A few months before,
I had ordered the deployment of seventy thousand men from Havana's
heavy battalions to occupy virtually every spring, crossroads, and hut in
the mountain range. In the language of the peasants of the Sierra Maestra, it was about cutting off their "feeders." It never fails. To capture a
guy in the mountains, put a nest of machine guns at every source where
there's food. We had to neutralize the Escambray's insurgent group. We
did so to avoid the *yanquis*, should they invade us, getting a hold of the
almost three thousand counterrevolutionaries taking up arms against us
there. In that operation—which we called La Limpia, the Cleanup—we
captured a good number of those elements. But the invasion had already
happened (and we had also already defeated it; it's the Playa Girón episode that you know so well) and the remaining insurgents who were in
hiding, waiting for the Cleanup *to move past them*—the prisoners said—
were perking up again. So I ordered the *compañeros* from the Army of
the Center—Escambray was part of its responsibility area—to reinitiate operations, but they had to do so with a more modest amount of
men and resources. For the time being, we had to apply our other principle of battle in the mountains: not leaving any free territory under
their domain. We had to have them on the run all the time. The reason I was in Trinidad was because of Mao's famous concept of taking
water away from the fish as a viable way to wipe out the rural counterrevolution. And since I had received word that a poor woman had lost
her son in a skirmish against the insurgents and that stones were being
thrown at her door as a sign of mockery of the counterrevolutionaries
around there, she was going to serve as my excuse to initiate my drain-
age campaign. I was thinking about this, about Mao and his theory,

when I saw Dalia. She was wearing a Literacy Campaign volunteer's uniform—black calf-length boots, olive-green cargo pants and a gray shirt with the plastic Literacy Campaign monogram hanging from the left shoulder—very clean, meticulously ironed. She was walking calmly and taking advantage of the shadows cast by the colonial houses over the narrow sidewalk and a short piece of the cobblestone path. I said, "What a pretty girl." Much later, Abrantes told me that at the time he thought, How does he know she's pretty if he's only seen her ass? Ass isn't a bad word in this context, nor is it disrespectful. In this context, to the average Cuban, ass means that I had only seen her from behind. And given that she is now my beloved wife and the mother of my children and that I will most likely spend the rest of my days with her, we have to be very careful about the words we use to describe her. She didn't pay any mind to our cars, which were barely moving at her pace, until she saw me to her left just a meter away, and with the windows rolled down, because— as I previously said—we never had air-conditioning in those Oldsmobiles, so I had time and space to nod my head slightly as a greeting and murmur, "Good afternoon, *compañera*," to which she responded with a similar gesture of her head, but without saying a word, although winning me over with her smile. The cars kept going and Abrantes, in the backseat, noticed that I wasn't turning over my right shoulder to take another look at that young literacy volunteer whom I could now see from the front. I remained inscrutable in the way that Abrantes called "absent while still nailed to the spot." So, I was saying that I was going through the streets of Trinidad when I saw this woman, very attractive, with a certain air like Naty González Revuelta, and I was dumbstruck. Very big ass. Very pretty. Move the car back to take a good look at her, I told the driver. She had to have heard me. But she didn't pay any attention. Abrantes noticed and got out and went up to her and introduced her to me. Fidel, come over here so I can introduce you to this girl. Later Pepe boasted of having been the "architect" of that relationship. The martyr's mother with her beaten-down door and the draining of the fish's water were going to have to wait.

On the blackboard, the sketch of an ambush, July 1979. The Sandinista guerrillas are on the verge of defeating dictator Anastasio Somoza. At the urban struggle training center Punto Cero, about thirty kilometers east of Havana, while he consumes one of his expensive and ever-present Cohiba cigars, Fidel outlines the ambush that should decimate Somoza's troops in the outskirts of Managua.

The Key Is in Dallas

///

CAMILO, KENNEDY AND ANDERSON. THE HOLY TRINITY OF MY crimes. We're talking about deaths that someone in the exile community or in the American government guessed would be profitable to blame on me. Camilo to stir up old revolutionaries a little and get them to come out against me, or because, being veterans of the Rebel Army with a history of executions or expropriating large landholdings, they needed a reason to land in Miami. Camilo's death persuaded them to turn against me. That's the logic behind assigning to me this first homicide. Kennedy because he could provide the ultimate pretext for the Americans to invade me. The common accusation that I was a communist, in the days prior to Playa Girón, had already failed, so they needed a large-scale assassination. A presidential assassination forged in Havana was (and would be still) deserving of a fair punitive operation. As far as the downing of Major Rudolph Anderson's U-2 was concerned, it should have represented a miniature Pearl Harbor. A Pearl Harbor with only one casualty. The disappearance of Camilo Cienfuegos, the head of the Rebel Army, is for Cuban national consumption, for those who have made a career out of hating me. Nothing is definitive with them. The assumption is that I am responsible for everything that happens in Cuba, including accidents, including casualties, including the disappearance of a Cessna due to a pilot's negligence in the face of a cumulonimbus cloud. But both Anderson's case and Camilo's case have an overwhelming amount of supporting information in publications and the Internet and it's not necessary for me to harp on them.

Kennedy. This is the thorniest one of the lot, as you can assume, but what worries me most is the disappointment I will most certainly cause in the reader upon not being able to lay out any more information than what has already been published, in overwhelming quantities, by the Americans. There's just one difference. That the tons of documentation the *yanquis* have made public was nothing more than a smokescreen covering up the truth. I, however, am committed to not going beyond some basic reasoning. At the end of the day, I fear disappointing my readers regarding a matter about which I have always taken great care to feign knowing only about as much as the average interested person. But I'll tell you what I can. And most importantly, I'll reveal my logic to you. To begin with, I'll say something that will surprise interested parties, not those who are interested in Kennedy's assassination, but those who are busy studying *us*. The State Security commanders have always been bewildered by what I have come to call their favorite topics of 1962 and 1963: the development of the October Missile Crisis and the famous presidential assassination in Dallas. The October Missile Crisis because it was when—according to their assessment—these commanders learned what *realpolitik* was. It didn't escape me that they viewed Nikita Khrushchev as that episode's hero. The Soviet leader's management of all the details, his excellent political calculations on the verge of nuclear war, his manipulation of Kennedy's hesitations and my fits of independence, were a model of shrewdness and well-carried-out conspiracy even in the unforeseen incidents and details. He put everything in the service of his goals. And he achieved them all. Naturally, my image would be tarnished by this interpretation. I accept it, fully aware that the element that excites them the most—although they have never dared pronounce it—is the fact that Khrushchev manipulated us, Kennedy and me, at his will. But if you really want them to be sharp and productive, you've got to give these intelligence organisms a wide margin of debate, and within the stagnant compartments of their management you have to allow imagination and irreverence to flow. I'm referring in particular to the action known as *intelligence* that, as I will explain here, in the early sixties was one of the tasks assigned to State Security's Department One. You can count on the counterintelligence services not only repressing others, but being repressive within themselves, animals keeping a watchful eye on each other. You cannot make this same mistake with intelligence, with officials *who work abroad*, because you'll lose the battle before you've even begun. There's something that my subordinates didn't notice, however, regarding Khrushchev's dirty tricks and the October Missile Crisis. It was also about what I learned then regarding how one had to manage in a game played only by superpowers, the only two that have ever existed, and how to avoid returning to the humiliating status of a banana republic in the eyes of the world. *Realpolitik.* You understand? I'll add something that is of utmost importance for me. Our intelligence's famous motto that when you have to make an analysis, you can't take sides, comes from that time period. It was a method I implemented, and the first time I laid it out, the phrase seemed very overwrought, but I ended up surprising myself when I came out with it in one of the first State Security methodology meetings, around 1963, when I said, "There's no flag that waves over information, *caballeros.*" I wanted to warn them not to become fixated on tailoring their analysis to meet a political objective, because if you manipulate information that way, the result is nothing more than a slogan, or at least it never exceeds that value. Kennedy and his head being blown off is a different matter and if our *compañeros* in State Security have kept themselves on high alert about all of its details, it's due to the considerable number of Cuban exiles and associated Americans, especially politicians from Florida and mafiosos divested of their casinos, who are mentioned in relation to the crime. The order to remain on alert came from my office. It's obvious that they had to be prepared to dodge any blows. Don't think it's an easy group to win over. We're talking about men with a high intelligence coefficient and very sharp intellect. The cream of the crop of our handlers, who worked within State Security Department One. This is the group that has successfully fucked up all of the CIA's operations in Cuba for a good half century. From very early on, we gave their activity the name of Direct Confrontation because they were the ones who went head to head with the CIA's spies and plans. I'll add that there was another name after the fact. They came to be known as El Cható's people because from 1967 on, they resided in a building that, in turn, came to be known as El Cható—a consequence of the pretentious name it was originally given as a tourist facility built on the coast to the west of Havana in the mid-fifties: El Chateau Miramar. From an operational point of view, they were in charge of the general management of State Security's main work, which at the time was counterintelligence or counterespionage. Since the Dirección General de Inteligencia (DGI) was still young and in formation, almost all of its work abroad in the sixties was managed by the counterespionage services—the Direct Confrontation folks. The handlers. Those are the people you have to watch all the time, because they're the ones who manage all of the operative games, and operative games are about infiltrating the enemy's ranks. This is the only thing Americans ask of the few deserters from our ranks as soon as they get to the United States. What operative game are you bringing us, amigo? All the deserters need is to report one operative game and they can fill their pockets and have the guarantee of a comfortable and peaceful retirement. What was that famous television program? *Have Gun—Will Travel.* Well, in the case of handlers who wish to desert, I would say that their motto is *Have Operative Game—Will Travel.* Because if you don't have anything in that Samsonite briefcase, amigo, you're better off finding a trade so you can make a living here in America. Therein lies the importance that Department One always had for me, because it was where the greatest number of handlers and operative games were concentrated. And because you had to learn to listen to them, while the norm was not to trust in them blindly. Don't forget that it's a two-way job and you never know for sure when the enemy has hijacked your operative game and started playing his own. In the case of Kennedy's assassination, and any attempt to blame me for it, the information coming from the department was very necessary, especially for my own *counterchecks* and while I was making inquiries through my own channels. You can imagine that, if a conspiracy in the United States was porous enough to have dozens of Cubans participating in it, I would expect a similar lack of trustworthiness in my own services. Certain clarifications must be made up front. The reader will have noticed during the course of these memoirs—part story, part pedagogy—that my maxim as a conspirator is to act only according to my own knowledge, and that is the path where my ideas unfold, between my being and my consciousness, where no one else fits and which allows me to state, after having survived for more than half a century despite over six hundred attempts on my life, that I conspire, therefore I am. Everything else is about delegating. I tell you what you have to do, but almost never explain why. I prefer to trust in silence and ignorance, besides which there is no better situation for an agent to be in, if he is captured and subjected to interrogation sessions of electric shocks with cattle prods and clamps attached to his testicles, than that of not having anything substantial to confess. You don't know how calmly you can face your torturers like that. In this regard, this doesn't stray too much from the classic use of maps during a war; the one that's in the hands of the squadron chief or the company is for tactical use and covers less territory; the one on the command post table is the strategic one. Fine, then, so what I've set out for myself now is to warn you that I was explaining a method and you should refrain from making a definitive judgment about the Cuban intelligence apparatus based on these precepts. The professional success of our intelligence missions —which are comparable to those of Israel's Mossad—lies precisely in the strict pyramidlike structure of these services and the extreme discipline with which tasks are carried out. It's one sole head and one sole army. And this one sole head is the one making decisions about how widely to disseminate information. Without a single crack. The only desertion of an active-duty officer in the special services that we've been hit with during the whole of the Cuban Revolution is that of Florentino Azpillaga. All of the others that the CIA has in hand, as the case may be, are still in Cuba and have most probably been retired after having received a ton of medals of commendation. As far as the Miami personnel are concerned, besides those who aren't worthy of any medals, the reader has the right to ask why I brought them up. I've referred to Miami because, in the first place, the *yanquis* themselves devoted to investigating the matter— amid journalists and politicians—deduced that if there were so many Cubans involved in the assassination, making little trips between Dallas, Miami, New Orleans and Washington and spending the CIA's money, ranting against Kennedy from the rooftops and loudly demanding his head on a platter, then I had to have known all of the details concerning the assassination, since many of those men—and they weren't lacking in common sense in this assessment—were actually double agents of mine. At the end of the day, where there are Cubans, there's the G2. So eventually it wasn't that I ordered my agents to encourage the assassins to kill Kennedy, but my men on the ground gave me all of the available information. Upon conceiving of me as a man with primal, visceral reactions, who wildly kicks everything in sight while frothing at the mouth every time he has been informed of another assassination attempt against him by the CIA, it follows that they would immediately designate me as the brains behind the presidential assassination. You can't deny that if there was an easy person to lay the blame on for all of this, it was me. Practically guilty by trade. But I wasn't going to stand for seeing the game repeated with Kennedy that Khrushchev played with me during the October Missile Crisis when he blamed me for shooting down Anderson's U-2. I'm done with superpowers blaming me for their sins. They kill and then try to make me pay the price. You've got to be fucking kidding me. To anyone who knows me or who has merely studied my behavior as a conspirator, the following reasoning should be enough to write off any participation of mine in the assassination of a North American president. Imagine me involved with those idiots in Miami for just one single second. I won't hide the fact from you that of course I knew something was brewing, although it was always buried deep in the mountain of reports that arrived about another assassination project, one that was infinitely more worrisome for me since, as you will understand, it had to do with my own assassination. The problem was that the so-called sign of attack was linked to an attempt on my own life. So we didn't learn about it because of Kennedy, but because of me. In any event, the news caught me by surprise. I was in Varadero, the beach resort town a hundred kilometers to the east of Havana, that afternoon of November 22, 1963. I was having lunch with Jean Daniel, the French journalist who had just flown down from the United States with a message from President Kennedy himself. I was savoring a strawberry ice cream and getting ready to share some fine Partagás cigars with the Frenchman, when the head of my guard dared to open the door to the ranch, in which the large stained-glass window overlooking the sea was always fogged up due to the effects of a powerful air conditioner, and I immediately knew there would be very bad news. I put down my spoon with a bit of ice cream still in it and said, "What is it, Chicho? Is something wrong?" He nodded, serious, pale, with that unmistakable mark of those who announce a war or death. "Forgive the interruption, Comandante. But the radio says they've just killed Kennedy." Jean Daniel and I had understood each other up to that point in a mixture of Spanish and English. But he understood the exact meaning of those words. As a courtesy, I added the title that Chicho overlooked. "¿*Presidente Kennedy?*" Chicho nodded. "Get the cars ready, Chicho," I ordered without hesitation. Then I got up slowly from my chair, and as an automatic gesture I took some cigars out of the box on the table and offered them to Jean Daniel, who was also standing up, and took another handful for myself, and then, standing and leaning forward with the tips of my fingers on the tablecloth, I lifted my gaze and told the emissary in a reflective tone, "I think your mission here is done. You are invited to accompany me to Havana, so I can leave you at your hotel."

His mission was over, but mine was just starting. You, open your eyes wide so that you can learn what hard-core conspiracy is all about. I hadn't walked three steps toward the exit with Jean Daniel in my wake, when all of a sudden I knew that I was being graced by a sort of divine revelation, it was one of those moments in my life in which my brain was able to produce something I would dare to describe as a moment of enlightenment. Only I could understand the immense value of the gift the Americans had just given me that afternoon, on which I still recall that I was deprived of my dessert. I didn't know who they were or where they were hiding or at whose behest they were working, but I had to make a real effort to not laugh with pleasure, to not let the happiness shine in my eyes, to adhere to my role of sorrowful foreigner at the far-off funeral of an adversary suddenly taken out of the game. The equation was simple. The *yanquis* were never going to dig up Kennedy's death again. Never. Because they were the assassins. My problem was to figure out the names. Until that should occur, until I had the little piece of paper in my hands on which were written all of the passwords and dates of the plots, I would remain on the defense. Hence I ordered Department One to stay on alert and track all of the Cubans with ties to the event. Knowing that those little Cubans in exile in any case were soldiers without any degree of responsibility, much less any knowledge of the very exclusive masterminds of the crime. I would begin my initial compilation of facts here. Here. And fit the pieces together. And never reveal the increasing size of this compilation of mine. For many months after Kennedy's death, I regularly reviewed all of the material relating to the case that came across my desk and that was placed in a special pile for me, to my left, under a paperweight with a white marble bottom on which rested a bust of Lenin. As I reviewed these documents and made occasional notes on them with my fountain pen, the *compañeros* in the office would put them away in a drawer that was specially designated for them, and they kept adding new material to the pile on my desk when it arrived. Of course, I'm talking about information that was classified as RESERVED or, in limited cases, TOP SECRET or ONLY FOR THE COMANDANTE'S USE. Of course, there wasn't a single piece of information that was valuable enough to destroy. It goes without saying that all of the really touchy details always came to me *in person and directly to my ear*, a whisper, an approving nod of my head, and a light pat of gratitude before removing my arm entirely from my interlocutor's shoulder. And that's it. But in those scant seconds of concentrated attention on my part, someone would have brought priceless information into my hands. Someone who showed up under a false name and passport at the international airport of Rancho Boyeros, in Havana, and who probably covered half the world to get to Cuba through Prague, Madrid or Mexico City to not leave any trace of his journey, would slip me some names in a fortuitous encounter in one of our most secret safe houses. Now I'll tell you something that could be of interest to you. The only thing I read regarding the attempt on Kennedy's life that really thrilled me was public information that reached Havana through the press agency teletypes in the first seventy-two hours after the events. The intensity with which I scrutinized every cable was equal to my ignorance about the episode. But everything began to go downhill after the shooting of Lee Harvey Oswald, the president's presumed assassin, in the basement of the police station. My interest waned because it was clear that they had started to eliminate any inconvenient witnesses and that this would be their modus operandi from then on. If they were already killing anyone in possession of any significant detail, then forget about going poking around. Just one Cuban document from that time period caught my eye about three or four months after having gotten enough of the subject. It came from the headquarters of the Bureau of Counterrevolutionary Bands in Oriente Province. I remember as if it were yesterday that it was signed by a first lieutenant named Jaime Santana and that, under the broken line of typewritten dashes, the signer identified himself as the second in command of the bureau. There were three or four pages of careful writing with an essay about the most important operations taking place in the country against those who had taken up arms. It wasn't directed to me but meant for a sort of study manual for a meeting the six provincial bureaus were planning. But Ramiro, who was acting as minister of the interior in those days, had casually looked over the document, which was among many papers he was reviewing one afternoon, and, knowing how interested I was in the subject, immediately sent me a copy with the paragraphs regarding Kennedy underlined. Lieutenant Santana's theory was very appealing. Perhaps it was only a rough idea. And, although it was partly mistaken, it awakened something dormant in my mind. It referred to a meeting that had taken place on November 5, 1962, in a hideaway in the

Escambray Mountains between an energetic CIA agent named Luis David Rodríguez González and the chiefs of staff of the counterrevolutionary insurgency under the command of the self-proclaimed Commander in Chief Tomás San Gil Díaz. Luis David, who had infiltrated Cuba a few months before and was clandestinely based in Havana and introducing himself to those of his kind as the secretary general of the counterrevolutionary organization Anticommunist Civic Resistance (Resistencia Civica Anticomunista, or RCA), appeared before Tomás San Gil as the CIA's direct emissary to ask the guerrilla chief to "try to be more aggressive" in his operations. The request, despite its inherent risks, was meant to spur the provision of new supplies and even reinforcement troops to the decimated guerrilla group. For the time being, he gave him money and committed to new and more frequent contacts. We will never know to what degree Luis David Rodríguez González was acting in good faith. But it is true—according to the information we obtained later—that he was the bearer of an authentic CIA request. The problem is that, given the situation of absolute degradation of the guerrillas and their increasingly reduced operative capacities, what was proposed to Tomás San Gil was a suicide mission. A man who was not only ambitious, and even charismatic, but also very brave, San Gil committed himself anyway to launching an offensive in the first quarter of 1963 and of doing so in principle with the munitions and weapons he already had and some logistics that Luis David would deliver from his organization in Havana. It goes without saying that, without any men, weapons or munitions, San Gil's offensive barely lasted a week, between the end of February and the beginning of March that 1963, the last date of which San Gil himself succumbed in a bend in the mountains called Las Llanadas de Gómez, and after verifying that his offensive effort—consisting of an attack on and the burning of some warehouses and sugarcane fields and a shoot-out on a Ferrocarril Central train—had exhausted all of his reserves. As far as Luis David Rodríguez González was concerned, he met a similar fate. Days after the Escambray battle, they proceeded to dismantle the RCA organization and its main assets, who had all been identified. This happened on March 8. Upon his being detained at the house where he was living in the neighborhood of El Cerro and being taken in a G2 operations patrol car to the Instruction Department in Villa Marista, a mansion to the west of Havana, the *compañeros* in charge of his transfer didn't thoroughly search him and didn't notice the short-barreled, .38-caliber Bulldog revolver that he was hiding in his ankle strap. Nor had they handcuffed him. When the Ford patrol car stopped in the villa's side arcade to identify themselves at the sentry post, Luis David drew his weapon and killed one of his custodians, combatant Orlando López González. It was the only shot he was able to fire, because the *compañero* assigned to the sentry post didn't hesitate for a moment in firing half a clip of forty nine-millimeter bullets from his Czech T–23 submachine gun into Luis David's neck and chest. At that time, our posts at Villa Marista had those weapons, now that I remember it. The conclusion that Lieutenant Jaime Santana reaches in his essay—and this was what activated my internal alarm system—was that the Americans had designed the operation with San Gil knowing that he would fail but with the deliberate purpose of increasing the gulf between the Cuban counterrevolution and the Kennedy administration. If his presumption is accurate, the lieutenant concludes, the definitive annihilation of the guerrillas in Escambray combined with the Bay of Pigs disaster was going to provide the mass of Cuban exiles with "necessary cannon fodder and a thirst for revenge" so that the CIA could use them in their Dallas conspiracy. "That's it!" I said to myself, smacking the papers with my index finger, "that's exactly it!" But, shit, he was looking at it in reverse. I already had the answer to one of the questions that had been dogging me since November 22, 1963. I had asked myself, And why are there so many Cubans involved in this? I knew from the beginning that it was a trap. To draw me into the problem or involve me at their whim. But suddenly I understood, I understood it all. Not only had Cubans been induced to participate in the task of killing Kennedy, but the CIA had likewise been used. We were all being used. All of us. I was tagged as guilty along with the Cuban counterrevolution and the CIA. That's why we would all remain standing. To implicate us together in someone else's crime. And don't forget to assign the Italian-American mafiosos that used to control Havana's casinos to me too. They started with Santos Trafficante, the Don of Tampa, and they didn't give it a break in all those sessions of Congress convened to investigate the presidential assassination. The idea was that he was bitter that Kennedy hadn't taken Fidel out of power, and so Kennedy prevented his return to Havana to resume managing his casinos. Here you have one of those marvelous advertising maneuvers that are only possible in political manipulation and to which I concede—especially in this case specifically—great credit to the *yanquis*. That is, they turned one of the men in the Mafia whom they hired to kill me, in one of those many plots to slit my throat, over-night into the perfect suspect to implicate in the assassination of their main contractor. So it's important for you to see the method that I used to shake these accusations off: simply, jump on the bandwagon of blam-ing the CIA and the Mafia.

I'll wrap up this segment of my memoirs here. I have to. Not out of respect for any commitment that I made to the assassins, I have none, but due to a much more pragmatic matter. *Because I found everything out, of course.* Because I know everything, of course. And because the man who is using his hands right now to type on this laptop the words with which he hopes to soften at least a part of the void that his death will produce, and who moves his fingers at average speed over the keyboard, believes it timely to confess to you that the only person—and the only foreigner—outside of that circle of conspirators (and their heirs, who are the ones still left), of a rough aristocracy safe and immune in the confines of the American West, who is in possession of the *whole* secret, is him. Ergo: is me. And that they know that I know, of course. That's the strategic value of having discovered them. Alerting them to my knowledge and tell-ing them that, as a guarantee, the information is secured in other secret depositaries placed many years ago in God knows what corner of this planet. It's the boat we're obliged to keep afloat together. Or sink with it. Do you understand? That's what I asked them and now I'm asking you. Do you understand?

Ever since then, I've enjoyed that incontrovertible life insurance. It extends to my family. That's why everything is following me to the grave. *For the time being.*

It's probably unnecessary to warn you, but from this point on you can speculate all you wish. At least you can make out the reason that, from the mid-sixties on, the *yanquis* abandoned all pretense of killing me. (Take a look at the last forty-five years to confirm it.) And under-stand how amused I am—on the rare occasions when fifteen days go by without my appearing in the press—after asking the *compañeros* in Intelli-gence to activate some of their useful links for me, that the Western press revives the old story of my participation in the presidential assassination in Dallas. We have two leading stories we usually use in the stockpile of trumped-up scandals. Kennedy and drugs. We alternate the use of these. And they never get old.

The Day That Never Existed. The Coda

It hadn't been three months since the assassination when I took advantage of the visit of that gringa Lisa Howard, a journalist for ABC television, to send to Lyndon Johnson the message that I wished to help him win the next presidential election and to that end I allowed, if it should be necessary, that he could launch any kind of attack against Cuba with the certainty that I would understand and also assuring him that he could count on my not responding with a similar action. Lisa herself had been a messenger in the exchange of my messages with Kennedy before the arrival of Jean Daniel. If I was directing myself to Johnson now, it was for a very specific reason. Because I harbored serious doubts about his innocence in Kennedy's assassination. I had just started my own investigations and I didn't want to waste any time in the least in showing Johnson that I was above any moral consideration concerning the assassination of a president (as long as—of course—I wasn't the president in question). And please don't get moralistic on me, in the United States they're always talking about the eventual need—and therefore the right—for the executive to order the assassination of a foreign head of state. You can't complain the day that the guns are turned on your own head. It was an oral message and they kept it secret for many years. In one way or another, however, the memo that Lisa wrote with the highlights of my message survived in the archives of Johnson's Presidential Library and was eventually made public along with other memos written by his assistants about this same issue. It's really one of the most enigmatic messages of my entire political career. While I'm telling Johnson that the doors are open to bomb any combat unit or town of ours at close range and I'll understand the reasons for this and won't even respond, I'm tempting him with poisoned bait. Like prior acceptance that he would put on his own Pearl Harbor, although of course his political career couldn't survive the consequences of such an action. You can't deny that it was the best way, at least in the eyes of the upper echelons of the Democratic Party, to deflect any attempt to implicate me in Kennedy's death. What greater proof of trust and loyalty to them could I offer than the banquet of a massacre in Cuba? On the other hand, upon asking the Americans to point out the time and place of the attack beforehand, I was giving myself undoubtable room to maneuver, to know, for example, which units or combat means should be kept in the designated destruction area, and to even assign to the place any commander or captain whom I was interested in getting rid of. There's nothing like the enemy's weapons to clean out your own backyard! Nonetheless, we had to make sure that they didn't fancy taking over the base at San Antonio de los Baños or Campo Libertad, where we had made a great investment in buildings and improving the old structures. Only in Campo Libertad were we making the largest repair hangar in all of Latin America. Don't forget about the Soviets either. What I could have milked them for, had a *yanqui* attack taken place against our country! The agreements from the October Missile Crisis would have run like water through their hands and Khrushchev would have turned into the laughingstock of public international opinion.

An unimpeachable plan. One of the many that have allowed me to survive to this day. Not only was I offering Johnson a test of unprecedented power, but it allowed me the luxury, when the time came, of sacrificing up an entire town.

Sierra de los Órganos training camp, Cuba, 1966. The next jungle is Bolivia. A proud group of guerrillas, but only three of these men will survive. It will happen within the year, and they will be wiped out in a rugged and foreign land. In the white pullover, with a pipe: Ernesto Che Guevara. The pleasant look of a balding bureaucrat out for a daytrip with his thick glasses is the work of—dental prosthesis and barber's razor in hand—Colonel Luis C. García ("Fisín," or "The Dentist"), Cuban Intelligence's master of disguise.

HEARING BIRDS PASS IN THE NIGHT

/ / /

There's a huge underground component to the history of revolutions which isn't widely known. Revolutions are not absolutely pure movements; they are made by men and brew amid inner battles, ambitions, mutual ignorance. And once this is overcome, it turns into a stage of history that, for better or worse, with reason or without it, is silenced and disappears.

—ERNESTO GUEVARA,
OCTOBER 28, 1963

THERE WAS A VERY OBNOXIOUS, VERY NEGATIVE COMMENT THAT Che made one afternoon upon returning from a flight. They had just managed to land after a storm had blocked all visibility over the runway at Campo Libertad and made them burst through the cloud. The tower at Libertad told them to find somewhere else because Libertad was closed and Che said no fucking way, he still had some visibility over the head of the runway and he was going to make his way however he could. And besides, the fuel they had left was a pittance, so they were either going to land the plane or it was going to drop out of the sky. It was after this landing that the Argentine uttered those words. He thought that only his pilot, Eliseo de la Campa, was listening. He didn't realize that the two engines were already turned off and that a mechanic was wedging a block under the Cessna's landing gear. Che said neither bad weather nor any son of a bitch was going to kill him in a plane, like Camilo. "Why do you think I've worked so hard to become a pilot?" he asked Eliseo. Che, of course, had no reason to know that the mechanic, who was one of the many communists planted in the Armed Forces by Captain Victor Pina, had heard him loud and clear. Thus the conversation was duly noted by the mechanic, who had the wisdom not to include it in his daily report but in a separate report that he sent immediately to Pina and that Pina delivered to me, directly to my hands, without commentary. But I couldn't bite my own tongue. "The Argentine is a piece of shit," I told Pina. "Trying to blame me for Camilo's death is a stab in the back. I'm not going to forgive this."

This wasn't the first comment he made of this kind that reached my ears, but it was the one that I still haven't forgotten to this day. It was still too early in the Cuban process for the Argentine to doubt my integrity. It was time to evaluate what we were going to do with him.

I sent Che on a trip on June 12, 1959. An extended tour meant to keep him out of the country for some time. At the airport, I assigned Vilaseca to him, that is, I instructed Vilaseca to keep an eye on him. An ideal Trotskyite to deal with Che's Trotskyism. That's what Ernesto Guevara was like. But he was an internationalist Trotskyite, not the kind who would help me consolidate my power. It was also the case that he was proving to be more of an adventurer than an ideologue. He hadn't achieved a single beneficial business treaty and he had wasted almost the entire tour on diplomatic gestures that rather favored the promotion of his own image, not that of the Cuban Revolution.

A few months after his journey, once the way was cleared for our rule to last for no less than twenty years (our estimate back then) thanks to the positive outcomes of Playa Girón and the October Missile Crisis, I undertook the task of involving Che in an expedition. I had to get rid of him. The island was too small for the two of us.

IT'S TRUE, NONETHELESS, that aviation accidents occurred with shameful frequency.

The same day as the burial of Juan Abrantes, due to an aviation accident, we lost another dozen *compañeros* who had traveled to Havana for the wake. We had commissioned Che to lead the mourning for Abrantes. He was being rather moderate, in all truth—"We can say with a clear conscience that we've tried to give the Rebel Army a technique. But these deaths could have been avoided. They are deaths that are more unfair than those at the hands of tyranny"—when his bodyguards grabbed him by the shirt, to get his attention. One of his bodyguards held out a piece of paper with the report about the latest accident. The Argentine stopped his speech and rifled around in his pockets, looking for a cigar. I think this was the first time in the history of funeral parlors that the ceremony was interrupted by the speaker searching for a cigar at the bottom of his jacket pocket, and upon finding it, he put it in his mouth, lit it, took a deep puff and blew out a thick column of smoke, saying sadly, with his face twisted in disgust, "We inform you that another Rebel Air Force plane has fallen." The Argentine had just invented a funeral speech with the evening news built in. It was something that I later repeated to mock him.

Many accidents. The *compañeros* were dropping like flies. Literally. It looked like a meteor shower. Men were falling out of the sky. Almost always, they were young and bearded and wore olive-green uniforms. I can't even begin to tell you about that year, 1959, especially those cumulonimbus clouds on summer afternoons. They took those light aircraft planes with our *compañeros* aboard and crumbled them like cookies. More people died in accidents during the Cuban Revolution than in combat or at the firing wall. In Angola, a third of our casualties were due to accidents. And if we add stray bullets, our number of accidents would be even higher. But in 1959, it was about light aircraft. The motor vehicle traffic fatality index remained steady despite a decrease in the number of cars in circulation. The importation of cars stopped for many years and the replacement-piece warehouses simply emptied.

THE STRANGER

I'm going to tell you about the time Che took a bullet to the neck and how I told him to get himself taken care of at the Bahía Honda clinic or in Consolación del Sur, two filthy little towns near the mountains in western Cuba. Don't think it was a joke, because I was absolutely serious. The truth was that I made him believe I was keeping him in Pinar del Río because of his symbolic value. My guess, on the eve of Playa Girón, was that it would be convenient in the case of a resistance war to have him up in that mountain range, at least at the beginning. It would be enormously attractive to achieve the distraction of any invading group, who would turn their attention to hunting down Che Guevara in those impassable mountains. His symbolic value was immeasurable in those circumstances. But during the October Missile Crisis, there was no plan. The actual situation was that of a gaunt, useless prisoner at the back of a cave, surrounded by a fresh group of guards that I myself had selected for the occasion and none of whom was going to disobey my orders to fight imperialism until the last bullet had been fired and the last drop of blood had fallen in that narrow cave. You don't believe me, right? Just go find out about the tantrum that caused him to pump his leg full of lead, taking care to only target his muscles. That the Stechkin fell out of his hands and went off pointing upward instead of down must have surprised him. My reasons for isolating him? One alone. Ernesto Guevara de la Serna was one of the two insiders responsible for the Cuban Revolution falling into the arms of the Soviet Union and being at their mercy. I say insiders because the outsiders, as you know, were the Americans themselves. The other insider, as you already know, was Raúl. But I had been able to control him from the time he was born and a brief scolding was enough to restore order. Besides, I had him so far away from Havana—in the province of Oriente—that it was as good as having him leading another country. So I assigned Che the Órganos Mountain Range, partly because of his presence as a standard bearer, and partly to get him far away from Havana.

He shot himself on April 18, 1961. According to our idyllic source of official history, Che had been in Consolación del Sur, Pinar del Río, since April 16. There he was leading the western command. Cuban intelligence thought there was an invasion in that area, the closest one to the continent. Upon experiencing *that accident* with his gun, he was seen by the chief of surgery at the province's hospital (Consolación was about twenty kilometers away from Pinar), Dr. Nicolás Pérez Lavín, who ordered him to shut up given his excited state and unstoppable loquaciousness and his need to control everything because he was Che. Of course, you'll never find this information in any of our pamphlets. My knowledge is based on the detailed reports that his guards made. His guards, my confidants.

THE DIFFERENCE BETWEEN knowledge and lies is that while knowledge barely requires a paragraph to be expressed, a lie demands a much larger production, even whole books. I was going over some of the existing literature about Che and I'm amazed as I leaf through page after page to find the authors' efforts to protect the CIA's image and exalt its executive officers in the region, especially Lawrence Devlin, the head of the Congo station who was accused of being the intellectual author of Patrice Lumumba's assassination. He—they write—*suspected, practically confirmed* and took for granted at CIA headquarters in Langley, Virginia, the presence of the Argentine in the Congo but—there's always a but!—the CIA *never found him.* If these writers are so adverse to us, one understands their efforts on behalf of the *yanqui* empire. For me, it's easy to understand what happened to Paco Taibo II and Jon Lee Anderson and all of Che's biographers. Their interpretations fail—especially regarding the Congo expedition and the tragedy in Bolivia—because, between me sending him to his death and the CIA hunting him down, they prefer to bet on the CIA; our adversaries credit the CIA because they're idiots and our friends do it as a form of attack.

For months I did everything I could so that the CIA would find out that Che was in the Congo, but they never caught on. I was the one who was transmitting the signals, not that fucking Lawrence Devlin, and they wouldn't react. One afternoon, I punched my desk while I was having one of my secret meetings with Commander Manuel Piñeiro, and exclaimed, "Goddammit, *gallego,* these people are so inefficient! When the hell are they going to realize that I am serving up the Argentine to them, that he's right there at their disposal?" Piñeiro had also done everything possible from the DGI. The only thing he hadn't done was leave a trail of bread crumbs from Langley to Zaire (Congo). Of course, we couldn't be that obvious. That was when I decided to read Che's famous farewell letter. In theory, its goal was to let everyone know that Che had left Cuba and, in passing, close off all possibilities for his return to the island. How could a hero like him abandon the battlefield where he was achieving one hypothetical victory after another, to go back to Cuba, tucking himself safely away in his sanctuary? On the other hand, according to the information that Piñeiro was processing, it was absurd to pretend that things were going badly for Che. Not at all. He had had some successes, attacking some barracks around there, in the deep jungle, and that could also be very dangerous—in this case for me, because the Argentine might then be able to come back through his own means and I could not allow that. If I opened the door for him to go to Africa, it was so he could be eaten by lions or crushed by elephants or bitten by snakes, not so that he could win an anticolonial war. But he was fucked, because I was the victim of my own superiority in the art of conspiracy. A conspiracy shows its excellence in relation to the public image that prevails. As you yourselves are confirming now—while you shake your heads and reject what you're reading—my plot to get rid of Che was a masterpiece, even if you still don't want to believe me!

Well, this work can't turn into a series of denials, not for our enemies or our apologists. But it's necessary to clarify certain matters. Let's start by saying that, in fact, we did an excellent job with the guerrilla forces—taken entirely from Cuba and placed in the Congo, more than twelve thousand kilometers away!—without anyone finding out. Eighteen days after my reading of his farewell letter, the CIA's main analyst in Cuba, Brian Latell, insisted on his story that he had found political discrepancies between the Argentine and me.* And without anyone in the Agency knowing that Che was in the Congo, in the company of a couple hundred Cubans.

But my strategic design failed somewhere. It had nothing to do with the struggle for power. It had to do with vanity.

The world was beginning to idealize my creations and did so because it wanted to start hating me. Camilo. Celia. Che sometimes. Che was the most independent. Not the most popular, but the most independent. Popularity does not determine independence. A popular guy is almost always easily manipulated. Che came with his own history, some reading and education and his adventure trips. He came with a history prior to me. All those people who joined me in the battle, their history began with me. Besides, the decisive point: Che didn't want power. Che wanted his ideas and to be the altruist in the process, that clean, candid image of change, of revolutions in Latin America. I am fucked here because I can't be president of the world while you pretend to be Bolivar and run around the rest of Latin America to perpetuate yourself as our latest saint. And that's how he beat me in the long run. On the surface, the dilemma of history's great men remains the same. Life or glory.

---

* It's one of the symbolic documents of the Cuban Revolution. In theory, it was to be revealed in case of his death. In his words, Che was freeing Cuba of all responsibility for his foreign adventures in insurrection and resigned from all of his responsibilities in the Revolutionary Government. He was still in the Congo but on the verge of packing things up, on October 3, 1965, when I read the material during a ceremony introducing the new Central Committee of the Cuban Communist Party, which was transmitted live and direct on TV. The Argentine had written it in Havana on April 5, 1965. Two weeks later, on April 19, he made his clandestine entry to the Congo. [*Author's note.*]

In the end, however, the best solution—as was proven—came about without my planning it and thanks to that farewell letter and its public revelation. If not for the fact that the African leaders themselves asked us to remove the Cubans, it would have been chaos for those troops. It was only a matter of time before the Cubans themselves did away with Che. When they realized that their mission had all indications of lasting forever and that they should forget about a speedy (or any) return to their homeland, the land of their birth, and about ever seeing their children grow or celebrating their oldest daughter's *quinceañera,* or, naturally, ever feeling their wives' asses, or ever sleeping with another white woman (or at least a light-skinned mulatta) again for the rest of their lives (the Argentine's letter stated it clearly: "Other lands in the world are clamoring for my modest efforts"), they immediately acquired the force of potential mutiny. He said *my* effort. His, dammit. Not *ours.* Che was never more of a stranger in his life than in front of those exiles—the Cubans in his contingent.

OUR FORMULA OF NOT exporting revolutions has counted on a formidable international subversion apparatus from the beginning, secret training camps and—at least concerning Latin America—networks of agents and officials planted in every country. This nonexporting position of revolutionary processes—sanctioned by Marxist theorists—is, of course, an exercise in rhetoric and is void of all significance. But it couldn't be any other way. Early on, the Cubans learned that language is also an instrument and that it can be profitable—and therefore useful— and that the language of war never means what it says and at the same time lacks importance because only actions are decisive. And so it was off to Bolivia with Guevara. Che trained in the guerrilla camps of the legendary General Division of Special Operations (Dirección General de Operaciones Especiales, or DGOE, also known as "Special Troops" or just "Troops").

From there—as they say—he went to eternity. Rather, *I made him go.*

OCTOBER IS A PROPITIOUS month for sailfishing. And cruising northeast of Havana, the *Acuarama* cutting light trails of foam on the current from the Gulf Stream, I found time to smoke a cigar and sip a little cognac. It was evening and we had had a downpour and had seen lightning coming down on the distant shadows of the city, about fifty kilometers from the stern, while we continued heading east. Two MPK-10 submarine hunters, sailing at a cautious distance, kept a diligent sweep with their radars, each one with a 57mm antiaircraft cannon turret uncovered and RBV-6000 antisubmarine launchers, two on the prow of each MPK, also were in combat position.

Those MPKs navigated well and I liked to watch them from a distance. The USSR had had them before the proliferation of huge enemy vessels, as part of their postwar defensive philosophy. They made these coastal crafts and then started to make masses of submarines with nuclear warhead missile launchers, reluctant as they were for decades to build aircraft carriers, a symbol of imperial power.

We had left Cubanacán, to the west of Havana, and the MPKs were navigating at the surface to not stir up the bottom. As a general rule—in my experience—only dolphins and sharks come up to ships in search of food. But sonar and antisubmarine radars tend to bother fish, especially the big ones, and they scare the fish away.

IT MUST HAVE BEEN around nine at night and I could already see the buoys of Varadero's military marina over the prow when the vessel's engineer cut the engine to enter the shallow waters and carefully approach the dock. As the motor decreased I heard flapping overhead. I was on my way to the cabin to sit in my reading chair and put on my boots. I recognized the curlews announcing the imminent winter fronts—the "*nortes*," in our meteorological language—and I have known these birds ever since I started fishing for sport after the triumph of the Revolution. Pushed by the masses of cold air, the flocks go south. I had learned that their flapping preceded the smell of land. There was no way you could get lost at sea if you followed their course because they always end up at a beach. They fly low and tend to rest in the ship's rigging and railings, like sparrows on power lines, which is the best way to identify them as land and not sea birds: because they need to perch on something steady. I counted seven flocks before night fell. But now you could only hear them if the engine was turned down. There was also a peregrine falcon. It must have been around five in the afternoon when it pecked at the prow in search of prey. You can hear the wind whistling beneath its extended wings and you know it's approaching. In its solitary, high-altitude flight the falcon is not identifiable to the naked eye as it makes its majestic crossing of the sky. You have to see it in its descent, when it reaches an attack speed of three hundred kilometers per hour. The arc of the firm trajectory, a splash at the prow and the predator barely brushes against the water as it changes its angle of attack and initiates its climb, its prey held firmly in its beak. We were below one of the migratory bird corridors that starts at the top of North America and runs down to Cuba, before splitting off toward Santiago de Cuba, crossing the Gulf of Mexico and reaching the Yucatán Peninsula to later join the Trans-American corridor that comes from the American West Coast. The other path reaches Cuba and travels along the Caribbean islands until it ends to the north of Venezuela or Colombia, where they spend the winter.

I was just pulling on my second boot to get myself ready for land when a mulatto from my guard, a large man in full uniform, stopped at my door and turned to me gravely.

"Comandante, with your permission."

This meant the news was very serious. I advised him without saying a word, by just raising my gaze and remaining expectant, to come out with it.

"A cable just came in about Manila, Comandante."

Manila was our code name for Bolivia.

"Che?

"Che," he responded.

I was preparing the expression I should wear upon receiving the news that the second largest modern symbol of the liberation of peoples had fallen in combat, when the officer added:

"Correct, Comandante. It's Che. He was captured this morning."

I couldn't hide my annoyance.

"Captured?" I asked.

"They've got him as a prisoner in an unknown location."

"*Cojones*," I said, not as a curse, but in a tone leaning more toward reflection. "Where did you say this cable is from?"

"Commander Piñeiro just read it to Mainé. Mainé is still on the phone with him. On the bridge."

"No, no. Tell Mainé to cut him off. All communications are over. Hold on."

The guard stayed at the door's threshold. Hold on means there are instructions coming.

"Listen, ready the cars. We have to get to Havana right away. No unencrypted language over the radios. But Piñeiro, Raúl and Osmany Cienfuegos should wait for me at the Central Committee and Piñeiro should have all the information as it comes in ready for me. Go on."

I looked at the calendar on the lit-up face of my Rolex GMT and memorized the date. October 8, 1967. At eight p.m., at Varadero's military marina. It was the moment at which I understood the enormous risk in which I would have put the Cuban Revolution if I had trusted Ernesto Guevara to carry out a very complex plot. He was too vain to understand the true nature of his Latin American mission. Despite the intelligence he boasted having, he was never in a position to know that his real objective was not to lead a guerrilla group, but to die. It was merely another instance of the Revolution's strategy to divest itself of its potential enemies by sending them abroad. One-way tickets. Never round-trip. For the future counterrevolutionary divisions gathering in Cuba, we opened the ports and authorized as many freedom flights as they wanted, as long as I could get them off my back and stick them in Miami. Nothing complicated. The Cuban counterrevolution, of bourgeois provenance, has always been an issue for sergeants or officers of little importance to attend to. Once the guidelines were established—execute some here, arrest a few there and let the rest leave the country—you didn't have to pay much more attention to them. But the revolutionary group, and especially your brothers-in-arms who stood out because of their intellectual gifts, inevitably became very dangerous and fearsome enemies. Pay attention to what I am going to say to you: no intellectual who has killed someone in the Revolution is a man whom you can ever trust again. They develop a strange mentality between their coming of age as assassins and their ascent to power. Raised on the Revolution's two supreme duties—homicide and ideology—they present an implicit risk. And in the end, the problem is that they don't know how to die. I never had those problems with the peasant veterans in my guerrilla group when I assigned them a mission no matter how suicidal. The peasant is already a butcher; he is surrounded by creatures that he sacrifices, twisting their necks or stabbing them until the deed is done. The same men who surrounded Che in his Congo and Bolivia campaigns—whom I took pains to select—were that type of mountain combatant and none of them jumped ship, despite the horrible deaths they faced. Who were the ones who were always causing trouble? Well, the three or four intellectuals who despite it all Che managed to bring along with him—Octavio de la Concepción y de la Pedraja, the guerrilla's surgeon (with his exasperating and in the end terminal slowness!); Tamara "Tania" Bunke, the liaison; and Régis Debray and Ciro Roberto Bustos, the visiting artists. And that's without even discussing the band of Latin American recruits that joined them, all of them at the halfway point between their happy university days and a moment spent betraying their comrades through uncontrollable sobs at the hands of an interrogator. In any event, our tendency to send abroad any revolutionaries who demonstrated a conflict with our politics or government almost automatically created a favorable image of Cuba. With these dispatches of trained personnel, we were fulfilling a kind of messianic destiny in our process: that of disseminating the Cuban project across the continent. When in reality it was something we undertook to get rid of our homegrown dissidents. Hence the legend of the Latin American Revolution sponsored by Cuba. From the use to which I put wasted personnel. I finished putting on my boots, I threw my jacket over my shoulders and clipped on the cartridge belt with the Stechkin APS in its black leather holster to my right side and the two double clip holders to my left. When I got up on deck and saw the movement at the dock of the silhouettes of my guard and cars, the curlews made their low flight toward the *Acuarama*'s port side for the last time that night.

SOMETIMES THE DAILY LIFE of an indefatigable guerrilla warrior becomes more tedious than that of a retired person. This would perhaps give us a justification for Che's presumptuous move to France, after the failure of his Congo war. just a few days after getting himself settled in the outskirts of Prague. Che would be in that remote place quickly dubbed the Little Farm by our *compañeros*, between February and July 1966. There were always a pair of Cuban guards with him, as you can imagine. The Czechs had given us the little house with its adjoining land so that—as we reasoned with them—some of our highest-ranking officers could rest upon returning from their studies at the USSR's military academies or from diplomatic tasks in Europe or Africa. We never told them Che's true identity. But, just after Che's arrival in Prague, I received the news of his unassailable desire to set up a cute, little apart-

Self-portrait of Ernesto Guevara in his room at the Hotel Copacabana, in La Paz, Bolivia's capital, November 3, 1966. He has just arrived and is fiddling with his camera while he smokes a special reserve habano. *He is still Adolfo Mena, Uruguayan citizen and Organization of American States official on his way through La Paz.*

ment for himself in Paris, an idea that had sprung from his imagination. Imagine this character in France, acting as intellectual critic of the Cuban Revolution. The André Malraux of the Cuban Revolution. Over there with Sartre and Régis Debray, relaying his guerrilla memories and criticizing the Revolution. Enjoying the Sorbonne, and all under the auspices of Paris's followers of Trotsky. What fools. They didn't realize that the Revolution—since it was me, that I represented it, that I embodied it, that I was its symbol—couldn't have anything above me. I have no way of explaining to myself how the Argentine could have harbored the dream of sitting at a little table in an open-air café, in jeans and sandals, after having killed so many people to advance my revolutionary justice or simply to save me from all harm. The number of times that I saw his face splattered with blood and brain matter after he had blown out the brains of some Batista supporter and spitting out pieces of bone that fell on his lips. Through Piñeiro's personnel, I had, at one time, pressing information on the measures that Che took to protect himself from our officials, my people, while he participated in a rather elaborate game that made it seem like he was protecting himself from Czech Security.

«FROM OJALVO* TO LEADERSHIP.

»SITUATION AT THE LITTLE FARM [APRIL 1966]:

»AFTER LEAVING THE HIGHWAY, YOU TAKE A NARROW COBBLED PATH. SINCE IT IS WINTER, IT IS PARTIALLY COVERED WITH SNOW AND THE TREES ARE PRACTICALLY BARE. AT ABOUT 25 METERS, A LARGE DOOR WITH TWO SHEETS OF WOOD PROVIDES ACCESS TO THE PLACE. AT A SIMILAR DISTANCE ONE CAN SEE A WHITE WOODEN HOUSE, WITH TWO STORIES, A TYPICAL COUNTRY HOUSE. AROUND, A LARGE GARDEN THAT IS WITHERING DUE TO THE SNOW.

»THE ROOMS, LOCATED ON THE SECOND FLOOR, ARE SMALL. DOWNSTAIRS IS THE LIVING ROOM, A HALL OR RECEIVING ROOM, THE DINING ROOM AND THE KITCHEN. THE HOUSE IS STAFFED BY AN OLDER WOMAN, EMPLOYED BY THE CZECHS TO COOK FOR THE GROUPS THAT GO THROUGH THERE. THIS WOMAN, BY THE LOOKS OF IT, DOESN'T SPEAK A WORD OF SPANISH AND IS NEVER SEEN ACTING SUSPICIOUSLY. SHE LOOKS VERY HUMBLE AND OF A LOW LEVEL, BOTH ECONOMICALLY AND CULTURALLY. WITH GREAT DIFFICULTY DOES SHE COOK ANYTHING EDIBLE, THE REASON FOR WHICH WE HAVE THE FOLLOWING ARRANGEMENT: IN THE AFTERNOONS, SHE MAKES US OMELETS WITH HAM, OR HER FLAWLESS VARIATION, SCRAMBLED EGGS WITH THE SAME INGREDIENT, A SALAD AND SOME FRUIT. WE BRING ALL OF THIS FROM THE CITY MARKET. AT LUNCH, ACCORDING TO OUR TREATY, WE ARE VICTIMS OF *GOULASH* WITH *KNELIKES*, THE POOR WOMAN'S ONLY DISH WITH ANY GASTRONOMIC LEANINGS.

»SOURCE: GENERAL INTELLIGENCE DIRECTORATE. PRAGUE MISSION.

«OJALVO.»

---

* José Luis Ojalvo. Head of the office of Cuban Intelligence in Prague. [*Author's note.*]

«From Diosdado* to Leadership.

»April 1966.

»By instructions from Commander Manuel Piñeiro, Vice Minister of MININT, who staffs the technical part [as we normally called Intelligence] and my immediate boss, I travel to Prague with the mission of coming under Che's orders. In the early morning hours of the following day, ready to depart, I have another meeting with Piñeiro at his house. He specifies my mission again, which is none other than to prepare the documentation to travel to the country of Guevara's choice, from where he hopes to go on to Latin America and reinitiate the armed struggle. I am not aware that Che is in the country, after having fought in the Congo. Piñeiro advises me that I should use tact and professionalism to try to convince Che of the danger it would bring him to live in another Western European country, as well as the operative difficulties and risks that go along with keeping up a clandestine link to him in these conditions.

»He [Piñero] tells me on more than one occasion that Che refuses to return to Cuba, where he can best see his plans through, but won't explain his reasons to me, nor do I ask. He gives me various sealed envelopes for Che. In Prague I am received by Ojalvo and as we arrive at the place where Che lives, I become happy since it's the farm on which I spent many months preparing Tania [Tamara Bunke, the girl of German origin who would later join Che's guerrillas in Bolivia]. Che is on the second floor. After responding to various questions he poses to me, I hand him the correspondence and he starts to read it. I remain in the room, and Ojalvo goes downstairs to make coffee and serves it to us. When Che is done reading, he and I go outside to converse in the ample garden in front of the house, since he makes a sign at the roof indicating

---

* Diosdado: pseudonym of José Gomez Abad. [*Author's note.*]

THAT WE CAN BE HEARD; THERE'S NO DOUBT THAT HE'S "GATO," AS WE SAY WHEN SOMEONE IS MISTRUSTING. BEFORE BRINGING UP THE REASON FOR MY TRIP, HE SHOWS INTEREST IN TANIA'S SITUATION [WHO HAD ALREADY BEEN DISPATCHED TO BOLIVIA TO ANALYZE THE POSSIBILITIES FOR A GUERRILLA MOVEMENT]; I INFORM HIM OF EVERYTHING I KNOW ABOUT HER AND ALSO TELL HIM THAT IN THAT SAME PLACE I HAD PREPARED HER FOR HER FRONT. HE STRESSES THAT HE SHOULD NOT BE GIVEN TASKS THAT ARE NOT RELATED TO HIS SPECIFIC MISSION.

»DESPITE HAVING REITERATED TO HIM ON VARIOUS OCCASIONS WHAT PIÑEIRO STRESSED TO ME, EVEN MORE SO WHEN I KNOW THAT THE COUNTRY HE HAS CHOSEN IS FRANCE, I DO NOT GET ANYWHERE, NOT THAT DAY NOR THE FOLLOWING; HE REMAINS STEADFAST IN HIS DECISION TO MAKE THE TRIP. IN THE REASONS I PROFFER, I NEVER MENTION THAT THE MOST LOGICAL THING IS RETURNING TO CUBA. THEN I TELL HIM THAT WE SHOULD WORK ON THE VARIATIONS OF POSSIBLE ITINERARIES FOR HIM TO GET TO PARIS, SINCE HE CLAIMS HE SPEAKS FRENCH AND THAT MANY LATIN AMERICANS LIVE THERE AND HE CAN BLEND IN AMONG THEM. UPON ASKING THAT NO ONE BESIDES THE TWO OF US CAN KNOW HIS TRIP ITINERARY, I HAVE TO TELL HIM THAT I CAN'T DO ANYTHING BEHIND MY SUPERIOR'S BACK, IN THIS CASE PIÑEIRO. HE UNDERSTANDS MY SITUATION AND ACCEPTS MY POINT OF VIEW. IN THE THREE DAYS THAT I SPEND WITH CHE, HE INVITES ME ON A WALK THAT IS LONG AND EXHAUSTING SINCE OJALVO AND I DON'T EXERCISE AND HE IS QUITE OVERWEIGHT. FINALLY, WE GET LOST AND SINCE I REMEMBER THAT THE HOTEL BALNOVKA IS NEAR THE LITTLE FARM, I GO OUT TO A ROAD AND ASK A YOUNG MAN COMING ON A BICYCLE; HE TELLS ME WHERE IT IS AND THAT'S HOW WE RETURN.

»THE DAY OF MY RETURN, CHE ASKS ME TO TRACK DOWN ALBERTO FERNÁNDEZ MONTES DE OCA (PACHUNGO), WHO WORKS IN THE MINISTRY OF INDUSTRY [IN CUBA], SO THAT HE IS READIED AND SENT TO HIM WITH THE GOAL OF ACCOMPANYING HIM AND STAYING WITH HIM AT HIS RESIDENCE IN PARIS. BACK IN HAVANA, I INFORM PIÑEIRO OF THE RESULTS OF MY MISSION AND HE ORDERS ME TO START WORKING ON CHE'S REQUEST IMMEDIATELY. AS FAR AS TRACKING DOWN PACHUNGO IS CONCERNED, IT'S NOT VERY DIFFICULT AND HE CHEERILY ACCEPTS THE MISSION, EVEN MORE SO

BECAUSE OF WHO IS ASKING. HIS PREPARATIONS, SO HE CAN COME
ACROSS AS URUGUAYAN, ARE CARRIED OUT AT MY HOUSE AND ONCE
THIS IS DONE HE RETIRES TO HIS OWN TO AWAIT NOTICE OF WHEN
HE SHOULD LEAVE.

»SOURCE: GENERAL INTELLIGENCE DIRECTORATE
«DIOSDADO.»

I LOOKED AT THE calendar on the lit-up sphere of my Rolex GMT
and memorized the date. October 8, 1967. At eight p.m. Che couldn't
check it on his identical watch because they had taken it away from
him. I had all of my bases covered and was only waiting, minute by
minute, for the inevitable outcome. Based on what I reviewed with
El Gallego Piñeiro, I knew that the Bolivian *compañeros* had received
their orders with enough time and that they were absolutely clear. My
convoy advanced toward Havana at high speed. We took the comfortable two-way road that hugged the northern coast and I had the windows rolled down and I enjoyed the autumn wind that beat against my
face. Every once in a while, mechanically, I looked down at the fluorescent sphere of my watch. I made my calculations. In Bolivia, the official
time in relation the Greenwich meridian is minus four hours (GMT-
4). Bolivia does not change the time, to save energy, and so there's no
difference in the time for summer or winter, it's the same all year and
doesn't vary between geographic areas within the country. We end up
having the same time as them since we have applied Daylight Savings
Time since 1963 (we go forward an hour in that period) and we extend
it from the last Sunday in March until the last Sunday in October. That
is to say that Che had started his Bolivian campaign with an hour's difference in his favor, 190 days, from Monday, November 7, 1966, to
March 26, 1967. But from then on and until his capture, today, Sunday,
October 8, 1967, and his upcoming death—which I estimated would
happen by dawn, Monday the ninth—during the 197 remaining days of
the 387 that his campaign had lasted, he had been trapped in the same
time zone as us and he would have still had twenty days left until Daylight Savings Time was lifted in Cuba, October 26, which was when
the last Sunday of the month fell this year. The time was the same—
for him and for me. Before me, in the distance, the glow, still tenu-

ous because of the distance, of Havana's lights and buildings started to reflect off of a sky full of low clouds.

I WAS THINKING a lot about *For Whom the Bell Tolls*, both the movie and the book. If given the slightest opportunity, I could have caused more damage than Gary Cooper did in the movie. The Argentine beat me to it. Che blew up about three bridges in December 1958 during the siege of the city of Santa Clara. He had that advantage on me because I didn't blow any up in the area under my control when I was advancing against the northern slope of the Sierra Maestra with my eyes set on the siege of Santiago. I blew up trucks with troops, as I've told you, but on the highway. That son of a bitch Argentine never read Hemingway. You protect yourself against Hemingway—I used to say to him, to bother him—the way a virgin protects herself from cocks. His attitude toward American writers in general was baffling to me. Being, as he was, a real fanatic about movies with gunmen and cowboys, you would think he'd appreciate literature in the same vein. Perhaps he saw a difference between the two. Movies were vehicles for entertainment, objects for matinees, to fill up a Sunday afternoon. But a book had a pretense of culture; it was a respectable and considerable article in and of itself, and maybe he felt there should be a rule against allowing those barbarians from the north taking their place in the pantheon of French writers he so admired. It was the deliberate behavior of an Argentine with intellectual ambitions who didn't want to see his cultural upbringing transgressed.

One day, just after the triumph of the Revolution, I invited him to a fishing tournament that Hemingway had put together—in May 1960. And he showed up on the yacht with a rambling stack of Soviet war novels and Stendhal's *The Red and the Black*. I remember it well because he read me a bunch of Stendhal's paragraphs. "Coño, Che. Don't be impertinent," I said, reproaching him. "Now the old man [Hemingway] is going to come on board to say hello to us and you're going to do everything you can to ignore him." Typical behavior of the Argentine. He preferred his irreverent stances over a well-orchestrated act of propaganda favorable to the Revolution.

I bring this up because I was thinking of his death. Or what should have been his last minutes of life, if we believe anything he wrote.

Rereading his chronicles of the struggle in the Sierra, I discover his fondness of a writer named Jack London. Wounded in the unfortunate battle of Alegría del Pío, and with very little hope of coming out of that ambush alive, Che recalled a character of London's who, in similar circumstances, decided to await death with the most dignity possible. Let's see what this London's got, I said to myself one day, and I ordered all of his books. That's when I found out, between the cover flaps and the introductory notes, that he was also American and had influenced Hemingway. Since I later continued this research, obstinate as I became regarding his literary tastes, I likewise discovered, although in the opposite direction, that the two French writers he most worshipped—Sartre and Camus—had recognized the influence exercised by Hemingway *on them*. And I won't even go into how desperate Sartre and his wife (Simone de Beauvoir) were to visit Hemingway at his Finca Vigía in the outskirts of Havana and show him their absolute adoration, like subjects before the pharaoh.

In sum, the most I was able to find out about his final moments, around noon on October 9, 1967, was that he suddenly paled when CIA agent Félix Rodríguez advised him that all of his efforts to save his own life had failed. Then he regained his composure a bit and even tried to put a bit of tobacco in the bowl of his pipe and smoke. He had already exercised the stupidest form of betrayal when he surrendered the previous morning to Captain Gary Prado's little patrol and introduced himself, with all his passwords, so that they wouldn't kill him.

Don't shoot. I'm Che Guevara and I'm worth more alive than dead.

Well, after exhausting all of the possibilities of betrayal, you can be as noble as you want.

HE SAT DOWN WITH great difficulty inside the classroom of La Higuera's little school. Leaning against the wall, he straightened out his shirt. With his legs extended and the unmade espadrilles in view, he started waiting. Once again he was like his favorite character from Jack London.

A flock of peregrine falcons—resting amid the trees of the nearby mountains, after crossing over La Higuera and descending in search of a puddle for their water needs and satisfying their hunger with the local diet of insects and reptiles and before continuing on their flight to the south of the continent at the end of their seven-thousand kilometer migratory trip from the American East Coast—went flying in all directions upon hearing the muffled boom of a burst of M2 carbine shots inside the little school.

USELESS LITTLE WOMEN

I told Aleida March, Che's widow, "Look, Aleida, what I want now, what the Revolution needs, is that you not marry again. We need your symbol. Or to put it more plainly, we need you *as a symbol*. The fatherland needs your pain, Aleida. A permanent pain. It can't burn out for many generations. I understand how big the sacrifice is that I am asking of you. But you'll have the reward of the solidarity and compassion of millions of people all around the world. This doesn't mean you can't have any relationships. I understand that you have needs to take care of. You're still a young and attractive woman, but what I'm asking is that you be discreet about it. The important thing, now and always, is the symbol that you and only you can represent. Do you understand? Do you understand, Aleiducha?" Well, no. She didn't understand. Her answer was not only unequivocal. She also had the *cojones* to be frank with me. First she reminded me of that trip around the underdeveloped world that I tried to send her on at the beginning of the Revolution. I had insisted that the Argentine take Aleida with him, in the delegation, and turn the tour into a honeymoon as well. They had just gotten married and the opportunity seemed unbeatable. But he refused. And Aleida had no qualms in reminding me. This meant, she said, that her deceased husband had taught her the necessary difference that had to be established between personal matters and Revolutionary matters. Second—and this was the critical moment in her dialogue with me—she asked me if I didn't have symbol enough with that German whore Tania who, with the knowledge of all of our *compañeros* in the Revolutionary leadership and probably even approval, had stolen her husband. I had the foresight then not to argue with the woman whose veins were popping from her forehead, such was her state of indignation, and swallow my pride as best as I could, as if I were swallowing my own Adam's apple, and excuse myself for having upset her that way, telling her almost in a whisper that my intentions had been purely political. Likewise, I had the foresight to not confirm or deny whether I knew anything about the Argentine's whoring around with that poor devil of a girl who was riddled with bullets in Vado del Yeso and whose corpse the water dragged for many kilometers until it appeared, days later, swollen like a giant mollusk and half eaten by the piranhas. Upon speaking with Aleida, I had committed the unforgivable mistake of confusing a woman consumed by jealous rage with a revolutionary willing to accept any task. And it was becoming obvious Che himself had made Aleida inclined to reject me. Never again did such a project occur to me. The women of those combatants' women, who were almost always coarse peasants, were unpredictable. That wasn't the case with Che, of course, who was the most convincing specimen of an intellectual that we had in the Rebel Army for a long time. Those girls, while very young, very pleasing to take to bed, with good bodies and their healthy and obvious country provenance, but bathed, perfumed, impeccable teeth, well dressed, girls taken by the Revolution before their breasts sagged and their teeth were destroyed, were at the ready. Their only, debatable defect was that they fornicated as if it were the most natural thing in the world, never allowing for the erotic effect of a sinful act, that possessing them was a secret offense. They became widowed when our *compañeros* were sent to their deaths and then continued on with their careers of being available to anyone who would enjoy them. (I'm not including Aleida in this bunch, of course.) It was unfair to compete with these martyrs. We are talking about young, strong, vigorous peasants, with cocks that could break a marble table. If you get together with a killer, it's very difficult later to have a relationship with an office typist. I'm serious. They competed in cracking the granite of the military camp tables, in chipping them with a whack of their members.

I decided to save myself a second confrontation with Aleida. In early 1968, Piñeiro and his men managed to recover some photocopies of the diary that Che had on his Bolivian campaign, along with his death mask and his hands, cut off before the rest of his body was buried at a secret site and placed in formaldehyde in a five-gallon Spanish olive oil jar. Antonio Arguedas, Bolivia's minister of the interior, who was an agent of ours and who was charged with the ultimate responsibility for making sure the Argentine didn't leave his country alive, sent them to Piñeiro. My dilemma was whether to give Aleida the opportunity to determine the possible uses of Che's artifacts or whether we should determine their fate according to what would be the best revolutionary propaganda. I took the shortcut of simply ignoring her and at the first opportunity, during a speech at the Plaza de la Revolución, I dropped the bomb that Commander Guevara's hands and the death mask taken at the morgue in Vallegrande's hospital were in Cuba and that we still hadn't decided what to do with them. The idea of placing them in a glass case for public display, at the base of the monument to José Martí, right there at my back (I pointed behind me with my finger), in the Plaza de la Revolución, was one of the options under consideration. The way in which this fit of loquaciousness of mine during the course of the speech affected Aleida or not is something I will never know because she didn't send us any sign. You have no idea how excited I was about that monument. We didn't have a full-bodied Lenin. But, at least, there were two hands. I held meetings with artists and sculptors and architects to hear their proposals. All they did was keep silent, go pale and look at me in horror. Two or three passed out. I thought we should put them inside some shirt cuffs. We didn't have cuff links. At least we didn't know how to get the appropriate cuff links. That was something that was clear from the commissioning sessions I held to that effect. That we were resistant to the concept of "cuff link." One day, Piñeiro told me what he thought obliquely, as he tended to do when he wanted to bother me. Those hands loose in a glass box were going to turn into a monument to the enemy's victory. "Don't you realize what this means, Fidel?" "What does it mean, *gallego*?" I pressed him. "What does it mean?" "Fidel, it means that they've cut Cuba's hands off in Latin America. That's what it means."

The Portuguese avoided colonizing the bare plain to the southeast of Angola. The landscape looks suspiciously pleasant in August 1982 when this group of experienced Cuban counterinsurgency troops combs it in search of Jonas Savimbi's guerrillas. In the forefront, this internationalist combatant wears a light Soviet-made RPK machine gun.

PART SEVEN

WHEN THIS WAR IS OVER

NIGHT FALLS IN LA PLATA ALTA

///

I HAD BEEN AT THE NON-ALIGNED MOVEMENT SUMMIT IN ALGIERS, where I had a fight with Muammar al-Gaddafi and Norodom Sihanouk, who couldn't swallow the bitter pill that the Non-Aligned countries were the natural allies of socialist countries.* It was during one of our idyllic moments with the Soviet Union, which was always due to the good offices of Leonid Brezhnev, who managed to establish an excellent relationship with me even before taking over from Khrushchev, since my first trip to Moscow, in April 1963. He had two capital defects in the eyes of a Cuban (I always refrained from pointing them out, as a basic courtesy): he was unaware of what it meant to have a Vuelta Abajo cigar between his teeth and he had never touched a mulatta's ass. But he managed to maintain a regular intelligent and friendly dialogue with me. My main foreign ally during almost all of the Revolution was immune to the seductions of an *habano*. I saw him smoke those appalling Papirosas made especially for him and throw back a good deal of vodka, but never hold a cigar. It was completely foreign to his way of being. As far as getting tangled up with a mulatta, what can you expect of the Party first secretary who rules from the Kremlin, such a long way from the world's most important enclave of mestizas and the whisper of palm trees? Well, I think it's time to go on to my Vietnamese tour.

Upon arriving in New Delhi, in a brief layover to meet with Indira Gandhi, I learned of the coup d'état in Chile.

---

* The summit took place in Algiers from September 5 to 9, 1973.

The view of a pitiful country home reduced to ashes by Batista's aviation led Fidel
to write this prophetic piece. The war in the Sierra Maestra is not yet over but he
already foresees what he calls destiny.

SIERRA MAESTRA
JUNE 5, 1958

Celia:
Upon seeing the rockets that they dropped on Mario's house,
I have sworn to myself that the Americans are going to pay
dearly for what they are doing. When this war is over, a
much longer and bigger war will begin for me: the war that I
am going to unleash against them. I realize that that will be
my true destiny.

Fidel

I had taken the necessary measures with two of my best men the night before leaving for the summit. They were also on the verge of boarding the plane, but toward Chile. The conversation with Patricio de la Guardia and Enrique Montero took place on the evening of August 27 at Piñeiro's house. Both were in the highest positions of our special services there. I couldn't tell you exactly what rank they had at the time, but I do know that just a few years later, Patricio ascended to brigadier general and Montero to colonel. That night we received the news that in Santiago, Chile, a "large bomb" had been placed and exploded at the door of Michel Vázquez, our commercial attaché there, and another one followed, on the doorstep of another of our officials, Félix Luna. I ordered the halting of the Il-62 that Patricio and Montero were supposed to board, until about nine when I spoke about Chile for the last time. This was literally what I said to them. "I am going to pronounce my last words about Chile."

I had arranged my ideas about the situation in Chile and what our conduct should be as follows:

1. Salvador Allende was going to be overthrown.
2. Allende had made too many concessions.
3. The Cubans had to get out of there in the most dignified way possible.
4. The Cubans couldn't get involved in any kind of street riots against the army if the masses weren't going to fight.
5. No commitment of help for Allende if the people weren't out in the streets.
6. All help to Allende had to be before a coup d'état and not after.
7. No support for underground groups. Only the central government (Allende).
8. The Cubans' mission was to defend our embassy.
9. Activate the military apparatus from Operation Quang Tri.

I explained myself in the following way to the *compañeros:* "Allende's downfall is going to take me by surprise while I'm traveling. He's a lost cause. Salvador has fallen into making a lot of concessions. Concessions can only be fixed with more concessions. To get out of concessions you have to make other concessions. It's like lying. In other words, you tell a lie and to cover it up you have to tell another lie. Let me warn you: The Cubans have to get out of there with their heads held high. We will only hit the streets there if the people are out on the streets. We can't go out on the streets to kill the people. Are you listening? I'll tell you one more thing. If Salvador asks for help, first you have to prove that the people are out on the streets, demonstrating in support of him. We can't be supporting the MIR,* either, or anyone, no other collateral group. All of our support needs to be for Salvador. But it has to be support beforehand, not something that is offered after the fact. I repeat. If there's a coup, you have to wait for the people to revolt. Your position, in any event, is to defend the embassy, just like the Vietnamese defended the Quang Tri bastion. Vietnam's irreducible hamlet. Remember that's how I baptized the operation at the onset. Remember that I told you, when we were gathered there, with our troops, selecting the personnel we were going to send to Chile, 'This is going to be like Quang Tri.'" And so I gave it that name: Operation Quang Tri. And so I wrapped up my last words about Chile. I took my leave of Patricio and Enrique and told them they could go get on their plane and that I was going to get on mine. Then I turned to Piñeiro, who had in his hand a glass of scotch on the rocks, and said to him, "And you better start thinking about where we get involved next, because you're running short on operations."

ON MARCH 10, 1977, I experienced something in the company of Libyan president Muammar al-Gaddafi. After being received with all honors and finding ourselves at a state dinner in my honor, Gaddafi confessed to me that his father, who was already very old, lived in a Bedouin tent next to an oasis in the middle of the desert and that he had once shown Muammar a picture of me in some wrinkled and dried-out old newspaper that he kept amid his cushions and had said to him, "My dear son Muammar. This is the only man I would like to meet before I die." Gaddafi looked at me, obviously anxious to hear a response he had guessed beforehand. Before I could even open my mouth, however, he gave me a hurried explanation. His father was not in the necessary physical condition to take an An-26 plane and make the long journey across the desert to Tripoli. That was why he wasn't at the dinner in my honor that eve-

---

* Leftist Revolutionary Movement (Movimiento de Izquierda Revolucionaria).

ning. So the next day, we were the ones who had to board the An-26 and fly over the desert for almost four hours, to a remote Libyan army base. Besides the runway over which sand clouds blew, and on which there was no other plane, there were several Soviet Kamaz tankers, like the ones we had in Cuba, waiting for us and providing the necessary fuel for our return. There was at least a battalion of T-62 tanks covered with canvas and the cannon barrels were also protected from the sandstorms with canvas muzzles. The troops were in formation and didn't tire of saluting their distinguished visitors. Gaddafi, with his agile, long strides and uninhibited juvenile gestures, plus his golden-thread cape floating from his shoulders, invited me to follow him. It goes without saying that I was accompanied by at least fifteen men from my guard and William Haber, one of our Arab language translators. But everyone else around us was a sea of Bedouins. In my quick operative study of the facilities, I saw a couple of average-sized fuel tanks semi-buried in the sand and also some camouflage canvas sheets over the circular lids. And there was a mobile electric plant, of French make, out of which a couple of thick feeding cables ran toward the armored battalion barracks building, and another cable, although this one was enigmatic and solitary and held to the ground by concrete posts, that came out of the camp and ran toward a dune. This son of a bitch, I thought, has this unit here only because of his father. And that cable is the one that brings electricity to the old man. Then, at the end of my reconnaissance scan, I saw what caused me the greatest concern, out of everything I could have seen on this trip: a crowd of Bedouins waiting for us with hundreds of horses dressed up with all fanfare for the occasion with colored pom-poms and cloth streamers and some refulgent pommels at the top of their saddles and unbearable silver bells and all other kinds of gaudy decorations. The problem wasn't the journey we then took on those galloping beasts, following the course of the cable from the French plant, which was raised by the cement posts here and there, nor that the distance to the old man's tent was about three kilometers; the problem was that those savage horsemen spent the entire journey howling and firing their shotguns into the air and forcing their horses to buck as the greatest salute they could offer in my presence. And Gaddafi dug in the spurs of his spirited white horse and looked at me from time to time with a smile whose excitement I did not share. Eventually, at first the old man's huge satellite dish appeared, one of the first ones I'd ever seen in my life, propped on cement buckets, and then the enormous canvas tent, with the thick electric cable going in like a catheter and, in the background, the palm trees of the oasis. Gaddafi went in first and told me with energetic gestures to follow him. Everyone else was to stay outside. I told Abrantes not to listen to him and to accompany me anyway and that William the translator should come, too. Gaddafi started to lift the flaps of cloth of the tent, which seemed infinite and the floor of which was covered by Tartan, and we could hear naughty little laughs that must have belonged to young girls, excited, contagious, but none of whom we ever saw, until we came to the center of a wide room under the tent in which an imposing Toshiba air conditioner was effortlessly at work. The old man, barefoot, in a white linen robe with a beard that was meticulously groomed by some professional and I would even say wearing makeup, was sucking God knows what material burning in a hookah. His eyes rose up to meet his son's. He looked at me. Without paying attention to the presence of Abrantes or the translator, he looked back, pleased, at Gaddafi. Finally, he cracked a smile of approval. That was when Gaddafi, with the same gesture with which you would display a trophy, said to his father, "Didn't I tell you that I would bring him to you?"

ALMOST FORTY YEARS of service by my dear tailor ended in Miami. Esteban Balcárcel. In the mid-nineties, he had the courtesy to ask my permission to leave the country. He wanted to retire and he had family in Miami. I gave him my blessing immediately. "I can't even thread a needle, my esteemed comandante," he said to me, his eyes barely looking out at me over the top of his glasses, which rested halfway down his nose. "How useful could I be to you?" Balcárcel had been the owner of one of capitalist Havana's most distinguished tailor shops, but he had no problems handing it over to the state at the very beginning of our Cuban process. I understand that, years later—when the effects of the *yanqui* economic blockade worsened—he wasn't one of these types given to walking by the desolate windows of his former business. "I've known two good tailors in my life," I used to tell Balcárcel in other times, "two different kinds." I was referring, in the second case, to old Fabio Grobart. It was a jocular way of talking to Balcárcel. "Yes," he would respond, but with a hint of gentleness in his voice as he marked something on the bottoms of my pants with his piece of chalk, "but that other tailor you mention, my esteemed comandante, is the only tailor in Cuba who has made Batista's suits and now wants to make yours." He was referring, of course, to the relations that the old communist guard leadership—with Fabio as one of his frontmen—had with the dictator. Years later, with Balcárcel already in south Florida, the position of official tailor to the *comandante en jefe* with all the necessary guarantees of his Personal Security Unit was occupied by a *compañero* named Antonio Pérez, whom Balcárcel had accepted as an apprentice for many years. As I understand it, Pérez spent that whole time conspiring against his teacher in order to get the coveted position of personal tailor. However, I don't think his slow victory was much good to him. Since 1994, some very, very expensive Belgian tailors travel to Havana to show me their luxurious models and take my measurements for my outfits.

MY LAST ENCOUNTER with El Chino Esquivel, on August 8, 1994, was not without its tensions. Three days before, on August 5, the people of Havana had just staged the first uprising in its history. There were dead, wounded and thousands of arrests. While I left the repression to Raúl and his tanks, I traveled to a continental meeting of presidents in Caracas, Venezuela. I returned immediately after to receive El Chino, whom I hadn't seen since the early sixties.

At first they put him in the Palace of the Revolution's great hall, surrounded by bodyguards and assistants, and also present were my childhood friend Bilito Castellanos and Havana's city historian—Eusebio Leal—and one of my veteran executive assistants, all of them dying to witness the meeting and concerned that I should not be killed by the excitement of it, concerned enough to have two cardiologists on hand (whom they kept hidden). It was almost midnight.

At last, after a long period of hugging and patting each other's bellies and practically kissing each other and confirming that we hadn't died, I was able to get El Chino into a small room contiguous to the main receiving room and I asked one of the bodyguards to leave us alone, but to bring us some croquettes and a bottle of wine.

El Chino, obviously worried by the counterrevolutionary protests, asked me what was happening. He mentioned the 1956 popular uprising in Budapest and I understood that in a very oblique way he wanted to know if there was any similarity. I would have been incapable of allowing El Chino to travel all the way to Havana just to find himself in the middle of a trap. But then I understood that the mistaken one must have been me, since El Chino had boarded his plane almost two days after the events in our capital, in other words, he was up to speed on everything and willing to assume all the risks. "No, Chino," I told him. "It's not Budapest. And don't forget that I am a veteran of the Bogotazo." My tone was ruthlessly self-sufficient, as if to make him understand that he was talking to his old friend and that I was never going to change.

His answer, likewise, brought my old friend back unscathed to me. He wasn't going to change either.

"*Sí, guajiro.* But back then you were on the streets. Now you're in the palace."

I approved with a smile and made a gesture with my index finger, as if to say, Write this down.

I let him enjoy things for a few moments. I had known how to appreciate his ingenuity, and, more importantly, his frankness.

"But there's something that never changes, Chino," I said. "And it doesn't matter where you are. No one dies before his number comes up."

"*Coño, guajiro,*" he said.

"No one," I stressed.

He remained silent. He wasn't going to argue with me. It was obvious that he hadn't traveled from Miami to get into a pseudophilosophical debate about the day it could be your turn to die.

So he forced me to continue the conversation.

"I think there are a couple dead, the only ones, and a kid who got his eye taken out in a brawl, although we have kicked a lot of asses. Don't worry. Everything's already under control."

RECOLLECTIONS BECOME WORKS of fiction from the moment you start to recall them from your memory. One second after events happen, when you begin to remember and reassemble what you saw according to your own personal interests, the doubts begin and then you start to fill in the gaps, and I'll tell you from the onset that you start rearranging the scenario according to what you remember a moment later.

I think the understanding of this phenomenon was most clearly revealed to me by the assumptions of Einstein's theory of relativity.

Because if anything has caused me great concern as I write these pages, it's proving that the past is as unfathomable as the future. The more I try to make my way through its labyrinth, the more I notice its vastness. I think of the past like digging a mine in Mount Everest. The future is symbolized by the openness of the sky from a summit like that of Mount Everest. Now look in any direction you choose, jump or dig, and you'll confirm that the only thing you can be sure of is the area between the ground you're stepping on and the bottom of your boots. The only certain and tangible thing after that lesson is, well, the present, that objective symbol of material that is as fleeting as a snap and that exists on the very border between the past and the future. Think of a ball of soft dough, putty, if you will, being smoothed into a string until it becomes very thin and then you will understand that you can't distinguish in which of these two camps your presence belongs, whether to memories or to the future, whether it is an echo resounding in the catacombs of the past or if it dissolves in the inconsistency of the future.

What's certain is that it was completely impossible for me during the course of any of the episodes I've relayed here to recognize what events would follow, despite their developing as a sequence and that one was a consequence of the other. Just as the past evades me in all of its details, let's use for example the moment at which Crescencio's son Sergio hadn't yet rested his finger on the trigger of his Garand up there in the mountains before the Revolution had triumphed—that finger that contained all the strength of working those hands like claws in the mountains, at the wheels and gears of the Diamond T—in a motion to fire, making me think I was as good as dead, it would have been impossible for me to imagine another instant of the possibilities of my existence.

Where are they, where are you, my sweet brothers? In what dark corner of the future could they be waiting for me, you, now the ghosts of my past? But what does it all matter now if I don't know any of them, if I can't see any difference between Rafaelito del Pino, who was marching at my side in Bogotá, or Pepe Abrantes, who (when we put him in jail in a dramatic proceeding in 1989) was imploring me not to kill him—I didn't even have the slightest notion of his name on the day of the triumph of the Revolution. It's a dilemma, although not one of life or death—as tends to happen with my affairs—as much as time and space.

Isn't it all the same in the end?

What a bastard, that Albert Einstein.

SO, LET'S RETURN to a subject that doesn't seem to have been duly clarified. That the Revolution is not the future, much less a legacy. The Revolution is about making it in that moment. And what will happen, comrade, when they ask you what has left so much blood and sacrifice behind? But the Revolution doesn't have to leave anything behind. What the Revolution needs is to be made. Because it happens. Because the Revolution didn't exist apart from my inventing it. Rather, because you, who owned this country, and later turned into my irreconcilable enemy, you bottled up the situation. Imagine. If after having it out with the Americans and having it out with the Soviets and having it out with the Cubans and having it out with Che and with Raúl, I have to have it out with the people waiting in the unfathomable future, I'm as good as gone. Oh, are you going to condemn me? Well, they're going to do it anyway. But I'm to die with the immense satisfaction that I will have to be judged in absentia. And when will such a process occur? In five hundred years? In a thousand? When is it that history judges definitively and without appeal? You've got to be fucking kidding. Or do you not realize that the dialectic of the past is the same as that of the future? Which is completely changeable?

The Revolution has given signs of an extraordinary pragmatism. Because of this, it lacks any ethical or moralizing intention regarding its passing and the measures of force it assumes. It is the modern event par excellence. And that's why it already knows that its relationship to the future is a dead letter. The same is not true with you, because the counterrevolution lives in the past and has all the space it wants there for its hopes.

AND I HAD THIS dream. We were all together at the foot of my little cave in La Plata Alta and there weren't any more than a dozen of us *compañeros* and Celia had gone inside to brew some coffee (I had asked her not to make it with the Italian *cafetera*, to not ruin the occasion, but to make good Cuban coffee, with only a cloth filter) and I had authorized her to open a bottle of rum to make the drink stronger and I was handing out cigars and couldn't contain my pride in saying they came from my reserves. And that they could take two each, so they would have one for the road, because we had to hit the road later. The way I handed them out was by passing the box to the Argentine, who was to my right, so that I wouldn't have to get up. We were seated in a circle, with our rifles on our laps, and a bonfire was burning in the middle. A bonfire in a cave. I was plagued by the worry that the remembrance of the war brought me and was aware of our prohibition on lighting bonfires so that we wouldn't be visible to aviation. Night was falling on the camp and the temperature was going down and a string of clouds remained unmoving around us. Celia was making the boiled coffee and all of my *compañeros* were focused on lighting their cigars, which is the moment in smoking that requires the most attention. They grabbed a piece of kindling from the bonfire, still crackling, and that was their light. Che was staring at me with some surprise. Was it Che or Pepe Abrantes? I thought, I don't think it's advisable to say it. So that they won't get mad. They are with me around a bonfire at the height of a Sierra night and they're dead. But the Remingtons and the Brownings with telescopic sights were resting on their legs and this means that they were commanders because there were only enough telescopic sights for the best men. The kindling was still going from one hand to another to light their cigars and they were making small jokes and I was surprised to hear the seriousness of my own voice upon asking for my men's attention, when I said something like, *Compañeros.* Listen here, *compañeros.* I came to understand something in that moment. It was in the dream but I have to make an effort not to forget it. The understanding that it's not imperative to survive. And I haven't forgotten it. I think it's due to the way I relate ideas to each other, although these happened in a dream. What happens in the subconscious also relates to the material world. Because, if you can manage to remember it, it's an experience all the same. Whatever I could have said in my dream, whatever matter about which I was calling for the attention of my *compañeros*, I can't transcribe it for you because I don't remember. My subconscious didn't consider it material that was worthy enough to be retained. What does remain firm in my memory is the certainty that one day I'll be reunited with my old troops. Then Camilo arrived, late as always, holding his Thompson in his right hand, and he said, "Fidel, make a little room for me next to you. Come on, Fidel." I moved with the heaviness forced on me by my weight, but in any event I made space for him and told myself, This is the best news I've gotten in a long time. Huh, *compañeros*? We'll meet again. Shortly.

COINCIDENCE. COINCIDENCE as matter. It's mysteriously elusive and the most religious form that I use for my own understanding of how things are. Coincidence leads me—us—to the limits of matter, what astronomers have called the Big Bang when they conclude that matter and the universe are the same entity and that they required a sum of coincidences and time and space to be made. And I, the pedestrian creature who came out of those sidereal dusts that navigate through the unconsciousness of the infinite, I feel moved and sad, sad in many ways—perhaps even perturbed because I am a conspirator, a man who plans—upon having to accept that I—everything surrounding me and all that I contemplate—am a result of coincidence.

History and how everyone manipulates it. This is the problem.

I see it as an eternal dilemma. History follows just one direction: the one that is convenient to you not because of tactical convenience, which princes need, but because of vanity, which is the mainstay of politicians, but which allows you to place yourself above it. So you can see the big picture, as they say. History is complete, it's comprehensive—it has its virtues and defects, but only in its overwhelming totality is it truly decipherable. The writer loses in the end because he's not a politician or because he wasn't in the key positions in which everyone, in all truth, has something to hide or has to choose; the politicians hide and change everything; writers accommodate. In the end—I say this due to my own experience—the decisions that one could delay just one second in taking, but that come relentlessly from reasons that accumulated in the past and that for the moment project themselves into the future like slowly extinguishing echoes, are interpreted by the weak and dispatched with a perfunctory phrase.

But writing a history of which one has been the main character but that has been interpreted by so many outside people, especially foreigners and many opportunists, forces you to go deep into yourself. I write in secret to save my text. But at the same time, the adversity or ignorance surrounding me allows me to turn the production of my book into a small conspiracy, and thus I like it and focus on it. The environment. I see the old *compañeros* at occasional political events or I receive reports about them as I am putting together these memoirs and I think, Everyone who knows a secret is compromised by it and won't disclose it. I'm invincible.

EVERY AUTOBIOGRAPHY is a second chance. Alone with his conscience, the author has the possibility of giving his existence the finishing touches. In this sense, it is also a teleological exercise, but fascinating as well. In addition, I can do it with full use of my intelligence and experience. If I can't modify the past, at least I can justify it through my words, and in the light allowed by the time that has passed but that was never at hand as the events occurred. It is not only a second chance, but a last chance. All human experience, all blood, all pain, all history, summarized in the light design of words.

THERE WAS NO WAR and I created one. There was no sectarianism and I created it. There was no history and I created one. It's the philosophical problem of nothingness that is resolved with absolutes. That's a fundamental part of my victory. And of squealing on each other.

I KNOW WHAT I am going to say when anyone asks me about what I might want as a last request. And I'll bring up the subject since a book of memoirs should finish somewhere around death. Why not enjoy that final pleasure of a cigar, since anyone could forgive me for it, if it's the innocuous pleasure of those sentenced to death and at this stage what does it matter if you're going to be executed or die of old age in a minute? What reason could there be for not asking for that prodigious stogie? I'm desperate to bring the splendid Lancero made for my sole consumption to my lips. Perhaps I wouldn't even have the strength to bring it to my lips. Perhaps someone would have to hold it for me. But it would be there, before the light even begins to make it burn, that I would turn it down with my last burst of energy and say that I don't want it. And I have the reason for my obstinate rejection. The same one I always had.

Because I don't fucking feel like it. *Cojones.*

Nicaragua, July 19, 1980, one year after the Sandinistas' victory. The Cuban Revolution at the height of its expansion.

On Resurrection

/ / /

PERHAPS SOMEONE HAS POINTED IT OUT BEFORE, BUT WHAT matters now is the idea and not an author's research. It's the notion that if a history book goes on too much about its material, it ends up being a report. You could say the same thing about an autobiography: once it goes beyond a certain point, it ends up being a diary. On the other hand, when I started this project, it was under the immense pressure caused by the disappearance of the Soviet Union and the imminent destruction of the Cuban Revolution. A bit in the tradition of Lenin, but in reverse. Lenin left the manuscript of *State and Revolution* unfinished before the arrival of the Russian Revolution, as is widely known: so it is logical to write about the Cuban Revolution after its unraveling was already a given. But things have radically changed in the last few years. The Revolution has been resurgent in the world and the most promising outbreaks are occurring in Cuba's area of historical influence: Latin America. Cuba, in all truth, has a lot to do with this novel situation, even if first it had to go through ruthless internal introspection and reestablish the old coordinates of solitude and voluntarism. We learned to live amid the ruins, we learned to elude the fainthearted and, above all, we learned the axiom that, in politics, nothing works fast, you have to make long-term goals. It's obvious at this point that there's a lot of ink left in my well, a lot left unsaid. A lot of material about the Soviets and about Che and about the rest of the internationalist paraphernalia. And about the surprising way, even for us, in which we regained control of the continent. In truth, there are many things left to be told. So, then, let's take our time with the book and avoid turning its final pages into a mere collection of daily notes.

First let's get out of the forest.

[Circa July 2001]

My fellow countrymen:

What can I grant you as we part? I believe I demonstrate how well I understand you when, in my final hour, I decide to regale you with the most precious object of your desires during all these years of inconveniences and obligations brought about by proximity to glory. It's simple: I leave you insignificance. The most banal, empty, insipid insignificance. Enjoy it now in the comfort of oblivion. Depart from the path of History and the spell with which we carried the world to the brink of nuclear holocaust, with which we set alight the continent to the south of us, bringing to its knees the most powerful empire since the origins of mankind, just ninety miles to the north of Cuba, and with which we took our undefeated troops through all of southern Africa. But I understand you. Now you need to enjoy the peace, happiness and prosperity that Hegel alluded to when he talked about the people who are the blank pages of History. Isn't that what all of you want? Isn't it what you aspire to? Well, you'll have it very soon because I am going to die. That is why I leave you insignificance in its entirety. The whole of insignificance.

Hasta la Victoria siempre.

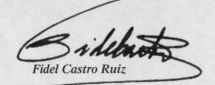

Fidel Castro Ruiz

August 13, 1926   Fidel Castro is born at Manacas Farm, in Birán, Mayarí, formerly Oriente Province (today Holguín Province). His parents are Ángel Castro y Argiz and Lina Ruz González.

September 1941 to June 1945   He attends Belén High School (from his second year until graduation), run by the Company of Jesus, in Mariano, Havana Province. Best athlete in his class, 1943–1944.

September 1945   He enters the law school at the University of Havana.

November 27, 1946   He delivers his first speech as a "political leader" to protest an increase in bus fares.

September 28 (or 29?), 1947   He swims across Nipe Bay to reach the island of Cuba and avoid being captured for his participation in the Cayo Confites adventure. He was part of a group funded by José Manuel Alemán and organized by the Revolutionary Socialist Movement (Movimiento Socialista Revolucionario, or MSR), which sought to invade the Dominican Republic and overthrow Rafael Leónidas Trujillo.

November 1947   He joins the Cuban People's (Orthodox) Party. He would have been nominated as candidate to the House of Representatives in the June 1952 elections, but they did not take place due to Fulgencio Batista's March 10 coup d'état that year.

March 31, 1948   He arrives in Colombia to organize a student congress of his invention, the object of which was to counter the Ninth Pan-American Conference, which opened on March 30, in Bogotá. He is fully supported by the Peronists. The morning of April 7, he meets with Jorge Eliécer Gaitán. He participates in the disturbances following Gaitán's April 9 murder, known as the Bogotazo.

October 11, 1948   He marries Mirta Díaz-Balart, whom he will divorce in December 1954.

October 13, 1950 He graduates with a degree in civil law and diplomatic and consular law from the University of Havana.

From 1950 to 1952 He works as an attorney in his firm at Number 57 Tejadillo Street, Old Havana.

March 24, 1952 He files an appeal before Havana's Emergency Court against Batista's coup d'état.

July 26, 1953 He leads the attack on the Moncada Barracks in Santiago. Of the 151 participants, 90 survived (6 died in combat and 55 were killed after being captured). On August 1, a patrol under the command of Lieutenant Pedro Sarría captures him at Las Delicias farm.

October 16, 1953 He gives the speech known as "History Will Absolve Me" before the court trying him and a hundred soldiers gathered at the Saturnino Lora Hospital. That same day he is sentenced to fifteen years in prison for "crimes committed against the powers of the State" and sent to the Reclusorio Nacional para Hombres prison in the Isle of Pines.

May 15, 1955 He leaves Reclusorio Nacional para Hombres prison in the Isle of Pines through an amnesty for political prisoners declared on the sixth of that month by Fulgencio Batista.

July 7, 1955 He arrives in Mexico to organize the uprising against Fulgencio Batista.

October 20 to December 10, 1955 He travels to various cities in the United States to collect funds.

December 2, 1956 He lands, in the company of eighty-one other expeditionaries on the *Granma*, near Las Coloradas beach, in the region of Niquero, on the southern coast of the former Oriente Province. They had left the Mexican port of Tuxpan in the early hours of November 25.

December 5, 1956 Along with the other expeditionaries, he is surprised by army and aviation forces in Alegría del Pío, in a sugarcane reed bed. They're scattered and suffer four casualties (the soldiers have three). Of the eighty-two men, twenty perished between the fifth and the eighth (three in Alegría de Pío and seventeen killed after being captured), twenty reached the Sierra Maestra, twenty-one managed to avoid pursuit and twenty-one were captured, tried in Santiago's Palacio de Justicia and sentenced to prison.

February 17, 1957 He is interviewed by Herbert Matthews of *The New York Times*, in the foothills of the northern slope of the Sierra Maestra.

July 11–22, 1958 He leads the forces to win the battle at Jigüe, the last and bloodiest of all the battles that took place during the army's summer offensive, which began May 24. About three hundred rebels defeated ten thousand soldiers under the command of General Eulogio Cantillo, head of operations in the Oriente Province.

November 12, 1958   Via Radio Rebelde, he gives the order to kick off the guerrilla forces' general offensive.

December 28, 1958   He meets with Eulogio Cantillo at the Oriente Mill, Palma Soriano, where they agree to sign a document on the thirty-first urging the army to join the revolutionary forces.

January 1, 1959   He meets with Colonel José Rego Rubido, second in command of the army's operations in the Oriente Province, who advises him that he will surrender Santiago before an attack planned for that afternoon. This allows the Rebel Army to enter the city without firing a single shot at one in the morning on January 2.

January 2, 1959   He calls a general strike under the slogan "Revolution, yes! Coup d'état, no!" and leaves for Havana in the so-called Freedom Caravan.

January 8, 1959   He arrives in Havana, and that night he addresses the country from Camp Columbia.

February 16, 1959   He assumes the office of prime minister.

April 15 to May 8, 1959   He visits the United States at the invitation of the Press Club. He expands the tour to Canada, Argentina, Uruguay and Brazil.

May 17, 1959   He signs the Agrarian Reform Law, which limits the possession of land to a maximum of thirty *caballerías* and does away with foreign ownership in general.

October 16, 1959   He creates the Ministry of Armed Revolutionary Forces (Ministerio de las Fuerzas Armadas Revolucionaries, or MINFAR) and names his brother, Commander Raúl Castro, minister.

October 26, 1959   He announces the creation of the Revolutionary National Militias (Malicias Nacionales Revolucionarias, or MNR).

February 13, 1960   With Anastas Mikoyan, he signs the first Cuban-Soviet commercial agreement.

March or April 1960   At some point he discovers that President Dwight D. Eisenhower gave the green light on March 17 for "The Covert Action Program Against the Castro Regime." In other words, war is coming.

April 16, 1961   He declares the socialist character of the Cuban Revolution in the memorial service for the victims of the bombings at the Pan American dock the previous day.

April 17–19, 1961   He leads the troops that fight and defeat Attack Brigade 2506 at the Bay of Pigs.

Summer, 1961 He meets Dalia Soto del Valle during the National Literacy Campaign.

May 29, 1962 He meets Marshall Sergei Biriuzov, head of the Soviet Strategic Missile Forces, who has the mission of proposing to the Cubans, on behalf of Nikita S. Khrushchev, the installation of forty-two mid-range and intermediate missiles equipped with nuclear warheads on the island, "so that the United States stops attacking."

October 28, 1962 Within the context of the so-called Cuban Missile Crisis, the United Nations is given access to confirm the dismantling and withdrawal of the medium-range Soviet missiles (a decision about which Nikita Khrushchev did not confer with him before informing John F. Kennedy), demanding, in return, five conditions as a guarantee that the Americans would not invade Cuba.

From the early 1970s until September 11, 1991 He governs comfortably under the shelter of Soviet subsidies, valued at about $6 billion annually.

November 10, 1975 He begins the greatest military intervention ever taken on by an underdeveloped country: the conquest of Angola, a country over eleven thousand kilometers from Cuba and eleven times as large as Cuba. A war that will last fifteen years and from which he will emerge victorious.

November 1977 He sends troops to Ethiopia at the request of leader Mengistu Haile Mariam. Two months after the Somalis capture Jijiga, he begins the deployment of seventeen thousand of his best men, including three combat brigades with experience in Angola, and Soviet logistics consisting of eighty combat planes, six hundred tanks and three hundred armored conveyors. He designates General Arnaldo Ochoa to lead the Cubans. On March 9, 1978 Somali President Mohamed Siad Barre declares the withdrawal of his forces as a result of Ochoa's crushing offensive in the Ogaden.

May 1979 From the General Division of Special Operations (Dirección General de Operaciones Especiales, or DGOE) Command Post, he leads the Sandinista National Liberation Front against the Nicaraguan National Guard under the command of Anastasio Somoza. This is the first war on the American continent that was controlled remotely. On July 20, 1979, he will consolidate the Sandinista victory with the entry of his columns in Managua.

May 1980 He initiates the doctrine of War of All the People (Guerra de Todo el Pueblo) as a response to Santa Fe I, the American government's program for the "capitalist restoration of Cuba." The doctrine consists of a group of survival measures in case of a military blockade, among which the highlights are the creation of the Militias of Territorial Troops and the organization of Defense Zones.

September 9, 1981 The Reagan administration's mounting threats cause him to send Raúl Castro to Moscow. Once again, the Soviets have to step in as Cuba's protectors. An unexpected response: the USSR is not going to risk itself to "go fight in Cuba, 11,000 kilometers away . . . to break our necks," according to Leonid Brezhnev himself. That the Soviets abandoned him to his fate then becomes a state secret. He calls it "Pandora's Case" and governs his own politics and strategic objectives while the USSR and the Cold War last.

November 7, 1987   He's in Moscow when the situation becomes more serious in Angola, due to the failed offensive on the Lomba by Soviet General Konstantin Ustinovich Chernenko, whom he opposed from the first. He orders Angolan and Cuban troops to establish a pocket of resistance in Cuito Cuanavale, an old and now devastated Portuguese village.

November 15, 1987   He makes the decision to reinforce his troops in Angola with five hundred T-54 and T-55 tanks sent from Cuba. The South Africans have three hundred. A correlation of force favoring him by almost two to one. In the coming months, he will lead the entire campaign from Havana.

February 14, 1988   The South Africans launch an attack to the east of Cuito Cuanavale against the Fifty-ninth Brigade (Angolan) and a company of mixed Angolan-Cuban tanks. Fourteen Cubans die and seven tanks are lost (only one can return on its mats). But they stop more than a hundred armored South Africans in their tracks. The defeat of this attack and the subsequent chaotic withdrawal of the enemy forces allows him to make sure that it is the beginning of the end of the South African forces of intervention in Angola and, as a consequence, the end of apartheid. He has achieved the last military victory of his life.

April 2–5, 1989   Mikhail Gorbachev's visit to Havana takes place, as Castro will later say, "in a strange and in no way happy manner." Castro comes to two conclusions: that the Soviets are too anxious to reach agreements with the Americans and that solidarity with Cuba is an obstacle to their achieving this.

From 1990 to 1991   He starts to publicly refer to the "falling apart" of the USSR and to urge the people to resist the severe effects on the country's economy and defenses caused by the double blockade—a reference to the United States' embargo to which is added the sum of ever greater cuts in the usual Soviet subsidies.

September 11, 1991   The Soviet Union announces the "modernization" of its relations with Cuba. In fact, this puts an end to the political, economic and military ties between both countries.

October 10–14, 1991   In a closed-door session of the Fourth Congress of the Cuban Communist Party in Santiago he advises those present to prepare themselves to govern the country as a minority.

December 8, 1991   Forced to entrench himself in the concept of resistance tooth and nail due to the dissolution of the USSR and the end of its copious economic and military subsidies, he again raises a forgotten nationalist sentiment and—of course—increases repression. He foresees the Revolution's worst years, even the possibility of its defeat. In conversations with those close to him, he says, "We need a year. One. If we can hold on this year, we'll be safe."

December 1991 The loss of the USSR and the socialist bloc's subsidies and markets brings about the so-called Special Period (which lasts a decade, until 2000).

December 5, 1999 He finds the vehicle to lift the spirits of a demoralized country when he makes a large-scale political battle out of the repatriation of a five-year-old boy, Elián González. Rescued by some fishermen on November 25 off the coast of Florida, he is the survivor of a group of *balseros*. His mother—Elizabet Brotón—was never found. On December 28, the Cuban government demands his return at the request of his father, Juan Miguel.

June 28, 2000 He achieves what may be his last international political victory: Elián returns to Cuba with his father after almost seven months of litigation in American courts and marches by the people in every corner of Cuba mirrored by seven months of demonstrations and street riots in Miami.

June 24, 2001 A certain period of economic growth begins, thanks to tourism and the association with China and with Hugo Chávez's Venezuela. But his health starts to fail him. He faints as he is delivering a speech.

October 20, 2004 He trips on a curb in the Ernesto Che Guevara Plaza in the city of Santa Clara. The accident causes a broken knee and hairline fractures in his arm. That's the immediate effect. Later, the excessive dosage of painkillers has a corrosive effect on his intestines.

July 26–31, 2006 He announces that he has undergone "complicated" emergency surgery and that he is temporarily delegating his main duties as a leader to his brother Raúl. A sharp intestinal crisis with sustained bleeding places him at the brink of death.

February 19, 2008 He makes public his decision to retire from public life and stresses that he will not run for or accept the office of President of the State Council and Commander in Chief. He will devote himself to writing. To working on his memoirs.

PHOTOGRAPH CREDITS

The photographic material often comes from worn negatives or originals that were stored, though not produced, without any professional consideration. The historic value of these images has increased the priority to restore them.

Approach to Havana. Over the right wing, Miami's lights are visible, per-
haps less than three kilometers away. Photo is taken in the flagship plane of the
Cuban fleet around eleven at night on October 4, 1986. An Ilyushin Il-62M
license number QT-52. Norberto Fuentes, Fidel Castro.

ACKNOWLEDGMENTS

THE AUTHOR WOULD LIKE TO EXPRESS HIS APPRECIATION TO THE following people, whose assistance has been inestimable throughout the creative process. First to those who were there at the beginning and demanded productivity: Silvia Bastos, Basilio Baltasar, Enrique Serbeto, Joaquín Palau, Ricardo Artola, Malcolm Otero, Richard Burton, Pau Centellas and Thomas Schultz. Followed by the unconditionals. The group. Álvaro Alba, Alberto Batista, Filiberto Castiñeiras, José Fernández Planas, Julia Gardiner, Brad Johnson, Caith Kushner, Amadeo López Castro, Rafael del Pino (and Laura Diego), Clive Rudd, Pedro Schwarze and Fernando Velásquez.

In the course of preparing this one-volume version for Norton, I've been fortunate to find two new friends, the translator Anna Kushner and the editor Tom Mayer. This is a note of gratitude to them, for their dedicated work and for their effort.

And Niurka. Niurkita. Always.